THE ANOTHER TRY COLLECTION

FAITH HART

THE ANOTHER TRY COLLECTION

Faith Hart

FOLLOW ME ON:
BOOKBUB

GOODREADS

COPYRIGHT

Published 2021 by: 2 Of Harts Publishing
www.2Ofharts.com

Individual Book Cover Designs by:
Sunset Rose Books

Box Set Cover Design by:
Rocking Book Covers

ACKNOWLEDGEMENTS

To Erin Wright, without whose guidance the magnificent transformation of the "Another Try" series might never have happened.

I appreciate you more than you'll ever know.

With Affection,

Faith Hart

OUT OF THE BLUE

Madeleine Nibless - Her husband's murder made national headlines – as did all his sordid secrets.

Heartbroken and humiliated, Maddie quietly takes back her maiden name and retreats into solitude – which deepens when she unexpectedly runs into the first unspoken love of her life, **Mason Gentries**.

Will Mason finally have the courage to tell Maddie how he feels? Will Maddie be able to overcome her past and allow herself to try for happiness once more?

PROLOGUE

June 2000

"I can't believe we're graduating," a breathless Madeline Smithing said as they walked into the holding room to line up for commencement. "It seems like just yesterday we were freshmen!"

"I know, Mad," Mason Gentries replied softly. "It flew by."

"*Get you some, Gentries!*" the class bully, Brock, yelled out as he moved past them.

Mason flushed deep red.

"Ignore him, Mason," Maddie murmured to him. "You know he's always been a rich, spoiled little jerk and he always will be."

"I'm just glad he leaves *you* alone, Mad," he told her sincerely. "I can take whatever he says to me."

She paused and looked around. "Okay, it looks like my spot's over there," she noted. "Gotta love a last name toward the end of the whole alphabet. See you after?"

He nodded and watched her walk away.

I love you, Mad, he almost said, as he'd wanted to every day since the fourth grade.

But as always, he stopped himself.

She'll never see me as anything more than a friend. I need to stop kidding myself and move on. Easier said than done, sometimes...

His train of thought was rudely interrupted by a shrill, grating voice.

"Hey, *loser*, you're blocking my way," Beverly Bennett, the head cheerleader and prom queen, snarled from behind him. He heard the snicker that meant Beverly's sidekick Stacie Frios was, as always, within inches of her ringleader.

He turned around and looked at them.

"Did I say you could make eye contact? No. I did not. Stacie, did you hear me say that?"

"Nope, sure didn't."

He crossed his arms over his chest and waited patiently.

After a few moments she rolled her eyes and stepped to one side.

"*Fine.* I'll go around you. I don't have time for this."

And she sauntered past, Stacie right on her heels like a faithful puppy.

***

Maddie took her place in line and looked back just in time to see Beverly say something to Mason.

Her hands clenched into fists as she watched from a distance, too far away to actually hear what had been said.

But knowing Beverly, it was condescending and rude, Maddie thought with a sigh. *It's a shame everyone's so mean to him. It's not his fault he wasn't born in this town like the rest of us. If they would just take time to get to know him, they'd see how brilliant he is.*

And cute, and funny, the part of her that had been crushing on him since elementary school chimed in. *Bet he's a good kisser, too...*

Stop it, she chastised herself. *We've been friends for years, and he's never made a move. Which means he doesn't see me that way, so, I need to get over this thing I have for him and move on. It'll ruin the friendship one day if I don't.*

CHAPTER ONE

March 2020

Mason Gentries scowled as he reviewed the data on a busy Monday afternoon.

"This here," he indicated one column. "This is *way* out of expected tolerances. Can we drill down into that, see what's going on there?"

"Sure thing," Toby said brightly.

Mason grinned as he returned to his office. Hiring Toby Mitting on full-time after his internship was turning out to be one of the best decisions he'd made. The kid's knowledge was off the charts, as were his intuitive problem-solving abilities. And Toby's enthusiasm was contagious.

He'd also blended seamlessly into Mason's established research and development team at a crucial point of a project that if successful, would greatly improve motor vehicle safety. Too many times Mason had seen news reports of fatal accidents caused by texting and driving. Austin, Texas based Gentries Unlimited was working on a solution.

A few more tweaks, a couple more rounds of beta testing, then a soft launch to gauge market interest, and if all that went as Mason expected, a full court press of marketing to round it all out.

He knew that Toby was at this very moment checking the code byte by byte to trace the variances that had presented in the reporting. But Mason settled in at his terminal, opened his own copy of the programming, and began to check it himself anyway.

It had to be one hundred percent perfect. No glitches, no mistakes. He'd made it his mission for no one else to die because of texting and driving. He had the knowledge and the desire to keep it from ever happening again - even if it cost him everything.

In most ways, it already had.

Focus, man, focus.

He blew out a deep breath, and with effort shoved the past aside and concentrated on each data point, looking for the troublemaker.

After forty-five minutes, as his eyes were beginning to fatigue, his desk phone trilled.

"Boss," Toby said triumphantly in Mason's ear, "I got it."

Mason's grin returned. "I'll be right there."

***

Madeleine Nibless was behind schedule, and she was frazzled as a result. She knew she'd have to hustle to get back on track to pull off the perfect date night. As she unlocked the front door of her two-story custom-built home, she resisted the urge to set her purse and coat down on the foyer table – Eric would have a fit if he saw a single item out of place.

And he notices everything, she reminded herself.

She quickly moved up the left staircase and into the master bedroom, hung up her coat, placed her purse on her nightstand, then took a quick shower.

Calmed, she went back downstairs and to the kitchen to prepare the meal she'd planned to surprise her husband. Eric's flight out was scheduled for seven a.m., and he'd be gone all week, so she wanted to make the night count.

With smooth, deft movements she set the needed ingredients for crab-stuffed filet mignon with whiskey peppercorn sauce on the counter, turned on the oven to bring it to temperature, and began to measure and dice.

Remember, Maddie, don't overcook his, she chided herself as she worked. *You don't want anything to ruin the mood tonight.*

She put together the crab stuffing and the peppercorn sauce first, then checked her watch.

Six o'clock. Good. He'll be home by seven, so this will all time out well.

Madeleine released a breath she hadn't realized she'd been holding and decided to take just a few moments to make sure she looked her best when he came home.

Sitting at her makeup table, she applied minimal amounts of blush, mascara, and lip gloss; just enough to enhance her smooth pale skin, complement her emerald-green eyes and whiskey colored hair.

Satisfied with her makeup, she traded her flannel robe for a silk one covering a negligee, added just a whisper of perfume, then returned to the kitchen to finish preparing dinner.

***

"That's it, Toby, I think we got the last of it," Mason crowed. "Fantastic!"

"This is awesome," the young man agreed. "I am so psyched to get this into the final testing round. You're gonna do so much good with this, boss."

"We," Mason corrected. "*We* are. Now, it's after seven. Go home. We'll reconvene at ten a.m. tomorrow."

"We're on tap at eight-fifteen on the calendar," his employee reminded him.

"Yes, we are. But since I'm the big boss, I'm telling you - sleep in a bit. You've earned it. See you at ten."

Toby's wide smile lit up the room. "Yes, sir."

Mason secured all the files and results before locking up the office and heading home. On the way to his car, he called the Chinese place he had logged into speed dial and ordered his usual for takeout. Within forty minutes he was walking triumphantly into his apartment with dinner, feeling like he owned the world.

It's finally coming together, he mused as he scooped out beef fried rice onto a paper plate. *After six years, it's finally going to happen.*

***

By seven p.m. Madeleine had candlelight flickering on a formally dressed dining room table and was plating the roasted vegetables alongside her husband's medium rare filet. That done, she plated her food as well, then sat down at the table to wait.

At seven-thirty she texted to confirm he was on his way home. He didn't answer. At eight p.m. she called, frowning when his phone went straight to voicemail. She ate alone, the candlelight now mocking instead of romantic. She called again at nine o'clock and tried to reach him a final time at two minutes past ten and got the same results.

Defeated, she cleared her place setting, put her dishes in the dishwasher, put his in the refrigerator, and changed into a t-shirt and yoga pants before settling in the living room with a book. By eleven-thirty, she'd fallen asleep.

***

The next morning, Maddie stirred, wincing at the stiffness in her neck she'd earned from dozing off on the couch. She glanced at her watch. Six-forty-three a.m.

Madeleine looked down at the open book on her lap and saw a note lying there.

Worked late, didn't want to wake you. I'll see you in a week. – E.

She crumpled up and threw the note in frustration as she stood.

Stomping into the kitchen, she gave a voice to her mood, slamming kitchen cabinets and drawers shut as she made coffee. By the time she'd finished drinking it she'd decided she was just pissed off enough to attempt the longer route again on her morning jog.

She took the staircase two steps at a time and changed into her workout gear, pulling her hair back into a ponytail for the run. She locked the door, tucked her house key in her hoodie's inside pocket, zipped up her jacket, and set out.

The morning was crisp and cold, and seemed to channel her anger to a fine point. She pushed through the first two and a half miles easily and was pleasantly surprised to find she wasn't even breathing hard yet.

By the time she walked back into her house from her morning jog, she was tired but pleased with herself. She'd achieved another goal. This morning was the first time she'd taken the longer route of four miles she'd previously tried and *not* been completely exhausted when she was done.

Building up the stamina! You go, Maddie! she congratulated herself.

And she did feel good about it. She'd only taken up jogging about five months ago; the first two months had been nightmarish – she'd had no idea until she started just how out-of-shape she was. There had been so many times the last five months she'd wanted to quit but kept going, and it was paying off.

Hell, I might even run a quarter marathon before the year's out, who knows? she speculated as she made her way into the master bathroom to clean up.

She turned on the shower, then stripped down, checking her body out in the mirror.

Not supermodel size by any stretch, but you're doing good girl, she told herself as she shook her hair loose from the ponytail holder and brushed it out.

She'd never been svelte, and she had realized long ago that at five feet six, with a stocky build she'd inherited from her father's side of the family, she never would be. Still, she could already tell a big difference, not just in weight, but in inches – most noticeably from her waistline and thighs.

Keep this up you're going to have to go get smaller clothes!

She grinned at her reflection. "I definitely don't mind having that problem," she announced to the mirror before stepping into her shower stall.

As she reached for her shampoo, she considered calling Eric after her shower, just to make sure he arrived at the conference safely.

But he can be so hateful to me sometimes, especially when he's working...I probably shouldn't bother him.

She sighed as she massaged her scalp.

Truth be told, he wasn't just snarky, and it wasn't just sometimes. He could and did crush her soul routinely with just a few venomous words, and lately it was much more frequent.

Maddie sighed again as she rinsed out her hair.

What the hell happened to us? We've drifted so far apart, she realized with sorrow. *And I have no idea what to do to fix it.*

By the time Maddie finished her shower, she'd decided to finally confide her woes to her best friend Kathy and ask for advice. She sent a text to make sure Kathy was home and immediately received an invitation to come have coffee. They had been friends for three years, and Kathy was aware of Maddie's tendency to keep her troubles to herself and present a happy façade to the world.

"Hell, she probably already *knows* how unhappy I am," she mumbled as she finished dressing and grabbed her purse. "She's just been waiting for me to talk about it."

And Maddie was right. The moment Kathy's front door opened, Kathy said, "Oh, honey. I was hoping you'd let it out at some point."

Maddie walked into Kathy's living room, sat on the couch, and burst into tears. Kathy grabbed a box of tissues and sat beside her, hugging her with one arm.

"I'm glad you're here, Mad. You've looked so unhappy lately, and I've been worried about you."

"Me too," Maddie sniffled as she wiped her eyes with a tissue. "I just don't know what to do."

CHAPTER TWO

"Let it out," Kathy repeated. "Don't keep carrying it around. You know I'm here to listen."

So, Maddie told her all of it. The hateful speech and wounding words, the distance that had grown in her marriage, not just emotional, but physical.

"Ouch," Kathy murmured in sympathy. "How long since... you know..."

"Years," Maddie blurted out. "We haven't had sex in four years."

"*Really?*"

"Really. And Kathy, I've tried everything. Sexy outfits, romantic date nights, even, you know..." Maddie trailed off as she blushed, "um... I've even suggested role playing. Nothing has worked."

She could see the understanding in Kathy's eyes when she risked looking over at her friend.

"Well, I know you, Maddie, and I know you're really shy about that kind of stuff, so, those were big steps for you. And you got no reaction?"

"I even went and bought this ridiculous red lace getup. It stressed me out just trying to figure out how to put the damn thing on. You know?" Maddie managed a small smile at that memory.

Kathy chuckled. "One of those 'is it lingerie or a puzzle rug' types?"

"Exactly! But I figured it out, and I put it on in the middle of a Saturday afternoon, and went downstairs into the living room. Eric was watching a show, and I stood in front of him and said something provocative, I don't even remember what exactly. Something sensual, like in those romances we read. You know what his response was?"

"What?"

"He said, 'Move, Maddie, I can't see the TV'."

Kathy's jaw dropped. "Seriously?"

Maddie's smile was gone, replaced with brimming eyes as she whispered, "Yep."

"Wow," Kathy breathed. "What an *ass*."

"So, I went upstairs, and took the red lace off and threw it in the trash, and put on sweatpants and a t-shirt, and I haven't tried anything like that since. That was four years ago. And I've gotten used to not having an intimate life anymore. But now, it's everything. He can't even bother to let me know he's working late anymore."

Maddie was transitioning back to anger as she spoke. "Like last night. I found a new recipe, decided to make us a nice dinner, with candlelight and everything. Had it plated and ready to eat at seven o'clock sharp. And he didn't come home, and he didn't return my text or calls. I wound up eating by myself, again, then falling asleep on the couch."

Her laugh was a bitter one. "I actually even put a negligee on last night too. Thank God I changed out of that! When I woke up this morning, he'd left me a note. A note, Kathy. And it just said, *'I worked late, didn't want to wake you, see you in a week.'* Not 'I love you', not 'sorry I made you worry', nothing else."

Maddie stood and began to pace, her anger growing.

"And I am tired of it, Kathy. I think I might be done with this whole damn thing. I think I deserve more. I'm thirty-seven, not dead. I'm no beauty queen but I am one hell of a good woman. I'm smart, I'm honest, I'm loyal, and I'm loving. There's got to be more for me in life than this."

"I agree," Kathy nodded. "Except for the 'no beauty queen' part. You don't give yourself enough credit, Mad. You don't ever notice it, but you do have men looking at you more than you realize. I think you're fabulous, and you deserve to have a man in your life that thinks so too!"

She reached out for Maddie's hand.

"Whatever you decide to do, just know, I have your back. If you need to crash here for a while, just say the word. Okay? You don't have to go through this by yourself."

"I know," Maddie answered as she hugged Kathy. "And I am so thankful for that."

"So, what's next?"

Maddie set her jaw, and her tone was soft but resolved. "I suppose it's time to find a good divorce lawyer."

***

"I think that went well," Toby said, as the research and development team members began to leave the meeting.

"Me too," Mason agreed. "And I believe we're actually ahead of schedule. Depending on this last round of testing, we should be good to soft launch."

"Mason, I just want to say thanks," Toby told him earnestly. "I am so grateful to be here, to be a part of all of this."

"Happy you're here, man," Mason clapped him on the shoulder. "You're a big asset to Gentries Unlimited."

The young man grinned.

"Now, back to work."

***

Maddie sat in the plush yet understated lobby of one Rebekah Blayne, attorney at law, absentmindedly toying with her watch as she waited for her appointment to begin. As usual, she'd arrived ten minutes early – a lesson learned from watching her father in his business dealings.

The anger that had fueled her making the appointment had dissipated, and an aching sadness had filled the vacancy. *Fifteen years, just... gone. I know this is what's right for me, but it still hurts.*

"Madeleine?" Blayne's receptionist called out. "Ms. Blayne's just about ready. If you'll come with me, please, I'll show you to the conference room."

Maddie stood, squared her shoulders, and followed the receptionist down the hall. As they walked, the woman said, "My name is Cheryl, it's nice to meet you. Would you like anything to drink? Water, coffee?"

"I'll take some water, please," Maddie answered. "Thank you."

Cheryl stopped at the second doorway on the left, and stepped to the side, saying, "Right in here. I'll be back with your water. Ms. Blayne should be just a few moments longer."

Maddie sat down, taking in the spectacular view of Lake Carolyn that only having offices on the eighth floor of a glass building could provide. *One of the many perks of having a thriving practice in Las Colinas*, she thought to herself as she waited. Moments later Cheryl returned with a bottled water, then gently closed the door behind her as she returned to the front desk.

Twisting the cap off the bottle, Maddie took a long drink to try to stem the tide of nerves she felt creeping in. Just as she put the lid firmly back in place, Rebekah Blayne entered the room.

"Good afternoon Mrs. Nibless, I'm Rebekah Blayne," she said, extending her hand.

Maddie rose, accepting the handshake, and answered, "Please, call me Maddie."

Rebekah took a seat at the end of the table at an angle from the chair Maddie had chosen and opened a notebook she'd brought with her. She looked at Maddie with sympathetic brown eyes for a long moment.

"Well, then, Maddie, please call me Rebekah," she said with a kind smile. "Now, tell me about your situation."

***

Once she'd shared everything with Rebekah, the lawyer had asked several questions, then explained, "Maddie, it sounds to me like we're talking what's called a 'no fault' divorce. Basically, it means the cause is irreconcilable differences. Now, do you think Eric will fight you on this?"

"I honestly don't know," Maddie murmured. "We barely even talk anymore. So, I honestly have no idea what his reaction will be."

"Okay. So, here's some things I want you to be thinking about. You don't have any children, and aren't expecting any, correct?"

Not unless pregnancy in humans now lasts over four years, Maddie thought bitterly, but only answered, "No, no kids, at all."

Rebekah made several notes as they talked, and at the end of their time together she'd concluded with, "I'm going to have Cheryl get all this into an outline and email it to you. You're going to want to be thinking about these things ahead of time. If you think he might contest the divorce at all, it's going to be better for us to have everything lined out as much as possible."

"One last thing," the lawyer told Maddie. "And I need you to answer me honestly. Do you have any concerns for your physical safety at all?"

"Eric is mean spirited, Rebekah, but he's never once been physically violent toward me," Maddie replied. "He prefers to use words as weapons."

Rebekah arched an eyebrow as she gazed at her client.

"No, I'm not worried about my safety."

"Good. I needed to hear you confirm that for me. When it comes to situations like this, you just never know." And the look of pain showing briefly on Rebekah's face let Maddie know she'd witnessed her share of abused clients.

By the time Maddie got home the document was ready and waiting in her inbox.

She ate a light supper – *no point in cooking for just me*, she reasoned – then settled in with a glass of sangria and the printed consultation summary and checklist of next steps.

***

Mason locked up and left the office just after eight p.m., tired but jubilant. If things continued to go well, Gentries Unlimited would be able to unveil their new technology before April arrived. He grabbed a drive-through burger on his way back to his apartment to relax and watch the hockey game.

***

As Maddie read, she made notes to herself, and then started on the lists Rebekah had mentioned regarding individual and joint assets.

Now that I think about it, we never truly shared anything.

At the time it had struck her as strange, but Maddie had shrugged it off as just another point of compromise in their relationship. Maybe the wine was starting to loosen her memory up – she remembered she'd done a *lot* of compromising over the last fifteen years.

She had desperately wanted kids, but did she have any? No. Eric didn't want them.

"Hell, I wasn't even allowed to have any *pets,*" she grumbled.

The more she thought about things, the madder she got.

The lists complete, she set down her pen, leaned back, and finished off the glass of wine.

One's usually my limit, but I think it's time to make an exception, she decided, staring at her empty glass.

Maddie went to the kitchen and poured herself another. Her cell phone, plugged into the charger, chirped at her from the living room, and she dutifully returned to retrieve it.

A new text notification. I bet fifty bucks I know who this is NOT from, she thought sourly. Pulling it up onscreen, her mood lightened to see it was from Kathy.

How did the lawyer's office thing go?

About like I expected, Maddie typed in response. *Made the asset lists like she suggested. Nothing much to do now but wait until he gets home so I can tell him it's over.*

A long pause, then another ping for a new incoming message.

I'm so sorry about all this, Mad. I have your back. Whatever you need, just let me know, okay? When does he come back?

"At least *someone* cares about whether or not I'm happy," Maddie muttered, then answered, *Friday night.*

CHAPTER THREE

When Mason finally did fall asleep, the same nightmare that always chased him started almost immediately.

I'm in the driveway, buckling Abagail into her car seat, those big blue eyes watching me as she coos and smiles. 'Da da da da,' she babbles, and I grin. Laura puts the diaper bag in the front passenger seat, then comes to me. I hold her in my arms and breathe her in; her hair is lightly scented like strawberries, from her shampoo.

"We'll be back tomorrow night," she tells me, as she kisses me.

But I know better, and I try to warn her not to leave yet, baby, don't leave yet! Wait ten minutes, that should be enough time.

Despite my efforts, the dream doesn't change. She doesn't wait. I stand outside myself, horrified, powerless, watching me blow Abagail a kiss, seeing her scrunch her tiny nose at me as she giggles. Waving at them as Laura backs out of our driveway.

Oh, God, Laura, please wait...

Mason moaned as the dream shifted.

A call. The office called me. So much for a quiet Saturday morning. I get in my car, buckle up, radio on, and head out. As I approach the large intersection, I am shocked to see red and blue flashing lights everywhere. The entire thing's shut down, all directions. Not surprising, accidents happen on a road this busy, especially when people aren't paying attention...

And I see it as I get closer.

No. Oh, please, God, *no.*

Our little beige Volvo with the distinctive bumper sticker. Almost completely buried underneath a cement truck.

I park my car in the middle of the street, I jump out, I'm running forward, screaming. Two policemen approach me, hands on weapons.

'Stay back, sir, you need to stay back.'
Darkness.

Mason came back to consciousness, soaked in sweat and sobbing.

***

Thursday morning found Maddie taking the long route again on her morning jog, and for the second time, she completed it without feeling like she was about to collapse.

Progress, I'm making progress! her mind exclaimed joyfully.

As she headed to the shower, she was thinking about her future. Maddie was about to have a whole new world in front of her.

No one to shoot down and belittle my dreams, she realized. *No one else's ego to have to cater to anymore.*

The notion exhilarated and scared her to death, all at once.

"So, what the hell *do* I want to do?" she asked her reflection.

Something with animals, I know that. And I have my MBA, so I am totally capable of running my own business. Anything I don't know, I'm sure I can ask Dad about.

"Yeah," she grinned at herself in the mirror. "Something that helps animals. Like a rescue shelter, where every animal gets placed in a new home."

Whistling, she continued her usual morning routine. Once breakfast was out of the way, she fired up her laptop and began researching what was required to own and operate a rescue shelter in Texas, taking thorough notes as she went along.

Before Maddie knew it, the morning had flown by. Her stomach rumbling caused her to glance at the time.

"Three o'clock? Good Lord, no wonder I'm hungry," she exclaimed.

She set her laptop to the side, stretched, and headed for the kitchen.

After a moment's hesitation, she opted to make a quick chef salad. As she ate, she texted her father, asking if he had time for some general questions about starting a company. The answer was immediate.

Happy to help, kiddo! Whatever you need. What did you have in mind?

Well, she typed back, *I am thinking about opening a rescue shelter. I'm researching specifics about what it would take to get one going, but I am going to need your input to help make sure I set it all up right, Dad.*

That would be perfect *for you, Maddie, I know how much you love animals,* her dad replied. *What does Eric think about it?*

"Oh, boy," she muttered. "Should have foreseen that question coming up. What do I say to that? 'Oh yeah, Dad, about that, forgot to mention I'm going to file for divorce so who cares what he thinks?' Not really something I want to break to my father via text message."

Before she could formulate her response, the doorbell rang. She texted *I'll fill you in more later, okay?* back to her father, hit send, and headed to the front door. When she saw who was standing there she was thoroughly confused.

"Hello, Mrs. Nibless?"

"Yes, that's me, but please call me Maddie. May I help you?"

"I'm Detective Kenney, and this is Officer Greene. We're with the Flower Mound Police Department. We need to speak with you. May we come in?"

"Um...sure, come in, please." She stood to one side as they crossed the threshold.

"Would either of you like something to drink? Coffee?"

"No, ma'am. Thanks."

"All right. If you change your minds, just let me know."

Maddie led them into the living room. She sat on one end of the couch, trying her best to calm her nerves. Officer Greene sat beside her as Detective Kenney took the adjoining high-back chair.

"Detective Kenney, Officer Greene, I don't wish to sound rude, but... Why are you here?"

The detective leaned forward and as gently as he could told her, "Maddie, I am so sorry to have to tell you this, but your husband Eric's been killed."

She could feel the color leaching from her face even as she struggled to process the words; she was positive that she'd misheard the man.

"I'm sorry, what did you say?"

"Your husband, Eric Nibless, was found murdered yesterday afternoon in Wyoming."

"It can't be him, he's not in Wyoming," she said immediately, almost defensively. "He's at a conference in Rapid City. Here. Let me find the number to the hotel, they'll tell you, he's attending a conference there..." She started to stand up to go retrieve her phone.

But Officer Greene laid his hand gently over hers. "Maddie, his wallet with his driver's license was at the scene, and they confirmed his identity this morning through fingerprinting."

She turned to argue with him and noticed the little crosses affixed to the collar of his uniform.

He's the police chaplain, she realized. *And they don't just randomly come to people's houses...*

Unless... unless...

"This is real...isn't it?" she whispered.

Officer Greene squeezed her hand. "I'm afraid so, Maddie. I am so very, very sorry."

A wrenching sob tore from her body as she began to weep. Greene handed her a tissue and patted her shoulder, trying to comfort her.

"Is there any one we can call for you, to come be with you?" the detective asked.

"My....my parents... and Kathy," she managed to get out in between sobs. "In my phone..." her voice failed her, and she pointed toward the kitchen.

Greene nodded solemnly and went to go make the calls.

Detective Kenney moved to sit on the edge of the coffee table in front of her.

"Maddie, I know this is hard, and I know now is not the best time, and I'm so sorry. But I need to ask you some questions, okay? It may help us find out who did this."

She nodded, still sobbing, reaching for another tissue.

"Can you think of anybody that would want to hurt Eric? Professionally, personally, anyone at all?"

"N-n-no," she stammered. "Nobody comes to mind."

Officer Greene returned to her side. "Your parents and Kathy are all on the way, okay?"

She nodded, whispering, "Thanks."

"I have to ask these next ones, Maddie, and I apologize. How was your marriage? Any problems between you two?"

"I still love him," she wailed. "But I haven't been happy in years. I went to see a lawyer yesterday. Eric's coming home Friday... was... was coming home Friday," Maddie swallowed hard, numb with shock, "and I was going to tell him then that I was leaving. That I still love him, but I just can't do it anymore."

"Do what, exactly?"

"Exist in a vacuum," she revealed, raw grief on her face. "Barely even speak to one another, much less any affection. We've been just roommates for a long time. I just didn't want to admit it until now."

She looked directly at Detective Kenney, and she could see he understood.

"But I didn't want this," she continued, fresh tears streaming downward. "I wanted us to part as friends and go live our lives. I never wanted anything bad for him. Ever."

A brief knock on the front door caught their attention, and Maddie's parents came swiftly into the room.

"Oh, baby," her mom Deborah said, and took her daughter into her arms.

Detective Kenney and Officer Greene stood and approached Maddie's father.

"Might we have a word in the other room?" Kenney suggested.

Her father nodded, and the three men traveled into the kitchen.

"I'm Chase Smithing," her father said. "What the hell happened?"

"I'm Detective Kenney, this is Officer Greene. Mr. Smithing, your son-in-law was found dead yesterday afternoon, in a motel just outside Sleepy Hollow, Wyoming."

"What in the hell was he doing there? He was supposed to be at an industry conference in Rapid City!"

"I know, sir, and authorities up there are trying to figure that out."

"Are you sure it's Eric?"

Officer Greene repeated what he'd told Maddie about positive identification through fingerprints.

"Wait – why couldn't they just match him to his driver's license photo?"

CHAPTER FOUR

The detective and the chaplain exchanged glances, and Kenney lowered his voice when he explained, "Mr. Smithing, Eric was beaten to death. The damage was such that visual verification wasn't possible. I didn't share that with her. I'm telling *you* this because Maddie may want to see him when he's released by the coroner's office. Trust me, she doesn't need that image in her head. None of you do."

Chase blanched. "I see. I'll make sure she's not subjected to that."

"Eric worked for you, Mr. Smithing, is that right?"

"Yes, he's my CFO."

"Do you know of anyone that might have wanted to harm him? Anyone you can think of?"

"No," Chase answered. "No one. Eric was well-liked by everyone so far as I knew."

Chase fielded a few more exploratory questions, and the three men moved back into the living room. Maddie's mother Deborah was seated beside her daughter, holding her hand.

"What happens now?" Maddie managed through her tears.

Officer Greene stepped forward, extending a card to her.

"Maddie, here's my contact information. Once they've done what they need to in Wyoming, they'll be able to send Eric home to Texas. I can help coordinate that for you, if you like."

"That would be very helpful. Thanks."

"Here's my card, as well," Detective Kenney offered. "If you have questions, or if you think of anything that might be helpful, please reach out. And again, I am so sorry for your loss."

Chase saw the policemen to the door and met Kathy as she was stepping onto the porch from the front walking path.

"Hey, Kathy, glad you're here. She needs you. Come on in."

"Thanks, Mr. Smithing."

They made their way back to the living room, where Maddie cried softly. Kathy sat next to her and hugged her.

"I'm so sorry, Mad."

***

Two days later, Maddie, her parents, and Kathy returned to Maddie's house from the funeral home. Eric had never agreed to any sort of pre-planning, although Maddie had told him repeatedly over the years that it was a good idea.

"Why? It's morbid," he'd snarled.

"Because," she'd sighed, "it will make it easier on the one left behind to not have to make all sorts of decisions during the worst time of their lives, that's why."

But she'd been unsuccessful, and he'd refused to discuss it further. Now, her prediction had become her reality. On top of the deep, stark grief came a myriad of choices to make, and Maddie had felt completely overwhelmed.

To make matters worse, Maddie's in-laws had shown up and attempted to take over all the funeral planning. When Caroline Nibless had shrilly and loudly announced to everyone present that no casket costing less than seven thousand dollars could *possibly* be good enough for her son, Maddie finally reached her breaking point.

I've always just put up with the way she treats me, because of Eric. No more, she thought, and set her jaw.

"We're going with *that* one," she'd said coldly and calmly, deliberately pointing to the lowest priced one.

"I hardly think—" Caroline started to protest but Maddie cut her off, with just enough volume to stop everyone in their tracks.

"I don't care *what* you think," Maddie said matter-of-factly to the woman who had treated her like a second-class citizen the entire marriage. "You know why? Because it's not your choice to make, Caroline. It's mine, and it's *final.*"

She'd turned back to the funeral director and spoke calmly. "Now, Mr. Gates, how about we continue this planning session in private, so there aren't any further interruptions?"

He'd swallowed, nodded, and escorted her to his office, leaving a visibly mortified Caroline in their wake.

I shouldn't have acted that way toward her, Maddie chastised herself the minute they walked away. *I know she's grieving too. But it was just too much. I've had enough.*

As if he could read her thoughts, Mr. Gates softly said, "No worries, miss, that's not the worst outburst we've witnessed here, believe me. Grief does strange things to people."

"I appreciate that," she'd replied, then sighed as they sat down in his office. "What did you need me to decide next?"

It was with relief that she sat in her living room that afternoon, surrounded by those she loved.

***

Mason sat in his office behind a firmly closed door with his head in his hands.

I still can't believe it.

When Mason had returned from lunch, he'd walked down the hall to the conference room for his two o'clock meeting with the team to finalize soft launch plans. But one person never arrived at the meeting. Toby Mitting had seemingly vanished from the face of the earth.

Mason had looked for him everywhere in the offices, then tried Toby's cell phone, and was dumbfounded to get a disconnected number message. He checked the number three times and got the same results.

Mason's stomach had turned to lead as he marched to his office again and sat at the desk.

"Please, dear God, no," he whispered as he attempted to call up files relating to the massive project that they'd all spent so much time and effort on.

The main server had been wiped clean. Even his personal folders on the secondary server - that no one else should have been able to even *navigate* to, much less *access* - were devoid of anything relating to the single most important project of his existence.

Specifications, timelines, testing, raw data, all of it. Gone.

It was like the last six years of his life had never happened. No obvious trace remained of Mason Gentries' dream to make the world a little bit safer.

***

"I'm glad that part's over," Maddie murmured as she rubbed her temples. "Although I should probably apologize to Caroline at some point."

"I don't think so, personally," Chase said. "She was out of line. But you do what you feel is right, Maddie."

"Here, sweetie," Kathy said when she came back into the house. "Thought I'd grab the mail for you."

"Thanks," Maddie told her, and began to leaf through the stack.

When she saw the thick manila envelope, her brows furrowed.

"Wonder what this is?" she wondered out loud. "And, who sent it. No return address on it."

"Only one way to find out," Deborah said.

"I suppose," Maddie replied, and opened the envelope to pull out the contents. She set the envelope on the coffee table and began to scan through the half-inch thick stack of pages.

Deborah turned to say something to Maddie and noticed her daughter had turned ghostly white.

"Maddie... What's wrong?"

"What... what..." was all Maddie could manage to say as she moved faster and faster, looking at page after page. "Oh...oh, no...."

She looked up at her parents and at Kathy.

"Look... look at all this...," her voice trailed off, and she thrust the pages toward them.

Chase reached out and took some from her.

"These... are these bank records?"

Her mother said, "Oh, my word... Kathy, look at these. What is this?"

Kathy scanned the twelve pages Maddie's mother had handed her.

"*Wow*," Kathy muttered, turning red. "Um... Deborah, those are screenshots of... um...some pretty explicit conversations in an ...um... alternative lifestyle chat room."

"And these pages," Maddie managed, "are filled with very disturbing and bigoted remarks..."

At the very last page of the stack, Maddie paused, then flinched as if she'd been struck.

"What, honey?" her father asked.

She held out the last page to him.

"*Dear Madeleine,*" Chase began to read aloud, "*I know you didn't know that your husband was into any of this, and I felt you deserved to know who and what he really was. Here's all his logins and passwords, if you would rather check it out for yourself. I know seeing all this hurts you, and I'm sorry for that. But you needed to know just how big a lie Eric Nibless was living.*"

"We need to get the police over here," Kathy piped up. "They need to see all this, take it into evidence, maybe. I'd say chances are pretty damn good it's related to his death."

"I'll go get the detective's card," Deborah said, and moved toward the kitchen counter where she'd seen it last.

Maddie nodded dully as her brain tried desperately to process everything she'd just seen. *Some of the most horrible, hateful things I've ever read.... and chatting with strange men to arrange hookups?*

From the corner of her eye, she saw her father's face turning crimson with rage.

"These pages here are only partly bank records. Some of these pages are screenshots of *my company's* accounting system. And they show money flowing out of my company and into an overseas account that I have no knowledge of," he thundered. "It sure as hell looks like Eric was stealing from me."

Maddie rose from the couch. "I don't feel well, I'm going to go lie down," she murmured.

She managed to take seven steps before the room began to spin and close in on her, then she lost consciousness and crumpled in a heap to the floor.

CHAPTER FIVE

Both the police and an ambulance were summoned to Maddie's home.

"I'm all right," Maddie protested weakly. "I just... got overwhelmed, is all."

"You went down hard, Mad," Kathy retorted. "Please cooperate, let them check you out. Okay?"

"Okay," Maddie whispered.

The emergency tech taking her vitals chimed in. "You have a pretty nasty bump on your head, ma'am. It wouldn't surprise me if you have a concussion."

***

"I have some news," Mason said through clenched teeth as his project team and upper management waited expectantly. "Some of you may have noticed that the server seems to be acting up. Can't access project files this afternoon that you could this morning, right?"

Several team members nodded.

"That's because they're gone," Mason announced solemnly. "All of them. Wiped clean. And Toby Mitting is MIA."

"That son of a *bitch*," Allen, Mason's business partner and VP of Operations, muttered loudly, then said, "Sorry, Mason."

"Don't be," came Mason's answer. "Because right now, I feel exactly the same way."

"What do we do now?" one team member asked.

"I've got some older copies of all those files on my home unit," Mason revealed. "But they're two weeks out of date, at least, and as we all know, the last twenty or so days we've really been moving and shaking on this thing. Tons of new stuff, good stuff, that we need is now history."

His accounting manager raised her hand.

"Mason," Jennifer said. "I know it may not help very much, but we recently enabled server backups to the Cloud, remember? So hopefully, at least part of what's missing is still intact out there. And, we also have coverage for this type of activity in our insurance policy. I think it would be a good idea to make some calls, file a claim."

"You're right, Jennifer, I'd forgotten about all that. Yes, let's get together right after this." He cleared his throat.

"Okay, so, if any of you have any file copies saved somewhere *other* than the main server – like your desktop – then I need to know as soon as possible. If you do, we might be able to salvage at least part of all this."

***

Meanwhile, at the Nibless residence, Detective Kenney was pulling on gloves before he picked up any of the pages Maddie had received in the mail. A member of Flower Mound's crime scene processing team was already sliding the manila envelope into an evidence bag.

"Pictures of each page, then bag them, please," Kenney directed, and the tech nodded.

Kenney stepped over to Chase and Deborah.

"Walk me through it," he said simply.

"There's not much to tell, really. We came back from the funeral home, and Kathy went and brought the mail in," Chase told him. "Maddie opened the package, turned white as a sheet and showed us the pages, and we called you."

"All right. We'll need fingerprint samples from each of you, to compare against any on the pages," Kenney told him, "so that we can eliminate them. Hopefully, there will be at least one good print somewhere in all those that won't match any of yours, and we'll have something to go on."

When the tech had bagged the last page, Kenney nodded. "I'll be in touch."

***

Maddie did indeed have a mild concussion, as it turned out. On the emergency room doctor's orders, she took it easy the next few days.

But in the middle of it all was the day of the funeral, which taxed her to her very limits.

She followed Mr. Gates as he led the family procession into the chapel where Eric's casket was on display. Closed, of course. Whoever had taken his life had done so much damage that Mr. Gates had gently told Maddie, "You really need to have a closed casket service, dear, trust me on this."

As she sat in the front row, staring listlessly at the flower arrangements, Maddie listened to the pastor talk about her husband's life, and it was all she could do not to laugh out loud.

If you only knew, Preacher, she scoffed internally. *He was a complete fraud! Managed to fool every single person he ever met. I wonder if there was ever anything* real *about him at all.*

She closed her emotions off to keep herself from screaming them out at the top of her lungs and derailing the entire service.

Cause boy howdy, wouldn't that just make old Caroline's day?

With effort, she stifled the giggle that thought summoned.

Keep it together, Mad. Keep it together. Fall apart when you get home, honey. You can do this.

She almost broke when the mourners in attendance began to file past the family and lie after lie of 'he was a great man' was heaped on her psyche like so many cement blocks.

The single thing that kept her from coming completely undone was the realization that all these people didn't know the truths about Eric that she did.

Only blessing in all this, really, is that at least the rest of the world doesn't know what he really was.

She managed to get through the rest of the service, and the graveside ceremony, and the house full of well-wishers.

At long last, the crowd dissipated, and she was finally among the ones she knew she could completely trust – Kathy, and her parents.

They all offered to stay overnight with her, but she declined politely.

"I love you, and I know you're worried about me," she told them. "But right now, I just want to soak in the tub with a glass or two of wine, then go to bed. I'm all right, I promise."

"At least come over for breakfast tomorrow," Deborah stressed.

"I will, Mom."

Maddie saw them out, grabbed a glass and the bottle of wine, and headed upstairs to her garden tub. She dropped a lavender bath bomb into the steaming water as the tub filled, then climbed in and poured herself a glass of sangria.

Fifteen years, she reflected as she drank. *Not just gone, like I thought when I realized I was going to get divorced. Nope. Gone was an understatement. A complete fabrication, is what they were...*

My whole existence all that time was built on lies.

The tears ran unchecked down her face and swirled unnoticed into the fragrant water.

***

Mason Gentries walked into his apartment, threw his keys on the kitchen counter, and headed straight to the liquor cabinet to pour himself four fingers of whiskey over ice before he slumped down in his armchair.

"Un-freaking believable," he muttered aloud to no one. He wanted to rant, yell, throw things.

But what would that accomplish? Precisely nothing. No good whatsoever. And this is partly my fault, for not thinking ahead enough to arrange daily back up of all the files onto a portable drive that I could keep at home. I overlooked a vulnerable spot, and they exploited it.

He ran his right hand over his face then through his hair as he considered his next move, but he felt adrift in the middle of a waking nightmare, with no safe harbor anywhere in sight.

And to make things worse, every spare cent of operating capital was tied to this project, he reminded himself. *Allen and Jennifer and I are the only three that know that. If I can't salvage this, Gentries Unlimited will have to shut down, and my entire staff will be out of work. They don't deserve that. None of them do. They've all busted their asses for this.*

But I can't think of any way to keep it from happening.

He threw back his whiskey, set the tumbler on his coffee table, and put his head in his hands.

***

Maddie woke the next morning and was surprised to realize she'd managed to get some sleep. Then she walked into the bathroom, saw the empty wine bottle on the counter, and remembered why restful sleep had come so easily.

I also, vaguely, remember dispensing with the glass at some point and finishing off the bottle directly...

"Yeah. Can't do that again," she murmured, as her head began to throb. "The aftermath isn't worth it."

She took as hot a shower as she could stand, then dressed casually for the morning meal at her parents' house she'd promised she would attend.

Moving swiftly down the staircase, she scooped up her purse and keys, and headed toward the garage before she remembered she'd parked her car in the half-circle drive in front of the house.

The moment she opened the door, Maddie was greeted with several flashbulbs going off and by her count at least eight microphones thrust rudely in her face. A barrage of questions shouted at her from the various national news media representatives rolled over her like a tsunami.

Overwhelmed, she immediately stepped backward into the safety of her home, closing and then deadbolting the front door with shaking hands.

Maddie backed away from the furor on her front lawn, eyes wide, breaths coming in gasps. When the house phone began to ring, she yelped, clutching her chest.

She moved back upstairs, away from the more brazen reporters and their cameramen now daring to peek in through the first-floor windows and called Detective Kenney from her cell phone.

"Please help me," she gasped. "There's reporters all over the place. I can't even leave my house."

"What?"

Maddie repeated what she'd said.

"Hang tight, Mrs. Nibless, we're on the way."

She hung up and called her parents' house.

"Mom," Maddie said, "there's people – "

"All over your front yard, too?" Deborah replied. "Same thing over here, honey. Something about Eric must have made the news. Your dad's flipping channels right now, trying to figure out what the hell's going on."

"I called Detective Kenney. He said he's on his way."

"Good thinking, hon. Maybe the police can get them to disperse."

"I'm stuck here until they're gone, Mom. I didn't put my car in the garage yesterday, I left it in the driveway. I couldn't even *see* it from the front door because of all the people outside. No way I want to try to shove my way to it."

Downstairs, the phone just off the kitchen continued to ring non-stop. Then Maddie noticed multiple unknown numbers ringing into her cell phone, disrupting her ability to hear what Deborah was saying.

"Mom. I've got call after call after call beeping in. I need to get off my phone. I will call you back when this is over, okay?"

"Maddie," Deborah said, and it was strained. "Your dad found something. Channel five. You might want to see this."

Maddie hung up the phone and switched on the television in the master bedroom. Then her knees buckled, and she slumped down, hand over her mouth in disbelief, her back resting against the footboard, as she watched and heard some of Eric Nibless' darkest secrets being openly discussed on a nationally televised newscast.

CHAPTER SIX

In his apartment, Mason Gentries had also happened upon the broadcast, and winced, partly from his hangover and partly from what he'd just heard.

"Man," he muttered. "Feel sorry for that guy's family. Their whole world must be turned upside-down right about now."

***

It took four officers each at Maddie's and her parents' residences to move along the hordes of trespassing reporters. Even then, the mass of fact-seekers didn't leave completely, just returned to the public easement side of the property line.

Man, I hope he never looks like that because of me, Maddie thought as she watched Detective Kenney's glowering expression. He was speaking to someone at Flower Mound's police headquarters, and Maddie could tell they were trying to figure out who had leaked information.

"Dammit. You sure?" he huffed, then listened a moment longer, then replied, "Got it," and hung up.

"Well, no one in our department leaked it, Mrs. Nibless," he told her. "Wyoming's officials swear they didn't either. I still need to confirm this, but we think the killer sent at least one network a full copy of the same packet you were sent."

***

Mason left the TV on as background noise while he worked through an idea to try to save both his project and his company. At eleven a.m. the broadcast repeated, using previously recorded footage from a residential area.

The on-scene reporter intoned, "Our attempts to speak with the victim's widow about the revelations that have surfaced have so far been unsuccessful," as footage from the morning's events scrolled across the screen.

Mason's jaw dropped when he glanced at the screen and saw whose shocked face had been captured briefly on camera. She'd only been visible for three, perhaps four seconds. But that was long enough.

I'd know that face anywhere.

After all, he'd been in love with Madeleine Kay Smithing since the fourth grade.

Maddie was in the back of his mind the rest of the day. Mason finally worked up the nerve to try to reach out to her that evening to check on her and offer his condolences, since he knew firsthand what being widowed was like.

But he couldn't find her. All her social media accounts had been closed, and he had no idea where she lived.

She'd disappeared from his life all over again.

***

"I can't do this anymore," Maddie told Kathy after three days of being hounded constantly. "I can't. I want to hurry up and sell the house and just... move away. Far, far away, maybe. I never even wanted this place to begin with. Besides, it's way too big for just me. I want to get rid of it and move somewhere where I don't have to deal with this... this..."

"Bullshit?"

"Yeah," Maddie agreed. "That's the word I was looking for. It's ridiculous. I didn't ask for any of this, and I don't want it. I'm done. The phone rings constantly now, Kathy. *It never stops.*"

"Hey, I just thought of something," Kathy said. "A realtor friend of mine has some cabins he rents out down around Lake Travis. If you want, I could give him a call. Maybe you can use one for a couple weeks until everything dies down. Take some time to decompress before you make any big decisions like leaving town for good, all right?"

Maddie contemplated only briefly before responding, "Deal. Make the call please, Kathy. I think that arrangement just might save what's left of my sanity."

Kathy called her back within twenty minutes.

"He says it's all yours, as long as you need it. And he offered the one that's the most secluded but still close to the water. It's got its own little dock, and the next closest cabin is a good hundred yards away. You'd have privacy, for sure. I've stayed in that one before. It's really nice, Mad. I think it's perfect for what you need."

"Kathy," Maddie sighed, "you're a lifesaver. Now all I have to do is hope no news people follow me out there."

***

The following morning, Maddie put her suitcase in the trunk, started the car, and opened the garage door. *Same stuff, different day,* she sighed to herself as the usual sharks circled just beyond where her property boundary ran.

"Keep up if you can," she muttered through clenched teeth, and pulled out of her garage, pausing only to make sure the door closed firmly behind her.

Then she rolled down her driveway, turned right, and sighed again as three news crews opted to follow.

But Maddie's spirits were high. In addition to her brilliant skills as a realtor, Kathy's natural ability to outthink most people in any given situation was a huge weapon in Maddie's arsenal.

"Here's what you do," Kathy had told her, before laying out a foolproof plan to evade the media.

"I love it," Maddie had grinned.

Per Kathy's suggestion, Maddie drove to Dallas-Fort Worth Airport. The media hounds tailed her, as both women thought they might, so for her pursuers' benefit Maddie did her utmost to make them think she was catching a flight.

She parked at the terminal, retrieved her suitcase, and walked inside. Her followers peeled off, and she giggled to herself as she surreptitiously watched them drive on.

She waited twenty minutes then returned to her car, left the airport, and headed south on I-35 toward Lake Travis and a long overdue break from her life.

***

"I'm sorry. There's nothing else we can do," the cybercrime specialists Mason had brought in told him. "The guy that did this burned all his bridges really well. There's no getting it back."

Toby had managed to not only steal from Mason's company but had also managed to hack and corrupt its Cloud storage – something that Mason could tell both frustrated and fascinated the tech geeks sitting across the desk from him.

Even more damning, Mason's copies he'd been keeping at home were, as he suspected, not recent enough to contain the last-minute breakthroughs they'd had to solve the last few glitches.

Allen knocked, then opened the door before Mason could respond.

"Hate to interrupt you guys, but you're going to want to see this, Mason," he said, his face red with fury.

Allen strode over to the large display monitor on the wall and turned it on, then fired up the keyboard and mouse, navigated to the industry's premier magazine's webpage, and clicked on a header to open the article.

Mason's heart sank to his knees. There it was, in black and white.

Toby Mitting had stolen all their data, all right – and judging by who he was posing with in the picture, he'd shopped it to their biggest competitor.

"We'll send our final report over," the leader of the independent IT team said. "I'm so sorry, Mason."

Once their visitors had filed out, Allen shut the door.

"What do you want to do next?" he asked Mason.

"I'm honestly not sure," came the weary answer. "All of our spare capital was tied up in this, Allen, you know that. We leveraged everything against this one project. I'm not even sure how we're going to keep the doors open, much less try to go after anybody in court."

"You need a break, Mason."

"I can't. I have to try to figure something out, man. I can't just run off somewhere."

"Mason," Allen intoned. "You've been beating your head against this rock since Toby skipped out on the meeting. You're wearing yourself out. Take a couple days, use my cabin. Unplug. Step away from this and take a break. It just might help you reset so you can figure this out."

"Nothing left to lose, right?" Mason said wistfully.

"Exactly," Allen said as he pulled out his key ring, took a worn silver key off the chain, and handed it over.

"Okay," Mason conceded on an exhale. "Okay."

"And if you drink all the whiskey in the cabin, just replace it before you leave, that's all I ask."

Mason grinned for the first time in over a week.

***

By mid-afternoon Maddie was carrying in the small bag of groceries she'd stopped and bought on her way down to the cabin. She put away the perishables, then looked around appreciatively at the small but cozy space.

A modest-sized television with DVD player and a three-tier bookshelf full of movies was strategically placed along the far wall to make any seat on the couch ideal for watching films. Another three-tier bookcase on the other side of the TV setup was crammed with paperback books.

The kitchen and little two-seater table were at the other end of the rectangular layout, and down a tiny hallway she found a double bed with a dresser to her left, and a bathroom complete with a claw-foot tub through the opposite door to her right.

This is perfect, she thought. *Just what I needed. Especially since there's zero cell phone reception in here. No one will bother me at all.*

She pulled her hair up into a ponytail, tucked the cabin key in the back pocket of her faded jeans, and walked the thirty feet to where the private dock began its run out onto the water.

When she reached the end of the dock Maddie sat down on the faded wood. *Too bad it's early March,* she thought. *Water's probably too cold to dip my toes in. Ah, well. Still a gorgeous view.*

Her dock was situated on a small inlet, where the lakeshore tucked around itself a bit before continuing westward into the open water. A line of trees to her right concealed the gravel road she'd turned onto from the two-lane road.

To her left she could just see the dock of the next cabin over that Kathy had mentioned, and she noticed someone fishing at the end of it.

While the person was too far away for any features to be readily seen, Maddie could tell by his movements that he felt quite at home with a fishing pole in his hand. She watched for twenty minutes as her mystery neighbor executed one perfect one-handed cast after another.

Fishing. Man, I haven't done that in years, she realized, then also realized how much she missed it.

Eric had no interest in fishing at all.

What else did I give up for him?

Now that it was all over, memories came flooding back with a vengeance in answer to that loaded question.

Overcome, Maddie stood and made her way back into her sanctuary to cry in private.

CHAPTER SEVEN

After a restless night, Maddie was awake for good by six-ten a.m. She shrugged on her running gear, pulled her hair up, tucked the cabin key into the tiny pocket of her jogging suit, and set out for an early morning run.

A low mist hovering delicately close to the water's surface lent an air of mystery to her surroundings. Her footfalls echoing off the gravel trail were only some of the sounds she heard as she went along. Birdsong was in full swing as the landscape around her came awake.

Sudden movement up ahead and to her left startled her and she stopped, heart racing. When the bushes parted, Maddie was face to face with a gorgeous doe. The deer looked at her for a long moment, then crossed the path in front of Maddie to continue her journey to the lake's edge for a drink. A dainty little fawn trotted along after its mother, pausing only to regard Maddie for a moment with its wide brown eyes before flicking its tail and disappearing, as the doe had, into the bushes on the trail's right side.

Smiling, Maddie waited until she could no longer hear their movements, then began to jog again.

***

An hour later, she'd showered and was making breakfast for herself.

I want to fish today, Maddie decided as she moved bacon around the skillet. *Need to check out this place, see if there's any gear here.*

To her surprise, there was not. But she'd seen a marina and general store on her way to the cabin and figured that was as good a place as any to start.

She finished her meal, washed the dishes and placed them in the tiny drying rack, then drove to the marina to get decked out with the supplies she'd need for fishing.

***

Can't believe I slept in, Mason thought to himself as he sipped his coffee on the porch. *I guess I didn't realize how much of a toll all this was taking.*

He heard a car start over to his right and turned his head in time to see the woman staying one cabin over pulling away.

At least, he *assumed* it was a woman. The neighboring setup was about a hundred yards away by Mason's estimate, so getting a good clear look at someone wasn't likely. But by the way the figure moved, it struck him as feminine.

When he'd arrived the previous day, he'd been dumbfounded to see anyone else in the area. Allen had mentioned that it would most likely be deserted this time of year, so it was with great surprise he'd noticed he had company in the cabin to his right.

Maybe they just needed a break from life, too, he mused, then returned to his cabin's kitchen to make himself some breakfast.

***

The marina's general store didn't open for another twenty minutes, so Maddie passed the time leaning against the dock, watching the miniscule waves crest to lightly kiss the shoreline.

Once the manager flipped the window sign from 'Closed' over to 'Open,' Maddie went inside. To her delight, she was able to buy a rod and reel, hooks, sinkers, worms, and a ten-day fishing license.

She traveled back down one more tiny aisle and found a little tackle box to round out her purchases.

In ten minutes, she was back at her cabin, and ten minutes after that, she was remembering what her father had taught her about how to properly string a fishing pole when using worms as bait.

Her first cast made her laugh out loud.

"Been a while," she mumbled as she grinned. "Definitely rusty. I can do much better than that."

She reeled in her line and tried again. This time, it traveled quite a distance, dropping down into the exact area she'd aimed for.

"There!" Maddie exclaimed, pleased with herself. "Now, we wait."

***

Mason's line had been in the water all of five minutes when he'd heard distant laughter pealing to his right. He whipped his head that direction and could make out his neighbor at the end of the dock.

Looks like she's reeling back in, he noticed. *Wonder what was so funny.*

He watched her cast, and his eyebrows raised. *Pretty damn good throw.* And he could tell she was pleased with it too, the way she pumped a fist in the air. He grinned as he watched her, caught up in her joy.

***

As she made herself comfortable on the dock, Maddie had a sense of being watched. She turned her head to the left and noticed the man was back on his dock again. Impulsively, she waved her hand, trying to ascertain if he was looking her direction or not.

And realized with a start that he *definitely* was when after a pause he raised his arm and waved back at her.

***

The figure in the distance waving at him caught him off guard for a moment, and Mason felt a pang of guilt, like he'd been peeping through someone's window.

Oh, well, what the hell, he'd thought as he shrugged and waved back.

***

After a few bites but no catches, Maddie opted to reel in her line for the last time just after one in the afternoon.

I seem to remember Dad and I always caught more when we fished closer to dark. I'll try again then.

She leaned her pole against the porch, set the tackle box down next to it, and went inside to make a sandwich for lunch.

***

Mason watched her pack up and head into her cabin. *Bye,* he thought. *Maybe she will be back out later.*

And he realized he already missed seeing her out there on her dock, throwing her line into the water.

Well, not her, *specifically,* he corrected himself. *Just.... another human being.*

He'd come out here to unplug, get some perspective. He had opportunity for both of those in spades. But he'd also spent the last six years by himself, and it suddenly dawned on him how tired he was of being alone in the world.

Tired of eating alone, going grocery shopping alone, watching TV alone, all of it.

Maybe it's time to start doing something about that, then, his inner self responded. *You've been barely existing for years now. No one will fault you for deciding to live again.*

And how would I even begin to do that? What, join some dating apps and hope for the best? And what would I even say to any woman I'm interested in? "Hi, I'm Mason and after my family died, I became overly obsessed with technology, but some asshole crushed my dream and I just lost my company?" Yeah, because that'll *cause the ladies to line up at my door,* he scoffed. *And I've never been one for one-night stands, either.*

But I need to make a change at some point, he realized. *And soon. Or I'm going to stay alone forever.*

***

Maddie woke from her afternoon nap – a luxury that she decided she could really get used to if she wasn't careful – then prepared to go back down to the dock and try her luck fishing again.

She pulled her hair up again, throwing on a baseball cap for good measure, then made her way back out to the end of the dock. She rigged another worm on her hook, cast out, set her line, and settled in to wait.

Just as the sunlight was beginning to fade, the end of Maddie's pole dipped sharply.

Hah! Got one!

She reeled in quickly, but the line stripped out. She set her teeth and tugged back against the brutal force pulling the top half of her rod toward the water.

Whatever it is, it's strong, she realized, and paid out just a bit of slack so the line wouldn't snap under the strain before slowly reeling it back in again.

She lowered the angle of her pole, then jerked sharply upward to make sure the hook was set. This caused whatever had swallowed her bait to thrash about even more, and she struggled desperately to keep her balance.

***

Mason, having no luck whatsoever, had just reeled in his line when he heard a yelp followed by a huge splash over to his right. He turned his head just in time to see his neighbor hit the water.

Without thinking, he raced that direction along the shoreline, using his flashlight to help guide his steps in the quickly gathering dusk. He reached the dock area, turned and ran to the beginning point so he could get to the termination point over the water.

Mason could hear the woman sputtering as she splashed about.

"Are you all right? Give me your hand," he said.

"Take the pole," came the response, and he couldn't help but grin.

"*You held on to the pole*? Why?"

"Because I've got a big one on there, I just know it," the mystery woman said. "Here. Take it. I'll be right up."

He chuckled as he reached down and grabbed the pole from her, and she swam to shore then came around behind him down the dock, her waterlogged tennis shoes sloshing as she moved.

"You've definitely got something big on here," he confirmed as he felt the weight of whatever was on the line straining to free itself.

"Y-y-yeah," she said, her face in shadow as her teeth began to chatter. "That water's f-f-freezing, too, I can t-t-tell you that much."

"Why don't you go change clothes, get dry? I can hold on here until you get back, then maybe we can work together to get this thing reeled in."

"Deal," she answered. "Be right b-b-back."

And Mason chuckled again as her squishy shoes sounded against the dock once more.

***

Back in her cabin, Maddie raced to get out of her wet clothes and into dry ones. *That was nice of him to come help,* she thought. *I'll have to make sure I say thank you.*

She stepped out to her car and grabbed her own flashlight so she could more safely navigate back to the dock.

"Hi again," she said. "So, what's the plan to land this monster fish?"

The stranger turned to look at her, his face plainly visible now in her flashlight beam, and Maddie's eyes went wide.

"*Mason*? Mason *Gentries*? Is that you?"

***

He heard his name, and with one hand pulled his own flashlight back out of his pocket and shined it toward her in disbelief.

For what felt like eternity, he didn't speak, just stared at her.

"Maddie Smithing," Mason finally managed to say. "What are you doing here?"

CHAPTER EIGHT

Mason was so shocked to see her that he almost set the fishing pole down, but he caught himself at the last moment.

"Um... hi," he murmured, not sure what else to say.

"Hi," Maddie parroted back, and he could see her cheeks turning red in the illumination of his little flashlight. "So... about the fish..."

"Yeah," Mason, with effort, returned his focus to the reason for them standing on the dock. "The way it's pulling I'm thinking it's either a pretty good-sized catfish, or an alligator gar."

"I thought so too. I remember catching a gar once when I was about eight," Maddie mentioned. "It fought like crazy. Dad had to help me with it."

Wow, her mind raced as she continued making safe small talk. *When did he get so tall? And how is it possible that he got even more cute? I don't remember his eyes being so blue...*

"Yeah. Either way, I think this may take a while. We'll have to let it tire itself out before we'll be able to bring it in, I think," Mason answered.

"Maybe set up something to brace the pole against?" Maddie suggested. "That way we can set it down for just a bit without it getting pulled in."

"I have an idea. Here, take this, I'll be right back," Mason said as he handed her the pole. "Let it do whatever it's going to do, but don't let the slack out."

Their hands grazed as she took control of the fishing pole, and Maddie shuddered.

"You all right?" he asked.

"Fine," she lied, unwilling to acknowledge the powerful surge of adrenaline caused by their brief physical connection.

He stepped around her, shining his light ahead of him, and disappeared into the dark.

***

As he walked swiftly toward his cabin, Mason's brain was on overdrive, replaying what he'd said to her so far. *Nothing stupid, right?*

Nope, don't think so.

Good.

He had so many things he wanted to ask her, to tell her, and he forced his thoughts into serenity.

Calm down. You haven't seen her in almost twenty years. No need to cover all of them in one night. Relax.

But God, she's just as beautiful as I remember – and tiny. Was she always that tiny?

He reached his cabin, rooted around and found what he was looking for, then started back over to Maddie's dock.

***

What are the chances of running into him again? A million to one? More?

And how the hell could I not remember how gorgeous he is?

Her mind's eye replayed seeing him in her flashlight beam. He still had that coal-black hair that just reached his collar, and those amazing blue eyes.

But the rest of him had changed quite a bit. In place of the five-foot-seven shy loner she'd known in school was a six-foot-two, very well-muscled specimen.

Just thinking about him was causing all sorts of very unladylike – and for her, atypical – thoughts of seeing him without a shirt on...

Without anything *on, actually... and in my bed...*

Whoa, Maddie, reel it in, she chastised herself, then grinned at the appropriateness of the thought given her current situation.

His approaching steps echoed down the worn planks as he returned to her side, and she willed her racing heart back into a normal rhythm.

"What's the plan?" she asked, and then cringed inwardly as she heard her voice sounding more husky than usual.

Mason went completely still for a moment before finally answering, "Gonna lash it to the dock."

***

God, that voice, he thought with a barely contained groan. *That whiskey-rough, bedroom voice...*

Hold it together, man.

He moved quickly to rig up the holder, then took the pole from her and fashioned it into place.

"There," he announced. "Now, we wait."

An expanding silence threatened to take hold, and Maddie shifted her weight nervously.

"So, Mason. How have you been?" she began. "We haven't seen each other since..."

"Graduation night," he finished. "Been a long, long time."

"I have to ask – when did you get taller?" she blurted out, then said, "sorry. I just... I remember you and I were about the same height."

***

Mason laughed, and the sound turned her to warm jelly.

"Yeah," he replied, running a hand self-consciously through his hair. "I had one last growth spurt while I was going through basic training."

Well, it looks good on you, she caught herself thinking.

Behave, Madeleine.

"Army, right?"

"Yep," he confirmed as he sat down cross-legged on the dock. "What about you? Last I knew, you were headed off to college."

"I did," Maddie answered as she sat down beside him. "Wound up getting my MBA."

"Nice! What do you do?"

She ducked her head and stared out into the night. "Nothing. At least, not yet. But I have a plan."

"What's wrong?" he asked before he could stop himself.

Maddie sighed heavily.

"Everything."

"Was it the news broadcast?"

She blanched. "Saw that, huh."

"Talk to me, Maddie," he said gently. "I want to help."

And his tenderness undid her. Before Maddie even realized what she was doing, she'd scooted over so close that their thighs were touching, leaned her head on his shoulder, and began to cry.

Mason responded by pivoting his torso and picking her up with no effort at all, swinging her over into his lap then folding his arms around her and holding her as she wept.

"Hey," he whispered against her hair. "Whatever it is, it'll be okay, Maddie."

She clung to him, face pressed against his chest, and cried even harder as he stroked her hair. He fell silent, letting his actions soothe and comfort her in a way that words could not.

After a while, she lifted her head and whispered, "Sorry."

"Don't be, Maddie. Don't you ever say sorry, honey. Not to me."

"You probably don't want to hear about my troubles," she sniffled.

"I absolutely do," he responded. "Whatever you feel comfortable sharing. Might help to talk it out."

"Okay," she said shakily after a long silence. "But not out here. It's getting cold."

He nodded, and gently set her off to the side again, then stood and helped her up.

"The pole's not going anywhere," he pointed out. "No need to stay out here with it."

She nodded. "Let's go."

They trudged up the dock toward her cabin.

"Want something to drink?" Maddie said. "I've got wine."

"I've got whiskey at my place," Mason offered. "And a fireplace. We could dry your wet clothes."

"You know what? Yes," Maddie decided. "My cabin doesn't have one, and I think this is gonna call for something stronger than wine."

She paused at her cabin long enough to scoop her wet clothes up into a plastic bag, and said, "Lead the way."

***

Within ten minutes, Mason was building a nice fire in the grate and arranging the screen so that she could drape her wet garments across it.

He moved to the small kitchen, then joined her on the couch, handing her one of the tumblers containing four fingers of amber-colored liquid over ice.

"Share whatever you'd like," he prodded gently.

Maddie took a small sip, and then a deep breath.

"I met Eric in college when I was going through grad school," she said. "Saw him walking across the quad, and he took my breath away. And I was completely shocked when he asked me out. At first, I thought he'd lost a bet. Eventually I realized he was serious, and I said yes."

"Why would you think he'd lost a bet?" Mason asked, genuine confusion on his face. "I mean, look at you. You're gorgeous."

A slow blush of pleasure worked its way across her features and made her green eyes sparkle.

"Anyway," she continued, once she was sure her voice wouldn't convey the deep want for him that she was suddenly overwhelmed with, "we dated for six months, then got married. And for a while, it was nice."

"I hear a 'but' coming up," Mason commented.

"And how," Maddie agreed. "It started with little things, and it was so gradual that at the time, I didn't notice. I see it all so clearly now, of course, but back then..." her voice trailed off, and she shrugged.

"Nothing I did was good enough. Nothing. Not the way I talked, not the way I dressed, my goals, my ambitions. None of it. And he... wore me down, after a while. I did what he wanted when and how he wanted, so I wouldn't 'embarrass him'," she snarled as she set down her drink long enough to make air quotes with her fingers.

"I gave up on children, because Eric didn't want them. I gave up on owning my own business – an animal shelter – because Eric had a problem with it."

She scooped up the tumbler and took a healthy drink this time.

"May I have another?"

"Sure," he said, and refilled her glass.

"Thank you. And that's the way it was, for years," she continued. "Finally, I decided I'd had enough, so, I went and retained a lawyer. I was planning on leaving. But the cops showed up at the house the next morning to tell me he'd been killed."

Maddie rose to her feet and began to pace. "But wait, it gets better. Two days before his funeral I got a packet in the mail, Mason."

"What kind of packet?"

"It had all sorts of stuff in it. Page after page after page of irrefutable proof."

"Of what?"

"Proof he had not only been unfaithful during our entire marriage, but that he definitely preferred men – which explains why we only had sex maybe six or eight times in fifteen years."

"Eight times... in *how* many years now? Fifteen? Did I hear you right?"

"You heard me correctly."

"Wow. Just... *wow*," he managed. "Sorry I interrupted. Continue."

"There were also documents proving he'd been embezzling from Dad's company. Proof that he was an all-around shit of a human being, and that the last fifteen years of my existence was a complete and total lie. Looking back, I think the only reason he ever looked twice at me was to worm his way into my father's company so he could steal from it," she finished.

Mason's jaw hung open. "I...I don't know what to say, except you didn't deserve that, Maddie. Any of it."

"You're right, I didn't," she nodded in agreement then took another drink that emptied her glass again.

"And to top it all off, evidently whoever killed him sent copies of what I got to at least one news station, and it's blown completely up. Everybody in the freaking world now knows all about his activities, and I've had reporters literally camped out at my doorstep ever since."

Mason winced. "Ouch. That must be awful."

"Yeah," she chuckled mirthlessly. "I had to pretend to catch a plane to throw them off long enough to be able to come here without any of them following me."

"So not only are you having to deal with being widowed," he said gently, "but processing the fact that he was a fraud, as well."

"Exactly!" she slurred slightly. "You know how hard that is?"

"About being widowed, yes, I know all too well."

CHAPTER NINE

"What?" she managed, as she stared at his wedding band. "I thought... you have on..."

"Yes, I still wear it," Mason told her. "But I lost Laura and our daughter Abagail in a car crash six years ago."

The revelation buckled Maddie's knees and she sank down on the couch beside him.

"Oh, Mason, I'm so sorry," she whispered. "What happened?"

"Cement truck driver that was too busy texting to pay attention to traffic, and he hit them so hard our car wound up completely underneath his truck."

Maddie paled as tears began to trace down her cheeks.

"They'd only been gone from the house about twenty minutes or so," he murmured, his blue eyes bright with pain from the memory.

"Laura was headed to her sister's house for a birthday party. I couldn't go, I was on call for work. Sure enough, my phone rang, and I headed into the office. When I got to the main intersection at the end of our subdivision, I noticed emergency crews everywhere, and then I noticed our car..." his voice, thick with emotion, trailed off.

He drained his own glass before putting it on the coffee table and resting his head in his hands.

"And you've been alone ever since," she stated softly.

His head bobbed slightly in answer.

Maddie set her glass down, scooted closer to him, and moved one hand under his chin to lift his head.

When he looked at her, she leaned in and gently pressed her mouth to his.

***

Once he got past being totally surprised, Mason's response was instant.

He snaked his arms around her, lifting her easily and pulling her into his lap facing him. He buried one hand in her hair to pull her even closer as he deepened the kiss. She parted her lips on a sigh, and he led the assault on her senses with his tongue.

He broke the kiss to murmur, "I've always wanted this," as his strong hands roamed her body.

"Be with me, Mason," she said huskily, her entire being alive with want. "Now. Tonight." And she leaned in to kiss him again.

"Wait...what..." he groaned as he reluctantly broke away from her mouth. "Maddie. Are you sure you want to do this right now?"

"I need this," she said simply. "I need you."

"Um..." his mind whirled. "I don't have any...protection with me..."

"Mason," she whispered. "I've basically been alone too. I haven't done anything in over four years. I'm clean."

He groaned against her mouth when she kissed him again.

"Maddie," he murmured. "Let's slow down just a minute here."

She leaned back, saw the conflict on his face, and climbed off his lap.

"Is it me?" she said in a small voice.

"God, Maddie, no. That's not it, at all, I swear to you," he stressed, cupping her face in his hands. "It's just... it's been a really long time. I don't want to be alone anymore. But you are dealing with very fresh trauma, and I don't want to add to it – or take advantage of it."

"I understand," Maddie managed to say, even though she really didn't. "I should go."

Crimson with embarrassment, she stood up and only barely kept herself from running out his door. She managed to hold it together until she'd locked her cabin's door behind her, then let the tears fall at will.

***

Mason sat on the couch, stunned, still trying to make sense of what had just happened.

What the hell? Why did you let her leave?

"I honestly have no idea," he whispered out loud in response.

He launched himself off the couch and out the door.

***

I can't believe I threw myself at him like that. I'm such an idiot. I mean, look at him. He's gorgeous. Mason Gentries could have any woman he wants. What could have ever made me think he'd want me?

Maddie was still sniffling as she started to pour another glass of wine, then paused, considering.

"To hell with it," she muttered, and tipped the bottle up to take a long swallow from it directly.

She'd just set the bottle down and wiped her mouth on her sleeve when a booming knock on the door made her yelp in surprise.

Trying her best to maintain her dignity, Maddie slowly opened the door.

"May I help you?" she said facetiously.

***

As soon as he saw her face, his willpower evaporated. Mason barreled through the open door, slamming it shut behind him, and in three steps he'd picked her up and pinned her up against the wall as his mouth ravaged hers.

***

Holy crap, he's got great arms, was all she could think at first as she ran her hands over them before wrapping her arms around his neck and her legs around his waist.

Mason broke the kiss to work his way down her jawline, then dipped to her throat, nuzzling tenderly.

She gasped as he bent his head down to nibble at her collarbone, and she interrupted him only long enough to pull up her t-shirt to give him better access.

"I wondered what you would sound like, how you would feel in my arms, what you would *taste* like," he whispered on his way down to do just that.

As his lips reached her left breast, Maddie moaned, arching her back when she felt his arousal pressing against her.

She worked her hands between their bodies and was just about to unbutton his jeans when he raised his head to whisper in her left ear.

"You need to understand," he growled softly. "I'm not interested in a one-night stand. Not with anyone, but *especially* not with you. If we do this, I want way more than that from you, Maddie. Are you ready for that?"

Her heart leapt into her throat as she processed what he was saying.

"You what?" she gasped.

"If we do this," he rasped, his voice full of need, "there's no turning back. This won't be a one-time thing and then you disappear on me."

"A relationship," she managed.

"Yes," he growled against her throat.

"I...I don't know if I'm ready for that," she admitted. "It's so soon. I don't even know exactly what I want to do with my life..."

He lifted his face far enough to gaze into her eyes. "Well, I *am* ready for that. So, it sounds to me like you need more time to figure out what you want."

With effort, he set her down gently and stepped back. "And that's what I was trying to tell you before. But you thought I didn't want you, so you ran away from me. I followed you back over here to make it crystal clear to you - wanting you isn't the issue, Maddie. Not at all."

He turned and started to walk toward the door.

"Wait. Where are you going?" she asked.

He turned back to face her, a scorching inferno of want blazing in his eyes.

"Back to my cabin," he said. "Where it's safer for both of us."

And he was gone.

***

What do *I want, really? And why do I care so much what people think?*

When Mason mentioned a relationship, Maddie's first thought was, *Oh, my. What will everyone think?*

But the more she thought about it, the more she realized she flat didn't give a damn what anybody else thought.

I should march right over there to Mason's cabin, and...

Okay, hold on a minute, her conscience retorted. *Why? Because you truly want to have a relationship with him, or just to prove a point to yourself? Which is it, Maddie?*

Does it matter? she fired back.

It absolutely does matter, came the response. *Because the wrong reason will only hurt Mason, and he's been through enough. If you can't figure out what you want right now, that's fine. Just don't wreck him in the process.*

She sighed as she moved to her suitcase, dug out one of the bath bombs she'd packed, and headed into the bathroom to soak in the clawfoot tub – and try her best not to think.

***

I did the right thing. I did the right thing, Mason told himself again and again as he paced back and forth in front of the fireplace.

She's not ready to get into another relationship, and I meant what I said when I told her I don't do flings. Therefore, walking out of there was the right thing to do.

Right?

But the way her lush, ripe curves had felt pinned between him and the wall was seared into his memory. He could still smell the faint scent of vanilla in the perfume she'd been wearing and hear her sweet moans of pleasure.

He sighed, raked his hands through his hair, and continued pacing, because he knew there were only two courses of action he could take at that moment.

Pursuing what I want – what I've always wanted - versus giving her the time and space that she needs right now.

It's as simple and as difficult as that.
I have to choose.

***

After a restless night, Maddie stepped out of her cabin at six a.m. sharp for another run. Mason watched her jog past his cabin, waiting until she was out of sight before he slipped out his door and made his way over to her car.

***

Forty-five minutes later Maddie was in the homestretch, passing Mason's cabin again, and she noticed his SUV was gone.

Hm, she thought. *Probably went into town for something.*

It wasn't until she reached her cabin door that she remembered the fishing pole they'd left overnight. She veered around the cabin, heading for the dock.

Maddie reached down and picked up the pole, frowning when she didn't feel the weight on the line that had been there the night before. She slowly reeled it in and was dismayed to find that whatever she'd hooked had managed to cut the line.

Lost a good one.

She sighed, picked up the tackle box, and walked back up to the cabin. As she opened the door, she glanced over at her car and saw something had been left on the hood.

Maddie set down the pole and tackle box and walked slowly toward her car. She reached out and grabbed the paper bag, then entered the cabin.

He brought back my clothes, she realized when she opened the bag and looked inside. *But that's weird. Why leave them on my car? Why not just knock on the door and hand them to me?*

It wasn't until Maddie took her dried clothing out of the bag that she saw the folded-up piece of notebook paper he'd placed at the bottom.

With a trembling hand she reached in and removed it, setting the empty bag down beside her.

She stared at the paper for a moment, then unfolded it to reveal a business card with a phone number and a short message.

Call me when you've figured it out. – Mason.

She sat silently for a while, lost in thought, digesting the fact that he'd left without saying goodbye.

And it struck her like a punch in the gut.

Maybe I just lost a good man, too.

CHAPTER TEN

"Hey buddy," Allen said when he walked into Mason's office the following morning. "Did getting away for a couple of days help?"

Mason just looked at him.

"What happened?"

"The last person in the world I ever expected to see again was staying one cabin over."

Mason ran his hands through his hair.

"Do tell."

"The good news is, she's single. And just as beautiful as ever."

"What's the bad news?"

"She's going through... a lot right now."

"I'm not following, Mason," Allen said as he made himself comfortable in the closest visitor's chair.

"Her name is Madeleine – Maddie," Mason revealed. "I've loved her since the fourth grade, Allen. And I *know* we connected again for a reason. I can feel it. But like I said, she's dealing with a lot right now. She recently buried her husband, for starters."

Allen winced. "That's rough."

"You don't know the half of it," Mason muttered. "Let's just say the guy was a complete ass and leave it at that."

"So, what happened when you saw her?"

Mason sighed.

"The short version is, I want to date her and see where it goes - and I told her that. And then, I left."

"You left?"

"Yep," he confirmed. "Because she has a *lot* on her plate right now, and the last thing she needs is to try to navigate a new relationship."

"You don't look happy, bro," Allen pointed out.

"I'm not. I want her in my life. But she needs space and time, Allen. Pushing right now will only push her away. It has to be her choice whether we move forward together or separately."

"So, what are you going to do?"

"It's killing me, Allen. But I'm going to honor what I told her, and I'm going to wait and let her figure out what she wants. And hope like hell she calls one day."

Mason exhaled heavily.

"Now, back to business. Any new ideas to save our sinking ship?"

***

When she returned to Flower Mound three days later, the first place Maddie went was to Kathy's house.

"How was the cabin? Relaxing, right?"

"Yes. And no," Maddie answered cryptically.

At the first sign of Kathy's brow furrowing in confusion, Maddie sighed and said, "Got coffee? There's a lot to share."

"Sure thing. Come on," Kathy said and led her into the kitchen.

Mugs filled, they sat at Kathy's kitchen table.

"Now," Kathy began once she'd passed the sugar, "spill it. What happened down there?"

"I ran into someone I haven't seen in years, Kathy. It was... surreal."

"In a good way or a bad way?"

A twinkle appeared in Maddie's eye.

"Well, for starters, Mason Gentries is even more of a hottie than I remembered. He's a lot taller now, too. Six feet, at least."

"Let me guess. He's dreamy," Kathy teased.

"*Definitely*. And the spark between us was instant. I've never wanted a man so much in my *life*."

"I'm not hearing a downside here, Maddie."

"Well..." she paused, remembering as she sipped her coffee. "We started to fool around, and then he stopped."

"Oh," Kathy said. "That's not what I expected you to say, to be honest. What happened?"

"He said he doesn't do one-night stands. If we get together, he wants more than just a night. He wants a relationship with me, Kathy."

Kathy's brows vaulted skyward.

"And you said?"

"I'm almost embarrassed to say it out loud, but honestly, my first thought was '*so soon? What will people think?*' I know how that sounds, but it was the first thing that popped into my head."

"Honey," Kathy chided gently, "you've *got* to stop living for others. It doesn't matter what anyone else thinks. You need to do what makes *you* happy for once."

"I know," Maddie sighed again. "And I've had a thing for him since fourth grade. Like, a *serious* thing. An 'I wrote *Maddie Gentries* over and over again in spiral notebooks all through high school' level of thing."

"Okay, so, go for it. What's stopping you?"

"I know he wants to be with me, but he said he doesn't want to add to the trauma I'm going through. And I don't want to hurt him by getting involved when my entire life is up in the air right now. I mean, I'm not even sure where I'm going to *live*, much less anything else. If I don't even have a home figured out, it's not fair to expect him to just be dragged along with me while I get my life squared away. You know?"

She leaned forward and rested her chin on her hands.

"And there's more. He's widowed, Kathy. Lost his wife and daughter in an accident six years ago. He's already been through his own version of hell – and I don't want to add to *his* trauma, either. As much as I want to see where this could lead, I really need to wait and get my own situation figured out. Diving in headfirst right now is not fair to him – *or* to me."

"I see," Kathy mused. "And based on everything you just told me, I agree with that, one hundred percent. So where did you two leave things?"

"He left my cabin that night, and sometime the next morning he left completely. No goodbye. I found this in the bottom of the sack he left on my car," Maddie announced as she retrieved the folded paper she'd tucked into her wallet and handed it to her best friend.

"Sack? On your car?"

Maddie relayed to Kathy the part about falling in the water and taking her wet clothes to dry them in front of the fireplace in Mason's cabin.

"And when he brought my clothes back, this was in the sack, at the bottom," she finished.

Kathy grinned. "What a great 'meet-cute'!"

"Meet-what?"

"A 'meet-cute'," Kathy repeated. "It's a phrase that screenwriters use to refer to the scene in a movie where the guy and gal first meet."

"Oh," Maddie said, turning a little pink.

She sipped her coffee as Kathy glanced over the business card and note.

"This sure does sound like he's willing to wait for you and give you the space you need, Mad," Kathy told her once she'd read it.

"Yeah," Maddie said, eyes beginning to brim. "And I know I need to work through my stuff first before I reach out to him. But I'll tell you something, Kathy. It really hurt that he just left the way he did, without a word to me in person."

"If I had to guess, I'd say he was trying to spare both of you," Kathy said. "Look at it from his point of view for a moment. There's this amazing woman that he knew long ago that's come back into his life, and he knows *he* feels ready to explore that, but he knows you're not. He probably figured it would be easier on you both if he just left you the note, and let you reach out to him when you're ready."

She reached over and patted Maddie's shoulder.

"So, do that," she prodded gently. "You control your own destiny now, and you have a chance to make a whole new start, Maddie. Find your center again, build your world, and when you're ready, *then* let him in."

"You know what? You're right," Maddie said, a spark coming back into her eyes. "And I'm going to start now. Kathy, help me get rid of the ridiculously pretentious house that I hate."

"I can have it listed and put a sign in the yard by tomorrow afternoon."

"Great! Speaking of that house," Maddie continued, "I wonder if it's safe to go back yet. What are the chances the media have decided to leave?"

"I'd say chances are good, since there was a *major* scandal that broke two days ago with an extremely well-known evangelist who's based down in Waco. They've probably all gone chasing that story."

"Well, then," Maddie decided, "I'm going to drive home and check it out."

As she rose and slung her purse strap over her shoulder, she looked at her best friend and said, "One more thing. I'm going to need you to find me some land, Kathy. Twenty or so acres should do it. And I'd like to stay in the area, so, it needs to be somewhere here in North Texas."

"You going to build your animal shelter?"

"I am."

CHAPTER ELEVEN

In the following months, the future Maddie had originally planned for herself finally began to take shape.

She'd moved to her parents' house only long enough to sell hers. After the sale was completed on the great big house in Flower Mound that she'd never wanted to begin with, she moved along to phase two of her plans - touring some plots of land Kathy had found.

She settled on the fifth location they explored, and paid cash for twenty acres in the countryside southwest of Fort Worth, Texas, with the intention of making her non-profit animal shelter a reality.

The land she chose already had two water wells and electrical lines running to it, so Maddie met with a builder.

"I'm going to live on the land," she told him, "but I also don't want everyone driving past my house to get to the shelter, either."

The man thought a moment, then said, "How about this?" and drew her a sketch that placed her private residence at the back of the property where she'd have optimum privacy.

She nodded her enthusiasm, eyes blazing with excitement, and replied, "Guess we need to go mark the location out and get started then."

She'd also drawn up a business plan, and between the financial backing from the bank, the proceeds from the sale of the house, and the payout of Eric's life insurance policy, she finally felt in control of her own destiny.

Apart from the short layover at her parents' place, she'd insisted on being completely self-sufficient, moving onto her property in a RV while construction of the house and facilities she desired got underway.

***

Mason and Allen had salvaged Gentries Unlimited. They'd been fortunate enough to find a lawyer specializing in corporate theft, who'd agreed to take the case pro bono.

In pulling files together, Mason had realized that he *could,* in fact, prove the origin of Toby Mitting's stolen data. The attorney had a field day in court with the defense witnesses who'd lied under oath and said that Harbinger Inc's text-blocking program had all originated in Harbinger's labs.

When the judge ruled to uphold the injunction barring Harbinger from using any of the ill-gotten data, Mason was overjoyed.

But he didn't know how to contact the one person he wanted to call and share the good news with – he'd never thought to get Maddie's number from her.

Instead, he celebrated with his office staff - all the while wishing he could hear Maddie's voice.

***

Late one September afternoon Maddie stood in Kathy's guest room, looking at herself in the full-length mirror that hung on the closet door.

"I really don't want to do this," Maddie grumbled.

"I know you don't," Kathy chided her. "But you promised me you would, so, you're going."

It was the night of Maddie's twenty-year high-school class reunion, and Kathy had talked her out of her usual routine of being a recluse.

"Do this *one* thing for me, and I swear I won't make you go anywhere else, hermit-lady," Kathy had pouted.

"Okay, okay, fine."

Now Maddie's eyebrows furrowed, and she frowned.

"Does this look all right?" she said, turning around to try to see what the back of the dress looked like.

"It flatters your shape, and it brings out your eyes," Kathy assured her, referring to the forest green wrap dress that hit just above the knee. "You look amazing, Mad, trust me."

For the millionth time, Maddie pulled out her cell phone and his note and started to dial Mason's number - and for the millionth time, she sighed and put them both back in her purse.

I waited too long, she thought mournfully. *It's too late now, I'm sure. I just hope he's not there tonight – especially with someone else. I couldn't bear to see that.*

Kathy could tell what Maddie was thinking by the look on her face.

"Are you *ever* going to call him?"

Maddie sighed. "I'm sure it's too late for that, Kathy. And what would I even say?"

"I don't know. Maybe just speak from your heart? It's not like you haven't had time to think about it."

Maddie shook her head. "I missed my chance with Mason Gentries. Now, I have to live with it."

She looked once more at her reflection and sighed.

"Okay, let's go," she murmured. "Let's get this over with."

***

Mason fixed his cufflinks in place, scowling at himself in the mirror.

I would rather take a beating than do this, he told himself for the hundredth time. *But I told Allen I'd go, and if I don't, he'll never shut up about it.*

Besides, maybe Maddie will be there...

He purposely forced himself off that train of thought. After all, he hadn't heard a word from her since he'd left the cabins that crisp March morning.

Guess she made her decision about her future, and it doesn't include me, he told himself once more. *God, I hope she's not there tonight with someone else. Seeing that would completely wreck me.*

He came out of his reverie and stared back at his reflection.

"Let's get this over with," he muttered, then turned on his heel and headed out his front door.

***

Maddie parked her car, then paused just for a moment to steel her nerves.

Kathy made you promise to go to this thing, but she never made any mention of how long you actually have to stay. So, walk in, take one lap around the room, and leave. Come on, girl. You can do this.

She willed her heart to stop racing as she climbed out of her car and slowly walked across the lot to the entrance.

***

Mason had scrawled his signature on the sign-in sheet, politely took the name tag thrust at him, then made his way to the far end of the long rectangular room where an open bar had been set up.

"Whiskey on the rocks, please," he said, handing the man one of the three tiny red tickets he'd been given at the sign-in table.

Drink in hand, he stood over against the wall, swirling the whiskey and glancing around to see if Maddie had arrived.

A shrill voice to his left made him cringe on the inside.

"Mason Gentries? Is that you? My, my, you got tall, built, and handsome, didn't you?"

He gritted his teeth even as he turned his head and casually remarked, "Hello, Beverly."

***

She signed in, took her name tag and peeled the paper off the back so she could affix it to her dress just under her right collarbone. Then she turned and walked into the ballroom.

"Wow," Maddie murmured under her breath as she stepped back in time. She recognized some faces, not others, and it amazed her to see all the people she'd last been around twenty years before.

"Maddie? You made it! I'm so glad!" a woman screeched as she barreled toward her.

***

From the other end of the room, Mason's ears perked up when he heard Maddie's name called out. He scanned the crowd looking for her.

Beverly Bennett touched his arm, pouting that the richest man in the room wasn't paying full attention to her.

"Mason, dear," she started to say, but he cut her off.

"Excuse me, please," he murmured and began to weave his way through the crowd, looking for Maddie.

***

"Hey, Stacie," Maddie managed to say before she found herself in a bone-crushing hug from a very inebriated former classmate.

"I was telling Beverly just the other day I hoped you would come," Stacie Frios slurred. "You poor thing. How are you holding up? That must have been such a shock, finding all that out about your husband, huh?"

The people in attendance around them got very quiet, watching and waiting for Maddie's reaction.

"It was," Maddie murmured, raising her chin defiantly and glaring at Stacie.

But her high-school alum failed to see the warning signs and continued to barrage Maddie with questions.

"I mean, wow. He was *gay*? How could you not *know* that?"

Maddie flushed scarlet all the way to her hairline, extricated herself from Stacie's grasp, and quietly said, "That's enough," then turned and walked away.

She heard laughter behind her, and picked up her pace, tears threatening. By the time she made it down the short flight of steps to the front door of the building, her breath was hitching in short, dry sobs.

***

"What the hell did you do to her?" Mason thundered at Stacie.

"I was just making conversation," Stacie gulped as she swayed. "Not my fault her husband was a fraud."

Mason snarled, stepped around her and moved toward the door he'd watched Maddie leave through.

"Mason, darling," Beverly purred as she placed her hand on his arm again. "Surely you'd rather stay here and talk to me."

"The stuck-up bitch that made fun of me all the time?" Mason shot back. "Don't hold your breath, sweetheart."

And he wrenched his arm loose and went after Maddie.

***

Mason threw the door open and raced into the night, desperately looking left then right to try to see where she went.

Movement across the street in the parking lot caught his attention, and the lights sprinkled through the lot illuminated just enough that he caught a glimpse of her.

"Maddie!" he shouted and barreled across the street.

She kept moving, never looking up.

"Maddie!" he yelled again, as he broke into a full run toward her.

She stopped, lifted her head, and slowly turned toward the sound of her name being called.

"Maddie," Mason panted as he slowed his gait, walking the last ten steps toward her. "Maddie."

"You should probably get back to your date," Maddie whispered.

"What date? I didn't bring one. Because the one I wanted to bring has had my number for months but never called me," he said, breathing heavily. "And I wasn't smart enough to get her number when I had the chance."

"I started to call you, so many times," Maddie admitted. "I just... thought I'd waited too long, and you'd moved on."

"Moved on? Seriously?" Mason asked. "Wow. But then again, it's my fault for never telling you."

"Telling me what?" Maddie questioned, completely confused.

"You remember Mrs. Caney's class? When we had to memorize the Preamble to the Constitution?"

Her brows knitted together.

"Back in like, fourth grade? Yes, I remember. Why?"

"And you got up there and sang it. You'd made up your own little song about it. Remember?"

Maddie blushed. "I remember. Why are we talking about this?"

"Well," Mason said as he took her in his arms, "we're talking about this because I've loved you since that very moment."

Her eyes went wide.

"You have?"

"I have. I just never had the courage to act on it, until now."

She tilted her head and looked up at him.

"You realize that makes both of us pretty damn stupid, then," she told him.

"How so?"

"Because I've loved you about that long, too."

He smiled.

"So, does that mean you've figured out what you want, Maddie?"

"It does. And it's you," she answered, and stood on tiptoe to kiss him.

He returned the kiss, then picked her up and swung her around with happiness.

"So, what's next?"

"Wanna come see the shelter I'm building?"

"I'd love that. But only if I can show you my place afterward. Come spend the weekend with me."

She grinned, and the sparkle in her emerald-green eyes warmed his heart.

"I'll say it again, just for the record. If we do this, Maddie, I want *way* more from you than a one-night stand," he whispered, nibbling at her bottom lip.

"I know. And I bet we can work out something."

EPILOGUE

The following April, Maddie wore a cream-colored suit and held a small bouquet of roses as she recited her marriage vows to Mason, whose blue eyes were bright with happy tears.

"I do," Maddie answered with a brilliant smile when the time was right.

A few moments later, they were pronounced husband and wife by the Justice of the Peace, and Mason's parents, Maddie's parents and Kathy were all misty. Allen passed Kathy his handkerchief, and she smiled as she accepted it.

Well, well, look at that. I think I see a little spark going on there, Maddie thought to herself as she watched her and Mason's best friends interacting.

"Are you ready to go eat?" she asked her husband.

My husband. That sounds so right.

"Yes, my love," Mason confirmed, holding his arm out to her. "I am completely ready to show off my beautiful bride to the world."

After a long and festive lunch, Maddie and Mason made their escape to the hotel room they'd booked in downtown Fort Worth for the night.

"What an amazing day," Mason announced, as he waited in bed for his wife to appear from the bathroom. "You coming to bed?"

"Just a minute," she said, her face glowing with excitement.

Oh my God.

"Hey, honey," she managed. "Can you come here a minute?"

"Sure," Mason called out from the other room. "What's going..."

His voice trailed off as he came into the bathroom and saw what Maddie was holding out toward him.

"Is that..."

"Yes."

"And... two lines on the little window means..."

"Yes," she gushed.

Mason gently took the positive pregnancy test from his new bride and set it on the bathroom counter, then picked her up in his arms.

"Let's celebrate properly," he growled against her throat, and Maddie Gentries giggled as he carried her to bed.

The End.

NEVER SAY SORRY

Trixie Benning– the no-nonsense Accounting Manager working her way up the corporate ladder. She is highly intelligent, introverted, and for the most part, steadfast about keeping personal and work separated – except when it comes to him.

Drew Alexander- the President and CEO that seems to be her polar-opposite in personality. A confident extrovert with the type of 'love- 'em-and-leave- 'em' history that the tabloids salivate over. He's used to getting what he wants – and he's not happy with being told 'no.'

When Trixie uncovers suspicious activity at the company, she and Drew must work closely together to repair the damage. But the deeper they dig, the greater the danger to them both.

They just might find the love of a lifetime – if they stop running from it long enough.

CHAPTER ONE

"I did it, Meghan. I got the assignment!" an exuberant Trixie Benning crowed into the phone. "The staffing agency just called me. I start on Monday."

"That's great! And knowing you and your skill set, you'll be full-time in no time," her best friend assured her.

"Here's hoping," she said as she kicked off her heels and wiggled her toes to restore the blood flow to her feet. "But right now, I'm just thrilled to have the opportunity. Alexander Limited is a *huge* company. And extremely stable, with plenty of space to advance later."

And boy, I am so ready for stability in my life again.

She blew out a sigh once she'd ended the call with Meghan.

Trixie had been one of the last employees laid off when her former company had unexpectedly been sold to a capital investment firm, who in turn gutted it to its core. Seven years of her professional life, forming deep bonds with great people, had vanished, trashed in a matter of weeks.

Except, of course, for her bond with Meghan, her best friend, college roommate, and the company's marketing genius at the time they'd been acquired. No longer working together wouldn't even put a dent in what Meghan always referred as to their lifelong 'wonder twins' relationship.

Now Meghan was unabashedly following her true passion – being an artist – and already, she'd made some sales of her sculptures. And Trixie was a strong enough person to admit that she was both proud of and a little envious of her best friend.

Wish I could be that brave. I've always wanted to work with animals. Then again, I'm the only financial support I have, so, it's not like I can just dive off into a huge career change whenever I want. At least being an accountant keeps the bills paid.

Her stomach rumbling broke her train of thought.

"Dinner, dinner. What to do for dinner," she thought aloud as she rummaged through her pantry and found very little to work with.

That's *what I forgot to do this week. Make a store run. I knew there was something I missed....*

She looked at the amazingly painful-to-wear high heels taunting her from her own living room carpet and sighed.

I so do not *want to put those back on....*

"Change, then store," she announced, and marched to her bedroom to strip out of the boring charcoal grey business suit she'd worn to yet another interview with yet another accounting firm in town.

She'd been going full tilt with sending out resumes and filling out job applications. The process had consumed her days for the better part of the last three months. With the extreme lack of luck in landing full-time employment on her own, she'd finally signed up with the temporary agency as a last-ditch effort to try to get income rolling again before her unemployment claim ran out.

I have some of my severance pay, still...

Trixie snorted at that thought.

"Not like it was much to begin with, just my unused vacation time and an extra five hundred dollars. And they're *required by law* to pay out vacation, so..." she admonished the hangers in her closet as she hung up her suit and reached for a sweatshirt and her favorite jeans.

Her phone rang while she had one leg in her jeans. She hurriedly finished putting them on, nearly toppling over in the process, then raced into the living room to answer her phone.

By the time she reached it she'd missed the call. But she noticed a new voicemail from Grant, her boyfriend of six months.

She played it back and frowned.

Hey babe. My trip got extended another week. I won't be back now until next Sunday. Hope you can still pick me up the airport. Love you. Talk to you later.

"That figures," she muttered. "I'm sure glad *someone's* career is going well."

She stalked back to her bedroom to grab her socks and tennis shoes.

***

Twenty minutes later she was meandering down the cookies and chips aisle of her local supermarket and willing herself not to fill her cart with junk.

Grand circle of irony, she mused. *Shouldn't come to the grocery store when you're hungry, but you can't eat beforehand when there's nothing at home to eat.*

She sighed and picked up her pace, determined to outrun the high carb and sugar temptations all around her, and heaved another sigh once she'd successfully run that gauntlet.

Vegetables, Trix. Make a stir-fry, even though you'd kill for a potato chip right now.

Resolutely, she worked her way toward the produce section, and was stopped dead in her tracks.

At seven-twenty-two on a Tuesday night, high traffic in the aisles wasn't the problem.

Nope. Not by a long shot.

The incredibly built, gorgeous man currently occupying space in front of the bagged salads was what had stopped her cold.

Trixie could feel her jaw hanging open as she stared at him. He was wearing shorts and a form-fitting muscle shirt, and even with his back to her she was plainly able to see his physique was cut, all the way down to tanned calves. Dark black hair grazed the collar of his blue top and looked so thick her fingers ached to run through it.

Then he turned around, and she barely managed to shut her mouth even as her pulse went into overdrive. Emerald-green eyes glanced her direction, and a lopsided grin appeared, causing a deep dimple in the man's right cheek to appear.

Oh, sweet Lord, Trixie thought, grateful the shopping cart was in front of her to hold on to when her knees went weak.

She'd just about regained her wits when the sculpted perfection in front of her— whom she dubbed 'Super-Hot Guy' in her mind - spoke.

"Sorry, am I in your way? There's just... so many different kinds to choose from," the vision admitted in a rich baritone, and Trixie blinked rapidly.

Say something, you dork! her brain screamed at her.

"I know, right?" she managed after a lengthy pause. "I mean, it's lettuce. How many choices do we really need?"

Super-Hot Guy's smile deepened, causing an equally sexy dimple to materialize in his left cheek.

I can't take much more of this...

He walked toward her, his every move graceful – *like a jungle cat,* she thought to herself – and said, "Exactly. I myself am good with regular old romaine."

Trixie's brain sputtered to a stop when she caught his scent.

Woodsy, with a hint of oh-my-God-he's-gorgeous... Walk away, Trix. Anything you say right now will just sound stupid...

"Question is," Super-Hot Guy murmured as he got closer, "what to put *with* the romaine to liven it up a bit?"

"Tomatoes," she managed, and was immensely proud she'd remembered a vegetable that belonged in salad.

Oh, wait... isn't a tomato technically fruit?

Shut up, brain!

"Avocado, purple onion. Maybe some yellow or orange bell pepper slices. Then..."

"Yes?" he leaned closer.

"If you want to live dangerously? Steak."

"What kind?"

"I prefer filets, myself," Trixie heard herself say. "A little pricey, but worth it. They're so tender."

Now he laughed. "Nice! Pretty much what I was considering when I walked in here. What about blue cheese?"

"Crumbles?" she asked, and he nodded.

"Classic choice, of course," she answered. "And a vinaigrette dressing."

"Of course," he agreed, dangerously close now. "But that seems like a lot to buy to feed just one person; after all, they don't sell single portions of avocado. So maybe we could have the salad together sometime."

Her mouth went dry.

Wow, he's gorgeous and *clever...*

"I... I'm flattered, mister...."

"Drew," he offered. "And you are?"

"Trixie," she answered before she could stop herself. She took a deep breath and continued.

"Drew," she echoed, "I really am flattered, but I can't share salad with you. I don't *know* you, and even if I did, I'm in a committed relationship, so..."

Her voice trailed off as she gazed into his eyes.

To his credit – and her sudden and unexpected regret – he nodded and stepped back immediately.

"That *was* kind of creepy of me, wasn't it? I'm so sorry if I made you uncomfortable," Super-Hot Drew said, sincerity in both his voice and his eyes. "I think you're beautiful, and I didn't see a ring, so..."

He thinks I'm beautiful? she thought, and barely resisted the impulse to look behind her to see whom he was actually speaking to.

Something on her face must have relayed her thoughts, because he smiled again. "You are, in fact, beautiful. Has no one ever told you that?"

She shrugged, unsure what to say.

"Well, you are," he finished. "And if the guy you're seeing hasn't ever told you that, than he's an idiot, plain and simple."

She flushed scarlet and looked down at her cart.

"Anyway, I guess I'd better be going," he said. "It was nice to meet you. Have a good night, Trixie."

And with that, Super-Hot Drew walked back over to the bagged salads, made his selection, and continued on his way.

That was surreal, Trixie acknowledged as she stood there for a few minutes to regain her composure.

And suddenly she knew what she had to do; the craving had been set in motion and there was no escaping it.

She pushed her cart around the produce section to grab lettuce, tomatoes, avocados and bell peppers before heading to the meat counter to select the smallest filet mignon she could find. After that she located a package of blue cheese crumbles and a bottle of vinaigrette. Her last stop was the wine aisle to pick up a bottle of Moscato before moving to the checkout line.

Forty minutes later she was sitting on her couch, her plated salad in one hand, and a glass of wine in the other.

"I hope you're enjoying your salad, wherever you are, Super-Hot Drew," she said aloud, raising her glass in the air.

***

"You're *kidding* me," Meghan gushed the next morning as she set a mug of freshly brewed coffee on her kitchen table in front of Trixie. "And you said no to Super-Hot Drew? Why?"

"Hell yes, I said no," Trixie retorted as she added creamer to her mug. "First of all, I have no clue who he is. He could be an axe murderer for all I know. Besides, I'm with Grant."

Meghan huffed. "I have to tell you, girl, Grant creeps me out. I don't like him, and I don't trust him."

"Why not?"

"I don't know, Trix. I can't really put my finger on it," Meghan admitted. "I just... *don't*. Please, please be careful with him."

"He's a good guy, Meghan, and he loves me. I really think we have something special," Trixie replied, not knowing how badly her defense of Grant would bite her squarely in the ass later on.

CHAPTER TWO

Almost three years to the day since she'd first walked into Alexander Limited, Trixie Benning had just about reached her limit.

She was home for lunch on a Monday from the job she loved – and feared she would lose before too much longer. *I've made a lot of rookie mistakes the last several months. It's a wonder Marjorie still has any patience with me at all.*

After all, as the accounting manager, her company depended on her to get her job done accurately. But lately, it seemed it was all she could do to arrive on time, much less present solid data.

She rolled her shoulders to try to dissipate some of the tension as she nibbled at the sandwich she didn't want.

Granted, she'd had a lot of distractions come her way since January, when her dad's health had begun to plummet. He'd been ill for some time with heart issues and diabetes, but it had quickly spiraled out of control. The dementia diagnosis had come not long after, and that news had ratcheted up the worry and stress to a brand-new level.

Then, suddenly, he was gone. While she'd expected it on some level, it still had blindsided her. But she hadn't been able to grieve yet. As the executor, she still had way too much to do.

Is it still called being an 'executor' when there's no money, just bills? Trixie pondered. *It's stressful, I know that much.*

And, of course, Grant just had to choose the same point in time to start acting strangely. *He's always been a bit eccentric, so that part isn't new. It's the working all hours suddenly. I'm not stupid. I know what's going on. What worries me is, after over three years together, I no longer care.*

"Yeah, that pretty much sums it up," she announced to her beagle, Joshua, who was sitting beside her on the couch giving her the look that meant he was hoping for a bite of sandwich for himself. Trixie tried to give him a stern look, but staring back into those big brown eyes, she just couldn't manage it.

"Fine, Josh," she chuckled. "Here."

The remnants of her lunch disappeared in mere moments. She patted his head, then scratched under his chin.

"I've got to get back, Joshie. I'll be home soon though, okay?"

A wagging tail was his reply as he hopped down to the floor and went in search of his favorite squeaky toy.

She carried her plate to the kitchen, grabbed her purse, and headed out the door to make the ten-minute drive back to her office.

***

Trixie was dumbfounded as she ran the reports again, then cross checked them – again – against her general ledger balances showing. She took off her reading glasses and rubbed her eyes.

Surely this is a glitch somewhere in one of the systems, either my accounting software, or the bank's reporting software.

She logged out of both, logged back in, checked her date selection, and ran all her reports again. Then she picked up her desk phone and called her contact at the bank.

And began to shake as she asked her question and was told the answer that she feared she would hear.

It wasn't a glitch.

Someone had initiated a transaction that lightened the company's bank account by five and a half million dollars sometime over the last seventy-two hours.

She verified the date and time stamp her contact showed for the transaction, then ended the call. Frowning, Trixie drilled down into the user maintenance log, cross-referencing the user ID tags involved in the group of general ledger entries whose total matched the missing dollar amount. And gasped when she found it.

WJones.

William Jones. The CFO. Her boss's boss.

"What the *hell*?" she muttered, trying to process what she'd just found. And she realized there was only one way she could possibly proceed.

She took screenshots and printed out everything that she'd need to show to Mr. Alexander, the President and CEO – including the email confirmation from her bank contact with the details *their* system showed. Then she dialed his secretary's extension and asked if Mr. Alexander had any timeslots available on the day's calendar.

"Only the next half-hour, I'm afraid. Beyond that he's booked until Friday," came the response.

"I'm on my way up," Trixie said.

She took a few deep, calming breaths to try to settle her nerves, then went to the elevator and pressed the button. Mr. Alexander's office was on the top floor.

It's a shame I get to finally meet him, and it's about his top finance guy stealing from him, she bemoaned. In a company of over ten thousand people, and with her starting as a contract-to-hire staff accountant and working her way up, she'd been much too far down in the hive to have any interaction with top management.

But she'd busted her ass the last three years; Trixie had been hired on permanently after eight months, was promoted to lead staff accountant right around her two-year work anniversary and had ascended to the accounting manager role just last November.

And now, on top of all the personal stress she carried, she was about to have to tell Mr. Alexander, in person, that someone close to him had stolen from him.

She had concerns he wouldn't believe her; after all, they'd never even met, and he'd been friends with William Jones since high school, according to the corporation's history section of the employee handbook.

Still, Trixie knew she had to bring this to his attention. *And if he blows it off, well, I'll cross that bridge when and if I get to it.*

The soft ping of the elevator as it arrived at its destination reminded her that judgement was possibly at hand. She swallowed hard, then stepped out of the car into the plush outer office, where Andrea, the CEO's assistant, sat behind a gleaming steel and glass console.

"Miss Benning?"

"Yes, that's me."

"I'll tell Mr. Alexander you're here. One moment, please." And Andrea rose and walked down the corridor.

Trixie thought about having a seat in one of the plush visitor's chairs, then decided she was too nervous to sit still. She wandered over to the window instead to take in the view.

Andrea reappeared in mere moments and stated, "Right this way, please."

Trixie followed her down the hallway that terminated in a single door, behind which sat one of the most powerful men in Texas. Andrea opened the door and stood aside for Trixie to enter, then closed it softly and returned to her workstation.

He was standing with his back to her, looking out over the city as he wrapped up the call he was on; she could see the Bluetooth earpiece blinking.

Trixie remained silent so she wouldn't disturb him and used the opportunity to take in her surroundings. Soft lush carpet of whisper gray ran the length and breadth of the room, all the way to the glass walls that afforded a spectacular view on three sides. The room was tastefully furnished in minimalistic style; a steel and glass desk, more plush visitor's chairs, a conference table and an impressive big screen hanging at an optimal angle to be seen easily from just about anywhere in the space.

He turned toward her as he thanked the person he was speaking with and disconnected the call, and Trixie could feel his intense gaze from across the room. He slowly walked her direction, six feet three inches of chiseled muscle draped in a very well-fitting suit, with coal black hair that went just past his collar and the greenest eyes she'd ever encountered....

Oh, my dear sweet Lord, Trixie's mind stuttered as she fought to keep herself from gasping. *It's Super-Hot Drew from the grocery store!*

God, he's even more gorgeous than I remember... I honestly didn't even think that was possible, was her first thought, and she felt herself beginning to blush despite her efforts to move her brain back over onto a professional track.

He raised an eyebrow, a slow smile coming to his lips, and said, "Miss Benning, isn't it?"

He doesn't recognize you. Be cool! Say something professional, you idiot!

"Yes, sir. Trixie Benning. I'm sorry to disturb you on such short notice, Mr. Alexander, but I've found something you really ought to know about."

"Please, call me Drew," he told her, and gestured toward his desk. "Have a seat."

Trixie sank into one of the visitor's chairs in front of his desk and was surprised when he did the same rather than settling behind his desk. Her nervousness threatened to undo her, and she focused very hard for a moment on her paperwork to steady her nerves.

"Are you all right?" he asked.

"I'm...um... I'm fine, sir. Just not sure how to tell you this." She took a deep breath. "So, I'll just say it. Our operating account is short this afternoon by five and a half million dollars."

Now both his eyebrows were raised. "You mean, a missed entry?"

Trixie squared her shoulders. "No sir. A theft. A deliberate wire transfer to an account I am not familiar with and can find no record of in our system was initiated within the past thirty-six hours. I noticed it when I was doing my daily bank to ledger reconciliations."

She began to relax as she lined out her evidence. "I ran the reporting seven times, sir, rechecked that no computer or software glitches were causing it, and I spoke to my contact at the bank, who confirmed the wire transfer did indeed occur. She sent me an email showing the bank's system details."

"Do you have any idea who could have done this?"

She shifted, uncomfortable with what she was about to tell him.

"Well? Do you?"

She took a deep breath, then looked him directly in the eyes. "I do. I drilled down into the user maintenance logs, and I discovered one set of transactions that total the dollar amount that's missing. Individually, they look innocuous, and I doubt anyone would have caught them unless they were drilling down line by line through the General Ledger module entries. But the total precisely matches what left our bank account. The user ID on every one of those transactions was WJones."

Drew started to protest, but Trixie said, "Here's all the documentation of both my research and what I've just told you," and handed him the file folder.

He took it from her and quickly glanced through the papers. When he looked up at her again, his green eyes gleamed with fury.

"Show me in the system, please," he instructed as he stood and moved around the desk to his computer. With a few quick strokes, he logged in, then said, "Come show me."

She came around to join him behind the desk, slipped her reading glasses on, leaned over, and navigated through the software as she had before, pausing at his direction to screenshot as she went.

When she was done, she stepped back, took off her glasses, and fell silent. Trixie could feel the anger rolling off Drew in waves, but she had no idea if it was due to the theft, directed at her, or both.

Finally, he spoke. "Miss Benning, I appreciate your diligence in bringing this to my attention. Trust me, this will be dealt with."

His tone, while polite, was ice cold, and she took that as her cue to leave. She nodded, stepped around the desk, and forced herself to walk calmly rather than run to the door.

CHAPTER THREE

Drew watched her leave, his interest in her petite, shapely form temporarily overriding his rage. He could still smell the faint linger of jasmine that he'd noticed when she'd come around and leaned in close to navigate through the accounting system. He could still see those full lips and rich brown doe eyes that had captivated him as she'd explained what she'd found.

Not to mention no sign of a wedding band... just like three years ago when I met her in the grocery store... she's not someone you forget...

I wonder if she remembered me?

He shook his head to clear it.

"Not where your focus should be *at all* right now, dude," he muttered, and reached for the phone to make the first of several phone calls that needed to happen. The first was via intercom to Andrea, asking her to reschedule everything that had been booked the rest of the day.

Three rings later, he was on the line with the managing partner of the law firm he kept on retainer. Forty-five minutes after that, he spoke in depth with his CPA firm.

Before he left the office, he sent an email to his traveling CFO, requesting a conference call at nine a.m. Tuesday morning.

***

Trixie got through the rest of her workday with no other surprises and headed home. But before she did, she sent an email to Drew, outlining tighter fraud prevention controls and specific recommendations she felt would prevent any reoccurrences going forward. She logged off her computer, locked up her office, and walked to the elevator.

When the doors opened, she found herself face-to-face with Drew, who looked pleased to see her. She stepped into the car, unsure what to say. So, she kept it simple.

"Hello again, sir."

"I *distinctly* remember asking you to call me Drew," he answered, a grin tugging at the corner of his mouth.

"I remember that," she admitted. "And I've not called you Mr. Alexander since – sir."

He chuckled, and the way his eyes held hers made her knees weak. Fortunately, they reached the bottom floor quickly, and the doors opened, providing her an escape route.

"Good night, sir."

"Good night, Miss Benning."

She smiled, nodded once, and headed to the parking garage, knowing she was going to think about him all the way home.

***

The moment she got out of the parking garage, she pressed the button on her steering wheel that activated hands-free calling, and said, "Call Meghan."

"Hey girl, what's up?"

"Meg," Trixie stuttered, "You're not gonna *believe* what just happened. I met the CEO today."

"Okay. And?"

"*Drew* Alexander. Meghan.... It's the *same guy.* My CEO is Super-Hot Drew from the grocery store."

"Get out! *Really?*"

"God as my witness."

"Did he remember you?"

"I don't think so."

"Small world, huh?"

"*Tiny.* What do I do, Meghan?"

A long stretch of silence.

"Honestly, girl, I really have no clue. New territory for me. But keep me posted, Trix. I'm *dying* to know how this turns out."

Me too, Trixie admitted to herself. *Lord help me, me too.*

***

Once again, Drew watched her go, and savored the light fragrance of jasmine she'd left behind in the elevator. *I wonder what her hair looks like when she takes it down out of that clip*, he pondered. *I would love to find out.*

"Just stop," he murmured to himself. Getting romantically involved with an employee was a supremely bad idea. He'd known men that did, and it had never ended well; some of the crash-and-burn scenarios had made national news. Besides, he had other more important things to worry about.

Yeah, best to leave it alone, no matter how attracted I am to her. It wouldn't be proper.

Drew Alexander grinned. He'd made most of his fortune by being a maverick who wasn't always proper and who went after what he wanted.

And he wanted Trixie Benning.

She just didn't know it yet.

***

The Tuesday morning call with his CFO went pretty much as he'd feared.

"Are you kidding me right now?" Drew was managing to hold his temper in check, but only barely. "How did she even manage that? She's not even employed here, much less set up as an authorized user, Bill."

A long silence, and Drew's stomach dropped to his feet.

"Bill?"

No answer.

Drew pinched the bridge of his nose in a vain attempt to rebottle his rage before the building headache he suddenly had exploded his head.

"Bill," Drew said, slowly and evenly, measuring his words. "*What did you do?*"

He heard a long exhale on the other end of the phone, then he heard Bill clear his throat to prepare to confess.

"Well," Bill began, "I was spending the weekend with Lola, and I'd forgotten my laptop in my hotel room, so..."

"Tell me you didn't. Tell me, William Jones, that you did *not* use your 'girlfriend-of-the-week's computer to access our secure mainframe, then forget to log out and clear the history. Tell me you didn't make a rookie mistake like that."

Another long stretch of silence confirmed Drew's worst fears.

"Bill, I can't talk to you anymore about this right now, or I will say something we will both regret." And Drew disconnected the call before Bill could reply.

Drew paced the length of his office, racking his brain to figure out a solution. *We're pressing charges against Lola, obviously, but what else? Bill and I have been friends since we were sixteen - he's family. Is there a way to salvage that?*

He'd never had to deal with anything like this before. Ordinarily, he would turn to his comptroller or CFO, but the comptroller was on vacation overseas, and his CFO was the idiot whose booty call had stolen from them...

Striding over to his desk, he dialed Trixie's extension. "Miss Benning, please come see me," he barked when she answered, then Drew hung up.

He told himself he'd summoned her for purely business reasons – as his accounting manager, she'd have the knowledge and ability to help the company work through this.

A tiny part of him acknowledged grudgingly he also just wanted to see her again.

***

Trixie was trembling as she replaced the receiver. *Wow, he's mad.* And she wondered if it was because of the theft, or if the mistakes she'd made over the last several months were finally coming home to roost.

At this point, she was fully prepared for her professional life to be in shambles too. Why not? She'd arrived at her house Monday night to find Joshua pouting on his dog bed, and a note on the kitchen counter beside Grant's front door key that confirmed what she'd suspected all along. Grant had met someone else; he was sorry if the situation hurt her, he hoped they could still be friends, blah blah blah. *Wasn't even man enough to tell me to my face. He came by when he knew I wasn't home, packed the few things he still had at my place, and bailed out.*

And don't they always say things happen in threes? Trixie mused bitterly. *My father died, and my cheating boyfriend finally officially dumped me. Only thing I have left is my job, and I get to kiss that goodbye now too. Great.*

As she got into the elevator and pressed the button to travel to the top floor, her self-loathing continued.

Idiot, she chided herself. *Yes, I've had a lot going on. Still no excuse. I brought it to work, let it distract me, and now, I'll pay the price for it.*

Determined not to cry until she made it out of the building and into her car, Trixie squared her shoulders, set her jaw and stepped off the elevator into the lobby outside Drew Alexander's office.

"Good morning, Miss Benning. Go on back, he's expecting you," Andrea informed her.

Trixie took a deep breath and ventured down the hallway. The door was open, but to be polite she paused. She'd planned on announcing her presence but found herself just watching Drew for a moment, taking in the sight of him.

No suit jacket today, Trixie noted. *Sleeves rolled up to the elbows. Work mode.* She particularly appreciated the way his tailored dress shirt molded to his torso, the corporate white enhancing his naturally tanned skin and muscular arms.

Got a thing for strong arms, she admitted internally. *I'd like to have his wrapped around me.* She felt her color rise as her mind wandered off course into very unprofessional territory, little snippets flashing across her brain of what it might be like to touch him, hold him, kiss him...she only just stopped herself from sighing aloud with longing.

Get a grip, he's the big boss! Totally off limits.

Drew glanced up and noticed her in the doorway. The scowl of concentration he'd been wearing was instantly replaced with a wide smile.

He's got perfect teeth was Trixie's next strange and very out-of-character thought.

Focus, dammit!

"Good morning, sir," she said in what she hoped to God was her most brisk, professional manner.

"Miss Benning." To Trixie, the way Drew said her name felt like a caress. He rose and stepped around the desk, then walked towards her, maintaining eye contact, his movements reminding her of a sleek and powerful jungle cat.

He reached past her and closed the door.

"Have a seat," he intoned gently, indicating the visitor's chair she'd occupied during their previous conversation.

She sat, and although she tried not to show it, she was surprised when Drew not only sat next to her again, but brought his chair closer, so that their knees almost touched.

"So," he began. "After we spoke yesterday, I consulted with both our legal team and our CPA group. They've each made recommendations as to next steps."

He leaned forward.

"The next steps the CPA suggested were identical to yours. I was able to tell him that my accounting manager had already made those *exact* recommendations to shore up this point of vulnerability. So, thank you so much for that. I like the way you think."

Trixie smiled.

"Now. As far as the legal piece. Can you please put together the data trail you followed, all your notes, work it up into a formal presentation, say, via Power Point? Speaker notes, the works?"

"Yes," she asserted. "I can do that rather quickly, actually."

"Good. I'll need it by mid-morning Thursday. I have a meeting set with the Board of Directors that begins at two p.m. Friday in Denver, and I will have to be able to lay out the entire scenario for them, along with my proposed course of action to handle the fallout of what's happened."

"What's going to happen next, sir?"

Drew grimaced at the 'sir' part.

"What? At least I stopped with the 'Mr. Alexander', didn't I?"

"You did," he conceded. "Doesn't stop my hoping you'll start just calling me Drew."

Trixie's gaze dropped to the floor so he wouldn't see just how tempted she was by him. "That wouldn't be proper. I work for you."

She could sense his grin widening as he watched her, and it was confirmed when she glanced at him through her lashes. She noticed his eyebrow twitch and was grateful when he relented and moved back onto strictly business-related topics.

"Anyway, the next steps are, I need you to coordinate with the CPA to book this transaction in a very specific way onto the general ledger. His words, not mine," Drew added hastily, hands raised in reaction to the *'you know accounting?'* look that she'd unconsciously let wash over her face.

She chuckled. "Okay. He probably will have me build two new GL codes, one in liabilities, one in expenses, then input an accrual recording the loss. Hopefully we'll be able to make recovery of at least some of it, and we'll just relieve the accrual at that time. What we don't get back we'll expense out."

"Greek. Complete Greek to me," Drew told her. "You guys do your thing."

He looks completely confused right now - and it's adorable, she realized. *In fact, it's hilarious.*

CHAPTER FOUR

Trixie forgot herself enough to tease. "What, hearing about assets and liabilities and debits and credits doesn't fire you up?"

He laughed out loud. "Lord, no. I look at the profit and loss statement, and I glance, occasionally, at the balance sheet. That's about all I can handle of that stuff. That's why I have people who *do* know it."

He shifted forward even further, looking intently into her brown eyes. "Like you."

Trixie held his gaze, seeing admiration, respect, and to her surprise a spark of lust, perhaps?

You're reading too much into this, stop it. You've got a crush on him so you're seeing signs that aren't even there.

She cleared her throat, then got to her feet. He caught her completely off guard by doing the same, which ended with them standing face to face, mere inches apart.

She watched his eyes break contact with hers and focus on her mouth for a long moment before he said,

"Yes, well, I have another meeting in about ten minutes that I need to prepare for."

"And I've got vendor payments to approve, in addition to getting with the CPA and lining out that entry," she replied softly.

Drew pursed his lips slightly, and Trixie would have given anything to know his thoughts at that moment, but she dared not ask.

Instead, she retreated to safe ground, both emotionally and physically, by taking a step backward and saying, "Okay, so, I will have that presentation done and emailed to you by ten a.m. Thursday. Is there anything else you need me to do? Anything else the lawyers or CPA group said that I need to be aware of regarding my duties here?"

"Probably," he told her. "But until the board meeting happens, I'm not ready to divulge anything. Let's see how that piece goes, then I'll fill you in."

An awkward silence ensued as he continued to look at her intently.

"Over dinner Saturday night," he added.

Her eyes went wide. "I can't do that."

"Strictly business, I swear. We'll even expense it," he remarked, a mischievous twinkle in his eyes that made her pulse race.

Did he just ask me on a date? was followed immediately by *Trixie don't be stupid, of course not, you're imagining things.*

"Lunch. *Onsite*. That, I can do," she countered, and his eyebrow raised.

"Don't you trust me?"

"It's not about trust. It's about perception. You're the CEO. I am an employee. Being out together after hours without other employees present would not be -"

"Would not be proper," he finished. "I agree, and I apologize. It was wrong of me to even ask that of you."

Given that he looked genuinely chastened, Trixie said, "Apology accepted."

See? Not a date. Hah.

He walked her to his office door, opened it for her, and asked, "When is Marjorie due back in the office, exactly?"

Trixie's brow furrowed as she tried to remember what specifics the comptroller's conversation about her trip to Italy contained.

"Tomorrow morning, I believe. I seem to recall her telling me the flight back from Milan would be coming in late this afternoon. I do know she logged it on the departmental calendar, so I'll double check that and let you know."

"Thanks. I need to get her up to speed on what's happened. Miss Benning, one more thing. Please keep what we've discovered about the theft to yourself, at least for now. We may have some delicate steps coming up because of this, but as I said, I won't be able to go into detail until after I meet with the Board of Directors."

"Yes, sir," she said, and watched him grimace again. And because she liked his laugh so much, she tacked on, "Drew," at the end, just so he would laugh again, before she walked away to the elevator.

***

Drew sighed as he shut his office door again. He did *not* have another meeting to prepare for, like he'd said. He'd needed to get Trixie out of his office.

When he'd teased her about calling him by his first name and she'd immediately looked at the floor, he'd found himself grinning.

I need to behave, I'm making her uncomfortable, he'd realized, and steered the conversation back onto proper grounds despite the rush he got from making her cheeks tinge a faint pink.

Proper. Whatever.

Being there, sitting in such close proximity to her, he'd been sorely tempted to say to hell with workplace rules and kiss her.

But his gut had warned him the results would have been disastrous. Possibly for him, but more likely for her. As badly as he wanted to pursue something with her, he knew how she felt about such things – she'd made it abundantly clear. Absolutely no fraternization outside of work unless other employees were present. He was intrigued by her, no question, but the last thing he wanted was to cross any line she wasn't comfortable with.

Not to mention, he hadn't seen any signs at all that the attraction was mutual. The look in her eyes when he'd foolishly tested the waters and asked her to dinner was surprise and confusion, not excitement.

He couldn't quite understand what he was feeling for Trixie Benning. He'd been attracted to women before, but not like this. This was different. Deeper. Something about just being around her caused a strange duality to well up within him – attraction, yes, but paired with a soothing feeling of calm in his soul.

It's unsettling, is what it is. I haven't experienced this in a long, long time...

Drew frowned.

Because he knew at some point, he'd *have* to cross that line she'd drawn to find out what was really going on, and they both could face serious repercussions if he did.

***

Trixie confirmed that Marjorie Evans was indeed scheduled to return to the office the following day. She fired off an email to Drew letting him know, then got to work on her regular Tuesday tasks, among them reviewing and approving the day's batch of vendor payments to be sent out. She went through four batches, one for each region, then moved to the theft-related task Drew had described, making sure to include the recommendations she'd previously lined out.

Before she knew it, lunchtime had come and gone. She grabbed her purse and rushed to her car. *Hang in there, Joshua, I'm on my way.* Her little beagle wasn't quite two years old yet and tended toward accidents when he was cooped up all day.

She could hear him baying as she worked to open the front door.

"Okay Joshie, sorry I'm late buddy, let's go," she called out.

He raced her to the back door, whining, while she removed the hard cover over the doggie door that led into the yard. Trixie barely got out of the way as he wriggled through.

That disaster averted, she pulled lunchmeat and cheese out of the refrigerator and began to make herself a sandwich. As she did, she thought about Drew.

And sighed. *God, am I attracted to that man. But I just can't go there. My career's all I've got. The last thing I need is to screw that up by getting involved with someone at work. And he's not just someone. He's the freaking CEO. Even* more *reason I can't do this.*

A whimper at her feet broke her train of thought.

"Damn, Josh," Trixie commented as she gave him a slice of turkey, "I know you just want food, but it sure seems like you knew what I was thinking. I know I have you too, buddy."

His whole body wriggled in thanks for the slice of lunchmeat, and he trotted away.

"Now," Trixie said. "Back to the topic at hand."

Which at its core was straightforward once she set her attraction aside and focused on it using logic rather than emotion. The inescapable fact was she needed to steer clear of Drew Alexander as much as she possibly could if she wanted to keep her career intact.

***

One-thirty found the man occupying her thoughts roaming the eighth floor. Drew had hoped to surprise her in her office and was shocked to realize he felt more than a little disappointment that Trixie wasn't at her desk. He helped himself to a post-it and pen and left her a message, then reluctantly returned to the elevator.

***

At one-thirty-seven, Trixie walked back into her office and immediately frowned when she saw her desk wasn't exactly as she'd left it. She picked up the post-it, scanned it, and paled.

There's been a development. Come see me. – Drew

"Crap," she muttered. "So much for steering clear."

She took a breath or two to steady herself, then grabbed a notepad and pen and headed for the elevator.

Andrea beamed at Trixie when she stepped out into the top floor reception area.

"Go on back, he's waiting for you," she said.

"Thanks," Trixie replied, trying to keep both her tone and expression neutral.

She walked slowly toward his open doorway, then rapped lightly on the frame.

"Miss Benning, come in," he said as he moved to meet her. "Have a seat."

"I got your note. What's going on?" she asked, barely managing to withhold the 'sir' as he shut the door then walked toward her.

"I just spoke to Marjorie," Drew said, as he once again settled in next to her in the other visitor's chair. "She's still in Italy."

Trixie's brows knitted with confusion. "But her flight lands in…" she checked her watch, "three and a half hours."

"I'm aware," Drew said. "Evidently, she broke her leg skiing in Chamonix, and the break was severe enough they did surgery. She said the doctors won't clear her to fly yet. She doesn't expect to be able to come back for at least another week."

"Oh," Trixie answered, eyes widening at the implications. "Oh. That's not good. What can I do to help cover things in the meantime?"

"Come to Denver with me," he said, and grinned when she physically shook her head as if to clear cobwebs away.

"I'm sorry, what did you say?"

He leaned forward to get even closer to her, and her heart did a strange double-thump.

"Come to Denver with me," he repeated. "I was going to take Marjorie with me, but that's out of the question now. For obvious reasons, I can't take Bill. That leaves you."

"But...but... why do I have to go?"

"Because you fully understand accounting, and I don't, and at least one board member will ask some deeper question that I might not be able to answer."

Trixie's mind raced.

"I thought that's what the presentation was for?"

Drew smiled. "That presentation is only a piece of what's happening. It's time for quarterly review anyway, so we tacked that on to the agenda. Typically, Bill presents the financials. Now, I need you to."

Her jaw dropped.

"Miss Benning?"

"Yes, sir?" her voice came out as a squeak, and she flushed scarlet with embarrassment.

"Are you all right?"

"Fine... I just... I need to make arrangements for Joshie."

"Joshie?" Drew echoed.

"Joshua," Trixie said without expanding further. "I need to get someone to watch him while I'm gone. How long *would* we be gone, exactly?"

"We can fly out Thursday afternoon, and the meeting starts at two on Friday," he answered. "Usually, we have a dinner afterward, so we wouldn't come back until sometime Saturday."

She nodded, her mind whirling as she plotted out who might be willing to dog-sit for her. *Damn sure not gonna ask Grant, I know that much,* she thought bitterly, and then realized her thoughts must have been displayed on her face when Drew reached over and took her hand.

Trixie almost gasped at the electric current his touch caused to flow through her, but she managed to stifle it.

"Something wrong?" he asked as he moved closer, his face filled with concern.

"No," she said, slowly pulling her hand back from his and hoping she didn't offend him in the process. "Just... trying to figure out something for Joshua."

"His dad? Grandma?" Drew asked. "Any family in the area?"

Trixie blinked repeatedly as she processed what he had said, then began to giggle before she pulled it together.

Drew thinks Joshua is a child...

CHAPTER FIVE

"He's my two-year-old *beagle*," she explained.

Drew grinned, and his smile lit up the green eyes she found irresistible.

"I love beagles," he enthused. "Had one growing up. Awesome dogs."

She smiled back at him. "Yeah, Joshie's pretty cool. I need to make a couple of calls and get something lined out for him."

She paused a bit, then nodded and stood. "Okay, I can figure something out. What time exactly are we leaving?"

"We'll be taking the company jet, so, whenever we're ready to go," came the answer.

"Then why not just wait and fly out Friday morning?"

"Because," Drew said as he stood up and gazed into her eyes, "I want a chance to go over that presentation of yours, ask you questions, get familiar with it. *Before* I have to talk about it to twelve other people."

"Twelve?" Trixie's voice began to squeak again.

"Twelve," he confirmed. "Why?"

It was all she could do not to squeeze her eyes shut as she willed her heart rate back to a normal level.

"Oh, no reason," she managed. "I just... I don't..."

What are you doing? Get it together, she berated herself. *No need to reveal all your insecurities right here in one conversation. At least keep your fear of flying to yourself, dammit!*

"Don't what?"

"I have a thing..."

"A thing?" he asked gently, with humor now in his eyes.

"Speaking in front of groups... terrifies me," she admitted on a whisper.

"Me too," he assured her. "Believe me. I get the whole 'mouth dry, palms sweaty, knees shaking' thing going. But I've learned some little tricks to help with it. I can show you."

"Really?" she answered. "You have difficulty with it too?"

"Really," he said earnestly. "It'll all be okay, I promise."

She nodded, then headed toward the door.

"Miss Benning?"

Trixie turned.

"Make sure you pull together the reporting to present the financials," Drew said. "They're going to want to review the quarter as a whole, but also each month separately."

"I know," she said. "Who do you think pulls them together for Bill?"

"I thought Marjorie did that."

"She uses my reporting, just tweaks the format. But I know the template she uses, so I can do that, no problem."

"Very well, then. I'll see you tomorrow. Plan on us leaving the office around two-thirty on Thursday."

"Yes, sir," she answered, a small smile playing on her lips as she let herself out.

***

Drew was silent for a long while after she'd gone, staring at his office door and replaying their conversation in his head.

I love the way her nose crinkles up when she makes that one face, he noted, and was grateful to have the room to himself so he could sigh aloud with no judgement.

While he had honestly intended to behave himself and respect the boundary she'd set, he felt it was more than just good luck that had resulted in her presence being necessary on this trip.

And it *was* necessary, no doubt about it. In every single board meeting for the past five years, he'd watched Bill field rather complex questions about the profit and loss statements. Each time, he'd been thrilled that he was only an observer in that scenario, not the one being queried. Therefore, Trixie Benning's coming to the meeting wasn't even a question. It was a legitimate need.

Better yet, he hadn't even had to try to orchestrate anything. While he was worried about Marjorie, he couldn't help but be pleased that spending lots of time with Trixie Benning had materialized of its own accord.

He was still smiling as he moved around his desk to work on returning some emails.

***

Holy crap was her first clear thought as she rode the elevator back down to the eighth floor, then escaped into her sanctuary and closed her office door. Trixie leaned against it for just a moment, eyes closed, focusing on her breathing. Once she felt steadier, she moved toward her desk.

Meghan. I'll call Meghan. She loves Joshie. I just hope she's not busy, Trixie thought. She tapped her fingers rapidly on her desk as she waited for Meghan to pick up the phone.

"Hey girl, what's up?" her best friend said after three rings.

"Well, I just found out I have to take a business trip," Trixie said. "I have to leave Thursday afternoon and won't be back until Saturday sometime. Can you watch Joshua?"

"Gee, let me think," Meghan replied with sarcasm. "Watch an adorable little doggie, or spend part of the weekend by myself? Hmm. Tough choice."

"By yourself? Why? What's going on?"

"Brad is taking Scott fishing this weekend. You know, father-son bonding time."

"Ah. What about Cammie?"

"Are you kidding? She's 'too girly for fishing' – her words, not mine. She got invited to spend the weekend at Julia's house and she jumped on it. She's ten now, so too cool to be seen with Mom," Meghan chuckled.

"You sure? I don't want to put you out."

"Whatever. Besides, Chester will be glad to have his own kind around for a change," Meghan said, referring to the three-year-old basset hound the Smiths owned. "You know he and Joshie are besties."

"That they are," Trixie confirmed. "So. I can bring him by tomorrow night?"

"Sure. As a matter of fact, come over for dinner. I'll make your favorite."

"Ooh! Carne asada and cheese enchiladas? I'm there. What time?"

"I should have it all done and ready by seven."

"Sounds good."

"Hey, Trix, one more thing."

"What's that?"

"What's with the tone?"

"What tone?"

Meghan snorted. "Your patented 'I can't believe that just happened' tone."

"Oh," Trixie said, wanting to bang her head on her desk. "Um. Yeah. This trip. It's with my CEO."

"Drew Alexander? Super-Hot Drew? The millionaire mogul who is so, *so* much eye candy?"

Trixie flushed scarlet again even though she was alone in her office.

"Yep, that's the one."

"Anybody else going on this trip?" Meghan asked.

"Nope. I mean, we're flying to Denver to go meet with the Board of Directors, so, there will be people when we get there. But we're the only two traveling from Las Colinas."

"Oh, my God, you get the eye candy all to yourself?"

"Jesus, Meg," Trixie muttered.

"What? He's hot. And I *know* you think so too. So, what's wrong with acknowledging that?"

"Nothing. Everything. I don't know..." Trixie trailed off. "Actually, I do know. He's the CEO of the company I work for, so doing anything but keeping it professional would be ridiculously stupid on my part."

"You have a point," Meghan agreed. "Not to mention all the rumors."

"What rumors?"

"I forgot you don't read the mags," her friend chuckled. "His love- 'em-and-leave- 'em reputation is well established, if you believe the tabloids. Supposedly he's left a trail of broken hearts from Amarillo to Corpus Christi."

"Ugh," Trixie exhaled. "If there's any truth to that at all, it's just more reason for me to keep my distance."

They chatted a bit more, then Trixie announced, "Anyway, I have to go. I have a lot to do before we leave."

"Yeah," Meghan said with a wicked giggle. "Like pack up some sexy lingerie, just in case."

"*Meg,*" Trixie hissed. "Stop it."

"Okay, okay, I'm sorry. I'll stop."

"Thanks. See you tomorrow at seven."

But as Trixie hung up and set her cell phone on her desk, her mind was already flinging itself down the rabbit hole Meghan's teasing had created.

Thankful she'd shut her door, she leaned back in her chair and just let her brain go there for a minute.

Fantasize about it all you want, but get it out of your system now, she told herself. *Because there's no place for any of it once you get on that plane.*

Plane. Ugh. That'll be another excellent time, she thought sarcastically.

She'd never managed to get comfortable with the idea of being contained in a long, pressurized metal tube thousands of feet off the ground and in the control of someone she didn't know.

A plane ride, then public speaking, and to top it off, being in very close proximity to the hottest man I've ever seen that I absolutely cannot get involved with, she summed up. *This is going to be the worst trip of my life. I just hope it passes quickly.*

She set her jaw and reached for her keyboard to pull the reports she needed to generate. As always, focusing on the numbers calmed her racing brain. She generated the July data and copied it over into the Excel template for that specific period, repeating the exercise with August and September, and then by third quarter to cross-check the figures. When she was done, she had a clean standalone file for each financial period to be discussed, and a cumulative summation to present for the quarter.

In front of twelve people. Just like a freaking jury, her mind murmured, and she clenched her teeth.

***

I wonder if she'd like to get dinner, since I didn't get to see her today, Drew pondered as he wrapped up his work on Wednesday afternoon. And he immediately chastised himself for the thought. *Don't go there, dude. Be patient. You're about to spend two days with her in a proper way.*

Proper. *That damn word again.* He grinned.

But the way I am starting to feel about Trixie Benning is anything but. Haven't been attracted to a woman this way in a long time. Not since Emily.

Emily. Had it really been twelve years? He was surprised to realize it had been – almost to the day.

"Time flies," he murmured, then immediately clamped down on the memories that threatened to wreck him. He turned off his computer, locked his office, and nodded to Andrea as he headed for the elevator.

***

"Auntie Trix!" Scott bellowed as he ran to hug her. "Hi! And Joshie! Hey, Joshie," the boy said in a singsong voice as he knelt down to love on the excited beagle.

"Hey, kiddo. You got taller," Trixie said with affection.

"Yep," Scott said proudly. "Dad says I'm growing like a weed."

Trixie laughed.

"Can I play with Joshie out back? Chester's already outside."

"That's fine. I'm sure Joshua will be glad to see Chester."

"Come on, Joshie, let's go," Scott yelled with the energy only a six-year-old could muster at the drop of a hat, and Trixie's smile grew as the little boy raced to the back door, Joshua's whole body wriggling as he followed.

CHAPTER SIX

"How have you been, Trixie?" Brad asked as he walked up to give her a hug.

"Not too bad, all things considered," she said. "You?"

"I'm good. Listen, Meghan told me about Grant. He's an asshat. I know it hurts, but I think he did you a favor, Trix. He was never good enough for you anyway."

"He is definitely an asshat," she agreed. "But you know what? Didn't hurt as much as I thought it might. I guess on some level I knew it was coming, and to be honest – I'm relieved."

Brad patted her shoulder. "That's good to hear."

"How's the practice going?" Trixie asked as they walked toward the kitchen.

"Pretty well, actually," Brad smiled. After spending several years paying his dues as an associate, he'd taken a gamble and opened his own law office. "Brought on another newbie a little over a month ago, and I've been really impressed with his work ethic and attitude."

"And how is the art world going?" Trixie asked Meghan as she hugged her.

"Fabulous!" Meghan announced as she pulled a pan of bubbly, hot cheese enchiladas out of the oven. "I just started a new line of sculptures Monday. I'm calling them the 'Infinity Refined' collection."

"Nice!"

"Is that Aunt Trixie?" Cammie asked, then squealed as she saw her. "I thought I heard you!"

"Hey, sweetie," Trixie said as she hugged the little girl. "Gosh, you've gotten taller too. Stop it. Stop growing, you're making me old."

Cammie giggled.

"Cam. Go tell your brother it's time for dinner," Meghan said.

"Yes, ma'am. Scott!" Cammie was yelling even before she made it out the back door. "Dinnertime!"

"Wash your hands," Brad told both children. Adding, "Especially you, buddy, since you've been playing with the dogs," as he pointed to Scott.

"Aw, *man*," the boy said before dutifully heading down the hall to the half-bathroom just off the living room.

They laughed and joked all through dinner, and for at least the hundredth time Trixie felt the little pang of longing, witnessing what Meghan had that she did not – a loving husband and children to share her life with.

Wish I could find that, she thought wistfully, and Meghan, sensing her melancholy, reached over discreetly and squeezed her hand, as if to say, *you will.*

***

After he'd eaten his fill of the pizza he'd had delivered – *no point in cooking for just one,* he reasoned – Drew placed the leftovers in the refrigerator and threw away his paper plate. Then he settled on the couch with a glass of whiskey and flipped through channel after channel, trying in vain to find something decent to watch.

His cell phone pinging with an incoming text message caught his attention. He idly scrolled to his messaging app and read what his Aunt Donna had sent.

Thinking of you, kiddo.

Thanks, he typed back. *Love you, Donna.*

Love you too, came the swift response.

But he really didn't feel like chatting any further, so he turned his phone off and tossed it to the far end of the couch.

Leave it to her to remember, he mused. *That woman forgets nothing. Must be in the genes. Cause I can't forget things either. Although this is one time I sure as hell would like to.*

Tears forming, he downed his whiskey and rose to go pour another.

***

Trixie arrived home late, and immediately felt more lonely than usual without Joshua there to snuggle up to on the sofa. Sighing, she stripped off her clothes in the bedroom and climbed into the shower, letting the steam soothe her troubled spirit. She stayed beneath the spray until the hot water began to fade, then stepped out and dried herself off.

Shuffling back into her bedroom, she pulled on her most comfortable pajamas, leaving a towel wrapped around her wet hair.

Ice cream, or wine? she contemplated as she went to her kitchen. *Hmmm. I think ice cream wins this time.*

She retrieved a bowl, the half-gallon of sea salt caramel swirl, and the chocolate syrup and was just about to start scooping ice cream when her doorbell rang.

Trixie frowned as she glanced at the clock above her stove.

"Who the hell would be here at eleven-thirty at night?" she wondered aloud.

Puzzled, she made her way to her front door and looked out the viewfinder. What she saw dropped her jaw wide open. She closed her eyes and took a deep breath before she opened the door.

"What in the world are you doing here?" she asked.

Drew smiled weakly at her from her front porch, then shrugged. "I'm not sure, to be honest," he admitted. "Can I come in?"

"Um... I guess so. Let me go change," she stammered, and stepped to one side for him to enter.

"No need to on my account."

"Sitting around in my pajamas while the CEO of Alexander Limited is in my living room isn't an option," she snapped. "Have a seat. I'll be right back."

"Thanks," he said, and the look on his face was indecipherable.

She huffed lightly, then turned and willed herself not to run down the hallway to her room.

"Oh, my sweet Lord," she gasped once she was safely behind her closed bedroom door. "Drew Alexander is at my freaking *house*."

Her first instinct was to call Meghan, but she fought it off. *No way I'm calling her this late unless it's a true emergency... which this is* – she sighed deeply – *not.*

Dammit.

Hands shaking, she took off her pajamas, slipped into her favorite old jeans, put on a bra – *no way in hell I'm gonna walk around without one while he's here!* she thought emphatically – then grabbed the nearest t-shirt and flung it over her head. It hung up on the towel still wrapped around her hair that she'd forgotten about, and she muttered a few choice words as she untangled the top from the towel, took off the towel, then tried again to put on her shirt.

Hair. I look like a drowned rat, she told herself as she barreled into the bathroom and looked in the mirror. She snatched up her comb and quickly worked the tangles out enough to be able to flip her hair up into a bun and secure it with a band.

There. Not great, but better, Trixie decided as she looked in the mirror again. *Now to get back out there and find out why the hell he thought coming to my house was even remotely appropriate.*

With her nerves only partially settled, she walked slowly back out to her living room, where Drew sat looking very relaxed and at home for someone who'd just barged in.

"Okay. Again. Why are you here?" she asked a second time, hands on hips, trying her best to not sound shrill.

He raised his hands, then let them fall to his lap. "I just... I didn't want to be alone tonight, and you were the first one I thought of."

She sensed his grief, and it struck her heart. She moved and sat in the chair next to the couch. "Are you all right?"

"Nope," Drew announced. "Not even close."

"Did something happen?"

He looked at her, and the sadness in his eyes burned right through her.

"You could say that. Got any ice cream?"

"What?"

"Ice cream. I tried whiskey earlier, but it didn't help, so now I'm thinking ice cream."

She smiled despite her irritation.

"As a matter of fact, I do," Trixie said. "Follow me."

He lurched to his feet, and she noticed his wobble.

"How much whiskey did you have?"

"Dunno. Five, six, seven glasses. Maybe more. Stopped counting."

"And you *drove*?"

"Nope. Uber."

Which means I get to figure out how to get him home. Great, Trixie realized.

"I usually go see Bill. I can't see Bill this time," he slurred as he followed her into the kitchen. "On account of he's a jackass."

"I see," she said.

But she didn't. She had no clue why this man – gorgeous, charming, and usually completely in control of himself– would be bobbing and swaying and grinning at her like an idiot in her kitchen at almost midnight.

She got out one more bowl and another spoon, scooped ice cream up for each of them, then turned to him.

"Want chocolate syrup?"

"Absolutely," Drew nodded enthusiastically.

She added the syrup then walked over to her dinette table and set the bowls down.

"There you go. I'll be there in just a second," she directed as she put the ice cream and syrup away.

Once she'd settled in across from him at the tiny table, she looked at him.

"Mr. Alexander.... Drew," she said gently. "Why are you here? What happened tonight?"

He was silent for a moment as he took another bite of his ice cream. Then he set his spoon down and stared into her eyes.

"I killed somebody."

"*What*?" Trixie thundered. "What the hell do you mean you killed somebody? Tonight?"

Drew shook his head vigorously. "Not tonight. Twelve years ago. It was an accident, but I still killed somebody," he said, and his eyes filled with tears.

She held his gaze. "Tell me," she said softly.

"Emily. My girlfriend," he began dully. "I took her to my uncle's ranch that weekend, as a surprise. I was gonna propose. Talked her into riding a horse for the first time. She was terrified of horses, but she finally agreed to try it, for me."

Drew ran his hands through his hair and took a deep shuddering breath, then continued.

"The horse she was on got spooked and reared up. She fell off, but she still had a hold of the reins.... she fell off and it pulled the horse backward, and he landed on her. She died in my arms, Trixie. Emily died in my arms. *And it's all my fault.*" And he laid his head on Trixie's wooden kitchen table and wept.

Trixie stood and slowly walked to his side, then started to lean down to wrap her arms around him. But he sensed her beside him, pivoted and clung to her, wrapping his arms tightly around her waist. She held him close, stroked his hair, and tried her best to comfort him as he grieved.

"It wasn't your fault, Drew," she murmured with tears in her own eyes as her heart broke for him. "Listen to me. It was an accident. It was a horrible accident, not your fault at all."

He didn't answer, only tightened his grip around her, and she continued to soothe him as best she could. Eventually his shoulders shook less and less, and he released her.

"I'm sorry. I shouldn't have come here. I...I should go," he managed, staggering to his feet.

"I'll take you home, if you want," she offered. "But you don't have to leave yet, if you don't want to."

He looked at her intently.

"What are you thinking right now?" she asked him on impulse.

Drew stepped toward her, and she instinctively stepped backward, her pulse racing. He took another step, then another, until Trixie was backed up against her kitchen counter. He closed the distance, never breaking eye contact, until his face was just a few inches from hers.

*Surely, he's not going to...*was all she had time to think when she noticed he'd begun staring at her mouth before his lips were on hers. Drew wrapped his arms around her and pulled her tight against him. She moaned and as she did, unwittingly gave him access with his tongue, which made her moan again. Trixie's hands traveled his chest, reveling in his muscular frame before fisting themselves in his hair to draw him in deeper.

Meanwhile his hands were doing some exploring of their own, running down her sides, traveling up to her breasts, then back down and around to cup her backside and pull her in so closely she could feel his arousal grinding against her.

And then it struck her – *I am standing in my kitchen kissing my CEO and his hands are on my ass. What the hell is wrong with me?*

With effort, she pushed away from him just as he slid one hand around to work the button loose on her favorite faded jeans, and they both panted as they stared each other down.

CHAPTER SEVEN

"We can't do this," she managed, her chest heaving. "We can't. I work for you."

"Right now, I don't care," Drew answered, his green eyes blazing with whiskey, unshed tears, and desire. "I want you."

"I want you too," she admitted. "But we can't do this. It's... dangerous. For both of us."

"You don't understand. I haven't been this interested in a woman in forever," Drew told her. "Twelve years, to be exact."

Trixie's eyes went wide.

"But... but... you don't even *know* me," she stammered. "Or anything about me."

"But I want to," he countered. "I haven't been able to get you out of my brain since you walked into my office."

Despite her best efforts she could feel herself blushing with pleasure. *Well, well. Guess it's not one-sided after all.*

Shut up, her self-preservation side hissed. *You do NOT need to get involved with the man who owns the company you work for. End of story. He needs to leave before you do something even more stupid than kiss him.*

"Mr. Alexander-"

He held up a hand. "I'm not so drunk that I don't remember you feeding me ice cream and us kissing and how nice your ass feels in my hands. I think we're past 'Mr. Alexander' now. Don't you?"

She stood upright and jutted out her chin. "That was a mistake, and it doesn't need to happen again."

Drew sighed, then ran his fingers through his hair again. "You're serious."

"Completely," she confirmed. "I cannot afford to be involved with *anyone* at work, but especially you.

My career is all I have left. Now. Shall I drive you home, or would you rather call another Uber?"

"I'll call for an Uber," he said as he swayed just a little. "May I use your phone? Mine's on my couch. I think. I hope it is, anyway," he finished as he patted his pockets and frowned.

"Never mind. I'll take you home," Trixie rolled her eyes in exasperation. "Come on."

Twenty minutes later she parked in his driveway and waited patiently on the front porch beside him as he fumbled to get the key into the lock on his front door. He finally waved with glee at her once he successfully opened it.

"Wanna come in?" he slurred lightly. "I promise to behave myself. Mostly."

"I need to go," she told him gently. "But thank you. Go to sleep. See you in the morning, okay?"

"Okay. You're gorgeous. Did you know that?"

"Um...," she stammered, and flushed red.

Should have let him take an Uber. I might never get out of here.

"Thank you," she said quietly. "But you need to go get some sleep. We have work tomorrow. All right?"

"Okay," Drew nodded. "Bye."

And he stepped inside and without looking back walked to his room. Trixie walked in far enough to grab the front door he'd left wide open and gasped.

Her CEO was stripping his clothes off and tossing them aside as he made his way through what looked to be a living room. By the time he'd reached the other side, only his underwear remained. He shucked them, turned around, waved to her wearing nothing but a goofy smile, and then continued on his way.

Holy crap that man is built, was all she could think.

Beet red at the eyeful she'd gotten, Trixie swiftly turned the little raised section of the door handle so that it would lock behind her and closed his front door firmly. She made it back behind the wheel of her car before she started to giggle.

***

The alarm sounding at five-twenty a.m. pierced Drew's skull like a screwdriver, and he reached out a hand to beat it into submission. He yawned, stretched, then gingerly opened his eyes and looked around.

Good. I didn't bring some stranger home. That's an improvement over some years, anyway, he told himself before slowly sitting upright to minimize the cacophony of drums pounding in his head.

He flung the covers back and staggered toward the shower, running his tongue over teeth that felt fuzzy and tasted like whiskey...and salt... and caramel?

He frowned.

Did I eat salted caramel last night? And why do I feel like I did spend time with someone?

He'd been under the shower spray for almost ten minutes when he remembered some of the previous night's events. A fragment of something Trixie had said floated to the surface of his memory.

It's dangerous... My career is all I have left...

"Man," he muttered in frustration. "I'm such an ass."

***

Trixie laid her suitcase on the bed and carefully packed her two best suits for the meeting in Denver and the dinner afterward. She paused, considering for a moment, then also gently placed an additional outfit suitable for a night out on the town. Next came socks, underwear, her pajamas and robe, as well as a casual outfit of jeans, t-shirt, and a light sweater, in addition to a swimsuit in the event the hotel had a pool or sauna. She briefly recalled Meghan's joking about frilly underwear, then shoved it out of her mind as she remembered the previous night's events with Drew.

The whole thing last night was just... surreal. Like a dream.

When she woke, that's what she'd thought at first – that it had all been a dream.

Until she'd gone into the kitchen and seen two bowls sitting in her sink, traces of chocolate syrup still visible around the rims.

Please, dear God, don't let this trip be awkward. I hope like hell he has no recollection of last night.

Once she'd arrived in the parking garage at work, she made her way to the lobby elevators, her eyes darting around for any sign of him. Trixie half expected the man to be waiting outside her office door and was pleased but also somehow disappointed when he wasn't.

She unlocked her door, flipped on the light, fired up her computer, and tried her best to concentrate on the day ahead. But she found herself glancing at her desk phone and her email to see if Drew had reached out.

Zero on both counts.

***

Drew resisted the urge to show up in her office doorway, shut the door behind him, and beg her forgiveness for his behavior.

Or kiss her.

Or both.

Instead, he purposely gave her space until it was almost time to go, then dialed her extension.

"Are you ready? Our ride will be here in fifteen minutes," he said.

"I need to get my suitcase from my car. Meet you out front, I guess?"

"Yes." And he hung up the phone before he said anything inappropriate.

***

She stared at the receiver. *Well, that was interesting. Kind of cold, too. Guess he realized last night was a mistake.* And was frustrated to realize that disappointed her a little.

Trixie logged off her desktop unit, picked up her laptop bag and purse, and closed her office door. The trip down to her vehicle was uneventful and before long she was striding back across the lobby level to get to the front steps of the building.

She was genuinely surprised when she saw Drew standing beside a limo. *I thought we'd be taking another Uber. So much for that.*

Drew's back was to her, and she let her eyes roam over him for a moment, remembering how his touch felt – and exactly how gorgeous the man was in his altogether. Then he turned, those piercing green eyes filled with... what exactly, she couldn't tell, and she couldn't risk letting her guard down enough to find out. With effort she composed herself, avoiding eye contact and working her face into what she hoped was a normal expression.

"Here, miss, let me get that for you," the driver said, reaching for her bags as Trixie came down to curb level.

She felt Drew's stare and was grateful for someone else to interact with.

"Thanks. What's your name?"

"Jack."

"Thanks, Jack. I'm Trixie. It's nice to meet you."

Jack smiled. "Nice to meet you, too," he replied, as he held the car door open for her and assisted her into the back seat. Drew walked around and got in beside her while Jack placed the luggage in the trunk.

"Would you like something to drink?" Drew asked. "We keep the bar in here stocked."

"Water, please," she answered, then turned her head to look out the window and willed her heart to quit beating quite so fast.

This is what you wanted, Trix, she reminded herself. *To keep him at arm's length. To remain strictly professional in your interactions. It's for the best. You know that.*

So why did it feel like she was dying inside?

***

Drew grimaced as Trixie accepted the water bottle with a curt nod, then turned back toward the window, her face a mask that gave away nothing.

She's closed off. And she's sitting as far away from me as she can. What the hell did I do last night? Although he could remember most of it, some parts were still fuzzy.

They rode to the airstrip in silence. Drew wanted to be the one to extend his hand to help her out of the car just so he'd have an excuse to touch her. But Jack, his very capable driver for the last seven years, beat him to it.

He clenched his fists and willed himself to act casually.

Maybe I can get her to talk to me during the flight. It can't stay this way between us the whole trip.

When he gestured for her to go first up the short flight of stairs into the plane, she nodded briefly, then grabbed the handrail tightly and made her ascent. Drew noticed the way Trixie's knuckles turned white and realized something else about the woman that already had him fascinated.

I'll bet all my money that she's afraid of flying. And she'll probably try her best not to let it show.

When he ducked and entered the plane's cabin, he immediately turned left toward the cockpit. After a moment, two men followed him back into the passenger area.

"Miss Benning, I thought you might like to meet our pilots. This is Thom Jenkins and Danny Oliva. They've been with me, what, gentlemen, five years now?"

Both men smiled and nodded.

"They're the absolute best, and I trust them implicitly. I just thought you'd like to know who's getting us to our destination."

He watched as Trixie stepped forward, extending a lightly trembling hand to each pilot.

"Hello there, it's nice to meet you. I'm Trixie," she paused, cutting a quick glance over to Drew, "and... um... I don't like flying. Makes me feel a bit better that I at least know who's behind the wheel of this thing."

Hah. I was right, Drew congratulated himself. *Now I need to be that observant about the rest of it where she's concerned.*

Thom and Danny both chuckled.

"If it makes any difference, Trixie, *we* don't like flying when someone else is behind the wheel either," Thom said with a grin as Danny nodded his agreement.

She laughed. "Actually, that does help, thanks."

"Have a seat anywhere you like," Danny said. "We need to get through the rest of our pre-flight checks, and then we can get going."

Both pilots nodded to her, then returned to the cockpit.

"Good call," Trixie finally spoke directly to Drew. "How did you know?"

"You gripped the rail so hard your knuckles turned white."

"Oh," she said, and her brown eyes widened as she blushed just a bit. "Gave myself away, I guess."

It was all he could do not to close the distance and plant a kiss on those full lips.

She looked around and chose one of the seats away from any windows and facing the rear of the cabin, buckling herself in and pulling the strap as hard as she could.

With a grin, Drew sat down beside her and fastened his seat belt too.

"It's going to be okay, you know," he told her. "I used to be terrified of flying. But at one point, growing my company meant I had no choice but to be on a plane several times a week. After a while, I just... got past it. I've probably logged over two million miles in the last five years."

When the steps raised and the cabin door closed, she shuddered, and when the sleek jet began to roll toward the runway to get in line for departure, her hands formed a death grip on her armrests.

CHAPTER EIGHT

"Trixie. It's okay. I'm here," Drew said, extending his hand.

She clutched it.

"Okay," she whispered.

"How many times have you flown?"

"Two. Including this one," she managed, going pale as the jet accelerated down the runway.

"Look at me. Trixie. *Look at me*," Drew urged. "Focus on me."

She slowly pivoted her head and locked eyes with him, and he could see terror building in hers that seemed to deepen their color from a chocolate brown to almost black when the plane's wheels left the ground.

On instinct, he leaned toward her until their foreheads were touching, maintaining eye contact as he whispered, "Breathe, Trixie. Come on. Deep breaths. In through your nose, out through your mouth. You got this."

She nodded against his forehead, then closed her eyes and focused on her breathing. A thumping sound reverberating through the plane made her yelp, and he murmured, "It's the landing gear coming up, that's all. Perfectly normal. Okay? You're doing great," as he stroked her cheek with the hand that wasn't being squeezed by hers.

Once the plane leveled off, she opened her eyes again.

"It's safe to move around now. Would you like some wine?"

"Whiskey and water," she said immediately, her voice trembling.

Drew grinned. "A woman after my own heart."

He left her side long enough to make the drinks, handing her one as he sat down again.

"I didn't cut off your circulation, did I?"

"Nope," Drew demonstrated by wiggling his fingers. "But I must say you have a hell of a grip for such a tiny little thing."

A smile flittered across her features as she took a sip of her drink.

Good. That's one. Maybe I can get her to smile some more.

"Are you feeling any better?"

"A bit," Trixie said, and he guessed the warmth of the whiskey was working through her system since she seemed to be more relaxed. "If I'd been thinking straight, I'd have had a couple of these *before* we got on the plane. Then maybe I wouldn't have embarrassed either of us by being so high maintenance."

"You didn't embarrass me, or yourself, for that matter. And you are the least high maintenance woman I've ever met."

"Wait until you get to know me," she said with a grin.

"I'd like to do just that," he countered, leaning toward her and gazing at her. "Very much. So. Let's talk about last night, for starters."

***

Crap, Trixie groaned internally. *What the hell did I say that for? 'Wait until you get to know me'? Seriously? That is the* last *thing that needs to happen between us.*

She looked up and met his gaze, her brain scrambling furiously as she sought a way out of the predicament her big mouth had just gotten her into.

"Oh," was all she could manage, as her brow furrowed, and her nose crinkled. "I... I don't think that's a good idea. At all."

"I do," he said, that unreadable expression in his eyes back in place. "And I'll start."

She sighed. "Okay, go ahead. After all, it's not like I can run away anywhere," she muttered, sweeping her hands around the cabin.

Drew chuckled. "Nope. And I think we need to talk it out."

He ran a hand over his face. "I remember most of it, I think. Things like, I showed up at your door unannounced and uninvited. I was amazed you even let me in."

"Me too," she admitted wryly. "Keep going."

"You had on cute pajamas. Those were teddy bears, right?"

She flushed scarlet and took a large gulp of whiskey.

"I take it that's a yes. And you fed me ice cream."

"With chocolate syrup," Trixie confirmed.

"And then, it's kinda fuzzy. I remember being in some random guy's car, then I woke up in my bed. But I feel like there's some things I missed. Some really big things."

"Um... yes," she said.

"Like what?"

"Well, you were in some random guy's car on the way *to* my house, but I took you home."

Trixie paused. *Should I mention the rest? How honest should I be?*

"I told you about... about Emily..."

She nodded. "And I meant what I told you about that. It wasn't your fault. It was an accident."

Just when she thought she was safe he suddenly blurted out, "I kissed you, didn't I?"

She nodded again, staring into her glass, wishing she could disappear inside it.

"For the record, I don't regret last night."

Her eyebrow raised. "Which part?"

Drew framed her face in his hands so that she had no choice but to look him in the eye. "Any of it."

Her mouth went dry.

"I remember you said something about your career was all you had left. What did you mean?"

"I really don't want to talk about this anymore," she whispered.

"Trixie. Let me in."

"I can't," her voice faltered as she began to panic.

"What are you so afraid of?"

"Nothing. Everything. I don't know. I... I can't do this," she pleaded, scrambling to undo her seat belt.

She stood and moved quickly toward the lavatory at the back of the cabin, willing herself to hold it together long enough to get the tiny door shut behind her. Her knees finally gave way and she buckled to the floor, tears streaming, her breath escaping her body in hard, racking sobs.

***

Drew watched, stunned, as Trixie lurched to her feet and almost ran to get away from him. After the lavatory door closed, he heard a thud, then what sounded like... crying?

He stood and quietly moved over to the door, listening intently.

No. Not just crying. Sobbing. Like her heart's broken.

The revelation pierced his soul, and he fought the almost overwhelming urge to wedge his way into the tiny cubicle and rock her in his arms.

But deep down he knew she'd never accept that. Instead of drawing them closer together, invading her space that way would only widen the gap between them. He reluctantly returned to his seat to wait.

But I promise you this, Trixie Benning, he told her silently. *I'll wait however long it takes for you to let me in.*

***

She reappeared after twenty minutes, her face as pale as it could be, and the only evidence of the tears he had heard were eyes that were a little red around the edges. She took a seat at the far end of the cabin from him, buckled her lap belt, and stared out the window, never once looking his direction.

It was a knife in his gut.

When the plane began its descent ten minutes later and she opted to endure her terror alone rather than let him help her through it, the knife twisted.

The ride from the airstrip to the hotel passed in silence, as did most of the check-in process. She received her room key from the woman at the registration desk, thanked her politely, and immediately proceeded to her assigned room on the eleventh floor without a backward glance.

Drew gave the woman at the counter his best smile and managed to get his room assignment changed to number 1110 - the suite adjoining Trixie's.

He wasn't fast enough to see her in the hallway of the eleventh floor, and his shoulders sagged as he let himself into his room. He went through the routine of unpacking his suitcase, then poured himself a double to keep him company as he paced the floor.

What does she need? What can I do to get her to trust me?

And why does it even matter to me so much?

The answer hit him like a two-by-four, buckled his knees and caused him to land heavily in the overstuffed armchair in his suite.

Because I think I'm falling in love with her.

***

Trixie unpacked her things, then headed for a nice long shower. As she ducked her head under the spray, she replayed the events of the plane ride.

Stupid, stupid, stupid. Fell apart. Not just fell apart. Fell apart in front of the big boss. The trip's not even four hours in, and I'm a complete mess.

And I owe him an explanation, at least.

The idea of that made her nauseous.

Why can't I just gloss it over, not talk about it?

But she knew the answer.

In just four days, he'd managed to get too close for comfort. Already, he was filling her thoughts, getting under her skin, working his way past her defenses - especially after the way he'd helped her through the flight. She'd never experienced a man so sincere. So tender. Between that, his kiss, and seeing his vulnerable side the night before, the heart she'd sworn to keep safely tucked away was in serious jeopardy of being stolen by Drew Alexander.

This isn't done. I have to face it. He deserves that much. And then? What happens after that?

She wished she knew.

***

Drew waited almost an hour before he screwed up the courage to go knock on her door, then held his breath, hoping against hope she'd answer.

The door to suite 1108 creaked as it opened, and there she stood. For a moment, he just gazed at her, taking in the way her long brown hair flowed across her shoulders.

She always wears it up. I wonder if it's as soft as it looks.

Those brown eyes he could lose himself in looked back at him expectantly as he searched for something to say, anything that wouldn't make her shut the door in his face.

After a moment that seemed to stretch into eternity, she broke the silence.

"We need to talk," Trixie said, her voice quaking. "Please come in."

***

He nodded and stepped inside. She closed and latched the door, then gestured to the couch in the sitting area.

"Drink?" she offered.

"Sure," Drew responded. "Just water, though."

She nodded, filled two glasses with ice and water from the bar, handed him one, then settled in at the other end of the couch from him.

"I'm sorry I ran away from you," Trixie said after a long pause. "That was wrong."

"Don't be sorry. I overwhelmed you, maybe. It wasn't my intention."

"You didn't," she smiled ruefully. "*I* did. And I think you deserve to know why."

She sighed and swirled her drink around absentmindedly.

"My mother and two little sisters were killed in a car accident when I was ten," she revealed with no warning. "My dad took it... well, let's just say, really hard."

She swallowed the lump that had formed in her throat.

"More accurate to say that the best parts of him left me when they did. It was like he'd died, too. He was never the same. He made sure I had what I needed, like clothes and food, but he never laughed again, never smiled again, we never really talked anymore. He worked, and he drank, and he visited the cemetery three times a week. Spent more time there than he did with me."

"I'm so sorry," Drew said tenderly.

She nodded her appreciation, then took a deep breath.

"Anyway, when I was sixteen, we had a falling out, and I left. I rotated through staying with friends and I talked my school into letting me double up on classes so I could graduate early. Then I put myself through college. Didn't talk to my father for..." she paused, calculating. "God, fifteen years, give or take. We finally reconnected about two years ago, and we'd been able to work through a small part of all of it. But he died in July, so..." she shrugged. "We never did get all the way back to reconciled."

"You haven't had a chance to grieve, have you," Drew observed as he watched and listened.

"Nope," she sighed. "First dealing with him being back in my life, then a solid six months of hospital visits. He was out of the hospital maybe three weeks total between January first and July eighth. By mid-June the doctors had also confirmed he had dementia, but he died before I could start the process of lining up long-term care for him. There's no one else, so, I had to handle all of it - his funeral arrangements, his estate, if you can call it that. Everything. Alone. Grant was no help whatsoever."

"Grant?"

CHAPTER NINE

"My ex," she murmured. "It's a long story. But the punchline is, he cheated, and then he left."

"When?"

She sighed.

"Unofficially? Two months ago. But he brought his key back this week. Monday, I think it was. Came home to a pouty beagle, a written confession, and a housekey on the counter. Thing is, I suspected it for months, so when he finally left, it didn't even hurt that much anymore. More just... sad, and maybe a little relieved, all at once."

Drew's eyes tinged with pain on her behalf, and seeing it made her duck her head.

"So now you see what I meant. My career. That's it. That's all I have. More than that. It's who I *am*. So. I can't do... whatever this is," she finished, waving her hand back and forth between the two of them. "I can't. It's not safe. If I let you in, you'll only leave at some point, just like everybody else, and then I won't have anything at all left, because I will have blown any professional credibility to hell. For a *fling*."

She fell silent, swirling her ice water and focusing on the way the cubes moved around in the mini vortex she'd created.

Careening out of control. Like my life.

Trixie could feel emotion radiating her direction from the other end of the couch, but she was too scared to look up and try to figure out what Drew was feeling.

She heard and felt him rise from his seat on the couch.

Good. Maybe he'll give up and go away.

She felt his presence right beside her, then his hand on her shoulder, and closed her eyes.

Or maybe not.

"I want you to know. I heard everything you said. And I understand why you're scared. I totally get it. But know this..."

"Please don't make me choose, Drew," she whispered, interrupting him. "Please don't do that to me. I can't be what you want. I...I can't be one of your good-time tabloid girls..."

His brow furrowed. "*What*?"

"You have a reputation as a 'love- 'em-and-leave- 'em' type," she told him. "And I don't play that game. Never have. Don't want to."

"You really think that of me? You really think that's all I'm after here, a good time?"

She shrugged. "You tell me if I should believe what they say."

"Look at me."

She shook her head, determined to keep her focus on the glass in her hand.

"Trixie. Please." He stood up.

The roughness in his voice was what made her look up at him.

"I've only been with five women since Emily. Five. *In twelve years*, Trixie. And each of them was a one-night stand that I picked up because I was drunk as hell on the anniversary of her death," he said stormily, eyes full of hurt. "Almost too drunk to function, much less make sound decisions. I'm not proud of it at all. But there's nothing I can do to change it. It is what it is. And that's not who I am normally. You have no idea how much more you are to me than that – so much more than a possible one-night stand. Although I am trying to tell you. To *show* you. This isn't a *fling* for me, Trixie. Not at all."

"I don't see how," she said, knowing he could see the honest confusion in her face. "If Bill hadn't done something stupid, or if Marjorie had been in town, we wouldn't even *be* here right now. You would still have no freaking clue I even *existed*. Much less be chasing me. And that's another thing I don't get. You could have any woman you want. Why chase *me*?"

"I don't believe that," Drew scoffed. "I believe something else would have put us together. *Something* would have made it happen. Because we are *supposed* to happen."

Trixie's eyebrows raised.

"Do you understand what I'm trying to tell you?"

"No..." Oh.... *Wait,* her mind whirled. *Holy crap. Is he saying what I -*

"Dammit," he growled, and he reached down, snatched her glass out of her hand, pulled her to her feet, and kissed her.

Trixie started to protest but her body betrayed her, molding itself against him, her hands clutching at him to hold him closer.

Her eyes fluttered shut and her knees weakened as she welcomed the feel of his hands on her body. He caressed her back at first, then his left hand traveled down and underneath her shirt, stealing under the bra to caress her breast while his right skimmed down her thigh then moved inward and cupped her. Instantly her core was aching with need, and it stole her breath completely when he suddenly moved both hands to her hips and lifted her off her feet.

She instinctively wrapped her legs around his waist, and his lips left her mouth to further explore her skin. He sprinkled soft, slow kisses down the side of her neck as he carried her across the room and pinned her between his rock-hard body and the wall. Trixie could feel his warm breath at the hollow of her throat, and his arousal was evident as he ground lightly against her.

"Drew," she whispered, panting, sensing that both of them were on the verge of losing control.

Drew nuzzled her neck and murmured, "You truly don't get it, do you? When you walked into my office Monday afternoon you brought the light back,

Trixie. I felt like I could see again, *breathe* again after twelve years of stumbling alone in the dark. *Does that sound like just a fling to you?*"

"I...I... no," she gasped with as much surprise as desire. "It doesn't. But..."

"No buts," Drew whispered against her mouth, then rested his forehead against hers, as he had on the plane. "I won't rush you, Trixie. I'll earn your trust, whatever it takes. I'll wait, for as long as it takes. But if you decide to let me in, know and understand that long-term is what I'm looking for with you. I can't and won't settle for anything less. Not with you. I refuse. If we do this, I need to know you're gonna go all in, because that's how *I'm* gonna go if you decide to give us a chance."

He kissed her one last time, then stepped back and set her down gently, the pain still in his eyes as he quietly walked towards her door.

He paused, one hand on the knob, and said, "I'd be honored if you'd join me for dinner downstairs at seven o'clock," before slipping back out into the hall and closing the door to 1108 softly behind him.

***

Trixie slowly sank back down on the couch, lips lightly swollen from his passionate kisses, her pulse racing, her head spinning.

I can't think. Need to turn off my brain right now.

Moving on autopilot, she pulled out her swimsuit, robe and tennis shoes. She changed clothes and quickly braided her hair to keep it out of her way, then headed for the indoor pool downstairs.

***

In the next suite, Drew heard her door snick shut and soft footfalls against the thick carpeting as she walked away in the direction of the elevator.

He shook his head in frustration.

Should I have gone ahead and said it? he wondered. *I'm not sure how much clearer I could have been, unless I just came right out and said, 'Hi, I know we only met four days ago but I think I might love you.' Yeah, that's not stalkerish or creepy at all.*

Running his hands over his face, he paced back and forth, back and forth.

"This is ridiculous," he muttered. "Need to burn off some steam."

He changed into workout gear, grabbed his iPod, headphones and room card, and headed for the hotel gym on the first floor.

Drew was relieved to find that the small gym was deserted. He stepped up on the treadmill, arranged the settings for varying grades, set his iPod to shuffle, and began. He fast walked the first half-mile, then pressed a button to kick the machine's speed upward. At the one-mile mark, he increased speed again, until he finally was at a run.

He lost himself in the rhythm of his movements, arms pumping, as his brain wandered wherever it liked. But he noticed it never took a path that didn't somehow lead back to Trixie.

***

Push it, Trix. Six more.

She flipped gracefully again at the far wall, churning through the water at breakneck speed as she marked off another half-circuit in her self-punishing regimen.

Her body was moving autonomously, leaving her brain free to roam. And every single thought it presented to her was of Drew. The way he'd looked. The things he'd said. His mouth on hers. How safe she'd felt tucked in his embrace.

At last, she finished her laps and turned over on her back to rest and float, her tears escaping unnoticed since they blended so well with the water droplets on her face.

***

Drew was physically exhausted when he finished the four miles, but his mind and heart were no less consumed by Trixie. He mopped the sweat off his face and arms, then left the gym, his towel flung over his shoulder.

He peeked into the adjoining pool area, and saw her floating gracefully on her back, her eyes closed, her haunted expression reflecting the same inner conflict he was having.

As he watched her, it shocked him to his very core to realize he'd been dead wrong. Drew didn't think he was falling in love with Trixie Benning after all.

He knew he already had.

A group of children pushed past him into the pool area and ran shrieking toward the water. He ducked back out of sight when he saw Trixie's eyes pop open, and he made a hasty retreat across the hall to the steam room.

Drew pulled off his socks, shoes, and shirt before climbing in and sitting down on the smooth wooden bench, noting that he had this amenity to himself, as well.

He leaned back and closed his eyes, taking deep breaths, trying his best to relax and adjust to the possible future his realization had just created.

***

The squeals of children interrupted her reverie, and Trixie sighed quietly to herself as she swam to the ladder and pulled herself up out of the pool. She toweled off as best she could, including her braid, then slipped on her robe and tennis shoes.

She paused in the hallway when she noticed the placard labeled 'steam room'. *Huh. The pool wasn't heated, so I am a little cold. Good way to warm up before I go upstairs.*

She walked into the outer room to set down her robe and shoes, then opened the door to the steam room. She cautiously made her way across the room, arms outstretched through the thick fog, and yelped when her hand grazed someone's knee.

"Oh, God. I am so sorry," she said, thankful that visibility was nearly nonexistent. "I didn't know anyone was in here."

"You're forgiven," a voice replied, one whose owner had already captured her heart whether she'd wanted him to or not.

"Drew," she breathed, and he materialized through the thick haze, stepping toward her as if her deepest unspoken wish had summoned him with a siren's call.

"Say the word, and I'll go and leave you in peace," he said gently, and she could see both the longing and the hurt that ravaged his eyes.

Trixie looked at him for a moment, then slowly closed the distance between them.

CHAPTER TEN

The passion and strength with which Drew suddenly held her body against his and plundered her mouth with his surprised her. He broke the kiss and made her groan as he traced his lips down her neck.

His fingers deftly unhooked her bikini's top clasp that rested against the nape of her neck, and pulled the flimsy material down, his strong hands gently cupping her exposed breasts.

She arched her back in response and was rewarded with his tongue circling her right nipple as his left thumb brushed the other one; she gasped aloud when he nibbled gently on the right side, then again when he switched direction and the left breast became the playground for his talented tongue.

His mouth worked his way back up to hers, as his hands continued to roam her body. He was slowly pulling on one end of the bowtie that held the left side of her bikini bottoms together when suddenly they could both hear someone outside the steam room's door.

In a flash, Drew changed course and set her bikini top back into place for her, threw her a wicked grin, and took two steps back before the newcomer even made it all the way into the space.

Trixie turned and fled the steam room, grateful that it gave her a plausible excuse for her suddenly very flushed cheeks.

Oh, my God, she thought to herself as she hurriedly shrugged on her robe and shoes. *What am I doing? What am I thinking?*

***

Forty-five minutes later she met him at the hostess station, and they were being escorted to a table in the corner of the restaurant where they'd be able to have quiet conversation.

After the wine selection had been made and appetizers ordered, Trixie said politely, "Walk me through how tomorrow's going to go."

All business, he thought to himself. *Okay. For now, I'll play along.*

"Well," Drew said. "Pretty straightforward, actually. Opening remarks, which are pretty much reviewing the minutes of the prior meeting. Then financials review. After that, please don't be offended if you're asked to step out so that the Board and I can discuss what's happened with Bill and the next steps regarding it."

"On the contrary, once I've run that gauntlet of public speaking, trust me, I'll *want* to get the hell out of there," Trixie assured him. "I neither need nor want to be privy to the rest."

"Is this really what you want to talk about right now?" he asked quietly.

"We're in a public place, where any member of the Board might decide to join us, so, yes," Trixie replied coolly, holding his gaze. "The rest can keep for now."

"Good point," Drew conceded. "And I agree."

"Good," she said. "Now, I'm thinking the pasta dish. Have you tried it? Is it good?"

For the remainder of the meal, they kept conversation confined to office related topics and surface information about personal items, such as education.

"I got my bachelor's degree from Tech," Drew revealed. "I had planned on getting my Masters' degree, but then the business took off, and I just never got around to it. What about you?"

"Hm," Trixie swallowed her sip of wine. "Bachelor's I completed at TWU. Once I started working, I got my Masters in accounting online, believe it or not. It was easier that way. I've worked full-time pretty much since I was sixteen. It was brutal working all those hours and taking onsite classes all through high school and for the first degree. So, when I realized I could pursue my Masters' electronically, I was relieved that I didn't have to try to figure out how to attend physical classes anymore."

"Online, huh?" Drew's eyebrows raised. "I might have to look into that. I really do want to get my Masters'."

"Go for it," Trixie said. "Every day is another chance to fulfill your dreams."

"I like your spirit," Drew chuckled.

***

Dinner over, Drew said, "Shall we?"

Trixie nodded, and they strolled back across the parquet floor of the lobby to the elevators. As he pressed the button for the eleventh floor he grinned and said, "This will sound so cliché, but - your place or mine?"

Trixie was startled. "For what, exactly?"

"To review that presentation," he reminded her. "We might as well get started on it. Unless you'd rather talk, or something."

"I think the presentation is a good choice. And I took the liberty of building some add-on slides for the financial review, as well. You know, to explain any variances that someone might want deeper detail on. I'd like to show you those, see what you think."

"Fine," Drew said with forced enthusiasm. *Damn, she's hardheaded. Gonna pretend earlier today never even happened, huh? We'll see about that.*

***

When he joined her five minutes later, he chuckled at them both having changed into jeans and t-shirts.

"If I could get away with wearing this all the time, I would," he announced.

"Me too," she sighed. "Unfortunately, that's not the way corporate America works."

"Maybe not yet," Drew held up a finger. "Want a drink?"

"Sure. Hey– Did you want to go over that presentation I built first, or the financials?"

"Can't we do all this in the morning? The meeting doesn't even start until two."

"I guess so," she said warily as she took her glass of whiskey and water from him. "So, I suppose you'd like to talk instead. About what, exactly?"

He shrugged. *I want to talk about us, but she's obviously not ready to discuss what I said earlier.*

"Your choice," he offered.

"Hmm," Trixie pursed her lips. "Ooh. Here's a good one. If you could have any career in the world, no limitations – what would you do?"

His eyebrows raised. "Seriously?"

"Seriously."

"Animals," Drew answered, his face alit with enthusiasm. "I love 'em. All kinds. But my interest is in rescues, particularly dogs. Locating good homes for them and caring for ones that can't be placed somewhere for whatever reason. A no-kill sanctuary."

"Aww. You big softie, you," Trixie said. "I love that idea."

"Good. In a perfect world, you'd come with me. Be my partner, side by side."

She blinked rapidly.

"Think about it. What I know and understand about accounting will fit in a thimble with room left over. I would really need your help and knowledge in navigating permits, getting the land bought and the facility set up, proper tax structure, all of it. And if we're in it together, that would remove the rule, don't you think?"

"It would," she said slowly. "But as it stands right now, that rule exists for a very, very good reason."

"It does," he agreed. "Which is how I first realized you were special to me. Of everyone I've ever employed, you're the only one that ever made me want to break it."

She smiled a little, even as her cheeks went red.

"Or you could stay at Alexander Limited, Trixie. Either way, I won't be your boss anymore if I sell."

Trixie almost dropped her drink.

"Nice catch," he teased.

"Thanks. Wasting good whiskey by spilling it would be a damn shame. Now. Can you please tell me what the *hell* you're talking about?"

Drew flushed with embarrassment and her eyebrows peaked.

"Did I just see Drew Alexander, the CEO of his own company, blush? *Wow.* I bet that hardly ever happens."

"You're right, it doesn't."

"That just slipped out, didn't it? The part about selling."

"Yes. But I've been thinking about what I'm about to tell you for months. I just haven't told anybody about it. Haven't had anyone I cared to share it with until now."

A frown creased her face. "Are you okay? What's going on?"

He swirled the amber liquid in his glass. "I got a buy offer about four months ago, from a private equity firm."

Her eyes went wide.

"I was already mulling it over, but now, I am seriously considering it."

"Why?"

"Because I'm tired, and to be honest, I'm burned out," he said. "Alexander Limited has gone from my passion to a huge... a huge...."

"A huge what?"

"I'm not even sure how to describe it. A pain in the ass? A chore?" Drew grimaced. "I built this...

thing... and I used to love it. And I just... don't anymore. It grew too big, doesn't feel like *me* anymore. I haven't been able to be hands on in years. I'm stuck at the top of the pyramid. I don't like it."

"What does the offer entail?"

"Basically, just buying me out. One of the stipulations I'd have is that no layoffs or restructurings occur for a minimum time period. But the company is rock solid, and this investor group knows it – which is why they want it so badly. They wouldn't mess with a winning formula. And, they've got the capital and backing to grow it even more, which would tickle the Board members to death."

"So... you'd just walk away."

"Yep, with a very healthy paycheck, and I already know what I'd want to do next."

"The sanctuary."

Drew nodded. "And I meant what I said. I'd love us to be in it together, side by side."

"Okay, I'll play along with this purely hypothetical scenario," she agreed, making it clear that she absolutely hadn't decided *anything* yet about the day's earlier events. "You don't think that's a really risky 'eggs in one basket' thing? What happens if I were to quit Alexander Limited to come with you, and we start to date, and then we don't work out? What then?"

"You still think I'd bail on you?"

"It happens. People leave."

"Not me," he growled, and pulled her into his lap. "I don't know what to say or do to reassure you, Trixie, except show you over time that I'm all in. But for me to do that, you must be willing to make the leap, too."

"I'm sorry," she managed. "I'm just...I'm scared."

"I understand. I really do," Drew murmured, tightening his arms around her. "It's new and a little scary for me, too."

"I'm not ready for this."

"I know that too. And we will go at whatever pace you need to, Trixie. I just want to be with you. You're who I want."

"You really mean that, don't you?" she asked as she searched his eyes and found no deception.

"One thousand percent," he answered. "But like I said, you have to be willing to join me out here on the ledge, or this won't work."

"Here's what I think," she said as she wriggled out of his arms, got to her feet, and paced, trying her best to steer the talk back to neutral ground. "I think that you need to make your decision to sell or not based on what's best for *you*, and I need to decide to stay where I am or not based on what's best for *me*. And maybe, those things will land on the same path."

"Well, if I sell, it won't be finalized before the end of the year, at the earliest. Possibly more like April or May of next year, depending on when the talks and due diligence starts."

"Okay, and?" Trixie said.

"How about this. You know, or at least hopefully have some idea, of where I want to see things go between us, right?"

She nodded. "We're talking hypotheticals, but the fact remains, I work for you. It's a big piece, Drew. It's important to me to keep that and whatever this is separated."

"Yes, and it's important to me too, just so you know," Drew admitted. "I've had the same rule as you have, my entire career. Don't date someone at work. It never ends well. I've seen several business owners go down in flames because of it."

"So," he blew out a breath. "I don't really like this, but it's the best way forward. Everything stays the same for now. Once I *officially* leave the company, if you decide you want to be with me then we won't have to worry about that damn rule anymore, regardless of if you stay there, or not."

"What's so bad about that?"

Drew ran his hands through his hair.

"I'll tell you *exactly* what's bad about that. The fact that I already want you so damn bad I can't stand it, and now, we're talking about no contact at *all* outside of work. Not even any more talks like this one. For months. If that's the path *we* choose, it would start immediately. Maybe even tonight. It would have to - for your sake. I don't give a damn about my reputation, Trixie, but I care a great deal about preserving yours. Not to mention, there's one other thing really wrong with that plan."

CHAPTER ELEVEN

"What?" She stopped her back and forth across the rug and waited. "What's wrong with it?"

"The fact that I'm selfish. I *like* kissing you. I *like* having you in my arms. Everything about you fascinates me," he murmured. "Absolutely everything, Trixie Benning. The way your nose crinkles up when you make a certain face. How your cheeks go rosy when you get embarrassed. That jasmine scent you wear. The way you slip on your reading glasses, and how you twirl your college ring when you're thinking about something. Your teddy bear-covered pajamas. Your raw honesty. Your independence. Your laugh. The way you cry. All of it. Everything I've discovered about you just makes me want to discover more."

She stood still as a statue, her eyes bright with emotion.

"You know where I stand, Trixie. You need to think about it and decide if you even want to give us a shot. Until then, there's not really any point in talking about a battle plan – even a hypothetical one."

Drew slowly raised his glass as he gazed at her with an inferno of need in his emerald-green eyes. After he finished off his whiskey, he rose to his feet.

"I need to leave now. If I don't, I'm going to want to kiss you again, and that's not fair to either one of us. I don't want to make you feel pressured, and quite frankly if I start kissing you again, I won't be able to stop. It's much easier on us both if I go back to my room now while I can."

He strode toward the door. "Let's meet at ten a.m. to go over the presentation materials. Will that be enough time?"

She managed a nod.

"Goodnight, Trixie," Drew said solemnly, and walked out.

***

At her wit's end, she'd called Meghan, and told her best friend everything that had happened.

"He showed up at your *house*?"

"Yes," Trixie confirmed, and continued to fill Meghan in about the plane ride, and everything Drew had said to her.

"Aww, that is so sweet," Meghan had said when Trixie had finished catching her up. "Are you going to take a chance?"

"I honestly don't know yet," Trixie admitted. "But I think I want to."

"Do it, Trix," Meghan had urged her. "Let go. It sounds like he's the real deal."

"It does, doesn't it?" and Trixie sighed with happiness.

By the time they got off the phone Meghan's eyes were brimming with happy tears. *Trixie doesn't even realize it yet,* Meghan thought, *but she's in love. And I'm so happy for her.*

***

It's ten-forty-seven, Trixie sighed as she glanced at the clock again. *I wonder if he's still awake too.*

She tried to watch television after her phone call with Meghan, but she found she couldn't even pay enough attention to make it worth the effort, and finally turned it off. She briefly considered reading, but even if she'd remembered to bring a book along with her, Trixie knew she wouldn't have been able to focus on that either.

She fluffed her pillow again and rolled over onto her back, staring at the ceiling and playing Drew's words over again in her head. And once more she felt that rush of warmth, her heart soaring at the memory of everything he'd said.

I want that, she realized. *I want him in my world. If I'm truly honest with myself about it - It's not even about that damn rule anymore. I'm just so freaking scared of letting my guard down and getting hurt.*

And he's pushed as much as he's going to. If I want this, I'm going to have to be the one to take the next step.

She grabbed another one of the four pillows that overloaded the bed, held it down tightly over her face, and yelled into it. Then she flung the covers back and got up.

***

Down in the hotel bar, Drew sat alone on a stool in the farthest corner, his head in one hand, the other clutching tightly to the tumbler on the tiny high-top table in front of him. From a distance it looked like he was on a bender, and Trixie's heart leapt into her throat.

He lifted his head and looked at her as she drew near, and the misery in his face had her fighting back tears.

She walked slowly toward him, the almost empty bar fading fast into the background.

"Can't sleep either, huh."

He tried and almost managed a smile. "Nope."

"What're you drinking?"

"Had two whiskeys then switched to club soda," came the wry answer. "No point in tying one on tonight. Big meeting tomorrow."

"Yeah, you need to be fresh for that," she said lightly. "Especially since your accounting gal is terrified of public speaking and will need your support to get through it."

Now he did smile, but to her dismay it didn't reach his eyes.

"I hope my accounting gal knows I'd go to hell and back for her," he said wistfully. "And that I'd do anything she asks me to, except walk away from her."

"Why did you have to say that?" she murmured.

"Because it's true, dammit," he whispered, breaking eye contact and frowning at the well-worn table. "You've wrecked me. I've known you all of four damn days, and you've wrecked me, Trixie. I can't sleep. I can't concentrate. All I can think about is you."

He closed his eyes and took a deep breath to rein himself in. "Why are you here? *Why?*"

She took a sudden intense interest in her shoes, and managed a barely audible, "Because you've wrecked me, too."

"What?" he growled softly.

I'm done fighting this, she realized.

She lifted her head and gazed at him with undisguised desire.

"You've wrecked me, too."

"Upstairs," he murmured, and she nodded once, then turned and walked across the bar toward the elevators as he settled his tab.

***

Trixie stepped off the elevator, her hands trembling as she quickly moved to her door and swiped her key card. She raced to the bathroom and nervously brushed her hair, staring back at herself with wide eyes and flushed cheeks.

What just happened, exactly? Did we just decide something? Because it sure feels like we did.

Drew's soft knock on the connecting door between their suites broke her reverie and she willed herself to stop shaking as she set the brush down and went to let him in.

No sooner had she slid the door open than he'd pulled her tight against his chest, his mouth plundering hers and kicking all her senses into high gear. They moved together, half-walking, half-stumbling, toward the sitting area of his suite, limbs and tongues intertwined. But they'd misjudged the distance, and the arm of the couch rose up sharply, colliding with the backs of his thighs and sending Drew tumbling backward. He landed on his back across the cushions, with Trixie on top of him.

"Ouch," he whispered against her mouth, and chuckled.

"Are you okay?" she whispered.

"I am so much more than just all right. I'm with you," he answered, and ran his hands up into her hair to keep her mouth pressed to his just a bit longer, then pulled her head gently to the side so he could explore her neck.

He nipped lightly at her collarbone, and she shuddered. He traced kisses back up her neck before gently nibbling on her earlobe, and she moaned.

"Drew..." she gasped.

"Hmm," came the answer as he moved his hands from her hair to her waist, then slipped them underneath the hem of her t-shirt and worked them up her back to unfasten her bra.

"Do you have any... um... protection with you?"

He stopped.

"I don't," he sighed. "I was absolutely certain that this would not be happening on this trip, so, no. I didn't buy any."

He said 'buy,' not 'bring', Trixie noticed. That surprises me. I thought all *single guys kept a stock of condoms ready... Interesting.*

"Oh," Trixie said. "Me either. Um..."

He sighed again, then maneuvered up and around until she was sitting on his lap.

"Dammit," he growled against her throat.

"Indeed," she replied, her voice husky with want.

"We should wait, then, until we're prepared."

"Yes," she agreed. "Although nothing says we have to like it."

He roared with laughter. "Eloquently put."

"Can we still make out a little, like high school kids?" she suggested with a mischievous twinkle in her eye.

"Well, well, aren't you the naughty one?" he told her before he kissed her again. "And then, I want to sleep with you. *Beside* you," he clarified. "I've been dying to know if those teddy bear pajamas were as soft as they looked."

She deliberately batted her eyes and whispered, "They're *softer*."

Drew laughed. "Well, go on then. Go change. Meet you back here?" and patted the couch.

"Yep."

***

After twenty-five minutes he began to get worried and was just about to check on her when she opened the connecting door leading from her hotel suite to his. Drew turned his head to look at Trixie as she walked into the room and his jaw dropped open.

She had on her teddy bear pajamas – and a box of condoms in her hand.

"Are you sure?" he asked.

"I am."

"Where did you-"

"Drugstore next door."

He looked at her, lost for words. He saw passion there in her eyes, and peace with it. Slowly, he crossed the room to her, lifted his hands to that beautiful face, then ran them up into that glorious hair she'd set free and brought his lips down to meet hers.

She sighed against his mouth, running her hands over his chest. He traced his hands down her back, to her hips, before he pivoted with her and walked backward into the bedroom, leading her with him and settling back on the bed so that she lay completely on him. Trixie reached out and set the box on the nightstand.

He wrapped his arms around her, then gently rolled her onto her back. Her hair splayed across the pillow and her hands moved down his back as he kissed her more urgently now, parting her lips with his tongue to take in her sweetness, using his hands and mouth to communicate the heat rising in him, an unspoken wave of need. Her hands clawed through his hair, then the sheets as he moved his mouth slowly across her jawline, searing the pulse point in her throat as his hands explored the new world hidden underneath her pajama top. She arched slightly as he undid the buttons down the front and flung both sides open, exposing her bare breasts.

"You're magnificent," he marveled as he stroked her skin. It was as soft, her body as lush, as he'd imagined. Dipping his head, he gently cupped her right breast with his hand while his tongue tantalized and teased her left, then switched over. Her eyes fluttered closed, a low primal noise humming in her throat, her hands gripping sheets so hard he thought they might tear.

She whimpered with pleasure as Drew's tongue traced sensual circles down her stomach. He eased her pajama bottoms down, then slipped them off. Whisper soft touches, kisses, met the leading edge of her black panties, followed by a slight scrape of teeth as those too gave way to his command. His mouth again, closer, hot breath against her inner thighs as he parted them, and he spun her world out of control as he opened her core to him and feasted.

"*Drew,*" Trixie moaned as the first jolt of release washed through her. Her fingers tangled themselves in his hair as she rocked and bucked against his tender onslaught. Gripping her hips, he did not relent. He couldn't. His white-hot need of her was too great. As her body lay quivering, Drew only moved away from her long enough to remove the remaining clothing between them and roll a condom into place. He stretched his frame back out over hers and wrapped his arms around her.

"Trixie. Look at me."

She opened her eyes. It inflamed him even further to see her raw desire for him, her need, had grown. He lowered his mouth to hers, never breaking eye contact as he slid into her, filled her. Her eyes went wide and dark, and she started to close them as her breath caught.

"No, Trixie. Don't close me out. Be with me. Jump off the ledge with me," he murmured against her lips as a sensual rhythm formed between them. Slow, deep rolling waves rocked them as they moved together as one flesh, building the pace, the heat, their eyes locked. And when hers glazed over, he knew he'd brought them both to the peak.

"Let go, baby," he said huskily, and followed her down into the abyss.

CHAPTER TWELVE

Drew's eyes popped open of their own accord just before six a.m. He tilted his head down to see that Trixie was still nestled against him, her head on his chest, and sleeping soundly.

He moved very carefully to extricate himself without waking her. She murmured and shuddered but stayed asleep, to his relief.

Drew went to the sitting area and turned on his computer after starting the small coffeepot. As he waited for the laptop to boot up, he replayed the night's events. They'd made love, kissed and talked and laughed, then kissed and made love some more. *One of the best nights of my life so far, even if we hadn't had phenomenal sex,* he realized. *And waking up beside her? Even better.*

The login screen finally materialized, and he entered his data to connect to the mainframe, then started wading through his emails. Thirty minutes later, he opened one whose contents caused a huge grin, and he picked up his cell phone and called his dad, who fortunately was also an early riser.

"Hey Dad, got some news for you," he said.

"Morning, son. What's going on?"

"You remember the Estalle Ranch, right?"

"The place in Nacogdoches that you've been going on and on about for years, saying if it ever came up for sale, you'd jump on it?"

"More than that. I've been pestering them on a regular basis for months now about selling it to me. And I just got an email. They've finally accepted my offer."

"Really?"

"Really. There was only one strategic thing I needed to get lined out, just for protection, and I was able to close the deal sooner than I thought."

"That's wonderful, Drew! I know how much you wanted that property. Perfect place for that animal sanctuary you're always talking about."

"I know, right? Such a sweet little piece of land, too. And yes, I can already see the sanctuary up and running in my mind's eye. You know what else? *You* get to pay up, you lost the bet. I *told* you it would happen eventually."

His father chuckled. "Yep, you're right. Since you were sixteen you've been telling me and anyone else that would listen that one day that place would be yours."

***

Trixie was vaguely aware when Drew got out of bed, but it wasn't until she heard his voice in the other room that she came awake.

He sounds so happy, even though I can't really hear what he's saying that well.

She smiled as she put her pajamas on and started to join Drew in the sitting area when she heard him say, 'protection, and I was able to close the deal'.

Then he was muffled, and she assumed he was pacing back and forth, moving toward then away from the door leading to the bedroom.

The next thing she heard was 'such a sweet little piece', then a bit later, '*you* get to pay up, you lost the bet. I *told* you it would happen eventually.'

Her smile faded into oblivion, and her blood turned to ice in her veins.

He... he... made a bet with somebody about getting me to sleep with him? Seriously?

Now, Trix, don't jump to conclusions, her rational side argued. *I'm sure that there is a logical explanation for what you just heard.*

Oh, sure there is, her self-protection mechanism snarled as it kicked into overdrive. *Lover boy in there can't be trusted, just like the rest of them. He saw you, wanted you, and bet his buddy he could have you. This was all a freaking game to him. That's all you ever meant to him – a game... winning a bet.... a* fling.

"No," she whispered, as tears filled her eyes. "No."

She held her breath, hoping against hope that Drew would detour to the bathroom, or better yet leave the suite completely so she could escape undetected.

Her prayer was answered when she heard the bathroom door shut, and she barreled quickly but quietly back into her suite, locking the adjoining door behind her. She hurriedly changed into her jeans and sweater and tugged on her tennis shoes. Flinging her suitcase on the bed, she grabbed her belongings up and packed them as quickly as she could.

***

Drew stepped out of the bathroom, and thought about waking Trixie up for breakfast, but decided to let her sleep a bit longer. He poured himself a cup of coffee, moved back to his laptop in the sitting area and continued checking emails, whistling happily under his breath so he wouldn't disturb Trixie.

Found the woman of my dreams, and now, I'm going to own the property of my dreams. Life doesn't get any better than this, he smiled to himself.

***

Within ten minutes she was at the reception desk in the lobby, checking out of the hotel.

"Can you please make sure Mr. Alexander gets this by ten a.m.?" she asked the woman behind the reception desk. "He needs it for the meeting this afternoon."

"Certainly, Miss Benning. Anything else?"

"Yes," Trixie answered. "Do you have a shuttle to the airport?"

***

By the time Drew noticed Trixie was no longer in his suite, she'd already caught the shuttle.

When she didn't answer his repeated knocks on both the adjoining door and her suite's main door, he called her room repeatedly. Then he bolted downstairs, looking in the pool, steam room, gym, and restaurant. And by the time he approached the front desk, worried sick that something had happened to her, the passenger van carrying her out of his life had dropped her off outside Denver International Airport's main terminal.

"Yes sir, Miss Benning checked out about..." she glanced at her computer screen, "forty minutes ago. But she asked me to make sure you got this before ten a.m." And the woman handed him a small manila envelope.

Drew was dumbfounded. "She *checked out*. Are you sure? Trixie Benning. Room 1108."

The woman nodded. "Yes, sir, she checked out and caught the shuttle to the airport."

Completely confused, he ripped open the packet while he was still standing in the lobby – and immediately wished he'd waited until he was back in a more private space.

Because inside was a thumb drive and a letter, folded neatly into thirds. Hands shaking, he unfolded the paper, and its contents skewered him through the heart.

Thumb drive has what you need for the meeting.

And nice try. You almost had me convinced this was for real. I heard you say you won the bet about me. Good for you. Hope you enjoy your reward.

Consider this my resignation. I never want to see you again.

***

Trixie stood in line at the car rental desk waiting her turn. Once she'd been dropped off at the airport, she'd realized that she absolutely could not face another flight. She researched the distance from Denver, Colorado to Irving, Texas on her phone. Once she'd realized it was only a thirteen-hour drive, she'd set her jaw and caught an inter-airport shuttle to the car rental area.

Drew had called four times and texted five times since she'd left the hotel. She'd ignored each one. Finally, she'd turned her phone off.

Within forty-five minutes she was driving herself out of the airport, her rental car's GPS programmed to take her straight to Meghan's house. She cranked up the radio and ignored the tears streaming silently down her cheeks.

***

Drew sat on the couch in his suite, head in hands, trying to figure out what the hell Trixie was talking about.

"Oh, shit," he breathed as realization finally dawned. "She heard parts of my conversation with Dad about the ranch, maybe? But what the hell did I say that would result in all this?"

He strained his memory to find *exactly* what he'd said to his father. Once he recalled it, he paled as he felt his heart break completely in two.

No wonder *she thought it was about her,* he grimaced as he scooped up his phone and dialed his father again.

"Dad," he managed.

"Drew. What's wrong?"

"Trixie. The woman I want to marry. I screwed up, Dad. There's been a huge misunderstanding, and she's gone. And I don't know how to fix it."

"Start from the beginning, and tell me what happened, son. And we'll go from there."

***

Thirty minutes later, Drew finished with, "And she left. Dad. What do I do?"

"If you really love this girl, you need to find her and explain, son. Hopefully, that will be enough."

"And if it's not?"

"Then you'll have to find a way to let her go, Drew."

"I can't. I won't. There must be something I can do to make her see." He paced up and down, his free hand raking itself again and again over his face and through his hair.

And stopped in his tracks as inspiration struck. "I have an idea. I just hope she's willing to talk to me long enough for me to make it happen."

He laid out his plan, to which his father responded, "Go for it, son. You have nothing left to lose. Good luck."

***

Four hours into her drive, Trixie's stomach was rumbling. Although she didn't feel like eating, she stopped at a little café in Springfield, Colorado anyway. *Stretch my legs, get a bathroom break, at the very least.*

She rummaged through her suitcase to find her hairbrush. Leaving the hotel so suddenly hadn't left any time to get her hair up out of her way. She deftly brushed it out, then formed a thick braid, securing the end with one of the small ponytail bands she always kept stashed in her purse. Then she went inside the café for some hot tea and food.

She used the ladies' room before taking a seat in the booth farthest from the door. The waitress took her order, then said, "You okay, honey?"

"I will be."

"Man troubles?"

"And how."

"Been there, honey. You'll get through it. Be right back with your hot tea."

"Thanks."

She sighed, then reached and dug her cell phone out of her purse. Against her better judgement, she turned it on.

Ten missed calls, the display read. *Twelve new text messages. Three new voicemails.*

Although she already figured Drew was behind them all, she scrolled through each app and confirmed her suspicions were accurate.

I can't do this right now, she realized, and turned her phone off again. *If I hear his voice right now, I'll lose it.*

***

Drew spent the rest of the morning pursuing his newly hatched plan with all the energy he could muster. Although he desperately wanted nothing more than to pack his suitcase and chase after Trixie, he still had a board meeting to get through.

But now, there would be an additional topic on the agenda. He gritted his teeth, willed himself to focus, and continued reviewing the files on Trixie's thumb drive.

***

At two p.m. sharp, dressed in his best suit, Drew Alexander walked in and stood at the head of the long oval table. Twelve heads swiveled to look at him.

"Good afternoon, ladies and gentlemen. Shall we begin?"

***

By the time she reached Amarillo, Texas, Trixie had hit her emotional and mental limits, and opted to stop for the night. She found a reasonably priced and safe looking motel next to a Waffle House, and paid cash for her room.

She turned the key, lugged her suitcase through and set it just inside the doorway, closed and locked the door, and headed for the shower.

***

By five p.m., the meeting was wrapping up, and as he glanced around the table, Drew could plainly see that he'd shocked the hell out of his Board of Directors. One by one they stopped to briefly comment and shake his hand, then left the room.

Well, that's step one, he thought as he loosened his tie. *Need to get moving on step two.*

He returned to the hotel, packed, checked out, and called for a ride to the airstrip where Thom and Danny were already waiting per his previous phone call to them. Then he checked for any new emails, texts, or voicemails. He had copious amounts of each, but none from the one person in the whole world that he wanted to hear from the most.

CHAPTER THIRTEEN

Trixie sat in the Waffle House just off Highway 287 and idly people watched as she pushed the remnants of her dinner around her plate.

What next? she thought.

Well, I have enough saved to cover everything comfortably for seven months, so there's that. I need to figure out where I want to start over. Her heart pinged at the thought of leaving Meghan, Brad, and the kids behind.

Not an option. They're the only family I have, she realized. *I don't have to leave town to start over. I just need to reset my career somewhere Drew Alexander isn't, that's all. You can do this, Trixie. Breathe.*

Do I want to keep the house? He knows where I live. What about selling it or renting it out, moving into something else? Bad memories there anyway thanks to Grant. And I don't need much room for just me and Joshua.

And do I really think he'd even care enough to try to find me? Based on what I heard this morning, I'd say not.

She sat, playing with her food as her mind raced, feeling simultaneously like the loneliest person on the planet and invigorated by the chance to reinvent herself.

Then Drew's words came flooding back to her, unbidden, like a massive tidal wave.

Everything about you fascinates me. The way your nose crinkles up when you make a certain face. How your cheeks go rosy when you get embarrassed. That jasmine scent you wear. The way you slip on your reading glasses, and how you twirl your college ring when you're thinking about something. Your teddy bear-covered pajamas. Your raw honesty. Your independence. Your laugh. The way you cry. All of it.

Trixie moved to the register, paid for her meal, and almost ran across the parking lot to her motel room, willing herself to get into seclusion before she fell apart.

That close. I was that close *to happy.*

And it was all a lie.

As soon as the door was secured behind her, she stumbled toward the bed and collapsed to cry herself to sleep.

***

When the jet landed at eight-thirty he scrambled over to Jake, barking out Trixie's address.

"Yes, sir. You okay, sir?"

"No," Drew admitted. "I'm not."

"Where's the young lady?"

"I'm a freaking idiot, Jake, and so we're headed to her place so I can try and get her back," he confided before he could stop himself.

Jake grinned as he placed Drew's bag in the trunk, then shut it. "Found the one, huh, sir."

"Yes, I did," Drew managed to grin back. "Now, I just need to get *her* to realize that."

Jake opened the back door. "Well, then. Let's get moving."

Twenty minutes later, after he'd pounded on her front door so hard that it rattled, he hung his head.

"She's not here," he said despondently. "She didn't come home."

Don't give up, dude. Think. Where else would she go?

"Jake, please take me to the office."

"Yes, sir."

***

Drew only barely restrained himself from running up several flights of stairs to get to the eighth floor. His patience ran thin as he waited for the elevator.

Are you freakin kidding me? It's after nine o'clock on a Friday night. No one's here. What's taking this damn thing so long?

At long last, the doors opened, and he flung himself inside, pressing the number eight key repeatedly.

But to his dismay, her office door was locked, the dark window making it obvious she wasn't in.

What next?

He returned to the elevator and headed for his office. Once inside, he threw his jacket across the visitor's chair she'd sat in, rolled up his sleeves, and fired up his desktop unit.

"Come on, come on," he muttered, willing the computer to hurry through its boot-up sequence.

"Yes!" he hissed in triumph as he finally arrived at the sign-in screen and logged into the mainframe. Navigating quickly, he found what he had hoped to – an emergency contact in Trixie Benning's personnel file that wasn't her ex, Grant.

Meghan Stevens, he noted on a small pad next to his keyboard, and he captured the address and phone number.

Okay, great. What's not *great is you showing up unannounced like some freaking stalker this time of night. Take a breath. Think this through. She hasn't come home. You know she's scared shitless of flying.*

She had to have driven, he realized. *She must be somewhere in between here and Denver.*

And if she stopped somewhere for the night, the earliest she'd be back in town would be sometime early tomorrow afternoon.

"I'll call Meghan Stevens in the morning," he muttered to himself, clinging to the hope that she'd be willing to help him. "Nothing more I can do tonight."

He shut down his computer, locked his office door, and headed home a broken man.

***

Trixie yawned and stretched, wincing at the stiffness in her neck. She moved gingerly, stretching muscles further before she decided a hot shower would be the quickest way to get relief.

She glanced at the clock on the nightstand. Six-twelve a.m.

Huh. I managed to get some sleep. Didn't think that would happen.

She rose, stretching her arms over her head, and headed for the bathroom. In a half-hour's time she'd dressed, packed, loaded her suitcase and turned in her room key. She saw a McDonald's sign not far away and made a run through the drive-through for breakfast.

Trixie left the drive-through lane with her food and pulled into an empty slot. She turned on her cell phone, synced it to her rental car, and dialed Meghan's number before she left the restaurant's parking lot.

"Hey girl, what's up?" Meghan said when she answered.

Trixie burst into tears.

***

Almost an hour later, Meghan said, "Okay, honey. Love you. Be careful, and I will see you in a while, all right?"

Trixie sniffled. "Okay."

Meghan hung up the phone just in time to answer the doorbell.

"Hi. You don't know me, but I need your help, Mrs. Stevens."

"I know *exactly* who you are. You're Drew Alexander, and I just listened to my best friend sob her heart out over you for the last hour. You've got a *hell* of a lot of nerve showing up here," she snarled, eyes flashing.

"Oh, thank God. She's alive. You talked to Trixie? Where is she? Is she all right?" Drew's face was creased and pale with worry, and Meghan's eyebrows raised.

"Why should you care? She told me what you said."

"She overheard parts of a conversation I was having with my father about some property I am buying. Parts that were taken extremely out of context."

"Why should I believe you?"

"Because I'm in love with her, Meghan."

The sincerity in Drew's eyes worked its way past Meghan's suspicion, and she sighed.

"Guess you'd better come in and tell me everything, then. Trixie won't be here for about six hours. She spent the night in Amarillo."

***

"So that's it," Drew wrapped up as he paced back and forth in front of Meghan's couch. "I went to wake her up, see if she wanted to go have breakfast downstairs or order room service, and she wasn't in bed."

He raked his hands through his coal black hair. "Then I thought maybe she'd gone back to her suite to take a shower. I knocked on the connecting door, no answer. Called her room several times. No answer. Went into the hall and pounded so hard on the main door that three other people staying on the eleventh floor stuck their heads out of their rooms to see what the hell was going on."

"And then," he sighed, "I looked every other place in the hotel I could think of. The pool, steam room, business office, gym, bar, and the restaurant. I went to the front counter to ask if they had some sort of paging system, and that's when I found out she'd left."

"Look. I've known Trixie since we were eight years old," Meghan told him. "She told you some of her history, but not all of it. She left out a couple of *huge* pieces. Once you hear them, you'll understand why she reacted the way she did."

"Will you tell me?"

"Yes, I will, because I believe you when you say you love her," she replied. "And if Trix gets mad at me for telling you, well, she'll get over it eventually. We go too far back for her not to."

"Now," Meghan leaned forward in her side chair as Drew settled back on the couch to listen, "the first thing she didn't mention to you was the *reason* she wasn't in the car with Debbie, Shayla, and Mia when the accident happened."

"Which was?"

"Her dad had taken her fishing," Meghan explained. "Trixie and her father were very close. He was her whole world, her 'very best friend', as she used to put it. When her mom and sisters died, it was hard enough, but then her dad just... drifted away from her. She really did lose her entire family due to that drunk driver."

"Oh, my God."

"Yeah. The other really big thing she obviously didn't mention at all was Trey."

"Who?"

"Trey Martani. We all went to school together. She'd had a thing for him since third grade, but nothing ever happened between them until about three years after we graduated high school. He was home on leave from the Navy, we bumped into him at a party, and they hooked up. He was leaving for Diego Garcia for a year, and he asked her to wait for him."

She exhaled heavily. "So, Trixie did. She didn't even look twice at another guy. For an entire year her life was nothing but her college classes, and work, and letter after letter she sent Trey. It was like pulling teeth to get her to go anywhere at all. She even borrowed my old portable stereo with the cassette tape deck, just so she could make mix tapes to send him."

Meghan paused when Drew smiled. "What's so funny?"

"Sorry...It's just... I remember how big a pain in the ass those were to make. You had to wait and listen for the song you wanted to come on the radio, and then you had to press the record button at just the right time, or you wouldn't catch the opening part. Huge pain. She must've *really* been into this guy to go through all that."

"I remember," Meghan smiled too. "And you're right, it was an all-day thing sometimes, just to capture five or six songs. And yes, she was absolutely head over heels for Trey."

"What happened?"

"His letters stopped coming. They got further and further apart, then stopped completely. Trixie was convinced it was only because he was stationed in the middle of nowhere. Anyway, about three days before he was supposed to come home on leave, Trixie called his mom's house to verify when his flight would be landing, since at that point she hadn't heard from Trey in over four months. His mom is the one that had to tell her."

"Tell her what?" Drew leaned forward.

"That Trey had already been home almost a week – and that he'd brought some woman home with him."

CHAPTER FOURTEEN

Drew's jaw dropped wide open.

"*Wow.* I honestly thought you were going to say he'd died... Hold up. Let me get this straight. Trixie put a huge part of her life on hold for a year, *at his request,* and then he hooked up with some bimbo he met in the middle of the ocean? And *then,* he didn't even have the decency to tell Trixie himself, his *mother* had to do it? Is that what you're telling me?"

"Yep," Meghan confirmed. "But believe it or not, it gets worse."

"I don't see how," Drew muttered, shaking his head.

"Here's how. When she bumped into him again several years later, he tried to spin it all, made it sound like he never *asked* her to wait, that she just did, all on her own," Meghan revealed. "Problem with that is, I'd personally read every letter he sent her. She shared every single one with me; she'd kept them all that time. And he was absolutely messing with her head. Every single letter she got from him was about them getting serious once he got home."

"He was lying about what happened back then to try to make himself feel better or look better, I guess," she continued. "All that did was hurt Trixie more. When she told me that, I got him on the phone and called him out on it all, and he catfished even more - until he realized I knew everything he'd said to her in those letters. I think *that's* what finally enabled Trixie to start to move on, hearing him on speakerphone with me when he didn't know she was listening. He showed his true colors, and she finally opened her eyes – to the point of finally getting rid of everything he'd ever sent her. But in the process, it broke her heart all over again."

"Jesus. No wonder Trixie's got trouble trusting people," he announced, anger flashing in his eyes. "Especially men."

"Yeah, that's an understatement," Meghan agreed. "It took her *years* to let another man past her guard again, and that was Grant – another complete jackass, if you ask me. And, well, Trixie already told you what happened there."

Meghan watched as Drew's eyes shifted, filled with pain and outrage on Trixie's behalf.

"She didn't deserve that. *Any of it*. But it certainly explains why she left me the way she did."

"Yep," Meghan confirmed. "That you got as far as you did? That's *huge*, Drew, because that's extremely difficult for her. I'm thinking she must love you, but she just doesn't realize it yet. Otherwise, she would *never* have allowed you to get that close."

"Tell me honestly, Meghan," Drew pleaded. "Do you think she'll listen to me? Give me a chance to explain what she heard?"

"I don't know," Meghan answered him honestly as she shrugged. "I know that's not what you want or need to hear, probably, but it's the truth. The ones that came before you didn't bother to try to explain themselves, so, I don't have a point of reference to go by on that part of all this."

She paused and stared at him a moment.

I'm being weighed and measured, Drew realized. *Please dear God, don't let me be found wanting.*

Then Meghan nodded; she'd decided his worth.

"But I know your intentions are good," she finished. "So, I'm willing to help you."

Drew smiled, and his eyes danced with hope. "And I appreciate that more than you could ever possibly know. I want to spend my life with her, Meghan. I really do."

"I know," Meghan smiled back at him. "I can tell."

Her cell phone rang, and she moved to the kitchen counter where she'd plugged it into the charger.

"It's Trixie," Meghan said before she answered the call, putting her finger to her lips to get Drew to be quiet so Trixie wouldn't hear him in the background. Drew nodded from the kitchen doorway and waited, holding his breath.

"Hey bestie! How far out are you?" she said, then paused, and frowned. "Yes sir, that's me.... uh huh... I'm sorry, I don't think I heard you right, did you just say... what?... *What*?"

Drew watched as Meghan's eyes went huge and her face drained of all color. He stepped forward quickly, brows furrowed, a questioning look on his face.

"Yes... yes...Where?... Oh *God*... okay... okay... Yes sir... thank you. I'm on my way," Meghan managed, and hung up.

"What? What's going on?" Drew said as she swayed, struggling to stay on her feet, tears already falling.

"Drew...Trixie's been in a wreck," Meghan sobbed. "They're transporting her by helicopter to United Regional in Wichita Falls."

***

As soon as Meghan said it, she raced upstairs to pack an overnight bag, and Drew whipped out his phone and called his pilots.

"I have an emergency; we need to be in the air as soon as possible. I'll be at the airstrip in thirty minutes. Be ready to go."

Drew drove as fast as he dared while Meghan called her husband Brad, who immediately assured his wife that he'd handle kids and dogs and anything else, and to keep him updated.

As she told Brad the information that the Texas State Trooper had given her, Drew's gut clenched tighter and tighter, as did his hands on the steering wheel.

The rental's front passenger tire had blown out on an elevated portion of Highway 287 just north of Wichita Falls, Texas, causing Trixie to lose control of the vehicle. The rim had hooked on the gravel shoulder, snapping her car further to the right, and she'd left the roadway, her car flipping several times as it barreled down the grassy embankment to the service road below before coming to rest on its wheels again.

Emergency crews had located her cell phone wedged in next to the back window of the demolished SUV and found Meghan's number listed as Trixie's emergency contact.

Forty minutes after they received the call, Alexander Limited's company jet was lifting off the runway, a frantic Drew and Meghan strapped in tightly in the passenger cabin and praying for miracles as they raced to be by Trixie's side.

"I can't lose her, Meghan," Drew mumbled, tears in his eyes. "I just can't."

She squeezed his arm, and her voice cracked when she said, "Neither can I."

***

When they landed, the car Drew had prearranged was waiting for them on the tarmac. They ran and climbed in.

"United Regional, as quick as you can, please," Drew almost shouted.

"Yes sir, Mr. Alexander," the driver said, and quickly wheeled the car around.

Drew pulled out his cellphone and called his father.

"Dad," he managed. "She's hurt, Dad."

"Where are you?"

"Wichita Falls. We're headed to the hospital now."

"Sir, we'll be there in fifteen minutes, tops," the driver offered helpfully.

"Our ETA is about fifteen, Dad. I'll keep you posted."

"Just say the word, Drew, and I'll head that way."

***

The driver pulled up in front of the hospital's emergency room entrance, and Drew and Meghan ran inside.

"Trixie Benning," Drew barked at the woman at the intake desk. "They said she was being brought in by chopper."

The woman, used to panicked relatives, remained calm and typed a few words into her computer.

"Yes, sir, she arrived about twenty minutes ago. If you will please take a seat just over there, I will try to get a status update for you on her condition."

"Thanks," he muttered, then dragged his hands over his face and trudged off in the direction the woman had indicated. Meghan walked side-by-side with him, her nervous tic of playing with her wedding band in full swing.

They'd only been seated a few minutes when a tall, thin man in scrubs approached and said, "Are you family of Miss Benning?"

They leapt to their feet.

"Yes," Meghan confirmed.

"I'm Dr. Baker," the man said. "If you'll come with me, I'll fill you in on what we know."

He led them past the double doors blocking the waiting area off from the triage units, then directed them into a small room off to the left.

Once the door was closed, he said, "Okay, we have quite a bit to cover here. You're aware Trixie was in a rollover accident this afternoon."

Drew nodded. "The trooper told us that when he called."

"I thought he might have," Baker said. "What he probably didn't mention was that the emergency

crews had to use the jaws of life tool to extricate
Trixie from the car. She took one hell of a ride.
Fortunately, she had her seat belt on, the front and
side airbags deployed as designed, and she rolled
down a relatively soft embankment. Had her vehicle
left the roadway fifty feet later, she'd have gone off
the bridge, and landed at a much higher rate of travel
on the road below."

"Now," the doctor took a breath. "I have to make
you aware that her injuries were quite severe. The
paramedics lost her pulse once at the scene, and once
more during the flight here."

Were?

He's using past tense... Oh, no. Jesus, please,
no.... Time stopped as Drew reached out blindly.

Drew and Meghan both began to shake, and
Meghan gripped his hand tightly for support before
the lanky surgeon's next words restored some order
to their upside-down world.

"But for now, she seems to have stabilized, and
we're prepping her for surgery. She broke her left leg,
her pelvis, her left arm and collarbone, and there are
hairline fractures of four vertebrae in her lower back.
In addition, the CT scan revealed a ruptured spleen, a
lacerated left kidney, and a broken rib that punctured
her left lung. She's also got a head injury; we're still
trying to determine how severe that is. All tests so far
show no sign of skull fractures or swelling on her
brain, which is excellent news."

"Is she going to make it?" Drew asked in a rush
with a tremor in his voice. "When can we see her?"

"She's still very critical, but stable at the
moment," Baker responded. "Like I said, they're
prepping her for surgery now, and we'll address the
injuries in order of severity. Because there's going to
be so many things happening in the surgical suite, I
can't give you an estimated length of time yet. What I
can do is have one of my staff come to the surgery
waiting area with updates as we have them. As far as

seeing her, there's just not enough time right now. We must get moving, quickly, to try to repair the damage she's suffered, and prevent more. But I promise that as soon as we're able, we will come get you and take you to her. All right? Hang in there, guys. We're going to do all we can for her, and I've got some of the best people in the business involved with her care."

A rap sounded on the door, and a petite woman in scrubs entered. "Dr. Baker, they're just about ready for you, sir," she said.

"Okay, guys, let me get to work. I'll speak with you personally once the surgeries are done, all right?" And he slipped out the door.

CHAPTER FIFTEEN

"Hello, my name's Julia. If you'll please follow me, I've got a room just outside the surgical unit where you can wait," the nurse told Drew and Meghan.

"Coffee and vending machines are just down the hall here," Julia indicated. "But I think you'll find this little room to be more comfortable than the main waiting area. Can I get you anything?"

"Take good care of her. She's my whole world," Drew managed.

Julia nodded, said, "I'll come out as often as I can to give you updates," and patted his shoulder before she walked out.

"I need to call Brad and update him," Meghan sniffled.

"I need coffee. You want some coffee? I can bring you back a cup," Drew offered.

"Yeah, with cream and sugar," Meghan replied as she pulled out her phone. "Thanks."

And after that, I'll need to make some calls too. This hospital just became the center of my universe until Trixie gets to get out of here, Drew thought as he made his way to the coffeepot. *Because I'm damn sure not leaving here without her.*

***

In the third hour, Julia appeared with an update.

"We've addressed the injuries to Trixie's spleen, lung, and kidney. She's holding up well under anesthesia, and we're moving quickly now to work on tending to all the fractures. Dr. Baker and the team are working to get it all done at once, so that we don't have to put her under a second time. Now, if her vitals show any sign of stress at all, we'll halt everything, and go back in later. But Dr. Baker thought you'd like to know her progress. Said to tell you both 'so far, so good'."

***

By the time Julia came out again three hours later, Drew's father had arrived with a suitcase, a phone charger, Drew's laptop, and some sandwiches.

"Your mom thought you might be getting hungry," he said as he stepped into the room and introduced himself to Meghan. "Hello. I'm Blake Alexander, Drew's father."

"Hi, Dad," Drew said, and hugged him.

Julia appeared in the doorway.

"They're wrapping up now. We'll be moving her to post-op within the next hour, I'd say, and it might take a bit after that to get her settled before you can see her. But I promise, as soon as she's set, I will come get you. Dr. Baker should be out in the next twenty minutes or so to give you more details."

***

At last Dr. Baker reappeared, tired but smiling.

"Hi folks. Couple things I want to get into, but I want to start off by saying everything went very smoothly, no issues. We'll be moving her to post-op here shortly, and once the anesthesia's out of her system, she'll make the trip to ICU. After that, we'll see how she does."

"Is she still critical?"

"In my view, she's downgraded to serious but stable. We had to put plates and pins in both her pelvis and her left leg. The arm was a simple fracture, no issues, so we've set it and put her in a gel cast, for now. The biggest problems were her spleen, which we did have to remove, and her fractured pelvis, which will take the longest time to heal – usually, three to five months. She's going to need physical therapy for a good while, and it might be a hard road back. But I am very optimistic that she can and will make a full recovery."

"Now," Baker added, "she might still be on the respirator when you see her. But don't let that alarm you. It's standard procedure. We're just making certain she's getting the help she needs to breathe until the anesthesia leaves her system completely and her breathing can happen naturally, okay? Just so you're aware."

"Thank you so much for everything, doc," Meghan said, and hugged him.

"Yes, thanks, doc." Drew shook his hand.

"I'll be back around later tonight to check on her, and I'll see you then," Dr. Baker said, and with one final nod, left the room.

"Oh, thank God," Drew managed before he finally broke down and cried like a small child in his father's arms.

He truly loves her, Meghan realized, fighting back her own tears enough to be able to dial her husband's number.

***

The next time Julia came to them, it was to escort one of them back to post-op.

"You go first," Meghan urged. "It's all right."

"Thanks," Drew said, and grabbed her in a fierce hug. "I promise I won't take up all the time."

Then he turned to Julia. "Take me to her, please."

He followed the nurse down the hallway to a set of double doors. Julia pressed the large square button set into the wall on the right, and Drew heard the soft hiss of the lock releasing to open the doors.

They walked in silence until they reached bay six, to Drew's right.

"Fifteen minutes, then we'll go back out, and I'll bring your friend in," Julia said. "We have to keep visits to a minimum in post-op."

"I understand," Drew told her earnestly. "I'm just happy I get to see her."

"I'll be back shortly," Julia added, and walked over to the nurses' station.

Drew took a deep breath and approached the bed. To either side, a battery of machines hummed, chirped, and buzzed. He could see the monitor that reflected her heartrate and blood pressure, and it buoyed his spirits to see healthy readouts.

He slowly took his eyes from the machines and gazed at her face, trying not to gasp as he took in the myriad of bruises and scrapes. She was still on a respirator, and although he knew it was helping her, it pained him to see the mechanical, forced motions of her chest, so unlike when she'd been curled against him in sleep.

"Trixie," he whispered, his voice breaking. "Trixie, I'm here." He moved to her right side and took her limp hand in his.

The tears ran unchecked down his cheeks as he squeezed her hand, stroked her hair, and told her, "I thought I'd lost you, and it devastated me, Trixie. I love you so, so much, and I'm going to be right here with you, baby, every step of the way. We'll do it together, Trixie. You and me."

He kissed the hand he was holding, then leaned down and kissed her forehead very gently.

When he stood upright again, he was shocked to see those big brown eyes he adored open and gazing at him for just a moment, then closing again.

Then she squeezed his hand back.

And Drew Alexander felt reborn.

Much too soon, his fifteen minutes with her had sailed by. He reluctantly let go of her hand and followed Julia back out to where Meghan was waiting her turn.

***

"Son, what can I do to help?" Blake said once Drew sat down heavily on the two-seat couch in the little room they'd spent all day in.

"I'm not sure," Drew admitted, his fingers raking his hair for the hundredth time. "I'm not leaving, Dad, I can tell you that much. I know they probably won't let me stay in ICU with her overnight, but once they get her moved into a regular room, they'll have to *drag* me out."

"Drew," his father said gently as he placed his hand on his son's shoulder. "You need rest, too. It doesn't mean you love her any less if you get some sleep and take time to shower and eat. It won't do her any good at all if the very first thing she sees is that you've run yourself into the ground."

Drew exhaled sharply. "I almost lost her, Dad. *And she doesn't know how I feel about her.* Not really. I hinted around about it, but I never just came right out and said that I love her. Now I've been given another chance to tell her, and I don't want to take it for granted."

"But you're right," he continued. "I need sleep, and food. I need to be at my best so I can be there for her, and right now, I'm not."

Meghan walked through the doorway. "Her face is so beat up," she whispered, looking emotionally and physically drained.

"Yeah," Drew agreed.

Meghan wiped her eyes and cleared her throat. "Julia said they won't be moving her to ICU for two more hours, at least, and she suggested we leave, go get some food, try to get some sleep, since visiting hours for the ICU unit are over for the night already. We can't see her until seven a.m."

"We were just discussing those very things," Blake replied.

"I know they have your number, Meghan," Drew said. "I want to give them mine, too, and then I guess let's go figure out where we're staying and what comes next."

***

They found a hotel two blocks from the hospital, and Drew booked two rooms for a week.

"Meet you guys downstairs in, say forty minutes, and we'll eat?" Meghan had asked, and the men nodded.

They parted company on the fourth floor, Meghan heading to her room to shower and change, while Drew and Blake walked further down the hallway and located Drew's room.

"Drew, I was thinking about it, and I wonder if I can be the most help to you by making sure Alexander Limited is running all right while you're away," Blake said. "I recall what you told me about Bill, and you mentioned your comptroller's overseas with a busted leg. Seems to me you might need to figure out who's gonna head up Accounting in the interim, since Trixie's the most senior after those two."

"Yeah, I need to. Gotta keep that department going, keep the employees and our vendors paid, at least. As I recall, you know your way around pretty good in that world, Dad," Drew said, and managed a smile. "I could really use the help, and I appreciate it. Having you involved means I can rest easy on that part of things, and just focus on what's happening here."

"Hey, what's the use of owning my own CPA firm if I can't use my powers for good?" Blake joked. "Consider it done. I'll head back in the morning, and I'll be at your office building bright and early Monday."

CHAPTER SIXTEEN

At six-forty-five a.m., they returned to the hospital. Blake had successfully talked Meghan and Drew both into catching at least a few hours' sleep.

"She was moved to ICU very early this morning," the helpful and friendly volunteer said once she'd looked up Trixie's name in the hospital database. "You've got good timing. Visiting hours start in just a few minutes. Fourth floor. You can take the elevators just over there to the left."

When they stepped off the elevator, they were greeted by another volunteer whose lapel tag said 'Valerie.'

"Hi, Valerie. We're here to see Trixie Benning."

She dutifully checked the system, then nodded. "She's in room 202. Here, you'll need these," and handed each of them visitor's badges with the room number written on them. "Only two back at a time, though."

"Is anyone allowed to stay overnight?"

"No," Valerie replied, "I'm so sorry. But once she's out of ICU, you should be able to. Just go right through those doors there," she pointed. "Room 202 will be on your left."

"This is where I'll say goodbye for now," Blake announced. "I'm gonna head back. Keep me updated, will you?"

"Thanks for everything, Dad," Drew gave his father one last bear hug. "And yes, I'll be in touch. Tell Mom I love her, all right?"

"I will. Meghan, I'm sorry it was under these circumstances, but it was nice to meet you. Hopefully we'll get a chance to visit again, in happier times."

"Likewise, Mr. Alexander, and thanks."

Drew and Meghan attached the visitor's badges to their jackets and walked through the oversize double doors. An alarm sounded, and they both froze as they watched medical staff scrambling into a room on the left side of the hallway. Meghan grabbed Drew's hand, and he wondered if they were thinking the same thing.

Please, dear God, don't let that be Trixie.

To their great relief, it wasn't. The patient in room 206's alarm had sounded, and from the slowing activity Drew could see, it wasn't a critical event after all.

He closed his eyes a moment and willed his racing heart to slow back down to normal.

"You all right?" Meghan murmured.

"Yeah," Drew whispered. "For a moment I thought... I thought..."

"Me too," she whispered back, and tightened her grip temporarily before she let go of his hand and they walked the rest of the way to Trixie's room.

Meghan went in first, while Drew leaned against the wall for just a moment to collect himself. He heard Meghan say, "Hey, honey, you're awake!"

"Yeah," Trixie rasped. "Hurting. Where am I?"

Her voice sounded rough and gravelly, but to Drew's ears it was music. *She's alive. She's awake and talking.*

The gratitude he felt overwhelmed him to the point it threatened to buckle his knees right there in the hallway. He wiped away a happy tear that had strayed down his face, then took a deep breath and stepped around the doorframe and into Trixie's room.

Trixie's eyes cut to the movement in the doorway, saw him, and narrowed.

"Hi," he managed, his green eyes bright with tears.

"Hi," she whispered, then frowned and looked sideways at Meghan. "Where am I, and why is *he* here?"

The pointed way she said 'he' felt like a bullet through Drew's chest.

"You had a car wreck, and you're in the hospital," Meghan told her. "And him? Well..."

"He's here because he is, without question, one hundred percent head over heels in love with you," Drew finished as he slowly walked to stand by her bed. "So, here is *exactly* where he needs and wants to be."

Trixie's brown eyes went huge, and she murmured, "Hallucinating. Must be."

"I assure you, you heard him correctly," Meghan said. "He loves you, Trix."

"You do?" she croaked, her gaze locked with his.

"Like I said. One hundred percent, no question at all."

She grimaced. "Hurting...leg..."

"I'll get someone for you, honey, be right back," Meghan volunteered, and skirted past Drew, who moved to Trixie's right side and took her hand.

Leaning forward, he lightly touched his forehead to hers, and whispered, "Trixie Benning, you have my heart. And I promise to never leave your side. I'll be with you every step of the way through this."

"We'll do it together. You and me," Trixie parroted back his words to her in post-op. "I didn't dream that. You really said that. You were here."

"No, you didn't dream that," he said as he tenderly kissed her forehead. "And I meant every single word I said."

"Don't understand... I thought... I heard..."

"I'll explain everything once you're a little bit better, I promise, Trixie."

"'Kay," she mumbled, as the nurse who'd stepped into the room added pain medication to her IV line. "Gonna sleep now."

"And I will be here when you wake up, baby," he said softly as she drifted down. "Every day, for the rest of our lives. I love you."

She surfaced again long enough to say, "Love you too."

He smiled.

***

The doctor finally released her from the hospital five weeks later, and Drew insisted on moving her into his house.

"What about Joshie?" had been her first concern.

"What about him? I have a huge backyard and multiple years' experience with playing fetch and giving belly scratches. He'll love it at my place."

"What about work?"

"It will still be there when you get back, Trixie," he said softly. "Or I can make sure you're completely set up to work remotely, your call."

She stuck her tongue out at him.

"Smartass," she teased. "I was talking about *you*. You have a company to run. You can't afford to be away."

"The hell I can't," he told her, and watched her brow furrow in confusion.

He knew the second she put it all altogether, because her eyes suddenly got huge.

"You took the buyout deal."

He nodded. "Ran it by the board and although they were surprised as hell, they voted one hundred percent in favor of moving forward with it."

"So... when does all that become official?"

"End of next month. And until then, I'm on leave to tend to my gorgeous girlfriend. At least, *I* consider her my girlfriend. I suppose I should probably ask her to *officially* be my girlfriend, huh?"

She swatted his shoulder. "You think?"

"Will you be my girlfriend?"

"Abso-freakin-lutely. So," she continued as he grinned at her, "let's talk lunch. I'm starving. And exhausted. That PT session earlier today wore me out. I wanna eat and take a nap."

"Not a bad plan, Benning. Think I'll join you. Hey, I have an idea," he said. "How about a nice salad? I can make you one. Someone gave me a great recipe once."

"Sure. What is it?"

"Well," he began, "It starts with good old romaine, but it needs stuff to liven it up some."

Her eyebrow raised.

"Then add tomatoes, avocado, purple onion, some nice colorful bell peppers, blue cheese crumbles, and strips of filet mignon. With vinaigrette dressing," he finished, and chuckled as her mouth dropped wide open.

"What? Did I forget an ingredient?"

"You *did* remember me from the grocery store."

Drew looked into her eyes and took her hand.

"Baby," he said softly, "that night was etched into my soul. I never forgot you in the first place."

***

Drew was by her side every day, cheering her on during her grueling physical therapy sessions. After five months, when she was fully healed and able to walk without a cane, he suggested, "Hey, let's go for a drive. I'd like to show you something."

"Sure, lead the way."

They drove leisurely, enjoying each other's company and a warm spring day, until finally Drew said, "Ah, here we are," and turned off the paved two-lane road onto a long gravel stretch.

"Where are we going?" Trixie asked, her curiosity piqued.

"You'll see," he said with a grin.

"Estalle Ranch," she read aloud when they got to the ornate sign hanging over their path.

"Not for much longer, it's not. But I need your help," Drew told her.

"I'm totally confused, honey. What are you talking about?"

"Just a little bit further," he said mysteriously.

Another quarter of a mile, and they rounded a corner to reveal a breathtaking view.

"This is… this is beautiful," Trixie gasped. "Is this a resort?"

"Sort of," Drew answered. "Remember that sanctuary idea I told you about?"

"Yes."

"This is where it's gonna be. I bought this place. I've wanted it for years, and I finally got it. This is the 'sweet little piece' you overhead me talking to my dad about when we were in Denver. That was the morning I got the email that they'd accepted my offer to buy the ranch."

Trixie's eyes welled up. "The day I ran away."

"The day I almost lost you," he acknowledged, squeezing her hand. "But that's past now, baby. We're together."

"I never said I'm sorry for putting you through that."

"No need, Trixie. Never say sorry. I'm in love with you, and you're in love with me. We're solid, baby, believe me."

He parked the truck, walked around and opened her door, then extended his hand to her.

"Now," he announced, "I have a really important thing I need your help with."

She clasped his hand and stepped out of the truck.

"And that is?"

"What to call this place. I didn't want to name it without you."

She mulled it over for a moment.

"How about 'Another Try'?"

He grinned. "I love it. It's perfect."

She leaned into him as he wrapped his arms around her.

"There's a lot of work to do out here to get this place ready, you know."

"I figured," she murmured.

"So, you with me on this, Benning?"

"You bet, Super-Hot Drew."

He raised an eyebrow. "Beg pardon?"

She snickered. "That was the nickname I gave you after we met in the store."

"Super-Hot Drew..." he looked down at her. "Huh... sounds kinda conceited. How about 'Trixie's Drew' instead?"

"I love it."

***

One year later, Trixie beamed with pride as Drew stepped up and cleared his throat.

"If I could have everyone's attention, please," he said into the podium's microphone on a perfect late fall morning in Nacogdoches, Texas.

The one-hundred-plus audience settled in to listen.

"We're thrilled you all could be here today," he began. "What started as a childhood dream so many years ago is at last now a reality. The facility we've built here will house animals that for whatever reason can't be placed in forever homes. I've loved animals as far back as I can remember, and I feel very blessed to be able to help, protect, and care for those that might otherwise be a tragic statistic. We want to thank you all very much for your support, and we welcome you to the grand opening of Another Try."

A strategically posed ribbon-cutting ceremony for posterity, and it was done. The double doors swung open, and the crowd made its way into the main building.

"I am so proud of you," Trixie said as she tucked her arm around his waist.

"Us, baby. *Us.* I couldn't have done this without you," Drew replied before leaning down to kiss her gently.

They stood, side-by-side, accepting congratulations and answering questions from those that passed on the way to tour the facility.

"We'll have two full-time veterinarians onsite to begin with," Drew responded to one query. "And we hope to add a third within two years."

"Mr. Alexander, Miss Benning, thank you for inviting us," a woman with green eyes and long brown hair said as she stepped forward. "My name is Madeleine, and this is my husband, Mason. We run a non-profit shelter up in North Texas, and unfortunately, we're already at capacity. I'd like to talk to you both about how we can get some of our long-term residents relocated down here at Another Try so that we can continue to help new cases."

"We'd be delighted to assist, Madeleine," Trixie said. "Do you two have plans this afternoon? We can talk some more while we have lunch, get a solid plan in place."

"That'd be great," Mason chimed in. "Thanks."

***

That evening, Trixie carried the pasta to the table while Drew sliced up the garlic bread and Joshua curled up contentedly in the corner on his doggy bed.

"I think today was a huge hit," she said. "And I really enjoyed meeting and talking with Madeleine and Mason. They've got the same mindset we do."

"Yep," Drew agreed. "And I think working with them will enable us to help even more dogs that need us."

Trixie smiled. "I don't know that things could get any better," she announced as she scooped pasta from the serving bowl onto their plates.

"I can only think of one more thing that would make it all completely perfect," Drew said behind her. "More... what's the word I'm looking for... *proper*."

"Really? What's that?" Trixie asked as she finished plating the pasta and set the bowl down.

She turned around and gasped to see him down on one knee, his arms extended toward her, holding an open box in his hands with a gorgeous ring in it that sparkled in the candlelight.

"Trixie Benning, will you marry me?"
Her eyes went wide, then filled with happy tears.
"Yes," she whispered. "Yes."

The End

Save Me a Dance

Evan and **Karli Anders** have been married for five years. She's making plans for them when he gets home from his business trip.

An unexpected knock at the door turns out to be **Jordan Baker** – confirmed bachelor, **Evan's** best friend, and the man she's convinced can't stand her – standing there, still in his EMT uniform, to give her the most horrible news of her life... **Evan's** been killed in a drunk driving accident.

Karli must now navigate burying her husband, then prepare to face an additional challenge alone - have and raise the child she *just* found out she's carrying. Or so she thinks.

What she doesn't realize is that **Jordan** would happily step up and be the loving partner she wants and needs for the rest of her life - if she'll only let him in.

But an unforeseen twist could dash all **Jordan's** hopes for good.

PROLOGUE

Jordan could still remember the very first time Evan mentioned her. They were juniors in college...

"You've *got* to meet this girl," Evan told him as they walked toward the quad after class one late September afternoon. "I think she might be the one."

"The one?" Jordan said, incredulous that 'Mister One-Night-Stand' himself would even think about monogamy. "You don't even know what that *means*. You go through women like water. You, Evan Anders, are a *poster boy* for players and heartbreakers everywhere."

"You're not wrong," Evan grinned. "But there's just something about this girl...anyway, I'm bringing her to the Omega party tonight. I seriously want you to meet her."

"Whatever, dude," Jordan replied, shaking his head.

"You're going, right? Jordan – tell me you're going. Too much studying isn't good for you."

"And *you* really *shouldn't* be going," Jordan shot back. "You really need to do *more* studying, Evan. Football's only gonna get you so far, man, and it's hard to find a team to play on if they kick your dumb ass out of college."

Evan looked at him for a long moment. "Remind me again how it is we're best friends?"

But Jordan honestly had never been able to figure that one out himself. He and Evan Anders were as opposite as could be. Evan was six feet two, with broad shoulders and the typical blond-and-blue Adonis-like looks women swoon over, not to mention a gifted football player. He was also extremely outgoing - he'd never met a stranger.

Jordan, on the other hand, preferred solitude and learning, thought his dark brown hair and eyes were boring, and was still hoping for the late growth spurt that would *finally* launch him past his current best-ever five feet eight inches tall.

But for whatever reason, they'd become fast friends in seventh grade, and it had stayed that way ever since.

"Come on, man," Evan sulked. "I really want you to meet her."

"Okay, okay, fine," Jordan said in exasperation. "But I'm not gonna stay long. Some of us actually *care* about our grades, you know."

"You're such a dork," Evan teased, and shoved Jordan lightly, like a brother might. "See you tonight, man."

And Evan veered off the sidewalk, moving over the grass toward the dorms reserved exclusively for the football team.

***

Four hours later, Jordan found himself in the middle of a collegiate Greek tragedy. The levels of drunkenness were already reaching epic heights by the time he arrived - even for Omegas.

Evan owes me big, he thought bitterly. *He's the only freakin' reason I'm here.*

He shoved his way through a mass of sweaty bodies jumping and swaying to a blaringly loud and seemingly endless techno grind, and finally made it into the frat house's kitchen where it was quieter – but not by much. Striding to the other side of the room, he took a chance but found only a single cold beer left in the fridge.

Frustrated, he closed the refrigerator door, then turned around and bumped straight into the woman of his dreams.

I'll be damned. Love at first sight does *exist,* he thought, then fought against the heat he felt creeping into his face.

She stood, watching him with her sapphire blue eyes, twirling a small strand of her long blond hair around her index finger. She stood maybe five feet six, at the most, with golden, sun-kissed skin and curves in all the right places. Even in a t-shirt and faded jeans, she owned the room.

"Anything other than beer in there?" she asked hopefully, and her sweet Southern drawl was as warm and rich as a fine whiskey.

Jordan stood gaping at her for a moment before he managed to find his voice.

"Nope," he answered, and it sounded rough and scratchy to his ears. He cleared his throat and tried again.

"No," he said. "Not even water."

"That's a shame," the angelic vision in front of him said. "I don't drink beer."

"Me either. Too bitter."

Her cute little nose wrinkled as she answered him.

"I know, right? The taste isn't bad, but the aftertaste..." her voice trailed off as she shuddered. "Blech."

"My name's Jordan," he said, then endured another stretch of unbearable silence during which they just stared at one another. To break it, he blurted out, "Baker."

"You're a baker?" she grinned in amusement, and her smile made his heart grow wings.

"No," he managed to say, and found himself smiling back at her. "That's my last name. Jordan Baker."

She held out her hand in greeting, and when he clasped it, he swore he felt an electric current surge through his body, so powerful he wanted to sing.

She began to speak, to tell him her name, but was interrupted.

"Jordan! My man!" he heard Evan shout from the kitchen doorway. "There you are. And hey, perfect timing. My two favorite people are here."

Oh no, Jordan thought. *Dude, don't say it...*

"Karli, this is Jordan, my best friend since what, fifth grade?"

"Seventh," he corrected Evan, his stomach filling with lead at what he knew Evan was going to say next.

"Jordan, this is Karli Bellows... the one I was telling you about."

Of course, she is...

As he watched them standing together, Evan's arm slung casually around Karli's dainty shoulders, Jordan realized that for the first time since he'd met Evan Anders, he wanted very badly to be in his shoes...

But it wouldn't be the last time. Not by a long shot.

Not when it came to Karli Bellows.

CHAPTER ONE

Seven years later...

Jordan Baker was a man on a mission. He'd already been lifting weights on a regular basis because it kept him fit for his work as a paramedic. But lately he'd taken up running, and he'd gotten serious enough about it that training for a half-marathon had crossed his mind more than once.

With his headphones in place, he pounded down the jogging trail that wound its way around the park across from his apartment complex, making his usual two circuits on a sunny spring afternoon. As he ran, he was ever watchful for that shapely figure with the familiar blond ponytail. And as always, his heart skipped a beat when he saw it.

One year earlier, Evan and Karli had bought their dream home in the subdivision on the other side of the park, and Jordan's sightings of Karli had increased. Normally, he only saw her from a distance and didn't have to interact with her. But this time, Karli was heading straight for him.

Lord help me... Game face, dude, he reminded himself.

"Hey, Jordan!" she said with a smile, waving him to a stop. "How's it going?"

"Fine. You?"

"Um, good, I guess," she said uncertainly. "We haven't seen you much lately."

The conversation faltered into silence, with Karli watching Jordan, a hopeful expression on her face.

What do you want me to say, Karli? You're married to my best friend, for crying out loud. The only way I can make sure I don't tell you I love you is not to talk to you at all, his mind answered. *Especially not when we're alone.*

But he kept a stone face and shrugged, even as he inwardly cursed Evan once more. *Dammit, dude, of all the subdivisions in Arlington, Texas... You just had to pick that one...*

"Work and training. Keeps me busy."

"Oh," Karli said, her smile faltering. "Okay, so, see you around, I guess?" she managed.

"Yeah," he replied curtly, and jogged away, with the hurt look on her face burning into his core.

He could feel her troubled eyes watching him as he moved away from her and down the jogging trail, and he kicked up his speed almost to capacity to outrun her gaze.

"I'm gonna propose, bro," Evan had said. "Will you be my best man?"

And six months after that, I had to stand there and watch the woman I'm in love with walk down the aisle – and marry the guy standing right next to me.

Neither of them had any clue what it cost me to stay quiet when the preacher asked for objections...

With a flood of memories chasing close behind him, Jordan sprinted until he was certain he was going to drop.

***

I don't understand it, Karli thought mournfully as she slowly jogged along the path. *He's never liked me, and I have no idea why. I've always been nice to him... he's Evan's best friend, so I know he's important to Evan. I just wish he and I could get along better.*

She recalled the first time she'd told Evan, "I don't think your friend likes me very much."

Evan had chuckled, then dismissed her concerns, saying, "That's just Jordan. He doesn't like anybody. Don't take it personally."

I didn't buy that then, and I still don't, Karli realized as she ran. *He couldn't get away from me quickly enough just now... I think Jordan Baker has a problem with me.*

I just wish I knew why.

***

Because he'd pushed so hard on the trail, Jordan took his time on the walk back to his apartment to make sure his legs wouldn't cramp up. He prayed he wouldn't run into Karli again along the way, and by some small miracle his wish was granted; she was nowhere in sight.

When he got back to his apartment, he threw his keys on the counter and took a long drink of water. Then he stripped off his sweaty clothes to head for the shower, and Jordan happened to glance in the bathroom mirror as he passed it. Even now, it shocked him to see his toned and muscled reflection – after all, he'd been a bit pudgy for most of his life.

All this exercising I'm doing has paid off, he noted. *Of course, finally breaching six feet helped too,* he concluded with a grin, and turned on the shower.

***

"So, when are you coming back?" Karli asked Evan on their nightly call.

"I should be home tomorrow night around ten," he said. "At least, that's the way it looks right now. If I have to stay longer, I'll text you and let you know. Okay?"

"Okay," she answered, even though it really wasn't okay at all. He had not spent more than two nights in a row at home in three months and counting. She knew he had no choice – as a regional sales manager, his career involved extensive travel – but it still irritated her how much time his job was carving away from a life together.

"I love you," she said earnestly, and didn't notice the brief pause before Evan replied, "I love you too."

***

"Another day, another dollar, right, Baker?" Tim quipped.

It was the twentieth day in a row that Tim and Jordan had been assigned overnight shift on Fire Station Number Two's EMT crew.

Jordan grinned. "Yep, that's what I hear. What *I* want to know is, who did you piss off to get us stuck with overnights for this long?"

Tim raised his hands in a gesture of defeat. "Not sure, but I'm sorry."

"Makes it hard to have an active social life, man," Jordan mock grumbled.

"Oh, totally, because I just *know* the babes are beating down your door," came the barbed response from his rig partner.

"Hey, you don't know for a fact they're *not*," Jordan fired back.

"Whatever, dude. Get clocked in, and let's go," Tim said. "We need to go fill up the rig – again."

"Seriously?" Jordan exclaimed. "Day shift can't be bothered to stop at a gas pump once in a while?"

"Guess not. Let's roll, buddy."

They climbed into the back of the ambulance and did the pre-run check of supplies before heading out to the gas station a few blocks away. Tim manned the pump while Jordan went in to pay the cashier.

Now armed with a full tank of gas, they pulled away from the pumps, and Tim waited for cross traffic to clear before pulling back onto the road.

From the corner of his eye, Jordan noticed a familiar car approaching from Tim's side of the ambulance.

Hey, that's Evan's car, he realized. *Thought he was out of town for work...*

Then he took a second look and frowned as Evan's car passed in front of them, and the rig's headlights illuminated the interior.

And who is that in the passenger seat?

His jaw clenched, Jordan pulled out his cell phone and fired off a text.

He didn't get an answer until after his shift was over.

***

Jordan climbed the stairs to his apartment at eight-forty a.m., emotionally and physically worn out from his night. What had promised to be a relatively calm Thursday overnight shift had turned hectic in a hurry. A four-car pile-up at three-forty a.m. involving eight passengers and four drivers had both he and Tim moving quickly to assess and assist the injured.

Two victims had been pinned in the wreckage for over an hour, and Jordan had tried his best to keep them awake and talking as the jaws of life were used to extricate them. But one, Kevin, a young boy no more than thirteen, had drifted into unconsciousness and died before Jordan could get close enough to help him.

He set his keys on the counter and ran his hands over his face, then through his hair. He reached for the decanter and had just begun to pour himself three fingers of whiskey when his phone buzzed in his pocket. He pulled it out and scanned Evan's messages.

"What the *hell* are you doing, Evan?" he muttered as he typed back a terse message. *You said you stopped. You obviously lied. Karli doesn't deserve this, Evan. Either you tell her – or I will.*

Disgusted with it all, Jordan plugged in his phone, downed his drink, and headed for a hot shower, then bed.

***

The alarm sounding later that afternoon caused Jordan's brows to furrow tightly.

"Already?" he mumbled, snaking his hand out from under the covers to press the snooze bar on the device and drifting off again.

But the machine's insistent beeping ten minutes later caused him to snarl and throw the covers back.

Come on, lazy, go run, he chided himself. *And then get ready for what will probably be a long Friday night.*

He staggered his way over to the dresser and grabbed shorts and a t-shirt. As he got dressed, he could hear his phone buzzing repeatedly from the kitchen, but it stopped before he could finish tying his shoes.

Jordan moved through his apartment toward the counter where he had plugged in his phone. He picked it up and saw multiple texts from Evan.

About time you came to your senses, he told his friend silently as he read Evan's words. But Jordan also noticed Evan had not mentioned any plans to confess to Karli.

Why not tell Karli what he's been up to anyway? his conscience asked. *Doesn't she deserve to know that she's been taking their vows way more seriously than Evan has?*

She does, he answered himself. *But I am the last person she needs to hear it from. I could tell her – but if I do, I need to make damn sure it is for the right reasons, not a selfish one.*

He sighed as he closed and locked his apartment door to head to the park, hoping he didn't cross paths with Karli during his run.

***

I don't feel like running. But it's gorgeous out. I think I will just take my time and walk and enjoy the sunshine, Karli decided. She changed into her jogging suit and headed for the park, hoping that physical activity would help calm her growing restlessness.

She meandered down the trail, watching a group of small children squeal with laughter as they took turns down the slide in the park's playground to her left.

Karli turned her face away from the playground to focus on the path in front of her and noticed Jordan some distance away but approaching quickly.

A strange thought popped into her head. *Maybe I just need to ask him what the hell his problem is.*

She waited until he was close enough, then waved to get his attention. But he never slowed his pace and moved past her without acknowledging her at all. Stunned that anyone could be that rude, she stopped and turned around, watching him as he disappeared further along the trail.

Wow. I know for a fact he saw me. What a jerk.

It was just enough to torpedo her mood, and Karli's eyes brimmed with tears of hurt and frustration.

***

He was so focused on his running and his music that he didn't see Karli until it was too late.

There she is, right in front of me, Jordan realized. *Dammit. What do I do?*

He could not take the chance of stopping and talking to her. Not right now. He couldn't trust himself to stay aloof and not bring Evan's deeds to light.

So, he'd taken the path of least resistance – which was not to even acknowledge her, much less talk to her, and he'd noticed the flash of surprise and hurt in her eyes as he'd run right on past her without stopping.

I am so sorry, Karli. But it's better for us all if you think I'm an ass. Trust me.

Even so, he completed the rest of his circuit with a heavy heart, knowing he had intentionally hurt her, and knowing he could never apologize for it. After all, apologies involved talking, and if he talked to Karli, all sorts of things might come to light that were much better off left unsaid.

Why can't I just move on, find somebody else? he shouted in his brain as he ran.

You know why, came the familiar answer. *Fool yourself all you like, but you already know exactly why.*

CHAPTER TWO

Since she knew Evan would not be home in time for dinner anyway, she indulged herself and made one of her favorites – angel hair pasta with chicken and mushrooms. Cooking had always been a favorite hobby of hers, and Karli had found over time that the simple motions of preparing a meal also soothed her soul when something was weighing on her.

And something was. Karli shook her head, still in shock about what had happened in the park.

Still cannot believe Jordan just raced on by like that. He's not even trying *to hide the fact that he hates me anymore. And I still have no idea what I have done to him to deserve that.*

She plated her meal, then poured herself a glass of the red wine she enjoyed occasionally. She had heard small amounts of wine could help settle an upset stomach, and hers had been acting up for the last couple of days.

Really hope it's not the flu, she thought as she moved to the living room. *I would like to be able to have a decent weekend with Evan – provided he gets to be home for once, that is.*

Karli curled up on her end of the couch, flipped on the TV and called up the recordings of her favorite true crime series. She scrolled down, finding the next one in sequence that she had not seen yet, and pressed play.

Seven o'clock, she noted, twirling pasta onto her fork and spearing a chunk of chicken to accompany it as the opening credits came on. *Evan will be home in three hours. But until then, I am unplugging my mind. Gonna enjoy my food and my show.*

***

"Ready for another one?" Tim asked.

"You know it," Jordan answered. "I just hope it's not *too* interesting tonight. Maybe the drunks will have the sense to let someone else drive."

"I hear ya. Hey – grab some more gauze rolls and tape, we're low on the rig," Tim requested.

"You got it. Anything else we need to stock before our shift starts?"

"And…" Tim rummaged through the last cabinet, "two more cold packs, please. We're good on everything else."

"On it. Be right back."

Jordan went and grabbed what they needed to stock the ambulance. His pre-shift tasks accomplished, he grinned at Tim and said, "Okay, buddy, take us out."

***

Karli had been so engrossed in her show she was not aware ten o'clock had come and gone until she paused the TV to get another drink.

"Wow," she exclaimed. "It's really almost eleven?"

She went into the kitchen and saw her cell phone still on the counter. Scooping it up, she noticed she had no new messages.

"I thought he said he'd text me if he wasn't going to be home by ten," she muttered, frowning, as she dialed Evan's number and waited.

But the phone rang five times, then went to voicemail. Karli hung up, confused, then dialed again. This time it routed straight to voicemail.

So, he saw it was me but didn't answer, and then turned it off? What the hell is that about?

She could feel herself shifting from confused to angry; it was crawling up her spine to tense up her shoulders and her chest and inflame her cheeks.

She dialed again, and this time left a message for him to call her. Then she refilled her wine, and settled back into the living room to wait, her phone within reach on the end table next to her glass.

***

Jordan's night went sliding off the deep end a little after midnight; dispatch sent them to a two-car accident on I-20, just east of Loop 820. A wrong-way drunk driver had collected an innocent victim in his path.

When they rolled up on the scene, Tim whistled at the two obliterated vehicles. "Wow," he said. "It's a bad one. We might need more than one rig here."

"I can hear them coming," Jordan pointed out, and looking in the passenger side mirror, he could see two more ambulances were seconds away from being on scene.

Jordan waited until his partner had come to a complete stop before he leapt out of the passenger seat to move to the back of the rig for the gurney. But he heard Tim call his name.

"Jordan, wait! There's a third car involved, and it's down there," Tim told him, pointing down.

"Went off the bridge?"

"That's what the chatter indicates," Tim confirmed. "Let's get down there."

Jordan scrambled into the cab again and they took off, taking the next exit and circling back onto the service road to reach the third passenger vehicle some good Samaritan had just called in.

The rig's headlights illuminated the scene of a mangled and rumpled car on its roof, its make and model rendered unrecognizable from the damage the vehicle had sustained. Tim and Jordan could see a Ford pickup parked off to the right side with flashers on, its owner on his hands and knees beside the upside-down car.

"He's not talking anymore!" the Samaritan called out to them. "I was trying to keep him talking, but he's not answering me now."

Tim rushed to grab the gurney and a kit, and they made their way to the driver's side of the victim's car.

"Sir, can you hear me?" Jordan shouted as he lay on his belly, shining his flashlight inside the vehicle to try to ascertain the position and condition of the driver.

And his blood turned to ice in his veins.

"Evan? *Evan!*" Jordan yelled, shoving his arm through the busted side window to try to feel for a pulse in his best friend's neck.

***

By twelve-forty a.m. Karli was mad down to her toes, and in a moment of spitefulness she used the lock chain on the front door before she went to bed, knowing Evan would not be able to get inside easily.

She heard pounding on the door around five a.m. that woke her from a sound sleep.

Hah, here we go, she thought, and put her robe on before marching to the front door. Karli flipped the deadbolt, undid the chain lock, and flung the door open, prepared for a fight with Evan. Instead, her jaw dropped.

"Jordan," she stammered. "What are you doing here?"

"Karli. May I come in?"

Karli blinked rapidly a few times, trying to absorb the fact that the man who had blown her off so easily the day before was now standing on her doorstep.

"Um, sure, I guess," she said, and moved aside to let him enter. "Evan's not here, though."

"Can we sit down?" Jordan asked, as though he had not heard her.

"Yeah. Come on," Karli answered, and led the way to the living room.

She curled up on her end of the couch, feet tucked under her, fully expecting Jordan to sit at the other end or in the recliner.

Karli was shocked when he sat right next to her.

"Jordan," she began, "what's up with you? You don't give me the time of day yesterday, and now you're plopped down *right beside* me on my couch?"

He reached out and took her hand.

"What's going on here?" she asked, trying desperately to interpret the look on Jordan's face.

"Karli," he said, and his voice broke.

He closed his eyes, cleared his throat, and tried again.

"Karli, there's no easy way to say this. Evan was killed in a car accident last night."

She yanked her hand away from his and jumped to her feet, coldly furious.

"That's not funny, Jordan, and Evan's an ass if he put you up to this," she snarled.

Jordan stood up and ran his hands over his face, then through his hair.

"I wish I could tell you this was some sort of prank, Karli. But I can't. I worked the scene last night...he's gone," Jordan told her, his eyes welling.

"You're... you're serious," she breathed, turning pale.

Words failed him and Jordan could only nod slowly as he watched the truth hit Karli like a freight train.

"No... no...," she whispered, her blue eyes huge with shock and disbelief. She took one step forward, swayed, then slumped toward the floor.

Jordan caught her as she fell, then moved to the couch, setting her on his lap and wrapping his arms around her as she began to sob, her face buried against his chest – but only for a moment. Then she wriggled out of his arms and staggered to the bathroom to be violently ill.

***

He followed her, concern lining his features, and called out to her through the bathroom door.

"Karli. You okay?" he asked, and immediately thought, *wow, what a dumb question, dude. She just lost her husband. How the hell can you even ask that?*

He tried the handle, and when he realized the door wasn't locked, he opened it and gingerly stepped inside. Karli was at the sink, taking handfuls of water into her mouth, rinsing and spitting.

Their eyes met in the mirror, and he noticed how pale her face had become, her blue eyes almost luminescent against a creamy white backdrop.

Without speaking, he moved to the linen closet, grabbed a washcloth, wet it, and placed it at the back of her neck. She flinched and closed her eyes.

"Tell me you were joking," she pleaded, gripping the sides of the pedestal sink so hard her knuckles were turning as white as her face. "*Please*, Jordan."

He put a hand on her shoulder. "I'm so sorry, Karli."

Now she turned, tears flowing again, and went into his arms.

I would give anything to spare her this. Anything, he thought, and he felt guilty that even though a devastating reason was behind Karli being in his embrace, he was still somehow savoring the feel of her cheek against his chest and her arms around his waist.

I'm a ghoul. A complete bastard.

But he couldn't bring himself to break contact.

"Does Madge know yet?" she managed.

"By now, probably," Jordan whispered against her hair.

"What happens next?"

"I'm not sure," he told her honestly. "But whatever it is, you don't have to do it alone. I will help however I can. You know that, right?"

"I thought...... you hated me," Karli murmured between great hitching breaths.

"I don't hate you, Karli," he told her gently. "I'm just... not good with people."

There. A plausible lie. Because this is not the right time or place to tell her I've loved her for seven years and counting...

She could hear her cell phone ringing in the kitchen and pulled away from Jordan to go answer it.

"His mom," she mouthed at Jordan before she answered.

"Yes, I just found out...No, Jordan told me. He's here now. Um, sure, hang on," she said, and held out the phone. "Madge wants to talk to you."

"Madge," he said softly, and closed his eyes as the woman who had been a second mother to him sobbed in his ear. "I know... I know... Yes, we can be there shortly, I think. Hang on."

Jordan muted the call and looked at Karli. "She wants us to come over there."

Karli nodded her assent, moving into her bedroom to pull on something other than pajamas and a robe.

"Madge, we'll be there in about a half-hour... Love you too."

***

While Jordan was wrapping up the call with Karli's mother-in-law, Karli was standing in her walk-in closet, tears still flowing, feeling adrift.

I can't leave the house in my pajamas... But what outfit do you put on when your world's been shattered? Never seen anybody blog about that, she realized. *I usually write about this year's hot hemlines...*

She frowned at her brain coming up with such strangeness amidst the worst morning of her life. In desperation she pulled her favorite sweatshirt and pair of jeans off their hangers, then flung them on the bed as she raced back to the bathroom to be sick again.

Once the extreme nausea eased up, she dressed and climbed into Jordan's truck for the drive to Madge's house. Every single bump in the road seemed to send her stomach into spasms, and Karli silently prayed she wouldn't get sick again along the way.

Madge met them in her front yard, opening her arms wide to embrace them both at once, and the trio cried together.

CHAPTER THREE

Eight days later...

Karli had somehow managed to navigate Evan's funeral service and burial, although she still wasn't quite sure how. A lot of that time was still blurry in her memory, a blessed numbing of senses mixed with adrenaline that she felt certain had carried her through that fateful Tuesday afternoon. She was grateful for it. Some things, she did not *want* to remember clearly.

Almost as a temporary cease-fire, her stomach issues had dissipated for a few days, then returned with a vengeance around midnight on Tuesday. By Wednesday morning, she had had enough, and at three p.m. she was sitting in her family doctor's lobby waiting for her name to be called.

The nurse collected her and walked her over to the scales, then handed her a specimen cup. Once Karli had completed giving a urine sample, she followed the nurse to an exam room. The woman took her vitals, made note of Karli's symptoms, then said, "Dr. Hollard will be right in."

Another twenty minutes passed, and the doctor knocked lightly on the door before entering the room.

"Hey, Karli," he said, and his pleasant voice calmed her, as always.

"Hi, Doc," she said. "I think I have the flu, or a stomach bug. I feel lousy."

"Well," he said, "You're in the right place to find out."

He asked a few questions, then performed the swab needed to check for flu. "Be right back," he told her, and stepped out.

When he returned, it was the second time in as many weeks that her world was completely turned upside down.

"You're joking, right?" Karli was stunned. "You're joking with me, and I actually have the flu...".

"No, young lady," Dr. Hollard chuckled. "It's not the flu. You are most definitely pregnant, according to the pregnancy test Loretta just did. We need to do a full exam to confirm."

"I can't believe it," she muttered. *Maybe the test was wrong. It happens sometimes. I've heard of false positives. Yeah, that must be what this is. I'll get some home pregnancy tests, and they will be negative, and I can move on from this...*

Karli's mind raced as she absorbed the news. She chewed her bottom lip as she tried and failed to navigate her new reality with a clear head. For once, she wasn't embarrassed during a gynecological exam. *Nope. I am way, way too stunned right now to be embarrassed.*

"You all right?" Dr. Hollard asked once the exam was over.

"Um... well...," Karli stammered, unsure what to say much less how to say it.

"Let me guess. This is unexpected," he suggested.

She nodded vigorously.

"So, you're not sure how to break the news to your husband," Hollard continued.

"He died last Friday," Karli revealed, and burst into tears.

The doctor patted her shoulder awkwardly, and she could tell he was not sure how to proceed, either.

"Karli...I'm so sorry..." he cleared his throat and was silent for several seconds.

"I want you to start taking prenatal vitamins," he finally continued, moving safely out of 'counselor' and back over into 'doctor' territory. "And we'll schedule your first sonogram for two weeks from today. I am betting you're around five, six weeks. But the sonogram will help confirm how far along you are. All right?"

A silent nod from Karli, and he nodded back.

"Everything's going to be okay, Karli," he told her in his grandfatherly voice as he patted her shoulder again. "You'll see."

Once he left the examination room, she took off the paper gown and got dressed, her mind still a blur.

We're having a baby. We're having a baby... I... I'm having a baby....

Doc Hollard said five or six weeks... she counted backward in her head as she drove back toward her home. *Yep, that's the last time we made love...*

Karli stopped at the pharmacy and purchased a pregnancy test, then went home and followed the directions. Sure enough, a huge dark plus sign appeared in the results window even before the recommended wait time of five minutes had passed.

Wow. Somehow, seeing that makes it even more real, she realized, and immediately felt butterflies in her stomach. She stashed the little stick for safekeeping.

Karli moved to the dining room table and fired up her laptop. *Well,* she thought as she opened her blog page, *I will have some new topics to talk about, I guess.* She had been a fashion merchandising major in college, then found her calling with her blogging site. But lately, she had wanted to try branching out and talking about other things.

A blog for moms-to-be, she realized. *From beginning to end, all the way through, and it can include fashion along with everything else. After all, I'm about to experience it all firsthand.*

She traced her hand over her still-flat belly.

By myself...

I don't know if I can do this...

She suddenly felt claustrophobic, so Karli changed into comfortable clothes and headed to the park for a walk to try and clear her head. And once again, she found herself watching the kids on the playground.

I get to do that someday soon - bring my child here to play on the slide. The thought caused her to well up with bittersweet tears. A stray one cascaded down her cheek, and she wiped it away absentmindedly.

Oh, God... help me...I don't think I can do this alone...

"Karli," came a deep voice from her right, and she turned her head that direction to see Jordan walking toward her.

"What's wrong?" he said as soon as he got close enough to see her welling eyes.

"Um... I don't have the flu," she stammered.

"Well, that's good, right?"

"Yes," she managed.

"Okay, so.... What's going on?"

I'm pregnant, she almost said, but held back.

I need to figure out how I feel about this before I tell anyone.

"Just... not a good day," Karli whispered.

He tilted his head, gazing at her intently.

"I know what will cheer you up. Food."

"Food?" she blinked.

"Yeah, you know. Food. Let's have dinner, my treat. Anywhere you want to go. I know you've been hiding away at home. Can't say I blame you. But I think a dinner out somewhere would do us both some good. What do you say?"

"You don't have to work tonight?"

"Nope," he confirmed. "Have a couple days off, and then Tim and I rotate to day shift."

"You're probably happy about that," she pointed out, grateful for the distraction from the maelstrom that was currently her thoughts.

He shrugged. "Just when I get my sleep schedule figured out, they change up the roster. It usually takes me a couple of days to adjust."

They stood quietly for a moment.

"Hey," he said softly. "I meant to ask you something..." his voice trailed off. "But you're already not having a good day, so, it can keep."

"What is it?"

"I was just gonna say... If you need help with packing up anything..." he trailed off again, uncertain how to proceed.

"You mean Evan's things," she guessed.

Jordan exhaled. "Yeah. I didn't know if you wanted to leave them in the closet for a while, or if it would be easier on you if they were removed, or what. I'm willing to help if that's what you want to do."

"To be honest, seeing his clothes still hanging in his closet hurts," she admitted. "Makes it feel like he's just on another trip and he'll be back. But he's not coming back."

Karli exhaled a shaky breath. "But if I clean out all his stuff it makes it more... final. I don't know..."

"No need to decide right away," Jordan reassured her. "I just wanted to put it out there. If at some point you decide to do that, I can help you."

She nodded.

"So, will you have dinner with me? I promise to provide sparkling conversation," he teased, trying desperately to rid her eyes of the shadows he saw there.

"I could eat, I guess," she replied. "Haven't had much of an appetite lately, but I can try."

He smiled. "Pick you up in an hour?"

"Okay."

***

Jordan arrived as scheduled, and his breath caught when she opened the door. She'd opted for jeans and a blue blouse that complemented her curves and brought out her eyes. He also noticed she'd applied a bit of makeup.

Not that she needs it, at all. She is stunning already.

Easy, dude. Keep a lid on it.

He schooled his expression into one of casual interest, and said, "Ready?

"Yep, just let me grab my purse," Karli announced, and moved to the coffee table to get it. She locked her door, and they walked to his truck. He saw her safely seated in the passenger seat, then moved around and got behind the wheel.

"Where would you like to eat?" he asked.

"Barbeque," she decided. "I've been craving it."

"Your wish is my command," he quipped as he fastened his seat belt, then put the truck in reverse and backed out of her driveway.

When they reached the restaurant and got in the serving line at the cafeteria-style setup, she asked, "Everything sounds good. What are you going to get?"

"Hm. Leaning toward the ribs and the jalapeno cheddar sausage. You?"

"Brisket," she replied. "Keeping it simple."

The man behind the counter moved swiftly with his carving knife and handed them their plates of meat. Continuing down the line, Karli opted for loaded mashed potatoes while Jordan went with coleslaw and cowboy-style beans.

They moved around the corner to the cashier, then headed to a booth with their trays.

"I'm going to get a roll," he said, pointing to the little station where freshly baked bread waited. "Want one?"

"Two, actually," came her answer, and he chuckled.

Once they got settled into the booth, Jordan asked, "How's the blog stuff going?"

"You care about that?" Karli was shocked.

"Yeah. Why wouldn't I be? It's what you're into, right?"

"Well... yeah."

"So why are you surprised I'd ask about it?"

She paused. "You're a guy, so... Evan *never* asked how it was going. Fairly sure he thought it was dumb."

"You mean he missed the entry about the must-have spring accessories?"

She narrowed her eyes. "Are you messing with me right now?"

Jordan grinned. "I can see where you'd think that, but no."

"You *read* that?"

Now he started to blush as he said, "We have never really talked much, Karli. And I wanted to be able to have something for us to talk about besides... you know... to give you a break from it."

"That is so sweet," she whispered, a slow smile warming her face.

"I can be people-friendly, on occasion," Jordan answered, his smile growing to match hers.

She's always had the best smile, he thought to himself as he watched her butter the rolls he'd snagged for her. *And I will do whatever it takes to make sure she keeps smiling.*

He pulled out of his reverie when Karli said, "You're right. We haven't really talked before. Let's change that. What kind of music do you like?"

***

Two hours later, Jordan's truck was pulling into Karli's driveway, signaling the end of one of the best days Jordan had ever had.

As they talked, they had discovered more and more common interests – music, writers, television shows, movies. Neither one really cared for sports.

"That was something that always drove me a little bit nuts about Evan," Karli had confessed. "Way, way into sports. Like, take-up-all-the-recording-space level of 'into.' Did I tell you about the time he erased the season finale of my favorite show so he could record a dart tournament?"

"*Darts?* Seriously?"

"Yep. I guess... I guess I can record whatever I want now," Karli had said as the smile was chased away by the sudden barrage of tears threatening to fall.

He had held out his hand across the table and tried not to gasp at the amazing sensation touching her caused him. Karli clutched it tightly with her left hand while she used her right hand to wipe her eyes with a napkin.

"I miss him, Jordan," she'd squeaked. "I thought we'd grow old together."

"I know, honey," he had murmured, squeezing her hand. "And I miss him too."

Oh, dear Lord. Did I just call her honey?

CHAPTER FOUR

Although she did not comment on it, her rapid blinking let him know Karli had heard it, and he'd winced internally. *What the hell do I say now?*

She'd stared at him for a long moment, then gently withdrew her hand and said quietly, "Are you ready to go?"

Dammit. I made her uncomfortable. Great job, Jordan, he berated himself in his head as he'd nodded and told her, "Whenever you are."

Now he sat in her driveway, putting his truck's transmission into park, and racking his brain for a way to undo the awkwardness he'd shoved into their perfectly nice time together.

"So," he began, "let me walk you to the door."

"You don't have to," she protested.

"I know I don't. But I want to," he answered, and in a flash was out of his truck, moving around to the passenger door to open it for her and extend his hand. She hesitated only briefly, then clasped it, and Jordan almost closed his eyes at the electricity that seemed to flow back and forth.

Breathe. Just breathe, he chanted in his head like a mantra as she gracefully stepped down out of the truck. Then she dropped his hand, and it felt like a physical blow to him.

They walked together up the sidewalk, and Karli pulled out her keys.

"Thanks for dinner," she murmured as she slid the key into the lock. "And the company. It was nice."

"You're welcome," he said earnestly.

She went still, seemingly conflicted about something, although Jordan had no idea what it could be. It was a complete surprise to him when she suddenly pivoted, closed the distance between them, stood on her tiptoes and kissed him on the cheek.

"See you later," Karli whispered, and went into her house, closing the door behind her.

He stood, feeling rooted in place, one hand slowly traveling up to his face to land softly where she had pressed her lips to him. It seemed like forever before his legs finally cooperated and he was able to walk back to his truck.

***

Karli shut the door, locked it, then leaned against it, eyes closed, her mind a battlefield of chaos and conflict.

He called me 'honey', her shocked brain repeated. *No one's ever called me that.*

Is it wrong that I liked it? It feels so... disloyal to Evan. Not to mention – I kissed him? Seriously? I mean, it was a peck on the cheek, but still... What the hell is wrong *with me? Evan hasn't even been gone two weeks and I am kissing someone else?*

With tears of shame running unchecked down her cheeks, Karli headed for the one place in the house that could usually soothe both her body and her spirit – her garden tub. But her cell phone rang as she moved toward her bedroom, and she returned to the couch where she had dropped her purse and answered it.

"Sarah," she managed.

She could hear the worry in her best friend's voice when Sarah said, "Oh honey. Need me to come over?"

"Yes," Karli gasped. "Please."

"On my way, girl. Be there in twenty."

"Okay," Karli sniffled, and disconnected.

***

Jordan brooded in his apartment on the opposite side of the park.

She kissed me. I still cannot believe she kissed me. And I should feel like I am betraying Evan – but I don't. I don't. Not after everything he did. My only regret is that Karli kissed me on the cheek, not the mouth. And I hope it happens again...

How big a jerk does that make me?

Shaking his head in frustration, he moved to his bedroom to change into running gear, grabbed his headphones, and prepared for three punishing circuits of the jogging trail.

***

Sarah grabbed Karli in a one-armed hug the minute she got through Karli's front door.

"I brought ice cream," Sarah announced, holding up the bag and shaking it. "Come on, girly. Let's talk it out."

"Sea salt caramel?" came the shaky but hopeful whisper from Karli.

"You know it."

They moved to the kitchen, and Sarah got out bowls and spoons. "Okay, Karli. Talk to me," she prodded as she began to scoop ice cream. "What's up?"

"Um... I kissed somebody," Karli said, her voice riddled with guilt.

"What?"

"Jordan and I went to dinner, and I broke down, and he called me honey. And I liked hearing him call me that, and I kissed him goodnight on the cheek, and I'm a horrible person," Karli wailed.

"Not horrible, Karli. Human," Sarah said softly.

"But I'm being disloyal to Evan," Karli protested.

"I can see where you might feel that way," Sarah observed.

Karli nodded. "There's more, Sarah."

Sarah handed her one of the bowls. "What's that?"

"I'm five weeks pregnant. I found out this afternoon."

"Oh," Sarah's surprise mixed with sympathy. "Wow."

"Yeah," Karli agreed. "Blindsided me, Sarah. Never even occurred to me."

"Well," her best friend said thoughtfully as she joined her at the kitchen table, "that's understandable. How do you feel about it?"

"Overwhelmed. Exhilarated. Scared to death," Karli confessed. "Everything at once. I always wanted kids with Evan... this is like some really cruel joke now that he's gone."

"What are you going to do?" Sarah asked, and Karli knew what she meant.

"Not even a question, I'm keeping it," Karli said firmly, one hand moving to her stomach. "I'm just not sure how I'm going to do this by myself. Whenever I pictured having kids in my head, it was with Evan *here*," she finished on a sob.

Sarah took Karli's hand. "You won't be by yourself, Karli. I have your back, and your parents will be there too. And you're going to be an awesome mom, I just know it."

"What do I do about Jordan, Sarah? I feel so guilty," Karli asked.

"Allow yourself some grace, Karli," Sarah told her. "There's no one right way – or timeline, for that matter - to grieve. Maybe with a bit more time, you'll find it's easier to forgive yourself for any misstep you feel you made."

"Do you think it was a misstep?"

"You gave someone who was comforting you a peck on the cheek," Sarah answered. "I personally don't think there's anything wrong with that."

"What about the other part?"

Sarah sighed. "Only you can decide to beat yourself up about that or not, Karli."

"But what's your opinion?"

Sarah contemplated. "I personally would have viewed him calling me that as comforting, and I would have appreciated it. Jordan was kind to you. It's okay to appreciate that. It does not mean that you love or miss Evan any less, Karli. One doesn't cancel out the other."

Karli fell silent, weighing Sarah's words as she took another bite of ice cream.

***

Two weeks later, Karli was back at Dr. Hollard's office, lying down as the sonogram tech spread warm, clear jelly across her abdomen.

"Here we go. Just relax, Karli," the woman said.

Karli nodded, turning her head so she could see the monitor.

Her heart skipped a beat when she saw the first images appear onscreen. *My child,* she thought fiercely, and fell completely in love.

I am ready for this, Karli decided.

"Nice strong heartbeat," the tech noted, and the rapid *whoomp-whoomp-whoomp* filled the air around them.

Karli beamed, wiping away happy tears.

"How far along?" she asked.

"Hollard will confirm," the tech said, pausing her motions with the wand to capture measurements and screen shots, "but I'd say eight weeks."

When she got home, Karli pulled out her laptop and began to build twelve blog posts to kick off her new series, saving them as drafts. She also worked out the frequency of the mom-to-be set – posting every two weeks felt right.

***

Jordan had purposely kept his distance since the night they'd had dinner. While he had no problem with what had happened between them, he figured Karli had felt guilty about it, and he didn't want to add to her stress. But when she called and told him she was ready to pack away Evan's things, he agreed to be at her house at eleven the following morning.

He stepped out of his truck and walked slowly to her door, knocking gingerly and steeling his nerves. *Help her with this, make sure she's okay, then leave,* he reminded himself. *And for God's sake don't call her 'honey'.*

He squared his shoulders when she opened the door, willing himself not to react when he noticed she was wearing the exact same t-shirt as the very first time he had seen her.

"Hi," he managed to say, his voice sounding rusty to his ears.

"Hi," Karli said softly. "Come on in."

"So, what's the plan?" Jordan asked as he followed her into the living room.

"Um, I went and got boxes yesterday afternoon," Karli answered, working her hair up into a ponytail as she walked in front of him down the hall. "And I guess we'll start in the closet?"

"Whatever you want to do," he said. *Honey,* his brain added, causing a small riot. He worked his impish grin back into a neutral expression before she turned to face him again.

In an hour's time, they had emptied Evan's walk-in closet, with Jordan carrying boxes to the living room when they were full.

"Now what?" he asked her.

"I think I want to sit for just a minute, then tackle the dresser and bathroom, then make a trip to donate the clothes. After that, the office. And I'll be honest – I have no freaking clue where to start in the garage."

"We'll figure it out. I'm going to load the boxes we've got done so far," he told her, and picked up the first one.

"You want something to drink?"

"Got any sweet tea?" Jordan answered.

"Coming right up," he heard her call out as she went into the kitchen.

After taking a small break, they turned their attention to Evan's dresser and his side of the bathroom.

"Okay," Karli said, hands on hips. "To the donations place, then food, maybe?"

Jordan nodded.

They rode along in an easy silence, and if Karli was remembering the last time they'd gone out for a meal together, she didn't let it show. Jordan, however, was having difficulty remembering much else.

They dropped off the boxes of clothes, and Karli's face lit up when Jordan suggested tacos for lunch.

He did a double take when she ordered five of them.

"What?" she said. "I'm hungry."

Jordan held up his hands. "Nothing, absolutely nothing."

Looking at the cashier, he said, "Double that order, please, and we're going to eat here."

When his name was called, he strolled back to the counter and grabbed the tray, setting it between them on the table. And was stunned when the tiny little woman across from him ate all five of the tacos she had ordered without blinking an eye.

"Where are you even putting those?"

"Huh?"

"You're so tiny... how do you have room for those?"

She snorted with laughter. "I told you. I'm hungry."

He raised his eyebrows in appreciation.

Lunch over, they headed back to the house to start going through everything in Evan's home office. The mailman had just pulled away from her mailbox, and Karli waved to him as she jumped down out of the truck and retrieved the mail.

They walked back inside, her detouring to the kitchen to open the mail, Jordan heading toward the office.

"What the *hell*?" he heard her exclaim and rushed to her side.

"What's wrong?" he asked, watching her turn red with anger.

"This," she said, and thrust the letter toward him. "According to my mortgage company, we're two months behind on payments."

CHAPTER FIVE

"How in the hell is that possible?" Karli said through gritted teeth. "Did he just not pay it?"

Jordan shook his head as he scanned the notice. "I have no idea, Karli. You need to call them."

"He wouldn't let me handle the bills. I offered to, and I am perfectly capable. But he said, 'no, Karli, let me worry about that. You focus on your blog.' *Jackass*," she snarled. "I wonder what else he failed to pay."

"Get them on the phone,' Jordan urged. "It could just be a misunderstanding."

"Believe me, I intend to," she answered as she dialed.

Jordan watched, a reluctant witness, as Karli turned progressively paler during the call with her mortgage loan servicer.

"Okay," she murmured quietly. "Thanks for the information. I'll be back in touch."

She hung up and looked at Jordan with disbelief in her eyes.

"The letter's accurate," she said flatly. "The last payment he made was late December. *Three months* before he died. The one I made for April? They applied it to February."

She leaned on the counter, trying to regain her composure.

"How can I fix this? He didn't have any life insurance," she lamented. "I don't have that kind of cash lying around to get it caught up. And even if I did, I would need to save it for..." she trailed off, suddenly looking self-conscious.

"Save it for what, Karli?"

She shook her head violently as she bit her lower lip.

"Karli... what is it? Maybe I can help. But you have to let me in."

"I'm pregnant, Jordan," she blurted out, and another tear escaped custody and rolled down her cheek. "I'm a twenty-eight-year-old widow, and I'm pregnant, and the COBRA coverage through Evan's work is too expensive, so I don't even have health insurance anymore."

He stopped in his tracks, watching her carefully. "How far along?"

"Doctor Hollard said eight weeks. And I don't know what to do," she continued stormily. "And now, I'm even *more* worried about being able to keep up with the bills. How am I going to do this, Jordan? How am I going to care for a child, when I'm not even sure how much longer I'll have a place to *live*?"

He closed the distance and rubbed his hands up and down her upper arms. "I told you before that you wouldn't have to do any of this alone, Karli. So, what makes you think you'd have to do *this* part by yourself?"

She gaped at him. "*What*?"

"My lease is almost up at the apartment," he explained, his voice calm and level. "Why don't I move in with you? I can take the third bedroom, cover the mortgage payment and the utilities, take some stress off you. If you are okay with it, that is. Or," he said, "if it is easier on you, sell or rent out this place, and come move in with me. I have plenty of space in my apartment – that second bedroom has nothing in it right now. We would just add you to the lease. Easy."

"Jordan...why would you do that?"

So much for 'make sure she's okay, then leave', his brain interjected. *Watch yourself, Baker. Thin ice.*

"Evan was my best friend," he said simply after a long pause. "What kind of best friend would I be if I walked away from you when you obviously could use some help?"

"I...I..." Karli's voice faltered.

"You don't have to decide right this second," Jordan told her. "Think it over. The main point I was trying to make is, you're not alone."

He glanced at his watch. "I really don't want to leave while you're upset, but I have to get ready for work soon," he said. "They asked me and Tim to come in at five today. Would it be okay if I come back tomorrow, bring lunch with me, maybe? And we can talk some more?"

She nodded, a small smile combating her tears. "I'd like that."

"It's gonna be all right, Karli. I promise," Jordan said, and hugged her. "We'll figure something out, okay? I'll see you tomorrow."

And he reluctantly turned and walked out her front door.

***

Jordan thought he'd done a rather good job of staying calm, sensing that calm was what she needed at the time. But his mind was reeling, his insides knotting at Karli's news. Not just the pregnancy, but the fact that Evan had failed her on yet another level by dropping the ball on the mortgage payments.

"If Evan was here right now, I'd punch him in the mouth," he muttered as he drove back to his apartment.

Wait, hold up, his psyche amended. *That is not exactly true... I would not only punch him in the mouth, I'd beat his ass,* he fumed. *How dare he put her in this position?*

Because Jordan was sure he knew what Evan had spent the mortgage money on. Not that he would ever tell Karli if he could help it. He saw nothing good at all coming from Karli finding out her dead husband had been keeping a mistress the last six months of their marriage.

***

By the time Jordan saw Karli again the next afternoon, she had contacted every single creditor she and Evan had accounts with. After she had finished the last phone call, she felt like someone had dropped her from an airplane with no parachute.

"It's bad, Jordan," she murmured as they sat at the kitchen table unwrapping the sub sandwiches he'd brought. "The only things he kept paid on time were the utilities and the car payment. Everything else – the house, credit cards, the school loans - is at *least* a month behind. All the stuff that I wouldn't notice right away."

"What about the bank account?" Jordan asked.

"I downloaded statements going back a year, but I haven't looked at them yet. And to be honest, I'm not sure I want to."

She put her head in her hands.

"What this means is, I can't stay here," Karli sighed. "No matter how much I want to. I just don't have the funds to handle everything. I've run the numbers four times already. Even if everything were current, I still wouldn't be able to afford this place anymore."

"Have you thought any more about what I said? About me helping you here, or your moving in with me?"

"I have," she hedged. "I've also considered moving back in with my mom and dad, too. Or Sarah."

"I didn't mean to make you uncomfortable," Jordan said quietly. "That was never my intention."

"You didn't, really," Karli answered quickly. "It's just...I don't think it would be proper, you and I living together."

"I get that, and I respect it," he assured her. "I just want to make sure you're okay."

"And I appreciate you for that," she told him with a smile as she reached over and squeezed his hand. "Now. I need to form a battle plan. We only bought this house a year ago. Even if I could sell it quickly enough to cover everything, I still owe so much on it that I wouldn't get very much out of the deal."

"Have you thought about renting it out?" Jordan asked. "My aunt is a realtor, and she's always saying she has almost as many clients asking about rentals as she does buyers. I can call her if you like."

"Do you think that could happen fast enough to help me out?"

Jordan shrugged. "We won't know if we don't ask, Karli. The worst she can say is you're better off selling."

"Okay," Karli said on an exhale. "Let's call her and see what she says."

Jordan pulled out his cell phone and dialed. "Hey, Aunt Kathy," he said when she answered. "You got a few minutes? We could use your expert opinion."

"Sure thing, kiddo. What's up?"

"Gonna put you on speaker," he told her, and set the phone down.

"So, here's what we've got going on," he began.

**

"Wow," Karli said a half-hour later. "I feel better just talking to her. She knows her stuff, huh?"

"Yep," Jordan said with pride. "She's excellent. I just knew she'd be able to help."

Kathy had asked a few questions, and once Karli had provided an address, the realtor had said, "Give me just a second."

They'd heard the sound of fingers moving swiftly across the keyboard, then, "That's what I thought. Karli, your place is in one of the most sought-after subdivisions in Arlington. Would not surprise me at all if we wind up with at least four people trying to be the first to rent it from you before the first week is out. And in this market, you would be able to not only make your mortgage payment, but you'd also have a healthy amount left over each month to use for other things."

They had chatted a bit more, and by the time the call ended Kathy was scheduled to be at Karli's home the following morning.

"Now then," Karli said, a smile back on her face, "you ready to tackle the garage?"

"Whenever you are."

***

It was close to dinnertime when Karli said, "I'm worn out, Jordan. I think the rest of this can wait, don't you?"

"Agreed," he said, interlacing his fingers and stretching his arms over his head to loosen up the stiffness in his back.

"Do you want to go out to dinner or have something delivered?" he asked her.

She considered for a moment. "Chinese food?"

"Sure thing. I'll call it in."

As they filled their plates forty minutes later, Karli announced, "I've decided to move in with Sarah."

"Yeah?"

"Yeah," she confirmed. "I know my parents would love to have me there, but it just doesn't feel right. I am too old to be running back home. You know? I mean, I know *they* don't see it like that, but I do."

"That's understandable," he said.

"Hey. I hope I didn't hurt your feelings earlier. I really do appreciate your offer. But I just... think it is best if we don't live together. Besides, the last thing you need is a pregnant roommate cramping your style with the ladies," she teased.

Wow... why did I even say that? she thought, then began to blush. She quickly rose from her seat and moved to the kitchen counter so he wouldn't see her suddenly flushed face.

***

He watched her, stunned into silence, even as his mind went, *Okay, that came out of left field. To be fair, how would she know I don't date much? I have never let her close enough to get to know me,* he realized. *Doesn't really matter though. I don't want anyone but her...*

Think of anything else, dude, anything, before she turns around.

Jordan cleared his throat. "Um. Yeah. No worries there," he managed. "Work, and training. Keeps me busy."

"I seem to remember you told me that before," Karli observed as she busied herself at the cabinet reaching for a glass.

"I did. And it's still true."

"Don't you get lonely?" The question escaped her lips on impulse.

Nope, nope, nope. Do not *go there. Just because she opened that door... Just don't.*

"I guess," he answered, as nonchalantly as he could. "On occasion."

You're killin' me, honey, his brain summarized.

"Oh," Karli said, and the strange conversation lapsed into an even more uncomfortable silence as she poured herself some tea and returned to her seat.

***

Finally, Jordan stood, carried his plate and fork across the kitchen and placed them in the dishwasher, then said, "I guess I should be going."

"You don't have to on my account. I like the company. I thought maybe we could watch a movie," Karli shared, and watched his eyebrows twitch for a split second and a flash of something she couldn't identify in his eyes. It was gone before she could analyze it closely.

"I...like spending time with you, too," he answered, after a long moment of gazing at her intently. "But it's getting late, and I want to get a run in."

I wish I knew what he was thinking right now, Karli thought, her own eyes widening a bit. *He gives nothing away.*

"Oh. All right," she said, disappointed. "Will you be here tomorrow when Kathy comes?"

"If you like."

"Yes, I would."

"Then I'll be here. You won't do this alone. That's what I told you, remember? And I meant it," he finished softly, with that unfathomable look in his eyes again.

She saw him to the door, resisting the impulse to kiss his cheek again, and gripped the door a bit tighter than necessary as she watched him smile at her, then walk down the driveway and climb into his truck.

CHAPTER SIX

Kathy showed up as scheduled at nine a.m. the next morning. As soon as she stepped across the threshold, she beamed and turned to Karli.

"Karli," she said, "we are not going to have any problems at all finding you stable renters, I can feel it."

Karli's shoulders sagged in relief. "That's so good to hear. How quickly would we be able to list it? And do I need to be out of here first?"

"Whenever you're ready, we post it," came the answer. "And yes, it's been my experience that empty places tend to rent more quickly. People are more easily able to imagine their own belongings in the space."

"And then what?"

"Then, we handle all of it. Screening tenants, completing the rental contracts, collecting rent, making repairs, the whole nine yards. It's all included in our monthly rate."

"Which is?"

When Kathy told her, Karli's jaw dropped.

"Wow," Karli exclaimed. "That's... that's a lot more reasonable than I was expecting, I'll be honest."

Karli swiveled to look at Jordan. "Sarah said she's got space for me whenever I'm ready," she said. "How soon can we get me moved out of here?"

Jordan grinned. "Let me see if I can line up some free labor, and we can have this place ready to rent out by the weekend."

"Really?" Karli answered, her face flush with excitement.

"Really," he confirmed, then staggered back a step as she rushed over and slammed into him, hugging him tightly.

"I feel like I can breathe again," she whispered against his chest. "Thank you."

He closed his eyes in contentment as he returned her embrace. *Anything for you, Karli,* he almost said, but amended it just in time.

"It's what friends do, right?" he told her instead. "Now, we need to get more boxes, and line up a storage unit."

"I'm on it," she said, releasing him and wiping away a happy tear as she went into the living room to grab her cell phone.

Jordan's aunt looked at him carefully once Karli had left the room.

"How long have you loved her?" she asked softly, so Karli would not hear.

"I have no idea what you're talking about," he muttered.

Kathy stared at him, a hand on her hip, eyebrow raised, waiting patiently for him to drop the act and confirm what she already knew.

"That obvious, huh?" he finally confessed quietly. "Years, Aunt Kathy. I've loved her for years."

***

By Friday morning, the move was in full swing. Jordan had used pizza and beer to bribe some of the guys down at the station who had the day off. Seven of them, including Tim, took him up on it, and it was all Karli could do not to clap with excitement at how quickly the house was being emptied.

By lunchtime, the rental truck containing items destined for storage was pulling out of the driveway headed to Karli's unit, with Tim behind the wheel. He was leading a convoy of helpers to go unload it all. The only things remaining were what she needed with her at Sarah's – namely clothes and personal items, since Sarah's second bedroom was already fully furnished.

"I think all that's left after I get my stuff to Sarah's is a deep clean around here, and then tomorrow, Kathy can come take pictures and post the listing," Karli announced with satisfaction.

"Yep," Jordan agreed. "Glad my guys pitched in with this."

"The pizzas should be here by the time they get back from the storage unit," Karli confirmed as she glanced at the order tracker on her cell phone. "Beer run?"

"On it. Be right back," he answered. "Want to come with me?"

"I'm going to start putting stuff in my car," she told him with a grin.

"You know," she continued, as they each carried a box to her SUV, "for the first time since Evan died, I feel hopeful about the future. I am still scared brainless about being a single mom, but I'm hopeful. Thanks to you."

"You're a strong person, Karli. You can get through anything. And you are going to be a great mom," Jordan said sincerely.

But she noticed that look was in his eyes again, hinting at something that he was unable - or unwilling - to share with her. Just for a fleeting moment... and then, the moment was gone, before she could form the question.

Next time I see that look, I am going to ask, she resolved, as she watched him leave to go get the beer that he'd promised his co-workers.

Sighing, Karli headed back inside to grab another box.

***

Friday evening.

Karli and Jordan stood in the front doorway, the empty pizza boxes and beer bottles in the trash bag in Jordan's hand.

"Back door locked?" she asked.

"Yep. Everything out of here?"

"Yes, I just double checked every drawer and cabinet in this place, right before you mopped the kitchen," Karli confirmed.

"This is it, then," Jordan stated. "Let me text Kathy."

A few quick keystrokes, and he hit send.

"Feel like celebrating?"

"I do, actually," she nodded. "But I need a shower first."

"Me too. I can meet you at Sarah's in an hour or so if you want," he offered.

"I'd like that," Karli smiled. "See you in an hour."

***

"So, tell me more about Jordan," Sarah said as she watched Karli decide what to wear.

Karli glanced at her, a little confused. "Like what?"

"You said he's Evan's best friend, right?"

"Yeah," Karli answered. "But we never really hung out much until now. I always thought he didn't like me."

"Why would you think that?"

Karli frowned. "Just... whenever Jordan would come around, it was always... I don't know... like he wasn't happy to see me."

"Interesting," Sarah murmured under her breath.

"What?"

"Nothing," Sarah said quickly, and darted down the hall to answer the doorbell.

***

"Hi," she said, when she opened the front door to find a tall, well-built, brown-eyed man standing there. "You must be Jordan. Come on in, I'll tell Karli you're here."

He smiled, and Sarah's heart palpitated. *Wowzer. He is a hottie with a thing for Karli and Karli is clueless.*

But maybe I can help her with that.

"Thanks," he said, and walked inside.

"Um, so... yeah. Have a seat," Sarah gestured toward the couch, then hurried back down the hall.

"Oh my God," she hissed in a stage whisper as she barreled into Karli's room. "You didn't tell me he was *gorgeous.*"

"I never really thought about it before," Karli confessed. "I forget you've never met him. You were out of town for the funeral, and that would have been pretty much your only chance. Like I said, he seemed to prefer not being around me."

"I still feel bad I wasn't able to be there for you," Sarah said. "But I couldn't get back in time."

"I know, Sarah. It's okay."

"So, back to Jordan," Sarah continued, her eyes sparkling brightly. "I wonder if he's single."

"He's not married, but I'm not sure if he's seeing anybody," Karli told her.

"Girl. Find out, and let me know," Sarah urged. *"Please?"*

***

Karli was surprised to realize Sarah's words had created a fierce surge of jealousy in her core, and she just stopped herself from shaking her head to rid herself of the sensation.

"Okay," she responded in a clipped tone.

Karli finished dressing, and together the women returned to the living room. Jordan stood as they entered.

Wow, Sarah's right, Karli thought, seeing Jordan for the first time as a man, not a friend. *He* is *gorgeous.*

His faded jeans clung to his muscled legs in all the right places, and the blue t-shirt he wore showcased his impressively built arms and torso. His wavy, dark brown hair tumbled down just past his collar, and Karli's hands suddenly itched to run themselves through it. She wanted to feel that hint of five o'clock shadow gently scrape across her throat, then her cheek, before their lips met...

Whoa... What the hell?

"Hi," Jordan said softly in that deep baritone, and Karli felt her knees go weak.

What's going on here? He's your dead husband's best friend, for God's sake. You cannot do this, her conscience shouted.

And another part of her brain reached over and turned her conscience off as Karli smiled at him and said, "You ready to go?"

He nodded. "Nice to meet you, Sarah."

"Likewise," Sarah purred.

***

As Sarah shut the door behind them, she smiled. *It is obvious they belong together,* she thought. *The way he looks at her... I cannot believe Karli has no idea. But maybe my feigning interest helped her see him better.*

You're welcome, Karli.

***

Jordan had managed to keep his expression neutral as he watched a confusing array of emotions roll across Sarah's and Karli's faces in the living room.

Wonder what that's all about?

Must be a girl thing.

He mentally shrugged, then focused himself on opening the door for Karli and seeing her safely into the passenger seat.

"Where to?" he asked.

"You choose, I'm good with just about anything."

"Italian?"

"Perfect. So, I figured out the first twelve entries of the new blog I'm starting," Karli volunteered as they drove.

"Cool! What's it about?"

"Being a mom," she declared. "I've got a front row seat for it, and I've been wanting to do something besides fashion anyway, so it seemed like a good choice."

"And you'll be fabulous at it," Jordan chimed in, and reached over and squeezed her hand.

***

As soon as he touched her, she had the sensation of being very warm. Karli almost wiggled in her seat a bit to try and restore balance before she stopped herself.

"You okay?"

"Yes," she managed. "It's just... a little stuffy in here, don't you think?"

"Here," he offered, and adjusted the truck's air conditioning controls. "Better?"

"Yes, thanks," Karli answered, then turned her face to the passenger window and watched the scenery as she tried desperately to stem the tide of new and unexpected emotion that she was feeling for Jordan Baker.

This is so wrong... isn't it?

Not to mention - what if it's one-sided, Karli?

What if he's only been nice to you because he is Evan's friend?

What then?

***

Jordan's phone chirped just as the hostess seated them. He scanned the text.

"Kathy says she can meet you at the house at eight a.m. tomorrow to take pictures, put the lockbox on the front door and set the sign in the yard," he relayed to Karli.

"Good!" she answered brightly.

He smiled at her, warmth in his eyes.

There it is again, she told herself. *Now's my chance.*

"I need to ask you something," she said abruptly.

"Go for it."

"What's with the look?"

His brows knitted. "What look?"

"There's been a couple of times you've gotten this... look on your face," Karli said. "And I don't know what it means."

She swore she could pinpoint the precise moment he clamped down on whatever he was feeling; Jordan's eyes went carefully blank, like a curtain had been lowered.

"I have no idea what you're talking about," he said gruffly. "Ready to order?"

Fine, don't tell me, Karli thought to herself as she gazed at Jordan. *But I will find out, mark my words.*

Jordan was increasingly distant through the meal; she could feel whatever was weighing on him rolling toward her, a palpable aura of tension blanketing them both.

They waved off dessert and prepared to leave. After he settled the bill Jordan escorted her to the truck, making sure once again to see her settled comfortably before he got in the driver's seat.

They rode in silence back to Sarah's apartment complex. It wasn't until Jordan parked that Karli spoke up and said, "We need to talk, Jordan."

"Okay," he muttered, visibly uncomfortable.

"Why have you been so nice to me lately?" she asked.

"You needed it," came the answer.

"Yes, and I appreciate it. But why *now*? Why go seven years acting like you hated me?"

"I don't hate you."

"Really? Because you always seemed distant toward me, like you were pissed off I was even around."

"I don't want to talk about this," he began.

"But I do, so, it's happening," she shot back, chin raised in defiance.

"I don't hate you, Karli. I've never hated you."

"Then why did you act like that?"

She waited, watching as his hands gripped the steering wheel until his knuckles turned white.

CHAPTER SEVEN

"Karli... I *really* don't want to talk about this," he said in a warning tone through clenched teeth.

"Too bad," she said. "I deserve an answer to the question."

"You want an answer?" Jordan growled.

"Yes," Karli snapped.

She was totally shocked when he undid his seat belt, leaned her direction, and reached for her. He gently framed her face with his hands, paused for a moment, then leaned in to plant an ardent kiss on her mouth.

Her senses reeled at his touch, his feel, the way his lips were both urgent and gentle against hers, and she felt every sliver of emotion that Jordan poured into their contact.

"*That's* why," he murmured when the kiss finally ended. "That's why, Karli."

"But...I..." she stammered.

"I wanted you for myself," Jordan spoke in a low tone, his words tumbling from the lips mere inches from her own, his dark brown eyes alive with what she'd only glimpsed before. "But not this way. *Never* this way. Not because he died. Do you understand? And you are *carrying his child*, Karli. I am trying to do the right thing here and not take advantage. Support you, but also keep my distance to let you grieve, let you heal. And then I see you...hear your voice...and I just...".

His words fell away as he kissed her again, and with a sigh Karli leaned into him and ran her hands through his hair before landing her palms on the back of his neck to pull him closer.

But he slowly lifted away from her mouth to whisper in her ear, "This is why I didn't want to talk about it. You should have left it alone."

Jordan gently lifted his hands from her face and retreated to his side of the truck, his expression guarded. He sat for just a moment, then got out of the vehicle and went around to open her door.

She swiveled in the seat, like she was about to climb down from the truck, and as he had before, Jordan held out a hand to assist.

Now it was Karli's turn to shock as she took his hand, then pulled him close enough that she could kiss him again. Jordan immediately closed the distance and wedged himself between her knees.

He fisted his left hand in her hair as he plundered her mouth, and his lips curved briefly into a smile when hers parted. He deepened the kiss as his right hand crept up under her shirt, under her bra to gently cradle her breast, and the feel of his touch on her bare skin caused Karli to shudder.

Jordan growled low in his throat as he dipped his head to blaze a trail of scorching kisses down the side of her neck before returning for another taste of her mouth.

Meanwhile, Karli's hands roamed his chest, then down his sides. She moved them down and around to his back, finally exploring the muscular physique she'd admired. When she gripped his ass to pull him in even more firmly against her core, he moaned against her mouth, and the sound turned her on even more.

"Karli. Wait," he managed, as she moved her hands back around to the front and started to undo the button on his jeans.

"What?" she whispered.

"I don't... I don't know if we should do this right now, honey," he whispered back, with both longing and pain shining in his eyes as he pulled his hand back from her breast. "You need more time...".

His words were more effective than a bucket of ice water. She released her hold on him, leaned back, and watched him take two shaky steps backward, both of them panting for breath.

"Maybe you're right. The last thing I need is to rush into anything right now," she conceded after a long silence.

He nodded, and she could see what it cost him to agree with her.

"Not that I'm not *insanely* attracted to you, Karli. That's not it at all, trust me. I have wanted to be with you for a long, long time. But I also don't want to see you get hurt anymore."

"Would you hurt me?" she asked, her eyes locked with his.

"Never, if I could help it," came the earnest response. "But if we are ever together, I need to know it's because you *want* to be with me. Not because of loneliness, or physical attraction... or grief."

She nodded silently, weighing her disappointment against the wisdom of what he was saying.

Then she hopped down out of the truck, whispered, "Thanks for dinner," and hurried past him toward Sarah's apartment, her cheeks crimson, her eyes welling up.

***

Jordan stood silently and watched her go, fighting the urge to run after her and scoop her up in his arms.

This is the right thing to do. It's the right thing. Even though it feels like hell.

He sat in his truck for a few minutes to try and clear his head before he drove away.

***

"You all right?" Sarah asked. "What happened?"

"We kissed," Karli revealed. "And it felt so right, and then Jordan stopped. Said I need more time, and to make sure this is what I want."

Sarah tilted her head, thinking.

"He's not wrong, you know," she told Karli. "You *do* need to make sure what your motivations are.

After all, you have more than just you to consider now. You have a child on the way."

"I know," Karli sighed. "But I never expected to feel this way about Jordan, especially not so soon after losing Evan. Part of me feels really guilty about tonight, Sarah, but part of me doesn't at all."

"Take your time to sort it out," Sarah suggested. "I saw the way he looked at you tonight. Trust me, Jordan Baker is not going anywhere. I'm kinda jealous of you about that part, by the way," she finished to keep up her charade, and was relieved to see Karli chuckle. "I'm not even joking – that man is *fine*."

"He is," Karli agreed. "And he's also a great guy. I don't want to hurt either one of us, so, it sounds like I have some thinking to do."

***

"Dude. You okay? You look like someone punched you in the gut," Tim observed as he and Jordan prepared for their Sunday shift.

"I'm fine. Let's go," Jordan groused, and Tim's eyebrows raised.

"Jordan, listen, if you need-"

Jordan cut him off. "I said I'm fine," he spat out. "Drop it."

"Hey," Tim snarled back, "don't be an ass to me. I'm trying to be a friend here."

"Sorry, man," Jordan's shoulders slumped as he ran his hands over his face. "Sorry."

"It's that girl, isn't it? The one we helped move?"

"Yeah," Jordan admitted. "Yeah. Karli."

"What's going on?"

Jordan looked at his rig partner for a long time, then began, "It all started seven years ago."

Tim listened as Jordan told him everything.

"So, when she kept pushing for answers the other night, I couldn't hold back anymore, and I kissed her."

Tim whistled. "What now?"

Jordan paused. "I told her I think she needs more time to be sure of what she wants," he finally said. "I didn't like telling her that, at all. *I'm* ready for us to be together right now. But it's not about me. It's about what's best for her."

"I get that," Tim reassured him. "And for what it's worth, I agree. She's going through a lot as it is – and that's just the stuff she *knows* about."

"Yeah," Jordan sighed. "And I hope she never finds out about what Evan did. Sincerely. It would crush her."

"So, what are you going to do?"

"Give her space," Jordan said, feeling like someone had stabbed him in the chest. "That's what."

"Nothing says you have to like it, bro. Even if it *is* the right thing to do," Tim commiserated as he patted Jordan's shoulder. "Come on, buddy. Let's get to work."

***

By midday Monday, Kathy called Karli with news. "It's rented, dear," she told her. "I had fifteen people call me about it just within the first two hours it was listed. All in all, we had over forty applications come through the website. We're wading through them now, and I should be able to place a tenant for you before the week is out."

Karli sighed in relief, leaning against Sarah's kitchen counter.

"That's wonderful news," she answered. "Thank you so much, Kathy, for everything."

"Not a problem at all. You need anything else, I'm as close as the phone, all right?"

Karli disconnected the call and instinctively began to dial Jordan's number to share the happy news. But she faltered, then stopped, frowning.

I really want to share this with him, but I don't know if I should. Things got awkward Friday night and I have not heard from him since.

Maybe I should text him? What should I do? Maybe he doesn't want to talk to me...maybe he is regretting Friday night...

The thought of Jordan stepping back out of her life again ripped at her chest, and she clutched it in surprise as unshed tears threatened to breach.

***

Four weeks later, Karli was surprised to see that the first three blog entries of her 'mom-to-be' series had resulted in her number of followers increasing tenfold.

Imagine that, she mused, as she scrolled through page after page of likes and positive comments. One entry, dated from just two days before, caught her attention and stole her breath. A simple thumbs-up icon, and the username... *JB-EMT.*

I miss him, she thought with sorrow. *I really miss him.*

Then she felt it. A tiny flutter, like gossamer wings floating into mist in her lower abdomen.

It moved, she realized, eyes widening as she caressed the belly that had started to reflect her condition. *My baby just moved.*

And she choked up as she remembered that the one person in the whole world that she most wanted to share it with had broken off contact.

***

I wonder how Karli's doing, Jordan thought as he ran. He had not seen or talked to her in almost two months. Aunt Kathy had relayed the news weeks ago about finding Karli a renter so quickly, and he had been tempted to make contact, but restrained himself.

Don't wimp out, Baker. Focus. Two more circuits, his mind commanded, and his body obeyed.

But running in the park wasn't the same anymore. Since he had helped Karli move across town, there was no longer any chance of catching a glimpse of her as he ran.

Didn't realize how much those sightings meant to me until now, he thought with sorrow, and kicked up his speed to try to outrun his feelings.

***

"It must be in storage," Karli muttered in irritation a few days later. "I can't find it anywhere in here."

"I bet it is," Sarah reassured her. "Just go get it. May have to open a box or two, but I am sure you'll find it, okay? Please don't stress."

Karli took a deep breath. "I'm trying," she said. "I'm headed to the storage unit. Be back in a bit."

She made her way to the storage facility, unlocked her unit, and pushed the garage-style door up.

"Okay," she murmured to herself. "Let the games begin."

She waded through box after box, finally finding the folder of papers she was looking for. She also noticed Evan's cell phone and impulsively grabbed it too before putting the box back into place and locking up the unit.

When she got back to the apartment, she found a note from Sarah on the counter. *With Jodie. Long story, will explain later - S.*

"Very well then. Pasta with chicken for one it is," she said, then chuckled as she felt another flutter from her baby. "Sorry, sir or miss, I meant for two."

After she'd made dinner, she sat at the kitchen table with her plate and Evan's cell phone, feeling nostalgic. But the battery had been drained, so she plugged it into the charger while she ate.

***

An hour later, his phone's battery fully restored, she sat on the couch, and began to scroll through his pictures.

Karli's eyes bulged, and she began to scroll faster, her hands trembling. In the more recent pictures, Evan was with some brunette, and from some of the poses it was obvious they were much more than friends. She paused long enough to check the date stamps of some of the pictures she'd uncovered so far.

October sixteenth through October twenty-second.

When he said he was being sent out to Midland?

The next pictures, in November, were with the same woman, and the dates corresponded with the week-long business trip to New Orleans he had supposedly been sent on over Thanksgiving.

After that, December, and that same woman smiling, arms wrapped around Karli's husband in what looked to be a tropical location – when he said he had to go to Kansas for work the week of Christmas.

She could not handle looking at any more pictures.

Her stomach lurched as she moved to his text message history and read line after disgusting line of sexy chats between Evan and his mistress.

But she also saw a thread with Jordan's name.

She opened it and scrolled, going more and more numb with shock as she read everything the two best friends had said to each other. The last entries were from the week Evan died.

I cannot believe you, man. You have a great *woman at home. What are you doing, Evan?* Jordan had typed that Thursday night.

Evan's responses were eye-opening, to say the least. He'd told Jordan he loved 'Melissa', that he wanted to be with her, that he'd tried to give her up and couldn't.

Jordan's last entry in the thread was on that Friday morning, Karli noticed, and it read *You said you stopped. You obviously lied. Karli doesn't deserve this, Evan. Either you tell her – or I will.*

She set the phone down and stared blindly into space, her heartbeat sounding in her ears, her hands beginning to shake with rage. The next thing she knew she was behind the wheel, driving to Fire Station Number Two.

"Jordan," Karli called out, walking through the open bay door beside the fire trucks. "*Jordan!*"

"He's out on a call, miss. Can I help you?" a voice to her right said.

"When do you expect him back?"

"I'm not sure."

"Fine," she snapped. "I'll wait."

"Miss, if you..." the fireman stopped mid-sentence when she whirled and glared at him.

Pregnant and *mad? Nuh-uh, buddy, no way,* he thought to himself.

"Okay, then," he said, hands raised and backing away slowly. "Okay."

CHAPTER EIGHT

Twenty minutes later, Tim and Jordan's ambulance pulled in and parked. Jordan did not see her right away; Tim tapped his shoulder and murmured, "You have a visitor."

"Karli?" Jordan exclaimed, walking quickly to her with a huge smile. "Hi! What a nice surprise. What are you doing here?"

"You knew, Jordan. You *knew*, and you didn't tell me."

"Tell you about what?"

"Evan and Melissa," she hissed.

His face and shoulders sagged.

"Did you even *think* I deserved to know?"

"You must have read the text messages, Karli. So, you tell me. Didn't it *sound* like I thought you should know?"

"It did," she snarled. "You just didn't give enough of a damn to protect me. You helped him cover it up."

"You wait just a minute," he said, his eyes stormy with emotion. "I couldn't bring myself to tell you, Karli. Lord knows I wanted to. But I knew it would crush you to find out."

"It has," she managed, tears streaming. "But right now, what hurts even more is that you let me stay in the dark, Jordan. You *knew* my marriage had turned into a joke. A lie. And you said nothing."

She turned and began to walk away.

"Karli, wait. Please wait," he pleaded.

She stopped but did not turn around.

"I didn't trust myself to tell you for the right reasons."

Now she turned to face him, still crying, and flung her arms wide.

"What the hell does that even *mean*?"

"Do you really not know, Karli?" he murmured as he watched her, his eyes blazing.

"No. What are you talking about?"

He swallowed hard, then closed the physical distance between them and poured his heart out at her feet.

"I'm in love with you, Karli."

She gasped. "But we only hung out a few...".

"It's been way, *way* longer than that," he interrupted, taking another step closer. "I fell in love with you the moment I saw you at that frat party seven years ago. But my feelings did *not* need to be the reason I told you. Was Evan's cheating wrong? Absolutely. Did you deserve to know? *Absolutely*. But I questioned my motives for wanting to reveal Evan's secret. Not to mention, I didn't want to tell you something I *knew* would hurt you. Does that make sense at all?"

"I...I can't be around you right now," she whispered, and slowly turned and walked to her car.

"Punch me," he offered, striding after her. "Scream at me. Throw things. Whatever you need to do. But please, Karli, please. Don't try to drive while you are this upset. *Please.*"

She whirled around again, and her face crumpled as she began to sob.

"How could you *do* that? How could you just... keep *quiet* like that?"

He put his arms around her, and she struggled at first.

"*No!* Get away from me!" she yelled.

"Karli, I'm so sorry," he whispered against her hair, pulling her to his chest. "I'm so sorry, honey."

Suddenly she clutched at him, leaning on him as the fresh grief of Evan's ultimate betrayal overwhelmed her.

"Oh, Jordan," she managed. "Why didn't he love me anymore? Why wasn't I enough?"

"It was his failing, not yours," Jordan whispered. "*You did nothing wrong, Karli.* You hear me? This is on *him*, not you, honey. Not you."

"I'm sorry I took it out on you," Karli wailed. "I'm just...so...".

"I know," he told her. "It's okay. I've got you, Karli. Let it out."

***

Later, they sat on the couch in his apartment. He had left work early and brought her home with him, since she'd mentioned Sarah wasn't around and he didn't want her to be alone.

Karli gripped her mug with both hands, sipping the tea Jordan had made for her.

"Is it all right? Not too hot?"

"It's perfect, thanks." She gazed at him over the mug's rim. "I'm going to ask you something, and I need you to be honest with me."

He nodded solemnly, moving to sit on the coffee table directly in front of her.

"This... *Melissa* person. To your knowledge, was that the first time he cheated on me?"

"I don't think so. I think there were others before that, Karli, but I can't prove it," he told her, wincing when she flinched as if she'd been struck. "I'm sorry, honey. But you asked me to be honest."

"I did," she agreed. "I just... was hoping you'd say, 'no way', or something."

"I wish I could, truly," he assured her. "I hate seeing you hurt."

"It's not your fault. Any of it. He knew what he was doing was wrong, he just didn't care. And I know you tried to talk some sense into him."

"For what it's worth, if I could go back in time and do all this again, I'd tell you the minute I found out. You deserved to be fully informed about things impacting your life. I felt that way then, too. I just... like I said, I couldn't figure out if my feelings were clouding the path, or not."

"You mean the fact that you're in love with me," she said softly, her blue eyes searching his.

"You caught that part, huh? Yeah... about that," he said with a lopsided grin as he raked a hand through his hair. "Well. Tonight's conversation is definitely *not* the way I ever, ever imagined telling you, but, yes, I am," he answered, turning red despite his best efforts.

"Is that why you acted like you hated me all that time?"

"Like I said before, I've never hated you. But I needed to avoid being around you so I wouldn't cross that line. You were off limits, married to my best friend. If I let myself be around you, I would have slipped up and told you how I felt. It was safer for me - for all of us really - for me to just stay away."

Karli gazed at him for a long moment.

"What happens between us now?"

He exhaled heavily. "I honestly have no idea. It really is not up to me, Karli. I just hope I didn't make it so awkward between us that you stop talking to me again."

She set her mug on the end table and took his hands in hers.

"Let me set the record straight right now. I was only stopping myself from exploring this thing between us out of loyalty to Evan. That ship has sailed now," she told him firmly. "I obviously didn't have his. He doesn't deserve mine."

"And? What are you saying?"

"That I want to see where this goes, Jordan. But I also do not want to hurt you, in any way."

"How would you hurt me?"

"What if... what if I can't say it back?"

"Karli. I did not tell you how I feel to try to force a response from you. I told you because I wanted to tell you. I didn't want it to be a secret anymore."

"Oh," she said suddenly. "There it is again."

"What?"

"I started feeling the baby move a couple of weeks ago. I really wanted to call you and tell you about it, but after that Friday night..." she shrugged. "I hadn't heard from you, so, I didn't think I should call."

"You wanted to call and tell *me*?"

"You were the first person that came to mind, actually," she admitted. "Same thing when your aunt found me a renter back in April. I started to dial your number."

"I miss seeing you in the park," he confessed.

"You do?"

"Very much."

"Oh, wow, there it is again," she noted. "That one was a lot stronger. Here. See if you can feel this."

She lifted her shirt, then grabbed his hands again and put them on her bare belly.

"Karli... wait...are you sure...".

"Shush," she admonished. "I want to share this with you."

They waited, and Jordan watched her eyes grow big.

"Really moving around now," she whispered. "Can you feel it?"

"Very soft, like a ripple, but I can feel it," he whispered back, and grinned. "That is just amazing."

"I know, right?" Karli's nose crinkled as she smiled.

He leaned forward and lightly touched his lips to hers, soft at first, then more insistent as she sighed and wrapped her arms around his neck.

"So," she murmured, "I guess this means we're talking again, huh."

He chuckled.

"And since we are," Karli continued, "I have a favor to ask."

"Name it," Jordan answered.

"Would you be willing to go with me to childbirth classes? Be my birth coach when the time comes?"

He took her hands and kissed each one.

"I'd love to," he told her, his eyes shining.

"Good! I was hoping you would say that. Because I already signed up for them, but I really did not want to do it alone," Karli said. "The first one's in three weeks."

***

The following Friday Karli had another sonogram to go to, but this time she had someone to share the experience with. Jordan came to Sarah's as scheduled and just stopped himself from picking Karli up and carrying her like a china doll to the passenger seat.

"You sure you can get up in there okay?"

"I'm fine," she chuckled. "May not be able to in another month or so, but right now, I'm good. Stop worrying."

"Can't help it," he said earnestly, and received a kiss for his concern.

At Dr. Hollard's office, Jordan held Karli's hand as the tech, Tracy, raced to keep up with an increasingly active baby.

"Trying to get good pictures, but this little angel won't cooperate," Tracy commented with a grin.

Jordan leaned down close to Karli's belly.

"Hey you in there," he murmured. "Can you please hold still for just a little while? We'd like to get a good look at you."

Karli gasped when she looked at the monitor, watching her baby slow its movements and turn its head in response to Jordan's voice.

"How did you do that?"

"Honestly? No idea," Jordan laughed. "I'm amazed that worked."

"Well, figure it out for when the little one decides to dance on my kidneys some more," Karli suggested.

"Do you want to know ahead of time if it's going to be a boy or a girl, or did you want to be surprised?" Tracy asked Karli. "If you want to know today, I can tell you."

Karli looked at Jordan, who said, "Totally your call, Karli."

"Tell me," Karli said mischievously.

"Okay...give me just a moment....and... looks like you're having a girl, Karli."

"And she will be beautiful, just like her momma," Jordan chimed in as he squeezed Karli's hand.

Dr. Hollard did a routine check-up once the sonogram ended, adjusted Karli's due date to October the fifth, and set her next appointment for two weeks out.

"Where to now?" Jordan asked as they walked back out to the truck.

"I'm thinking ice cream first, then, would you like to come with me and look at baby clothes?" Karli mused. "Now that I know I'm having a girl I have this need to go pick out cute pink stuff."

"You got it," Jordan said as he helped her into the truck.

They ordered two scoops each - sea salt caramel swirl for her, mint chocolate chip for him - and settled into a booth to enjoy their afternoon treat.

"I was thinking, after the baby's born," he began, "how would you feel about a spa package?"

"A spa package?"

"Yeah, you know. Manicure, pedicure, massage, all that stuff. Just go get pampered one afternoon. I bet all that feels pretty good, right?"

"It does. What's your point?"

"My point is, let me do that for you," he said gently. "Let me give you that."

"Why?"

"Because I love you," he told her. "And because I think you deserve an afternoon of just relaxing and doing the girly stuff. The only reason I haven't lined it up for you already is because I know you can't lie down on your stomach these days."

Karli laughed out loud. "Nope, not even close. It's like trying to lay on a medicine ball. Not to mention I am getting less graceful by the day. It's all I can do to get out of bed some mornings when she's over to one side."

"Think about it, at least," Jordan finished.

"Oh, there's no need to think about it. That sounds fabulous, and I am so ready for all that," Karli smiled. "But yeah, it's probably smarter to hold off until I can tie my own shoes again."

"Deal."

After they finished their ice cream, they shopped for baby clothes. Karli found four tiny outfits she fell in love with and bought them. Before they left the shop, she excused herself to the ladies' room.

"I'll be outside," Jordan told her, and she nodded.

She met him on the sidewalk and noticed his beaming smile. "What?"

"Nothing," he said. "Just happy to be with you, that's all."

When they got back to Sarah's, he walked her to the door, kissed her, and said, "I'm on overnights the next three weeks, starting tonight. But I should still be able to do the childbirth classes. When do they start?"

"Two weeks from today," she answered. "From two to four p.m."

"That works well," he confirmed, "because I don't have to be on shift until ten."

It wasn't until after he had left that she noticed two extra items in the shopping bag. A three-pack of tiny pink and purple onesies, with 'Little Miss Perfect' inscribed across the front of each, and a velvety soft footed sleeper with 'Princess' embroidered on it.

Aww... he bought baby clothes, too...

Karli's heart melted.

CHAPTER NINE

"Check out this bassinet I found," Jordan said excitedly two weeks later. "It should fit nicely in your room."

He pulled up the picture on his laptop, then scooted over to show her the screen.

"Yeah, space is kind of tight, so that should work pretty well. Nice catch!" Karli answered, then glanced at her watch. "Oops. Better get going. The sonogram's in forty minutes."

"And after that, our first childbirth class," he reminded her. "You excited?"

"Yes, and no," she said. "I think it's going to be good to learn some breathing and relaxation techniques, but I have no desire to watch a video. I'm already gonna feel it, I don't need to see it."

He laughed. "I'll tell you what. When the time comes, I will have them cover the mirror in the birthing suite."

"There's *mirrors*? In a *birthing suite*? What sadistic lunatic came up with that?" she exclaimed, horrified. "I don't want to watch myself go through this! Good Lord!"

"You are so damn cute when you make that face," he rejoined, still chuckling.

"What face?"

"That..." he scrunched up his nose, "face like that. It's adorable."

She rolled her eyes and smiled. "Okay, you ready to go?"

"Yep," Jordan stood up, moved in front of her, and held out his hands to help her up off the couch.

"Ow...ouch," Karli yelped. "Settle down, kiddo," she murmured, rubbing the sides of her belly.

"Is she tap-dancing again?"

"It sure feels like it," Karli confirmed. "Feel."

He placed his palms on either side where Karli had been rubbing. "Wow. Our little angel is rocking right along today, isn't she?"

"That, or she's sideways again," Karli grimaced. "*Ow.*"

"Hang on, I got this," Jordan announced, and he sat on the coffee table, his face close to Karli's belly, and began to talk in a low murmur to the baby.

Karli stood, running a hand through his soft, thick, dark hair, listening and smiling as he worked his magic. Her child was calming inside her.

She is probably as entranced as I am by that smooth baritone of his, Karli thought. *It does a number on me too. Not to mention the way he says 'our' when he is talking about the baby. I don't even think he's aware of it when he says it. But I absolutely adore it – and him. I am so happy he's in my life...*

She sighed in contentment without even realizing it, and Jordan spoke to her and brought her out of her reverie.

"Honey?"

"I'm sorry. What were you saying?"

"I asked if it's better now."

"Yep, she calmed right down the moment you started talking. You *have* to tell me how you do it."

"I still have no idea," he chuckled, then kissed her. "But I'm glad it works. Now, let's get to the sonogram before she gets all wound up again."

Their time with Tracy went smoothly, and Doctor Hollard nodded in approval as he quickly scanned the sonogram pictures and then Karli's chart.

"About six more weeks, I'd say. You're almost in the home stretch, and everything looks great, Karli. Bloodwork, weight, the baby's size, all right where they should be. How is everything else going? Any problems sleeping?"

"Other than not being able to get comfortable for long, no," she answered. "But I am starting to notice more frequent heartburn, even with mild foods."

"Not uncommon," Hollard assured her. "Fortunately, over the counter medications, such as Tums, are perfectly safe to take while you're pregnant. But you may find the *liquid* versions of calcium carbonate are more effective."

***

"So, that wasn't so bad," Karli decided as they left their first childbirth class later that afternoon. "A lot of that stuff I already knew, and I am *totally okay* with the idea that watching the video isn't required."

Jordan grinned. "I thought that might make you happy. I've had to watch it, as part of my EMT training. It's pretty, um, intense."

"You know what else is intense? This heat," she observed, fanning herself with the welcome pamphlet they'd been given. "Late summer in Texas is always a beating, but being almost eight months pregnant in mid-August? That sucks on a whole new level."

"Sounds like you could use air conditioning, a bowl of ice cream, and a foot rub," Jordan mentioned. "And I just happen to know a place that has all three."

"Lead the way," she urged. "Before we melt."

In a half-hour, Karli was stretched out contentedly on Jordan's couch, a bowl of her favored sea salt caramel ice cream in her hands. She was also moaning lightly as Jordan gently worked a knot out of her right foot's arch.

"Man, that feels *so* good," she sighed. "They hurt all the time now."

"I can imagine, honey," Jordan replied. "But just think, not much longer, and our little angel will be here."

She smiled. *He said it again. 'Our'. I love hearing it. I hope he never stops.*

"What?" he asked.

"Nothing," she answered. "Just happy to be with you, that's all. You have to work tonight?"

"Actually, no, I don't," Jordan revealed. "And I was thinking stay in tonight. Chinese food and that new action flick we saw the ad for. It's out on Netflix now. Wanna watch it with me?"

"Absolutely," she grinned.

"And after that, stay with me, Karli. Spend the night," he said, almost bashfully.

"Um... I really appreciate the invitation to... *you know*... but I kinda can't right now," she stammered, waving at her belly like a model might gesture at a shiny new prize on a game show.

"Oh my God, no, not like *that*," Jordan exclaimed, his eyes wide, his discomfort growing exponentially as he turned beet red. "I mean, not that I don't *want* to... What I'm saying is I've *always* wanted to when it comes to you... Geez, now I sound like a perv *and* an idiot...Um... no, I meant just sleep, Karli."

"You've thought about us... *together* like that?" she queried, also blushing now, even as she thought *oh good, it's not just me.*

"Every day, for the past seven-plus years," Jordan said without hesitation, the raw want flashing in his eyes. "Are you *kidding* me? Look at you. You're *gorgeous*. But I am willing to wait for as long as it takes. And not just because you are pregnant, Karli. Being with someone that way... it's a big deal. A big step, for both of us. One that only needs to happen if, and when, we are both ready for it to. You know?"

If I weren't already falling for him, that right there would have done it for sure, she thought as she nodded, blinking back happy tears.

"Now," he directed, "you wait right here. I'm gonna order the food, cue up the movie, and then, you're gonna give me your left foot to work on."

***

Two and a half hours later, she'd nodded off on his couch. He sat, gazing at her, her feet in his lap, her long blond hair spilling over the miniature couch pillow. Karli was making a little wispy sound as she exhaled, and a rush of emotion almost overwhelmed him.

God, I love this woman. Even when she snores.

Jordan's heart was suddenly so full it felt like it would burst right out of his chest.

He gently eased himself out from under her feet, stood, then slowly scooped her up off the couch and carried her into the bedroom to lay her gently on the bed. Karli sighed once and gradually turned on her side but did not wake.

He turned off the lights in the living room and kitchen, then made his way back to his room and lay down next to her. He snuggled up behind Karli and draped one arm protectively over her, his hand splayed like a shield over the unborn child that he already loved as his own.

Jordan smiled into the dark, reveling in the feel of Karli's body in proximity to his, and faded into sleep.

***

But by the time Labor Day weekend approached, Jordan had become very secretive, including ending calls abruptly whenever she walked in the room. Karli had begun to worry that maybe he'd changed his mind about the two of them.

Maybe the reality of a 'ready-made' family finally sank in, and he just can't figure out how to break it to me, she worried as she washed dishes at Sarah's sink.

The doorbell ringing caught her attention, and she shuffled to answer it.

"Hey," Jordan said nonchalantly when Karli opened the door. "I have some errands to run. Want to come with me?"

"Um, sure, I guess," she shrugged. But she could tell he was holding something back, and the realization hit her like a ton of bricks.

Oh, my God. He's breaking up. He doesn't want to see me anymore, her brain concluded, and it almost buckled her knees.

She moved to his truck on autopilot, tears already threatening, trying her best to steel herself for the conversation she just knew was imminent.

"I need to swing by the station right quick," he murmured, and she only nodded, focusing her attention out the passenger side window in a desperate effort to keep it together.

Jordan pulled into the station's visitor parking lot, then went around and opened her door. "Come on," he said. "This won't take long, I promise."

Karli reluctantly took his hand and let him help her down to the ground.

"Just through here," he pointed, holding the door open.

She walked in front of him down a narrow hall, turned right where he indicated – and jumped with both surprise and a little fright as a room full of people, including Madge, her parents, and Sarah yelled out, "Happy baby shower!"

"Wait...what..." Karli's mind was reeling.

"I wanted you to have a baby shower," Jordan whispered in her ear, his arms around her as he stood close behind her. "Cool surprise, huh?"

"Is *this* why you've been so secretive lately?"

"Yeah," he admitted. "I really wanted it to be a surprise."

"So... so... you're not breaking up with me?" she whispered back.

He slowly turned her around to face him, and she gasped as she saw a flicker of hurt in his brown eyes.

"Honey. Is that what you honestly thought?"

She nodded.

He squeezed her to him gently. "You're the love of my life, Karli," he told her in a low murmur meant only for her that thrilled her to her core. "I'm not going anywhere. Ever. I promise."

***

Cake, punch, party games, and an avalanche of opened baby gifts later, it was time to go.

Madge approached Karli and enveloped her in a huge hug. "You two are so good together," she whispered. "This is the most I've ever seen Jordan smile. And I am so happy to see *you* happy again too, Karli."

"Thanks, Madge. Truly."

"Call me if you need anything," Madge said, and walked away.

Karli looked at the mound of gifts once everyone had left. "No way all this is going to fit in my room," she lamented.

"About that," Jordan said as he came back in from putting another box in the bed of his truck. "Why don't you move in with me? Think about it. You're at my place most of the time now anyway, and that second bedroom is completely empty. It would make a great nursery."

She tilted her head and considered. "You know what? Yes. Let's do it."

"I was hoping you'd say that," he grinned before he kissed her. "I'm the luckiest man on the planet, did you know that? And it's because of you."

"When do you want to move stuff around?"

"Well, maybe it's just me being selfish, but I vote the sooner, the better," he announced. "But for right now, let's head back to my place, and I can unload all *this* stuff into the nursery."

***

When she got back to Sarah's apartment a couple of hours later and announced she was moving out,

Karli was surprised that Sarah was *not* surprised to hear the news.

"Are you kidding me?" Sarah said as she hugged a smiling Karli. "I'm amazed it took you guys this long. He's head over heels in love with you, you know."

"I know," Karli sighed in contentment. "And I've fallen for him, too."

"So, when are you going?"

"He has to work tonight, so, probably tomorrow afternoon," Karli confirmed.

"Sounds like we need one last chick flick and chocolate night," Sarah pointed out. "Send you off right."

"Deal."

CHAPTER TEN

At two-twelve a.m., when her daughter began to bounce on her bladder once again, Karli lumbered out of bed and made her way to the bathroom. As she began to get back into bed, she glanced at her cell phone on the dresser.

"Missed calls? How did I miss calls?" she wondered out loud. Then she realized she had once again forgotten to turn the ringer back up to normal volume after an appointment.

"Ah, *that's* how," Karli said.

Stupid pregnancy brain. I thought people were making that up, but they weren't. I can barely remember my own name.

She stared at her phone, frowning. Six calls, all in the past half-hour, from a number she did not recognize, but whoever had called her left no voicemails.

Intrigued, she called the unknown number back, and waited.

"Hello?" a male's voice answered after just one ring. "Karli? Is that you?"

"Yes," she said, confused. "Who's this?"

"Thank God. I've been trying to reach you," the man said. "This is Tim Fresco, Jordan's rig partner. He's been hurt."

"Where is he?" she stammered as she grabbed clothes to put on.

"Medical City, just off Matlock Road," Tim told her.

"I'm on my way."

She hung up the phone, changed clothes as quickly as she could, then pounded on Sarah's bedroom door.

"What's wrong?" Sarah asked, eyes wide with panic.

"Something's happened to Jordan," Karli cried. "I need to go."

"Give me two minutes to get dressed. I'll drive you."

Please, God, please let him be okay, Karli chanted again and again in her head as she wiped tears from her face. *Please don't take him. Please.*

***

Within twenty minutes of the phone call, Sarah had pulled her car up at the emergency room entrance to let Karli out.

"Go on, I'll find you in there," Sarah urged.

When the attendants saw a crying, extremely pregnant woman walking in so quickly, they started to bring a wheelchair over for her, thinking she was in labor.

"No... no," she sobbed, trying to wave them off. "Not me... Jordan... where's *Jordan?*"

"Karli," she heard someone call out, and she swiveled her head to the left. A man in an EMT uniform with light brown hair and storm grey eyes was coming toward her.

"Hey. I'm Tim. Drove your moving van, remember? Come with me, Karli. This way."

"Wait, Sarah's coming," she managed, and he nodded.

Sarah blasted through the door a few moments later, saw them, and paused for a split second before walking over to where they were standing.

"Take me to him, Tim," Karli pleaded.

As they moved, Sarah quietly asked, "What happened?"

"We got called out to assist with some injuries sustained during a barfight," Tim replied, running a hand over his worried face. "Jordan was working on one guy who was drunk as hell and got combative. When Jordan went to strap him down on the gurney, the guy pulled a knife and stabbed him."

Karli went ghost white and began to sway.

"Is he... is he..." she went silent, tears obscuring both her voice and her vision.

"They took him into surgery about five minutes ago," Tim told her as he put his arm around her waist to help steady her. "We're heading to the waiting room upstairs just outside the surgical unit."

When they entered the room, Karli was stunned to see it was packed with police officers and emergency personnel. A few of the other firemen who had helped her move in the spring waved solemnly to her in recognition.

"Have a seat right here," Tim offered, pointing to the chair that one of the officers immediately vacated when she walked in. "I'm going to see if I can get an update. Okay?"

"Okay," she sniffled.

Dan, another crew member from Fire Station Number Two that she had met before, approached her with tissues and a bottled water.

"Hi, Karli," he said gently as he handed her the items. "Jordan's tough, all right? I'm sure he's gonna be fine."

She nodded, dabbing at her eyes. "Hi Dan...I...hope so," she wailed, her breath hitching.

"Karli look at me," Dan said, crouching down in front of her and taking her hand. "I know you're upset, but I need you to try to breathe normally for me. Last thing you or your baby need is to work yourself up to the point that you go into labor early. All right? Come on, big deep breaths."

Karli closed her eyes and focused on her breathing, even as she willed Jordan to be okay. With each inhale she felt more and more certain that Jordan Baker had captured her heart, and with each exhale, she sent up a prayer for him to be spared.

***

After three hours, the general surgeon came out to the waiting room.

"I'm sure you all will be glad to know EMT Baker should make a full recovery," he began, and the room erupted with cheers. The surgeon smiled and waited a moment before motioning for quiet so he could continue.

"The surgery went well. The knife missed all major organs, thankfully. He did have muscle and ligament damage that required repair, so you all will have to do without him wrestling a gurney for a little while. We'll keep him for a few days, then send him home."

"How soon can we see him?" Tim asked.

"Immediate family only until he's out of ICU," the doctor replied. "He's in post-op right now, and we'll be moving him to ICU within the next two hours."

"His girlfriend's right here," Tim pointed at Karli. "Can she see him in post-op?"

Karli lurched to her feet and came to stand beside Tim with hopeful eyes. Tim put an arm around her.

"Give us ten minutes," the surgeon said, "and I'll send my nurse out to come get you, miss."

"Thanks, Doc," Karli told him sincerely. "That's great news."

Then she broke down, overcome with relief and gratitude.

"Oh, thank God," she said into Tim's shoulder as the surgeon walked away. "Thank God."

After a short time, an older woman appeared.

"I can bring you back for about fifteen minutes," she told Karli with a kind warm smile. "You'll be able to stay with him longer once we get him into ICU. Come with me, dear."

They walked through the double doors and down a narrow corridor, then turned left.

"He's in bed three, just down and to the left," the nurse told her. "My name's Abagail if you need anything. I'll be around to collect you when it's time to head back to the waiting room, all right?"

"Thanks, Abagail," Karli whispered. She took a deep breath, then walked in the direction Abagail had pointed.

When Karli peeked in Jordan's room, another nurse greeted her. "Hi. I'm just checking his progress," she said. "He's drifting in and out still."

Karli nodded, moving to the other side of the bed, and clutched his hand in hers.

"Hi, sweetheart," she murmured as she stroked his hair. "It's me, Jordan. It's Karli."

He moaned a little and turned his head toward her voice. His eyelids fluttered open, and he smiled at her and squeezed her hand before he slid back under.

"You're going to be all right," she whispered, and leaned over to kiss his forehead. "And I will be right here with you."

His eyes opened again, and he croaked, "Hi, honey," then drifted once more into sleep.

She leaned down again, put her forehead on Jordan's shoulder, and cried.

***

Abagail came and got her much too quickly; Karli was amazed at how fast her fifteen minutes had gone.

As they walked back toward the waiting room, the nurse patted her hand and said, "Don't worry, dear, he's in very good hands, and as soon as they get him settled in upstairs you can see him again, all right? Give me your cell phone number. I can text you when they move him."

"Thanks for taking care of him," Karli managed, another tear rolling down as she walked back out toward the waiting room.

When she got there the crowd had begun to dissipate; the surgeon advising that Jordan would be okay was enough reassurance for most. She found Dan, Tim, Sarah, and a handful of others awaiting her return.

"We were thinking you could probably use some food," Tim suggested. "They probably won't have him settled in for a while yet. What do you say?"

"I have zero appetite," Karli admitted, "but yeah, I probably ought to try. I gave the nurse my number, and she's going to let me know when I can go back up and see him."

The group rode the elevator to the ground floor and headed for the hospital's cafeteria. While nothing sounded appetizing, Karli forced herself to grab a small portion of scrambled eggs and toast, smiling wanly when Dan announced, "Nope, put your money away, I got this."

They sat and ate, making conversation all around her. But Karli was only partially listening. Her mind was on the man in the hospital bed two stories above their heads, and how close she had come to losing him forever.

"You all right?" Sarah murmured.

"Just...so relieved," Karli murmured back. "So relieved."

Her best friend gave her an appraising look.

"I can see that you love him, Karli," Sarah said softly so that no one else at the table could hear her. "And you should tell him, as soon as possible. Trust me on this. When you find the one, you should never, ever let them go."

Sarah's face took on a weird expression, but before Karli could react, her phone buzzed.

"They've moved him," she announced after she scanned the text. "I'm going back upstairs."

***

It was late afternoon before Jordan blinked his eyes rapidly, then opened them and frowned.

"Where the hell am I?" he rasped.

"ICU, but just as a precaution," came a voice from his right.

He swiveled his head and looked into the sapphire blue eyes that had captivated his heart so many years ago.

"Hi, honey," he said. "What happened?"

"Jackass stuck you. The one you were working on," Tim told him from the foot of his bed. "Got you pretty good, but the doctor says you're gonna be okay."

"Well, that explains why my gut hurts," Jordan observed. "They do surgery?"

"Yep, had to," his partner confirmed. "But you should only be out of commission for about three weeks. I swear, dude, if you wanted a break, you could have just filled out a vacation form, like normal people do."

Jordan grinned at the words, and nodded at the underlying sentiment coming from Tim. *He is relieved, I can tell.*

"Anyway, I'm gonna get out of here, I need to get some sleep," Tim continued. "Karli, you need a ride?"

"They won't let me stay past visiting hours," she explained mournfully to Jordan. "So, I will have to leave here in a bit, too. But I will be back first thing in the morning."

"I'll give you guys a moment," Tim offered, and stepped out.

"Karli," Jordan said, cupping her cheek. "You've been crying."

"Of course, I have," Karli managed, leaning into his palm and closing her eyes. "I thought... I thought you..."

"Karli, it's okay, I'm going to be fine, honey," he reassured her.

"There's something I need to tell you before I go," Karli said. "I didn't realize it until last night when Tim called me...and..." her voice broke, so she took another deep breath and pressed on. "Told me you were hurt. And the thought of losing you was like the world ending all around me. *I love you*, Jordan Baker. I didn't realize it until last night, but I love you, and I will make sure every single day you know how much."

His eyes went wide. "You do?"

She nodded, and the tears that flowed this time were happy ones. "I really do. With all my heart."

***

In the early morning hours of October tenth, Karli woke from a deep sleep and nudged Jordan's shoulder.

"Baby," she said through gritted teeth.

"Hmm," came the sleepy response.

"No. *The baby.* I think I'm in labor," she told him, her pitch rising as the next contraction almost stole her breath away. "And I think my water just broke."

Jordan went from mostly asleep to wide awake in an instant, scrambling for his watch.

"Tell me when this one is over, okay? And breathe, honey. In through your nose and out through your mouth," he directed, moving around the room to get dressed and grab her hospital bag.

"It's gone," Karli said, and motioned to him to help her sit up and maneuver to the side of the bed. "But I think another one's pretty close behind it."

When the subsequent contraction began, she panted, "Now," and he noted the time then coached her breathing through it.

"A little under five minutes apart," he calculated once it had passed. "I think we need to get going."

She nodded, holding still while he slipped her shoes onto her feet, then helped her stand.

Two more contractions happened between the bedroom and the truck, with Karli clutching his hand through each.

"Jordan."

"Yes, honey?"

"We might want to hurry," she said.

Jordan drove as fast as he safely dared to, then threw the transmission into park at the patient drop-off zone. He leapt out of the truck and ran around to her side to bodily pick her up and carry her into the emergency entrance. A quick sign-in while an attendant brought forth a wheelchair, and away to the birthing suites they went.

As soon as she was wheeled into the room, Karli laughed.

"*Wow*," she said. "How bizarre. You weren't kidding. That is one big mirror."

"I'm on it," Jordan assured her, and rummaged up an extra blanket to drape over it.

***

She had waved off pain medications, determined to see a natural childbirth all the way through. Twenty-three hours later, after some of the worst pain she'd ever experienced, it was finally time to push.

"Come on, Karli, just one more," Doctor Hollard urged, and she strained with all her might, yelling through gritted teeth as she braced against Jordan's chest.

For a split second there was an immense silence, and then the most beautiful sound Karli had ever heard – her daughter sucking in a lungful of air, then wailing.

"She's here, honey," Jordan murmured in Karli's ear as tears streamed down his cheeks. "She's here. And she's beautiful."

Karli slumped back against him, exhilarated and exhausted.

Hollard deftly handed the newborn to his nurse, who promptly weighed and measured the baby and cleaned her up a bit, then wrapped her in a tiny pink blanket and brought her to Karli.

"Here you go, Mommy," the woman said with a warm smile as she lay the baby in Karli's arms. "She *is* beautiful. Congratulations!"

EPILOGUE

A little while later, once the aftermath had been tidied up and the doctor and nurse had left, Jordan sat on the edge of the bed, cradling the infant in his muscular arms and talking to her in his low murmur.

Karli smiled as she watched them together, the baby's expression serene but occasionally smiling at Jordan as he spoke.

"You're the most gorgeous little baby ever," he crooned. "Our little angel."

"What should we name her?" Karli asked.

"We?"

"Yes, Jordan. We. What should *our* daughter's name be?"

He blinked rapidly.

"I like Grace," he managed to say after a long pause to try to regain his composure.

"Emily Grace," Karli mentioned, and smiled. "I love that. What do you think?"

Jordan looked up at Karli.

"What do I think? I'm so in love with both of you," he proclaimed, his voice thick with emotion. "I want us to stay this way forever. Please say you'll marry me, Karli."

"Yes," she answered, beaming with happiness. "Yes, Jordan. I'll marry you."

***

Four months later, Jordan and Karli arrived at Madge's house as scheduled.

"This is gonna be alright, right?" Karli said nervously. "It's her first time away from us."

"I'm having trouble with it too, honey," Jordan admitted. "But it's gonna be okay."

"It should be fine," Madge assured them. "But if you need to, swing on by and check on her in between your running around. Or come pick her up right after dinner. No harm in it. I was a new parent too once, so

I know how this feels, guys. It can be a little nerve-wracking the first time."

"Thanks, Madge," Jordan said.

They got back into the truck after giving Emily copious kisses on her chubby little cheeks.

"Okay," Jordan began. "Dinner, and then whatever else you'd like to do on our date."

Karli turned her head to look at him.

"I already know *exactly* what I want to do tonight," she said, toying with the solitaire he had put on the third finger of her left hand.

"Whatcha got?"

"You remember when we were talking that one time about... you know... and you said it's a big deal, a big step, and it only needed to happen when we were both ready?"

"Yes, I remember."

Karli leaned across the cab and kissed him, then whispered against his lips, "I'm ready, if you are."

"Straight back home it is then," he growled against her mouth.

The way she laughed with delight as he gunned the motor was music to his ears.

The End.

Falling into Place

<u>Sarah Genard</u> – Karli Anders' best friend and fellow blogger. Three years earlier, she made a rash decision that left her with a tattered heart. While she acts like her life is going exactly as she planned it, she secretly longs to reconnect with that one special man, someone she genuinely loved - not just in body, but also in mind, heart, and soul.

<u>Tim Fresco</u> - Jordan Baker's friend and co-worker who has sworn off women after a runaway bride left him standing alone and emotionally gutted at the altar. The mere thought of Sarah Genard both intrigues and terrifies him. Only he can decide whether to let fear keep him lonely or follow his heart and reach out for her - again.

PROLOGUE

"You nervous, buddy?" Kevin asked him as they stood at the front of the First Baptist Church in Adrian, Texas on a gorgeous late May morning.

"Nope, not at all," Tim told his best man without hesitation. "I love her, and I'm ready for this."

Tim Fresco and Sarah Genard had dated all through high school, remaining as strong a couple as ever when he left for the Army. By the time he had gotten through boot camp, he'd decided to ask her to marry him, and she'd accepted, her entire face alight with happiness.

Ten months later, he was home on leave, standing in his best dress uniform in front of all their friends and family members, just waiting for the music to start and his bride to appear on her father's arm.

He glanced at his watch. Three minutes past ten.

Not a big deal, he thought. *I'm sure I will see them walking in any minute now.*

At fifteen minutes past ten, people in the pews began to whisper, and the pastor leaned over to him and murmured, "Everything okay, son?"

"I'm sure it's fine," he murmured back.

At ten-forty-two, the door at the back of the church opened, and Tim's eyes filled with hope, but it was dashed when he saw it was Jenny, Sarah's maid of honor.

Jenny nervously made her way down the aisle, the whispers in the audience increasing to a loud murmur as she moved to the front of the church where Tim still stood resolute but beginning to turn pale.

"What's going on, Jenny? Where's Sarah? Is she all right?" he asked, with fear in his eyes.

"She's gone," Jenny answered as quietly as she could. "But I found this. I'm so sorry, Tim."

And she handed him an envelope.

He opened it to find two things, both of which caused a lump in his throat. He held one of them in his left hand, and with his right hand unfolded the paper. As he scanned its contents, he felt his knees give way, and sat down heavily on the altar step in complete shock.

"What the hell is she *talking* about?" he whispered, completely confused, clutching the engagement ring that he'd had custom made just for Sarah as his eyes filled with tears.

But she was already gone, and no one, not even Jenny, knew where she was headed.

So he couldn't ask her.

CHAPTER ONE

Right around the time Tim was reading the short note she had left for him, Sarah was frowning as she fiddled with the radio, searching for a new station to keep her company on the drive. She'd spent a restless night in a Motel 6 just south of Lubbock, Texas, passing part of the time in her room setting up a new email account before falling into a fitful sleep. By nine-thirty a.m. she'd left the motel and was walking into a Verizon Wireless store to get a new cell phone with a new number.

He probably won't even bother *to try to find me,* she had sighed to herself. *Still, better safe than sorry.*

Now, she was back in the car and heading east, her fingers idly drumming in tempo with the random pop song playing in the background.

She glanced at the clock display on her dash. Almost eleven a.m. *We would have been pronounced man and wife by now.* Tears glistening, she looked at her reflection in the rearview mirror and willed herself not to cry.

"Come on, Sarah, you got this," she muttered aloud. "You know it had to be this way."

Sarah already knew her parents must be worried sick, and she resolved to call them as soon as she got to Arlington. Not before then. She could not risk reaching out before this afternoon. By then, everyone would have gone their separate ways. She hoped so, anyway. She also knew that Marty and Bethany Genard would never reveal their daughter's location to anyone if she asked them not to – not even Tim.

Especially not Tim. If he even cares enough to ask, that is.

Sarah set her jaw, blinking rapidly to see the road through the tears she couldn't hold back anymore, and cranked up the radio before gripping the steering wheel like it was her lifeline.

***

"I don't understand," Tim said as he sat on the Genards' couch beside his parents, Patrick and Paige Fresco. "I have no idea what she's talking about, I really don't."

He lifted devastated eyes to Bethany and Marty. "Do you have any idea where she is? If you do, *please*, tell me. I have to find her and talk to her."

"No one's heard from her, and her phone's going straight to voicemail," Bethany replied softly, her voice catching. "Marty had to work last night, and I went to bed early, so we didn't even know she'd left the house, Tim. When I got up this morning and she wasn't here, I just assumed she'd gone to Jenny's house or the church to get ready."

"But-" Tim started to say, and Marty held up his hand.

"She didn't tell us anything either, son," he said gently, his face creased with worry. "She never said a word. Didn't even leave us a note. When I went to work last night, she was here, and she was happy, and I was gonna walk her down the aisle to you this morning. We're just as surprised as you are, and we have no damn clue where she is."

Tim closed his eyes for a moment and hung his head. With a heavy sigh, he stood up and shook both their hands.

"I have no idea what happened," he repeated, "but I love your daughter. She's my whole world. If you happen to talk to her before I do, can you please tell her that for me?"

Marty nodded, and saw Tim and his parents to the door as Bethany dabbed at her eyes.

***

Sarah stopped for food in Abilene. While she waited for her take-out order, she made a call and confirmed that registration for the summer semesters would begin on Thursday morning. She made an appointment with an academic advisor for Wednesday morning, then ate her lunch at a picnic table just outside the restaurant before getting back in her car.

That gives me a few days to find a place to live and get settled in, she told herself. *Better get going.*

Almost three hours later, once she'd passed the Arlington city limits sign and taken the exit she needed, she pulled into a strip mall parking lot and called her parents' house.

"Sarah!" Bethany exclaimed, and burst into tears. "Sarah, where are you? What's going on?"

"Mom, I just...," Sarah took a breath to compose herself. "I had to get out of there. I had to."

"Why? What happened?"

"I don't want to talk about it, Mom, I really don't. Just... let's just say Tim is not who I thought he was, and leave it at that, okay? Please?"

In the silence she could hear her mother sniffling, followed by, "If you want. But honey – *where are you*? We're all worried sick!"

"Is he there right now?" Sarah asked, her bruised and battered heart in her throat.

"No. Tim and his folks left a while ago. I'm not sure what happened between you two, but he's devastated, Sarah."

"He's the *last* person in the world who should have the nerve to be surprised by this," she snarled before she could stop herself.

"Oh, honey. What did he do?"

"You can ask *him* that. Like I said, Mom, I don't want to talk about it."

"Are you coming home?"

A long pause, then, "No, Mom, I'm not. I'll tell you what I'm doing, but you can't tell Tim. Promise me."

She heard a click and then her father's voice on the line too. *He must have picked up the phone in the study,* she realized.

"Sarah. Are you okay?" he asked, and Sarah winced at the pain in his voice. "And where the hell are you?"

"I'm in Arlington, Dad. I am going to find a place to live and enroll at UTA. And you guys cannot tell Tim where I am, all right? Promise me you won't tell him if he asks. Although I'm probably not even on his mind anymore."

"You're wrong about that," Marty retorted. "Dead wrong. That young man is completely distraught, Sarah."

Sarah's brow wrinkled in confusion as she listened to her parents' words. *Why would he even care? I know what I saw.*

"It doesn't matter," she replied shakily, her heart breaking in two all over again. "He made his choice, and I've made mine. I'm just sorry I worried you both in the process."

She gave them her new phone number and email address, then swore them both to secrecy. After another round of 'I love you' and a promise she would tell them her address once she had one, Sarah disconnected the call.

Next, she drove to the city's library and signed in to one of the computers, then began her search for housing. She wrote down several choices, all within a three-block radius of the campus, then began making calls.

She hit gold with her fifth call. The complex had one unit available, and the woman's voice over the telephone line was warm and soothing, reminding her of her beloved Grandma Peggy that she'd lost in March.

"I can show it to you today, if you'd like to come see it, dear," the woman had said.

To which Sarah replied, "I can be there in twenty minutes."

***

Once they had gotten off the call, Marty walked back into their kitchen.

"I think there's been a huge misunderstanding," he observed as he looked at Bethany. "It's a shame, too. They're great together."

"Yes, they are," Bethany agreed. "But they're grown, and it's between them, and she doesn't want to talk about it, dear."

"I know," Sarah's father sighed. "I just wish there was something we could do."

"Me too, but there's not," his wife rejoined. "We made a promise not to share her location, and we need to keep it. And if they're meant to be," she continued as she moved into Marty's arms, "then it will happen at some point, honey. That's the best we can hope for."

***

Across town from the Genard house, Tim sat on his parents' couch in a stupor. *Sarah and I should be cutting our wedding cake and laughing and having our first dance as husband and wife right now,* he realized, and a fresh wave of pain stabbed him straight in the heart. He raked his hands over his face and stood.

"I can't do this," he mumbled aloud to his mother and father. "I can't just sit here and wonder what the hell went so wrong. I'm heading back to my unit."

"Right now?" Paige asked.

Tim's jaw set. "Yes, Mom. I love you both very much, but right now there's just too many ghosts in this town." He leaned over and kissed her on the forehead. "I'm going to go change and pack my gear."

His father watched him walk down the hallway, then rose and followed his son, stopping in Tim's bedroom doorway.

"Did you ever tell Sarah you're deploying to Afghanistan, son?" Patrick murmured.

"No, I didn't." Tim's shoulders sagged. "She knew it was a possibility, but not that we've been issued travel orders. I was going to tell her tonight."

***

"How soon did you need the place, dear?" Mrs. Richardson asked sweetly as they toured the two-bedroom second-floor unit.

"As soon as possible, although it might take a bit to find some furniture," Sarah told her honestly. "Everything I own is in my SUV."

"I think I can help with that," the old woman beamed. "My grandson works in a furniture store. He's about your age, too, and he's handsome. And single," she added with a sly grin.

"I appreciate that, Mrs. Richardson, but I'm only looking for furniture. I, um... well, I just got out of a relationship, so..." Sarah faltered as her face filled with hurt.

"Now, now, dear, no worries," came the response along with an affectionate pat on Sarah's hand. "And please, call me Jodie. I didn't mean to upset you, Sarah."

"You didn't. It's just a very recent breakup." *Like the 'not-even-forty-eight-hours-old' kind of recent,* Sarah concluded in her head.

They returned to the office and filled out the lease paperwork, and Jodie tilted her head when Sarah mentioned she was enrolling in UTA.

"Really? That's delightful. What are you majoring in?"

"Accounting," Sarah replied.

Jodie regarded her a moment longer, then leaned forward and whispered, "Maybe we can make a deal."

"What kind of deal?" Sarah asked, amused at the twinkle in the complex manager's eye.

"Well, I'm not getting any younger, my eyesight's not what it used to be, and I'm supposed to be putting all of my bookkeeping onto the computer. But I'm just not comfortable using the darn thing. So, let's trade. If you will work here part-time and help me out with the books, I'll put you in the two-bedroom unit at the one-bedroom rate, and I can deduct what you work from the rent. How does that sound?"

"Jodie," Sarah smiled, "you have a deal."

"Excellent!" the grandmother clapped her hands with glee. "Now, let's get this paperwork done, and then I can reach out to Larry, and we can get you some furniture."

That night Sarah, wearing one of Tim's oversized t-shirts and wrapped up in her favorite blanket, leaned back in the overstuffed recliner she had picked up on clearance and cried herself to sleep in her new apartment.

***

"You take damn good care of yourself, you hear me, son?" Patrick intoned.

"Yes, sir," Tim answered as they hugged.

"Come back safe to us," his mother said as she threw her arms around him. He returned Paige's embrace before he threw his duffel bag into the truck and climbed behind the wheel, watching his parents move back to the porch to wave goodbye.

God, I miss you, Sarah, he thought as he glanced over at the empty passenger seat. *You should be here with me.*

He pushed the love of his life from his mind, waved to his parents, and pulled out of the driveway to begin the eight-hour drive back to Fort Hood.

His teammate, Dack Abrams, was still awake when Tim arrived back at the barracks at one-thirty a.m. They had met and bonded during boot camp and were almost inseparable.

"Dude! I didn't expect you back for a couple of days. You an old married man now, or what?"

Tim clenched his jaw but only said, "No."

"What happened, bro? You get cold feet?" Dack teased.

"I don't want to talk about this," came the clipped response.

"Tim... you all right?" Dack asked, all traces of humor gone now.

"No," Tim admitted, "but maybe someday I will be."

"You know I got your back, right? You can talk to me anytime you need to," Dack said, clapping his friend on the shoulder.

"I know it, Dack. Not right now though, okay?"

Looks like his entire world has come crashing down, Dack realized. *But if he doesn't want to talk about it there's not much I can do to help.*

And his friend watched him thoughtfully as Tim walked away to stow his gear.

***

By the end of the week the two men, along with the rest of their platoon, had departed for the Middle East. Leaving Texas, they had flown to Germany before boarding Army transport planes to go take their turns wading through hell. As their C-130 left the runway to head into Afghanistan, Tim held his breath and said a prayer, not just that he would make it back safely, but that he would reconnect with Sarah someday.

CHAPTER TWO

Nine days later, Sarah was surprised to see her parents on her doorstep on a bright Saturday morning.

"Hey, kiddo," Marty said as he hugged her. "We figured you could use some furniture, so, we packed up your bedroom and brought it to you."

"Hi!" she exclaimed. "I found a recliner, and a table and chairs, but that's it so far. I was planning to hit some more garage sales to try to find some cheaper stuff, but I haven't had much time."

"Well, now you don't have to worry about what to sleep on, at least," Bethany said, as she held out three envelopes. "Here, honey. These came to the house."

Sarah's chest tightened as she recognized Tim's slanted handwriting on one of them. "Thanks," she managed as she took them from her mother. "I'll open them later."

She took a moment to regain her composure, then put on a cheery smile and said, "So, come on in and take a look at my place!"

"Lots of space here, honey," Bethany mentioned. "Have you thought about getting a roommate to help with the bills?"

"Actually, no," her daughter answered, and told them about her arrangement with Jodie, finishing the story with, "I think you'll both like her. She reminds me a lot of Grandma Peggy, Mom."

"I miss that sweet woman," Marty chimed in. "She was a great lady. Best mother-in-law ever." He paused, cleared his throat, and said, "How about we get your stuff unloaded and set up?"

Within twenty minutes Sarah's master bedroom had been transformed from an empty square to a fully functioning space.

"Now then," Bethany said, rubbing her hands together, "how about we go eat, then shop for some things for your apartment?"

***

By early afternoon Sarah's mother stood with her hands on her hips, nodding in approval. "*Now* it's a proper kitchen," she announced to her husband and daughter.

And she was right. In addition to cookware, the cupboards contained matching plates, bowls, glasses and mugs, and Sarah now owned pretty much every cooking utensil known to man in a decorative canister that matched the oven mitts and little towels Bethany had discovered.

Mr. and Mrs. Genard had also insisted on taking their only child to the grocery store and filling a cart almost to overflowing with not just food, but other household staples like aluminum foil, paper towels and sandwich bags.

"Mom," Sarah had started to protest when Bethany approached the cart with a family-size package of chicken breasts. "Mom, it's just me living there. No reason to buy enough to feed an army."

"I know that," came the response. "Break the package up into smaller portions and freeze them, honey. I just want to make sure my daughter has enough to eat."

"Mom," Sarah began again, but Marty's hand on her shoulder stopped her as Bethany went off in search of more items to buy.

"Let her go," he murmured. "You may be almost twenty, but you're still our baby, Sarah. No way we are leaving here without a whole cart full of stuff. If your mom hadn't already insisted, *I* would. All right?"

"Thanks, Dad," Sarah whispered as she kissed his cheek.

"You gonna tell me what happened, kiddo?"

"Maybe someday, Dad," she admitted. "Maybe someday when it doesn't hurt so much."

"Fair enough, honey. Just know you can always talk to me."

"I know," she'd squeezed his hand. "I know, Daddy."

"There's one thing I feel like you need to know, Sarah."

"What?"

Marty hesitated, then looked into her eyes. "I talked to Patrick Fresco yesterday. Tim's unit deployed to Afghanistan last week."

***

"Are we having fun yet?" Dack called down to Tim from the gunner's turret as they rode.

"Tons, can't you tell?" Tim answered before returning his attention to his supplies. Dack grinned and resumed scanning their surroundings carefully as the platoon made its rounds.

As the group's medic, Tim usually had the back of the MaxxPro MRAP ambulance to himself while the patrol convoy was in motion. He only occasionally had to step out while route clearance was underway in case someone got injured as they swept for landmines and IEDs. Everything he'd imagined about this place was spot on, including the ever-present sense of foreboding that had seized up his gut on their first patrol and had never let go.

As they made their way down the narrow road, with all senses peaked to maximum alert, Tim continually hoped for just another routine run, but remained ready should the worst happen. It wasn't until their group reached the other side of the small village that he allowed himself a full breath. The convoy of five armored vehicles turned left to continue its circuit before returning to base.

***

Her mom and dad met and visited with Jodie while Sarah finished making dinner with her brand-new cookware.

"It's ready," she announced as she carried the casserole over and put it on the table. "Help yourselves."

Marty leaned forward, sniffing the air. "Is that Grandma Peggy's recipe?"

"Yep," Sarah said proudly. "She taught it to me."

"Jodie, you're in for a treat," Marty exclaimed. "This recipe goes back what, three generations, Bethany?"

Bethany nodded. "With a few alterations along the way."

They ate and talked, and Sarah tried her best to maintain a happy expression, but her mind kept replaying her father's words in the grocery store.

Tim's unit deployed to Afghanistan.

***

Once they'd completed another patrol safely, Tim settled into his bunk, his thoughts full of home, and Sarah.

I'm not going to stop trying to get her back, he told himself, his jaw clenched with determination. *No matter what.*

One bunk over, Dack watched Tim, and recalled their conversation from the prior day. Tim had finally confided in Dack about everything that had transpired on what should have been the happiest day of his life.

"Man, that's rough," Dack had commiserated. "You sure you have no idea what she meant?"

"No," Tim lamented. "No clue. And because she took off the way she did, I never got a chance to ask her what the hell was going on."

"Hey," Dack said to Tim now as he watched him, recognizing the glint in Tim's eyes that meant he was focused. "When we get this tour over and get back home, you'll find her, and talk to her, and I'm sure it will work out, bro."

"I sure hope so, Dack."

"I know so, man. I can *feel* it," Dack reassured him.

***

She offered her parents her bedroom for the night and was pleased when they accepted.

"I didn't want you guys driving back late," Sarah explained. "Besides, I've gotten used to the recliner. One more night is fine."

"I really like Jodie," her mother mentioned as she rinsed plates before putting them in the dishwasher. "And you're right. She's a lot like my mom."

"Yep," Marty agreed. "I'm glad you met her, kiddo. Nice to know you've got someone here you can count on."

"She's great," Sarah nodded. "And she was also telling me about this local writers' group. I may go see what that's all about at some point."

"Oh, most definitely keep up with your writing, dear. It's brilliant," Bethany told her. "As a matter of fact, I'm a bit shocked you chose accounting as your degree path."

"Because at least with an accounting degree I know I can find a stable full-time job," Sarah pointed out. "It's going to be a lot easier to support myself. Besides, I can still write. I'm not giving it up; I'm just not counting on it to pay my bills. *Yet.*"

"That's smart," her father said, and patted her shoulder. "Really smart, Sarah. I'm proud of you."

***

Once her parents had retired for the night, Sarah sat down in her recliner with Tim's letter in her hand. She stared at the envelope a long while, noticing it had been postmarked from Fort Hood over a week earlier. She turned it round and round in her hands as she summoned the courage to open it.

Sarah closed her eyes briefly and took a deep breath, then eased the single page out of the envelope and began to read.

By the time this letter gets to you I will probably be overseas, Sarah, it began. *I wanted to be able to tell you face-to-face that I was being deployed, but that chance is gone now.*

What the hell happened to us, baby? I've re-read the note you left me so many times now, but I still don't understand it. Whatever you heard was wrong, Sarah. It's always been you, always – and it always will be.

I lie awake at night wondering where you are, if you're safe, if you're happy. I miss everything about you, and the thought of never seeing you, never holding you again hurts so bad I can barely breathe.

I just hope that once I get back, we can talk this out. Because I am still head over heels in love with you, Sarah Genard, and I still want to spend the rest of my life with you.

I still have your ring. I'll keep it safe until the day I get to put it back where it belongs – on your left hand.

Sarah gently set the letter down in her lap, her heart yearning to believe him while her mind raced, replaying what she had witnessed that contradicted everything he said. Conflicted, her soul in tatters, she covered her face with her hands and cried.

***

The next morning, Marty made his signature pecan waffles and sausages for his wife and daughter, as he had on so many Sunday mornings before. He cast a glance at Sarah, noticed the dark circles under her eyes, and raised an eyebrow. But she only shook her head sadly.

"Coffee?" he offered, attempting to break the silent tension thickening the air.

"Yes, please," Bethany said.

"I'll stick with juice, I think," Sarah replied.

"One coffee, one juice, coming up."

Marty set each drink on the kitchen table before pulling the last waffle from the iron and adding it to the stack. Then he carried the food to the table and took the seat next to Sarah.

"Rough night?" he prodded.

"I read Tim's letter," she mumbled.

"Oh," Marty answered, unsure whether to ask more questions.

Sarah let out a sigh. "Here's what happened," she began, and told her parents her side of the story.

"Oh my," Bethany said, her eyes wide with sympathy. "I can see why you reacted the way you did, then."

"Yep, completely understandable," Marty confirmed. "Sounds pretty black and white to me. Except for the fact that Tim was..."

"Crushed," Bethany filled in the gap. "He was absolutely crushed – and *genuinely confused*, Sarah."

"I don't understand why, given what I just told you."

"There must be some piece of the puzzle that's missing," her mother suggested. "Something we aren't aware of. And you two talking it out may provide that piece, honey."

"But he's overseas now, so we *can't* talk about it. And what if... what if something happens to him and he doesn't come back?" Sarah managed to say before she broke down.

Marty put his arm around her shoulders as her mother reached over for her hand.

"You just have to have faith he'll come home safely," Marty told her. "And when he does, you two need to talk. That's the only way you're going to know if what you witnessed is what it seemed to be."

CHAPTER THREE

One year later found Sarah Genard printing out her assignment to take with her to her next class. Sarah glanced at her watch and grimaced. *Get a move on or you're gonna be late,* she chided herself. She hurriedly stuffed her homework, laptop and notebooks into her backpack and headed out the door for her Advanced Accounting class.

As she walked, she felt grateful. Taking accelerated courses in her hometown's high school had earned her college credits as well, and as a result her time spent on UTA's campus began with Sarah having already met the core requirements. Now she had enough credits to reach junior status and was taking as many classes a semester as possible and working part-time at the campus bookstore. Her goal was to finish her bachelors' degree in three years instead of the usual four, and the college fund Peggy Mitchell had set up for her only grandchild enabled Sarah to focus on school and not worry about how to pay for her education.

The other blessing had been meeting Jodie. The little old woman had taken Sarah under her wing, and for Sarah it was almost like having her Grandma Peggy back again, so she made it a point to spend some time with Jodie every day. And thanks to their arrangement, Sarah had been able to use the money she had saved up from her summer jobs during and after high school for other things than paying rent.

Win-win all around, especially since when I got here I had pretty much nothing, and I didn't know a soul.

The only thing that had not changed in the past twelve months was the heartache. She missed Tim down to her core. Sarah had no idea how to reach him on deployment, so she'd been sending letter after letter to him by way of his parents' house, knowing they would forward them to Tim. Since her letters had not been returned, Sarah assumed they were being delivered successfully. But to date she had never received a reply.

I wonder if he's even reading them...

She shook her head vehemently to get her mind off that track and quickened her pace. *Focus. Now isn't the time to wallow, Sarah.*

***

Paige Fresco walked out to her mailbox at the end of the driveway, waving at Edna Laney, her next-door neighbor, along the way. She opened the metal box and withdrew the day's mail, frowning when she saw yet another letter addressed to Tim from Sarah Genard.

Her brow furrowed, she quickly walked back into her house and headed straight for the little office Patrick had set up for her in the third bedroom.

She bowed her head and silently asked the universe for forgiveness, then set her jaw and fed Sarah's latest attempt to contact her son into the shredder - just as she had all the others that had arrived at her home.

I'm doing the right thing, she told herself. *Sarah Genard has hurt my boy enough. No more.*

I'm doing the right thing.

***

Her class over, Sarah gathered up her things and stepped back out into the warm sunshine to make the short walk back to her apartment. As she wandered down the sidewalk, she stopped suddenly, palms sweaty. A man just ahead and to the left of her was talking with some other students.

It can't be him, Sarah's mind raced. *It can't be.*

But from her vantage point the partial profile of his face sure looked like Tim's, and her heart leapt at the thought despite her best efforts to reel it in.

"Move quickly," she muttered under her breath, and resumed her course at a brisk pace. Just as she had drawn alongside the small group, the man glanced over at her and smiled.

It's not Tim, she realized, and forced herself to smile politely back when she felt like crying. She ducked her head and hurried back to her apartment to fall apart in private.

Before long, she heard Jodie knocking softly. She stood, wiping her eyes, and went to let her in.

"Oh, honey, what's wrong?" Jodie asked.

"Just... not a good day," Sarah sniffled.

"I bet I have something that will cheer you up," Jodie replied with a twinkle in her eye. "Freshly baked brownies. What do you say?"

Five minutes later Sarah was seated at Jodie's kitchen table with brownies and milk, unburdening her soul to the kind old woman.

"So, I ran," Sarah finished. "But I miss him so much, Jodie. He is on my mind all the time. I know now I made a huge mistake by leaving without talking to him at all."

"Reach out to him, then," Jodie urged, and Sarah sadly shook her head.

"I tried. I've sent so many letters, but he hasn't responded to a single one. Too much time has gone by, I guess," she whispered as two more gigantic tears rolled down her cheeks. "It's too late, Jodie. I've lost him."

***

That evening Tim Fresco pulled into his parents' driveway, put the truck in park, and sat staring at the house he had grown up in. *Funny how it looks so much smaller now,* he found himself thinking as he looked back over the past year. *Funny how much bigger the world got.*

Just over eight months into their tour, Tim's platoon had been on routine route clearance patrol and had been ambushed, taking heavy fire. He vaguely remembered shouting as the first wave of chaos unfolded all around them, then seeing Dack collapse to his left.

But as he lunged toward his best friend to check Dack's injuries, an enemy soldier's round pierced his left shin, shattering Tim's lower leg and sending him writhing in pain to the ground. The next thing Tim remembered was hearing someone call for a nine-line medivac as they tied a tourniquet just above the knee, then being airlifted out of the hot zone and back to Kandahar Airfield.

It wasn't until he reached Landstuhl Regional Medical Center in Germany that Tim learned Dack and four more of his teammates had been killed, and another seven severely wounded. The nurse on duty had held his hand and cried with him as he grieved the loss of his brothers.

Three surgeries had followed, and he was forever grateful that the skilled Army doctors working on him had been able to save his leg. Fifteen weeks after being wounded, he was shipped back to the States, his lower limb held together with plates and pins.

Next on his horizon was intense physical therapy at Fort Sam Houston's medical facilities while he awaited word about whether he would be medically discharged or returned to active service. By mid-day on day one, Tim had been registered and settled in at the inpatient facility on base.

"Get some rest," his therapist, Mark, had told him. "We're gonna get started first thing in the morning."

And Mark hadn't been joking. Almost immediately, Tim found himself wading through exercises that were exhausting.

"Come on, Tim, give me just two more if you can."

Having been fitted with a walking boot that reached all the way up to his knee, Tim at last was allowed to try and use the lower leg that had been so badly damaged months before. With sweat already dripping and his face tense with concentration, he'd taken another step forward with his right foot, temporarily placing all his weight on his left leg, then quickly shifted it back to his right as he took the final step requested.

"Not bad!" Mark had said with a grin. "Look behind you."

Tim glanced over his shoulder, leaning on the bars on either side of him for support. "About a fourth of the way."

"Which is better than I thought you'd do on the very first day. But we don't want to push *too* hard, either, or we'll cause more damage, and it will take longer to heal. Understood?"

Tim nodded, reached for the towel Mark offered, and mopped his face. "You don't realize how much you take simple things like walking for granted until you can't do them," he'd observed.

Mark's grin widened. "I know, right? Gives you a whole new appreciation. Now, let's move over to the stationary bike and get a baseline of where you're starting from on strength and leverage."

"Busy first day," Mark had observed when his session with Tim was over. "You did great. I think if we can keep this pace without causing further injury, you can be out of here within three months and get back up to eighty-five percent of the use of that leg. Sound good?"

"Sounds great," Tim replied with a smile. "I'm ready to get back to normal, that's for sure."

"I like hearing that. Just make sure you're honest with me - and yourself - about your limits. We won't get there overnight, Tim."

"I know that. But I'll put in as many hours as it takes."

"I figured as much. Just, no more today, all right? Back on your crutches until morning."

"You're the boss."

Eighty-two days later, just before he completed his physical therapy regimen, Tim Fresco received official word that he was being medically discharged from the U.S. Army. For the second time, the future he'd envisioned for himself had taken an unexpected turn.

***

Tim's focus returned to the present when he saw his parents approaching and waving at him. He smiled, opened his door, and slid out of his truck, immediately finding himself wrapped in his father's embrace.

"Welcome home, son, we're so proud of you," his father managed to whisper against his ear before his voice failed him. Releasing him and stepping back, he looked Tim over, then cleared his throat and said, "You look good, kiddo. Let me get your bag."

Tim pivoted in time to see his mother coming forward, arms open wide, and made his way over to her for another huge hug.

"Oh, my boy," was all she could get out before she too burst into tears and sobbed into his chest.

"It's all right, Mom. I'm fine, I promise," he murmured as he patted her back.

So many others got handed so much worse, and some did not get to come home at all. I got lucky, he reminded himself, thinking once again of Dack, who had been walking beside him when all hell had broken loose. *I got so, so lucky...*

To lighten the mood, he cocked his head toward his dad, and added, "And man, I am so glad you talked me out of buying a truck with a manual transmission like I wanted. I wouldn't have been able to drive myself *anywhere* for a really long time."

Tim felt his mom chuckle against his chest as his dad smiled, eyes still bright with emotion.

"Come on, kiddo, dinner is just about ready," Paige managed as she finally turned him loose and wiped her eyes. "I made your favorite."

***

When she left Jodie's apartment, Sarah found herself in a melancholy state of mind. She poured a generous glass of wine and set both it and the bottle on her coffee table, then went into her room and retrieved an old shoebox from her closet.

Before she sat on the couch and opened the box, she queued up the playlist and put on her headphones. As the first song began, she took a deep breath, then a large drink of wine, and opened the only tangible thing in her current life that connected her to a painful past.

***

After dinner, Tim excused himself and went to his old room, citing exhaustion from the drive. *But it's more than that,* he realized. *I kept looking at the chair next to me expecting to see Sarah.* Like it or not, he was strolling down memory lane.

He walked over to his dresser and retrieved a tiny velvet box from the top left drawer. Then he dug out his iPod and headphones and laid down on his bed.

Tim queued up Doug Stone's "I Thought It Was You" and set it to repeat, then stared at Sarah's engagement ring as the song that seemed to be written just for him played over and over.

Everything in this town reminds me of her, dammit, he admitted to himself. *Everything. The school, the store, driving down Main Street, everything.*

I should go see her parents, demand to know where she is, he thought. *But then again, I haven't heard a word from her since she left. Maybe she's moved on. Maybe I need to give up. But I don't want to.*

Oh, Sarah...

***

Piece by piece, Sarah waded through the box of memories. Picture after picture of them together, happy, always smiling in the Polaroid snapshots taken so long ago. A dried rose from the first bouquet he had ever bought her, a snippet of ribbon from that first high school homecoming mum she'd worn that still had both their names on it in sparkly gold letters. Handwritten notes to her, still safely tucked in their envelopes, from when he'd gone away to boot camp.

She managed to hold it together a bit longer this time, until the one item that always broke her surfaced. Their wedding invitation.

She did not have a copy of what she'd written to him that fateful night. But she didn't need one. She still remembered word for word what the note she'd left behind for him said. They had been seared into her brain and heart for all eternity.

I think you meant to give this ring to someone else.

I hope you two are incredibly happy together.

The tears seemed to run down her face to the tempo of the song currently assaulting her senses – the very song she had chosen so long ago to have playing when she walked down the aisle toward him.

I don't want to miss him anymore. Help me not love him anymore, God. Please.

When her third glass of wine was empty, Sarah rose from the couch, stumbled to her bedroom, and escaped into sleep.

CHAPTER FOUR

Sarah yawned, stretched, and rubbed her eyes the next morning. *A little too much wine, for sure,* she thought as she made her way to her kitchen for two aspirin and a glass of juice. *No wonder I have a raging headache.*

She blinked rapidly, trying to rid herself of the tracers that were starting to blur her vision. "Please, oh *please,* don't let this be another migraine coming on," she muttered. "I have way too much to get done today."

As she went back past the couch, she spied the open shoebox, with its contents still strewn about as she had left them the night before. With a heavy sigh, she carefully restored her box of memories, put it back in her closet, and headed for a hot shower to try to clear her fogged brain.

***

"I beg your pardon?" a shocked Paige said as she, Patrick, and Tim sat down to breakfast.

"I said, I'm not staying in Adrian," Tim repeated firmly. "I only came home to visit for a few days, Mom. I'm not moving back here. I want to be an EMT. To do that, I have to attend specialized training, and it's not available here. I'm leaving on Friday."

"But... but..." Paige faltered, close to tears.

"Mom," Tim said, the edge leaving his voice. "You and I both know there's nothing here for me anymore."

She sat silently with her head bowed for a long while. When she did finally make eye contact again, Tim could see his announcement had devastated her.

"If you'll excuse me," Paige murmured, and left the table.

Tim watched her leave the room, then looked at his father.

"Son, you have to do what's best for you," Patrick reminded him. "And you're right. There's nothing for you here. You need to make your own way. Don't worry about your mom. She'll be all right."

On Friday morning Tim packed up his clothes, and his father helped him get it all put into his truck. Paige, still in disbelief that her son hadn't come home for good, opted to stay in the house and not watch her only child leave again.

Patrick hugged Tim tightly and said, "At least *try* to come back for Thanksgiving, all right? She'll be over it by then. I think."

Tim chuckled. "Okay, Dad."

***

Just before ten a.m. Saturday morning, Sarah walked into the library and approached the circulation desk.

"Hi. I'm here for the writers' group?"

"Through there, hon. Meeting room B."

"Thanks."

She stepped inside the room and looked around, trying not to be overwhelmed by the fact she was surrounded by strangers.

"You can sit with me, if you like," someone called out.

Turning her head to the right, Sarah made eye contact with the person who had greeted her.

"Thanks," Sarah said, and pulled out a chair to sit down.

"First time with one of these?"

"Yep," Sarah answered. "I've been meaning to come before now, but with school it's been a little hectic."

The petite blond laughed. "I don't miss those days. I'm Karli, by the way. It's nice to meet you."

"My name's Sarah."

***

"Hi, I'm Tim Fresco," he said to the receptionist at the training facility in Irving, Texas. "I'd like to get registered for your program, please."

"Which one?"

"EMT, and Advanced EMS after that."

"Certainly," the young lady responded with a warm smile. "Let me get you an enrollment packet, and let John know you're here. He's our program director."

A few minutes later a tall, muscular man with closely cropped hair came into view, hand outstretched.

"Nice to meet you, Mr. Fresco. I'm John Duncan. Right this way, please."

John led the way back to his office.

"So, tell me about your situation," John prompted once they sat down. "Why do you want to be an EMT?"

Tim cleared his throat. "Well, sir, I was a medic in the Army, and I loved it. I'd like to pursue that path in civilian life."

"Honorable discharge?"

"Yes sir, a medical separation. I was wounded in Afghanistan."

John leaned back in his chair. "It sounds to me like you weren't happy about being discharged."

"No, sir, I wasn't. I'd planned to retire from the Army twenty years from now. But it is what it is."

"I wasn't either when it happened to me," the program director confided. "I was in the Marines. And like you, I planned on being a career man. But small arms fire during Desert Storm altered my path."

***

"So how long have you been writing?" Sarah asked her new friend over lunch.

"I've always been interested in it," Karli replied as she dipped a French fry into her ketchup. "My degree's in fashion merchandising, though. I did some hands-on stuff for a couple of places, but I didn't enjoy it as much as I thought I would. Then I stumbled across the writers' group. Meeting them helped me realize I wanted to focus on writing about fashion. So, I finally worked up the courage and built a blog site about three weeks ago and got started. And I hit one hundred followers yesterday."

"That's great! It will be in the thousands before you know it."

"Here's hoping," Karli smiled. "What about you?"

"I'm an Accounting major," Sarah revealed. "I like it, and I'm good at it. But it's not my passion and it never will be. I'm getting that degree so I can pay the bills, but I long to be an author. That's the dream."

"How much further do you have to go?"

"If I maintain the pace I've been running, I should graduate next summer," Sarah announced. "The goal was to try to get it done in three years."

"Impressive!"

"I'm ready to be done, that's for sure," Sarah said with a smile.

"I felt that way too," Karli confessed. "And then when I graduated and got my job and it just didn't make me happy the way I thought it would, I felt so lost. But with the blogging angle, I'm excited again, even though Evan isn't."

"Evan?"

"My husband," Karli explained. "He's not really into any sort of fashion-related stuff. Calls it 'cute'."

"Ouch," Sarah said. "That must sting, feeling like you don't have his support."

Tim always supported my dreams no matter what they were, Sarah thought wistfully before stopping herself. *No. Don't go there, girl. Have a nice time for once.*

"It's not that he's not supportive," Karli clarified. "It's just more like, he can take it or leave it."

"Let me guess – he'd rather watch pretty much any sporting event than even *think* about stuff like fashion."

Karli laughed. "Every day of the week. So, what about you? You married?"

"I was engaged once," Sarah murmured, but didn't offer details, and her tone conveyed that the subject was not a happy one. "Anyway – how often does the writing group meet?"

"Twice a month," Karli answered, shifting gears smoothly when she felt Sarah's discomfort. "Usually every other week. The first meeting of each month is at the library, and the second one is typically at one of the restaurants nearby. We have lunch and talk writing, and sometimes we do timed writing sprints or play themed games. It's fun."

"Sounds like it," Sarah agreed.

"So, why don't we plan on riding together to the next one? I'd be happy to swing by and pick you up."

"Are you sure? I don't want to be any trouble."

"No trouble at all," Karli assured her. "Because I really don't know anyone very well in that group, either. I figure if we team up, it will be even *more* fun."

***

When Tim was done filling out the application, he handed it to John.

"Everything's in order," John pronounced once he'd reviewed the packet. "The next round of classes starts June fifteenth, a week from Monday. That gives you time to line out a place to rent and get settled in."

"Yes, sir. I'm actually in a pretty nice extended stay hotel at the moment, so I may just stay there. I haven't decided yet. That's next on my list to figure out."

"Well, there's no shortage of apartment complexes in the area. Most are not too pricey and they're all pretty safe. If you need some leads to work with, let me know."

"Thanks," Tim said as he stood up. "See you on the fifteenth, sir."

"You're welcome, Tim," the program director replied as he shook Tim's hand. "And please, call me John."

***

"Hey kiddo, guess what I found for you?" Jodie called out to Sarah on Sunday afternoon.

"What?"

"A new daybed! Frame, mattress, sheet set, the works. Never even been used. And it's *free*. All you have to do is go pick it up!"

"But I already have a bed," Sarah pointed out.

"I know that, silly," Jodie chided her. "But you also have a second bedroom that's still completely empty, and it's just so sad looking, dear. A daybed would brighten it right up!"

Sarah chuckled. "All right, Jodie, all right."

Jodie clapped her hands together with excitement. "Here's the address," she exclaimed, and handed Sarah a piece of paper.

Forty-five minutes later Sarah was backing into her parking space to unload her newfound treasure. Jodie met her at the curb.

"I asked Jack to come help you unload it," she told Sarah.

"There's no need to, really. The frame came apart easily, and none of it is heavy at all," Sarah replied. "Besides, isn't he fixing the sink in unit fourteen?"

"I'd forgotten about that," Jodie admitted. "You sure you don't need help?"

"Nope, I can manage," Sarah smiled as she patted Jodie on the shoulder. "I'm good, I promise."

Once she was done lugging all the pieces into her spare bedroom and reassembling them, she made the bed, then stepped back and viewed the results from the doorway.

I'll be damned. Jodie was right. It does *cheer this room up,* Sarah decided, and grinned.

***

Tim spent Sunday reviewing his finances, and by Monday morning he had decided an apartment was the more economical choice. He signed a six-month lease for a one-bedroom apartment on Tuesday afternoon, and spent Wednesday shopping for furniture.

After some deliberation, he settled on a dark gray sectional sofa with matching recliner, a coffee table, a bistro table with two chairs, and a full-size four-piece bedroom set. Satisfied with his choices, he arranged for weekend delivery of his purchases. Then he headed to Best Buy to select a television, entertainment console and surround sound system, booking them for delivery as well.

By mid-day Saturday, he'd checked out of the hotel and was unloading groceries and other household necessities from his truck. The furniture arrived as scheduled at one-thirty, his electronics at two-thirty, and by five o'clock in the afternoon Tim's apartment had been transformed from a hollow hull into a livable space.

Saturday evening found Tim Fresco humming along to his iPod playlist as he cooked his first meal in his new home, then settled in on the sofa to watch a baseball game on his brand new seventy-inch television. But the loneliness settled in as well, almost palpable as it filled the room all around him. Tim caught himself glancing at the empty space beside him. He moved to the recliner, but the ache followed him.

I wish Sarah was here. I wonder where she is and what she's doing right now. I wonder if she ever thinks about me at all.

Little did he know that the woman who still held the keys to his heart – and who still loved him - was less than twenty minutes away.

CHAPTER FIVE

Sixteen weeks had flown by, and Tim arrived at the training facility at seven-forty-five on a crisp October Friday morning, even though his last day of class to complete his EMT program didn't start until eight a.m. The final written exam and practical he'd studied for was mere moments away.

He strode with purpose toward the front door, the laptop he'd invested in tucked safely as always in the backpack slung across his right shoulder.

"Hey, Stacy," he called out as he passed the reception desk on his way to the classroom. "Looking forward to the weekend?"

"When am I not?" she answered with a smile. "How about you?"

"Yeah, me too," he grinned. "Hey – when does the Advanced EMS set begin?"

"We won't schedule you into that program until the test scores come back," she advised him. "Should know something in a week or so."

"A week of downtime," Tim said thoughtfully. "I may not know what to do with myself."

***

Sarah sighed as she saved her cost analysis paper and then printed it out before closing her laptop. *One more major assignment done. Not gonna miss those, I have to admit.*

She could see the light at the end of the tunnel. Six months. That was all that was left of her degree program.

Sarah Genard was more than ready to move on and start the next chapter of her life.

She checked her watch, frowned, and loaded up her backpack to go turn in her work.

***

The practical came first, and Tim sailed through each hands-on demonstration with ease. By mid-day, all that stood between him and his first goal of certification as an EMT in the state of Texas were two hundred questions comprising the written exam.

Tim took his time, carefully reading each question and making a selection from the multiple-choice answers. Once he'd answered the last question he scrolled back to the top and reviewed his answers to make sure he hadn't missed anything. Satisfied with his performance, he pressed the 'submit' button on his final exam and logged out.

"All done?" John asked as Tim stepped out into the hallway.

"Yep," Tim confirmed. "And now, we wait."

"I'm sure you did fine, Tim. Your performance has been stellar throughout the program," John reassured him. "Check your email. You should have your scores within a week."

"Will do," Tim said. "In the meantime, I think I'm going to take a road trip."

"Have fun."

Tim waved as he headed toward his truck.

I wouldn't necessarily call where I'm going 'fun', he thought to himself as he drove back to his apartment to pack a bag. *But I've put it off for far too long.*

When he got home, he made a sandwich and ate before grabbing his small duffel bag and putting in enough clothes for a week's trip. Then he opened Google Maps on his cell phone and typed in an address. He clipped his phone to his belt, hoisted his duffel bag and backpack, and closed and locked his apartment door.

Once he was settled into his truck, Tim moved the phone from his hip to the holder on his dashboard and pressed 'start' for turn-by-turn navigation.

Corpus Christi, Texas, here I come.

***

Sarah got back from her class and walked into the apartment complex's office just in time to see Jodie scowling, her tiny hands holding a claw hammer high in the air above her head as she stalked toward her desktop unit.

"What are you *doing*?" Sarah exclaimed.

"This damn thing is the bane of my existence, and it needs to *die*," Jodie muttered between clenched teeth.

Trying her best not to laugh, Sarah moved swiftly to intercede on the machine's behalf. "Jodie, calm down. Let me take a look at it."

"Fine," Jodie growled. "But if you can't fix it, I'm gonna put *it* out of *my* misery."

She's a tiny little thing but Jodie is terrifying when she gets mad, Sarah thought to herself. *I sure hope she never looks like that because of me!*

She forced down the chuckle she felt coming on and turned her attention to diagnosing the problem as Jodie mumbled continued threats of physical harm to the computer under her breath.

"The anti-virus software is about to expire, that's all," Sarah announced. "Give me just a few minutes and I will have this thing good as new."

"That's it?" Jodie asked ten minutes later when Sarah pushed the chair back and stood up.

"Yep, all done. Want to know what I did?"

"*No,*" Jodie shook her head back and forth as she dropped the hammer on the desk. "I don't care. It's fixed, so it gets to live another day. Now, how was your class?"

***

While Sarah was rescuing Jodie's computer from being bludgeoned beyond repair, Tim was passing through Waco, Texas. Although the total drive from his apartment to his destination was less than eight hours, he'd decided to relax and take his time on the journey. So, he diverted over to the less traveled US-77 from I-35 for a more scenic route south. He stopped for dinner and a motel room in LaGrange and fell into restless sleep.

***

At eight-thirty the next morning Karli called Sarah to shore up their plans for the day.

"I'll be there around eleven-fifteen. Is that too early?"

"That's fine. See you then."

Promptly as scheduled, Karli arrived to pick Sarah up for the writers' group meeting.

"You ready? Got your laptop, right?" Karli asked as Sarah buckled her seat belt.

"Yep, it's in my backpack. And I'm looking forward to this."

"Me too. I wonder what they've got planned today?"

***

Tim yawned, stretched, and looked at the alarm clock next to the bed.

Eight-forty-two, the red dials read.

"Better get going," he mumbled to himself, and threw back the covers to head for the shower.

***

Just after noon, Tim turned left, parked in the main building's visitor lot and went inside to get further directions. The kind woman manning the desk checked her computer records, then retrieved a map of the property and indicated Tim's desired destination.

"Thank you very much," he said solemnly, and returned to his truck. He glanced at the map for a moment to get his bearings, then pulled out onto the narrow strip of pavement that led into the wide open. He passed under the archway and took the third right onto another slender strip of asphalt until he came to the section he sought.

He parked his truck and closed his eyes for a moment, then stepped out, shutting the driver's side door gently behind him. To his left was a small fountain, and the sound of gently flowing water was soothing as he began to scan ahead and slightly to the right, walking between the rows.

At last, he found what he was looking for. A somber light gray granite stone, polished to a deep sheen, with a simple but heartfelt inscription:

Dack Abrams. Soldier. Son. Brother. Friend. You are missed.

Tim stood for a long while, just staring at his friend's headstone. Then he gently cleared his throat and sat down beside it.

"Hey, buddy," he tried to say, and instead burst into tears.

***

"That *was* fun," Sarah said with a smile when the group disbanded around two-thirty p.m. "And I loved the exercises we did. They really got my imagination flowing. I think I'm gonna keep going when I get home, get some more thoughts out of my head and into written form while they're fresh."

"Yeah, those sprints really help me, too," Karli chimed in. "I was really intimidated the first time I did writing sprints. Now, I look forward to them."

She pulled into Sarah's complex and parked. "Hey. Want to come over and have lunch with us tomorrow? Evan's going to put steaks and brats on the grill."

"Sounds good. What time?"

"Come over whenever you're ready. The food should be done around one."

***

Tim sat quietly, one hand on Dack's headstone, listening to the fountain and watching the sun moving lower in the western sky. He'd cried and talked for over four hours as he'd unburdened his soul to one of the best friends he had ever had.

He told Dack about his future plans, and about the gaping hole in him that still existed from Sarah's abrupt departure. He talked about his injury and working his way back. And he talked about the nightmares he'd kept to himself that had chased him almost daily since they'd come under fire on patrol that fateful afternoon.

"And *you*, buddy. I really miss you," Tim whispered after a long silence, his voice almost spent. "Man, I wish you were here, Dack. I wish I'd been able to get to you when you were hit. Maybe...maybe you'd still be here if I'd done my job better."

"I know it feels that way, honey. But probably not," came a soft soothing voice from behind him.

Stunned, Tim rose to his feet and turned around, wiping his eyes. A petite, slender woman with long flowing blond hair was gazing at him with the same intense hazel eyes that she'd passed down to her son Dack.

"You must be Tim, dear," the woman said, and moved toward him as she held out her arms. "I'm Mary. I was hoping I would meet you someday. Dack told us so much about you."

When she'd closed the distance between them, she hugged Tim and said earnestly, "There's not *anything* you could have done differently, honey. Please don't put that burden on yourself. It's not your fault. None of it."

And Tim, who thought his tears had all been spent, laid his forehead on her shoulder and cried some more.

***

When Tim left Corpus Christi that evening, his soul felt lighter than it had in a long time. Mary had insisted he join them for dinner, and he'd reluctantly agreed, afraid that others in Dack's family might not be so welcoming.

But he couldn't have been more wrong.

The moment Dack's father, Charlie, was introduced, Tim found himself wrapped in a big bear hug.

"Thank you for being such a good friend to our son," Charlie told him.

At dinner, Mary, Charlie, and Wade, Dack's older brother, asked Tim questions about himself, and slowly he felt his tension melt away. By the end of the meal, he felt more at peace within himself about the events of that day so long ago.

"You're welcome back here anytime," Mary told him as she and Charlie walked him to his truck.

"Thanks, Mrs. Abrams, I appreciate that."

"Safe travels, Tim."

When he stopped for the night, it was the first time in over a year that restful, dreamless sleep found him. He awoke refreshed and ready to embark on the next chapter of his life.

***

When Sarah arrived at Karli and Evan's house for lunch, Karli greeted her with a hug.

"Hey there! Come on in," Karli said with a bright smile. "I want you and Evan to meet."

Karli led the way out onto the back patio where Evan stood, a beer in one hand and a pair of tongs in the other, talking to two other people.

"Babe," Karli called out. "This is my friend Sarah."

"Nice to meet you, Sarah," Evan offered, showing a smile Sarah would have bet money he'd practiced in a mirror. "Would you like a beer?"

"I'm good, thanks."

For the next few hours, Sarah tried her best to maintain a pleasant smile whenever she noticed Evan looking her way. But he made her deeply uncomfortable.

I don't know what it is, she thought to herself, *but something about Evan Anders creeps me out.*

***

On Thursday morning, Tim's cell phone pinged to let him know he had a new email.

He opened his browser and logged in, scanned the message, and smiled.

For the hands-on assessment, he'd scored a perfect one hundred out of one hundred possible points. And out of a possible one hundred points on the written exam, he'd earned ninety-seven.

Tim Fresco was now a certified EMT in the State of Texas.

"Hot damn!" he exclaimed, pumping a fist in celebration before he called John Duncan to ask how soon he could start the next program.

Ten days later, Tim began the six-hundred-hour journey to attain his Advanced EMS certifications.

CHAPTER SIX

By the following November, Sarah had graduated with honors and was almost two months into her new entry-level job as an inventory accountant. While the pay was infinitely better than the wage she'd made working part-time at the bookstore, it was also already obvious to her that writing would be the only thing that kept her from being completely bored to death.

She was frowning as she reviewed the prior week's reconciliations from the company's Denver branch on a typical Monday morning. Then her cell phone rang, and Sarah's mood lightened to hear Karli's voice.

"Hey, you," she said. "What's up?"

"Not much," Karli sighed. "I was gonna ask – Are you going anywhere for Thanksgiving?"

"No. Our office is only closed Thanksgiving Day, and I don't have any paid time off built up yet. I would have to leave work Wednesday afternoon and drive straight through to Adrian, eat with my folks Thursday and then drive straight back. Why?"

"Well," Karli said wistfully, "Evan just told me his company's sending him to New Orleans to work next week."

"Seriously? Well, just go with him," Sarah suggested.

"I already mentioned that to him," Karli told her. "Evidently Evan's company frowns on spouses tagging along. So, I am gonna be by myself. Mom and Dad are on that cruise."

"That's right," Sarah recalled. "Two weeks in the Caribbean. And didn't you say the other day that Madge was down with the flu?"

"Yep. So, what do you say? Wanna make it a bestie lunch?"

Sarah chuckled. "Sure thing."

***

Tim Fresco pulled into the parking lot at Fire Station Number Two, ready to begin his first day of work as a full-time permanent member of the Arlington Fire Department. His time as a medic in the Army had set him on a path that led him directly to a new career as an EMT in the civilian sector.

Civilian. Still not sure how I feel about that, to be honest. I thought I would be in until retirement.

He took a deep breath before grabbing his duffel bag and heading into the building.

"You must be my new partner," a baritone sounded from his left as he stepped through the main entry.

"Yep. I'm Tim Fresco," he said, extending his hand to the tall stranger.

"Jordan," came the reply. "Jordan Baker. Nice to meet you, man. Follow me, I'll show you around."

"How long have you been here?" Tim asked as they moved down the hallway to the lockers.

"Four years," Jordan responded. "Pretty great group here, too. Everybody gets along."

"Good to know," Tim observed. "Especially being the FNG."

"FNG?"

"Freaking New Guy."

Jordan laughed. "Expect a bit of hazing but nothing over the top."

He stopped and pointed. "These two lockers here are unoccupied. Pick which one you want and get your gear stowed. Then we'll go see the captain, and after that we'll take the grand tour."

"Sounds like a plan. Meet you at his office?"

"You got it, Tim," Jordan said, and strolled away.

Forty minutes later Jordan had introduced him to all the guys onsite, and he and Tim were doing a spot check of inventory on the rig before their shift started.

"Hey, new guy!" Dan called out as he passed. "You're on kitchen duty this week. What's for supper?"

Without missing a beat, Tim responded, "Pizza, and it should be here in five...four...three...two...," as he looked at his watch, then at the door.

Sure enough, a teenager wearing the local pizza chain's uniform wandered into the bay with ten boxes and announced, "Order for Tim?"

"Yep, that's me," Tim said, and took the boxes to the station's kitchen before returning to sign the slip and tip the young man. "Thanks."

"You're all right, Fresco," Dan murmured in approval as he moved past to go grab himself a slice. "You're all right."

Tim grinned.

***

Sarah arrived at Karli's on Thanksgiving Day with a bottle of wine. "Here," she said, holding it out. "I thought this would go well with our lunch."

"Absolutely!" Karli exclaimed. "Speaking of which, it is just about ready. Come on in."

"So, how's your week been, girl?" Sarah asked as she followed her into the kitchen.

"Not bad," Karli answered. "Got some surprisingly good feedback from my readers about my latest blog. For the most part, it was positive. What about yours?"

"Well, I may have to start making regular trips up to Denver at some point," Sarah revealed. "There's an anomaly in the monthly reporting they want me to physically ferret out. I was hoping I would be able to research it remotely. You know how much I hate to fly."

"I do know," Karli confirmed, her nose crinkling at her friend's predicament. "But keep the faith, Sarah. One day your writing will take off, and you'll be able to walk away from inventory accounting and be a full-time author like you've always dreamed."

Sarah sighed. "From your lips to God's ears," she muttered as she poured wine into two glasses. "Here's to eventually seeing dreams realized."

The women stood silently for a moment after the toast, each lost in her own thoughts. Sarah's tall, slender frame, darker hair and brown eyes provided an interesting contrast to Karli's shorter, curvier build and blond-and-blue combination. But that was the only difference between them, and since they'd met, they'd become as close as sisters.

"I mean it," Karli said quietly after a long pause. "You're a brilliant writer, Sarah. Your time is coming, I can feel it."

"Yours is, too," Sarah replied. "I know you want to do more than blog about fashion. So, step out on faith and try something new. Why are you holding back?"

Karli shrugged. "I'm not sure what else to write about yet," she admitted, biting her lower lip. "And I also don't want to alienate the few loyal readers I *do* have."

"You're so funny," Sarah teased with affection. "Five hundred and seventy followers? That's way more than 'a few'. But I get where you're coming from."

The oven timer went off, and Karli grinned.

"Lunch is ready! Let me get it out," Karli said as she pulled on her oven mitts and opened the door.

***

"So, what happened to your previous partner?" Tim asked as they settled in for their sixth overnight shift together.

"Moved away. His wife works in finance, and she took a promotion with her company that meant moving to Seattle," Jordan explained. "He had family up there anyway, so, I think it worked out for them all around."

"And what's your story? You from around here?"

"I grew up in Decatur, about forty minutes northwest of here," Jordan said. "Came to Arlington to go to college. I had every intention of becoming a doctor, but I couldn't afford all the schooling. So, I got a Bachelors in Paramedic Studies, then sat for the certification exam, and landed here instead."

"Married?"

"Nope," Jordan said with a strange look on his face. "Not dating anyone, either. I focus on work. What about you?"

"I was engaged once," Tim answered, managing to keep a light tone. "But it fell through."

"Sorry to hear that, man. So, where are you from?"

"Adrian, Texas. And yes, it's as small as it sounds. I graduated and went straight into the service. I had planned on staying in until they retired me, but a bullet shattered my lower leg and that was it for me, man. I was a medic in the Army, though, so after I got my EMT certification I went ahead and did the Advanced EMS program, too."

"John Duncan's group?"

"Yep."

"Nice! That's who I went with to take the exam. And here you are," Jordan said with a flourish.

"Yep, here I am," Tim agreed with a chuckle. "Not exactly what I'd planned, but I like it so far."

The crackle of the radio coming to life stopped the chit chat.

"We're up," Jordan said solemnly. "Let's get going."

***

"Really? It's not enough we didn't get to spend time together for Thanksgiving?" Karli lamented to her husband Evan on their call.

"Sorry, babe," he told her. "You know they've expanded my territory. I can't not go."

"I know," she said, eyes closed in frustration. "Any chance at all you and I will at least see each other on Christmas Day?"

A long pause, then, "I'm just not sure."

When she got off the phone she paced back and forth across the living room, finally giving in to the urge to vent to Sarah.

"Hey," she said when her best friend answered. "Got a minute?"

"Sure, what's up?"

"I'm thinking ice cream and girl talk, if you're free tonight."

"I don't know, let me check my schedule," Sarah said mischievously, then paused on purpose for several seconds before saying, "yep, the Chippendale dancers canceled on me tonight so yeah, I'm free."

"Smartass."

Sarah laughed. "You know you love me."

"You're right, I do. I'll be there shortly."

Per their custom they settled in with ice cream, and Sarah added chocolate syrup to hers as she listened to Karli rant about Evan's work.

"It's ridiculous," Karli said between bites. "It's gone from once a month or so on the road to now I'm lucky if I even *see* him once a month."

"Well, what can you do?" Sarah asked. "If his company's making him travel that much, what can you do about it really, except look into going with him?"

"I've tried," Karli sighed. "I've mentioned it several times. He keeps telling me it's not allowed."

Something sounds fishy here, Sarah thought to herself. *I think Evan's feeding her a line of crap. Unfortunately, I can't tell her that. It will just upset her more, and I have zero hard evidence to prove anything, just a gut feeling.*

"Bummer," Sarah commiserated. "And it also doesn't make much sense, especially if you two covered your plane ticket out of pocket."

"I know, right?" Karli chimed in. "It's not like I would expect his company to cover my travel costs." She paused for a moment, then said, "I think this might call for chocolate syrup."

Sarah pushed the bottle toward her. "Help yourself."

***

Unbeknownst to Sarah, the man she still loved was pulling into his apartment complex on the other side of the city, exhausted after a hectic shift.

Thank God I decided to relocate closer to work, he realized. *I can't imagine driving more than ten minutes after the night we just had.*

He parked his truck and wearily climbed the stairs to his apartment door. Once inside, Tim kicked off his shoes, then wandered down the hall to the bathroom.

Fifteen minutes later, he was standing in front of his refrigerator in his sweatpants, trying to decide whether he had enough energy left to cook himself something to eat. A random thought popped unbidden into his tired mind and set every nerve ending alight.

One of Sarah's omelets would be perfect right now.

"Damn. I haven't thought about that in forever," he muttered with a scowl, running his hands over his face and then through his still damp hair.

But the thought, once loose, could not be bottled up again, and Tim found himself rummaging through his fridge and pantry for the ingredients needed for an omelet. As he did, his mind replayed one of many favorite moments he had shared with the woman of his dreams.

What are you doing? he'd asked her on a rainy Saturday morning at her parents' house. *You know I'm not a big fan of eggs.*

Just trust me, Sarah had giggled. *You will like this, I promise.*

Tim had watched, transfixed, as Sarah had diced green onions and ham, sautéing them together in a tiny pan while the egg mixture cooked in another. She had deftly flipped the egg mixture and cooked the other side, sprinkling a bit of steak seasoning over it as she went. At last, Sarah added the onions, ham, and a handful of shredded cheese before she folded up the omelet.

Now we give it just a minute, let the cheese melt, she'd said, covering the pan with a lid.

Three minutes later, he'd scooped up a forkful of heaven, and grinned at her once he'd chewed and swallowed.

This is outstanding, he'd told her. *You're gonna spoil me rotten, you know that, right?*

She had beamed with pride. *That's the plan,* she'd said, and kissed him.

"God, I miss her," Tim found himself saying with a sigh as he cracked the eggs into a bowl.

CHAPTER SEVEN

The next morning Sarah absentmindedly pushed the cart down the cereal aisle. *Cannot believe I forgot my freaking list,* she grumbled to herself as she tried desperately to remember a single thing that had been written on the tiny dry-erase board hanging on her refrigerator. *Oh, well. Keep circling, maybe I will see something that jogs my memory.* But nothing did.

She was almost to the end of the aisle when a completely unexpected memory came at her out of nowhere – her and Tim, smiling, walking closely together as they shared cart duty.

Captain Crunch? she'd suggested.

With berries, he chimed in, and she had nodded and put a box in their cart.

We need to do this more, he'd announced.

Come shopping? Well, yeah, otherwise the food runs out, she'd teased.

Yeah, come shopping, but together. Everything is more fun with you, Sarah. Even trying to pick out cereal. I can't wait for us to get a place together, and I wanna pick out cereal with you for the rest of our lives...

"Are you all right, sweetheart?" the little old lady asked.

Sarah came back to the present and was horrified to realize she was standing in the middle of the aisle with tears streaming unchecked down her cheeks. She looked at the woman who had spoken to her for a long moment before she managed to whisper, "No."

Then she abandoned the cart with a lonely yellow cereal box in it and made a beeline for the door.

***

"What's wrong?" Karli exclaimed with a gasp when she opened her front door and saw Sarah standing there.

"It's never gonna go away," Sarah blubbered, and fell forward into her best friend's outstretched arms.

Karli was shocked. Out of everyone she knew, Sarah Genard was usually the most together, the most level-headed, and the most laid-back woman of any group. To see her so obviously distraught tore at Karli's soul.

"Oh, honey," she murmured softly in Sarah's ear, "come on in and let's talk it out. Okay?"

"O... okay," Sarah said in a whimper.

Karli reached around and closed the door, then guided Sarah to the kitchen table.

"Coffee?" she asked.

Sarah nodded, still crying.

"Coming up," Karli confirmed, pausing only to place a box of Kleenex in front of Sarah before heading over to grab two mugs from the cupboard.

A few minutes later Karli was seated next to her best friend.

"Okay, hon, what's going on?"

"The past is kicking my butt lately," Sarah managed.

"What do you mean?"

"I told you I was engaged once, right?"

"You mentioned it," Karli said carefully, "but the look on your face told me you didn't wanna talk about it."

"I think... I think I need to," Sarah admitted.

"Let it out, honey. It's a safe space here, you know that."

Sarah smiled gratefully at Karli before taking a sip of her coffee. She closed her eyes and took a couple of deep breaths, then opened her eyes again and began to speak.

"Tim was my everything," she told Karli. "We started dating the summer before our freshman year. When we graduated, he went into the Army, but by the time boot camp was done he proposed, and I said yes. Because I knew he was my one and only. So, we planned our wedding, and it was supposed to be perfect," she sighed. "And then..."

"And then, what?"

Sarah swallowed hard. "It was the night before the wedding. I knew Tim and Kevin were gonna have one last boy's night out, and I was fine with that because I trusted him, you know?"

Karli nodded.

Sarah continued, "We were out of milk and butter. Dad had gotten called in to work and Mom was already in bed with a migraine, so, I drove to the store. I parked and got out of the car, and I noticed movement across the street in front of the pool hall, so I glanced that direction. And I saw them."

"What? What did you see?" Karli whispered.

"My fiancé kissing the town slut," Sarah mumbled. "It was already dark outside, but they were under a streetlight, and it sure looked like he was into it. I couldn't think, couldn't speak, couldn't breathe. I got in my car, and I drove back to my mom's house. I packed up my things, and I put my engagement ring in an envelope with his name on it and left it where my friend Jenny would find it. I waited until I was certain my mom was asleep, and I left town."

Karli was stunned. "You didn't confront him?"

"No," Sarah told her. "It crushed me. He was my entire world. He was my first... you know...everything. And all I could think of was to get away."

"Did he try to come after you or find you?"

Sarah shrugged as she stared into her coffee mug. "No idea. I changed my email and phone number the next morning, and I didn't tell anyone where I was going. I called my parents later to let them know I was okay, but I made them promise not to tell him they'd heard from me," she confessed quietly. "All I could think was that I didn't want to be stuck in that tiny little town where I'd have to see them together. Seeing her live the life with him that should have been mine would have killed me."

Now she lifted her eyes to glance at Karli, and it hurt Karli's heart to see the haunted look on Sarah's face.

"And then I started to regret not at least talking to him before I left. My mom brought me a letter he'd sent to the house letting me know he'd deployed, but that's the last time I heard from him. I sent letter after letter but never got an answer, so I figured I was too late. That was over two years ago, Karli, and I still love him. I still miss him. It's like a bad dream I can't wake up from. I want to move on, but I can't. I don't know how."

"Is that why you don't date?" Karli asked her gently.

Sarah nodded. "I've tried a couple of times, but I just... I can't get Tim out of my head."

She reached over and grabbed Karli's hand. "But I need to. I *need* to move on from this. Help me think of a way to move on, Karli. This is killing me."

***

"You don't look so hot," Jordan observed that evening. "You getting sick? There's a bug going around."

"Could be," Tim admitted. "Didn't sleep worth a damn, either."

Jordan cocked his head to one side and gazed at his rig partner. "Yeah, you do look tired. What's going on?"

"Shades of the past," Tim muttered, then waved his hand when Jordan raised an eyebrow in concern. "Never mind, dude. I'll be fine."

"You know I'm here if you need someone to listen, right?"

Tim smiled. "I know. And I appreciate that. Maybe I'll take you up on that sometime, but I'm not ready to talk about it now."

Jordan held up his hands. "Fair enough, man. The offer stands."

"Thanks," Tim answered. "Now, we gonna get to work or what?"

***

"What about a dating app?" Karli mentioned a few days later when they met up for lunch.

Sarah frowned as she toyed with her cheeseburger.

"Well," Karli said, "I know you don't want to go the whole bar scene route, and I don't blame you. So that leaves work, places like the grocery store, and dating apps."

"Yeah. Strike work off the list," Sarah pointed out. "That's just dumb, to mix work and personal."

"Agreed. And as a result, I think a dating app or two is the way to proceed. Kind of 'set it and forget it'. Check out any matches every couple of days and go from there."

"Ugh. I really, really don't want to do this," Sarah protested. "I really think I am better off just staying by myself."

"Just try it out," Karli suggested. "What's the worst that could happen?"

***

Two days later, Sarah called her best friend. "What's the worst that could happen, that's what you said to me, right?"

"Uh oh," Karli answered. "What happened?"

"Oh, not much," Sarah said. "Only twelve unsolicited pictures of complete strangers' private parts."

"*Ew!*" Karli could not help but chuckle. "Why do guys think we'd find that attractive at all?"

"I have no idea," Sarah murmured, "and those twelve... did I mention that that was just the *first* hour my profile was active? And I lost count of how many 'hey baby wanna hook up' instant messages I got. I've deleted my profile already."

"I'm sorry, hon."

"Yeah, well, we can definitely draw a big ole line through 'dating apps.' What else do you suggest?"

Karli blew out a sigh. "I guess you're gonna have to meet someone nice at the grocery store, or something."

"*Or*," Sarah chimed in, "I can just say forget the whole thing. There's no guarantee of meeting a normal guy that way any more reliably than the dating app."

"Oh, Sarah," Karli said.

"It is what it is, Karli," Sarah told her. "I guess I just need to figure out a different way to get through this. The last thing I need is to get tangled up with someone new and get hurt even more. It's just... safer if I keep doing what I've been doing."

A long pause, then Karli asked, "Sarah, did you ever think about trying to find Tim?"

"What? *No*," Sarah's response was forceful and immediate. "I don't *wanna* know how happy he is with her. Nope. Besides, what would I even say if I *did* manage to find him? '*Hey, remember me, the runaway bride? I know it's been a while, but I still love you, how have you been?*' No thank you."

"But what if – "Karli began.

"*No*, Karli. I'm not going to try to contact him ever again, and that's final."

"Okay," Karli responded quietly. "Your life, your call."

They chatted a bit more, and Sarah said, "Well, I'm going to go figure out something for dinner. Talk later?"

"You got it," Karli confirmed and disconnected the call.

As Karli moved to her kitchen to get her own dinner underway, she reflected on the conversation that they had just had.

Sarah is so convinced he never even looked back. But I don't think so. My gut says she's got it all wrong. I can understand why she does not want to reach out to him, and I respect that.

But that doesn't mean I can't dig around a little bit, see what I can find out about a guy named Tim from Adrian, Texas.

***

One week in, and Karli was not having much luck. Sarah's Tim either wasn't much for social media, or he was hiding in plain sight. She had tried tracking him through Twitter, Facebook, and Instagram with no luck – plenty of guys named Tim whose profiles mentioned the Army, and Texas, but not a one listing Adrian as his hometown.

"It sure would help if I knew his last name," she grumbled under her breath.

Well, duh, her mind slapped back. *But how are you gonna get that without making Sarah suspicious?*

"I have no idea," Karli answered aloud.

"No idea what?" Evan asked as he walked through the living room, his fingers flying on his phone's keyboard.

"Nothing," she answered, and frowned as he kept moving, his attention riveted on whatever he had going on his phone.

Even when he's here, he's not completely here, Karli thought to herself in disgust. *Makes me wanna throw his phone out the window.*

"Hey," Evan said as he came back into the living room. "About Christmas."

"We're supposed to be at my parents' house Christmas morning, then spend the afternoon with your mom," Karli reminded him.

"Yeah... about that. I just found out I have to go to Kansas next week. I might not even be home for New Year's. I just don't know yet."

"Seriously? Are you kidding me right now?" she rejoined, hands fisted on her hips. "But we always spend Christmas with the family. What am I supposed to tell them?"

"Tell them duty calls," he snapped, and walked back toward his home office.

Karli could only stare, fuming, as he shut the door behind him.

***

"I can't," Karli answered, when Sarah suggested the two of them take a girl trip Christmas week. "Evan may not care about letting our families down, but I do."

"Okay, so, I'll be your plus one," Sarah offered. "I'll go with you, and we'll do the things you usually do Christmas day, and *then* we'll head out of town on the girl trip. I just found out my office is going to close down for the whole week, and I know we both could use a break."

"What did you have in mind?"

"Honestly? I was thinking Vegas."

"Ooh, that does sound fun," Karli's tone had turned wistful. "But what about *your* family?"

"They won't be in town," Sarah revealed. "Mom and Dad are heading up to my aunt's place in Kentucky and they're not coming back until after New Year's Day. And Jodie's still in Florida taking care of her sister."

"You know what? Yes. Let's do it," Karli agreed. "And we can drive it. It's not that far, and we can see the Hoover Dam, and maybe the Grand Canyon on our way there."

"Deal! This is gonna be great!"

***

"So, are you heading to Adrian for Christmas?" Jordan asked him.

"Nope," Tim said. "I kinda figured with me being the new guy I'd get put on the duty roster first. What about you?"

"I usually volunteer to work so the guys with kids can have the time off," Jordan answered.

"Sounds like a plan. Me and you, holding down the fort," Tim agreed.

CHAPTER EIGHT

"I really, really don't want to go, but I don't have a choice," Sarah lamented to Karli on their way to the airport on Wednesday morning. "I absolutely *hate* to fly."

It was mid-March, and Sarah had been tasked with traveling to Denver yet again to get a handle once and for all on the inventory counts coming out of the company's second largest manufacturing facility.

"I know," Karli said as she reached over to pat Sarah's hand. "But it will be over with before you know it."

"I thought that four months ago," Sarah sighed. "Still hasn't happened yet."

"Well, the sooner you get your first book out there in the world, the sooner you can get some traction," Karli reminded her. "And eventually, it will grow to a point where you can write full-time. You just have to keep working at it."

She saw the drop-off area just ahead and moved to the right to pull up at the curb.

"You'll be fine, Sarah. And I'll pick you up when you land Friday night."

"Thanks, bestie. Wish me luck."

***

After a turbulent ride, and a miserable landing in snowy conditions that only enhanced Sarah's negative opinion of air travel, she trudged to the baggage carousel and waited in a horde of people for her suitcase to finally appear.

And waited.

And waited, until only she was remaining from flight 156 that had arrived from Dallas-Fort Worth International Airport.

Her left eyebrow raised as she watched the carousel grind to a halt and her flight number disappear from the overhead monitor.

Well, that figures, she thought with a grimace, and pivoted to stride over to the concierge station.

"Hi. I think maybe my bag got lost," she said, and offered the attendant her claim stub.

"Let me take a look," the woman, whose name tag read 'Cyndy,' said with a smile.

A few keystrokes later, Cyndy confirmed Sarah's assumption. "Yes, ma'am. I'm so sorry, but it seems your suitcase got sent to New Hampshire by mistake."

Now both eyebrows arched skyward.

"Oh, boy. How do we fix that?" Sarah asked politely.

"I'm just double-checking to make sure they already know to re-route your luggage," Cyndy said briskly. "And... yes, I can see they've already noted it."

"When do you think it will arrive?"

"That, I'm not sure of," Cyndy answered apologetically. "You see, with the storm that's coming in, I don't know how many more flights in or out there will be today."

Cyndy pulled a form out of a drawer, and continued, "But fill this out for me with your contact information, and we can call you when your suitcase arrives."

Sarah completed the form, and when she handed it back to Cyndy, she mentioned, "I'm not from around here, I'm up here on business. The first address I listed is the hotel I'm staying in, but I'm supposed to fly home Friday afternoon."

"Yes, ma'am. I'll make sure they call you once it arrives."

***

Almost three hours after landing in Denver, Sarah was standing in the checkout line at the Wal-Mart about a mile from her hotel. She'd decided to purchase two outfits, just in case her lost luggage never showed up, and she picked up new toiletries, undergarments, and sleepwear in addition to a new suitcase to put it all in.

By the time she got back out to her rental car, the wind had picked up tremendously, with oversized flakes whipping furiously past her face at a forty-five-degree angle. It seemed to take forever to drive the rest of the distance to her safe haven for the next two days, and she sighed with relief when she walked into the hotel lobby.

Check-in went smoothly, for which she was grateful, and she thanked the desk clerk as she accepted her keycard and made her way to the elevator. Once she was safely in her room, she called Jodie, then Karli, to let each know she'd made it to her destination. She spent the rest of Wednesday cross-checking the reports she'd run back in Fort Worth and identifying which inventory items would be part of the impromptu cycle count she was planning in the morning.

***

"Overnight shifts are my least favorite," Tim muttered to Jordan as they pulled back into the station at seven a.m. "Takes me forever to get to sleep once I get home."

"Yeah, me too," Jordan agreed. "And just about the time I get used to them, we switch around again."

"But not lately," Tim pointed out. "This is how many in a row now?"

"Eighteen, I think."

Tim sighed. "Meet you back here in twelve hours." And he walked to his truck to make the short drive home and fall into bed.

***

Sarah showered and dressed, then sat on her bed, only half-listening to Denver's most popular morning newscast as she brushed out her hair and put on her shoes.

It wasn't until the meteorologist came on that the television got her complete and undivided attention.

She grabbed the remote and increased the volume just in time to hear his words in conjunction with a very gnarly looking satellite photo of the state of Colorado.

"And if these two storm systems converge, ladies and gentlemen, we could see record high snowfalls over the next few days. The bottom line here is, use caution, and if you don't have *to go out in this stuff, don't. Back to you, Steve."*

"Great," Sarah muttered. "That's the last thing I need is to get stuck up here."

She sent up a quick prayer for the weather to hold until her flight left town on Friday afternoon, grabbed her purse, room card, and briefcase, and headed for the elevator.

***

Sarah finally made it back to her hotel around seven p.m. Although the plant was only fifteen minutes away, the weather had deteriorated so much that it had taken her almost two hours to make the drive back. By the time she slowly eased her rental car into the lot and parked, her nerves were shot.

Not to mention I'm not used to all this, she grumbled internally as she headed for a hot shower. *I live in Texas, for Pete's sake. When we get weather even remotely like this, we stay home.*

She showered, changed, and just made it to the restaurant downstairs before they closed for the night. Knowing the staff was probably anxious to get home, she ordered her dinner to go, and made small talk with the hostess until her order was brought out to her.

"Ya'll be safe," Sarah said, and headed back up to her room.

As she ate her sirloin and loaded baked potato she reflected on her day. Inventory was definitely missing based on the cycle count she'd overseen.

And I don't think it's a receiving or unit of measurement error either, she acknowledged as she chewed. *I think someone's taking it home with them. Maybe more than one someone. I just can't prove it. Yet.*

***

The next morning brought the realization of Sarah's biggest fear. The two storm systems had indeed merged in spectacular fashion as the weatherman predicted they might. Worse, the mega-storm stalled directly over Denver and the surrounding area and churned out inch after inch of heavy snow.

She got a flight update notification shortly after eight a.m. that confirmed what she already suspected – no one would be flying into or out of Denver International Airport for at least the next two days, much less her now cancelled flight that was supposed to depart at four-thirty p.m.

She sighed, shook her head, and dialed a number.

"It's me," she said when Karli picked up the call. "You don't have to worry about coming to the airport to get me tonight. Everything up here is shut down. The way things are going, I'll be lucky to be out of here by Sunday."

A call beeped in, and Sarah said, "Hang on a second, Jodie's calling."

"Call me back, okay?" Karli said and disconnected.

Sarah swiped right to accept and said, "Hi Jodie, how are things there?"

"Hey kiddo. I figured you might want to know – your suitcase made it home safe and sound. A nice young man with the airline just dropped it off. Now, when are *you* coming back?"

***

It was just before midnight on Friday, and Tim and Jordan were hoping for a quiet shift. But it was not meant to be.

The alarm sounding had them racing to their rig, responding to a wrong-way driver crash on Interstate 20.

"Let's roll, man," Jordan urged, and Tim pulled out of the bay and hit the sirens and lights.

In mere minutes they'd arrived on scene. Jordan went to the back of the unit to grab the gurney just as Tim got a call over the radio.

"Come again?" he said, then, "Roger, we're on it."

"Jordan!" he yelled out the window as two more ambulances arrived.

"What?"

"Just got word there's another car involved. Down there," Tim told him, and pointed off the bridge. "Let's go."

Jordan double-timed it back to the passenger seat and they made their way to the service road below, where an overturned car awaited them.

Tim could hear the man that had called it in telling Jordan he'd been talking to the driver trapped in the car.

"But he's not answering me anymore," the man lamented, and Jordan started toward the wrecked vehicle while Tim got the gurney and the kit.

He'd just about made it over to Jordan's side when his partner began to yell at the top of his lungs.

"Evan? *Evan!*"

"Jordan – what's going on?"

"It's my best friend...*dammit,* Evan, don't you die on me. Don't you freakin *die* on me, man," Jordan babbled as he felt desperately for a pulse.

He whipped his head around and looked at Tim, his eyes wide with adrenaline. "We gotta get him out of there, man. We gotta...but he's pinned. We need the jaws, Tim. Call it in."

Tim stepped away and keyed the mic on his collar to request the extrication tools needed to free Evan from his car. Then he hurried back to Jordan, who by now was in tears.

"I can't feel a pulse..." he managed. "No pulse."

"Move," Tim commanded, and Jordan wriggled out of the way.

Tim, being the smaller of the two, was able to push his upper body through the drivers' side window and get closer to Evan. A lack of carotid pulse and no sign of breathing, followed by checking the pupils' reactiveness to light, confirmed for Tim what he already suspected – Evan was beyond helping.

By the time the extrication equipment had arrived, Jordan was sitting on the ground with his back up against the ambulance's rear tire, pale and glassy eyed with shock and grief.

"What's with Baker? He all right?" Dan asked as he approached the car with the jaws of life.

"He knows him," Tim murmured. "That's his best friend."

"*Jesus.* Get him out of here, Tim. He doesn't need to see this."

"I tried," Tim answered, shaking his head. "He won't go."

***

At four a.m. Tim and Jordan were back at Station Number Two, sitting in the kitchen with cups of coffee.

It had taken over a half-hour to remove Evan's body from his crumpled car. After that, Jordan had insisted that he and Tim be the team to transport Evan to the hospital, where the emergency room doctor made the official pronouncement. Then he'd asked to be the one to notify Karli, Evan's wife.

"I've known both of them for years," he'd said earnestly. "Please. I really need to be the one she hears this from."

And his superiors granted his request. He'd inclined his head in thanks, then gone back into the triage room to stay with his friend until morgue transport arrived.

Now Jordan sat, coffee untouched, leaning over the table with his head in his hands, trying to prepare himself for one of the worst conversations anyone could have.

"Seventh grade," he told Tim, his voice hoarse with emotion. "He's been my best friend since seventh grade."

"I'm so sorry, buddy," Tim murmured, his hand resting on Jordan's shoulder.

I know how this feels, Tim acknowledged to himself. *All I can do is be there for him and let him know he's not alone.*

"I'm glad you're here," Jordan rasped before emotion overcame him again.

"You're my partner, man. Here is where I'm *supposed* to be. Do you want me to go with you to tell her?"

Jordan sighed heavily. "No. But thanks, Tim."

***

Saturday morning brought little relief from the massive storm system still spinning slowly in place over the greater Denver area. When Sarah's cell phone rang at seven a.m., she pounced on it, eager to communicate with someone back home.

"Hey girl! What's up?" she said cheerfully but was greeted by sobs.

"Karli? Karli, what's wrong?"

"Oh, Sarah... Evan's dead."

"What happened?"

"He...he died in a car accident last night," Karli blurted, then cried even harder.

"I will find a way to get home, Karli, as fast as I can," Sarah said with determination.

"No, please don't. I don't want anything to happen to you too," came the answer. "Please, Sarah. Don't get out in that storm. Wait until it's safe. Promise me."

"I promise."

***

Evan's funeral service was held on Tuesday at two p.m., a pale and somber Karli sitting between Jordan and Evan's mother Madge in the front row of the chapel. But it was Tuesday night before Sarah was finally able to fly back to Dallas-Fort Worth International Airport.

Karli met her at baggage claim, and the two friends cried together.

"I'm so sorry I wasn't there for you," Sarah told her as she hugged Karli tightly. "I'm so sorry."

CHAPTER NINE

"So, I ran into Jordan in the park. We're going out to dinner," Karli told her over the phone the following week.

"That's good. You need to get out of the house once in a while," Sarah chided. "Get some air."

"Yeah," Karli agreed, then said, "Oh, that's the doorbell. He's here. Call you when I get back?"

"Sure," Sarah replied, and hung up.

I need to organize another girl trip, even if it's just a weekend away, Sarah realized. *She could use the break.*

She opened her laptop and began a Google search using the term 'weekend getaways within three hours of DFW,' then began scrolling through the results and fine-tuning her planning.

Before Sarah even realized it, two and a half hours had passed. She'd settled on three possible destinations; now, she needed to run them by Karli.

She dialed her best friend's number and waited.

"Sarah," Karli said with a tremble.

"Oh, honey. You don't sound okay. Need me to come over?"

Within five minutes, Sarah was in her car, armed with the one thing that always seemed to make them both feel better – sea salt caramel ice cream.

She grabbed her best friend in a one-armed hug as soon as she walked through Karli's front door. "Brought reinforcements," she announced, directing Karli's attention to the ice cream. "Come on, let's talk it out."

Sarah listened to Karli relate the details of what had happened between her and Jordan. When Karli asked her opinion, Sarah gave it honestly. *There's nothing to feel guilty about here,* she thought to herself, and told her friend as much.

Next, Karli confided in her about the pregnancy she'd just had confirmed, and Sarah's eyes widened.

"What are you going to do?" she asked, then reminded Karli she had a support system in place to help her.

"And you're going to be a fantastic mom, okay?" Sarah assured her. "You can do this. Now, in the meantime, I have an idea. How about another girl trip?"

Sarah presented the choices and Karli's face lit up.

"I've never been to Lake Murray! That sounds like fun."

"Done! I'll book it for this weekend."

They talked a bit more, and Sarah waited until she was absolutely sure that Karli was okay, then suggested, "Hey. Go run a bath and soak. You know that always makes you feel better."

Karli chuckled. "It really does."

"Okay, so, shoo," Sarah gestured. "I'll wash the bowls and let myself out. You need a soak and some sleep."

Karli stood and grabbed Sarah in a fierce hug. "Thank you," she murmured.

"For what?"

"Being the best friend I've ever had."

***

Two weeks later, Sarah was dumbfounded as she sat at Karli's kitchen table again and listened.

"Holy crap! What was he thinking?" she exclaimed.

"I have no idea. He just quit paying stuff, Sarah. Almost every bill we have is behind," Karli ranted as she paced. "I'm gonna lose this place."

She paused and ran her hand over her face. "And then Jordan surprised the hell out of me and offered to move in here and help me out or let me move in with him."

Sarah's eyebrows knitted.

"He was here when I opened the letter from the mortgage company," Karli explained when she saw the look of confusion on Sarah's face. "He's been helping me figure out what to do with Evan's things."

"Ah," Sarah replied, even as she thought *sounds to me like someone just might have a thing for Karli.*

"So, what are you going to do?"

"I don't feel comfortable living with Jordan. It wouldn't be... proper. And I love my parents, but I really, really don't want to move back home."

"Okay, then, so, come live with me," Sarah announced. "I have that second bedroom that already has a bed in it, and I've been meaning to put a dresser in there anyway, I just haven't gotten to it yet."

"I'd pay you."

Sarah waved a hand. "I get such a good rate on my place it's not even funny. Pitch in for food, we'll call it good. All right? At least think about it."

***

By the time Sarah got home from work on Friday, Karli was moved into Sarah's second bedroom and was trying to decide what to wear for a dinner out with Jordan.

I think it's time I give her a nudge, Sarah decided, and started asking about Jordan. But their conversation was interrupted by the doorbell.

When Sarah opened the door and saw Jordan, all doubt was removed from her mind as to his intentions toward her best friend, particularly when she mentioned Karli and saw Jordan's face light up with a brilliant smile.

Oh yeah, he's definitely interested in her. Time to make sure Karli sees him as more than a friend.

Sarah politely pointed Jordan toward the couch then rushed back to Karli's room to sprinkle some seeds of realization in her best friend's mind. When she asked Karli to find out if Jordan was single, Sarah saw a flash of jealousy spark in Karli's eyes.

There we go. Now let's go see what happens, she thought, and followed Karli down the hall to the living room where Jordan waited.

Her heart swelled with hope for the two people standing in her living room staring at each other, each one obviously crushing on the other.

Mission accomplished, she thought with satisfaction as they left smiling at one another.

She closed the door behind them.

Jordan looks at Karli the way Tim used to look at me, she realized, and closed her eyes from the sudden stab of heartache.

***

A crying Karli was the last thing Sarah expected to walk through her door just over an hour later. When Karli managed to tell her what had happened, Sarah realized not only did Jordan care about Karli, but that he was putting her well-being above his own.

He's not just interested in her, he loves her, Sarah mused to herself as she and Karli talked it out. By the end of the conversation, she had Karli calmed down.

***

When Tim realized the mood Jordan was in, he attempted conversation, but Jordan snapped at him.

"Hey, don't be an ass," he growled back. "I'm trying to be a friend here."

Jordan's shoulders sagged as he heaved a sigh and then filled Tim in.

Girl trouble, Tim acknowledged silently. *Boy, do I know about that.*

He listened, assured Jordan that under the circumstances giving Karli some space was best, then moved his partner's focus to work.

But as the shift progressed, he found himself wanting to share his personal experience with matters of the heart.

"I know how you feel more than you think I do," he said abruptly, startling Jordan.

And he told him all about Sarah, from their first date through the present day.

"And you've never seen or talked to her again?" Jordan was incredulous. "Why? Why didn't you try to find her?"

"At the time, I loved her enough to respect her space," Tim shrugged. "I don't know if that makes me the biggest fool on the planet, or what. But now so much time has gone by. She's probably moved on."

"But you don't *know* that for sure," Jordan protested. "Not unless you try to find her. Can you honestly live the rest of your life with not knowing?"

"She walked away from me with only a two-sentence letter, and I never heard from her again, Jordan. I'd say that's pretty damn clear."

"That why you don't date?"

"Yep," Tim admitted. "No point. No one will ever measure up to Sarah."

***

The next two months found Sarah and Karli settled into a natural rhythm as roommates. Sarah realized how lonely she'd sometimes been before Karli moved in, and she was grateful her best friend was now just down the hall instead of across town.

They shared a love for romantic comedy movies, so they developed a Friday night routine that Karli dubbed 'chocolate and chick flick' night. Jodie would sometimes join them, and the three would talk and giggle until the wee hours of Saturday morning.

"She is such a sweet woman," Karli said of Jodie after one such evening.

"She really is," Sarah agreed. "She was the first person I met in Arlington, and she's been my rock."

"She's good people, as my dad would say," Karli grinned.

"Yep. Hey, I'm turning in."

"See you in the morning," Karli said as she attempted to leverage herself off of the couch.

Sarah snorted. "Having issues?"

"Help," Karli laughed, holding out her hands, and between the two of them working at it she was finally standing upright.

"Geez," Karli breathed. "I'm not even really that big yet and I'm *already* having trouble getting around?"

"And you have what? Four more months, something like that?"

***

A few days later Sarah could tell Karli was frustrated.

"What's wrong?"

"I must be losing my mind... I could have sworn I put the mortgage closing documents in my box of stuff that came here, but I can't find them," Karli fumed.

"Karli, calm down. I'm sure they're in the storage unit. You'll find them."

"I'm going to go look."

"Okay, be careful."

Karli had been gone about twenty minutes when Jodie called, and her voice sounded very strange.

"Can you come down to the office please?"

"Sure, be right there," Sarah said, and locked up her apartment before heading downstairs and to the front of the complex.

She opened the door to the office and her eyes went wide. Jodie was on the floor beside the desk.

"Jodie? What's going on?"

"Hey, kiddo," Jodie gasped, her eyes glazed with pain. "Thank God I was able to pull the phone down off the desk. I think my hip is broken, honey."

"What?? Then why did you call me and not 9-1-1?"

"Because I need you to gather up my medicines, Sarah. They're going to want to know everything I take and the doses."

Sarah yanked her cell phone out of her pocket and dialed 9-1-1 to get an ambulance en route.

"What happened?"

"Tripped over that damn cat," Jodie growled, referring to the stray she'd been feeding.

Sarah stayed with her until the paramedics arrived, then went to Jodie's unit to gather up her medications. Before she went back to the office, she swung by her own apartment to leave a note for Karli – *With Jodie, will explain later* – then hurried back to Jodie's side.

As they loaded Jodie into the ambulance, Sarah told her, "I'll follow you in the car."

Jodie nodded, and answered, "Call Larry for me please. And my sister."

***

Sarah returned home around one a.m. and a concerned Karli launched to her feet from the couch.

"Where have you been? Is everything all right?"

"Jodie fell and broke her hip," Sarah said wearily. "They took her to the emergency room, then admitted her. They're doing surgery at nine."

"Oh my God. Is she gonna be okay?"

"I think so. When she finally chased me out of there, she was in the process of trying to set the night nurse up with her grandson," Sarah answered with a chuckle, then glanced at Karli. "Something's different with you. What's going on?"

"Get comfortable, it's a long story," Karli said with a gleam in her eyes.

Sarah sat, her eyes growing wide as Karli relayed discovering her late husband's infidelity and her confrontation with Jordan.

"And? What happened?"

"He told me he's in love with me," Karli smiled.

Hah! I knew it, Sarah crowed in her head.

"So, what are you going to do?"

"Jordan's a great man, and I am going to see where this goes," Karli announced. "I was holding back because I felt guilty about Evan, but after finding out about everything he did, I don't feel guilty anymore. I deserve to be happy and being around Jordan makes me happy."

"I agree one hundred percent," Sarah answered. "You glow whenever his name comes up."

"I do?"

"Yes," Sarah smiled at her best friend. "Yes, you do."

She yawned and stood up. "I need to get some sleep. I want to be back at the hospital in time to visit with Jodie before they take her into surgery."

"Let's both try to get some rest, and I will go with you," Karli replied.

CHAPTER TEN

Five weeks later, the surprise baby shower that Jordan had enlisted Sarah's help with had finally arrived.

"I'm glad this is almost over," Sarah told him. "It's been hard keeping secrets from her."

"I know. It's been difficult for me, too," Jordan confessed. "But I really, really want it to be a complete surprise for her. She deserves that."

They talked a bit more, laying out last-minute details, then Jordan said, "We'll meet you there. I'm on my way to go pick her up now."

"See you in a bit," she confirmed, and hung up. "Well," she said to Jodie, "I need to get moving."

"I wish I could be there," Jodie frowned. After her surgery the doctor had insisted on placing her in an inpatient rehabilitation center, and Jodie was out of patience with the pace of things.

"I know," Sarah said as she patted her hand. "But it's better to go slow and make sure everything heals right, remember?"

"I remember," Jodie grumbled. "Bring me some cake."

Sarah laughed. "Of course, I will. I'll come back by with it this afternoon." And she leaned over and kissed Jodie's cheek. "Love you."

Jodie's features softened at the sentiment. "Oh, kiddo. I love you too."

***

When the baby shower was successfully concluded, Sarah dutifully wrapped up a chunk of cake and returned to see Jodie.

They spent some time visiting, and when Jodie began to yawn, Sarah gently said, "I'm going to get out of here so you can take a nap. But I'll be back tomorrow."

Jodie nodded sleepily, and Sarah hugged her before leaving.

She'd been back in the apartment about an hour when Karli launched herself through the door.

"Um, I'm moving in with Jordan," she announced with a huge grin on her face.

"Took you guys long enough," Sarah teased, and hugged her. "I'm so happy for you, Karli, you two are great together."

"We are, aren't we?"

"So, when is the move happening?"

"He has to work tonight, so, sometime tomorrow."

"Well, then," Sarah declared, "I think it's time to have a mid-week chocolate and chick flick night, don't you?"

"I couldn't agree more."

They went back and forth before settling on *The Holiday* with Kate Winslet and Cameron Diaz.

"I know it's not Christmastime, but it's just such a good movie," Sarah reflected.

"I agree," Karli said. "And after that, how about *Fifty First Dates*?"

"Done," Sarah proclaimed. "Popcorn, or just the chocolate?"

"It's a celebration," Karli answered, "so let's do both."

***

It was almost midnight before the second movie wrapped up, and Sarah and Karli were both yawning as the credits began to roll.

"Okay, I'm headed to bed. Long day tomorrow," Sarah told her.

"See you in the morning," Karli said cheerfully, and waddled down the hall to her room.

Sarah turned off the TV, placed the DVDs back in their appropriate slots in her alphabetized collection, carried the empty popcorn bowl and candy wrappers to the kitchen, then headed for bed.

As she brushed her hair and then her teeth, she reflected on the fact that within the next twenty-four hours she'd be alone again in her apartment. The thought did not appeal.

I am so happy for Karli, I truly am, she told her reflection. *I just wish I could find that, too.*

Sighing, she changed into her pajamas, then turned off the light and climbed into bed. She snuggled down underneath her blanket and willed her mind to think of anything but Tim. But it wouldn't cooperate at first.

She finally was able to drift off around one a.m.

***

Meanwhile, Tim and Jordan had their hands full. They were one of three units called out to a scene of utter chaos. Two very drunk individuals had gotten crosswise at a popular watering hole and succeeded in getting themselves thrown out, but not before causing quite a bit of damage.

The fight had moved to the parking lot, with friends of each man deciding to wade into the melee, resulting in twelve people with injuries before the cops arrived to break it up.

Tim applied a butterfly bandage to the patient he was triaging, while to his right Jordan was attempting to take vital signs of one of the men that had caused the whole mess in the first place.

"Sir, I need you to hold still," Tim heard Jordan say for the second time, with steel in his voice. "I'm going to have to restrain you if you don't hold still so I can work on you."

"Like hell you will!" the drunk man bellowed, and for Tim time seemed to stop as he glanced over and watched Jordan's patient pull a knife out of hiding and ram it into Jordan's upper abdomen.

"Jordan!" Tim cried out, then, "Need some help over here!" to the policemen standing a few feet away interviewing witnesses.

Tim bolted over to where Jordan now lay on the ground, the hilt of the knife protruding from his midsection.

"Easy, buddy, easy," Tim soothed, as he tried to approximate the length of the blade.

"Pull it out," Jordan gasped.

"Not yet. Right now, leaving it in is keeping you from bleeding out," Tim told him. "I have to get you to the ER."

He lifted his head and barked, "Somebody get me a gurney over here. *Now*."

Within minutes Jordan was loaded. Dan, one of their co-workers, got behind the wheel while Tim rode with Jordan.

He's going into shock, gotta keep him talking.

"Hey buddy," Tim growled, lightly patting Jordan's cheek. "No sleeping. Stay awake. Talk to me."

Jordan moaned, and Tim noticed that in addition to an erratic pulse, he was turning more and more pale.

"Step on it, Dan!" Tim yelled.

They arrived at Medical City in short order, and Jordan whispered, "Call Karli," as they wheeled him into the emergency room triage unit.

"You got it," Tim answered, and he stepped back outside to try her number. He called six times and each time her phone rang and rang, then went to voicemail.

Oh hell no. Voicemail is not *going to be how she finds out about this,* Tim asserted, his jaw set with determination. *I'll try back in a little bit.*

And he stepped back inside to check on not just his rig partner, but one of the best friends he'd made in his lifetime.

After twenty minutes, Tim stepped back outside to try to reach Karli again, and was relieved when his phone rang.

"Karli? Is that you?" he asked, and when she confirmed, he told her Jordan was hurt and what hospital they were in.

***

At two-eighteen a.m. a frantic pounding on her bedroom door startled Sarah out of a very sound sleep. She opened it to find a hysterical Karli.

"Something's happened to Jordan," Karli sobbed. "I need to go."

Sarah was instantly awake and already reaching for the t-shirt and yoga pants on the top of her dresser.

"Two minutes, and I'll drive you," she said, and Karli nodded.

Sarah beat her promise by forty-five seconds, and they locked the front door and headed to Sarah's car. She made sure Karli was buckled in, then swiftly moved through the parking lot to leave the complex.

"Which hospital?"

"Medical City, off of Matlock."

"Okay. Breathe, Karli, he's gonna be all right."

"I... hope...so...," Karli managed between huge gulping sobs.

Sarah reached over and held Karli's hand tightly as she drove through the night. At last, the hospital was in sight, and Sarah turned in at the Emergency Room entrance and drove up to the passenger drop-off doors.

"Go on," she said, squeezing Karli's hand. "I need to park, and then I'll be right in, okay?"

Karli only nodded, tears streaming, and maneuvered her hugely pregnant frame out of the car then waddled as fast as she could into the building.

Sarah watched her go, then looped around and pulled into the first spot she could find. She got out, grabbed her purse, locked her car, and jogged toward the same entrance Karli had gone through.

When she walked through the doors, already slightly out of breath from adrenaline, what she saw stopped her in her tracks and almost dropped her jaw wide open.

Karli, her best friend, was standing beside and talking to a man in an Arlington Fire Department EMT uniform. It was none other than Tim Fresco, the man Sarah had left at the altar. And he hadn't noticed her - yet.

What... how... Sarah's brain completely failed her, and for a moment she could only stare as she fought the overwhelming urge to run into his arms.

Focus, Sarah. Karli needs you more than ever right now.

Somehow, she managed to compose herself and slowly continued forward until she was standing by Karli's side.

***

Tim had been waiting in the main lobby of the emergency room for Karli to arrive so he could take her to the room where everyone had gathered to wait for news. She'd mentioned needing to wait a few minutes for someone named Sarah, and he'd nodded in acknowledgment.

He did a double take when he finally noticed the woman approaching them, thinking at first he'd seen a mirage. Karli's Sarah was *his* Sarah. It was all he could do not to grab her, kiss her, and never let go.

Not the right time or place, he reminded himself. *This is about Jordan and Karli right now. But we're damn sure going to talk before either of us leaves here.*

He sharpened his focus as Sarah asked, "What happened?"

Her voice... it's as sweet as I remember... I missed hearing her voice so much.

But he kept his attention focused on Karli as they walked down the hall, leading them to the elevator. As they moved, he explained the night's events that had led to Jordan's injury, then slipped an arm around Karli when she went pale and began to sway.

379 | P a g e

He guided them off the elevator and to the right, where a room of police officers and firemen waited for word on Jordan's condition. Tim saw Karli seated, then moved to the desk to ask for an update. He noticed Dan walk over and squat down in front of her.

That's good, he thought. *He'll be able to calm her down, so she doesn't go into labor early.*

And he took a moment to stare at the woman beside Karli who'd remained the love of his life, even after all this time.

***

Sarah, meanwhile, was patting Karli's shoulder, trying her best to be a comfort. She felt someone watching her and lifted her head to make eye contact with Tim from across the room. There was an unmistakable 'we need to talk later' vibe in his stare. She nodded once in acknowledgement, then returned her focus to Karli.

***

Once Dan had gotten Karli's breathing under control, he left her under Sarah's watchful eye and sauntered over to Tim.

"Any word?"

Tim shook his head. "Not yet, I'm afraid."

"By the way - who's the brunette? She's cute."

Tim growled before he could stop himself.

"Dude, what the hell," Dan muttered, clearly confused, and wandered back over to check on Karli.

After three hours, the surgeon arrived with an update, and shortly after that Karli was being escorted into post-op for a brief visit.

The moment Karli left to go see Jordan, Tim looked at Sarah, an almost imperceptible head motion indicating he wanted her to step out into the hall. He moved that direction, and she sighed, then followed.

Dan grinned as he watched them leave the room. *Ah,* he thought. *That explains him growling at me. Guess she's spoken for.*

* * *

Tim strode to the far end of the long hall to be assured of some privacy, then leaned against the wall and watched her approach.

Just as gorgeous as ever, he thought, and frowned.

Sarah stopped in front of him, gazing at him with big brown eyes clouded with emotion.

"What the hell are *you* doing here?" he grumbled.

"Karli's my best friend, Tim," Sarah said quietly. "I wasn't about to let her come up here by herself. Not as upset as she was."

"Oh," he snarled, when what he really wanted was to touch her. "So, you don't run out on *everyone* you supposedly care about, just *me,* is that it?"

Her eyes went wide with pain and surprise before narrowing in anger.

"I don't have time for this right now," she snarled back, giving him a surprise of his own. "Karli needs me."

He grabbed her elbow, but she yanked it out of his grasp.

"Be sure and say hello to *Lilah* for me," she sneered, then turned on her heel to stomp away.

But she wasn't fast enough. He noticed the tears beginning to form.

CHAPTER ELEVEN

Lilah? What the hell is she talking about?
He raced after her.

"We're not together," he told her.

"Aw, you two broke up? I'm so sorry. Sucks for you, I guess," Sarah's voice dripped with derision.

"Will you please stop walking for one minute and just *listen* to me?"

She whirled, and yes, there were definitely tears in her eyes that he could see, but also a huge dose of hurt.

"You have one minute," she hissed, arms folded defensively across her chest. "Go."

"We're not together. *We were never together.* I don't know what the hell you were told, but it was wrong."

"You don't understand... *I saw you myself*, Tim. I *saw* you kissing her the night before our wedding. I was driving to the store, and I saw the two of you in front of the pool hall."

"There's nothing to understand, Sarah. I have never, *ever* been involved in any way with Lilah Tucker. Not that she didn't try. That's what you saw. She was drunk as hell, and she followed me and Kevin outside and planted one on me. If you'd kept watching, you'd have seen me shove her away and put her in her place, because I was with *you*. I love... loved *you*," he corrected after a brief pause. "I wanted to marry and spend my life with *you*. But you didn't trust in me, trust in *us* enough to *ask* me what was going on. Instead, you assumed, and I got an envelope with your ring and a scrap of paper with two sentences on it that broke my heart."

He paused, his gray eyes alight with feeling as he watched her.

"And so here we are, almost three years later. Three years that we could have shared and been happy together, Sarah. But you bailed out on me because of a few seconds of a situation that I didn't start and damn sure didn't want."

Sarah took a stumbling step backward from him as the import of what he'd just said hit home. She blinked once, slowly, sending tears cascading as she stared at him silently.

"I've missed you every single day," she finally whispered. "I thought you betrayed me, and it crushed me, and I ran. But I never stopped loving you, Tim. Never. Not even a little. I just..." she paused, swiping at her eyes with her sleeve, "I couldn't handle staying in that little town, knowing I might see you out in public with her. I just couldn't face that. So, I left. And then when you didn't answer my letters, I figured you were probably still with her, and happy."

"I'm sorry," she told him as her voice began to quaver. "I love you. I still love you, Tim, and I hurt you, and I'm so sorry... I just... I just hope one day you can forgive me."

Tim balled his fists to keep himself from reaching out for her, even as his heart soared.

She still loves me.

Sarah turned, her breath coming in great hitching gasps, and walked unsteadily back down the hall. Tim stood slumped against the wall in her wake with his head bowed. Because he knew he had just lied to her.

He'd never stopped loving her, either.

And then one sentence she'd uttered finally registered in his brain and sent a surge of confusion through his system.

Letters? What letters?

"Sarah," he called out, pushing off the wall and starting down the hallway after her. "Sarah, wait."

***

Sarah veered off sharply to the right and headed into the ladies' room to pull herself together. *I can't let Karli see me like this. She's got enough to worry about right now.*

She stooped low over the sink, cupping water in her hands and splashing her face, then stood upright and gazed at herself in the mirror, her red-rimmed eyes widening with realization.

Wait just a damn minute. I wrote him at least twenty letters. If he was as heartbroken as he claims, then how come he never wrote back?

"This isn't over," she whispered to her reflection.

She rolled her shoulders to try and dissipate some of the tension that had formed there. Then she dried her face with a paper towel, flung open the door and stepped back out into the hallway.

And was immediately swept into Tim's embrace, his mouth crushing hers with all the pent-up passion of the last three years. Her heart leapt with joy, and she wrapped her arms around him, pulling him in more closely and returning the fiery kiss as he backed her against the wall.

***

"Sarah," he whispered against her mouth when he finally pulled his lips away from hers. "I missed you so much."

"Then why didn't you write me back?" she managed through her fresh tears. "Why?"

He pulled his face back from hers just enough to be able to look directly into the brown eyes he adored.

"Baby, I never, ever got any letters from you," he said softly as he wiped a tear from her cheek with his thumb. "Not a single one. If I had, believe me, I'd have answered them by showing up on your doorstep. I've missed you every day, too."

She could see his sincerity, and she frowned, completely confused.

"But none of them were returned to me... I don't understand..."

Tim's stomach clenched at the thought that was creeping into the forefront of his mind.

"Sarah – where did you send them?"

"Your parents' house," she said earnestly. "I didn't know how else to reach you on deployment."

Tim's jaw set and he was silent for a long moment.

"I think I might know what happened. But I really hope I'm wrong," Tim's voice took on an edge as he spoke.

"What?"

He shook his head. "Later. Karli will be back soon, and we need to be there for her right now. But can we continue this talk in a little while? Please?"

She nodded, and he kissed her again.

They separated, then made their way back down the hall. As they approached, they could see Karli opening the door to walk back into the waiting room, and they quickened their pace to rejoin the group.

***

Once Jordan had been moved to ICU, Karli was allowed to go see him again, and once again Sarah and Tim found a more private space to continue their discussion.

"Are you giving her a ride home?"

Sarah nodded. "I'd planned on it. She still lives with me right now, so that makes the most sense."

"We need to figure out something," Tim murmured against her ear. "I want... I *need* to be alone with you for a while."

"I also need to go check on Jodie," she pointed out.

"Jodie? Who's Jodie?"

"Long story. The short version is, she's like a grandma to me, and she's in rehab. Fell and broke her hip a little over a month ago."

"Rehab. Been there. No fun at all," Tim commiserated, and watched Sarah's head tilt with a questioning look.

"I got shot in Afghanistan," he explained, and tightened his arms around her as she began to tremble.

"You mean... you almost... and I would never have known..." her voice faltered.

"I'm fine, I promise," he soothed. "And I'll tell you everything, okay? Just not here."

"Okay," she breathed. "How about this. I need to check in on Jodie, and we both know Karli won't leave his side until visiting hours are over."

Tim nodded his head in agreement.

"So, I am going to go see Jodie. You bring Karli home when she's ready, and then you and I can go somewhere. All right?"

***

It was early evening when Tim and Karli pulled into the parking lot at the complex and made their way to Sarah's unit.

"Hi," Sarah said softly when she saw Tim walk in behind Karli.

Even though she was exhausted, Karli's ears perked up at the tenderness in Sarah's tone. She whipped around and studied them both, and her eyes bulged as it occurred to her what was going on.

"*You're* Sarah's Tim?"

Tim nodded.

"Holy crap. Talk about a small world."

He grinned. "You could say that."

Karli glanced back and forth between the two.

"Okay, you two definitely need some alone time, and I need some sleep."

She turned her attention back to Tim. "Thanks for everything," she said, and moved forward to hug him, then stepped back.

When she pivoted her gaze to Sarah, the look was unmistakably one of *OMG, tell me everything later!*

A single nod from Sarah was sufficient to make Karli smile, and she turned and went to her room.

"Let's go to my place," Tim offered, and Sarah smiled.

"Just let me get my bag."

***

A few minutes later, as he pulled out of her complex's lot, Tim said, "So I take it you're not seeing anyone."

"No, I'm not. You're who I want. There's never been anyone but you."

"Same here," he told her earnestly. "I didn't even bother to try. You're who I want, too."

He reached over and took her hand in his.

They rode in silence the rest of the way to Tim's apartment, and Sarah gasped when she realized how close he'd been all along.

"When did you move here?" she asked as they parked.

He shrugged. "About a year ago, I guess, give or take."

She followed him up to his front door, and as he turned the key in the lock, he heard her sniffling.

"Sarah. What's wrong?" he asked as he stood aside and held the door open for her.

She stepped through into his living room and set down her bag.

"I... I can't believe you and I have been living so close to each other..." she said, then burst into tears. "All... all that *heartache*... wasted time..."

"Baby," he murmured, taking her into his arms. "Please don't cry. It all worked out. We're together now."

He reached down and gently lifted her chin to look into her eyes. Wiping her tears away softly with his thumb, he whispered, "What do you need, baby?"

"You," she answered, "I need *you*. Be with me, Tim."

He picked her up in his arms and carried her into his room, laying her down gently on the bed before he joined her there. The moment he got close enough she threw her arms around him and drew him in.

Tim kissed her softly, slowly, and it felt to her as if he was slowing time itself to an exquisite crawl. He broke contact with her mouth to kiss her cheeks, her forehead, then trailed down her neck to the base of her throat to lightly trace his lips across, before moving back up to her mouth again.

"God, I missed you, Sarah," he murmured between kisses, "I missed everything about you."

She fisted her hands in his hair, and she could feel her heat rising with each tender kiss he placed, with each heartfelt word he spoke. When his lips found hers again, she moaned, parting the way for him to deepen the kiss.

And when he lifted away again, she said only one word.

"Please."

Tim gazed into Sarah's eyes as he slowly lifted the hem of her t-shirt, his hands exploring, working their way up as hers left his hair to travel down to the waistband of her yoga pants. Moments later she lay on his bed, waiting, wanting, as she watched the man that she'd never stopped loving undress as well.

He came back, kissing her softly once more before he slid down her frame to lavish attention on her breasts. She moaned with pleasure as he caressed and kissed her body, and she tightened her grip on his sheets as he slowly moved back up to claim her mouth again.

"Please, Tim. I love you, and I need you. I need *us*," she gasped as he wrapped his arms around her.

"I love you," he whispered in her ear as he filled her. "I've always loved you. Only you, Sarah. Forever."

Later, they drifted off to sleep, arms and legs intertwined, both of them whole again, *home* again, at last.

***

"Are you hungry? You must be. I noticed you hardly ate anything in the cafeteria last night," Tim observed as they walked hand-in-hand into his apartment's small kitchen the next morning.

"I am, actually, now that you mention it. What did you have in mind?"

"Well, I have this excellent recipe for omelets, if you're interested."

Sarah smiled at the memory he'd invoked. "Got you hooked on them, huh?"

"And how," he agreed, pulling out ingredients. "But mine never taste as good as that first one you made me."

She giggled, and the sound pierced his core. He abruptly set down the items he'd gathered up, moved around the counter, took her in his arms, and kissed her passionately.

"I missed that," he murmured. "Hearing your voice. Hearing your giggle. Holding you close to me. I missed *us*."

"Me too," she sighed, laying her head on his chest.

He reluctantly turned her loose so he could cook them breakfast.

As he did, they began to talk. Sarah filled him in on her life since the last time they'd seen each other.

"My day job's all right, but you know I want to be a writer," she concluded.

"I do know. You've always been passionate about it. I think you should go for it," he said, smiling at her tenderly.

They sat at his little bistro table, and it was his turn to talk. He told her about being deployed and about being scared pretty much the whole time. His voice broke as he talked about Dack, and she reached over and took his hand as he relived one of the worst days of his life.

He shared his journey through rehab and training and how he'd come to be in Arlington. By the time he finished, her eyes were glistening.

"I'm so sorry I wasn't there for you through all that," she whispered.

He shrugged. "But you're here now. I'm just thankful we found each other again, Sarah."

"I am, too," she said, but her face was troubled.

"What are you thinking?"

"I'm thinking... I'm thinking that I can't believe we lost so much time over a misunderstanding. *My* misunderstanding," she confessed.

"Baby," he said gently as he stood and pulled her into his arms. "Please don't do that to yourself. We're *both* at fault in this. I assumed, wrongly, that you didn't want to hear from me, so I didn't make a nuisance of myself at your parents' house. I could have. I *should* have. But what's done is done. We're here now. No point in looking backward. We're together again, that's what counts."

"But I still want to know what happened. Why didn't you get my letters?"

He sighed. "I have a theory. I'll be right back."

Tim ducked into his bedroom for a moment, and when he returned, he said, "Whatever happens next, we'll get through it together, okay?"

She nodded, and he pulled out his cellphone, dialed a number, put it on speaker, and motioned for Sarah to remain quiet.

His mother picked up on the third ring.

"Hey, Tim," she exclaimed. "What a pleasant surprise! What's up?"

"Hey, Mom, I have a question for you. You got a minute?"

"Absolutely, son. Anything for you."

"Mom," Tim said softly, his eyes locked with Sarah's, "Did I ever get any mail at your house while I was deployed?"

A long pause, then, "Well, some junk mail, but nothing else."

"You're sure that was all?"

"Um...," Paige hesitated, and Tim knew he was on the right track.

"Never got any letters from anyone?"

"Um," came through loud and clear over the speaker.

"Mom."

"Well, you did get several letters from Sarah, but I knew you wouldn't want them. So..."

Tim cut his mother off mid-sentence.

"What did you do with them?"

"I shredded them," his mother snapped. "She caused you enough embarrassment, leaving you standing up there in front of all our family and friends. I refused to let her embarrass you further."

Sarah's eyes gaped in surprise, and her hands flew to her mouth.

"Me, or *you*?" Tim's voice was razor sharp.

Paige began to sputter. "This isn't *about* me."

"Isn't it? If it was about me, you'd have let me make up my own mind about Sarah. But it's not. It never was. It was about your reputation in the community."

"I always felt she was beneath you, and she proved me right by running away," Paige huffed, and Tim reached out a hand to steady Sarah, who had turned white.

She was never anything but kind to me, Sarah's mind reeled. *Was it all an act?*

"Well let me tell you something, Mom," Tim said, his eyes never leaving Sarah's and his voice strong with conviction. "I've found her again, and I still love her, and if she'll still have me, I will gladly make her my wife."

Tim hung up the phone, then reached into the pocket of his robe and brought forth Sarah's engagement ring.

"But...but...what about..." she began.

"The *only* opinion I care about is yours," he replied, love shining in his eyes. He got down on one knee and softly said, "Sarah Genard, I've always loved you, and I always will. Are you willing to give us another try?"

Sarah nodded, beaming with happy tears, as Tim gently clasped her left hand to place her custom-made ring back where it belonged.

EPILOGUE

Three weeks later, Sarah was standing outside the courtroom of the Justice of the Peace, with Jordan, Karli, Jodie, and her parents in attendance. As per tradition, she and Tim had last seen each other the evening before.

She stood in a small alcove out of sight of the courtroom doors, wearing a simple sheath gown and fingertip veil, waiting anxiously and clutching the bouquet her mother had made for her.

"You look beautiful, honey," her father said and kissed her cheek.

"Thanks, Dad," she answered, and hugged him. "Um, what time is it?"

"Two minutes to ten," he answered.

"Is he here yet?"

"I'll go check."

Her father disappeared around the corner and returned moments later.

"Not yet," he confirmed. "But I'm sure he'll be here any minute, Sarah."

"Okay," she exhaled, trying to calm her nerves. *Why am I nervous? I'm marrying the love of my life, my best friend. Nothing to be nervous about.*

A hugely pregnant Karli came around the corner a few minutes later.

"Any sign of Tim?" Sarah asked.

"Not yet," Karli said. "You want Jordan to call him and see if he's on his way?"

"Yes, please," Sarah answered. "I don't have my cell phone."

"Okay, hang tight," Karli said, and then added, "You look beautiful, by the way."

Sarah smiled softly.

Another ten minutes passed, and still no Tim. Karli reappeared several minutes later to confirm Jordan had called multiple times but was not getting an answer.

Oh, no, she thought, tears beginning to form. *Is he... is he leaving me at the altar this time as payback?* She shook her head trying to force the fear from her mind, but it started to take root.

At ten-thirty, just as the first round of tears began to fall, she heard a commotion from around the corner.

"Where is she? Is she mad? There was a wreck, and I stopped and rendered aid; I couldn't just drive by."

She stepped out into the hallway and relief flooded her to see Tim walked slowly toward her.

"You... you're an absolute vision in that dress," he whispered as he looked at her. Then he noticed her brimming eyes. "What's wrong, honey?"

"I thought maybe..." Sarah began, then faltered.

"You thought... maybe I wasn't coming?" he guessed, and she nodded as twin tears streaked down.

"Oh, Sarah," he said, taking her in his arms. "Honey, the *only* thing in this world that's going to keep me from marrying you today is if you tell me 'no'. I passed a minor accident on the way here. There was a pregnant woman who was already in labor involved in the accident, and no emergency crews were on scene yet, so I stopped to help her. I'm so sorry I made you worry."

She sniffled even as she smiled. "You delivered a baby?"

"I did," he confirmed. "A beautiful, healthy baby boy. But I still should have taken two seconds to let someone here know what was going on so that you wouldn't worry. I'm so sorry, Sarah."

"It's okay," Sarah told him, love shining in her eyes. "You're here now, that's what counts."

"So," Tim murmured, "you ready to do this?"

"With all my heart," she replied, and together they walked into the courtroom.

They stood, hand in hand, looking into each other's eyes as they recited their vows. Tim's voice was husky with emotion as he said, "I do" and slipped the band he'd had made to match her engagement ring onto her finger.

Then it was Sarah's turn, and Tim felt and saw the sincerity of her words as she recited them to him, then placed his ring on his left finger as well.

The Justice of the Peace pronounced them husband and wife and Tim grinned ear-to-ear as he leaned in to kiss his bride.

At the end of the ceremony, Sarah turned and gasped as she saw Patrick and Paige Fresco walking toward them. Tim, following her gaze, instinctively stepped in front of Sarah to protect her.

"I'm so sorry," Paige began, reaching out as she began to cry, her voice heavy with sincere regret. "I said that out of anger, and I didn't mean it, and I am so sorry I let my pride keep the two of you apart. I'm so sorry I put myself above your happiness. I know I have no right to ask this of either of you, but please, please forgive me."

The group was silent, watching and waiting, as Sarah slowly moved around Tim and contemplated his parents for a long moment.

Then she stepped forward and wrapped her arms around her new mother-in-law.

"I'm so glad you could come," she said earnestly as she hugged her, and Paige sobbed on her shoulder.

One year later...

"You did it! I am so, so proud of you," Tim said as they opened the box containing the proof copies of her first novel.

Sarah giggled. "Did you know your mom was the first one to say she wants an autographed copy?"

"Did she now? Too bad. The very first autographed copy is *mine*," Tim told her before he kissed her.

"I can handle that for you right now. Hand me a Sharpie," she gestured, and he quickly located one and passed it to her.

She opened the cover, thought for a moment, then wrote an inscription.

"Here you go, honey," Sarah beamed as she held out the book.

He opened it and read what she'd written, and his jaw dropped open.

"Really?"

"Really."

"How far – "

"Two months."

Tim tossed the book aside, scooped her up and twirled her around. The book slid off the couch and tumbled to the floor, coming to rest open-faced so that what she'd written to him was plainly visible.

To my husband Tim - My rock, the love of my life and the father of my child.

The End.

Love Notes

<u>Shannon Rivers</u> - The striking twenty-four-year-old with a heart of gold who's running from trouble. Her main focus is surviving the life-or-death scenario she's been unwittingly cast into the middle of. But when she meets Pete Jenkins, sparks fly despite the desperate circumstances that introduce them.

<u>Pete Jenkins</u> – The twenty-eight-year-old U.S. Marshal living and working in Fort Worth, Texas. His routine pre-shift morning ritual is upended when he is assigned to hide and protect two young women - Shannon Rivers, the target of some very ill intentions, and her roommate. Smitten with Shannon at first sight, Pete resolves to keep her safe - at any cost.

CHAPTER ONE

It was a typical mid-October night in Chicago, Illinois, and Shannon Rivers was getting ready for her date. Her free-spirited extrovert roommate, Leah, lounged in the doorway, keeping her company as Shannon tried to figure out what to wear.

"Ten dates already, huh?"

"Yeah," Shannon confirmed.

"Think tonight's the night to *finally*... you know...?" Leah teased.

"Stop that," Shannon admonished, even as she giggled and blushed. "And for the record, probably not."

"Seriously?" Leah's tone turned incredulous as she came and sat on Shannon's bed. "Still not yet?"

Shannon shrugged. "I'm not ready."

"Robert's tall, built, cute, and is steadily employed," Leah reminded her. "Pretty good catch."

"I know," Shannon sighed. "And he's very attentive and sweet. I just don't...," and she trailed off.

She'd met Robert at the coffee shop on campus two months earlier. She was almost done with her double Bachelor's in Finance and Accounting. He'd just graduated with his Master's in Business and was studying for the CPA exam when he wasn't working at Creach & Langford, one of the most prestigious investment firms in the nation.

He was handsome, smart, funny, charming, and completely besotted with her. The fact that she felt no spark whatsoever when he kissed her bothered her a great deal.

"Don't, what?" Leah asked.

"Think of him like that," Shannon confessed, then sighed again. "He's a great guy, and I like spending time with him. But something's missing, Leah. I'm just not attracted to him that way, at all, and I have no idea why. Unless that changes somehow, I don't know how much longer I will see him. I know he wants more than just a goodnight kiss."

"If that's really how it is, you should tell him, Shannon," Leah said somberly. "You can't help what you don't feel. It's not anybody's fault. It's just the way things go sometimes."

Shannon nodded. "Yeah. And like I said, he's a great guy. Robert deserves someone who can be more than a friend to him."

"So, talk to him. And after that, give him my number. I think he's hot, and I'd be happy to 'more than friend' him as many times as humanly possible."

Leah grinned as she watched Shannon's eyebrows vault skyward.

"Girl, *please*. I'm kidding. You know I'd never do that. I mean, depending on the circumstances, I probably *would*, but not to *you*. Just trying to get you to loosen up and at least smile."

"You're talking like I haven't seen you in action after a few too many Jell-O shots," Shannon teased.

"I like to play the field. What's your point?" Leah said primly.

Each of them managed to keep a straight face for a few moments before they both roared with laughter.

***

When Robert picked her up, he looked exhausted and tense. Shannon chalked it up to all the hours he'd been putting in. *He's been working so hard lately,* she thought. *He deserves a night of fun. Our talk can wait a day or two.*

Over dinner they both slowly relaxed - until he brought a tiny square box out of hiding, and Shannon's heart leapt into her throat.

What is he doing... is he... oh, no.

That was followed immediately by enormous relief when he opened it and showed her its contents, saying simply, "I saw this today, and thought of you."

It was a small silver locket, intricately engraved with a swirling pattern.

"Please accept this, as a token of friendship," he continued softly, and his eyes told her that he wanted more, but would settle for being friends - for now.

Shannon didn't want to hurt his feelings, so she accepted, and he smiled as she fastened the braided chain around her neck.

"It looks good on you," Robert observed, and she blushed. "Now, how about a movie? The one we were talking about the other day is showing at the theater not far from here. Show starts at seven. You want to go?"

She smiled and nodded.

***

"That was quite an ending! Didn't see that twist coming at all," Robert announced as they left the movie theater a little over two hours later.

"Me either," Shannon agreed. "What do you want to do next? It's only nine o'clock."

"Hmm," he pondered. "How about that new nightclub that just opened? Wanna stop in, see what all the fuss is about?"

She shrugged. "Clubs aren't really my thing."

"Come on, it'll be fun," he goaded, and smiled the smile he knew she couldn't resist.

"Oh, all right," she conceded, and couldn't help but grin back.

She realized just before he opened the passenger side door for her that she'd left her purse in the theater.

"I need to go back in, I forgot my purse. Be right back."

"No problem. I'll pull up to the curb and pick you up," he answered.

She smiled, nodded, then pivoted and started to walk back toward the movie theater's entrance. Behind her Shannon heard Robert's driver side door open and close, then the cranking noise as he started the car.

She'd gone about fifty feet when suddenly the earth trembled, followed by the loudest *boom* she'd ever heard. The next thing she knew she was flying forward through the air, landing with a massive thud face down almost twenty feet from where she'd been. She gasped, disoriented, trying to draw in a breath, but the impact had knocked the wind out of her.

Shannon struggled to pull her arms in and under her chest to leverage herself up off the ground, and she felt something slapping at her back.

"Hold still," a voice said. But he sounded muffled, miles away, and she shook her head, not comprehending what he'd said.

"Hold still, your shirt's on fire," the stranger yelled, and used his jacket to smother the flames licking at her clothing.

Once he'd put out the fire, he crouched down next to her head where she could see him more clearly in the dark. Deep brown eyes, filled with worry, were staring intently into her aquamarine ones, and correctly read shock and confusion in her gaze.

"Are you hurt?" he asked, and she realized she had to watch his lips move to understand the question, because she couldn't hear much of anything at all.

"Don't...think...so," she wheezed, still trying to regain her breath.

Slowly, he aided her in turning over, then sitting up. The motion, combined with the smells of gasoline, melted plastic, charred cotton and burned flesh, assaulted her senses and made her nauseous, and she leaned to one side and vomited.

The wave of nausea finally passed, and as Shannon sat upright again, she blinked rapidly several times, trying to make sure the scene unfolding in front of her was real.

It was Robert's car.

Or what's left of it, anyway, her brain observed. Still sitting in the same parking spot. *Kind of.* Mangled, and in flames...

What the hell just happened?

The Good Samaritan beside her stood up and waved his arms frantically at the ambulance and fire trucks pulling into the lot.

"Over here!" he cried out. "She's hurt!"

"Robert," she croaked, looking up at the man who had helped her and noticing he was wearing a mall security uniform. *"Where's Robert?"*

The guard looked down at her, his expression full of concern, and Shannon squinted to try to see his lips better so she could understand the answer.

"I don't know."

I have to find him, her brain screamed.

The man tried to get her to remain where she was and wait for the approaching EMTs, but she shook him off. Shannon struggled to her feet, staggered four steps forward, and slumped toward the ground as unconsciousness took her.

Luckily, the first paramedic was only steps away, so he raced forward and caught her, then scooped her up and placed her on the gurney his partner had just wheeled over.

Her next awareness was sometime later, lying on her side in the back of an ambulance, being tended to by one of the emergency workers.

"Can you hear me?" he asked her.

"I know you're speaking to me, because I can see your mouth moving," she said loudly. "But I can't hear you."

He held up a finger, then scribbled on a notepad and handed it to her.

That's because both your eardrums are ruptured from the blast, the note said.

"Blast? Are you talking about an *explosion?*"

He nodded.

"*Seriously?*"

He nodded again.

A knock on the back of the ambulance, then the door opening, revealed the same security guard that had come to her aid earlier. He held up her purse where she could see it.

This yours? he mimed to her, and she nodded. He held it out to the paramedic, who took it and handed it to her.

"Thank you," she told him, and he gave her a smile and a thumbs-up, then closed the ambulance door.

"Anything else wrong with me?" Shannon asked the paramedic, and he took the pad back and wrote some more, then showed it to her again.

A probable concussion – you've got a hell of a goose egg on your head. Scrapes on your chin, nose, torso, hands and knees, and you've got some second-degree burns on your back. All in all, you got really lucky.

She reached up gingerly and winced as she felt a huge knot bulging prominently in the dead center of her forehead.

"Where's Robert? Is he okay?" she asked.

And she noticed the man hesitate.

"What aren't you telling me?"

He sighed, then slowly drew his pen again across the page.

He's still in the car... I'm so sorry.

Shannon's emotions spilled over in an instant, and the paramedic took her hand and held it as she sobbed.

"I want to see him," she exclaimed.

He squeezed her hand to get her attention, and when she raised her tear-stained face up to look at him, he made sure she understood what he'd written next when he showed it to her.

NO. Trust me. You REALLY don't want to see that.

Her eyes went wide with realization, and the realization made her nauseous again. Her caretaker anticipated it and was ready, holding back her long auburn hair as she retched violently once more.

Once the nausea was gone, Shannon Rivers lay on her side again. Her right hand was wrapped tightly around the tiny locket she'd now wear in remembrance of the sweet man she just hadn't been able to love, and she shed silent tears en route to the hospital.

CHAPTER TWO

Leah came bursting into the triage room.

"Are you all right?" she exclaimed as she looked at Shannon.

"They said I burst my eardrums," Shannon told her. "Can't hear much of anything at all right now. Grab a notepad and write down what you wanna ask me."

Leah nodded, pulling her favorite pen and a full-size spiral notebook out of the huge handbag that Shannon always teased her about.

Guess the cavern she insists on lugging around isn't useless after all, Shannon realized, and grinned despite the circumstances.

Leah uncapped her pen and scribbled furiously for a moment, then whipped the notebook around where Shannon could see the result.

First – Are you okay?

Second – What happened???

A tear slid slowly down Shannon's cheek, and she took a deep breath before she started to tell Leah the evening's events.

But the man in the black suit that knocked on the doorframe then strolled casually into the room stopped her short.

"Miss Rivers?"

"Her eardrums got screwed up, she can't hear you," Leah snarled. "And *you* are?"

He held up his hands to show he wasn't there to harm.

"Easy, Miss..."

"Culverton," Leah snapped. "Leah Culverton."

"Miss Culverton," the man said, and smiled. "I am just gonna reach for my badge, okay? It's all good."

Moving slowly, never breaking eye contact, he dipped his thumb and forefinger into his interior jacket pocket and pulled out the folded leather containing his shield and ID card. Holding them flat in his palm, he stepped slowly forward and extended his hand to her.

"I'm here to help, I promise. My name is Larry Fuller," he said gently. "I'm with the FBI."

Leah reached forward and took his offering, then scrutinized the photo ID closely, comparing it against the man standing in front of her. Satisfied, she nodded once, handed it back, then wrote '*his name is Larry Fuller. He's FBI*' and showed it to Shannon.

Shannon nodded her understanding, and said, "Come on in, Agent Fuller."

"I hope you don't expect me to leave," Leah stated.

"No, Miss Culverton," he said. "Not at the moment."

Her eyebrows raised.

Shannon snapped her fingers to get their attention, then said, "What's going on?"

He's letting me stay, for the moment, Leah wrote out and showed her.

"*Letting* you? *For the moment*? Let's get something straight right now, buddy. After the night I've had, I'm not talking to *anybody* by myself," Shannon announced, the monitor she was hooked up to beginning to beep rapidly as her heart rate and speaking volume both increased. "She's my best friend, and whether she hears it now, or later, she *will* know all about it, regardless. She stays. Now, write down what you want to know."

Agent Fuller shrugged, then nodded.

"I take it you want her to start from the top?" Leah asked.

"Yes, please."

Leah held up the notebook and pointed to her second question she'd written, and Shannon noticed that Fuller pulled out his own, much smaller notebook to record her answers, as well.

Shannon closed her eyes briefly, then began to speak, walking them both through her date with Robert all the way through to its fiery conclusion.

"You mean he's..." Leah's voice trailed off, her dark brown hair looking almost jet black now against her pale face. Then she realized Shannon was frowning at her and muttered "sorry" before presenting the statement in written form.

"Yeah," Shannon said sadly. "And if I hadn't had to go back inside for my purse, I'd have been sitting right next to him in the car when it blew up. Being forgetful is the only reason I'm still here."

Leah's hand flew to her mouth as she paled. She was silent for a bit, then started to write another question, but Agent Fuller beat her to it.

"Did she notice anything unusual? Anyone following them, or paying a little too much attention to them at dinner or at the movies?"

Leah scribbled his question instead.

Shannon's brows knitted together as she thought about it, then answered, "Not that I noticed."

"What was Robert's mood?"

Shannon read Leah's written version.

"When he first picked me up, he looked... haggard. Haunted. Seemed really, really tense. Over dinner he seemed to relax, and by the time we left the theater he was his usual smiling self. I just thought maybe all the hours he's been putting in had taken their toll."

Now Shannon's color fled again as she mentally assembled puzzle pieces, and exclaimed, "You don't think it was an accident. Otherwise, the FBI wouldn't be here. Am I right, Agent Fuller?"

Before he could answer, the three-way interview was interrupted by medical staff, who had come to collect Shannon for a CT scan.

"We'll have her back here in about forty-five minutes," one of the nurses said. "You're welcome to wait in the lobby."

"Meet you back here," Shannon called to Leah and Agent Fuller when she saw them leaving the room.

***

"Where are we going?" Shannon asked nervously.

CT Scan, the nurse wrote on the whiteboard hanging up on the wall.

"Oh, yippie," Shannon mumbled. Closed-in spaces didn't terrify her *quite* as much as rodents and heights, but they came pretty darn close.

The nurse at her right shoulder could see Shannon's stress level rising and patted her arm as a way to try to comfort her. Shannon, meanwhile, focused on her breathing, and then on the light fixtures as she was wheeled down the hall, through a sharp left turn, and into what looked like a service elevator. One floor later, the doors opened, and two more right turns signaled the end of their trip.

She looked at the machine, with its menacing, gaping maw, and shuddered.

"I really, *really* don't want to be in that thing," she stammered.

The tech, having been told of her hearing loss, grabbed a clipboard, paper, and pen, and wrote a note to her.

I know, Miss Rivers. It's going to be all right, I promise. There's more room in there than you think. And I will go as fast as I can, okay? We're just looking at your head, so, there won't be any need to hold your breath or anything. But you will *need to stay completely still.*

She read his note and gave him a shaky thumbs-up.

The tech and one of the nurses assisted her in moving from the gurney to the platform.

"Is there any way we can put some padding down for her?" the nurse asked him. "She's got second-degree burns across her upper back, and I don't know if she'll be able to put pressure on them *and* try to hold still for you for very long."

The tech thought it over, and answered, "I don't see why not, as long as we position it properly; it's not like we're scanning her chest or anything, just her head."

Although Shannon had no idea what was being said, she figured it out once they folded a blanket and lined it up with approximately where her upper back would come to rest on the platform once she laid down.

She leaned back slowly and winced.

"She needs more. What about a pillow?"

The nurse helped her sit up again and the tech maneuvered a pillow into place, then indicated for Shannon to recline.

It was still uncomfortable, but the pain was down to a manageable level, and she gave them the 'okay' sign.

I just wanna get this over with, she thought to herself, and gritted her teeth when the platform began to slide into the imaging unit.

Shannon tried her best to hold still and not succumb to claustrophobia during the thirty-minute CT scan of her head. When the tech finally pressed the button that moved the hard, uncomfortable platform back out of the mouth of the machine, she sighed in relief, then sat up quickly to take the pressure off of her back.

But the quick motion combined with the ache of lying on burned skin made her lightheaded, and her upper body swayed as the room swam in her vision. She blinked rapidly several times as she took deep calming breaths. Eventually, the sensation passed, and with the tech's help she maneuvered back over onto the gurney for her trip back down to triage.

***

She'd been settled back in for almost fifteen minutes when Leah and the agent returned. Shannon immediately sensed the tension between them. She started to ask about it but opted to wait when she saw the attending physician had stepped in right behind them.

Leah explained the setup – written questions – and the doctor nodded.

"First let me say, your hearing should return within a couple of weeks," he said. "I didn't see anything that would lead me to believe your ruptured eardrums won't heal themselves."

Shannon smiled, giving him a thumbs-up after she'd read his message.

"The burns and scrapes should be completely healed in the next couple of weeks, as well," he continued, and Leah wrote it out and showed her, earning them all another thumbs-up from the patient.

The doctor went over wound care and forty-eight-hour concussion protocols with Leah, then announced, "Okay, let's get you out of here, young lady."

When it was relayed to her, the last statement garnered applause from Shannon, and the doctor chuckled as he left the room.

"Can't *wait* to be home," Shannon said, then frowned when she saw Leah and Fuller exchange a glance.

"What?"

Yeah. About that, Leah wrote. *We need to make a detour.*

Shannon grumbled as Fuller stepped out to give her some privacy, but she kept her questions in check while the nurse was removing her IV.

"Detour? What detour? Why?" Shannon asked as soon as the nurse left.

Leah wrote, *He will explain it all, but we need to get going* and showed her friend, then handed Shannon underwear, yoga pants, and a baggy t-shirt to put on.

"What aren't you telling me?" she asked Leah, as they worked together to pull the t-shirt down gently across her wounded back.

Please don't freak out, but our apartment was broken into tonight. Massive destruction, Leah scribbled then shared.

"*What?*" Shannon's mouth formed a small 'o' in surprise.

Leah nodded, then wrote, *Place was trashed.*

"Does Fuller think it's all connected?"

Leah wrote, *He won't say so, but yeah, I think that's exactly what he thinks. He said he'd explain everything, but we need to get moving.*

Shannon fell silent as she pulled her yoga pants up over her hips, then sat on the edge of the thin mattress. Leah bent to help her put on socks and tennis shoes, then grabbed Shannon's purse for her and they stepped out into the hallway.

"Ladies," Fuller said, sweeping his arm out in front of him to indicate the direction they needed to go.

CHAPTER THREE

Twenty-five minutes later they were sitting in Agent Fuller's office visitor chairs.

"What you're about to learn stays in this room," he began, and paused so Leah could write out his words for Shannon.

She read, then nodded.

In turn, he handed Shannon a previously typed file summarizing the situation so she could read at her own pace while he verbally brought Leah up to speed.

"We've suspected for some time that Robert's employer, Creach & Langford, is a front for a massive money laundering operation, but we've never been able to gather any solid evidence. About four weeks ago, Robert reached out to us, and I was assigned to interact with him. He had stumbled across some documents at work that piqued his curiosity, and he'd begun to dig. Once he realized what he was looking at, he called us. He and I met, and he agreed to help us build a case against them."

Fuller paused for a moment to take a sip of water. "The plan was, he would copy as many files as possible, then hand them over to me on a set day and time."

"What happened?" Leah asked, as Shannon gasped to her right.

Leah and Fuller both turned to look at Shannon, who had already completed her reading and was staring at the agent with scared eyes.

"I think they figured out he was digging around, and had him killed," Fuller stated with frustration. "Robert had mentioned all the files he thought we would need were probably on their most secure server. One of our IT guys walked him through the best way to make the copies and *not* get caught. Evidently, something didn't go right."

When she saw he'd stopped talking, Shannon blurted out, "Why did they break into *our* apartment? Robert and I weren't serious, Agent Fuller. We only met two months ago. This was only our tenth date, and he's never even been *inside* our apartment."

Fuller shrugged. "The only thing I can think of is that they started watching him as soon as they became suspicious. And I got confirmation earlier that Robert's place was ransacked tonight, too," he answered, and Leah wrote it down and showed her.

Visibly shaken, both Shannon and Leah were silent for a long moment.

"You have to hide her, don't you?" Leah murmured. "She could be a target. Right?"

Fuller nodded.

"What did you say?" Shannon pleaded.

Leah wrote it down and showed her. *It's not safe for you to stay here right now, Shannon. He thinks you're a target, too.*

"But I don't *know* anything!" she exclaimed in frustration, plopping her face into her hands.

Leah tapped her shoulder, and when Shannon looked up, she saw Leah's note.

Whatever happens, I'm coming with you. I insisted. You're my best friend, and I am not gonna let you do this alone.

Shannon's smile was shaky.

"How long will we have to hide?" she asked.

"To be honest, I'm not sure," Fuller said, and Leah relayed his words with her notebook and pen.

Shannon's eyes narrowed. "What about our jobs? Our classes? I only have two months until I finish my degree! And what about our family? Our friends? Do you really expect us to just leave town without telling anyone where we're going?"

Fuller snapped, "That's *exactly* what I need and expect you to do. I'm much more concerned with keeping both of you alive."

"You're an ass, you know that, right?" Leah muttered to him, then sanitized his answer for Shannon's perusal.

He said he's so sorry, and he knows it sucks, but his number one priority is our safety, and part of that is that no one else can know what's going on.

Shannon's shoulders sagged and she hung her head in despair.

"When do we leave?" she managed.

Fuller checked his watch and leveled his gaze at both of them before saying to Leah, "Tell her we need to get going now, actually."

"At four a.m.? Where are we going at four a.m.?" Leah responded.

"South."

"South... um... you mind being a little more specific?"

"Texas."

"Texas?"

"Yep, Texas. Now if you don't mind, we have a plane to catch."

***

U.S. Marshall Pete Jenkins arrived home from his pre-dawn run on schedule; it was a habit ingrained in him from his Army service. He whistled as he made his way into the bedroom to get ready for work.

He quickly showered and toweled off before shaving, then put on his jeans, button-up shirt, and boots. The last thing he added to the belt around his waist was his department-issue Glock 22. He was just about to make breakfast when his cell phone rang.

"Jenkins," he answered, then listened. "Yes, sir. He asked for me, specifically? Okay. What time? Okay. I'll be there."

He hung up the call, put the bacon and eggs back in the refrigerator, and grabbed his keys.

"Looks like drive-thru again," he muttered as he locked his door and headed to his truck.

Twenty minutes later, with coffee and a breakfast sandwich secured, he steered his vehicle toward Meacham Airport on the north side of Fort Worth to rendezvous with Agent Fuller as instructed.

He pulled into the main lot and checked his watch. *Flight won't land for another fifteen minutes or so,* he noted. *It'll be good to see Larry again.* Not many people knew it, but Pete Jenkins and Larry Fuller had served together; they'd been in the same platoon in the Army.

His phone rang again, and it was his boss again, but this time reading him fully into the situation.

Pete's eyebrows raised as he listened.

"Car bomb? Wow. Not the most subtle method, for sure. Do we know how long she's going to... *they?* There's two? Interesting. All right... No, I think Beta will work just fine for this. We'll head straight there. Who else is in on this?"

***

In the tiny aircraft, Shannon squirmed in her seat. The high-powered pain medication she'd received at the hospital had left her system, and her entire body ached.

"You can get up and move around if you need to," Fuller pointed out, and when she frowned in confusion, he took off his seat belt, stood, and gestured to her.

Shannon nodded her understanding and followed suit, wincing.

"She's hurting," Leah observed. "Guess the good stuff wore off."

Fuller mimed *you okay?* and received a mirthless chuckle from Shannon.

"No, and you wouldn't be either if you'd been thrown twenty feet and landed on concrete on your face, then caught fire," she griped. "*Everything* hurts."

Leah rummaged through her handbag and pulled out an economy-size bottle of Tylenol, holding it up in triumph to shake it at her roommate.

"I absolutely love you," Shannon sighed with relief and held out her hand. "Gimme twelve of em."

Leah solemnly shook her head and held up two fingers.

"Fine," Shannon muttered. "Just... anything, *please.*"

Leah handed two pills over, then scribbled *you're loving my great big ol' purse* now, *aren't ya?*

"I really am," Shannon agreed before swallowing the Tylenol. "But it still cracks me up that it's almost as big as you are."

"If we're going to be hiding out longer than a couple of days, we're going to need extra supplies - bandages, surgical tape, and aloe vera," Leah mentioned to the agent. "I don't think what the hospital sent her home with will last very long."

"Once we get there, we'll go get whatever she needs," Fuller responded. "The biggest thing is, when you get where you're going, you'll need to stay put, and stay inside as much as possible."

The 'fasten seat belt' sign flashed on, quashing any continued conversation, and the three retook their seats for landing.

***

Pete was leaning against the side of the hangar when the plane landed and taxied into the structure. Fuller exited the aircraft first and walked over to meet Pete, who had moved toward the plane.

"Hey Pete, long time no see. How ya been?" Fuller said, hand outstretched.

"Not bad, buddy, how about you?" Pete responded as they shook.

"Pretty good, all things considered. Your people read you in?" Fuller asked as they approached the plane.

"Yep, for the most part. I have a couple of questions, though. Why are there two of them with you?"

Fuller grinned. "Her roommate insisted on coming along. She's quite the little firecracker, too. You'll see for yourself in just a moment. What's the second question?"

"Why didn't you deal with our office up there?"

Fuller leveled his gaze at his old friend. "It's a long story, and I'll fill you in on the details later. Let's just say I need someone I know I can trust working this."

"Fair enough. Shall we?"

Agent Fuller led the way back up the short steps into the passenger compartment, with Pete right behind him.

Pete ducked to enter the cabin, then stood upright. As he did, he was immediately accosted by a tiny woman with closely cropped dark brown hair, whose hazel eyes flashed a challenge as she stood blocking his path.

"Badge and I.D. please," she barked, and he raised an eyebrow but complied.

She reviewed them carefully then returned them, pivoted, and wrote the third passenger a note. When she held up her notebook, Pete's eyes moved to the woman being shown the message.

He only barely stopped his jaw from dropping open as his heart melted. Standing before him was the most beautiful woman he'd ever seen.

Pete stared, taking in her long, dark red hair and brilliant aquamarine eyes. He noticed her tall, willowy frame, the light smattering of freckles across her nose and cheeks, and her naturally long eyelashes.

And he felt his fists clenching as he also noticed the scrapes marring her milky white skin along her chin and nose. His rage built inside him to see the large and already bruising knot on her forehead, and

the pain and fear showing in those amazing eyes. He
was suddenly obsessed with finding whoever had
hurt her so he could strangle them with his bare
hands.

Swallowing down his unexpected anger took
every bit of self-control Pete Jenkins possessed, and
he knew at that moment that he would, without
question, be willing to die to protect her if that's what
it took.

"Ladies, this is Pete Jenkins with the U.S.
Marshals," Fuller announced. "He's taking point on
keeping you safe until this is over. Pete, this is Leah
Culverton, and Shannon Rivers."

Shannon, who nodded that she'd seen Leah's
message, stepped forward and held out her hand.

"Pleased to meet you," she said quietly, and the
touch of her skin against his sent a vibration
throughout Pete's system.

He watched her eyes go wide for a moment, and
thought to himself *did she feel that, too?*

Get it together, dude, you're on the job, he
reminded himself, and murmured, "Likewise," before
reluctantly letting go of her hand.

CHAPTER FOUR

Shannon just managed to stifle a gasp of surprise. The moment she'd locked eyes with the stranger she'd felt her pulse quicken.

He's tall, over six feet for sure. And built. Those blue eyes of his are amazing, she'd thought to herself before she could help it. *I want to run my fingers through that coal-black hair...*

Seriously? Now is not the time, girl! Get a grip!

She'd inwardly focused on restoring her heart rate to a reasonable level, then stepped forward with much more confidence than she felt, greeted him, and offered to shake hands.

His large, strong hand had wrapped warmly around hers, and the sensation of electricity sparking between them had almost buckled her knees. Next came the realization that something big and unexpected and, well, *intense* was happening, and it made her eyes widen.

She saw a flash of something – *recognition? acknowledgement?* - in his arctic blue eyes as well, then watched it disappear as he shuttered away whatever he was thinking.

His lips moved, saying something in a voice that she just *knew* would have made her pulse ratchet up again if she could hear it, then pulled his hand back.

He paused, then spoke again, this time to Agent Fuller. "We should get going. It's about a forty-minute drive. Let me get your suitcases."

Fuller pulled the bags down from the overhead compartment, handing one to Pete and keeping the other.

"Let's go," Fuller said, gesturing with a wave.

***

He stood with his back to his visitor, gazing out across the downtown Chicago skyline as he willed his temper into submission.

"Let me get this straight," he stated, his voice hard as steel. "I asked you to handle it, and I trusted you to understand the need to keep it very low-key; a burglary gone wrong. Something that happens by the thousands in this city every year, so that it won't stand out. But you? *You* opt for a car bomb. *One of the most public ways possible to handle my private business.* Do I have that right, Charlie?"

Charlie's reflection in the glass confirmed his visitor swallowed hard before answering.

"Yes, sir. I just thought – "

"And there's our problem, Charlie. You *thought*," he sneered, cutting the man off. "You *thought*, and the results made both last night's and this morning's news. Idiot."

He paused, rubbing his temples with his index fingers to try and calm himself.

"Did you at least manage to find the copies he made?"

A pause, then, "I grabbed all three laptops, and any thumb drives I could find, boss. Gabe is reviewing them all as we speak."

"Where is the woman now?"

Another hard swallow.

"I don't know, boss. Our contacts are looking into it."

"Don't bother me again until you have her location," came the brusque command, and Charlie gratefully fled the room.

***

Boy, he's pissed, Charlie admitted as he waited for the elevator to take him to safety. *I'd better make this right, and soon.*

He pulled out his cell phone and dialed.

"What have you got for me?" he barked, then listened. "What do you mean you don't know? Don't tell me you don't know, man. I *have* to have it as soon as possible."

He frowned as his contact spoke some more, and Charlie finished the call with, "I'm calling you back in four hours, and you'd better have something for me, or we're *both* in deep trouble."

Frustrated, he shoved his phone into his pocket, stepped into the open elevator and stabbed the button for the lobby.

***

The man in charge sighed.

Charlie's been with me a lot of years, and he's never, ever screwed up like this, the part of his brain that placed a high value on loyalty pointed out.

Then the all-business, self-preservation side kicked in.

Yeah, but this? This is huge, and you know it. He might as well have taken out a billboard ad inviting the Feds to waltz right in and crawl all over us.

He sighed again as he made his decision, then pivoted and strode over to his desk. He snatched up the phone receiver, punched in a set of numbers, and waited.

"Hey," he said when the person he sought answered. "I'm going to need you to plan a retirement party."

A few carefully phrased instructions later, Archibald Creach, the founding partner of Creach & Langford, smiled like a well-fed cat as he set the receiver back into its cradle.

***

"Hey, can we stop at a pharmacy somewhere along the way? We need to pick up some things," Fuller told Pete as the four of them climbed into his crew-cab truck.

"Yeah, we can do that," Pete confirmed.

Within twenty minutes, they had the supplies Leah had mentioned, and were on the way to what would pass for home for the foreseeable future.

"I called and made sure it was stocked up with food," Pete mentioned. "Another marshal should be out there already, and you can catch a ride back to your plane from him. I assume you're not staying, right?"

"That's right," Fuller confirmed. "I need to get back, get up to speed on evidence collected from the bombing."

In the back seat, Shannon sat quietly, oblivious to the conversation, and contented herself with gazing sleepily out the window. The surge of adrenaline that had carried her through most of the prior night's events was long gone, and she had every intention of taking a nap as soon as it was safe to do so.

She perked up slightly as the truck turned right, off the asphalt road and onto gravel, then traveled up a slight slope.

Pete pulled up in front of the structure and put the truck in park.

"Here we are," he announced.

It was a small but lovingly kept old farmhouse about eight miles north of the Decatur, Texas city limits. The farmhouse sat at the top of a small hill, about one hundred yards from the narrow farm-to-market road that led back into town. It was flanked on three sides by a grove of trees, and the nearest neighbor was just over a half-mile away, which provided some additional privacy, as well.

Pete climbed out of his truck, opened Shannon's door, and frowned when he saw how exhausted she looked.

"Need help?" he said, and she pointed to her ears and shook her head.

Puzzled, he looked past her at Leah, who explained, "The blast ruptured her eardrums. Doctor said it could be a couple of weeks before her hearing returns."

Come here, he gestured to Shannon, and when she climbed out, he gently scooped her up, marveling at the feel of her in his arms.

"Watch her upper back, she got burned," Leah warned him, and he adjusted his hold accordingly so as not to cause Shannon any more pain.

She was so worn out she didn't protest being literally swept off her feet. Instead, Shannon linked her arms around Pete's neck and laid her head on his shoulder like she'd known him all her life.

He fought back a smile as he carried her up the porch steps and through the front door.

"Hey, Duffy, it's me," Pete called out.

"Hey there," Duffy answered with a grin. "Good timing. I just got the groceries put away."

His grin faltered when he saw Shannon. "She all right?"

"Yeah, she will be. She's been through a lot," Pete said. "I'm about to go put her in bed. I think some sleep will do her good."

"She hasn't eaten since about six o'clock last night," Leah interjected. "Neither of us have. Stop walking around with her for a minute and let me ask her if she wants food first, or sleep."

Leah wrote it out and showed her.

"Food would be good, but I'm exhausted," Shannon answered, her head still leaning on Pete's shoulder. "Can it be something quick?"

"I just stocked this place with everything you might want for a sandwich," Duffy revealed, and Leah smiled.

"Perfect! I'll make her one, and then she can go lie down."

Shannon swiveled her head up to look at Pete just as he was glancing down toward her, and their lips almost touched before he stopped his forward motion.

It surprised her to feel disappointment that she had not just been kissed by a complete stranger.

"I think you can put me down now," she said softly. "At the table. And I can make it from there to the bedroom okay."

She was shocked to see disappointment peek through on his face too, briefly, before he composed himself, nodded, and set her gently on her feet.

So... he was enjoying that too, huh? her right brain crowed as she shuffled over to a dining room chair, surreptitiously scoping out Pete's left hand for any sign of a wedding ring.

UGH, the left side of her brain railed. *Really? SOOO not the best time for this. You almost got blown up last night, remember? Bad guys chasing you, remember?*

Focus!

Leah brought over two plates, each with a sandwich and chips, and Shannon turned her attention to her meal.

***

Whew, that was close, Pete thought to himself as he watched the fascinating woman before him dig into an oversized sandwich. *I almost kissed her right here in front of everybody... if I do that, I say 'goodbye' to any professional credibility at all.*

Yeah... but did you notice she looked kind of let down that you didn't *kiss her?* his inner voice pointed out. *Because I sure noticed. And I think you ought to remedy that the first chance you get.*

"Hey, Larry," Pete managed, in an effort to quell his internal struggle. "Step outside with me for a minute?"

"Sure," Larry answered, giving him a strange look before leading the way out onto the front porch.

"What's with you?" Larry asked, as they walked out into the front yard for a bit more privacy. "You seem... off."

"Yeah. I am," Pete admitted. "Um... Shannon... she's..." his voice trailed off.

"Just between you and me? I feel that way about the other one. Leah's feisty as hell, and I don't think she likes me very much. But I'm just... fascinated by her, is a good word for it," Larry confessed. "She's tiny, and fearless, and I'm in awe of her. Not that I'll do anything at all about it until all this is over."

"Yeah," Pete agreed. "Yeah. Gotta focus on keeping them both safe. Once this is over, then maybe." He shrugged. "Or maybe not. You know how it is in our line of work, man. Relationships don't last a lot of the time."

"The right ones can," Larry pointed out. "But for the moment, let's get back to business. You asked me why I didn't go through the marshals in Chicago. We have a leak somewhere, Pete. I don't know how far-reaching it is, and I just couldn't take that chance with these two. You and I have known each other for what, ten years now?"

Pete nodded. "Almost eleven, actually."

Larry grinned. "Yeah. So, I know I can trust *you* with all this. With *them*."

"So, what's the plan?"

"I'm gonna go back to Chicago and keep digging. I'm not working with a team on this one, Pete, so nobody but me should be contacting you, at all."

"And if someone else reaches out?"

"Then get Shannon and Leah out of here, as fast as you can," Larry urged.

"What's our code sequence? The usual?

Larry pondered, then nodded. "And the old place as the fallback?"

"Sounds good to me."

They shook on it, then went back inside.

CHAPTER FIVE

Shannon had managed to finish half the sandwich but was yawning.

"Come on," Pete said, and motioned to her. She nodded, stood, and followed him out of the kitchen and up the stairs.

He opened the second door on the left, then stood to one side to let her through.

This okay? he mimed to her and got a thumbs-up in reply after she'd surveyed the bedroom. He held up a finger to indicate he'd be right back and moved quickly downstairs to retrieve her suitcase.

"May I borrow a piece of paper?" he asked Leah.

"Sure," she said, and tore a clean page from her notebook for him.

"Thanks," Pete answered, and returned upstairs.

He entered her room, holding her suitcase up with a questioning look. She pointed at the dresser, and he set her luggage down gently on it.

Then Pete fished a pen out of his back pocket and wrote, *you've been through a lot, and you look like you could really use some rest.*

She read it and nodded.

Next, he wrote *I will be downstairs, if you need me.*

Shannon smiled and walked over to him. Before Pete could react, she'd wrapped her arms around his waist and tiptoed to kiss his cheek.

"Thank you," she said simply, then moved to the bed to lie down.

He set the paper and pen down next to the bed and was almost back to the door when she said, "Will you stay with me?"

Pete went still, his heart somersaulting in his chest. He turned slowly and walked back across the room, gazing at her, before he picked up the pen again.

I don't know if that's a good idea, he finally wrote.

Shannon read it, then turned crimson when she glanced up at his face again and saw the unmasked desire he couldn't hide quickly enough.

"I didn't mean... I just meant sit with me until I'm asleep."

They stared at each other for a long moment, and then it was Pete's turn to blush as he wrote *Oh. Sure.*

Feeling awkward, Pete sat on the edge of her bed as she took off her shoes and crawled under the covers. Shannon turned on her side so she could see him.

"Sorry I embarrassed you," she whispered, smiling back at him when he began to grin.

Hardly anyone I know manages to do that to me, he wrote, and showed her.

"Really?"

He nodded, then scribbled, *Get some sleep. You're safe here.*

She yawned, nodded, and blinked slowly twice, her lids heavier with each attempt to keep them open. On the third blink, she was out.

He stayed a few minutes longer, watching her breathing become deep and even, a sure sign she was heading into restful sleep. As he lingered, he fought and conquered a sudden, powerful impulse to gently stroke her hair.

Time to go, he told himself, and reluctantly crept out of her room, pulling the door closed behind him.

***

"How is she?" Larry asked when Pete stepped back into the kitchen.

"Out like a light," he revealed. "Where's Duffy?"

"He stepped outside a bit ago," Leah said.

"Probably radioing in. Any more sandwich stuff? The one you made her looked really good."

Leah smiled and pointed, then swiveled her head back to Larry as Pete went to help himself to food.

"So, what's next, Agent Fuller?"

"Can you just call me Larry? Please? No need to be formal."

"Fine. What's next, *Larry*? We just... camp out here forever?"

"Well, hopefully not forever," he told her. "That's why I've got to go back. By now, the techs that pulled evidence from the scenes have at least *something* I can chase. I hope they do, anyway," he finished, running his hands over his face and then through his hair.

"What if they don't?" Leah pressed.

Larry looked at her and could only shrug.

"Seriously? We're just in some big random holding pattern, with no guarantee we ever get to have our lives back?" she fumed, rising from her seat. "Great. That's just *great*."

Pete and Larry exchanged raised eyebrow glances across the room, and Larry stood and approached her, placing his hands gently on her shoulders.

"Hey," he said softly. "I am gonna do everything in my power to solve this as soon as possible so you and Shannon can be out of danger, okay? Please trust me."

"I do trust you, oddly enough," she replied. "I'm just frustrated. I *hate* not being in control of my situation."

That earned her an ear-to-ear grin from him.

"Oh, Leah. You and I have more in common than you know," he said. "I can be a major control freak."

"I can attest to that," Pete said, after he swallowed the huge bite he'd just taken. "I just *knew* he was gonna get tossed out because of it."

"Tossed out of what?" Leah's confused eyes traveled from Pete to Larry. "You guys go further back than today?"

"Yep. We met the first day of basic training," Larry confirmed. "Did our whole stint together in the same platoon."

He looked over at Pete. "I've been looking at your hideous face for what, eleven years now?"

"You're no prize either, sunshine," Pete retorted, making Leah snicker while he took another bite.

Duffy strolled in a few minutes later and told Larry, "I'm ready to leave when you are, just say the word."

"Let's get moving, then," Larry said. "The sooner I get back the faster I can work this case."

Pete had just finished his last bite of sandwich, and was standing up to see Larry out, when a blood-curdling scream barreled down to them from Shannon's room. In a flash, Pete was around the table and up the stairs, flinging her bedroom door open.

Shannon was sitting upright in bed, eyes huge and glassy in a pale face, and was swinging her arms wildly to ward off whatever she was battling in her mind. Her right hand brushed against Pete's right shoulder as he sat on the edge of the bed, and she shrieked, recoiling in horror.

Pete gathered her carefully into his arms so he wouldn't touch her burns, then began to rock her, gently stroking her hair and murmuring to her even though he knew she could not hear him speaking.

Her screams turned to sobs as she clutched at him, taking comfort in his warmth.

"Is she okay?" Leah's worried tone carried from the doorway.

"Nightmare," Pete told her as he held Shannon close to him. "I wondered if she'd have any, with everything that's happened. Not to mention the blow she took to the head."

"That blow to the head is the *only* reason I'm not giving her a strong drink to help her sleep and not dream," Leah revealed. "She's a lightweight when it comes to booze, so it wouldn't take much at all. But the doctor said no caffeine or alcohol for a couple of days."

"I think she's awake now," Pete observed, as Shannon lifted up from his chest so suddenly that she almost caught him under the chin with the crown of her head.

"Wha...what's going on?" Shannon mumbled as she looked down at the muscular arms encircling her, then at the three people gazing at her from the doorway.

Leah stepped forward and grabbed the pen and paper from the tiny bedside table.

Nightmare, she wrote.

"Oh," Shannon said in a small voice, and she flushed scarlet all the way to her hairline as she wriggled her way out of Pete's grasp. "I'm all right, really. But thanks."

"I'll stay with her a while," Leah murmured to the men. "She'll feel less self-conscious if you three quit staring at her and move along now. Besides, I need to check her bandages."

"Guess that's our signal. Larry, Duffy," Pete said as he stood, "I'll walk you guys out. I need to get my duffel bag from the truck anyway."

***

"Did I yell?" Shannon asked as soon as the men were out of sight.

Leah nodded, and Shannon squeaked.

"Really?"

Leah gave her a sympathetic smile as she wrote *it's nothing to be ashamed of. You've had a traumatic experience.*

"Don't I know it," Shannon muttered, then her eyes lit up. "Ooh! I know! They have liquor around here, right? I'd be sound asleep in no time with some of that."

They do, was Leah's response on paper. *But the doc said no alcohol and no caffeine for forty-eight hours.*

"Seriously?"

Yep.

"Aw, man."

Leah laughed, then wrote *sounds like something I would say! That's the first time since I've known you that you've been bummed out about NOT drinking.*

Shannon chuckled at the comment. "I know, right?" Then she sighed. "A hot bath, maybe? As long as I don't get the bandages wet?"

Let me go see what we're working with, Leah scribbled. *I bet we can make* that *happen for ya, at least.*

"Thanks," Shannon said, her eyes beginning to brim. "I know being here sucks, but I'm so glad you came with me."

Love you, girl. Be right back, okay? was Leah's answer, and she left the room before she teared up as well.

***

"I'll be in touch when I can, Pete," Larry was saying as they walked toward the four-door sedan Duffy had driven out to the farmhouse.

"Here's hoping you find something useful," Pete replied, and they shook hands.

Duffy climbed behind the wheel, and Pete watched them head down the driveway and turn left back out onto the paved road. Then Pete went to his truck and grabbed the 'ready bag' he always carried with him for situations precisely like the one he now found himself in.

When he walked back inside the house, Leah called out, "Hey, bring in the Epsom salt, will you? I think it got left in your truck."

"Sure thing," he called back, and dutifully u-turned to go fulfill the request.

He came back in as Leah was coming down the stairs.

"Thanks," she said as he handed her the package. "I think this will really help her relax."

"It should," Pete replied. "I know it always does wonders for me. This place has a nice, deep clawfoot tub, too. Perfect for soaking."

"That's the plan, since I can't ply her with liquor to put her to sleep," Leah said, and grinned.

"Okay, so, I'm just gonna stay down here for a while," Pete advised. "Let you two have the run of the whole upstairs. I think there's a bathrobe or two in the hall closet, if she wants one when she's done."

"I'll check it out," Leah answered as she headed back up.

Pete moved to the couch and grabbed the remote, settling in for what he hoped was an uneventful afternoon and evening.

But his mind kept drifting upstairs to the woman with mesmerizing eyes.

CHAPTER SIX

"Oh," Shannon moaned as she sat down in the tub and leaned back a little. "This feels *so* good. I didn't realize how banged up I truly was until just now."

She turned her head to the side to look at Leah, who was sitting cross-legged on the floor, leaning back against the wall.

Comfortable? Leah wrote then showed her.

"Most definitely. I just wish I could sink lower in the water."

Your bandages start just above where the back of your bra would normally be, so, just don't go higher than that, is all, Leah answered via written message.

"Are the burns bad?"

They actually don't look too bad at all. I think if we do what the doctor said regarding wound care, they should heal up in a couple of weeks, came the answer.

"I'm lucky I didn't get burned worse," Shannon conceded. "Or over a larger area."

Definitely, Leah agreed.

Shannon's tone turned wistful. "I really wish I could hear. It's got to be getting old, having to write everything down for me."

Leah chuckled. *It's not so bad, really.*

Silence for a bit, and then Leah, with a mischievous smile, scribbled furiously for a moment.

So, her note read, *tell me ALL ABOUT how it felt being in Pete's arms* twice *in as many hours. He is so hot. And I think he likes you.*

"You think so?"

Leah nodded vigorously.

"He *is* cute," Shannon said, "but I am sure he's just being nice. I mean, he's charged with keeping us safe, after all."

Whatever. I know he's into you. I can see it.

"And?"

And? You lost your hearing, not your eyesight, so I know you've seen how hot he is. I say go for it!

"Have you lost your mind?" Shannon retorted. "There's no time for that right now. Way, way more important things to worry about lately."

She leaned back a little further and closed her eyes for a while. But Leah's prompting had started her mind down a very specific road.

Shannon sighed, and looked again at her roommate and best friend.

"What does his voice sound like?" she asked.

Girl. His voice is as smoking hot as the rest of him. If his voice were a drink, it would be twenty-year-old scotch.

Shannon read, then frowned. "No clue what you mean by that. Let's try it this way... What famous actor might he sound like?"

Leah contemplated the question, tapping the top of the pen against her bottom lip as she mulled it over.

Okay, I have it... think a mix of Liam Neeson and Daniel Craig – but American.

"Ooh!" Shannon's eyebrows raised. "So, like, a baritone?"

I guess so.

"Nice," Shannon sighed, and closed her eyes again as she thought, *I hope I get to hear it for myself soon.*

She soaked until the water was lukewarm, then pulled the plug. Leah helped her out of the tub, then helped her bundle into the soft, fluffy robe after her bandages were changed.

When Shannon ambled over to the mirror to brush her hair, she shrieked in surprise at her reflection.

In mere moments, Pete was knocking on the bathroom door.

"Leah, is she okay?"

"*Wow.* You heard that all the way downstairs? What are you, part bat?"

She could hear him chuckle. "I'm attentive, is all."

"Yes, she's okay. She's a little shocked right now," Leah told him through the closed door. "She just got her first look at the scrapes and bruises on her face."

Pete sighed in relief. "All right. I'll be downstairs," he announced, and Leah could hear him walking away.

Leah turned away from the bathroom door to look at a puzzled Shannon.

"What just happened?" Shannon asked.

That man has amazing hearing. Heard you yelp and came to check on you, Leah wrote.

"He did?" Shannon's nose scrunched up as she smiled. "That's sweet."

He is definitely into you, Leah penned next.

***

Pete resumed his place on the couch, trying and failing to pay attention to the television. He had to admit, even he was amazed he'd heard Shannon from such a distance.

Something about her, he mused. *All my senses are sharper somehow when it comes to her.*

He allowed his mind to drift along the direction it had been yearning to go, which was thinking about what might happen once all this was over.

Ask her out? Sure. Then what? Her life's in Chicago and mine is here, he pondered. *Not to mention my job. It's dangerous sometimes.*

His brain promptly replayed the last conversation he'd had with Molly, the woman he'd been seeing up until February.

I'm so sorry, Pete. But I can't do this anymore, she'd said. *Every time you go to work, I'm terrified you won't come back. I care about you... but I can't live like this. I thought I'd be okay with it, but...*

And I can't give it up, he'd answered. *Being a U.S. Marshal isn't just my job, it's my calling, Molly. It's my passion.*

So, this is it, then, Molly had said sadly, as she packed up the few belongings she'd kept at his place.

And he'd held his breath as she'd walked out his door, a single thought looping in his mind.

I guess I am meant to be alone.

From that moment, he'd thrown himself into his work even more fiercely, as a shield against the loneliness that threatened to consume him.

But if I'm honest with myself, he admitted, *the loneliness went away the moment I laid eyes on Shannon Rivers.*

The only question is – should I do anything about it?

***

"I think I'm going to try the nap thing again," Shannon told Leah. "If I'm not up by seven, come get me, okay?"

Leah nodded. *Either way, when you wake up, we'll figure something out for dinner,* she wrote.

"You got it," Shannon said through her yawn, and went to her room.

She considered it, then opted to stay in the robe and lay down on top of the covers. As per her usual habit, she started off on her back, then winced as she felt the result. Sighing, Shannon turned onto her right side, pillowed her cheek in her hand, and drifted off.

***

Downstairs, Leah settled in with a book in the overstuffed recliner, while Pete casually flipped channels from the couch.

"So," she began, and he glanced over.

"So... what?"

"What do you want to know?"

Pete's brow knitted. "About what?"

Leah laughed. "I get the feeling you've got a ton of questions about Shannon, but you're either not sure how to ask them, or you don't think I'll cooperate."

His left eyebrow arched. "Interesting. And how, exactly, did you arrive at all that?"

"Never mind how. My point is, I can see you're interested in her," Leah stated with conviction. "So, fire away. If you're out of bounds, trust me, I'll tell you."

"Are you always this direct?"

"Life's too short not to be."

"Fair enough," Pete murmured, and thought, *yep, she and Fuller are* made *for each other.*

"Here, I'll even get the ball rolling for you," Leah offered. "She's twenty-four, single, almost done with her degrees, and despite the circumstances of how it happened, I'm sure she's tickled to death to be back in Texas."

At his puzzled look, Leah explained, "She's *from* Texas. Shannon grew up down around Ennis. She just wound up in Chicago for school."

Well, well, would you look at that, his mind pointed out gleefully. *She's actually based down here. There's one obstacle out of the way...*

"Degrees? What's she studying?" Pete latched on to the most neutral of the data bits Leah had thrown out.

"She's a double major. Finance and Accounting."

"Interesting."

"Glad you think so," Leah grinned. "I myself would be bored out of my skull."

"Really? What are *you* studying?"

"Criminal justice and psychology," she said. "And nice try. But this conversation is about *Shannon*, remember?"

Pete's jaw twitched. "You're like a bulldog with a bone. You are just *not* gonna let this go, are you?"

"Nope. And you know why?"

Now he paused the TV to make eye contact.
"No. Why?"

"Because I think you'd be good for each other."

"How can you *possibly* know that? You two just
met me today," Pete pointed out. "Like, not even
twelve hours ago."

"Call it a hunch."

He waved his hand, even as his heart soared at
everything she was saying. "Here's the thing, Leah.
My job? It's not just a job. It's what I was *meant* to
do. And it's not the safest profession on the planet.
That's a lot of worry to put on somebody that you
care about."

She leaned forward and stared him down.

"Luckily for you, Shannon is used to that."

"What do you mean?"

"She has three generations of military and law
enforcement in her family, Pete. She knows all too
well what it means to put on a uniform or wear a
badge."

Timber! Pete's mind called out. *Excuse me, sir.
Am I mistaken, or is that another barrier you built
coming down?*

"Okay," he said grudgingly. "But here's
something else. I don't mix work and personal. *Ever.*"

"And I admire that. But it's not like you're gonna
be babysitting us until the end of time, Pete. I'm just
saying."

"Fine," he challenged, and turned the tables on
her by bringing up her and Larry.

Shocked and speechless, Leah huffed as she
opened the book she'd selected and began to read,
while Pete found himself with a lot to think about.

CHAPTER SEVEN

Shannon yawned, stretched, and looked at the alarm clock by the bed. *Six-thirty-seven.*

Got a good five hours in, she realized. *And I'm starving.*

Then she realized what had caused her to wake. A tantalizing aroma had made its way up the stairs to tempt her back to awareness.

She stood, stretched again, and moved to her suitcase to rummage for something to wear beside the robe. *Oh good, she grabbed it for me,* Shannon thought as her hand found a sleeve of her favorite oversized sweatshirt. She slipped it on along with yoga pants, pulled her hair up into a ponytail, and made her way downstairs.

"Something smells fabulous," Shannon exclaimed as she walked into the kitchen. "What *is* that?"

Beef stroganoff, Leah scribbled, then added *He's cute AND he can cook? Double bonus for you!* and smirked as Shannon turned red and mouthed 'stop it'.

Pete's back was to them as he busied himself at the stove, and Shannon focused on returning her color to normal before he turned around. She managed it, but only barely.

Then he turned to look at her, and she felt the heat creeping right back into her face when his eyes locked with hers. She saw his mouth move, and Shannon blinked to distract herself from the fact that she wanted to know what it would feel like pressed to hers.

He asked if you got any rest, Leah showed her as she nudged her with an elbow to get her attention.

"I did, thanks."

Unsure of what else to say, Shannon broke eye contact and made her way to the table. Pete plated her food and brought it to her, smiling softly as their eyes met again.

"Thank you," she said, and noticed the dimple that appeared when his smile grew wider.

***

Charlie settled into his seat over the wing, smiling to himself. *My guy came through, thank God,* he thought once again. *Maybe this will get me out of Dutch with the old man.*

His contact had relayed good news when Charlie called him back as scheduled.

"I think they went to Dallas," the man said. "I had to dig around in the system to find it. The lead agent is playing stuff close to the vest."

"You got someone down there you can reach out to?"

"Yes, I do. By the time you land, I'll have more information for you."

"Good work. I'll call you when I get to Dallas."

Then he'd walked into Archibald Creach's office long enough to say, "I've got a lead, boss. Need to fly out."

Creach had stared stonily for a moment, then finally answered, "Very well. I'm giving you one chance to fix this, Charlie. *One.* Understand?"

"I understand, sir."

Creach waved a hand in dismissal.

***

Dinner was over, the kitchen had been cleaned, and Shannon, having slept earlier, was wide awake.

She sat in the living room, contented and full, watching the movie on television that Pete had so thoughtfully turned on closed captioning for. Pete was stretched out in the recliner with eyes closed, and even Leah had turned in for the night, her seemingly boundless energy reserve finally depleted.

As he slept, Shannon had the luxury of studying Pete more closely while she warred within herself about her attraction to him. Pete's long, lean muscular frame was draped nicely in jeans and a button-down shirt. Thick, coal-black hair swept back from his face and trailed down just past his collar. A hint of five o'clock shadow lingered on his chiseled jawline. Long eyelashes framed what she already knew were the most beautiful blue eyes she'd ever come across.

Suddenly a vision popped into her head of her and Pete tangled together in bed, her legs wrapped around him, and his fingers interlaced with hers as he nuzzled her neck and murmured things meant only for her...

And her cheeks flushed as the living room's temperature seemed to soar.

This is neither the time nor the place to be having romantic thoughts, her inner matron intoned. *You're in danger, and he has a job to do. A distraction could get all three of you killed.*

Fine, the part of her brain where attraction resided chimed in. *But what about after all this? You're going to do something about it then, right? Don't you want to know what being with him would be like? Feeling that fantastic body of his pressed hard against yours? Running your hands through his hair as he kisses his way down to your...*

"Enough. Shut up," Shannon whispered to herself, then jumped when she saw Pete sit upright suddenly.

"I'm sorry, did I wake you?" she asked.

He shook his head and pointed to the cell phone clipped to his belt.

"Oh," she managed, alarmed at the expression that came over his face while he read whatever he'd been sent.

***

Pete was having one of the best dreams ever.

It was him and Shannon, walking along hand-in-hand on a long, deserted stretch of beach as the sun dipped into the water.

In his dream, he swept her into his arms, then leaned down and kissed her passionately before laying her down on the beach towel and undressing her slowly.

When his lips closed around her right breast, she moaned and arched her back, and when she guided him into her warm and waiting center, he could feel the tingle of their connection surge throughout his body...

Wow, his subconscious exclaimed. *I can feel that to my core.*

Then he frowned.

That's weird, why is it starting at my hip?

My phone...

The thought immediately jolted him awake, and he realized that his phone was indeed buzzing with a new message.

He lowered the footrest of the recliner abruptly and stood, noticing that Shannon jerked as he did so.

Note to self – no sudden movements around her if I can help it. She's still jumpy from the blast.

He plucked the phone from its holster, and his blood turned to ice as he read the message from a number he didn't recognize.

Hey, baby blue.

He stood, set his jaw, and typed back *Gone fishing.*

Pete whirled around, looking for Leah's notebook. He found it on the kitchen table and couldn't help but smile when he noticed what Leah had written to Shannon about him.

He's cute AND he can cook? Double bonus for you!

"Little matchmaker's working both ends," he murmured, and returned to the living room to communicate with Shannon.

She turned beet red when she noticed that he'd written just below Leah's last message.

Oh, good Lord. There's no way he didn't see what she said! she realized, horrified, and the twinkle in his eyes confirmed her supposition.

Then she went stark white when she looked back at the page and focused on *his* words.

Go wake up Leah and pack up your stuff. We have to get moving. NOW.

"Why? What's happened?" Shannon asked, her eyes huge with fright.

We've been compromised.

She nodded and bolted up the stairs, while Pete hustled out to his truck to retrieve the burner phone that he too had bought for emergencies, then stashed in his glove compartment.

He turned it on and sent *Sitrep and ETA?* back to Larry's unit.

Larry sent him the intel he had so far, ending with *he's on the flight landing at DFW at one-forty a.m., give or take. No telling if he has help down there. I'll be at Omega within seven hours, eight at the most. I'm in route now.*

Meet you there, Pete replied. *I'll signal when we're an hour out.*

Stay safe, brother, Larry fired back. *I'll turn the porch light on for ya.*

***

Meanwhile, a distressed Shannon was shaking Leah awake, then ducking as her best friend came up swinging.

"It's me. Leah, it's me," Shannon told her. "Listen, we have to go."

Shannon didn't need a pen and paper to decipher Leah's *what the hell?*

"Pete got a message, and told me we're compromised, and we have to move, quickly," Shannon relayed. "I'm gonna go pack up my suitcase. Meet you downstairs."

She moved swiftly to her room, wincing with discomfort as she added a bra to her ensemble, then switched out her yoga pants for jeans and a belt before she put on socks and her sneakers. She made sure the few things she'd scattered around – her brush, toothbrush, and toothpaste – were tucked safely back inside her luggage, then closed and fastened it to haul it back down to the living room.

Leah met her at the top of the stairs, and they walked down together to where Pete waited.

"You guys get everything?" he asked.

Leah said, "All good. Let's roll."

By seven minutes past ten, Pete Jenkins was steering his truck down the long gravel driveway leading back to the blacktop farm-to-market road. Instead of turning left to head back into town, he turned right.

"Guess we should have used the bathroom before we left, huh?" Shannon quipped.

"Tell her we'll stop somewhere in Oklahoma. And after that, you two might as well try to get some sleep," he instructed Leah.

***

By two-thirty a.m. Pete's truck was across the border into Arkansas and continuing east on US-70 for the next leg of the trip. They'd stopped at a twenty-four-hour truck stop in Hugo, Oklahoma for gas and snacks. When they'd climbed back into the truck, Shannon had opted to move to the front passenger seat, and Leah had promptly stretched her tiny frame across the back seat and was sound asleep.

"I can help with the driving, you know," Shannon told Pete as he turned the ignition key. "I may be temporarily deaf, but I can still operate a vehicle just fine. Besides, I have a feeling you need to be rested for what's coming next."

He grinned and gestured for the notebook. Shannon handed it to him, and he wrote his answer.

I'll take the help. How about we switch out when we get to Little Rock? I will wake you up, I promise.

"Deal," she said.

***

At around three a.m. a very pissed off Charlie Zavier paced back and forth, back and forth across the front yard of the recently vacated farmhouse north of Decatur.

"They must have gotten tipped off somehow," his point of contact repeated. "But it's all good, man. We can track them."

"And how do you propose we do that?" Charlie snarled. "They could be *anywhere* right now."

"Simple," Duffy answered with a smile. "I put a tracker on Jenkins' truck."

Charlie smiled. "Welcome to the club, kid. I had my doubts about you, being new and all, but you're all right."

CHAPTER EIGHT

As promised, just before they reached the Little Rock city limits, Pete pulled into a roadside rest stop and gently shook Shannon awake.

Follow the signs to head toward Nashville, and wake me when we get there, all right? he wrote and showed her.

She nodded and smiled, then exited the truck to make use of the rest stop's facilities before trading seats with him.

Leah yawned and stretched from the back seat.

"Bathroom break, yay," she said blearily, and Pete chuckled as she followed Shannon to the ladies' room.

His burner phone buzzed, indicating an incoming text from Larry. Pete glanced at the message and was dumbfounded.

Duffy? Seriously? Are you sure about that? he typed back.

Positive. He was mentioned by name, Pete. How far out are you?

About halfway.

Get a move on. Need to form battle plan as soon as you get here.

Roger that.

"Holy crap," Pete murmured, just as Shannon and Leah returned to the truck.

"What?" Leah asked him.

"Duffy. He's in Creach & Langford's pocket."

Leah stared in amazement as Shannon pleaded, "Will one of you please tell me why Pete looks majorly stressed out right now?"

Leah grabbed the notebook from the front seat console.

Duffy's in with the bad guys, she wrote.

"Great. That's just great," Shannon remarked. "Now what do we do? Does he know where we were going?"

Pete shook his head no.

"Oh, thank God," Shannon said. "Let's keep moving, then. I'll drive." And she waved her hands to get them into gear.

Leah resumed her spot in the back seat, and Pete climbed in on the front passenger side.

"You still need to sleep, you know," Shannon told him as she clicked her seat belt into place.

He nodded, his mind racing. *Not sure how successful I will be at that, but she's right. I need to at least try.*

"So, you two switch places. Leah up front, you stretch out in the back," she commanded, and raised an eyebrow when he opened his mouth to start to protest. "Now."

Pete started to argue, then thought better of it.

"Here," he said, handing Leah the burner phone as they traded places. "Fill Larry in. I'm going to try to sleep."

Shannon pulled out of the rest stop and quickly gained speed as she got back out on the road toward their destination. Leah, nicely settled into the front seat, opted to entertain herself by texting an update to Larry.

In the meantime, Pete stretched out as much as he comfortably could, given his height, and began to scheme as they continued to tick off the miles. Before twenty minutes had passed, he was sound asleep.

***

"Where are they now?" Charlie demanded.

"Just a second...and... yeah, heading east out of Little Rock," Duffy confirmed.

"Let's roll," Charlie urged.

"Why? I say we wait for them to stop moving," Duffy suggested. "Once they do, we'll know *precisely* where to hone in. There's no point in *us* moving around until *they* stop. They could change direction at any time."

Charlie reined in his temper enough to consider that the kid had a valid point.

"All right," he muttered. "But the moment that dot stays in the same place for longer than forty-five minutes, we're moving. Got it?"

***

Shannon delivered them to Nashville without incident, and Pete resumed the driving duties. He glanced at his watch as the three changed up seating positions in the vehicle.

"Four more hours, and we're there," Pete announced. Another round of bathroom breaks and a gas stop, and then Pete's truck rejoined the flow of traffic heading north on I-65.

From her position in the backseat, Leah relayed the latest update from Larry.

"He says he just heard Duffy is nowhere to be found," she read aloud, and Pete's grip tightened on the wheel.

"If he's in the wind, then chances are he's trailing us."

"How could he be trailing us?" Leah asked, as the scowl on Shannon's face revealed she wasn't happy with being left out of the conversation.

Leah scribbled it all down and showed her.

Suddenly Leah had a flash of inspiration. "Wait! Pete, Duffy went outside for a little while, remember?"

"Yeah, I remember."

"And you said he was probably radioing in. What if he put a thingy on your truck?"

"A thingy?" Pete smiled despite his best attempts not to.

"You know, a thingy, like you see in spy movies. A... what are they called?"

"You mean a *tracker*?" The smile left Pete's face.

"Yeah. A tracker."

Pete took the next exit, pulling into the first parking lot he came to. He slammed the transmission into park, got out, and immediately moved to the back of his vehicle.

Reaching his hand down under the back bumper, he frowned, moving from side to side.

"I don't feel anything," he murmured.

"Here, let me," Leah offered, and before he could stop her, she was on the ground, peering up underneath the chassis.

She whistled, took her phone from her pocket, and snapped a picture.

"What is that?" she asked, as she showed Pete and Shannon the photo.

Pete's jaw set like granite.

"That is definitely a tracker on my truck," he growled.

Shannon snapped her fingers then flung her arms out in a *what's going on* gesture.

Pete grabbed the notebook and wrote, *Duffy put a tracker on my truck.*

Shannon's eyes darkened as she finally completely lost her temper.

"I'm done with this," she exclaimed, hands on hips. "I'm done running, and I *refuse* to be afraid anymore. This is bullshit, and it stops now. So, here's what we're gonna do. We are gonna leave that tracker right where it is, so they can follow the signal. We are gonna go wherever it is you and Larry agreed on, and we're gonna set a trap for however many jackasses decide to show up."

I think I just fell in love with this woman, was Pete's immediate and heartfelt realization.

"You two with me?" Shannon challenged.

A thumbs-up was the reply she got from each of them.

"Good."

They climbed back into the truck with Pete behind the wheel. As he navigated back to the interstate, Leah typed furiously to pass the new battle plan on to Larry.

***

By five p.m. Pete was turning onto the county road that would lead them most of the way to the farm. Four miles down, he took a sharp left onto the narrow strip of gravel that wound its way two miles further back before ending in front of a small cabin.

Larry stood grinning at them from the front porch as he watched them park and climb out of the truck.

"So, the little creep tagged your truck, huh?" Larry quipped as he stepped forward to help grab their bags.

"Yeah," Pete said. "I definitely owe him one."

Shannon stood for a moment, taking in the landscape.

"This will be perfect," she observed. "One way in and out. We can pin them down, make sure they can't leave." And she walked away toward the cabin.

Larry's eyebrows raised. "O...kay... I am loving her attitude. Where did it come from?"

"She's pissed," Leah volunteered, a huge grin on her face. "Those guys won't know what hit 'em. They messed with the wrong woman."

"I thought *you* were the feisty one," Larry teased.

"Oh, no, we both are," Leah corrected him. "I just let mine out to play more often than she does. And it takes a *lot* to set her off. That's how I know these guys chasing us are in serious trouble. In fact, I almost feel sorry for them. Almost."

"Well, we most likely have an hour or two, at least, to get organized before our uninvited guests show up," Pete said.

"What makes you say that? How do you know that?" Leah asked.

"If I were the one tracking, I wouldn't bother chasing until the beacon stopped moving for a while," Pete told her, with Larry nodding in agreement. "Let's get inside, make some food, and line it all out."

"Way ahead of you, man," Larry answered. "The grill is nice and hot. The only thing I need to know is how everyone likes their steaks."

Within a half-hour they were gathered around the table with their plates.

"Here's what I had in mind. Tell me what you think," Shannon said, and all three paused to watch and listen to her. "I vote we go up into the tree line on either side of this place in pairs. Me and Pete on one side, you two on the other. Leave the vehicles right where they are, in plain view. Leave a couple lights on, maybe the TV, too. Watch and wait and let them come on in. They'll think we're in the cabin and try to ambush us, but the joke's gonna be on them."

"I like the way she thinks," Larry told Pete, then asked Leah, "You sure she's never done this before?"

Shannon guessed the question by the stunned look on Larry's face.

"You're wondering how I came up with all that," she stated, and Larry and Pete both nodded.

"There's a bunch of cops and soldiers in my family," she said simply. "I've been shown and told a thing or two over the years. Speaking of which, I hope you two have extra guns with you, because I was also taught how to shoot, and I fully intend to play offense, not defense, when these guys get here."

Leah laughed out loud at the way both men's jaws dropped open at the same time. Shannon noticed it too and grinned mischievously.

"So, did either of you bring any long-range stuff, or are we just doing this with handguns?"

In response, Pete stood and motioned for her to join him. They walked over to his ready bag, and he brought forth his Remington rifle and his extra 9mm semi-automatic pistol for her inspection.

"Nice!" Shannon said, nodding in approval as she expertly checked to make sure each was unloaded, then tested the sights.

"Those will do nicely. I don't suppose you brought night vision gear, did you?"

Yep, I love her, I'm sure of it, Pete's brain shouted triumphantly as he grinned down at her. *And as soon as this is over, I'm gonna kiss her, and I don't care who sees.*

"Larry," he called over his shoulder. "You still have the ATV's around here?"

"Of course, I do. They're in the shed out back."

"When is sunset tonight? We're going to want to be in place in the trees before dark, right?" Leah asked.

"That's right. We have about forty minutes of daylight left, so we'd better get moving," Larry announced. "There are two deer blinds already set up on either side of us in the tree line. I think they'll do nicely for this. Should be able to drive the ATV's right up to them but still have plenty of cover. And you can't see them at all from the driveway."

Leah wrote down what Larry said and showed it to Shannon.

"Cool," was Shannon's response. "Let's finish our food and go get in place."

CHAPTER NINE

"It hasn't moved in the last forty-five minutes," Duffy announced. "It's time to take a plane ride."

"You arranged a plane?"

"I have a buddy that's a pilot, and he owes me one," Duffy explained, as he dialed and waited.

"Mark? Duffy. Hey, I need a lift, man. You ready? Great. We'll meet you at Meacham in a half-hour."

He hung up and grinned at Charlie. "Let's go."

***

The quartet firmed up their plans, and Leah insisted on changing out Shannon's bandages before they traveled to separate sides of the property.

"All good," she pronounced, giving Shannon the 'ok' symbol.

They moved quickly out to the shed to liberate the ATVs from storage. As they did, Larry tossed Pete a walkie-talkie.

"Channel two," he said, and Pete nodded.

"Meet you guys back here," Shannon said with a smile as she climbed up behind Pete, hooking her arms around his waist.

"Wait," Leah told Pete, and rushed back into the cabin. She reappeared a few moments later with a pen. "I can't find my small notepad."

"Here," Larry pulled his out and handed it over.

"Thanks," she said, smiling softly at him, then pivoted and handed both to Pete.

"That way you guys can still communicate," she confirmed.

Pete grinned as he tucked both items into his shirt's breast pocket, then turned the ignition key. With a wave, he surged the ATV forward, and his heart thumped double-time as he felt Shannon's arms tighten around him. She let out a surprised and delighted *Whoop!* as he turned to take them toward the blind on the far side of the clearing.

Shannon looked back just in time to see Leah settle in behind Larry, throw her arms around his waist and rest her head against his back, and she smiled at her petite but fiery friend.

She's in good hands. And they look cute together, Shannon thought warmly.

She sighed, snuggling closer to Pete as they traveled along across the valley floor, and tightened her grip when they reached the narrow, barely visible trail that began to lead them upward at a steep angle. At one point she was convinced gravity would win out and they'd go tumbling back down the way they came.

But the anxiety was short-lived as the trail leveled out again, and she realized with satisfaction that Pete had brought them straight to the base of the blind.

He turned off the ATV and patted her hand to let her know to dismount. She reluctantly released him from her embrace and climbed off, standing to one side so Pete could swing his long leg over and dismount as well.

Pete hefted the ready bag across his shoulders by its strap, then gestured to her to climb up first. She paused, looking at the homemade blind with its steep wooden ladder leading straight up. By her estimation, the platform looked to be a good ten feet off the ground, and she felt her hands getting clammy.

Heights. Not crazy about heights, she admitted, and she started to mention it to Pete when she noticed he was holding out the notepad.

Don't like heights, do you? Don't worry, I don't either. We'll get through it together, he'd written.

"I was hoping it wasn't on a stand, I'll be honest," she confessed. "This makes it a little more... challenging."

Pete reached over and squeezed her hand in solidarity, and she was amazed at the way his touch both calmed her nerves and made her heart race all at once.

Smiling, she boldly stepped to the base of the ladder, took a deep breath, and began to climb. She'd gotten about four steps up, hugging the ladder tightly, when a protruding nail caught her swinging necklace at just the right angle and ripped the chain apart, sending the locket tumbling to the ground below.

"My locket!" she cried out, risking a look down to see where it landed.

Pete watched it fall and picked it up, holding it in his palm to show her he retrieved it, then gestured for her to keep going. She nodded and continued to climb, shaking slightly when she reached the platform. In moments Pete was beside her, showing her a note.

Did you know this thing opens?

"Really? No, I didn't notice that."

He scribbled some more, then handed her the notepad.

Who gave you this? You need to take a look at what's inside.

Puzzled, she examined the locket he'd placed in her palm more closely and noticed a tiny notch on one edge. Sliding part of her fingernail into it enabled her to open the locket, and she stared, stunned.

"That...that's a... *microchip*?"

Pete nodded.

"Robert gave me this," Shannon stammered. "At dinner, right before we went to the movie. Before the explosion."

Pete's next message was somber, as was his expression when she looked back up at him.

I think your friend was successful in getting those files copied after all. I think we're looking at what got him killed.

"We have to tell Larry," Shannon breathed, her eyes huge. "Like, *now*."

Pete nodded and keyed the walkie-talkie's mic.

"What?" Larry responded loud and clear, and Pete turned down the volume before he repeated himself.

"Keep it safe," came the clipped response.

"Roger that," Pete said, and put down the two-way device to write Shannon another message.

Tuck that locket away somewhere safe.

She nodded, closed it, and shoved it down into the left front pocket of her blue jeans.

"Are you okay?" she asked, noticing Pete's jaw clenching and unclenching rapidly.

He looked at her for a long moment, then wrote.

Actually, no. I'm furious that a so-called "friend" of yours put you in harm's way like this. If he were alive, I'd punch him.

"Surely there's a good reason he did this."

His reason doesn't matter. There was NO excuse to tangle you up in this mess. None.

"Pete, calm down. I'm fine, really," she soothed as she laid her palm against his chest and looked up at him.

There's no way I can wait until this is over, he realized, as he glanced down at the delicate hand whose touch made his heart surge into overdrive.

Pete looked into Shannon's eyes, then gently cupped her face in his hands, leaned down, and kissed her. She sighed, moving toward him, her eyelids fluttering closed as she felt the passion behind his kiss all the way down to her toes.

At long last he lifted his mouth from hers, grabbed the notepad, and wrote.

Does that *adequately explain why I'm upset?*

"Oh," Shannon murmured, then, "*Oh,*" in realization, her lips curving slowly into a warm smile. "Yes, I guess it does. But only if you do it again. You know, just so we're on the same page about things."

He smiled and pulled her into his arms, kissing her again, and she parted her lips to give his tongue access as she fisted her hands in his hair and moved even closer to him.

He trailed kisses down her jawline, down her throat, and she shuddered in his arms, gasping with pleasure when one hand snaked up under her shirt to caress her right breast.

"Yes," she whispered as he lifted her shirt enough to be able to duck his head and trace his tongue over her left nipple. She moaned with desire and could feel his breath against her skin as he growled with want.

Suddenly he stood upright again, gently lowering her shirt, and Shannon breathlessly asked, "Why did you stop?"

He stepped back, grabbed their source of communication, and wrote, *I want you, Shannon. Badly. But not here, and definitely not with you injured. I want us to do this right. I want you to be able to hear me, not just feel me. I want our first time to be spectacular. So, it's better if we stop - for now. But trust me when I say, I really don't like waiting.*

She read his note, then looked into his eyes.

"I agree," she murmured, her aquamarine eyes filled with passion. "Just so you know – I *hate* waiting."

He laughed.

Me too, he wrote to her. *But something tells me it will be well worth it – for both of us.*

***

Duffy's friend made good time in the air and was depositing his passengers at Blue Grass Regional Airport just after sunset.

"Another fifty or sixty miles to go," Duffy informed Charlie as he checked his laptop to verify Pete's truck hadn't moved in the last two hours. "Get us a rental car."

Kid better watch his mouth, he ain't running this show, Charlie grumbled in his head even as he walked away to do Duffy's bidding.

***

Shannon and Pete sat side-by-side, their backs against the wall of their tiny deer blind. Pete used a penlight to illuminate his words to her, and she softly spoke her answers as they waited in the dark for trouble to arrive.

He flipped back through Larry's notepad, grinned, and showed her what Larry had written.

Shannon gasped. "So, he's got a thing for Leah?"

It sure seems that way based on this, doesn't it?

"It does," Shannon agreed. "Well, don't tell her I told you this, but I know for a fact she's got a crush on him, too."

Get out. Really?

Shannon nodded.

Huh. I wonder if they're having as much fun in their blind as we are here.

She laughed as quietly as she could, and to Pete's ears it was the finest music he'd ever heard.

He thought for a moment, then shrugged, and wrote *Do you plan to stay in Chicago?*

"Nope. I *never* planned to stay up there," she murmured, enjoying the feel of his hand lightly caressing the back of her neck. "I'd always planned on moving home to Texas once I was done with my degrees."

You don't know how happy I am to hear that.

She smiled. "So, should I expect you to ask me out in the near future?"

Why wait? I'll ask now. Is it all right if I take you out sometime?

She giggled. "What day?"

How about all of them?

She swiveled her head to stare into Pete's eyes.

"Fine by me," she whispered, and kissed him.

***

"Showtime! Headlights coming this way," Larry's voice crackled through the speaker of the walkie-talkie, and Pete jumped.

At Shannon's questioning look, he pointed at the twin beams of light in the distance.

"Here we go," she muttered with her game face on, loading two magazines for the pistol as she watched the headlights grow closer.

"Half-mile out, at the most," Larry advised via walkie, and Pete chirped the mic once as an acknowledgment.

Pete handed her a pair of night vision binoculars as he loaded his rifle, then peered through the special scope he'd attached for nighttime viewing.

Suddenly Pete was snatching up the walkie and rapidly speaking into it, pausing to listen, and speaking once more before he set it down again and hurriedly scribbled on the notepad.

Shannon noticed his frantic movement and raised an eyebrow.

We've got a problem. That's Larry's great-aunt and uncle that just showed up. I have to get down there and get them somewhere safe before Duffy gets here.

"Here," she said, not missing a beat as she offered him the 9mm and its magazines. "Switch with me. I'll stay here with the rifle and cover you."

He kissed her, grinned, mouthed "I'll be back," and disappeared down the ladder into the growing black.

***

"Okay, four miles up, take a left," Duffy instructed from the passenger seat, and Charlie did as he was told.

CHAPTER TEN

It seemed to take forever for Pete to get back down to level ground so he could accelerate the ATV on his way to the cabin.

He came screeching to a halt near the couple, scaring the hell out of them in the process. The woman shrieked and ducked behind her husband.

"Lynda, Montie, hi. I'm so sorry I startled you. I'm Pete, Larry's friend from the Army, remember?"

"Good Lord, child, you gave us a fright!" Lynda exclaimed, one hand on her heart.

Pete dismounted from the ATV and approached them. "Again, I am so sorry for that. Listen, we have a problem. It's not safe for you to be here right now."

"What's going on?" Montie demanded.

"Bad guys will be here any minute. The kind that shoot first and talk later and don't care who they hurt," Pete told them honestly. "You can't be here."

A glimmer far in the distance confirmed his worst fear.

"As a matter of fact," he pointed past the couple, "I think they're coming in now. You need to hide. Quickly. Here, take the ATV. Is that other cabin still further back on the property?"

"It is," Montie confirmed.

"Go there. Now. I'll send Larry down to you when this is over, okay? Please. You have to trust me."

Montie went to the trunk of his car, pulled out a double barrel shotgun and a box of shells, and said, "Come on, honey, let's get going."

To Pete he said, "I'll make sure they don't get past ya," and winked. Then he handed his wife the shotgun and shells before climbing on to the ATV in front of Lynda and steering them out of harm's way.

***

From her perch in the tree line, Shannon could only watch through the scope as the older couple took off on the ATV. She swiveled back to the right to watch a new arrival approach, and her heart leapt into her throat as she realized Pete wouldn't be able to make it back to her side in time. The second vehicle was traveling much too quickly for that.

Breathe, and remember what you learned about shooting a rifle. You got this, she told herself, and made sure the butt of the weapon was properly cradled into her upper body.

She sighted in and waited.

Shannon watched Pete, the man who had captured her heart, as he turned on his heel and ran as hard as he could back toward her position. He was moving perpendicular to the car's path, using the darkness as a natural shield to cover his retreat.

He's gonna make it back to the trees, she thought. *He's gonna be okay.*

Then time seemed to slow to a crawl as the next events unfolded before her eyes.

Because Pete Jenkins ran out of time to get to safety.

Charlie swung his rental car hard to the left to avoid hitting the three parked cars, and Pete was as visible in the high beams as if it were daylight outside. As soon as he was silhouetted, Pete began to run in a zig-zag pattern, turning around occasionally to fire his pistol at the men shooting at him.

Shannon watched anxiously as he seemingly dodged every round. Then he turned yet again, and she saw him fly backward, then crumple to the ground.

No! Shannon's mind screamed as she zeroed in on Duffy, gun still in his hand, running to where Pete had gone down.

She said a prayer, took a breath, focused, and squeezed the trigger, taking out Duffy's right knee. His pistol flew from his hand as he collapsed to the ground clutching his leg, his contorted face in her scope proof of his screams carrying through the still night air.

She watched as Charlie also went down, presumably from Larry's rifle.

Fighting back a sob, Shannon flung the rifle across her back by its strap and hurried down the steep ladder, not caring how many times her motions sent the steel across her back crashing against her existing wounds.

I have to get to Pete, was all she could think.

She stumbled and almost fell down the length of the trail, but caught herself, and kept moving forward at breakneck speed. Some part of her noticed that although it was well into nighttime, she could see where she was going – the moon had opted to come to her aid long enough to get her to level ground. It ducked behind some clouds just as Shannon finally reached the flat, and she began to sprint through the diminishing light, crying, calling out to Pete as she went.

Motion off to her right caught her eye, and she veered that direction. It was Pete, who'd heard her yelling and raised his hand up to try and signal his position.

"Pete!" she yelled and skidded to a stop on her knees, running her hands over him to try to figure out where he'd been hit. When she touched his right shoulder, her hand was sticky and wet when she pulled it back.

She rummaged through his pocket for the penlight, turned it on, and gasped. Pete's blue eyes were huge and glassy, his face a deathly pale – he'd been shot somewhere around his right collarbone, and it was gushing blood.

"Hang on, baby. Hang on, Pete. You hear me? *Don't you dare leave me, babe.* Hang on. Help is on its way."

Over and over again she urged him to stay awake, focus on her, as she ripped the gun strap off her body, then removed her sweatshirt and pressed it to his wound to try and staunch the flow.

A hand on her shoulder made her scream with fright, and she jumped and looked up. It was Leah, with the cabin's first aid kit and a flashlight.

The moon reappeared, and now Shannon could make out Larry securing Duffy's hands behind his back with handcuffs. The fight had left Charlie the moment Larry had quite literally shot the pistol out of his hand. But just in case either one of the intruders got twitchy, Montie seemed to be taking great pleasure in leveling his shotgun at both intruders to ensure they remained cooperative.

Shannon saw the lights of police cars and ambulances coming down the long driveway toward the cabin, and she stood and waved her arms.

"Over here! He's hurt, please help him," Shannon screamed, then knelt back down at Pete's side.

He reached up and cupped her cheek, wiping at her tears with his left thumb. He gazed into her eyes and spoke to her, and she shook her head in frustration.

"I wish I could hear you!" she sobbed. "Oh, Pete, please don't leave me. Please. You promised we'd have *all* the dates, remember? No takebacks, Pete. Stay awake, stay with me, baby."

Two EMTs raced up with a gurney and gently moved her aside to work on Pete, while two other crews tended to Duffy and Charlie's gunshot wounds.

Come on, Leah motioned to her.

"I'm not leaving him," she said firmly.

Leah held up an index finger, then ran toward the cabin.

Shannon remained on her knees close to Pete's head, watching them work on him, sending up prayer after silent prayer for him to be all right. She was only vaguely aware of Larry and Montie speaking with the senior police officer on the scene, and Leah walking her direction with another shirt for her to put on.

"I can't lose him, Leah. I can't," Shannon cried, and Leah wrapped her arms around her.

When the EMTs lifted the gurney, she rose as well, and trotted right beside it to the ambulance. They started to bar her from climbing in the back with him, but Pete reached out for her, and they relented.

She sat to his left, the medic to his right, as the ambulance turned around in the grass, then sped down the long gravel driveway to get to the closest hospital as quickly as possible.

***

Larry and Leah arrived at the hospital about a half-hour after Pete's ambulance did. They found Shannon in the emergency room lobby waiting for word of his condition.

"They wouldn't let me go back there with him," she said, fresh tears streaming. "They made me stay out here, and they won't tell me anything."

Larry scribbled *We'll just see about that. Leave it to me!* on Leah's oversized notebook they'd brought with them, and Shannon managed a thin smile.

"Thanks," she whispered, and Larry winked before heading to the sign-in desk to raise hell on Shannon's behalf.

Within a few minutes Larry came back over.

Come with me, he gestured, and led Shannon and Leah to the elevator.

"They already took him into emergency surgery upstairs," Larry told Leah. "The bullet clipped Pete's brachial artery, and they've got to get in there fast."

Leah relayed the message to Shannon via her notebook, and watched, alarmed, as Shannon went pale and began to sway. Larry stepped forward just in time to catch her as Shannon's vision swam in an ocean of gray before plummeting into black.

***

When Shannon regained consciousness, she was dismayed to find herself in a hospital gown with an IV needle in the back of her hand.

"What happened?" she mumbled, blinking her eyes rapidly to try to focus them.

She turned her head to the right to see Leah's anxious face.

"What happened? Where's Pete?"

You fainted, and he's in surgery still, Leah answered.

"How long was I out? And why am I hooked up to an IV?"

About a half-hour. The IV is because you are a bit dehydrated. A precaution only, don't worry. Although, you did do quite a number on your burns, bouncing that rifle off them like you did.

"Where are my clothes? I put my necklace in the front pocket of my jeans," Shannon whispered as she sat up frantically.

Leah held up the white plastic bag containing her belongings.

Shannon nodded and exhaled a sigh as she leaned back.

"What's next?"

They're about to turn you loose as a patient, and you will get dressed then come upstairs with me to the surgical waiting room.

"Okay. Any word on him yet?"

Leah shook her head.

The nurse came by twenty-five minutes later to take out her IV and lecture both of them about taking better care of Shannon's preexisting injuries.

Leah listened politely, and then rolled her eyes and conveyed the gist to Shannon in a not-so-polite summation once the nurse was gone.

Shannon struggled not to giggle as she read Leah's creative writing. It was hard not to, given that Leah had led with '*Nurse Squeaky Shoes said*' and wrapped up with '*let's see how well* she'd *do in a freaking deer blind shooting at bad guys.*'

Once she was dressed again, Shannon walked with Leah to the elevator, and they proceeded to the third floor to reconnect with Larry.

It was another two hours before the lead surgeon came out to update the trio.

"A delicate surgery, very little room for error. But it went well," he told them. "He got really lucky. Two centimeters higher, and the bullet would have shattered his clavicle and shredded the artery instead of just nicking both. He may have some physical therapy he'll need to do to build strength back up in the muscle tissue that was damaged, but I expect Marshal Jenkins to make a full recovery."

When Leah relayed the surgeon's news, relief washed over Shannon like a flood.

"How long will he be here?" Shannon asked.

"At least a week, maybe two," came the response, and Leah once again passed on the doctor's answer.

"Can she see him?" Larry asked, pointing to Shannon. "This is his girlfriend."

"Sure, as soon as he's out of post-op and settled in a room."

Shannon beamed at this last statement Leah shared with her.

They thanked the surgeon, and once he'd left Shannon said, "Now what do we do? Pete's truck is at the farm, and he's going to be in here for at least a week. You have to go tie up loose ends for your case, right?"

Larry sighed. "Yeah," he said, nodding so Shannon would know his answer.

"So, how do we do this? I don't want to leave him, but I don't have anywhere to stay. And I've still got classes for another two months."

Actually, you do have a place, Larry wrote to her. *You're welcome to stay at the farm, Shannon. Lynda and Montie already suggested it, as a matter of fact. Said they could tell you 'wouldn't want to be far from your fella', as they put it.*

She smiled. "They're right, I don't."

And as far as your classes. If I can get you situated with a laptop, can you do your last two classes remotely for a little while? Larry asked. *Not forever, Shannon. Just until I can get the key players at Creach & Langford into custody. Two, three weeks, tops. Then it will be safe for you to go back to Chicago.*

"I think so. I'd need to email my professors and find out. I don't see any reason I couldn't. Leah, what about you?"

Leah looked at Larry. "When are you heading back?"

"Sometime tomorrow. Why?"

"Can I catch a ride? I want to get back, put my apartment back together."

Larry's gaze was unreadable. "Sure."

Shannon tapped Leah's shoulder. "What's your plan?"

I'm going to ride back to Chicago with him, Leah wrote. *Get our apartment cleaned up.*

"When are you leaving?" Shannon asked them.

Tomorrow, probably in the afternoon, Leah wrote.

Shannon's eyes went wide as she remembered, and she stood, digging her hand down into her pocket.

"Here, while I'm thinking about it. You're going to need this," she said, and handed him her locket.

Larry gently pried it open and gazed at the microchip nestled inside before looking at each woman in turn.

"I think with these, we'll have an airtight case," he said, and smiled.

"Excuse me," a young woman in scrubs said from the doorway. "We're settling him into a room now. Follow me, please."

CHAPTER ELEVEN

Two weeks later...

Shannon stretched and yawned, blinking as the morning light through the cabin window bathed her face in its warmth.

She'd spent every moment she could by Pete's side since he'd been settled into his room on the hospital's fifth floor – so much so that she knew, by name, every nurse on every shift that had helped with Pete's healing.

Pete's getting out today, she remembered, and the thought spurned her to joyful action, flinging back the covers and heading for a quick shower.

She checked out her face in the bathroom mirror. The scrapes and bruises were just about gone, and the burns she'd suffered had left little trace behind as well – Lynda had insisted on tending to them.

She retrieved a set of clothes from her suitcase, then turned on the water in the shower so it could warm up. She was just about to brush out her hair as she waited for the hot water heater to do its thing when she stopped short, stunned.

"I can hear the water running," Shannon realized, and laughed.

She powered through her morning routine and grabbed a set of clean clothes from his ready bag for Pete to put on before driving Pete's truck to the hospital to pick him up. She knocked on the door to his room, then swung it open.

Pete saw her and his face creased into the smile she loved so much. He immediately scooped up the notepad and painstakingly wrote, *Good morning, beautiful. I missed you,* as best he could with his right arm in a sling.

"I missed you too," she replied with a twinkle in her eye, trying to keep her secret just a bit longer. "How did you sleep?"

Pretty good, I guess. Ready to be in a real bed again.

"I bet," she said, and wickedly thought to herself, *I know I'm ready to have you in a real bed...*

But she kept her expression neutral and told him, "I brought you some clothes. Didn't think you'd want to wear your designer backless ensemble outside the building."

He laughed, shaking his head.

Mabel, one of her favorite nurses, walked into the room, hugging Shannon and greeting Pete with, "Good morning, Pete. You ready to get out of here?"

"I am beyond ready," he said. "Get this IV out of me, already."

Mabel chuckled, and swiftly completed that task.

Meanwhile, Shannon was trying her best to hold it together.

Sweet Jesus, he sounds sexy, just like I thought he would, Shannon thought, her body instantly primed for him, and she fought to maintain her composure.

"I'll be right back with your discharge papers," Mabel told him.

"Thanks, Mabel. I appreciate you," Pete answered as she left.

Shannon waited just a moment until the door shut again.

"So," she purred, a megawatt smile on her face, "*that's* what you sound like."

"You can hear me?" Pete stood, his face alight with joy, and immediately crossed the room to her.

"Every single sexy baritone syllable."

He wrapped his left arm around her waist and kissed her.

"Good. Then listen very, very closely," he murmured in her ear. "I love you, Shannon."

"I love you too, Pete," she answered, her heart flooding with joy as she wrapped her arms around his waist. "I love you too. And let me guess. Now we need to wait until *you're* all healed up?"

He leaned down and pressed his lips against the pulse point just under her jawline.

"I don't think I can wait that long," he growled. "Can you?"

"That would be no," she confirmed. "So how about you let me lead this time? I promise to be very, very careful with that right arm."

He stood upright again and looked into her eyes, a smoldering smile beginning to curve his lips.

"I'm intrigued," he murmured. "And *seriously* turned on by that."

"I can tell," she murmured back as she giggled, feeling his arousal pressing against her.

"Come on with that paperwork, Mabel," he called out. "We've got somewhere we need to be."

Shannon laughed.

"You wait right here," he told her. "I'm gonna get out of this damn gown."

He kissed her again, then scooped up the clothes she'd brought him and stepped into the bathroom to get changed.

***

Twenty minutes later, Pete had the papers signaling his freedom in his possession and they were heading to his truck.

"I'll drive," she volunteered, and climbed behind the wheel. "You need to save your strength."

The seductive look she threw his way sent his pulse into overdrive.

"Yes, ma'am," he drawled, searing her with a sultry look of his own.

To assist him with keeping his hands to himself while she drove, he got out his cell phone and called Larry.

And when Larry answered on the sixth ring, out of breath, he grinned.

"This a bad time?"

"Um... yeah. Can I call you back?"

"Sure. Sometime tomorrow, please," he said to his friend as he cast a glance at Shannon. "Tomorrow works better, actually."

She nodded, holding back a snicker.

Still grinning, he hung up the phone and looked her direction again.

"I think I might have interrupted something," he told her.

"Good for them," Shannon replied, then added, "and nice call, telling him to wait until tomorrow. Today, you're all mine."

The flames of desire she saw in his eyes when she looked over at him made her want to break the speed limit to get back to the cabin.

***

Pete was dismayed to see that Montie and Lynda's car was parked at the cabin when they pulled up.

"We have visitors. Guess we have to behave ourselves," he observed.

Her nose crinkled up when she said, "Yes – but hopefully not for long."

Pete roared with laughter and told her, "If it helps, honey, I feel the same way. They're sweet people, but I need some serious alone time with you."

Lynda stepped out of the cabin as they approached the door.

"Hey, Pete! Glad to see you back," she exclaimed as she moved forward and hugged him. "I was just dropping off some fresh towels and some groceries. You two are all set, and you're welcome to stay as long as you need. How's the arm?"

"Better all the time, Aunt Lynda," he replied. "Doc said no lifting, pushing or pulling for a while, but other than that, it's going along pretty well."

"Good! Well, I'll get out of your hair. You two need some quiet time alone together," she said, and winked, then left.

"My thoughts exactly," Pete murmured as they waved to her from the porch.

He turned to Shannon.

"After you," he said softly.

***

As they walked in, Shannon's hands felt clammy.

I sure talked a big game earlier, but now, I'm nervous as hell. And it's been so long.... what if I don't do something right?

Pete picked up on her nervousness.

"We don't have to do this now, if you're not feeling comfortable with it," he told her. "We can wait. The last thing I want to do is pressure or rush you in any way, Shannon."

"It's not that, it's just that... um..."

"What? You can tell me."

"Um... I haven't done this in a really long time," she admitted, flushing a deep scarlet.

Pete's eyebrows raised. "Oh," he said. "Well, I haven't either.... and I just realized something. I don't have any protection with me."

She went into the bedroom and came back with a small box.

"I... I... went and got these," she stammered, and showed him.

"Honey," he murmured, and closed the distance between them. "Only if you're sure."

"I'm sure," she told him softly, then looked into his eyes and felt her nervousness dissipate. "I'm sure. I want to be with you, Pete. Make love with me."

He reached out, took her hand, and led her to the bedroom.

***

Later that evening they sat in the hot tub on the back porch, watching the sunset disappear behind the mountain to their west.

Shannon glanced over and saw Pete watching her intently.

"What?"

"Just enjoying the view."

"You must be talking about the sunset. I'm just.... average," she said, and shrugged.

He moved toward her through the water. "You are most definitely not average. Let me prove it to you."

"Pete, your shoulder..." she began to say, but he kissed her.

"I'll be careful. Now then, where was I? Oh, I remember," he said as he placed his hands on her shoulders.

"Soft creamy skin," he began, as he ran his hands up and down her arms.

"High cheekbones, delicate features," he continued as his hands mapped out the journey he was narrating.

"Inviting, full mouth." He brushed a thumb over it.

"The most mesmerizing aquamarine eyes I've ever seen, with long lashes."

"Next, a supple neck." His fingers trailed down her throat as he continued, "and collarbones that beg to be nibbled on. Leading down to amazing breasts, God given, not too big, not too small."

"Slender frame into a tiny waist," he spread his hands around her midsection, measuring, to prove his point.

"Curving out into great hips. Toned legs," he announced, and noticed her breath hitching as his hands slid toward her inner thighs.

He cupped her and watched her head loll back, lost in his touch. He saw the passion ignite again in her eyes.

"I love the way you respond to me," he told her, teasing her with his fingers as he brought his left hand up to support her head. "I love the way you feel, the way you taste and sound, the way you tremble like you are right now."

Now Shannon arched toward him, breath coming in gasps as she rode the wave of feeling, her arms circling his neck.

"Let's continue this outside the tub so we don't drown," Pete suggested, and she nodded.

He stepped out, helped her out, wrapped her in his robe, then led her inside to the living room. Once she was lying on the thick rug in front of the fire, he opened her robe and pounced.

The flickering flames cast their shadows on the far wall as he teased her and tasted her before he filled her. The pace was slow and languid, their bodies relaxed, floating in the feelings of just being one. Reaching the peak was both exhilarating and deeply peaceful, an understood and expected bliss between them, and she sighed with pleasure, fulfilled.

As they lay together afterward, her head on his chest, Pete murmured, "Shannon."

"Hm?"

"Marry me."

She turned her head to look at him.

"Come again?"

He looked down at her, his eyes brimming with emotion.

"I'm in love with you, Shannon Rivers, and I want to spend forever with you. I don't have a ring to give you, but we can take care of that anytime you want. Will you marry me?"

She smiled, warm and slow, her eyes sparking with happiness.

"Yes, Pete Jenkins. I will marry you."

***

Seven months later, on the third weekend of May, Pete Jenkins and Shannon Rivers stood in front of friends and family and exchanged vows and rings. The beaming smiles on their faces when they were pronounced man and wife almost brought Leah, Shannon's maid of honor, to tears.

After a sweet, earnest kiss, they joined hands and walked back down the aisle as those in attendance clapped and cheered.

Read My Lips

<u>Leah Culverton</u> – Shannon Rivers' roommate and fiercely loyal best friend. A stubbornly independent and free-spirited soul, Leah takes orders from no one, least of all a bossy FBI man...no matter how attractive she finds him...

<u>Larry Fuller</u> – The FBI agent working to bring down a huge money laundering operation. With Shannon Rivers in harm's way, it's his job to make sure she's safely hidden until the bad guys can be caught. But he has his hands (and his heart) full when he meets her feisty roommate, Leah.

PROLOGUE

Leah Culverton had officially now seen it all.

She was standing in a triage room of the emergency department at Chicago Memorial, witnessing her best friend in the world starting to yell.

Leah's eyebrows hit their highest peak as she thought, *Wow. Shannon never sounds off like this.... I am so proud of her right now...*

In all fairness, it had been a very rough night.

It had started with Shannon's tenth date with a man she just wasn't into - and wasn't sure about how to let down gently - and ended with some sort of explosion.

"You need to tell him how you feel, Shannon," she'd said when Shannon had confided in her, then cracked a joke about tagging in to try to get the shadows out of Shannon's eyes. Luckily, it worked, and they'd laughed together before Shannon left.

Leah had settled in with a bowl of popcorn and five as yet unseen recordings of her favorite crime show, and was merrily entertaining herself when her cell phone rang at almost ten p.m. She'd paused her show and picked up her phone, noticing Shannon's number flashing on the screen.

"Let me guess. He didn't take it well, and I need to come and get you," she'd said.

"Um...," a man's voice faltered on the other end. "I'm trying to reach a Leah Culverton?"

"This is she," Leah had answered, frowning. "Who's this, and why do you have Shannon's phone?"

"Miss Culverton, my name's Danny," he'd told her. "I work at Chicago Memorial, at the intake desk. Your friend Shannon was involved in an... incident earlier, and she was brought here for treatment. She asked me to call you."

"I'm on my way," Leah babbled, then she'd hung up as she raced to put shoes on and grab her handbag.

She'd made it to the hospital in record time and barreled up to the information desk in the emergency room.

"You Danny?" she'd barked at the young man behind the counter.

"Yes."

"I'm Leah Culverton. Hand over Shannon Rivers' phone, and take me to her," she'd commanded, and he gulped and obeyed.

"This way, please."

***

Leah had been standing next to Shannon just long enough to realize her best friend's hearing had been damaged, and she had pulled out her notebook and begun writing.

Shannon had started to explain what had landed her in the emergency room, then stopped, staring over Leah's left shoulder at the doorway. Leah had turned to see what she was looking at, and almost froze in place.

It was a man, tall, built, with light brown hair and stunning blue eyes, dressed in a very well-fitting suit the color of night sky.

Wow, he's pretty, had been her first thought. But her protectiveness had kicked in as he drew closer, and when he'd said, "Miss Rivers?" it sailed into overdrive.

"Her eardrums got screwed up, she can't hear you," Leah snarled as she'd stepped directly into his path to keep him from coming any closer to Shannon.

"And *you* are?" she'd challenged, hands on hips and hazel eyes blazing.

"Easy, Miss..."

"Culverton," she snapped. "Leah Culverton."

"Miss Culverton," the man had said, and smiled, and Leah's heart had thumped in double-time for a moment when she saw his dimples and the way his blue eyes sparkled.

And when he'd offered his credentials for review, Leah tried her best to ignore the rush of attraction she'd felt when her fingers brushed his palm.

Not now, she'd chastised herself. *Focus.*

CHAPTER ONE

Wow, she's gorgeous, was Larry Fuller's first thought as he looked at Leah, followed immediately by *and, she thinks I'm here to hurt her friend.*

As a result, he made certain that his every movement was deliberately benign. Her petite frame stood rigid, angry, ready to battle to protect her injured friend, and Larry found it endearing.

She can't be more than five-foot-five at the most, he realized. *But she's fearless.*

Leah Culverton had already captivated him, and they'd met not even two minutes before.

Larry watched as Leah took her time and carefully reviewed what she'd been handed. Since she was so focused on vetting that he was who he claimed to be, he seized the opportunity to stare openly at her.

The dark hair worn in a pixie cut flattered her slender neck, strong cheekbones and sparkling hazel eyes with naturally long lashes. White teeth chewed at the full bottom lip that he suddenly longed to nibble on himself. She was a good six inches shorter than him, and it brought to mind a vision of lifting her up off her feet and into his arms to be able to kiss her properly.

He found that while he was totally okay with that idea, he was shocked to be having those thoughts while working.

At last, she arched one eyebrow, then nodded, and he schooled his face back into nonchalance before she resumed eye contact and gave his badge and ID back to him.

Within two more minutes, he was unwittingly the direct cause of Shannon Rivers' outburst.

***

"*Letting* you stay? *For the moment*?" Shannon said, and then veered out of orbit.

It was the first time in the four years they'd known each other that Leah had ever heard her yell, and it was impressive to the point of almost rendering Leah speechless. By the time Shannon was done, both Leah and Agent Fuller – and likely everyone occupying the two rooms on either side of them - were very well aware of her wish that Leah remain present.

Once she calmed down again, Shannon walked them both through the night's events, and Fuller just stopped himself from putting an arm around each of them to comfort them when Shannon talked about the car exploding.

Fuller could see both women were shaken up and uncertain what to say or do next, so he jumped in and steered the conversation, asking Shannon questions that would help her focus.

At one point, Shannon asked *him* a very direct question – one he wasn't quite prepared to answer yet. Leah swiveled her head to look at him, and he opened his mouth to deflect, but at that moment a tech came to take Shannon for an imaging procedure.

***

Leah stepped out into the hall to give them some space to work, and Fuller followed suit.

"I need to go get her some clothes," Leah said. "Whatever wasn't ruined from the blast they ruined here, cutting them off of her to treat her."

"Happy to drive you," Fuller said, and she cut a sideways glance at him, then shrugged.

"Fine, whatever," she answered in what she hoped was a solid 'I don't care' tone to combat the giddiness she felt when she saw him grin.

They walked to his car, and he held the door open for her before getting in behind the wheel.

"Where to?"

Leah gave him the address, and he pulled out of the visitor lot. They pulled into her building's lot fifteen minutes later, and this time she purposely bailed out of the car before he could make it around to her side to open her door.

They were in the elevator before Leah turned to him and abruptly asked, "So, do you?"

"Do I what?"

"Think Robert's car exploding was accidental?"

He held her gaze but remained silent.

She pressed the button for the fourth floor, and concentrated on the lights illuminating the panel, trying not to be drawn in by his presence.

At last, the doors opened, and she led the way down to her apartment. Leah rummaged for her keys as they walked, and she'd just pulled them out and stepped forward toward the lock when she found herself flung backward, and his strong, wide frame blocking her view.

"What the..." she started to say, but Fuller softly said, "It's already open. Stay out here."

She watched, partly fascinated and partly uneasy as he silently drew his weapon, then eased the door all the way open and slipped inside.

Leah realized what he was doing, and also realized that the direct line of sight from her front door was probably not the wisest place to be, so she stepped to the left, leaning her back against the hallway just beside the door.

Although he'd caught her completely off guard, she managed not to jump and yelp when his head suddenly appeared through the open doorway and he said, "All clear. Come on in but watch your step."

"Watch my step? That's just dumb! Why would I need to...?"

Leah's questions trailed off and she began to shake as she took in the view. A malevolent force had ripped her and Shannon's apartment to shreds. Everywhere she looked, something was smashed, broken, or otherwise vandalized. Immediately inside and to her left, all the kitchen cabinets were flung open, with broken dishes, spices, and cans and boxes littering the floor.

Four steps further in was the living room, where it looked like the overstuffed couch and recliner had simply erupted. Every single part of them had been slashed open and stuffing strewn everywhere. The entertainment center had been knocked over completely, breaking the TV screen as it fell, and their meager DVD collection lay scattered around the room.

She moved swiftly through the living room, picking her way around debris, then turned right to check out the bedrooms. They, too, had been torn to pieces; mattresses and pillows shredded, bureau drawers thrown haphazardly, closets rifled through.

And she went pale as she also realized *I haven't been gone that long. An hour, maybe two, tops. If I hadn't gotten the call from the hospital, I'd have been home watching TV when they broke in...*

Get it together. Don't lose it in front of the FBI man...

The idea of what might have been made her lightheaded, and she leaned against the hallway wall until it passed.

***

Leah's mind reeled as she moved on autopilot back to the living room where Agent Fuller was on his phone reporting the break-in. *What happened here? Is anything salvageable? Our renters' insurance will cover this, right? I hope?*

He finished with, "We'll meet you there," and disconnected, then looked at her.

"Is anything missing?" he asked sternly at just the wrong time and managed to push her buttons without even trying.

"Are you kidding me right now?" She twirled around, gesturing like a model on a game show. "Do you not *see* this? There's pieces of my couch everywhere!"

She scooped up handfuls of the stuffing material and shook them at him.

"Look at this place! I have *no freaking idea* what might be missing, because I'm too busy noticing that everything we own is destroyed!"

Two long strides were all it took, and he was in her personal space, hands on her upper arms, his jaw ticking with irritation. He pulled her so closely to him she had to lean her head back to maintain eye contact with him due to the seven-inch difference in height.

"Think, and focus. This is serious," he told her, his face within kissing distance of hers, his voice deadly calm in contrast to the raging storm in his eyes. "I need to know if anything is missing. *Now.*"

For a millisecond, she toyed with the idea of closing that distance, but her intense attraction to him was overwhelmed by her indignation at being manhandled.

Leah saw red.

***

"*Let. Me. GO,*" Leah hissed between clenched teeth.

Fuller immediately released her and took a step back, not knowing whether to feel more surprised at her reaction, or guilty at his behavior.

"Miss Culverton, I'm so sorry," he said tenderly, and meant it. "I should not have done that. Please forgive me."

She stared at him silently.

"Can you please just take a look around, let me know if you notice something's missing? Please? It's important."

"Fine," she snapped, still trying to rein in her temper. She took a calming breath and began to focus on her surroundings.

"Now that you mention it, I don't see either one of our laptops anywhere in this... mess. What is going on here?"

Fuller bit the inside of his cheek to keep from smiling at the sight of Leah, standing in the sea of ruin that once was a functional living room, with her hands on her hips like a tiny pixie warrior.

"I promise I will tell you more in just a little while," he answered. "But we need to get back."

"Wait a minute... This is all connected, isn't it? The car exploding, and then this... none of this is random. Am I right?"

He stared at her.

"Fine, don't tell me," she huffed, turning to move to Shannon's bedroom. "I'm gonna grab her some clothes."

***

"Hey," he called out, "pack enough for two weeks."

That brought her right back, not only out into the living room, but standing toe to toe with him again.

"*Why?*"

He pinched the bridge of his nose, then ran his hands through his hair in an obvious effort to align his patience level.

Good, she found herself thinking. *Why should I be the only one sick of this crap?*

"I swear I will explain everything," he muttered. "The condensed version is, she's not safe here, okay?"

"You think she's a target," Leah guessed, her eyes filling with concern.

His look was indecipherable.

"You're not sending her off somewhere by herself. I'm going with her."

"Oh, no you're not."

"I go where she goes," Leah asserted, thrusting her chin out in defiance.

"That is *so* not happening."

"Like hell it isn't," she snarled. "Hide and watch, mister. She's gonna need me. She can't reach the wounds on her back. Who's gonna change out her bandages? *You?*"

And the pixie warrior crossed her arms firmly and tapped her foot as she awaited his answer.

***

Holy crap. She's even more stubborn than me, he realized. *I honestly did not think that was even possible.*

I kinda like it.

He sighed and relented, rolling his eyes at her as he muttered, "Fine. Go pack for both of you."

"Thanks, that's more like it," she grinned, and started to saunter down the hall in victory.

"Miss Culverton? One more thing."

"Yes?" she called back, her voice dripping with sugar.

"We don't have a lot of time here."

"You're the boss, Agent Fuller," she said with an undercurrent of giggle in her tone.

Which was ironic, since they both knew all too well that at the moment, he was the boss of precisely nothing.

CHAPTER TWO

They were both quiet on the ride back to the hospital.

Leah sat with her hands folded neatly in her lap and a neutral expression on her face as she gazed out the window. She was trying her best not to think about how attracted she was to the extremely handsome man to her left.

And bossy. Don't forget amazingly, infuriatingly bossy, her psyche threw in.

***

Meanwhile, Larry was deep in thought about his two biggest problems, the first being how he was going to keep them safe in a very dangerous situation. But his brain refused to stay on task and was trying to gauge just how badly he'd damaged any chance of getting to know the fascinating woman beside him.

It chafed his pride as a federal agent to have to admit he was struggling with keeping those problems in that order of priority at the moment. He was in completely new territory. Leah was the first woman he'd looked twice at in years – and it was happening at the worst possible time.

Pull it together, dude, he thought to himself. *Focus and do your job. You're responsible for their safety. If you make a single wrong decision, it could get them both killed. Remember that. Save the high school antics for later.*

With an effort, Fuller shoved his concerns about Leah Culverton's opinion of him into a box in the corner of his mind – and padlocked it.

He pulled into the hospital lot, parked, and said, "Okay, let's get back in there," in his best professional manner.

But he couldn't help but notice that this time, Leah waited and let him open the door for her.

***

After Shannon was discharged from the hospital, the three traveled to Fuller's office. He gave her and Leah his take on what had happened to Robert, answering the shocked questions they each had the best he could as he went. More importantly, he impressed upon them the very real danger Shannon Rivers was in.

He maintained his professional demeanor throughout, but inside, his emotions were churning.

Being ripped away from everything you know, through no fault of your own... it's got to be really hard on them, he thought to himself, and vowed to get them back to their normal lives as quickly as he possibly could.

Once he'd told them all he knew, and answered the questions they had, the trio left his office to head to a small regional airport in the suburbs for their flight to Fort Worth, Texas.

On the drive to the airport, Leah asked abruptly, "Are you staying in Texas with us?"

"I will see you safely to your destination, but no, I can't stay," he answered, and gazed at her in the rearview mirror as he thought, *even though I'd really like to spend more time with you.*

He stared so intently at Leah that she finally blushed and looked away.

***

After they landed, the ladies were introduced to Pete Jenkins, U.S. Marshal, the man who'd be their primary guardian. Leah blocked his approach and demanded to see his identification. Only when she was satisfied did she move out of his way so that he could get close to Shannon.

And Leah immediately noticed the heat radiating between the newcomer and her best friend, and barely stifled a grin.

Pretty big fireworks going off there, she observed.

She felt Fuller, who was standing to her left and just behind her, staring at her, so she slowly turned to face him. He was focused completely on her, and Leah was shocked to her core to see tenderness in his expression.

Pete saying "Likewise" in response to Shannon's greeting pulled both Leah and Fuller back to reality, and the men grabbed the suitcases and led the way out of the plane and over to Pete's truck.

They left the airport, Pete behind the wheel, Fuller in the front passenger seat, and the roommates in the spacious back seat of the crew-cab truck. Which was fine with Leah and Shannon, because they used the notebook to gossip back and forth about the men in their company during the first part of the drive.

Don't look now, but I think mister FBI dude has a thing for you, Shannon wrote first, her face twisting into a smile.

Whatever. He's bossy. You know I don't do well with that! Leah had responded.

Whatever, yourself. He's given you some really, really steamy glances a couple of times. I'm deaf, not blind, you know. And you two are cute together.

He is SO not my type!

Shannon had to stifle a giggle at that one. *Let me see. He's tall, he's built, he's handsome, with a steady job, and he seems to have an actual personality. What did I overlook that's NOT your type?*

I'm not doing this right now, Leah shot back. *My focus is you, that's why I'm here. The fact that there's a pretty boy around doesn't hurt, but that's not what this is all about.*

Famous last words, Shannon wrote, and then their conversation was interrupted so Fuller and Leah could go into the pharmacy Pete had stopped at to get the medical supplies.

***

Later, when they arrived at the farmhouse and a tall, dark and handsome Pete scooped an exhausted Shannon up into his arms to carry her, Leah almost squealed with delight for her friend.

That's what she deserves. Someone who looks at her that way. Like she hung the moon, Leah thought, and it made her a bit wistful as she started to try to reach over the side of the truck bed and grab luggage.

"Let me get those for you," came a voice from her right. She swiveled her head to find Larry standing beside her, his head cocked slightly to one side and a warm smile on his lips.

I wonder what he kisses like was her next thought, and her eyes went wide as she imagined it.

"You okay?" he asked.

"Um. Yeah, fine," she stammered. "Just, you know... the suitcases."

"Again, let me get those for you," he offered. "Or would you rather climb up the side of the truck and try to reach them yourself?"

It was the wrong thing to say.

Ears back, she tiptoed and stretched as far as she could, grinning in triumph when her hand closed around her suitcase handle.

"Hah!" she grunted as she hefted the luggage high enough to clear the side of the truck. "One down, one to go."

On her next pass, she found she was only grabbing air. Undeterred, she stepped around him to move to the tailgate, lowered it, and clambered up into the bed of the truck to retrieve Shannon's suitcase.

"I would have helped you," he said softly as he held out a hand to her to assist her descent.

"I can handle things just fine by myself, Agent Fuller," she retorted, and ignored his hand and jumped.

"I have no doubt of that at all," he replied sincerely, and caught her off guard.

Feeling oddly pleased by his comment, she grabbed one suitcase and let him take the other one, and they followed Pete and Shannon into the house.

They walked in just in time to hear Pete say he was taking Shannon upstairs so she could rest, and Leah immediately stopped him.

Leah barked, "Hold still for two seconds and let me ask her if she wants food or sleep first."

When Shannon chose food, Pete gently set her down as Leah strode into the kitchen to make her something to eat. As she brought two plates of food to the table, Leah noticed the two men stepping outside, while Duffy, the agent that had been at the house when they arrived, moved into the living room.

The women started to write notes back and forth between them again as they ate, but Pete and Larry returned before they had a chance to delve into much of anything serious.

***

When Shannon and Pete went upstairs so he could show her to her room, Fuller sat down in the chair at the end of the table to Leah's left. He reached out and pulled the bag of chips within reach, then grabbed himself a handful of them.

"So," he began. "You think there's any way I can get you to just call me Larry, not Agent Fuller?"

"You're here on business, aren't you?" she asked, an eyebrow raised.

"Yep."

"Then no, Agent Fuller. I think we ought to keep it professional."

He laughed, and the sound warmed her soul. Leah fought very hard to keep her reaction to it out of her expression, but when she glanced at him, she lost the battle, and smiled.

Pete's interruption to ask for a piece of paper was a relief, and Leah tore out a clean page for him to use before closing the notebook's cover to prevent Fuller from seeing what had been said about him.

"So," she pursed her lips. "How long have you been with the FBI?"

"Let's see," he began. "I spent six years in the Army and applied to the FBI right after I got out, so... four and a half years now that I've been an agent."

"Have you always been in Chicago?"

"Nope, that's a pretty new posting," he told her. "I transferred to that office just under a year ago."

"Why?" Leah propped her elbow on the table and rested her chin on her hand.

The moment she asked, she knew she'd struck a nerve. His blue eyes darkened with emotion, but what kind it was precisely, she couldn't tell.

"I wanted a change of scenery," he muttered. And his tone made clear that the current topic was closed to further discussion.

Interesting, Leah thought to herself. *I wonder what that's about?*

She filed it away for a later time and started to steer the conversation back toward a more neutral topic, but he beat her to it.

"So, are you going to school, or working?"

"Both, actually," she said. "I'll be done with my Criminal Justice and Psychology degrees in the spring, and I work part-time."

"Nice," Larry answered.

CHAPTER THREE

Pete returning to the kitchen a short time later altered the trajectory of their conversation, and a screaming Shannon altered it again.

Leah was surprised at the speed with which Pete reacted. He was upstairs and opening Shannon's bedroom door before she, Larry and Duffy even made it to the base of the stairs.

The three skidded to a stop in the open doorway, watching, worried as Pete gathered Shannon up and tried to calm her.

"Is she okay?" Leah asked.

"Nightmare," came the answer.

I was afraid of that, Leah thought to herself.

"Well," she said to them, "I was gonna ply her with booze to help her sleep, but that's a no-go. She can't have any caffeine or alcohol for forty-eight hours due to the concussion."

Shannon woke up at that moment.

"What's going on?" she said, confused, and Leah could tell that everyone staring at her was making her uncomfortable.

Leah shooed the men out of the room and took point on making sure her best friend was okay.

***

Later, after Shannon went back to sleep, Leah wandered downstairs and into the living room. Pete was sitting on the couch, flipping through television channels.

Now's my chance to sound him out, see what might be going on between him and Shannon, she realized. She'd already had a similar conversation with her best friend as Shannon soaked in the tub, so Leah knew Shannon was interested in Pete but was trying her best not to focus on it.

Leah selected an intriguing title from the three-tier bookshelf, then parked herself in the recliner that sat at a right angle to Pete's position.

"Did Agent Fuller leave already?" she asked.

"Yeah. He was anxious to get back, talk to his lab guys."

He left without telling me goodbye. Really? That was rude...

"Huh," she said, then casually began, "So...", and proceeded to completely fluster Pete by talking about Shannon.

"Oh," he said when Leah mentioned Shannon was from Texas, and Leah held back a grin.

I knew it. I knew he was doing some weird 'this-can't-work-we-live-too-far-apart' thing in his head.

"Degrees?"

Huh. Leave it to him to seize on the least emotionally challenging thing I've said.

She answered his question, then swerved the topic firmly back over to him and Shannon.

"Fine," he finally snapped. "So now, let's look at you and Larry."

Uh oh, didn't think this through... She fought to keep from turning red.

"I have no idea what you mean," Leah said breezily, feigning a sudden deep interest in her reading material as her heart began to race.

"Oh yes you do. I think there's something going on with you two, as well," he retorted, and grinned at her obviously flustered state as he used her own phrase against her. "Call it a hunch."

She just kept her voice from squeaking as she shot back, "There's *nothing there.* He's bossy. And he's not even my type."

"*Now* who's in denial?" was Pete's parting shot before he turned his attention back to the television show.

Crap, she thought. Pete had definitely picked up on her view of Larry, all right.

But it doesn't matter, she told herself. *Even if he hadn't left, he still has a job to do. I just need to put whatever this is aside and get Larry Fuller out of my head.*

And even as Leah thought it, mental snapshots began to move in a carousel around her consciousness.

First up was the moment he'd first stepped into Shannon's triage room. The grin as he'd approached that had widened into a smile, revealing two perfectly placed dimples. The intense blue color of his eyes, and the surge of... *something* that had almost taken her breath away when he'd held his badge out on his palm and she'd made contact to take it.

Next, the apartment, as he'd physically shielded her once he realized her door was standing open when it shouldn't be. The rush of him striding forward and pulling her close to him, so close she'd had to look almost straight up to make eye contact. Seeing the wave of concern – *of worry,* she realized now – on his face at that moment was what had made her ache to kiss him.

Then it was the moment on the airplane, when she'd looked up and over at him and caught him staring at her in such a way that it made her insides flutter.

And finally, standing at the side of the truck, him with a slanted grin as he watched her every move. She hadn't been able to decide whether to punch him or grab two handfuls of his suit jacket and pull him down so she could plant a kiss on him. To her credit, she'd done neither. Then he'd completely surprised her with that softly spoken compliment.

She fought back a quiet chuckle as she admitted that although Larry Fuller could definitely be bossy, for some reason she found it exhilarating coming from him.

Which is so out of character for me it's unreal, she also admitted. *Maybe because I can tell he only uses it when he has to, and even then, it's for a purpose. It's not just to be a jerk, like my ex.*

Her ex.

Or as she liked to refer to him, 'The Dink'.

Ten months had passed, and her soul still bore some scars from that relationship. He'd tried his best to kill her independent, free spirit – and he'd almost succeeded. Because of The Dink, she'd built an impenetrable fortress around her heart, vowing to never let anyone get close enough to wound her heart – or attempt to commandeer her life - like that ever, ever again.

But Larry Fuller was wired completely differently – she could feel it to her core. His bossy streak wasn't borne of arrogance, or zero self-esteem, or sociopathic tendencies. His was rooted in a genuine desire to keep people he cared about safe. It made her want to dismantle some bricks from her carefully constructed wall and get to know him better...

And it clicked in her head.

That's what it is. Being around him makes me feel safe, and warm, and desirable, and just... really, really happy, Leah realized, and her eyebrows raised as it sank in.

"I think I'm in deep trouble," she whispered to herself.

"I'm sorry, what?" Pete asked, glancing over at her.

"Nothing. Thinking out loud," she replied.

***

Meanwhile, Duffy had returned Larry to Meacham Field to catch his plane back to Chicago. He said goodbye to Duffy in the parking lot and called his office prior to boarding to get a battle plan lined out once he arrived. Then he climbed aboard the jet, grabbed a bottled water, and settled into one of the seats next to a window.

Larry's plane had reached cruising altitude after ten minutes, and with nothing more he could do regarding the case until he landed, he closed his eyes and allowed himself to re-open that padlocked box.

Leah Culverton, he sighed. *She's something, all right. Tiny. Fearless. Gorgeous.*

Yes, all those things. And so much more. Tenacious. Loyal. Caring. Independent. Tough, but with a soft side, too.

Every single tiny piece that he'd learned about her so far just made him want to know more. About her family and her childhood. About her hopes, her dreams, her goals and fears. Even her favorite food, color, and flower.

I want to experience the way she kisses, and how she looks in moonlight. I want to see her dance, make her laugh out loud and watch her eyes sparkle. I want to feel her in my arms and make her moan with desire for me and me alone...

"I think I'm in deep trouble," Larry Fuller murmured as he gazed out the window at the clouds and wondered if Leah Culverton was thinking about him, too.

***

By the time Shannon woke from her nap, Pete was almost done with dinner.

"Wow, you cook?" Leah had exclaimed when he got up, moved to the kitchen, and pulled out a skillet and saucepan.

"I do," he confirmed. "You two like beef stroganoff?"

"Oh," she sighed. "That sounds so good! I haven't had that in ages."

"Coming right up," Pete said with a smile. "Grab the steak and an onion from the fridge, will you?"

A half-hour later, Shannon padded into the kitchen on bare feet.

You look rested. I'm glad, Leah wrote to her, and she smiled, sitting at the table.

"Something smells awesome. What is that?"

Beef stroganoff. He's cute AND he can cook. Double points for you! Leah teased with her notebook while Pete's back was turned, and Shannon flushed beet red.

***

While dinner was underway at the farmhouse in Texas, a tired Larry Fuller was standing next to a lab tech in Chicago.

Among other things, they'd managed to salvage a partial palm print from the burned-out hull of Robert's Mazda, and they'd lifted two more fingerprints from both apartments – Robert's had also been burglarized. Now, all three prints were being scanned in for comparison against the national database.

"This could take a while," the tech said. "Might want to go grab a bite and come back. Or I can call you if there's a match."

"I'll hit the vending machine, but I'm not going far," Larry answered. "Because we're gonna narrow the search parameters to Chicago and the surrounding area. Something tells me we're going to have a match sooner than later."

"Man. You're either really tired or you don't care about taste if you're settling for vending machine food. That stuff is legendary, and not in a good way," the tech retorted.

"Yeah, well. Perks of the job," Larry joked back, and headed down the hall to make what he hoped was a safe selection from the available choices.

Forty-eight minutes later, the tech turned to Larry and smiled.

"Got a match on all three, same guy," the man said. "Charles Allen Zavier."

"I know that name," Larry muttered. "Thanks. Keep working on the other pieces, okay?"

"You got it."

***

Ten minutes after that, Larry was in his office, at his terminal, calling up all his notes about Creach & Langford.

"I *knew* it," he exclaimed in triumph, and reached for the phone.

"Hey, boss," he said. "I've got a lead. I'm heading out now to chase it down."

But he was destined to be disappointed when he arrived at the last address on record for Charles Allen Zavier. Larry had no way of knowing, but the man he sought was the last-minute passenger who boarded the nine-fifteen p.m. flight out of O'Hare to Dallas-Fort Worth.

CHAPTER FOUR

The three sat down to their meal, purposely keeping the conversation light as they ate. When they were done, Leah insisted on clearing the table and cleaning the kitchen up while the other two settled in the living room. Pete leaned back in the recliner while Shannon got comfortable on the couch.

I'm beat, I'm going to bed, she wrote to Shannon and vocalized to Pete before she headed upstairs to the second room on the right, where her suitcase and a very comfortable-looking bed waited.

Suddenly exhausted, Leah changed into pajamas then crawled under the covers, and was sound asleep in less than five minutes.

Almost immediately, her brain began to play some very interesting scenes – her and Larry, laughing over dinner together. Her and Larry, walking hand-in-hand. Her and Larry, tangled in an embrace in candlelight as a light rain spattered against the bedroom window.

***

When Larry returned to his office, he found his lead IT man, Bruce, waiting for him.

"Hey," Bruce said without preamble. "You remember when you had me spike those files, so we'd know if anyone accessed them who shouldn't be?"

"Yeah," Larry answered, his belly growing heavy with dread. "And?"

"Lit up like a Christmas tree," Bruce revealed, and showed him the printout. "Every single one of your files on Creach & Langford has been accessed in the last twelve hours."

Larry scanned the report. "Really?"

"Yeah," Bruce sighed. "I knew you'd want to know."

"Same user ID?"

Bruce pointed it out, and Larry's jaw dropped. "*Him*? Really?"

"Really. I know. I was surprised, too."

Larry stood and put back on the suit jacket he'd just taken off. "Do me a favor," he said, and wrote Zavier's name down. "Check this guy out, let me know if he's booked any flights tonight. And let the big boss know you found the leak. I need to get moving."

"You got it," Bruce answered. "Be careful, man."

***

The first place Larry stopped was his apartment to change into more casual gear and grab his own, very meticulously stocked 'ready bag'. His combat kit – a sturdy duffel bag – contained, among other things, two walkie-talkies and a disassembled M-16 rifle with a night vision scope. He moved to his dresser and tossed a burner phone into the bag, as well as two changes of clothes.

Larry locked up his apartment, got in his car, and purposely drove in a random pattern to shake any tail he might have grown. Then he pointed his car southwest and drove to Bolingbrook, where he kept his four-wheel drive truck in storage. He pulled the truck out of and the car into his oversized unit, moved his bag to the truck, then rolled down and locked the unit's garage-style door. His work phone pinged, and he read the latest update from Bruce just before he pulled out of the storage lot.

Charles Zavier booked a seat on the nine-fifteen flight. Flight was delayed, left at nine-thirty-two. Two connections. He'll be in Dallas around one-forty a.m.

Larry checked his watch. *Nine-fifty-eight.*

"I hope you got a nap in, buddy," he muttered as he pulled up a new text window to Pete on his burner phone. "Because it's about to be a very long night."

He sent Pete the prearranged signal that trouble was brewing. Then he shifted his truck into drive and headed toward the meeting place.

About seven hours, he thought. *And it will take Pete twice that to get there, at least. But it's the safest place I know.*

***

Leah was in the midst of possibly the best sleep – and possibly the hottest dream sequence - of her life when she felt someone shaking her. Panicked, she came awake with hands bunched into fists, swinging wildly.

"Leah, it's me," Shannon soothed, and Leah dropped her arms and blinked rapidly.

"What the hell?" Leah managed.

When Shannon filled her in, Leah was instantly awake, tearing off pajamas to put on yoga pants and a t-shirt, and pulling on socks and shoes. A quick glance around the room confirmed she had all her things – she'd been so tired when she'd come upstairs that she hadn't even bothered to unpack. Within three minutes of Shannon waking her up, she was standing at the top of the stairs, suitcase at the ready.

***

By the time the women came downstairs, Pete had already used his burner phone to reach back out to Larry and get more information.

"Here's what is going on," he told Leah, handing her the notebook and pen so she could write it out for Shannon. "Larry sent me a code that means we've been compromised, and we're no longer safe here. Someone in his office told his main suspect in the car bombing where the two of you are. That guy is on a plane heading here as we speak. We need to get moving; we have a sixteen-hour trip ahead of us."

Leah scribbled furiously, then showed Shannon, and watched her best friend go ghostly white.

They piled into the truck, Pete and Shannon up front, and Leah in the back seat. Pete reached back, handing Leah the burner phone.

"Let me know if Larry sends any more messages, all right?"

"You got it."

They pulled back out onto the farm-to-market road, heading north to start their journey away from what had, up until that point, been a safe and secure location eight miles north of Decatur, Texas.

* * *

By two-thirty in the morning they'd crossed over into Arkansas. Both Shannon and Leah were sleeping soundly as Pete continued the drive toward Little Rock, where he and Shannon had agreed to switch places.

It was just about seven a.m. when he pulled off the highway into a rest stop, and gently woke both of them up.

"Time to switch out," he said, and Leah handed him the phone as the ladies went to the bathroom.

* * *

By seven a.m. Larry was roughly ten miles from his destination. Suddenly his work phone pinged repeatedly, signaling message after message coming in. He pulled over to review them. They were all from Bruce, and they were alarming to say the least.

All hell had broken loose overnight at the FBI's downtown Chicago branch. C.W. Picking, the third-in-command, had been taken into custody, and during interrogation admitted to passing information to a lackey connected directly to Creach & Langford.

During questioning, he also began to talk extensively about just how many people were in on the investment firm's schemes, naming participants as far away as Houston – and Fort Worth.

And there was other disturbing news.

Zavier's plane landed about fifteen minutes behind schedule, but we missed him at the airport. He could be anywhere by now.

Bruce's last text was *One name Picking mentioned was a guy with the U.S. Marshals, Larry. Some new kid named Duffy.*

"Holy crap," Larry muttered under his breath, and pulled out his burner phone.

Duffy's on the take, he texted to Pete's secure means of contact, then kept moving.

***

Pete handed Leah the phone after he'd confirmed Larry's messages and shared the latest news with Leah and Shannon.

"Here. Fill Larry in on where we are," he said, before stretching across the back seat to try to sleep.

Hmm... This could be fun, Leah thought, and smiled as she typed.

So, hi. It's Leah, she began, then continued *I guess I am supposed to update you. So here goes. Shannon is driving, Pete's trying to sleep, and I am staring out the window trying to be patient because I am beyond ready to be out of this damn truck. How's life there?*

***

Larry sighed with relief as he turned onto the barely two-car-wide gravel lane leading to the farm. As he slowed his speed to match the road conditions, he took careful note of his surroundings.

This will work well, he realized. *Only one way in and out, unless you're a mountain goat. Easier to see them coming, especially with the dust kicking up from the road.*

The farm was over four hundred acres, nestled between two mountains, and backed up against the Daniel Boone National Forest, an area strictly off-limits to anyone not employed with the Forestry Services. The property had been in Larry's mother's family for over four generations, and he felt confident that Shannon and Leah would be safe here until he and Pete could thwart the danger threatening them.

Leah, his mind echoed. *It's crazy how much I am looking forward to seeing her again.*

His burner phone buzzed just as he stopped in front of the cabin, and he grinned when he read the message.

***

In no time at all, the phone buzzed in Leah's hand.

Well, I was ready to be off the road, too, if it helps. I just got here, actually. How far out are you?

Just east of Little Rock, she answered. *But since I don't know where we're going...*

Okay, Larry responded. *You have another eight hours, give or take.*

Seriously? You guys couldn't pick something closer?

LOL, was Larry's response, followed by, *trust me the drive will be worth it. Not only is it beautiful here, but it's safe. I guarantee it.*

I just don't understand why you took us all the way to Texas in the first place, she wrote.

Fair question, Leah. Pete told you guys about the leak, right?

Yeah.

That's why I took you to Texas. The only one I knew I could 100% trust to keep you both safe is Pete, because I've known him for years.

"Makes sense," she murmured, then typed back, *Okay I get that. And I appreciate it.*

She paused, contemplating her next move.

So, what are you wearing? she asked.

Three dots appearing and disappearing cycled for close to a minute, and Leah grinned as she imagined the look on Larry's face while he worked out the safest way to answer the question.

Finally, she was rewarded with an answer.

...um...

Leah snickered, covering her mouth with her hand so she wouldn't wake up Pete.

"You are having way, way too much fun over there," Shannon said dryly from the driver's seat when she caught Leah's movements from the corner of her eye.

You don't know the half of it, Leah thought to herself.

Sorry, couldn't resist, she messaged Larry, followed by a smiley face.

You really asked me that? I thought it was Pete messing with me, he answered.

Now she did laugh out loud, albeit as quietly as she could.

CHAPTER FIVE

Leah had been spot-on in her assessment. The question had caught him completely off guard.

Larry read it, blinked, read it again, and then again, and frowned, trying to figure out if Leah had asked the question or if his old Army buddy was goofing around.

After several rounds of typing then backspacing, he finally typed the only thing he could think of that wouldn't land him in trouble and hit 'send'.

Then she responded with an apology and a smiley face, and he grinned.

"She's got a goofy sense of humor like me. Nice," Larry observed. "So here we go," and he began to type.

I thought about packing the gorilla costume for the week's adventures, but it's just so high maintenance, you know? I mean, it's hard to see out of the mask, and the material doesn't breathe well AT ALL. Gets really stuffy in that thing. So, I kept it simple. Jeans, boots, and so on. But I think it's very important to note for the record – I did stash the inflatable dinosaur suit in my bag, just in case.

He hit 'send' and waited.

Several 'rolling on floor laughing' emojis were sent his direction. They were followed almost immediately by, *it's a shame I didn't think to pack my tutu, you'd have looked fabulous in it!* and a picture of Jim Carrey in a tutu from *Ace Ventura.*

He roared with laughter at her response.

Yep, I can't wait to see her again, he confirmed.

A flash of inspiration struck, and he typed furiously.

Do you like steaks? I cook a mean steak.

Do you now? Leah responded. *I believe I'd like to test that.*

Done, he sent back. *By the time you guys get here, I'll be ready to put them on the grill.*

Still grinning, he put his truck in reverse, turned around, and headed back down the driveway toward the town of Ravenna on a grocery run.

He was back at the cabin in an hour, unloading enough food for three days – including steaks he'd had the butcher cut especially for him.

Once that was done, he typed *I am gonna try to get a nap in. Text if you need me* and sent it to Pete's phone.

Leah responded immediately. *I was going to ask you when you last slept.*

Oh, I don't know...I'd been up since five a.m. when I got the call about the car bomb, so...a day, or so?

Wrong. Forty-eight hours at least, by my calculation. Set an alarm and go to sleep, Larry. You need it, was her answer.

Yes, ma'am, he typed back before he did exactly what she suggested.

***

Leah was still giggling off and on about Larry's costume comments four hours later. Just before Shannon pulled over so they could switch out drivers, Pete stirred.

"What are you giggling about?"

She showed him, and he chuckled.

"You asked him that? That's *hilarious*. I bet it took him a while to respond, huh?"

"Yep."

"Yeah, Larry's got a great sense of humor," Pete said as he grinned. "Get him to tell you about him cracking wise while we were in formation sometime. It was epic."

"What happened?"

"Nope, I'll let him tell you. He tells it better. Let's just say I personally thought the extra pushups we all had to do were worth it."

***

He took her hand and said, "May I have this dance?"

And as he pulled her into his arms and they began to sway to the music, the light fragrance of jasmine she wore tickled his senses. Larry looked down at her with a warm smile.

"What?" Leah asked.

"Nothing," he replied. "Just enjoying being with you. You look beautiful tonight."

She blushed, glowing with pleasure.

He guided her expertly around the floor, focused completely on her, delighting in her giggle when he dipped her low without warning.

"Nice moves," she said, looking up at him through her long lashes. "Very nice."

"You think so?"

"I do," she answered.

"Well, then," he murmured. "Check this out."

And he gently lifted her and kissed her as the slow, sultry music drew to a close.... and began to ping?

What?

His brows furrowed together before he realized it was his work phone, which launched him to wakefulness.

He snatched the offending object up from the bureau and scanned the latest messages from Bruce.

Bad news, his IT man had written. *Duffy is off the grid. Fort Worth team went to pick him up, but they can't find him, Larry.*

The next message a minute later read *I cross-checked his name against all flights leaving DFW and Love Field in the last twelve hours. Wherever he went, he didn't fly there – at least, not commercially.*

"My money says wherever Duffy is, Zavier's with him," Larry observed to himself before he read Bruce's last text.

So, heads up, you might wanna include unexpected company showing up in your plans – B.

"Great," Larry muttered under his breath, and picked up the burner phone to warn Pete.

***

Pete pulled his truck back out onto I-65. They hadn't gotten very far when the phone buzzed in Leah's hand again.

She read it and frowned.

Just heard from my guy in my office, Larry had written. *Fort Worth crew went to go take Duffy into custody, but he's nowhere to be found.*

She solemnly relayed the message to Pete, and suddenly remembered something that at the time seemed innocuous. Now, with more context, it struck her as sinister. She voiced her concerns to Pete, and it led to them discovering that a tracking device had been placed on the underside of Pete's truck.

Shannon's temper unleashed for the second time in as many days, and again Leah found it amazing to watch, if not a little scary. The three formed a battle plan, and Leah communicated it back to Larry as Pete drove.

Hey, she said. *We're gonna bring the fight to them!* and proceeded to give him the summary of Shannon's rant.

Sounds like a plan. How far out are you guys?

Pete says about four hours. We just went through Nashville.

Okay. Get here safe, and we'll line it out.

You going back to sleep?

I'll try, he admitted. *No guarantees.*

Leah chewed her lip, then typed *I'm worried about you. You need to be rested. I have a feeling what's coming is gonna be huge and being tired won't help.*

"She's worried about me?" Larry said out loud as he stared at the screen. She'd stymied him with that statement almost as much as her playful 'what are you wearing' question.

I'm good, I promise, he finally typed back.

If I get there and you look tired, you're in big trouble, mister.

I'll try, okay?

Okay. See you soon.

Larry put the burner phone on the charger right next to his work phone and stretched out again on the bed, thinking about the dream that had seemed so real.

Funny part is, I have absolutely no idea how to dance, he acknowledged. *But for her, I'd definitely be willing to learn...*

He drifted back to sleep still thinking about it. His next dream of spending time alone with Leah was set in a dimly lit bedroom, watching her face come alive with passion as his hands and tongue explored her body.

***

His alarm went off at ten minutes to four, and he purposely set the water temperature to cold when he turned on the shower to help combat the erection his dream of Leah had caused.

Larry showered and changed, then prepped the potato packets and put them on the grill before turning his attention to seasoning the steaks.

A little after five, he glanced out the window and saw Pete's truck moving down the long driveway. He smiled, moving to the porch to watch them as they pulled up and parked.

"Hey, you," he told Leah when she walked up to the porch.

"Hey, yourself," she said shyly, and smiled, and his heart picked up its pace.

***

Ten minutes later, Larry and Leah were standing side-by-side at the grill, carefully placing steaks so that each would more evenly cook to order – medium for Shannon, medium well for himself and Leah. He'd put Pete's steak down first, since he knew from prior barbeques that Pete preferred his well done.

"Not burnt," Leah said of her preference. "Just, not pink."

"I heard that," he agreed. "I don't do pink in the middle, either. And now," he waved with a flourish, "now we wait."

He grinned at Leah. "So, do I look rested enough?"

She eyed him carefully and nodded. "Yes, you actually do. I'm glad to see it."

Silence between them for a moment, then Leah asked, "How long until we eat?"

"Half-hour, maybe forty-five minutes, tops."

"You mind if I take a shower? We weren't at the farmhouse long enough for me to get one."

"Go for it," he answered. "Fresh towels in the linen closet just outside the bathroom door."

Leah didn't know it, but he watched her all the way to the door while pretending to look after the grill.

***

"I saw that," Pete murmured as he approached.

"She's...something," Larry murmured back.

"Yeah. I really admire the way she looks out for Shannon," Pete observed. "You don't see that level of loyalty very often. Not to mention, I think Leah's got a crush on you."

"Do tell," Larry said, as he turned the steaks.

"She came at me last night telling me all sorts of stuff about Shannon, and how we'd be so good together," Pete divulged.

"Had your number, did she?"

Pete chuckled. "And how. She just wouldn't let it go – until I brought *you* up."

Now Pete had Larry's full attention.

"Really? Um... what happened?"

"Well, among other things, she turned red as a beet and stopped talking."

Larry's eyebrow raised. "So..."

"So," Pete echoed. "So, I think you've got a shot, from what I can tell. Just don't goof it up."

"Yes, Poppa," Larry smirked. "Speaking of goofing it up– what *is* going on with you and Shannon?"

When Pete smiled slowly, Larry grinned. "You really, *really* like her, huh?"

Pete sighed. "Yeah. I really, really do. Actually, I'm pretty sure I *more* than like her."

Larry clapped him on the shoulder. "That's awesome, man."

"I thought so, too."

CHAPTER SIX

Leah was humming to herself as she washed her hair.

We just met, and we weren't apart that long, but I really missed him, she thought, and was shocked to realize that instead of scaring her the way she expected it to, the statement made her feel warm all over. She sighed as she rinsed out her hair, then dried herself off and dressed.

When she stepped back out into the living room, Shannon was ready and waiting.

"You *glowed*," she told Leah once she confirmed the men were out of earshot. "You were actually glowing when you got out of the truck and saw him. Did you even realize you were smiling that big?"

You noticed? Leah wrote out. *I'm shocked, what with you being in Rambette mode when we got here.*

Shannon gasped, then laughed as she swatted Leah's shoulder. "I was not!"

You were too, Leah answered. *I wish you could have heard yourself. Very G.I. Jane sounding.*

"Yeah, well, nice try, but we were talking about *you*. I wish you'd just go ahead and admit you like him," Shannon told her. "I mean, it's not like it's not already obvious. And you *deserve* to be happy, Leah. Especially after what you went through."

You think?

"Yep, I really do," Shannon confirmed. "No one deserves it more."

The idea of letting someone else in scares me to death, Shannon.

"I know, honey," Shannon told her, squeezing her hand. "But I think Larry Fuller is unlike anyone else you've met, and I think you two could have something amazing together. You just have to be willing to step toward him and try."

Overcome, Leah hugged her tightly.

I'll think about it. Okay?

"Fair enough," Shannon said. "Now, let's go check on the guys – and the food. I'm starving."

***

Larry brought the steaks in on a platter and pointed to one. "Shannon, that's yours there," he said with a smirk. "You know, the one that's still half-raw."

Leah winked at him then wrote, *He said yours is the one on the left.*

They each grabbed their steaks and a potato packet and headed to the table. Shannon had already set out the butter, sour cream, and shredded cheese she'd found in the refrigerator.

"I've never seen potatoes done this way," Leah remarked.

"Yeah. They cook more quickly like this," Larry told her. "Dice them up and put them on some foil, put whatever seasonings you want in there, plus some butter, then close it up."

She took a sniff. "Garlic? Nice!"

"I didn't know if anyone else would want jalapeños in theirs, so I just did mine that way," he told her, pointing at the portion on his plate with diced peppers in it.

As the four began to eat, Shannon spoke up, telling them her ideas about how they could utilize the layout of the farm in their favor.

Larry could tell by Pete's demeanor that he was impressed. Larry was too. But the big surprise came as she announced her ability to handle firearms – and then requested one.

Leah had to laugh at the identical expressions of shock on the men's faces.

***

When Pete and Shannon stood and went over to his ready bag so she could see the firepower he'd brought, Larry leaned over and whispered, "Match made in heaven, aren't they?"

"I sure think so," she whispered back as she observed the topic of their quiet discussion. "Listen to her go. And look at his face as *he* listens to her. I can feel Pete falling in love from all the way over here."

Larry smiled. "Yeah. And it's so good to see that. I think he thought he'd always be alone after Molly left."

"Molly?"

"I'll tell you later," he murmured. "I'm just glad he found someone."

"Pete, alone?" Leah said, hand on heart. "That would have been so sad. Now I'm *really* glad they met."

She turned her head, and noticed she and Larry were leaning toward each other, their faces mere inches apart. She looked into his eyes, seeing something resembling – *interest? attraction?* She really wasn't sure. All she knew was that it was pulling her in...

***

Pete called out at that point, asking about the ATVs he knew Larry's family kept on the property, and the spell was broken; the chance for a meaningful moment of their own had vanished.

Maybe later, he thought. *After all, Shannon did make a point of saying we're splitting into pairs, so I'm about to get some alone time with this fascinating woman.*

I just hope I don't do anything stupid.

"Oh, I meant to tell you," Leah said, scampering back to emotionally stable ground as Shannon and Pete rejoined them at the table. "You were right. You do cook a mean steak, Larry. This is really, really good. What seasoning did you use?"

"Classified," Larry quipped, and winked. "I could tell you, but then... you know...".

She laughed, and he sighed to himself.

I love the way she scrunches her nose.

***

Pete and Larry were ready to take up their stations the moment dinner was over, but Leah was having none of it.

"Come on, guys. Walking wounded, remember?" she reprimanded, pointing at Shannon. "We need to change out her bandages before we all go traipsing through the forest."

She crooked her finger, gesturing for Shannon to come with her, and they went into the bathroom. Leah moved swiftly, applying the aloe vera then taping new bandages into place.

With Shannon's burns tended to, they joined the men outside at the little shed where the ATVs were kept. Shannon had just climbed up behind Pete when Leah realized that without a pad and pen, they wouldn't be able to talk back and forth.

She rushed into the cabin, and for the first time ever the size of her purse was a hindrance rather than a help.

"I know I've got a tiny notepad in here somewhere," she grumbled as she fought the urge to dump the contents out onto the couch.

Defeated, she grabbed the pen she'd found and went back outside, where Larry surprised her by offering *his* notepad to the couple.

Pete took the pad and pen, secured them, and took off, Shannon holding on tightly behind him and yelling with delight as they steered across the property to the far hillside.

***

"Uh oh," Larry said, as he felt Leah climb on behind him.

"Uh oh, what?"

"Well," he said, "Pete got going so fast I didn't get a chance to remind him."

"Remind him of what?"

"That the deer blind on that side is ten feet off the ground."

"Shannon doesn't like heights."

"Pete doesn't either."

"What about the one on this side?"

"It sits on the ground."

"Should we use the walkie, let them know, see if they want to trade?"

"They're halfway to it by now," Larry said. "So, you and I will take this side, and if they reach out about it, we'll trade."

Leah shrugged. "Works for me."

"Hang on tight," he told her as he fired up the ATV. "It will get a little steep."

He was just about to get rolling when he remembered that the notepad he'd loaned to Pete and Shannon contained some things he'd never meant for anyone else to see... in particular, thoughts that had popped into his head about Leah.

Crap.

Maybe they won't see those, Larry's right brain said.

Yeah, right, came the retort from the analytical left. *Pete is meticulous. He misses very, very little.*

He shook his head without realizing it.

"Everything all right?" Leah's voice pierced above the motor noise.

Larry gave her a thumbs-up, then started forward to take them to their assigned spot in the tree line.

***

Leah yelped when their ATV started upward at almost a forty-five-degree angle.

"You weren't kidding!" she called out.

"Nope," he called back, and Larry grinned as she clutched him even more tightly.

Holy crap, we're going to fall! Leah's brain screamed, and she barely kept that conviction to herself as they continue to climb upward. Just when she thought the angle would prove more than the ATV could handle, she felt the pitch coming back down to a more manageable level, and she exhaled the breath she didn't know she'd been holding.

"You all right back there?"

"Um... yeah, fine," she managed.

About ten yards further, and Larry swung around in a tight circle, then stopped the ATV and turned the motor off.

"We're here," he told her.

Oh, thank goodness.

Leah slid off the side of the vehicle and watched Larry pull his combat kit from the tiny rack on the back.

"After you," he said with a smile.

They opened the door to the blind and walked in. Larry set his bag down, pulled out the pieces needed, and had started to reassemble his M-16 rifle when the walkie-talkie crackled to life.

"Larry, you copy?"

Leah picked it up and answered, "He's right here, hang on a sec," then handed it to Larry.

"What's up?" he asked.

"Well, Shannon's necklace got hung on the ladder, and the chain broke."

"Sorry, man."

"No, that's actually a good thing. We took a closer look at her locket. It opens, Larry, and you won't believe what was inside."

"What?"

"A microchip."

"A *what*?"

"A microchip. And Larry? *Robert gave her the locket.*"

Larry and Leah looked at each other, stunned.

"Keep it safe," Larry told Pete. Then he set down the handheld device and looked back at Leah, immediately sensing that she was not okay.

"That.... *bastard*. Robert put her in danger. And he did it *deliberately*," Leah was seething, so angry she was shaking and on the verge of tears. "He made the copies of his own free will, and he *knew* what he was doing was dangerous, and then he *purposely* hid them in something he gave to *her*?"

She glanced up at Larry and saw the understanding and the empathy shining back at her in his eyes, and she began to cry.

"Why would he *do* that? I thought he cared about her. You don't *do* stuff like that to somebody you *care* about."

Without a word, Larry held out his arms and she moved into them. He held her tenderly, one hand on her back, the other stroking her hair, as she sobbed into his chest.

Stay quiet and listen, his instinct told him. *This goes beyond what she and I just heard. It's much deeper than that.*

Someone wounded her once, too.

CHAPTER SEVEN

Leah sniffled after a while, then tilted her head up to look at him.

"I'm sorry," she whispered. "I got your shirt all wet."

"It's fine," he murmured, and started to wipe her tears, but she flinched, withdrew from him, and did it herself using the hem of her t-shirt.

Seeing her flinch hurt his heart.

What happened to you? he started to ask but caught himself. *No. Don't force it. She'll share when she's ready.*

"I think I see lights," she said, sniffling one last time. "Are they here?"

Larry pivoted to follow where she pointed.

"Looks like it," he confirmed, and grabbing his night vision binoculars, took a closer look.

"Pete," he said on the walkie. "Headlights coming in."

To Leah he said, "You take these, and keep watching. I need to get the rifle ready," and handed her the binoculars.

He turned his attention back to his weapon and had it fully assembled and ready to use in under sixty seconds. He moved to the half-window opening in the blind and attached the night vision scope, then took a quick peek.

"Tell Pete they're about a half-mile out from us," he told Leah, and she got on the walkie and relayed the message.

"Now what do I do? What can I help with?" she asked Larry.

He grinned. "In my combat kit there's a box of ammo, and an extra magazine for this thing. If you could load that magazine for me, that would make things faster later."

"You got it," she replied, and got to work, grateful for the opportunity to focus on something else besides her embarrassment at crying like a baby in his arms.

She jumped as Pete's panicked voice came across the walkie.

"Larry, it's Lynda and Montie that just pulled up. I'm heading down to warn them."

"Send them further in," Larry answered. "They should be safe there."

"Roger that, I'm on it," Pete said.

"Who is Lynda and Montie?"

"My great-aunt and uncle," Larry explained. "Sweet, sweet people, with terrible timing to come visit. There's another cabin further back on the property, out of sight from our cabin. It's the best place for them to go."

"Can they not just leave completely? Wouldn't that be safer?"

"Zavier and Duffy could be here in three hours, or any minute," he answered. "There's just no way to know. The last thing I want is for Montie and Lynda to run into them, I know that much."

"How did they even know you were out here to come visit with in the first place?"

"My second cousin, most likely," Larry told her. "He waved at me when I was pulling into the grocery store parking lot earlier today."

"Ah," Leah said, and smiled. "Small town charm."

She held up the binoculars again. "Oh, I see Pete's made it to them. Your uncle's moving to his trunk?"

Larry laughed. "Probably to grab the shotgun he carries around. He's a laid-back man – unless you're trespassing. Then he can be hell on wheels."

Leah looked again, and chuckled. "Yep, the gun *and* a box of shells."

Then she gasped.

"Larry," she stammered. "There's more lights coming really fast. And Pete's on foot! Montie and Lynda are driving off on his ATV."

"I'm sighted in," he said solemnly, as he finished fine-tuning his scope's settings. "This is it."

"Here's your other magazine," she pointed out, setting it on the little windowsill beside where he had his gun resting.

"Thanks. Hey, there's earplugs in the side pocket of my bag. Might want to put some in. This could get loud."

"What about you?"

"Earmuffs in the main part of the bag. Bring them over, please."

She retrieved them and walked over.

"Hold still," she said. "And keep watching Pete. I'll put them on you."

Leah situated them for him. "Good?"

He gave her the thumbs-up symbol, and she grinned as she wedged the small foam-like pieces down into her ears.

Man, this probably doesn't even come close to what Shannon's been going through, she contemplated, noticing immediately that everything she could previously hear clearly now sounded like it was underwater.

She raised the binoculars again and watched, horrified, as Pete began to run, with the two men in the car both firing out their windows at him.

She watched Pete get shot and fall, and she cried out. His pursuers left their car and started toward him on foot. Then she heard a faint *crack* rolling through the air from across the valley, followed by a second and *much* louder one coming from the rifle six feet from her.

Hands trembling, she stayed the course and kept watching, and saw both men that had been firing at Pete were down on the ground.

"We've got to get down there. Pete's been hit," she heard Larry say as she pulled the plugs out of her ears. He took off his earmuffs, pulled two sets of handcuffs from a side pocket of his kit and led the way to the ATV.

"Here, hold this," Larry said, and handed her the rifle. They climbed on the four-wheeler, the rifle wedged between them, and Larry drove as quickly as he safely could down the steep incline.

"Lean back," he told her, and he did the same until they reached the valley floor where he could accelerate.

"Let me off at the cabin, I'll grab the first aid kit," she shouted, and he nodded, skidding to a stop in the gravel just long enough for her to bail off and hand him back his rifle.

***

She located the kit and a flashlight and was about to step out onto the porch when she shrieked in fright – a slender, gray-haired woman was standing in the doorway.

"I've called emergency services, they're on the way," the woman said as she held up a cell phone, and Leah nodded, and continued past her to head out toward where she thought Pete might be.

That must be Lynda, Leah thought almost in passing. *I'll have to introduce myself later.*

She could hear Shannon yelling Pete's name, and it broke her heart to hear the fear and pain in her best friend's voice. She turned on the flashlight, and following the sound, she located where Pete had fallen.

Leah touched her hand to Shannon's bare shoulder, and Shannon screamed in fright. Leah noticed that Shannon was using her favorite sweatshirt to try and stop the bleeding. She knelt beside her friend and opened the kit, sifting through its contents. She found three huge rolls of gauze and handed them over before starting to open the oversize cotton pads she'd also found.

She watched with tears in her eyes as Pete cupped Shannon's cheek and gasped, "*I love you.* I want to make sure I tell you now, just in case."

And Leah's tears spilled over when Shannon sobbed even harder because she couldn't hear him.

Please, God. Please don't separate them. They just found each other. Please, Leah prayed over and over again.

When the EMT crew arrived to work on Pete, she tried to get Shannon to come back to the cabin to put on another shirt, but Shannon refused to budge. So, Leah ran back to the cabin and grabbed a loose t-shirt that she knew would be comfortable for her and went back to hand it to her. She helped her put it on, then hugged her best friend tightly as Shannon completely fell apart.

Leah stayed with her until she climbed into the back of the ambulance with Pete, then watched as it raced down the driveway out of sight. She wiped her eyes and turned around.

Ahead and to her right, Duffy was being loaded onto a gurney by the second of three ambulance crews that had arrived. As she moved closer, she saw that he'd taken a round through his right knee.

She felt no sympathy. *Traitor, and a dishonor to the badge. He had it coming.*

Not far from him was the man she presumed to be Zavier from Chicago, also being treated by emergency personnel. His hands were cuffed together in front of him since he'd been shot through the right one.

She recognized his type all too easily and shivered.

Leah walked over to Larry, who alongside Montie was filling the local policemen in on the night's events.

"I'll be in the cabin. Let me know when you're ready to head to the hospital, okay?" she said softly, and Larry nodded.

She stepped onto the porch and entered the cabin. Lynda looked up from putting the last of the dinner dishes in the rack to dry, and said, "I've got coffee already made, unless you'd like some tea, dear."

"Yes, coffee, please," Leah said, and took a seat at one of the barstools at the counter. "Sorry you had to clean up after us. Things moved... a little quickly."

"That's all right, dear," came the warm response. "You all had your hands full."

"I'm Leah, by the way. You must be Lynda. It's so nice to meet you."

The next thing she knew, Lynda had moved around the counter to hug her as she began to cry.

***

When Larry walked in a few minutes later and saw them, he was immediately concerned.

"Is she all right?" he asked his great-aunt.

"I believe so," she murmured as she comforted Leah. "Just – a very eventful night, you know."

"I'm... it's just... a little overwhelmed, is all," Leah managed as Lynda stepped back. "I'm all right. Worried about Shannon being up there by herself, though. We really need to get going."

"At least get some coffee to go," Lynda suggested, and fixed two travel mugs for them.

"I need to head back to the blinds, get mine and Pete's gear," Larry said.

"You'll do no such thing," Lynda scolded. "Take your young lady and go check on your friends. Montie and I can handle bringing your stuff back down."

"Yes, ma'am," he said, even as he thought *my young lady... I like the sound of that.*

"You tell Pete Aunt Lynda said thank you. He got us out of harm's way."

"I will."

"And you tell that other young lady if she needs a place to stay, she can stay right here, no trouble at all."

"Yes, ma'am," he said, and kissed her cheek, then looked at Leah.

"You ready?"

"Yes," she said. "Let's get going. I don't want Shannon to be alone right now."

They climbed into Larry's truck, and he maneuvered around Pete's truck, Montie's car, and two police cruisers, then started down the driveway.

"So," he said softly. "*Are* you all right?"

She shrugged.

"You know you can tell me anything, right? Anything at all. I'm here for you."

Leah didn't answer, but she reached over and took his hand.

CHAPTER EIGHT

When they arrived in the hospital parking lot, she turned her head and looked at him.

"Not right now, but, later, I want to share some things with you. Okay?" Leah said softly.

"Anything you want to share, I'll listen," Larry answered as he gently squeezed her hand.

She slipped her hand out of his and waited, letting him walk around and open her door. Leah climbed out, and they moved side-by-side into the main entrance of the emergency room.

As they walked, Larry glanced over at her, and was amazed that he could almost *see* Leah shoving whatever tonight's events had stirred up back into the emotional Pandora's box within herself. Her posture became straighter, her face schooling into a determined set, eyes clear and focused.

Putting her game face on to be strong for Shannon, he realized.

They spotted Shannon immediately, sitting in a corner closest to the intake desk. She was staring off into space, holding a wad of paper towels, rubbing them over her hands absentmindedly.

Shannon blinked, then looked up when they approached her.

"I had to wash up. I had Pete's blood on them," she whispered, and began to cry again. "They told me I had to stay out here, and no one is giving me any updates, Leah."

"You bring the notebook?" Larry asked, and Leah nodded and brought it out of her handbag.

Larry wrote *We'll just see about that, leave it to me!* Then he handed Leah the notebook, pulled out his badge and ID, and moved swiftly to the intake desk.

"Agent Fuller, FBI," he said tersely. "U.S. Marshal Pete Jenkins was brought in with a gunshot wound. I want to know his condition, and I want to know *why* his girlfriend" – he pointed to Shannon – "has been left out here by herself with no updates. *Now.*"

In moments, he had the latest information, along with the man's sincere apology to relay to Shannon. He muttered an abrupt "Thank you, I'll take her upstairs," before he pivoted and walked back over to Shannon and Leah.

As they moved toward the elevator, he updated them. Leah scribbled what he said and showed Shannon, then cried out, "Larry!" as Shannon began to slump toward the floor.

He scooped an unconscious Shannon up in one fluid motion, turned and headed back to the intake desk.

"Get somebody out here who can help her," he growled. "*Right now.*"

Leah was pleased to see Larry's demeanor light a fire under the man, and instantly two staff members arrived with a gurney. He placed Shannon on it very gently, then barked, "Lead the way."

Larry stayed in the triage room with them until he was convinced Shannon would be all right, then he turned to Leah.

"I'm going upstairs to the surgical waiting room to try to get an update on Pete," he announced. "You going to be all right here without me?"

"Go," Leah said, and smiled at his question for what it was – genuine concern. "I've got this part covered. As soon as they finish checking her out, we'll come find you."

He took two steps before she called out.

"Hey."

He turned. "Yes?"

"I appreciate you," Leah said, and meant it to her core.

He winked. "See you two upstairs," he replied, and was gone.

***

An hour later, the three were reunited in the third-floor surgical waiting room. Shannon was a bit dehydrated, but otherwise doing pretty well under the circumstances. Leah had even managed to make her laugh when she'd mimicked the staunch nurse's directives as only Leah could, referring to 'Nurse Squeaky Shoes' and barked orders.

Larry traveled over to the small table in the corner, returning with two coffees for himself and Leah, and a hot tea for Shannon. Then they sat, Shannon in the middle, and waited for someone to bring them news about Pete.

Finally, the lead surgeon appeared. And when he told them Pete would make a full recovery, Leah almost cheered.

He also conveyed recovery time – one to two weeks – then let them know they'd be able to see Pete once he left post-op.

Next came a bit of planning. Shannon had no intentions of going anywhere until Pete was released – and said as much. Both Larry and Leah could see the relief in her eyes when Larry passed on Lynda's invitation to stay at the farm.

When Shannon mentioned her classes, Larry had a solution for that, too – he'd already planned to bring her a laptop so she could finish them remotely.

"Seems like you've been lining stuff out," Leah remarked, and he grinned.

"When are you heading back to Chicago?"

"Tomorrow," he answered.

"Do you think Lynda would be willing to help Shannon with her bandages?"

"Absolutely. Born nurturer, that one. Why?"

"I want to drive back with you," Leah told him, her face carefully neutral. "Our apartment's still a wreck. I need to get all that sorted out."

He gazed into her eyes. "Sure."

She let Shannon know her plans via written message.

Shannon stood and reached into her pocket, bringing forth the locket Robert had given her. She solemnly handed it to Larry.

He carefully worked it open and stared for a moment at the tiny piece of circuitry that had gotten Robert killed and Shannon placed in so much danger.

Larry snapped the locket shut again, tucking it into the front pocket of his jeans just as a surgical tech arrived to take them to Pete.

***

They stayed as long as hospital visiting hours allowed, then returned to the farm. Larry managed to convince Shannon to eat before sending her off to bed.

"She'll be okay, now that she knows Pete's going to be fine," Leah assured him. "She's strong. And stubborn."

"Maybe that's why you two are best friends?" he teased, and she laughed.

"Probably. We met the first day of freshman orientation, standing in line to get registered. Later, when we got to the dorm, we found out we'd been assigned as roommates. Small world, right?"

He nodded.

"Anyway, she and I just hit it off immediately," Leah continued. "We got along so well that once freshman year was done and we weren't required to live on campus anymore, we found an apartment together."

Larry sensed there was more to the story, but he kept quiet.

"Hey, I noticed there's a fire pit out back," she said suddenly. "Could we build a fire, maybe sit out under the stars for a while?"

"Coming right up," he said, and smiled.

Larry deftly arranged bigger and smaller pieces of wood in the pit, added kindling, and got the fire going. Then he grabbed two lawn chairs, plus a blanket for Leah in case she got cold.

They settled in as the night sky deepened and the millions upon millions of stars began to twinkle overhead.

"That is so beautiful. Peaceful," she murmured as she looked up.

"It is," Larry agreed from the chair to her left. "When I was little, we used to come up here every summer. Best months of my life. I lost count of the crawdads I've caught in the creek over there. And smores. Packed away a ton of smores that were made right here, over this fire pit."

Leah smiled at the memories he was sharing with her.

A long silence drifted in as they watched the flames, then the sky.

"A little over a year ago, I started seeing this guy named Gregg," Leah said quietly. "And at first, everything was fine."

Larry turned his attention from the stars to her and waited patiently for her to continue.

"We'd been dating three, maybe four months? Something like that. And things had started to turn. He became jealous, paranoid, obsessive. Tried to tell me how to dress, how to wear my hair, what classes I should take."

She took in a huge shuddering breath, then kept going.

"Shannon was worried about it, and she tried to talk to me, but he'd convinced me it was all in my head," she said. "And then one night, everything became crystal clear. I was working as a waitress at the time, and I'd finished up a night shift and was walking to my car. A man approached me, pulled a gun, and forced me into my car and told me to drive."

Larry held his hand out, and she clutched it.

"I was scared to death. I didn't know what was going to happen to me. And then, I got mad. I had put on my seat belt out of habit. And I noticed he didn't. So, I accelerated to about forty-five miles an hour, then drove into a light pole on purpose."

Larry gasped in surprise. She took another deep breath, and he squeezed her hand in solidarity.

"After the airbag deflated, I shoved my door open and undid my seat belt and ran, screaming for help. Luckily, a police cruiser had just turned onto the block, and they stopped and helped me."

"What happened?"

"They took him to the hospital to get checked out, and then they took him to jail. And that's when the real nightmare came out."

Leah glanced over at Larry, saw his concern, and continued.

"Come to find out, he was Gregg's dealer. Gregg was hooked on cocaine, and I had no idea. He told the cops questioning him that he and Gregg had made a deal."

Her voice was turning hard and cold, and Larry tightened his grip on her hand, somehow sensing he hadn't heard the worst part yet.

"He told them Gregg owed him a lot of money. And then... then he told them that Gregg had offered *me* up as payment," she said, a single tear streaking down her face as she stared into the flames. "Like I was a bargaining chip. Like I was a piece of *property*."

She looked over again at Larry and saw and felt the outrage threatening to consume him.

"I thought he cared about me. But he didn't. I was disposable. That's why what Robert did with the locket made me so angry. It felt like he was using her, the same way Gregg tried to use me."

"Understandable," Larry murmured, caressing the back of her hand with his thumb.

"I pressed charges, and I testified, and they're both in prison now. And Shannon never left my side through any of it, Larry," she revealed. "She kept me safe, and she kept me sane through it all. As a matter of fact, it was *her* idea for us to move to a different apartment, just in case anybody else who knew Gregg came around."

Another deep breath.

"Shannon stuck with me, when a lot of other people would have bailed. So, when we went to my place to get her some clothes, and I saw it was wrecked, I almost lost it. I thought somehow Gregg had managed to find out where we'd moved to and sent someone. And I was terrified that by sticking with me, she'd been put in danger, too."

That's why she's so protective of Shannon. It also explains why she reacted the way she did that day, he realized with sorrow - and shame.

Leah immediately noticed his change in demeanor.

"What?" she asked.

CHAPTER NINE

"I grabbed you that day," Larry managed as he replayed the scene in his head, his throat choking with emotion as he tried to speak. "Leah, I..."

She stood and moved in front of him, taking his face in her hands and making eye contact.

"Look at me," she said sternly. "Larry, listen to me. You're *not* Gregg, and you're *not* the man that tried to kidnap me. I *know* you're not. You're *nothing* like them."

"I'm so sorry," he whispered, full of remorse.

And in that moment, she led with her heart. Leah leaned in and touched her lips to his, kissing him gently, and noticed his eyes went wide with shock.

She stepped back and softly said, "I'm turning in for the night. See you tomorrow." And she walked back into the cabin, leaving a restless Larry Fuller behind to stare at the flames and think.

***

Leah entered the cabin as quietly as possible so she wouldn't wake up Shannon. She thought briefly about crawling into the bed – she knew Shannon wouldn't have minded bunking together. But she decided against it.

"I'm probably going to toss and turn all night, and that's the last thing she needs," she said to herself. She stretched out on the couch, pulling the blanket that was spread across the back down over her, and stared at the ceiling.

It had felt really good to tell Larry about what she'd been through, she realized. She hadn't known just how liberating sharing all that with him would be. It had been a much-needed catharsis for her soul.

But then I kissed him. And I think that was a major mistake. He didn't react like I hoped he would. Maybe I read it all wrong, and this is one-sided after all, she thought, and the thought made her melancholy.

She wiped her cheeks, willing herself to banish the new wave of tears that had come unbidden to the surface, and sometime later, she drifted off.

***

By mid-morning, Shannon was preparing to climb behind the wheel of Pete's truck to go spend her day with him. Leah made a last check that Shannon's bandages were staying in place, then hugged her.

Text me if you need me, and I will get back here as quick as I can, Leah wrote. *Unless you need me to stay. I can stay, you know.*

"I love you, and I appreciate your concern," Shannon said. "But I'm good. I've got this. Okay? Go."

Larry stepped out of the cabin with his and Leah's bags, putting them in the back of his truck before walking over to Shannon.

Gonna overnight you a laptop so you can do your classes, he wrote. *You'll have it tomorrow.*

"Thanks," Shannon said, and hugged him too. As she did, she whispered, "You take care of her. She needs you."

He winked at her once she'd turned him loose.

Shannon got in the truck, waved, then turned around and headed to the hospital.

***

Larry looked over at Leah.

"You ready?"

"I am," she confirmed. "Let's get rolling."

They settled into Larry's truck to begin the journey back to Chicago.

"So," she began, "what's the plan, exactly?"

"Well," he mused, "I do need to get this locket to Bruce as quick as I can. But Zavier won't be transported up to Chicago for another day or so, at least. And Duffy? Shannon got him pretty good; he might be in the hospital down here even longer than Pete."

"Meaning?" Leah's eyebrow raised.

"Meaning once I hand the locket over, I should have a day or two of down time. And I'd like to help you get your apartment put back together. If you want, that is."

"You don't have to do that."

"I know. I *want* to do that," he answered.

She smiled. "Okay. Thanks."

"Don't mention it."

They traveled into and through Ravenna on KY-52, heading toward US-75.

"What's our travel time?"

"Seven hours, give or take."

"Huh," she said, and fell silent again for a while. Then she took a deep breath and spoke.

"About last night…"

"Yes?"

"Thanks for listening to me."

"Absolutely. Thank *you*, for feeling comfortable enough with me to share that."

A few more miles down the road, she spoke again, but he noticed that she hesitated first.

"You were going to tell me about Molly," she reminded him.

Uh, he thought. *I was hoping maybe we could talk about that kiss, but okay.*

"Yes, I did say I'd tell you later, didn't I? Well. Molly and Pete dated for almost a year. Out of the blue she up and left about eight months ago, I think it was."

"Poor Pete! What happened?"

"She told him she couldn't handle him being a U.S. Marshal," Larry revealed.

"Really? That's kind of selfish on her part. I mean, I'm sure his job wasn't a secret when they met, right?"

"Nope, it wasn't," Larry confirmed. "And that's what shocked me when he first told me. But looking back, I think she was fascinated by his career. All mysterious, you know. I think initially, it attracted her to him. But then the reality of being with someone whose job can be really dangerous set in, and she just couldn't do it."

"I get that, but still. That must have crushed him."

"It did."

Leah pursed her lips. "So, what about you? Married? Seeing anybody?"

"Not anymore, and no," he said, a little abruptly.

"Sorry," she murmured. "I didn't mean to upset you, Larry."

He sighed. "You didn't. It's just... that is why I transferred to Chicago."

"Oh," she said, eyebrows raised, then hastily added, "You don't have to tell me. Really."

Now he softened. "I don't mind sharing. It's just... it's still hard to talk about."

He thought for a long moment, then shrugged.

"We met right before I got out of the Army. Whirlwind courtship, and so on. Got married three months later, and not long after that, we were expecting a baby."

Leah saw his jaw clenching and unclenching and extended her hand. He took it and held it tightly.

"Anyway, she had a son."

Okay, he said 'she had', not 'we had'... that can't be good, Leah thought.

"And I was ecstatic at being a dad. It was something I'd always wanted, someone that *I* could bring up to the farm in the summertime and teach how to catch crawdads and make smores. You know?"

"Sounds nice," Leah agreed.

"Only when they did the test to determine the baby's blood type, the truth came out. I have type O blood, and she had type A. The baby turned out to have type B."

Larry looked over at Leah and she winced in sympathy.

"So, no possible way the child was yours," she said, and he nodded.

"Exactly. So, I demanded a paternity test, and that proved it. She finally broke down and confessed. She hadn't been faithful from day one. She'd just *hoped* the baby was mine, because, and I quote, 'you have better benefits', end quote. And then she made it a point to tell me she never loved me to begin with."

Leah's jaw dropped. "I am so, so sorry."

"Yeah," he said. "Unfortunately, I couldn't get an annulment, since we'd been married longer than a year. I had to file for divorce. She tried to fight me on it, but once the paternity test was submitted to the judge, it was finalized pretty quickly. I'd already broken off all contact with her and moved on with my life. During that timeframe I'd left the Army, completed the FBI Academy and been assigned to the regional office in California not far from the last base I'd been stationed at when she and I met."

Larry only released her hand to take a drink of the iced tea he'd brought with him for the trip. He set the glass back in the cup holder, reached for Leah's hand again, and continued.

"And things were good for a while. She left me alone for over a year, and then it started, out of the blue. She would call and leave message after message for me. Then, she started showing up at my office demanding to talk to me. I tried switching up shifts, you name it. She just would not stop."

"And to get away from that, you had to transfer," Leah summarized.

"Yep. But wait, there's more before I even get to that point in the story. She went so far as to threaten and harass a really nice woman that I had just started dating. Needless to say, that woman - understandably - decided that we didn't need to hang out anymore. And then, it got bad."

"It got worse than *that*?" Leah was dumbfounded.

"Much worse. She filed a bunch of complaints against me – and some of them were really serious ones. Like, career-ending, jail time level accusations. But I got really, really lucky, Leah. I had people I worked with who knew the whole situation and who had independently witnessed her behavior. Between their sworn statements, the formal notes I'd kept about all the bizarre stuff going on, and video footage from the surveillance cameras at work, her claims were proved to be false. I filed a restraining order and stalking charges, and then I applied for a transfer, and had to wait until it came through."

"She eased up at that point, and I heard later she'd found another guy to focus on. But by then, I was beyond ready for a change. When the chance came to relocate to Chicago, I took it, and I haven't heard anything from or about her since I made the move. Ask Pete about it sometime; he had a front row seat for most of that."

"Her behavior reminds me of Gregg, to be honest. Maybe she was strung out on drugs," Leah observed.

"Or as Pete likes to say, maybe she was just whackadoodle," Larry chimed in, and Leah giggled, which made him laugh.

It's good to hear him laugh, she thought. *I was hoping sharing his story with me didn't bring him down.*

They rode in a comfortable silence for the next several miles, and when they got to US-75 Larry steered the truck north toward Chicago.

"Let me know when you get hungry, and we'll stop," he told her, and she grinned.

"I already know *exactly* where I want to eat," Leah exclaimed, her eyes twinkling.

"Really? And where is that?"

"Portillo's."

"You're in luck, then," Larry said with a grin, "because I just happen to know, there's one just south of Indianapolis."

"We don't have to wait until we get to Chicago?"

"Nope."

"Nice!

***

Once they were roughly ten miles from Indianapolis, Leah pulled up directions to the nearest Portillo's and cued up her GPS.

"This will take us straight there," she announced.

A half-hour later, they'd placed their orders and were waiting for their food. When their number was called, she beamed.

"I'll be right back," Larry said, and promptly returned with her chopped salad and his Italian beef sandwich.

"I propose a toast," she said, raising her lemonade. "To surviving crazy exes."

He clinked his glass against hers, and added, "And here's to new beginnings."

CHAPTER TEN

As they ate, they learned more about each other.

"I'm originally from Texas," Leah told him. "I was born in Killeen, but we moved all over the place; my dad was Army, too. When he retired from the service we settled in Tulsa."

"What made you choose Chicago for college?"

"It wasn't my first choice," she said. "But I got a scholarship that covered the first two years of school, so, it was kind of a no-brainer at that point."

"I can see how that would influence the decision," he admitted, and she grinned.

"But I can't handle the winters up there," Leah said, and shrugged. "As soon as I'm done with my degrees, I'm out of there."

"Where were you planning on going?"

"Back to Texas, actually. Out of everywhere we lived, Texas was my favorite."

"Interesting."

"What about you? Where are you from?"

"Born and raised in Tampa, Florida. I'm the oldest of four - two brothers and one sister. It was *never* quiet at my parents' house growing up. I'm amazed they survived all that noise with their sanity intact, to be honest."

Leah grinned. "Sounds like fun, though. I was an only child."

"Maybe you can meet them sometime," Larry said. "They're a lot of fun."

Wait... I'm confused. I thought there was a spark there, and then I kiss him and get no reaction, and now he mentions meeting his family?

"What?" he asked, seeing her frown.

"Nothing," she said, "I just noticed I'm low on lemonade. Be right back."

***

Leah got up and left the table abruptly, and Larry was left pondering what had just turned sideways between them.

She returned and they finished their meal, then walked out to the truck.

"Ready to keep going?" he asked, and she nodded as she put on her seat belt.

Uh, oh. What did I goof up? he wondered.

"You okay?"

"Sure," she said, a little too brightly.

"Okay," he replied, and backed out of their parking space.

But I know that tone, he thought, *and things are not okay.*

***

They had traveled another fifty miles when Leah cleared her throat.

"Um," Leah stammered, flustered, and Larry glanced over.

"You all right?"

"No...yes... I guess, what I mean is..." she trailed off.

"Leah," he murmured. "Just talk to me."

"I just... I kissed you last night."

Now Larry's lips curved into a smile.

"Yes, you did. And?"

"And I was thinking... maybe I shouldn't have."

"Oh." His smile faded.

"Man, I am messing this up," she muttered under her breath, and tried again.

"I didn't kiss you just to make you feel better. And I didn't kiss you because of what I told you. I kissed you because I *wanted* to."

"Okay, so, why are you saying you shouldn't have? I'm confused."

"Well, I kissed you, and well, you just... kind of... *sat* there. So, I'm thinking maybe you didn't want me to, and I made you uncomfortable?"

He whipped his head to the right to stare at her. "You think I *didn't* want to kiss you?"

"Well... yeah," Leah turned her face to the passenger side window. "And if not, that's okay. I thought there was something going on between us, but, I mean, if you don't feel what you don't feel... but *then*, you mention maybe meeting your family? So now, I am completely confused. Are we just agent and roommate-of-target, or friends, or what?"

The screech of tires had her looking over at him as he swiftly took the next exit, traveling down the service road until he found a strip mall parking lot, and turned in to the first empty spot he came to.

He shifted the truck into park as she nervously twisted her hands in her lap, looking out the window again.

"Hey," he said softly, and she slowly turned her head to face him.

When she did, Larry cupped her face in his hands and planted a passionate kiss on her mouth that took her breath away.

He pulled away, but only to rest his forehead on hers. "Leah, I've wanted to kiss you since the very first moment I saw you," he said. "But I've had to hold back, for two reasons."

"Okay... the reasons being?"

"One, I'm still on the job here. Until I get everyone at Creach & Langford into custody, I *have* to stay focused. If I don't, the situation still poses a risk – to Shannon, and now also to *you*, because I care very much about you. And the wrong people could use that, use you to get to me. Does that make sense?"

"Yes," she said softly. "What's the second reason?"

"I thought you didn't like me," he said simply. "And who in their right mind would try to kiss someone they think hates them? Surefire way to get slapped, if you ask me."

She giggled.

"So, what about last night? I would have thought that would have cleared up the second reason, at least."

"Honestly? Last night, you shocked the hell out of me. All I could think was 'man, this gorgeous woman is kissing me. She must *really* need her eyes checked'. By the time I realized it was intentional on your part, you'd gone inside."

She laughed. "You're a goofball."

"One hundred percent. But don't ever, *ever* think I'm not interested in you romantically, Leah. Because you'd be so very, very wrong."

"Okay," she smiled, and kissed him again before pulling back. "Okay. So, now what?"

"We're going to my office, and we'll need to play it straight," he said. "We found one leak. That doesn't mean that there couldn't be more. Everyone I work with, even Bruce, needs to think that you and I are interacting in a professional capacity *only*, agent to material witness, or as you put it, agent to roommate-of-target. Okay? It's the *only* way I know I can keep you safe until this case goes to court besides take you back to the farm."

"And after that? After all the bad guys are rounded up?"

"After that, be prepared to be kissed. A *lot*."

She smiled. "I can hold out until then."

"Ready to keep going?"

"*I'm* not the one who skidded us into a parking spot," she teased, and he laughed.

"Hey, *I* needed to put a certain misconception to rest, and I didn't think *you'd* appreciate me kissing you while driving seventy miles an hour," he shot back with a grin.

"Fair point. Onward."

***

Thirty miles from his office, he picked up her hand and kissed it tenderly, then set it back down.

"What was that for?" Leah asked, even as she was glowing from his affection.

"Trying to stock up on how kissing you feels, to get me through while we're in game mode," Larry told her honestly, and made her heart do that crazy double-thump thing again.

He glanced over at her, and grinned.

"You have about twenty-five miles to stop blushing."

"I'm working on it. Stop making me feel so good, will ya?"

Ten miles out, she could feel the shift in his demeanor, the emotional equivalent of discarding worn jeans to shrug on an impeccably tailored three-piece suit.

"Almost there," he muttered.

"We can do this," she assured him, even following up with, "Agent Fuller," in her most professionally detached voice.

The corner of his mouth twitched.

***

He arrived at the Bureau's parking garage entrance and was vetted by security. The remote-controlled gate lifted, and he drove in, pulling into his assigned spot. Then he went around to open her door.

"Miss Culverton," he said, and gestured.

She stepped down gracefully and said, "Thank you, Agent Fuller," in a spot-on 'you-bore-me' tone.

"Right this way, please."

They moved into the elevator, standing several feet apart, as two strangers would, for the ride up to the Director's floor.

***

"I'm sorry you guys had to scramble like that, Larry," the Director of the Chicago division said once they'd been shown into his office and seated in his visitor's chairs. "And to you, Miss Culverton, my apologies. How is Miss Rivers?"

"She's well, sir. She opted to stay... where we were, and watch over U.S. Marshal Jenkins, sir."

"I see," he said, fingers steepled. "Larry, it's my understanding both were directly involved in the events of the last forty-eight hours?"

"Yes, sir, right in the middle of it, unfortunately. There wasn't a chance to get them out before trouble came, sir."

"Relax, son. You did good," the Director said, and smiled. "And I hear tell Miss Rivers is quite a shot with a long gun. I'd have liked to have seen that."

"Beg pardon, sir?"

He leaned forward. "Larry," he murmured. "I know where you were, and I've heard all about what happened. I've got family up that direction myself; I grew up in Lexington, you know, and I have a third cousin that's a cop in Ravenna."

"I actually did *not* know, sir."

"Yes, well, now you do," he said, chuckling, then turned his attention back to Leah.

"So, young lady. What are your plans?"

She was momentarily confused. "My plans, sir?"

"Your plans," he repeated. "I understand you'll be done with your Criminal Justice and Psychology degrees in the spring. Have you considered working for the Bureau?"

"I hadn't until now," she answered candidly. "I'd planned to move back to Texas in the spring."

"Think it over," the Director suggested. "Something tells me you'd be quite a tenacious asset."

"Now, before you two get going, I have one more piece of business. We've investigated this group top to bottom, Larry, and C.W. was the only mole here. He did name other parties in other branches of law enforcement, mind you. And a thorough... cleaning of houses is well underway."

Larry nodded his understanding.

The Director nodded back. "Just so you're aware, Larry. There shouldn't be any more problems here.

Go get your evidence lined out, and get your official report done. I want it on my desk no later than Thursday morning so we can request warrants and present to a grand jury for indictments as soon as possible. Understood?"

"Yes, sir."

They rose to leave, and the Director said, "Oh, and one more thing. I'm assigning you personally to watch over Miss Culverton here until all arrests have been made. As part of that, I expect you to take her out for a nice meal or two. It's the least we can do for her. Use the company card."

"Yes, sir."

As they left his office Leah almost gasped in surprise; she could have sworn she heard the old man softly mutter, "And when the time comes, I expect a wedding invitation, young man."

She risked a glance at Larry, whose expression gave away absolutely nothing, and they took the elevator down to the lab.

CHAPTER ELEVEN

"Larry!" Bruce exclaimed, and gave him a fist bump. "Glad you're back in one piece, man. Was that intense, or what?"

"Just a bit," Larry grinned. "Bruce, I'd like you to meet Leah Culverton."

"Hello," she said, and shook his hand.

"Okay, don't keep me waiting. What have you got?" Bruce said with excitement, and his eyes grew wide when Larry opened the locket and showed him what was nestled inside.

Bruce immediately put on latex gloves, and gingerly took the entire locket out of Larry's hands. "None of you touched that, right? Just the locket?"

"Nope, just the locket."

"Good. I'm on this," Bruce said. "I'll get started on it right away. What's the turn time?"

"The Director asked for my formal report and supporting documentation by Thursday morning."

"I can do better than that," Bruce said. "You'll have my results within the next twenty-four hours."

"One more thing, Bruce," Larry said. "I need a laptop. Got any spares?"

"You know I do."

"Can I get you to overnight it for me? I promise it will come back safely. I'll even sign for it."

"Where do you need me to send it?"

***

"What was *that*?" she exclaimed as soon as they left the parking garage. "Does your big boss always act like that?"

"Yep," Larry grinned. "I really admire that man. I'll tell you something else, too. He's usually much more... colorful. The *only* reason he didn't cuss a blue streak when he was talking about C.W. was because there was a lady present. But he knows his stuff, and he's the best boss I've ever had. He really cares about his people."

"Did he say what I think he said as we were leaving?"

"What are you talking about?"

"You didn't hear him say... oh, never mind," Leah said. "So, what's next?"

"Well, it's a little after five," he pointed out. "And we had a late lunch. What about heading to your apartment? We could start going through things, see what can be salvaged and what needs to be replaced. And when we get hungry, we'll figure something out."

"Sounds like a plan."

***

When they arrived at her door and Leah saw the 'Do Not Cross' tape strung across it, she frowned.

"We're clear to go back in there, right?" she asked.

"Yes," he said. "Please, allow me."

He reached out, yanked the tape down, and gestured.

"After you."

She stepped forward and unlocked the door, then walked in and looked around, sighing.
"Yep, it's still horrible, and I still didn't dream it," she muttered.

He put an arm around her shoulders just as her phone pinged.

"It's Shannon," she said, and started to read the message.

"She says Pete is being a little bit grouchy."

"Well, he got shot. I can see where he wouldn't be a beam of sunshine," Larry quipped as he stepped over shattered dishes and looked under the kitchen sink for trash bags.

"Aww," Leah said, hand on her heart as she read some more. "It's not that. He's upset because they're not letting him use that arm for a couple of days, so he's not able to write to her as much as he wants to."

"How much do you want to bet those two will be married in a year's time?" Larry asked when Leah came to the narrow doorway.

"Seriously? I don't even think it will be *that* long. My money is on a May wedding. Mid-June at the latest."

"One question - why can they not *text* back and forth?"

"Pete's arm, remember? Not to mention, Shannon is constantly forgetting to charge her phone."

Another ping, and Leah laughed.

"She says Mabel, one of the nurses, volunteered to be the messenger whenever she can."

"And true love finds a way," Larry drawled in his best Southern accent, making Leah snicker.

"Okay, funny man, focus. Where do we start with all this?"

"Well, I'd say the bedroom, maybe? Since you're going to need a place to sleep at some point."

"At some point?"

He shrugged. "If the beds are too torn up, you can always crash at my place until we can replace your stuff."

Leah decided to mess with him a bit and narrowed her eyes. "That's moving a little fast, isn't it?"

"Not like that!" he stammered, then chuckled when he saw she couldn't keep a straight face. "You can have my bed, and I'll take the couch. I mean, the fluff all over your living room is what made *your* couch usable, right?"

"Fair point," she conceded. "But seriously - wouldn't me staying at your place break that whole 'we have to maintain appearances' thing? Just saying."

"And the boss said I am to guard you personally, remember? Easier to do that if we stay together. Just saying."

She looked up at him and batted her eyelashes. "You are so stubborn, Agent Fuller. It's a good thing you're cute."

He belly-laughed, and said, "Come on, let's go see how bad the damage is in the bedrooms."

***

Twenty minutes later, Leah threw up her hands in disgust. They'd put bureau drawers back in place, then put the scattered clothes away in both rooms. But Leah's and Shannon's beds were a complete loss, all the way down to the box sets.

"Whoever carved these up wasn't hugged enough as a child, or something. It was a really angry person with *way* too much time on their hands that did this."

"I would have to agree," Larry said. "They were very, very thorough. My bet is, they sent a crew here, not just Zavier. Faster that way, even though it draws more attention."

"Yeah, *but*," she countered, "it was after ten p.m. on a Saturday night. Most of the tenants on this floor are single and go clubbing every weekend, so they weren't home to see anybody break in. And anybody that *was* hanging out at home, like me? The bad guys didn't bust down the door, they picked the lock, remember? Less noise. The loudest part of all this would have been the entertainment center falling over, but other than that, not much to give them away at all."

"By the way - we haven't even talked about a major part of all this cleanup," she continued.

"Which is?"

"How many trips do you think it will take to haul all this downstairs to throw it away?"

"You figure out what can be kept, and I will handle the rest of it. I've got connections, you know," and wiggled his eyebrows at her.

They separated, Leah starting in the kitchen while Larry tackled the debris pile in the living room.

"Pretty much every dish we had is destroyed," she called out, once she'd swept up all the remnants and dumped the dustpan for the last time. "Cookware, utensils, a few spices, and some cans. That's about all that's still good from the kitchen."

Shaking her head, Leah pulled the magnetized dry erase board off the fridge and began to make a list of items to replace. When she finished, she grabbed two cold bottles of water from the fridge and went out to the living room to offer Larry one.

"Nice work," Leah said, nodding in approval.

He'd gotten all the stuffing corralled and into bags, righted the entertainment center, and gathered up the DVD collection, putting them back on a shelf.

"The TV is toast, and so are any places to sit," he reported. "But other than that, not too bad."

"Yeah. The three most expensive things to replace, not including the beds," she pointed out. "It's gonna cost me two, two and a half grand, at least."

"No, it won't."

"Yes, it will," she protested.

"Did you not hear me earlier? I've got connections," Larry said again, and smiled.

"What time is it? I'm starved."

He checked his watch. "Eight-forty."

"Food time?"

"Food time," he confirmed. "We can order takeout and pick it up on the way to my place. And just plan on staying there for a week or so. All right?"

Leah smiled softly. "All right. Let me grab some more clothes first, though."

***

They hit a drive-thru for subway sandwiches then headed to Larry's apartment.

She started to grab her suitcases and Larry immediately said, "Nope. I've got them. You're in charge of sandwiches."

She stuck out her tongue but didn't argue, and they made their way together up the stairs to his front door.

"Nice place," she said when she stepped through the door that he'd opened for her. "Comfortable. With stuff you can actually sit on in the living room, unlike my place at the moment."

He grinned. "I'm just going to set your bags down in the bedroom. Be right back."

He returned in short order and led her into the kitchen.

"What would you like to drink?"

She shrugged. "What have you got?"

"Whiskey?"

She smiled. "Works for me. On the rocks?"

"One on the rocks, coming right up."

He poured out two and handed her one, and they sat at the dinette table by the window, eating their sandwiches in companionable silence.

When they finished, Larry said, "I'm just going to grab my pillow and a blanket right quick, and then the bedroom's all yours."

"All right," Leah replied, even as she thought to herself *boy, are you about to be so, so surprised.*

She smiled sweetly as she watched him arrange his bedding on the couch, then asked, "Mind if I use your shower?"

"Go right ahead."

"Thanks, I'll be out in a little bit. And make me another drink, would you?"

"I'll have it waiting for you when you return."

She sauntered into his room and shut the door behind her, then moved immediately to the second suitcase she'd brought and rummaged through it until she found her sexiest negligee.

Leah hummed to herself as she showered, then toweled her body off and slipped into the nightie. She brushed her teeth, towel-dried her short dark hair, then put on her terrycloth bathrobe to keep her plans a surprise for as long as possible.

She gazed at herself in the mirror, nodding in approval before she tied the robe shut and headed back toward the living room.

"Thanks," she said silkily when he handed her the glass.

Leah sat on one end of the couch, feet tucked underneath her, and sipped her whiskey as she gazed at him.

CHAPTER TWELVE

All Larry could concentrate on was the jasmine scent wafting his direction. *The same as in my dream,* he realized, and felt his arousal kicking in.

He watched her as she finished her drink and set the glass on the end table.

"Well," she began, "I guess I'll turn in."

She stood, then walked over until she was standing in front of him.

"Larry," she murmured.

"Yes?" he replied.

She held his gaze and smiled seductively as she slowly untied her robe and let it drop to the floor.

"I think you should join me."

His jaw dropped as he took in the dark blue satin and lace nightie she was wearing.

"Are you sure about this?"

She nodded solemnly, her eyes bright with want.

Once he realized she was serious, he wasted no time at all. He leapt from the couch, scooped her into his arms, and carried her to the bedroom.

"Woman," he growled against her throat, "I've wanted you since the first time I saw you."

"Well, here I am," she whispered against his mouth. "Be with me, Larry. I need you."

He kissed her passionately before he gently laid her down on the bed, stepping away from her only long enough to shed his clothing. He rejoined her, pulled her close, and kissed her deeply again as their hands splayed across each other's bodies.

His breath caught when her hands slipped down from his washboard stomach and closed around him. Leah smiled against his mouth as she made little motions with her hands, and watched his eyes go dark with pent up desire.

Larry returned the favor by drawing his right index finger downward, between her breasts, down her stomach, cascading lower then turning and moving up under her short satin gown until it met her center and made her breath catch as well.

When he saw the glow of passion in her face build to a crescendo, he knew it was time. He separated from her to roll protection into place, then slid into her effortlessly, his eyes locked with hers, and he saw and felt the inferno blazing in her as he buried himself.

Leah's entire body quivered with each movement. "Larry," she breathed. "Oh, *Larry...*"

"Yes?" he whispered against her ear as she wrapped her legs around his waist.

"Take me there," she gasped, drunk with the sensations he was causing.

Larry covered Leah's mouth with his as he finally lost control. All he could see, smell, touch, hear, taste was her. Nothing else existed. Nothing else mattered. And when she cried out his name, she took him with her into oblivion.

***

The next morning, she stretched and yawned, reveling in the feel of him snuggled up behind her.

It feels so natural being beside him, Leah realized. *So perfect.*

And she sensed he must have had the same thought, because he pulled her closer, turned her over, kissed her deeply, and murmured in her ear "I want you," as he maneuvered her body onto his for a proper good morning ritual.

***

Later, after they'd showered and dressed, Larry said, "Which store did you want to hit first?"

"Well, I'm not sure, to be honest," she said. "The furniture place, I guess? And then the grocery store for some things. But I can hold off on the perishable stuff until I'm moved back in over there."

"Makes sense," he said, even as he thought to himself *although I think it would be awesome to have you here all the time.*

***

They selected the couches and beds and arranged to have them delivered, then headed to the store to replenish the badly gutted kitchen.

It was almost seven p.m. before all the new dishes were washed and stored in the cabinets.

"Not bad, though," Leah said appreciatively. "All that's left is to restock the refrigerator stuff, basically. What time is it?"

"Seven," Larry told her. "I'm thinking takeout. I don't feel like cooking. Do you?"

"That would be nope, I don't either."

They talked out their options, then decided on Japanese cuisine, and Larry called and placed their order with the place he frequented that was close to his apartment.

***

"I have to warn you, I am not good with chopsticks, at all," Larry told her as they drove to go pick up their food, and she giggled.

"I'm serious. It's horrible. The last time I tried using the things in public I wound up flinging a *huge* piece of sushi halfway across the restaurant. They brought me a fork, and smiled, and *they took away my chopsticks*, Leah. Does that tell you anything?"

"They did not!"

"Did so. And they've called me 'no-stick-man' ever since. Just wait, you'll see."

They entered the establishment and almost every single employee in the place yelled "Hey, no-stick-man!" at the same time.

Leah thought she was going to cry from laughing so hard.

He shrugged, grinning. "Like I said. Something of a legend here, just, not in a good way."

"That's.... *hilarious*...." She managed to get out between bouts of breathlessness.

They got their food, paid, waved goodbye, and returned to the truck. Larry opened her door for her and handed her the takeout bag once she was seated.

***

He had just closed Leah's door when he heard his name called from behind and to the right of him.

I know that voice... You've got *to be kidding me...*

He turned slowly.

It was her.

"You followed me across the *country*?" he yelled as he took a step forward. "What part of 'stay the hell away from me' don't you understand?

"Who's the slut, Larry?" she hissed.

"That would be *you*," he scoffed. "We proved that a long, long time ago."

Neither of them noticed Leah climb over the console and quietly exit Larry's truck from the driver's side. She ducked down and crept silently along the length of the bed, working her way around past the tailgate.

"This has gone on long enough, Larry. You need to come home now."

"My home stopped being with you the minute that kid's blood test came back. Now, you can leave, or I can call the cops and *make* you leave."

Her eyes were even crazier than he remembered, and a lead weight filled his stomach when he saw the knife in her hand.

Larry reached down to his hip and unbuckled the strap that held his firearm in place.

"Nancy, don't do anything else stupid. I don't want to hurt you, but I will if I have to."

She took two menacing steps forward.

"Hey, you bitch!" Leah yelled.

When Nancy turned Leah's direction, she was met with a roundhouse kick that sent the knife skittering across the pavement. Leah followed swiftly with a right cross and a left uppercut before another spinning kick caught Nancy squarely in the left side of her head and knocked her out cold. She slumped to the ground like a rag doll.

Leah stood, eyes blazing, chest heaving, glaring down at the crazy woman lying unconscious in a heap at her feet.

"*Nobody* messes with my man," she growled.

***

"Where did you learn that?" Larry asked, watching as the paramedic who'd checked Nancy's condition turned her over to the cops who'd arrived on the scene.

"After that guy tried to kidnap me, I started trying out different self-defense classes. I liked kickboxing the best," Leah answered with a grin.

A detective walked over, took their statements, and wished them a pleasant evening.

"Don't you need us to come to the station?" Leah asked.

"The restaurant owner's cameras got the whole thing on tape," the detective answered. "I'll be taking a look at that, and if I have any more questions, I know where to reach you both."

After the man walked away, Larry looked at her and said, "So... I'm your man, huh?"

"Caught that, did you? Well... I mean...if you," was all she got out before he silenced her words by kissing her.

"You already have my heart, Leah," he murmured against her lips. "You know that, right? For as long as you want it."

"That sounds like a fair trade," she whispered. "Because you have mine."

EPILOGUE

True to his word, within twenty-four hours Bruce had confirmed that the contents of the microchip were priceless; just about everything the FBI would need to shut Creach & Langford down permanently had been saved on that tiny wafer. Warrants were being issued for individuals throughout the organization, based on what Robert had found and made copies of, with indictments soon to follow.

And there was one lone paragraph in a Word document, penned by Robert himself, explaining his panic at the sensation of being watched, and his decision to stash the microchip in the only safe place he could think of – the locket he'd bought to give to Shannon.

With luck, I'll be able to get this back, with no one the wiser, the paragraph had ended, and Larry shook his head sadly as he read it.

***

Charles Allen Zavier was transported back to Chicago on Thursday afternoon, and Larry started the interview process Friday morning. Charlie, as he was known, had started off being extremely uncooperative – until he learned of the hit placed on him, that is.

C.W. Picking had been the recipient of Creach & Langford founding member Archibald Creach's phone call requesting Charlie be 'retired'. He'd mentioned the conversation during his interrogation. Larry, in turn, blindsided Charlie with it.

Then Larry got a surprise of his own. Charles Allen Zavier, it seemed, wasn't just another lackey – he was Archibald Creach's illegitimate son.

When he realized his own father had ordered him killed, Charlie conferred with his lawyer for all of three seconds before he looked across the table at Larry.

"Make me a deal, and I'll tell you everything I know," he said quietly.

It was the final nail needed.

***

Nancy was arrested and charged with assault with a deadly weapon. Given the documented history of stalking Larry Fuller, she was denied bail, and eventually sent to prison.

One Year Later...

Larry, Leah, Shannon and Pete were sitting around the fire pit at the farm outside Ravenna, Kentucky on a gorgeous October night. Pete stretched back, putting an arm around his wife. Leah's guess had been spot-on; it had been a May fifteenth wedding.

"I have to say, I like *this* trip to the farm much, much better," Pete announced.

"Agreed. No bad guys coming down the road any minute," Leah chimed in. "Plus, we made smores this time, so, that right there makes it *automatically* better."

Larry grinned at her.

"Anybody want another beer?" he asked.

"I'll take another one," Pete replied.

"Be right back," Larry said, and went into the cabin.

Shannon and Leah were talking back and forth, with Pete listening and occasionally jumping in.

"Larry's been gone a while," Leah noted at one point.

"I'm sure he's fine," Pete told her.

Several minutes passed, and then a loud rustle behind Leah had her eyebrows raising quickly. She stood, turned, and began to laugh.

It was Larry, all right.

In a gorilla suit.

With a bright pink tutu around his waist.

"Dammit," he said, and pulled the mask off. "Can't breathe in that thing, and this is important."

Suddenly he went to one knee and held up a tiny box, and she gasped.

He took her hand and looked into her eyes.

"Leah Culverton, my tiny pixie warrior, kicker of asses, my best friend. You are the love of my life. Will you do me the honor of becoming my wife?"

"Yes," she whispered, trembling as he slid the ring on her finger.

He rose, took her in his arms and lifted her off her feet, kissing her as Shannon and Pete clapped and cheered.

When he set her down again, he said, "Now don't forget, we have to make sure the Director makes the guest list."

She stood, dumbstruck for a moment, and then swatted his arm.

"You've been holding out on me. You *did* hear him say that too!"

Larry laughed and kissed her again.

The End.

One Last Try

The Extended Story of Faith and Rick, two characters in my thriller series Vital Secrets

<u>**Faith Thomas**</u> – Thirty-six-year-old accountant and closet romantic whose marriage implodes when she catches her husband of ten years cheating. Devastated, she moves home to Texas, determined to never let another man into her heart ever again.

<u>**Rick Connor**</u> – The handsome thirty-nine-year-old retired Navy cryptologist making a new start for himself after a crushing loss four years earlier. He's alone, and he's made peace with it – until Faith Thomas wanders into his bookstore and into his heart.

CHAPTER ONE

Faith Thomas Tucker scanned the menu, then placed her order.

"And may I please have an amaretto sour?"

"Absolutely. I'll have that right out."

When the young man returned with their drinks, Faith held hers aloft.

"To surviving another week at that place," she intoned, and Trisha and Melanie both said 'hear hear' as glasses were clinked together.

Their customary Friday night toast accomplished, they settled in to talk. They'd all started in Clover & Grimson's accounting department within a week of each other and had become fast friends.

"Hey, don't you have an anniversary coming up?" Melanie asked Faith. "How many years now?"

"Kevin and I have been together for twelve years, and married for ten, come next Saturday," Faith confirmed.

"Aw, a milestone anniversary," Trisha exclaimed. "Doing anything special?"

Faith shrugged. "He puts in even more hours than I do. To be honest, I'm not even sure he remembers when our anniversary is."

The waiter brought out their meals, and Faith had just picked up her fork to begin eating when her phone chirped loudly.

Setting her fork down, she pulled the device out of her purse, and her brow furrowed when she read the text that she'd received from an unfamiliar number.

You might want to head home now.

Sorry, I think you've got the wrong number, she texted back, and went to set down her phone. But it immediately chirped again.

If your name is Faith Thomas Tucker, then I've got the right number. Trust me on this. You need to head home. Now.

Who is this?

Someone who's doing you a solid. Go home, Faith.

"Guys, I need to go," she said.

"Everything okay?" Melanie asked.

"I'm not sure," she admitted, and waved the waiter over.

"I'm so sorry, something's come up and I need to leave," she told him. "May I please have a to-go container, and the check?"

***

Twenty minutes later, she was pulling onto her block when her phone chimed again. She pulled into her driveway, killed the lights, then looked at her phone.

Might wanna hit 'record'.

"What the hell?" she muttered, as much creeped out as she was irritated.

She got out of her car and let herself in through her front door, and immediately noticed something wasn't right. There was something lying on the carpet in the hallway.

She set her purse down on the foyer table, pulled her phone out of it, opened the camera feature, and pressed 'record' before she walked any further into her home.

When she reached the object in the hall, she began to shake. It was a woman's silk blouse, and it wasn't hers.

Twelve steps further and a left turn led down another short hallway to the master bedroom, where a noise that turned her stomach was already assaulting her ears.

Hands trembling, she held up her cell phone and pointed it at the bed, making sure that her husband and the skank he was in the middle of banging were still in frame, and she captured almost a minute of quality video and audio.

Then she cleared her throat loudly, and when that didn't get their attention, she yelled.

"How could you?" she screamed at the top of her lungs.

Kevin's head whipped around, and his eyes went huge when he saw her.

"I don't want to be married anymore," he babbled.

"Wish granted, you bastard!" Faith snarled, turned, and marched to the closet to grab a suitcase, staying in the same room as her betrayal only long enough to grab a few changes of clothes and some toiletries.

"Faith. Faith, wait. I didn't mean it," he said plaintively as he followed her back out into the living room.

"Didn't mean what, Kevin? Which part? Screwing someone else in our bed, getting caught, or what you said? Because I gotta tell you, you just messed up big on all three counts."

He reached for her, but she batted his hand away.

"Stay away from me. We're done," she hissed.

She looked over his shoulder at his mistress, who had wrapped up in a sheet and was standing in the doorway.

"He's all yours, honey. Good luck with him being faithful," Faith sneered, and took great satisfaction in slamming the front door on her way out.

She drove three blocks, then pulled over and texted her anonymous tipster.

I don't know who you are but thank you. You just did me the biggest favor of my life.

The answer was swift.

I'm her soon-to-be EX husband, and if you need any further proof, I am happy to send it to you.

Faith attached what she'd recorded as a file and typed back *Deal. Let's trade. I think you can probably use this too* then hit 'send.'

The next thing she did was call the lawyer that she and Kevin had used for years.

"Marty," she began, "I'd like to retain you as my divorce attorney."

CHAPTER TWO

One year later, on a sunny spring afternoon, Faith Thomas sighed and rubbed her eyes.

I love what I do, but damn, it's hard on my vision sometimes, she thought, as the spreadsheets blurred together.

A lot had changed in twelve months. She'd gone from being an accounting drone in Clover & Grimson's office in Philadelphia to transferring to their Dallas branch. Now, she was working as the Accounting Manager / CFO at a privately-owned regional manufacturing company in Fort Worth, Texas.

Faith hadn't planned to make any more changes for a while, not after the tumultuous recent events. She had sent them a resume on a whim months ago, then forgotten about it.

But they'd called her at the beginning of the year, out of the blue, and made an offer she literally could not refuse. Not to mention it was closer to her home in Pantego, and her new role allowed her to use more of the MBA she'd acquired significant student loan debt to complete.

Despite having only been on board three months, she'd already identified several cost saving opportunities as well as plugged some gaps that had concerned her from a fraud prevention and segregation of duties point of view. The drone work she'd endured so long at the mega-corporate level was paying huge dividends, because she now was overprepared in dealing with GAAP compliance from being in a public entity before. Her successes so far had greatly bolstered her confidence, and that of the President, to whom she reported directly.

Now, she was wrangling her first quarter end close; one of the few times at her new job that called for Saturday work. *Still, a nice change from every*

Saturday all-the-time, like at the other place, Faith reflected.

She stretched her arms, got up and flexed her leg muscles, rubbed her eyes again, and rolled her shoulders trying to work out the kinks caused by being hunched over a keyboard for so long.

"Okay, break's over, back to it, girl," she chided herself. "These general ledger reconciliations aren't going to do themselves."

***

It was another steady Saturday for customer traffic, and Rick Connor was pleased. His little store had officially been in business for two months and things were going even better than anticipated.

This keeps up I'll have to hire some help, he thought with a grin as he worked the cash register swiftly to keep the line moving.

It was just after six o'clock before the crowd began to thin out and he finally had a chance to move around the store and tidy up some shelves.

***

I'm not really hungry yet, and nothing sounds good right now anyway, Faith realized as she stared vacantly at her pantry.

Sighing, she moved to the couch, with every intention of flipping channels until it was time to go to bed. But it seemed that plan wasn't viable, either – nothing even remotely interesting appeared through one full circuit of the channels.

"Okay," she said to herself, "how about emails or YouTube, maybe?"

You could read, you know, her mind chimed in. *Or – gasp! – actually leave your freaking house and go spend time outside. Just sayin'.*

And she needed to. If she spent one more Saturday night like this, she might just have to pull her hair out. A year of these kinds of Saturday nights was beginning to weigh heavily.

She glanced down at her phone's screen, and noticed she'd inadvertently opened her pictures app. And a photo of that no-good cheating bastard Kevin was staring back at her.

Oh hell no. That's gotta go! Geez, how long as it been since I've cleaned out my phone? she realized and began deleting every single picture with Kevin in it.

He'd swept her off her feet, then broken her heart when she'd caught him a year ago (*Jesus had it already been a year?*) in their bed in the middle of a younger, big chested blond bimbo. She'd filed for divorce immediately. Ten years of marriage was obliterated in an instant.

And twelve months later, it still hurt.

Man, I wish I could clear out the memories in my head as easily.

That accomplished, she looked around. *Now what? Still nothing on television...*

She didn't feel like unpacking more boxes, although she'd been in her new place now for almost six months. She also didn't feel like going out, although both a work friend and Jandy had called to check on her and invite her to do just that. In the aftermath of the biggest betrayal she'd ever felt, she had turned severely inward.

Her life had become her work as an accounting manager from Monday through Friday from eight to five, and this damn townhouse filled the other hours, with almost nothing in between. She had very effectively placed herself in solitary confinement.

Worth it if it keeps me from getting hurt, she thought cattily.

Not if it keeps you from being alive, her heart seemed to respond all by itself. *Go out. Do something. Stop rattling around this place like some godforsaken ghost.*

Her temper flared a bit.

"Fine," she said aloud to no one. "You win. Just shut up about it."

On the way home from work one day, she had noticed a new bookstore had opened a couple of blocks away. Maybe she could burn some time there, find something to add to her growing collection.

Faith strode to her closet, pulling out her favorite jeans and sweatshirt. Reluctantly she parted with her comfy pajamas, changed, and slipped on her boots. She swept her chocolate brown shoulder length hair up into a ponytail, then frowned at the streaks of silver beginning to wind their way through.

Be grateful, she thought. *At least they're silver not yellowish gray.*

Grabbing her phone and purse, she took a deep breath, locked her front door behind her, and forced herself out of her self-imposed exile from the world.

She turned left and went down the sidewalk, enjoying the early evening air as she strolled. May evenings in Pantego tended toward perfection in her opinion. Not cold, and not as hot or muggy as it would be when summer bore down once more.

It wasn't until she was almost to the building's front door that she noticed the sign hanging over the street from delicate chains.

"*Book Keepers*", she read aloud. "How clever."

Grinning, she stepped over the threshold into her personal nirvana.

Books.

They were everywhere, as far as she could see, and she barely resisted the impulse to clap her hands together and giggle like a little girl.

I could stay in here forever, Faith thought with contentment, walking up to the nearest rack of books and inhaling deeply as she closed her eyes.

I just got here, and I already love everything about this place.

She was so absorbed in relishing her environment that she almost jumped out of her skin when someone gently cleared his throat and in a rich baritone said, "Welcome to Book Keepers. May I help you find something special?"

CHAPTER THREE

You just might. Jesus, he has a sexy voice was her unbidden and unexpected first thought. She opened her hazel eyes and slowly turned the direction that voice had come from, and her jaw almost hit the floor when she saw who had spoken to her.

He was a bit taller than her and lightly tanned, with smoldering brown eyes, chiseled features, dangerously sexy goatee, and dark hair she wanted to fist her hands in.

Temporarily struck dumb, she managed only to nod as she also noticed his very built frame – broad chest, muscled arms peeking out of short sleeves, narrow waist. She had no doubt whatsoever that blue polo shirt concealed one hell of a six pack, and she could tell by the fit of his jeans across his thighs that the muscular build continued all the way down.

Now he stood, tilting his head slightly as he gazed into her eyes. Then he smiled at her, and her heart threatened to burst out of her chest.

Say something, you idiot, the part of her brain that wasn't on sensory overload demanded. She managed to find her voice, hoping she didn't sound as awestruck as she felt.

"Um, hi. I had heard this place had opened nearby," she said after a long pause.

His smile brightened.

***

"Well, welcome to my store. I'm Rick. Would you like me to show you around?" even as he thought to himself, *Christ, she's breathtaking, and she doesn't even know it.*

"Historical? Biography? Sci-fi? No, wait," he said, eyes narrowing as he met hers again. "Let me guess. Spy thrillers and murder mysteries."

Now Faith's jaw did drop.

"How did you know that just by looking at me?"

The expanding smile caused Rick's brown eyes to twinkle. "Kindred spirits. I just felt it."

Her eyebrow raised slightly, but she couldn't help but smile back. "Do tell."

And he felt something stir deep inside his soul.

***

Neither one spoke for a few moments; they simply stared at one another, at a loss of what to do next. Rick cleared his throat again, and that seemed to break the spell.

"I've got spy thrillers and murder mysteries over here, by author," he managed, gesturing to the right. "Next sections down the right side are sci-fi, romance, and the other fictional genres. Left side is all the nonfiction, biographies, and so on."

Faith chuckled.

"Makes perfect sense to me. Our creative selves are right-brain driven so this layout is spot on."

Now it was Rick's turn to be momentarily dumbstruck. He gaped, blinking.

"That is *exactly* why I set the store up this way; you're the first person to notice."

She laughed and echoed back to him. "Kindred spirits. I just felt it."

The moment was broken by the telephone at the front register ringing.

"I'll be right back," he said as he hustled to answer it.

She nodded, watching him walk away, and noted those jeans of his fitting nicely from the back view as well.

She just stopped herself from diving behind the closest aisle of murder mysteries almost as a shield.

What the hell's gotten into you? she scolded herself. *Have you lost your mind? No way in hell, Faith, don't even think about it. You know nothing about him. Nothing. You know his first name, he likes books, and that he's hot, and that's all. What if he's married? Or a murderer? Get a grip!*

Faith took several deep breaths to try to slow down her racing heart, then began to look at the books surrounding her. And her jaw dropped again when she realized that not only was he carrying all fifty-three of J.D. Robb's *In Death* series written to date, but also that he had arranged them in chronological order rather than just lining them up alphabetically. She was a huge fan and collector, with books one through thirty-two in her possession already, so his presentation impressed her.

Well, she mused, *I know where I'm taking myself as my birthday present this year. Right here to this row to buy whatever I still need to complete my collection at home.*

Faith started to move around the end cap to her right so she could walk down the next aisle, and her focus failed her as once again she was face-to-face with the handsome bookstore owner.

A yelp escaped her.

"Sorry if I startled you," he said, beginning to grin.

"Damn you're quiet," she muttered, hand on heart. "Do you always sneak up on people?"

"Only when I see they obviously have a favorite author in common with me," his grin grew as he pointed to the set she'd just been looking at. "My favorite series ever, hands down. J.D. Robb rocks. I've read them all at least once. It never gets old."

"No spoilers!" Faith laughed and mimed covering her ears. "I've only gotten a bit over halfway through them. But yes, the ones I own I have read at least once, too."

She ran a loving hand lightly across the spines.

"I was just admiring the way you organized them. Every other bookstore I've been in insists on displaying them in alphabetical order. It's maddening. Don't they know there's a reading sequence involved here?"

"I know, right?" Rick exclaimed. "You can't read book one, then skip ahead to book twenty-three, you won't know what the hell's going on."

"Yes! Someone besides me gets it!" she smiled in triumph.

"You have a great smile and an even better laugh," he said softly. "Miss....?"

"Faith." She extended her hand.

"Faith," he repeated, clasping her hand in his. "Beautiful name for a beautiful woman. It is Miss, isn't it? Not Mrs.?"

The question caught her off guard.

"I'm not married. Anymore," she stammered, a brief flash of memory moving across her features. "You?"

"Was," he said, and his eyes lost their spark for a moment. "Not anymore."

The jingle of the silver bell over the door marked another intrusion. He reluctantly let go of her hand.

"Excuse me one moment more," he said and went to greet the new patron.

***

Faith stifled a sigh as she pondered again what the hell was happening here.

She'd just met this man – *don't even know his full name, for Christ's sake* – and just touching his hand had her thinking, well... *all manner of thoughts,* her inner voice said, *and not even one of them puritanical in nature.*

"Shake it off," she whispered to herself. "You don't need this right now."

Before I get myself into real trouble, I had better go, she thought. *Besides, I'm starving.* She glanced at her watch. Almost eight p.m.

She turned back and picked up books thirty-three and thirty-four in her favorite series, paused, and grabbed thirty-five too.

"There! This should get me through next weekend, at least," she murmured, making her way to the counter.

Rick's new arrival was just setting her purchases down to be paid for, so Faith stopped a respectful distance to wait her turn.

That's the little white lie she told herself, anyway.

In truth she was taking advantage of an opportunity to watch the fine specimen before her in more detail while pretending to skim the back cover of book thirty-three. His hands were strong but graceful as he keyed the purchases into the terminal, wrapped them, handed them to the buyer, and made change.

Remembering how his brief touch had felt led to wondering what those hands could accomplish running through her hair, down her sides to her waist, up to her breasts...

And she realized she was blushing furiously.

CHAPTER FOUR

Faith was so preoccupied with self-recrimination that she failed to see the customer before her leave. It was Rick coming around the counter, placing one of those magic hands gently on her arm, that pulled her back into herself.

"You're my last customer of the night, Faith," he said with a wink.

"Oh," she said, unable to think clearly. "Sorry. I didn't mean to keep you."

"I don't mind it at all," he replied.

He rang up her books, wrapped them, and handed them to her. As they waited for the credit card machine to print her receipt he said, "I'm starving. Hey, there's a little bistro down the street from here. Really good sandwiches. You wouldn't want to join me for dinner, would you?"

"You must be talking about Mama J's. Their sandwiches are legendary."

"Oh, so you know it?"

"Yep, one of my favorite places around here."

"Good to know," Rick said. "So, will you join me?"

No! What are you doing? Run! her wounded side screeched, then wailed in her head as she looked into his eyes and answered, "Yes, I'd like that."

"Great!" he beamed. "Just let me close the store, and we'll go. About twenty minutes?"

"I don't live far. Let me take these books home right quick. Meet you back here?"

"Absolutely."

He let her out, closing the door behind her. And couldn't stop himself from smiling as he watched her stride away.

"Definitely didn't see that coming," Rick said to himself.

***

A million thoughts raced through Faith's mind as she hurried home to drop off her books.

"Don't get stressed out over this," she told herself out loud. "Okay, so he's pretty, and he likes sandwiches. Don't read into this what isn't there."

Pretty doesn't even come close to describing that man well enough, her psyche retorted. *And why don't you believe he's into you? He asked you to dinner, didn't he? Not to mention asking if you were married! He's interested, trust me.*

Back and forth the war within herself raged as she opened her front door on autopilot, set down her purse, unwrapped the books and put them in their proper order with the rest of the collection.

Faith moved to the bathroom, checking her appearance again. And the war increased in intensity, a very loud drum in her ears – *Oh my God girl please tell me you are at least going to put on mascara!* – with her battered self-esteem shouting out in response *Why? He's just being polite.*

She closed her eyes, hands gripping the sink for balance, and willed the storm into silence.

"I am terrified," she admitted aloud, lifting her head to stare into her own soul in the mirror.

***

Rick moved quickly through shutting the store down for the night, then set the alarm and locked the door. He stepped out onto the sidewalk and looked the direction she had gone.

What if she doesn't come back? Then what? he asked himself.

Guess I will just eat alone as usual, came the answer. *But I hope she does. Man, I hope she does.*

He pulled out his phone, started to check a couple of emails he hadn't gotten to yet, but he found that his focus kept returning to the woman he had just met.

The most gorgeous woman I've seen in a long, long time, he admitted, and when he closed his eyes, he could see her face as clearly as if she was still standing right in front of him.

Hazel eyes that seem to miss nothing framed with naturally long lashes, dark brown hair with beautiful silver strands cascading through, high cheekbones, lightly sun-kissed skin I would kill to touch, a mouth made for kissing. I bet underneath that baggy sweatshirt her body is lush and ripe... I wonder what it would feel like pressed against mine...

Sighing, he forced himself to concentrate. He responded to his distributor's notice about a pending shipment, and three more emails that he'd received in the past half-hour. He had just hit 'send' on the last one and closed his email browser when he noticed a flash of movement coming toward him.

He looked up and felt breathless, like he'd been struck by lightning.

She had come back.

"Hi again," Faith said. "I hope I didn't keep you waiting long."

"Your timing is just about perfect actually," Rick replied, hoping he didn't sound like a lovesick teenager. "I just wrapped up the last emails of the day. You hungry?"

"Yes," she said and smiled as he extended his arm to her.

"Okay," he said and willed his muscles not to tense as she linked her arm around his.

They strolled the two blocks further down to Mama J's. Rick noticed that the bistro had placed a couple of small tables with chairs out on the patio.

"Indoors, or out?" he asked Faith.

"Out," she answered. "It's the perfect time of year for it."

"Couldn't agree more," he said, and pulled out her chair for her.

***

"Rick! Faith! Nice to see you again! Didn't realize you two knew each other," Mama J said with a big smile, and hugged each of them in turn.

"We just met tonight, Mama J," Faith told her. "At Book Keepers."

Wow, look at the sparks we got flyin' between these two here, Mama J thought to herself with a smile before she asked, "Usual drinks?"

"Sweet tea with lemon," they said at the same time, and glanced at each other.

"And are you ready to order?"

"I will have my usual, Mama," Rick replied. "Hot pastrami and provolone on marble rye, with spicy mustard."

"Ooh," Faith piped up. "I love their pastrami, but I've never tried it with spicy mustard."

"Well, you should, it's awesome," he said.

Faith turned to Mama J.

"Sounds good, I'll do that too."

Mama J chuckled. "Peas in a pod. I will get those right out for you," she confirmed, and made her way into the kitchen.

***

"So," Faith began, "um, how long have you been around here?"

"Moved to Pantego about five months ago, after my uncle died. He owned the building Book Keepers is in, and he left it to me."

"Oh! Your uncle was Mr. Connor?"

"You knew him."

"I did. He lived across the street from me. I only moved in about six months ago, and only talked with him a couple of times. But he was a really nice man."

Rick sighed. "Yeah, he was. I hadn't seen him in a long time. Being active Navy tends to keep you moving around a lot. I found out he had passed when his lawyer called."

He paused, taking a sip of his tea.

"He and I were the only family left. I had been planning a trip to come see him after I officially retired from active duty back in October. Life had other plans, I guess."

CHAPTER FIVE

He smiled at her.

"Uncle Jack and I had talked several times over the years about taking that building of his and opening a bookstore. I moved here, sold the townhouse, spent the first four months or so rehabbing the bottom floor for the store, and converting the top floor as my living space, and I opened doors for business March thirtieth," he finished.

"Yeah, I noticed the moving van come into the neighborhood and people in and out over there by my place," Faith mentioned. "Wondered what was going on."

"Yeah, well, Uncle Jack was shrewd with money. He owned his townhouse free and clear, same with the bookstore building. I couldn't see holding on to both for just me. We shared a love of literature. I couldn't think of a better legacy to remember him than Book Keepers."

She placed her hand over his and squeezed it gently.

"What a sweet way to honor him," she told him, then pulled her hand away, blushing slightly, as Mama J approached.

"Here you go," Mama J said, setting two plates piled high with sandwich and fries in front of them. "Enjoy."

***

Companionable silence ensued for a bit as they both started on their sandwiches while Mama refilled their glasses.

When they were alone again, Rick asked, "So. Faith. I want to hear about you. What's your story?"

She took a deep breath then exhaled slowly.

"Well," she said, "you want the long or short version?"

"I have nowhere I have to be," he replied. "Share whatever you'd like."

"Remember, you asked me," she warned. "Let's see. I have an MBA with Accounting Concentration, and I've been working in accounting almost fifteen years now. I transferred down to Fort Worth about eight months ago with my old company."

She paused for a moment, absorbing the sudden realization that she found herself wanting to bare her soul to this man she'd just met.

"The weird thing is, being a bean counter is NOT what I planned to be when I grew up. I had every intention of becoming a best-selling novelist or screenwriter or teaching Shakespeare to college kids. But life had other plans for me too, I guess. I kind of fell into the career I have, discovered I am good at it, and people need accountants wherever you go, so no worries about job security."

"Well, that certainly explains you catching my right brain/left brain setup so easily. Where were you before you moved here?" Rick asked.

"Philly area," she said, a little tersely. "For four years. Hated it. Too damn cold up there for my tastes. But," she sighed, "that's where Kevin's career took him, so off to freaking Pennsylvania we went."

"Kevin?" Rick's eyebrows raised.

"My ex-husband," she said.

"Oh. Well, I remember you mentioned earlier you weren't married anymore. What happened, if you don't mind me asking?"

"Um...well......," she sputtered.

"You don't have to share this, if you're not ready," Rick said quickly, hand raised. "No pressure."

"No," Faith shook her head. "It's okay. It still hurts to talk about it, but it is what it is."

Taking a deep breath, she continued.

"The short version is, he turned out to be extremely allergic to being faithful," she stated, gazing at Rick as she sipped her tea.

"We were together twelve years, married for ten. I came home early from my Friday night dinner out with friends and found him in our bed with some trampy twenty-two-year-old waitress. As a matter of fact, it was a year ago today I caught him."

"Ouch," Rick said, and his eyes filled with sympathy.

"Yeah," Faith muttered, "and I found out later she was just one of many. Looking back, I don't think he was faithful the whole time we were together."

She sighed and picked up a French fry.

"I wanted to kill him, but I held it together. I packed my stuff, filed divorce papers, and lived out of a motel until my transfer came through. Funny part is, it took longer for the transfer to happen than the divorce to be granted. Those proceedings tend to speed up when you're able to submit videotaped proof of adultery. Go figure," she said sarcastically.

"Anyway, the transfer finally got done, and I drove down here with all my stuff, then camped at my sister's place for a while until I found my own place. And here I am."

She sighed again then took another drink.

"So, yeah. That's my sad little story. And I'm amazed I shared that much. I've never really talked details about it, not even with family."

Despite her best efforts, tears suddenly welled, and a single stray tumbled down her cheek.

Rick reached out carefully and gently traced her cheek where the tear had fallen.

"I am so sorry you were betrayed like that. You didn't deserve that. Can I tell you a secret? Your ex is an idiot."

Faith chuckled through the tears. "Yes. He is. It's no secret."

"Part of me wants to thank him for being such a colossal screwup."

"Why?"

"If he'd been the man you deserved, you wouldn't have come to Texas, and I wouldn't have met you."

Now he leaned in a little closer, his eyes never leaving hers.

"And I am so very, very glad I did. My next question to you is, I've been here for about five months, you've been here for about six, and we don't live that far apart. Why is it we are just now finding each other?"

She broke eye contact to fiddle with her glass.

"I've done nothing but work pretty much since I moved in, to be honest."

Easier that way. Safer, she added silently.

He nodded in understanding.

"Can we change topics? This is bringing the mood way down," she said, a little too brightly.

"Agreed. No need to cover absolutely every topic on the first date," Rick grinned. "But I'd like to, eventually. If you'd like to go out again, that is."

"Wait a sec, let me check my social calendar," she said in mock seriousness as she pulled out her phone. "Hmmm, the national bean counter's convention isn't until July, they haven't published the cotillion schedule yet...."

Faith's sentence trailed off as she looked up; Rick had leaned in further, and framing her face in his hands, he tenderly pressed his mouth to hers.

All coherent thought fled as her nervous system danced with the electricity passing between them, and she felt the blood in her head rush toward her shoes. Lust, long dormant, once believed extinct, had been resurrected in her core.

Oh, sweet Baby Jesus, her inner self moaned.

CHAPTER SIX

Mama J appeared at the table, and grinned as they broke apart suddenly, both blushing furiously.

"Ahem. More tea? Any dessert?"

"I'll take a lemon bar, Mama," Rick said, "and some coffee." He glanced at Faith. "You?"

"Lemon bar, absolutely. And you still got that English Breakfast tea?"

"Coming right up," Mama J said, and beamed at them both before she turned away.

I do love seeing that, she thought to herself. *They just fit, don't they?* It made her misty.

***

They kept to small talk as they savored their desserts. When Mama J brought the check, Faith insisted on paying her half. He started to argue the point, saw the way her eyebrow shot up and jaw set stubbornly, and let it go.

As they strolled together back toward the bookstore, Rick casually took her hand, and said, "Faith, I have to see you again. Have dinner with me tomorrow night. You pick the place."

"I can't," she shook her head. "I fly out tomorrow afternoon for a week-long conference."

"Oh," he murmured. "Rain check, then?"

Silence, and Rick could feel her hesitation. So, he met her halfway.

"Why don't we do this? You know where I am. When you're able, and if you want to, come to the store, we can figure it out from there."

"Great. Well, here you are," Faith said, stopping underneath the Book Keepers sign. "I should probably get going."

"Happy to walk you there," Rick said sincerely. "It's only two blocks."

"I appreciate the offer. I really do," she began. "But..."

"But you're not ready for me to know which townhouse is yours yet."

"Probably sounds silly."

"You've been bruised. I understand."

"Rick..."

"Faith," he said, gently taking her in his arms. "I get it. I really do."

And he just held her for a moment.

He could feel the muscles in her shoulders and back coil instinctively at first, then gradually relax again. Slowly she brought her arms up and hugged him back briefly, then broke contact.

"So, yeah...um... see you later?" she asked, taking a step back.

And he smiled at her. "Absolutely."

"Okay then."

She smiled back, then turned, striding away towards home.

He watched her go, then grinned like an idiot as he went upstairs for the night.

***

Faith sat through the final day of conferences on Friday, taking copious notes. Although she was extremely versed in accounting already, the company she'd joined was in manufacturing, an industry she had no prior experience in.

So, she was absorbing as much as she possibly could, from the guest lectures, from the Q&A sessions, and from the mixers each evening. She'd made an amazing number of contacts, and was pleasantly surprised to discover more than one established, industry-specific resource group available to her that consisted of seasoned pros.

The week to date had been filled to bursting with activity – at least, until it was bedtime.

Then, like clockwork all week long, Rick popped unbidden into her mind without fail.

Rick Connor.

She sighed as she returned to her hotel room for the final night.

He was so amazingly hot. But also, he just seemed to bring something out of her. This inexplicable urge to just tell him anything and everything about herself, that made her want to fling open the door to her psyche, her inner sanctum, and invite him all the way in.

That part made her very, very nervous. That part was what had her wound so tightly, if she was being truthful with herself.

As smooth as Kevin was, he never even came close to getting in all the way, Faith realized. *And look at all the damage he still managed to do.*

That. That right there. *That* was what had her on the ragged edge.

Her delicate features took on a scowl.

Even though she had never fully lowered her guard with him, Kevin had handed her the biggest hurt she'd ever felt, one that almost killed her soul.

And now, she realized, she'd met a man who if allowed in all the way would have the capability to decimate her, not just wound her.

No wonder she was on the verge of panic when it came to Rick Connor.

She frowned, considering her choices as she prepacked some of her things in preparation for her morning flight home.

Should she just put a stop to this, avoid it altogether? It was so, so tempting to crawl right back inside herself, and just learn how to somehow be okay with being alone forever.

But she remembered how Rick had looked at her, the way his lips felt on hers, the shock she felt at first when he had held her, followed by a flood of feeling protected and cherished and well, *home,* like in his arms was exactly where she was meant to be. She didn't know how else to describe it. The sensation had almost buckled her knees. She'd never known that intriguing combination of primal lust and deep trust before, with anyone.

Not that you've gotten around that much, her inner voice teased a bit.

Faith's eyebrows peaked in response to that. There'd only been three men, in total, she'd been seriously interested in through her life up until now, and only two lovers, one in college, and then the idiot now ex-husband of hers.

But, she admitted to herself in the privacy of her mind, none of them had stirred anything in her that even came close to what she felt right now. And she knew she'd have to clamp down on the crippling fear somehow to explore her feelings.

Resolved, she pulled out her phone, navigated to the Book Keepers website, clicked the "Contact Us" button and created a message. Then she held her breath, hit "send" before she could chicken out, and headed to the shower.

***

The topic of Faith's internal discussion had changed into sweats and his favorite t-shirt and cracked open a beer.

Rick was midway through the third page of a project he was working on when he heard the chime that meant a new email coming through the store website.

He went over to his computer, called up the Book Keeper's company email, and grinned from ear to ear as he read the newest one. He typed a response and hit send.

***

Twenty minutes later, Faith stepped out of the shower, wound towels around her wet hair and body, and went to the sink to brush her teeth. A buzz indicated new email activity on her phone. She opened her email browser, read Rick's response, and giggled like a teenager.

Faith now had a dinner date for Sunday at six p.m.

CHAPTER SEVEN

It was absolutely, positively never ever going to arrive. Rick was sure of it. It seemed like an eternity had passed since he had flipped the Open sign on and unlocked the door at ten a.m. Sunday morning.

It was now a little before two.

Four hours down, four to go.

Four.

Jesus.

He ran his hands through his hair. The reverie was shattered by the delicate peal of the doorbell. He fixed a polite grin on his face, willed himself to concentrate, and bid his customers welcome.

***

Down the block, Faith was already driving herself crazy trying to decide what the hell to wear. She sincerely hadn't given a tinker's damn about her appearance in over a year - and her self-esteem was so battered she was on the verge of a panic attack over it.

In desperation she called her sister Jandy, and paced, listening to it ring and ring.

"Come on, come on, pick up, I need you, dammit," she grumbled. And swore when it went to voicemail.

She left a message, hung up, and almost threw the phone in frustration - then almost flung it from fright when it rang in her hand.

"Hey little sis, what's up?" Jandy said.

"Oh my god, I am glad you called. Can you come over? I need you."

Concern crept into Jandy's voice. "Honey, what's wrong?"

"I have a freakin date and I have no freakin clue what to wear."

A long pause.

"You. Have a date. Like, you finally ventured out of your little cocoon, and met somebody, and you have a *date*? *Seriously*?"

"Smartass. If you don't want to help, just say so."

"No, no, no, come on now, you know I didn't mean it like that. I'm just...surprised is all. I'm on my way, okay? Go take a hot bath, calm down, we'll get you looking fabulous. Love you, kiddo, see you in a bit."

Faith smiled, despite her current mood. Jandy always seemed to know exactly how to say exactly what she needed to hear.

Best big sister ever, she thought as she headed upstairs to draw that hot bath. As the tub filled, she added a lavender and jasmine bath bomb, and the scent wafting up with the steam soothed her troubled spirit.

She stripped down and climbed in slowly, sighing as the heat worked its way into her bones. She leaned back, closed her eyes and let her mind drift, although she had a hunch where it would go.

Thirty minutes later, Faith reached for the drain, opened it, and stepped out onto the bathmat. She had toweled off and had just slipped into her robe when she heard Jandy come in downstairs.

"Hey kiddo," her sister called up.

"Hey," she called back. "Thanks for coming. Be right down."

"No rush. Got coffee, or would you rather have tea?"

"The English, please."

As she went downstairs, she heard Jandy milling around in the kitchen, humming to herself. Faith paused in the doorway and watched her for a moment.

Jandy was the oldest, but most who saw her would have never guessed she was over forty. Brown eyes that always smiled, closely cropped hair the same color, and a lively and sweet spirit. At twenty-four she had become the second mom to her siblings when their mother had gotten sick.

Her sister noticed her and came over with arms outstretched.

"Come here, girly," Jandy said, and scooped her up in a big hug. "Now. Tell me all about this guy. He must be pretty damn special."

Faith grinned, sat at the kitchen table and propped her face in her hands.

"He is. He's literally tall, dark, and handsome, and runs the bookstore two blocks from here. I got bored with myself last Saturday night, and I could hear you in my head telling me to not be a shut-in. So, I got dressed, and went to check out the place."

"Ah, yes, you and books," Jandy smiled as she handed Faith a cup. "A love affair that's well documented."

She sat, sipped, made a face and reached for the sugar. "Continue."

"Yes, well, that place is amazing," Faith said. "I was standing there just taking it all in, and he spoke to me, and I turned around. And Jandy, my God, he's pretty."

Jandy laughed. "You're blushing!"

Faith's shoulders hunched a bit. "If you saw him, you'd understand."

"Hmmm. One of those that cause naughty thoughts?"

Now Faith laughed. "Geez, you know me way too well. Anyway...," she drank, contemplated.

"So, what's the problem? Why the panic over what to wear? Knowing you, you probably just threw on that ratty sweatshirt and pulled your hair up. So, anything you pick tonight is going to be an improvement," Jandy teased, jostling Faith with her elbow.

"Well, he wasn't deterred by that sweatshirt, or the ponytail, or even no makeup," Faith sighed. "We wound up going down to Mama J's for dinner, and talking a while, and he kissed me. Then, he asked me out for the next night. I couldn't go, I had that trip this week. But we're meeting for dinner tonight."

"I say again, what's the problem here? Sounds like a nice guy, and you're obviously attracted to each other. What's going on with you?"

"Tonight's a real date, like, an official date. I insisted on going Dutch last weekend."

"Oh," Jandy said, understanding. "And you are terrified."

"Completely."

"Oh honey," Jandy said, holding her hand. "Faith, you can't let what Kevin did cripple you. You didn't deserve that. Any of it. I know you've been hurt, and that you are scared to let anyone else in, but you've got to try to live again at some point. You'll miss something, someone, wonderful if you don't."

"And," she continued, holding Faith's gaze, "the heart that's meant to love you will know your worth, as a person, as a woman, and that heart will heal yours, if you let it."

Jandy rose decisively.

"But for tonight, it's just a meal, right? No major decisions to make tonight. So, let's chillax a bit, and let's go see about what to wear, okay?"

Faith straightened her shoulders. "Thanks, sis. You always know just what to say."

Leading the way up the stairs, she said, "I was thinking the royal blue sweater... and 'chillax'? *Really*?" and laughed.

***

By four forty-five, Faith had picked out something that she felt confident about. Jandy hugged her, wished her luck, and left. But instead of immediately heading home, she opted to take a little walk.

Reconnaissance.

She wanted to see exactly what creature had her baby sister so excited and terrified all at once.

Being overprotective, I know, she told herself. *But she's been through so much already. I really hope for Faith's sake that this guy is the real deal.*

She entered Book Keepers and looked around the place, nodding approvingly. She turned toward the front counter where a dark-haired man was finishing up a phone call.

Wow, she thought. *Baby sis has good taste.*

He ended the call, then looked at her. "Hi, welcome to Book Keepers. I'm Rick, the owner. How can I help you?"

"Just browsing," she said.

"Oh, ok, sure," he said distractedly, and checked his watch. "We close at five on Sundays, so about five minutes from now. But you're welcome to return anytime. We're open Wednesday through Saturday from ten a.m. to eight p.m., and from ten to five on Sundays." And checked his watch again without realizing it.

"I'll come back," she said, and left.

"Geez, he looks as nervous as Faith did," she murmured. "That's kind of cute."

She sent up a silent prayer on her sister's behalf as she returned to her car and drove away.

CHAPTER EIGHT

Rick locked the door behind the last customer.

Oh my God, finally, he thought. *It's almost time to see her again.*

He ran on autopilot as he closed out the register, shutting everything down. Then he headed upstairs for a shower. He wanted to look his absolute best.

***

At five-forty p.m. Faith stood in front of her mirror, checking the results. She'd contemplated leaving her hair loose, a silver and brown waterfall down her back, then opted to pile it high into a loose bun instead. She kept her makeup to a minimum - eyeliner, a hint of shadow, mascara, just a bit of blush, and nude lips. The royal blue sweater fit nicely, showing curves without being tacky or revealing. Slightly faded jeans ran down to her boots.

Jewelry. She pondered it. Typically, she didn't wear much at all, only her college program ring on her right ring finger. But she found tiny diamond studs she'd forgotten she owned, and those she put on before opting to add a simple gold chain and tiny cross that had been her mother's.

She thought about, rejected, reconsidered, and finally consented to just a touch of perfume on her wrists and at the base of her neck. Then she stood a moment, eyes closed, willing herself to remain calm.

Jandy's voice echoed in her head. *It's just a meal, right? No major decisions to make tonight. So, let's chillax a bit.*

Chillax.

That still cracked her up. Must've been something Jandy picked up from the kids. Faith's niece and nephew were what? Nineteen and twenty-one now?

Jesus, time flies, she thought wistfully. She glanced at her watch. Five-fifty.

It does indeed.

She grabbed her phone and purse, overcame the couch calling to her telling her to play it safe, and firmly locked her front door.

As she walked toward Book Keepers, the knot in Faith's stomach seemed to grow and grow.

Just a meal, it's just a meal, she chanted in her head as if it were a talisman warding off evil. Her palms were sweaty. Absentmindedly she scrubbed them on her jeans as she walked. She arrived at the door just as it was opening.

Seeing him standing there made her stomach knot shrink some.

He looks nervous too, she thought, and the realization calmed her further.

He reached out and took her hand.

"Hi," he said, as he stepped outside. "Let me just lock this, and we'll head out."

She watched as he secured the door. Long sleeve button-up shirt, sleeves rolled to halfway, and damn if it wasn't the exact same color as her sweater.

It looked good on him.

He turned, caught her gaze, looked down at himself then back to her.

"Great minds, huh?"

"I believe you called it 'kindred spirits' the other day."

"That I did. Shall we?"

And they began to stroll back the direction of her house. The restaurant she'd chosen was about six blocks down and was a favorite of the neighborhood residents.

"Have you been to Jade's before?"

"Not yet," Rick admitted. "To be honest, I haven't really gone more than four blocks this direction since I got here."

"Well, you're in for a treat," Faith said. "Great food, nice atmosphere, and the people that own it are friendly but also give you your space, you know?"

"Sounds great," he said.

Then he caught her completely off guard by turning to her and stating, "I missed you."

"I missed you too," she said, smiling, and made his night.

They arrived and were seated quickly. Within moments, their drinks were served, and their dinner order placed.

"So," he asked, "how was the conference?"

"Amazing!" she said. "I have quite the learning curve about the manufacturing industry to work through, so it was nice to go be steeped in it for a week and be surrounded by others in my field. I made a lot of good strong contacts. So now, if I see something that's particular to manufacturing that I don't understand, I have people I can reach out to and ask if needed."

Faith took a drink, then asked, "How was *your* week?"

"Well," Rick answered, "pretty interesting. Met a guy named Max Jones."

"He came back?" Faith interrupted.

"You know him?"

"Kind of," she said. "He was looking for your Uncle Jack the day before Thanksgiving. Saw me on the street and asked me if I'd seen him lately. Said they were supposed to meet but your uncle wasn't answering his phone."

"Yeah," Rick said. "Uncle Jack always tried to answer, even if it was just to say, 'I can't talk, I'll call you back'. And he never failed to return a call."

"Anyway, long story short, Mr. Jones is the one that sensed something was wrong, called the police and had them check it out, and that's how they found him. Oh, and, sorry I interrupted you."

Rick grinned. "You're forgiven. So, you must be the 'attractive younger woman' Max was referring to when he told me that exact sequence of events. Small world."

Faith blushed.

Their conversation was paused as their food arrived and was placed neatly before them. After the waiter refilled their iced teas and left, Rick leaned over slightly and inhaled.

"Smells and looks fabulous."

"And the best part is, it tastes just as good."

"As I was saying," Rick resumed, "Max came down and introduced himself. He said he used to work with my Uncle Jack, then asked if I'd be interested in a little consulting work since Jack was gone."

"Really? What kind?"

"Solving puzzles."

"How weird. Why would he ask you that?"

"Remember when I told you I was retired Navy? Well, I was active service for twenty years – as a cryptology technician."

"That is seriously cool '007' sounding type stuff," Faith stated. "But what the hell would you need codebreaking skills for in the civilian world?"

Rick leaned in closer.

"It's not for the civilian sector," he whispered.

"Oh," she said, then her eyes widened as understanding dawned. "Ohhh..."

"Yeah," Rick grinned, and took another bite. "Anyway, it's classified, I can't share more than that, but suffice it to say it's damn interesting work. I got all the relevant files sent to me this week. A lot of stuff to dig into. I live for this kind of thing, and I get to put everything I learned from my Navy career to good use."

"Wait, aren't you going to get into trouble for even telling me this much?" she asked, panicked.

"No," Rick chuckled. "Besides, I trust you completely."

"You barely know me."

"That's not true. Kindred spirits, like I've said before."

With dinner done and the table cleared, they ordered coffee and hot tea, and shared dessert and further details.

He'd been an only child. She told him about her brother and sisters. He talked about his time in the Navy, describing some of the places he'd seen around the world in twenty years' time. And she walked him through the recent job change that had revitalized her professional life.

They talked birthdays – Faith had her thirty-sixth coming up at the end of June, Rick had just turned thirty-nine in February.

But Faith had a nagging feeling as they went along that he was holding something back from her, something vital. She couldn't shake it.

Finally, she summoned up the courage and asked the question weighing on her.

"What aren't you telling me?"

He gazed at her intently for a long time.

"Not here," he said, and signaled for the check.

CHAPTER NINE

They walked back toward his store, mostly quiet. Rick unlocked the front door, held out his hand, and brought her inside. He locked the door behind him then pointed to a door at the back of the store.

"I'm not really a fan of this setup," he explained as he led the way, "but, if I want to put direct access to upstairs from the outside, I have to get permission from the city, permits, yada, yada."

"However," he continued as they reached the door, "I do think *this* part's pretty cool."

He opened the door to reveal an old-fashioned lift with a sliding grate door.

"Don't worry, it's up to code. I made sure of it before I settled in here."

"I love it," Faith replied sincerely. "Love the history, and the fact it's still here so we can experience it."

"After you," he gestured, stepping in behind her.

The old mechanism groaned and creaked a bit but never missed stride as it gently brought them up to the second floor. Rick opened the grate, and Faith stepped out into a massive space.

"Wow," she managed. "This is absolutely gorgeous!"

"Welcome to my humble home," he said. "Would you like the grand tour?"

"Yes please," she smiled, and moved forward a bit, turning slowly. "You did all this remodeling on your own?"

"Sure did," he answered proudly.

He'd opted to leave most of the space open all the way to the rafters rather than put in a drop ceiling. This led to a cathedral effect and had enabled him to install skylights for natural lighting. Rich wood flooring the color of mahogany stretched the length and breadth of the area, meeting tile in a wide doorway to the left of her that Faith presumed led to the kitchen and dining room.

Across the expanse of the living room Faith could see another door over to her right, leading to the bedroom and bath area. An old and by its looks lovingly restored fireplace lent both warmth and charm to the sitting arrangement and beautiful area rug placed in front of it.

A wide screen TV, the biggest she'd ever seen, was mounted on the adjoining wall, and equipped with surround sound speakers. At the opposite end was a sleek workstation with dual monitors, and in its own space was a workout area boasting a treadmill and bench with free weights. She noticed that the treadmill was angled for its user to be able to watch the big screen while running.

"Help yourself to a drink if you'd like. There's wine in the fridge, sweet tea, and I have a fully stocked bar just through there," – he pointed back toward the living room area – "if you'd like something else. I'll be right back." And he went into the bedroom for a bit.

"Hmm. To be honest, I'm not much of a wine drinker," she called out to him. "I'll scope out the bar offerings. What would you like?"

"Amaretto sour, please, if you're in a mixing mood."

"What?"

"What, what?" Rick said, a bit confused, sticking his head through the bedroom doorway.

"Did you just say amaretto sour?" Faith asked.

"Yeah. Why?"

"Oh, no reason, it's just my preferred mixed drink, is all. I don't recall ever meeting anybody else that likes them."

Rick grinned. "Get out."

"I'm serious."

"Interesting. There may be something to that whole kindred spirits thing. Mix us a couple."

Smiling, Faith made her way to the bar.

"Disaronno. Nice!" she said, locating glasses, ice and the sweet and sour mixer. She mixed the cocktails and sat on the couch. Rick joined her a moment later.

"I'd like to explain my question, if that's all right," Faith began. "The other night you made the mistake of asking me my story. Kind of got out of hand. I didn't intend to share that much. Something about you, though. You're easy to talk to."

He grinned.

"So, your turn," she said directly. "You said you weren't married anymore either. What's your story, Rick? I sense a huge data gap here. What haven't you told me?"

The haunt in his eyes was palpable, and she immediately regretted the question.

Gently, she said, "I'm so sorry, I didn't mean to pry."

"It's okay," he replied softly, "I want to share with you. I need to get it out. You're easy to talk to, too. Give me just a moment please."

Rick took a long drink to steady himself. Then he reached for her hand, took a deep breath, and began.

"I was married for sixteen years to Becky, my high school sweetheart. We were happy. Had two kids, Ethan and Ellen, that were the center of my world. Four years ago, I was on deployment in Sigonella. They didn't come with me for that posting because Ethan had just started high school and made the varsity football team as a freshman, and we wanted our kids to be able to do all four years of high school in one place."

He closed his eyes but kept going.

"Long story short, I got notified that they, along with my parents, had all been killed in a car accident coming home from one of Ethan's games. Some dumbass kid decided to drink and drive, crossed the center line and hit them head on."

Rick glanced up at Faith and saw raw grief for him in her shimmering eyes. She reached out and quietly placed her other hand over his. Her breath caught in a sob, and she squeezed his hand.

"Rick, I am so very sorry."

He squeezed back, then exhaled deeply.

"I came home on emergency leave, and Uncle Jack met me at the airport and stayed with me, and he and I made all the service arrangements and stuff. He and I got really, really close through all that. He's the one that kept me level. He talked me out of going AWOL and pulled me out of the downward spiral I was headed into. I owe the last four years of an honorable Naval career to him."

He raised his glass in a silent toast, took another long drink, and continued.

"So, I know what it feels like to have your heart ripped out through your throat and your world turned upside down in an instant. And I know what it feels like to want to shut everyone and everything out and keep people as far away as possible. Up until lately, that was easy for me to achieve. I was still active Navy; I still had a job to do."

Another drink.

"But retiring. Man. Suddenly I could go wherever I wanted to, whenever I wanted to. It hurt too much to try to go back and build a new life in the town they died in. So, I didn't go back. I reached out to Uncle Jack and asked if I could come stay with him once my discharge was complete, and I sold the house that I'd held onto all that time."

Rick finished, "Finalizing the sale took almost a month longer than I'd planned. There were some issues that delayed the process. By that time, the lawyer called and let me know he was gone. I've told you the rest of it from there already."

He turned to Faith with a sad smile.

"You're the first person outside of me and Uncle Jack that now knows the entire story, start to finish, no omissions, no varnish. Uncle Jack only knew because he had a front row seat for it. In my chain of command, only my CO knew that I lost my family, but I didn't go into details with him, and I told no one else I worked with."

Faith was at a loss for words. When Rick rose and walked to the fireplace, she cleared her throat, and spoke her heart to him.

"I want to thank you," she said sincerely. "I know that wasn't easy at all for you to tell me about. It means a great deal to me that you feel comfortable enough with me to share yourself like that."

He nodded in acknowledgement as he watched the flames but did not speak.

I'm amazed he shared that with me, she admitted to herself. *That explains the unsettling feeling I was having about him. Which I just realized is gone now.*

CHAPTER TEN

She came out of her reverie when Rick asked, "Would you like another drink?"

"No, one's usually my limit, to prevent my saying or doing anything stupid," she admitted.

He laughed. "Sweet tea it is then. I'll be right back."

Rick went into the kitchen, returning a few minutes later with two tall glasses.

He handed her one, then said, "I'd like to propose a toast. To the amazing woman sitting beside me, who I hope I haven't scared off, and who I hope says yes to more dates."

She smiled as she clinked her glass to his, and they took a drink.

"There's more I need to say," he told her.

But it looked like the weight of the world had already been lifted from him, so Faith was confused as to what there possibly might be left to reveal.

Rick gently took her hand.

"What I didn't tell you yet is that when I came here it was with the intention of running my bookstore and being a hermit. I poured all my energy into this -" Rick swept his arm out indicating their surroundings "-to build a nice place to hide myself. My own fortress, as it were. Because I'd given up. After four years alone, I'd given up on feeling anything that deep ever again."

He turned to face her, putting his hands on her shoulders.

"Until last Saturday night just before eight, when you walked into Book Keepers, and turned my life upside down all over again, but in a great way."

"Me?" Faith's jaw was slack with shock.

"Yes, Faith. You."

"Rick. You don't want me. You barely know me. You must have me mixed up with someone else."

"Nope. No mistake. I knew the first time I looked into your eyes."

"I'm broken. *Seriously broken*. I'm not a good bet."

"This isn't a bet, or a game to me, Faith. And I'm broken, too. Kindred spirits. Remember?"

"Why? Why are you saying this to me?" she pleaded.

"Because it's the truth."

He touched her face lovingly.

"I'm scared," she stammered, trembling as she stepped back.

Rick took her hand and placed it on his racing heart.

"Feel that? So am I. Scared brainless. But I'm on the same ledge you are, Faith, and I am taking your hand and asking you to trust and jump off with me."

Words failed her for the second time in one night.

Faith lowered her head to Rick's chest. His arms went around her, and he touched his lips to her hair. He could sense, feel, the warring factions within her, the turmoil as she weighed which path to take.

When she raised her head to look into his eyes, and he saw the molten desire in hers, the control he'd fought to maintain gave way. He pulled her tighter to him, plundering that full mouth with his, gentle at first, then more and more insistent.

Her hands slid up his back, into his hair, as her soul awakened to his kiss. He ran his hands up first, unleashing her hair to let it fall, then gently down the sides of her face, her shoulders, down her sides just grazing her breasts, her ribs, settling on her hips for a moment as the kiss went deeper, deeper.

She gasped and clung to him as he broke the kiss and lowered his lips to trace the supple beauty of her neck.

"You smell so good," he murmured, placing strategic kisses as his hands slowly worked up underneath her sweater, under her bra. When he gently cupped her breast, she moaned.

"Rick," she managed.

"Hmm?"

"I...we... this is too fast...."

He stopped, withdrew his touch from her skin, and waited, his smoldering eyes locked with hers.

Faith took a step back, breathing heavily, trying to will her knees not to buckle.

"I am unbelievably attracted to you," she said. "And that felt really good, just, too fast."

It came easier now, she realized, because with him she didn't have to filter, just say it, and he would follow.

So, she told him.

"Rick, you don't even know my last name. My favorite color, my favorite food. I know this sounds stupid, but I don't want to just hop into bed with you right off. I want it to mean something more than that."

He tilted his head slightly. "I never had any intention *other* than being completely with you, not just sex."

Faith's eyes widened. His eyes never left hers, and she could see the want now tinged with anger and, she was surprised to note, hurt.

"Faith, I don't know what you're used to dealing with, or what you take me for, but I'm not wired that way. There's a reason why I've been alone so long. If it was just sex I was looking for, that itch could have been thoroughly scratched multiple times over the last four years."

Now he stepped forward.

"When I told you that you turned my world upside down, I meant it. I don't say those things lightly. I don't take these feelings lightly. I am trying, very hard, *not* to be offended that you think I would."

"I didn't mean it that way," Faith stammered.

His eyes flashed. "You've locked yourself away from the world, intentionally, so you don't get hurt ever again. I understand that. I've *lived* it. But you think I'm like every other man you've ever known, that after I bed you, use you, I'm going to just walk away without thinking twice."

She looked back at him with raw eyes and couldn't hold back the flood of emotion anymore.

"Exactly. That's *exactly* it. A large chunk of my life turned out to be a complete fabrication, one great big cosmic joke, and I am almost forty, and I am starting all over again, alone. I don't have enough armor left to survive another round of war. And *you scare me*. I want you, but I don't want to. I am putting up wall after wall to keep you out and you keep knocking them down. You scare the living hell out of me...."

When he saw the tears begin to fall, Rick enveloped her in his arms to try to comfort her, but it only lasted a few moments. Faith broke off, stepping away, arms wrapped around herself to try to stop shaking.

"I need to go now," she whispered, then fled.

***

Rick stood in his living room with his eyes closed and his head down, trying to process what had just happened between them.

She's so much stronger, sexier than she realizes, yet so fragile.

Her whole body shaking in his arms as he'd held her sobbing frame against his chest had gutted him to the core. It made him want to just wrap around her and protect her from absolutely everything, made him want to locate that idiot ex of hers and pound him into little, tiny pieces with his bare hands.

She's been through hell. But she's worth waiting for. So, I'll wait. As long as it takes. And she needs to know that.

He started after her.

***

Faith was trembling so much she almost couldn't get the front door to Book Keepers open.

"Faith, wait. *Please*. Wait just a minute," Rick called to her as he stepped off the lift.

Finally, her fingers cooperated enough to turn the latch, and she yanked the door open and raced down the sidewalk out of sight.

By the time she reached her townhouse, she was crying so hard she could barely see the lock well enough to insert the key.

Fate pitied her, and in between great gulping sobs the key somehow found its way into the slot. She barreled through then locked the door behind her before she sank to her living room floor.

CHAPTER ELEVEN

When she got home from work the following afternoon, Faith walked upstairs, traded in the business gear for yoga pants and her faithful sweatshirt, and took her hair down. She had just made it into her kitchen when the doorbell rang. Confused, she peeked through the viewer, then smiled and flung the door open.

"Sarah!" she cried, scooping up her little sister into her arms and making her drop her luggage.

"Oh my God it's good to see you! Get your skinny butt in here," Faith exclaimed as she let go of Sarah long enough to help retrieve suitcases and shut the front door. "You look fantastic!"

"Thanks," Sarah said, hugging her again. "You too."

Stepping back, she looked around. "Cool place, Faith, it suits you."

Faith looked at her little sister lovingly. Sarah was the only one of the siblings that didn't inherit the brown-on-brown variations. No. She was the only one that had bright green eyes and fair hair, like their father's side of the family.

Growing up we called her the milkman's kid, because she looked nothing like the rest of us, Faith remembered with a smirk. *But the shape of her eyes? Pure Mom.*

"What are you doing here?"

"The gig in San Fran wrapped up finally. And I was headed back to Manassas for a breather, and decided I just had to stop in Texas and see you."

Now Sarah narrowed her eyes and stepped closer. "Oh. My. God. Faith, you have a new fella."

"What?"

"I can just tell. Spill it, girl, I'm all ears."

Before Faith could speak, there was a brief knock on the door, and then Jandy let herself in. She stopped, gaping for a moment, then smiled as Sarah rushed her for a hug.

"Well, well, it's our little Cali girl," Jandy beamed.

Faith asked, "Hey big sis! What are you doing here? I wasn't expecting you."

"Are you kidding? Tony's working, kids are working, and I wanted to hear how the big date night went, so here I am."

At this, Sarah's ears perked up. "I *knew* it. The gut doesn't lie."

She looked at Jandy. "I was just this instant telling her to spill it because I could tell she has a new guy."

"Fine," Faith said, in mock defeat. "Let's eat too though. Who wants Chinese?"

***

The Chinese food arrived in about twenty minutes and was quickly divided onto three plates. The three sisters sat around Faith's table, wine glasses in hand, like old times. Sarah brought Faith and Jandy up to speed on her finished job in San Francisco.

"Lots and lots of hours, the entire holiday season went by in a blur. Was so busy I couldn't even look up," she sighed, then took a sip. "But worth it. They've already mentioned throwing me their *entire* fall campaign this year, not just the Christmas one."

"Good for you!" Jandy said, raising her glass in salute. "You've found your stride. We're so proud!"

Glasses clinked; sips were taken.

"And what did you think of Bella? Didn't they come see you over spring break?" Faith asked Sarah.

"They did," Sarah confirmed. "And she's an absolute doll. Perfect for Nathan. They just fit, you know?"

All at the table agreed.

"Now," Sarah said, pointing at Faith with her fork, "you've stalled long enough. Spill already."

Sighing, Faith told them about Rick. How they met, the entire sequence of events.

Before she got to the official date part, Jandy chimed in.

"Sarah, I can report he is a complete hottie, just like Faith says."

Faith's eyebrows went up as her jaw went down. "OMG. No. You didn't."

"I did. Are you kidding me? You were so wound up. Had to see for myself what the fuss was about. Don't worry, I didn't threaten him or anything," she added, hunching her shoulders a bit at Faith's growl. "I just went down, looked around the store. Said maybe five words to him. He had no idea who I even was. I can tell you this, he was acting just as nervous as you were. It was really sweet to see, actually."

"Aw," Faith's face got dreamy. "You're forgiven."

"Wow, what a look. Okay, Faith, keep going," Sarah prodded.

So, she did. But she prefaced it with a solemn, "Next part stays between us."

They both nodded - both remembered the sister code they'd created as kids.

"Oh my God, that is so sad," Sarah murmured, hand on heart, when Faith got to the part about his family.

"You do realize he's way beyond just 'into you', right?" Jandy pointed out. "Guys don't share that kind of stuff with just anyone."

"Oh, I know he is, because of what happened next." And she continued the story.

Now Sarah had tears sliding down her cheeks.

"You mean...," she swiped at her eyes and took a breath to calm herself, "he *actually said* all that?"

"Yeah, he did," Faith sighed.

"Good man right there, kiddo," Jandy told Faith earnestly, her own eyes starting to brim a little. "Don't be afraid to take a chance here, honey."

"That's the sweetest, most beautiful, most romantic thing I have ever heard, ever," Sarah sniffled. "I mean, to have a man be that open and honest, Faith. Just, *wow*. I am so happy for you and so jealous at the same time. What did you do when he told you that?"

Faith's nose crinkled as she hunched her shoulders.

"I ran."

"What? *Why*?" Sarah gasped.

"I... I got overwhelmed."

"Oh, honey," Jandy murmured as she patted Faith's hand. "We talked about this."

"I know we did. It's just... He was so..."

"Romantic? Passionate? Amazing?" Sarah offered.

"Not to mention if and when the sex *does* finally happen between them, it will probably be explosive and earthshattering," Jandy boldly predicted with a wicked little grin.

Silence for just a moment as Sarah's mouth hung open and Faith turned beet red.

Then rollicking laughter all around.

Three sisters. Like old times.

***

Jandy glanced at her watch.

"Geez, it's almost ten already, I'd better get going."

She pulled out her phone and texted Tony to let him know she was about to head back from Faith's.

"He worries," she smiled as she hit send.

"And I think it's sweet," Sarah piped up. "Hey Jandy, can I go back and stay over tonight with you? I'd love to see Tony and the kids before I fly out tomorrow night."

"Absolutely! Grab your gear, meet you outside." Jandy gave Faith a hug and stepped out.

Sarah wrangled her luggage toward the door, then paused.

"Hey, Faith."

"Hey, yourself."

"I want to say I'm proud of you."

"For what?"

"For trying again. I know the dink cratered you, pretty damn bad, even though you put on a brave face and stuffed it down like you always do. So, I know how big a step it was to go on that date."

She leveled a look at Faith.

"But please don't let the past continue to dictate the future for you, Faith. Something tells me this Rick guy is worth taking that leap. Promise me you'll at least consider it."

"I promise," Faith replied, and hugged Sarah before she walked out the door.

Faith softly closed and locked it behind Sarah, then leaned against it.

"I know he is," she whispered to herself. "I just need to get past being terrified to take that chance."

CHAPTER TWELVE

It was four months before Faith found the courage to return to the little bookstore down the street.

She waited until just before five o'clock on a pleasant September Sunday afternoon, then walked the two blocks to Book Keepers, her heart beating so loudly she was certain every pedestrian she passed could hear it.

She paused just out of sight of the front windows, closed her eyes, and focused on her breathing.

I haven't been able to get him out of my head. I need to see him. I need to know if he still feels the way he said he did.

And what if he doesn't? What then?

Well... then I guess I'll know I blew it.

She talked herself into walking through, rather than past, the entrance and noticed the look of complete surprise on Rick's face when he glanced over and saw her standing in his store.

"Hi," he said softly, and made her stomach turn to butterflies.

"Hi," she whispered back. "Is it all right if we talk?"

"I'd like that," he answered, and started to come around the front counter, but stopped as two patrons approached the register with their purchases.

She nodded to him once, then made her way to the mysteries and thrillers section to collect her thoughts while she waited.

***

While his hands busied themselves ringing up his customers and packaging their books neatly, Rick's mind raced.

I can't believe she's here. And I hope to God she doesn't leave until we can talk.

He thanked his customers and watched them leave, then walked over to the door, locked it, and flipped the sign to 'Closed.'

As he inched his way toward the rack that he knew she'd be standing in front of, his heart began to pound.

***

She'd just picked up the latest Paul Austin Ardoin novel and begun reading the back cover when she sensed Rick was nearby.

Faith turned slowly and looked up into his brown eyes.

He took a tentative step forward.

"Faith, I.." he started to say, then stopped.

"I missed you," she said simply, resisting the sudden urge to wrap her arms around him and not let go.

He smiled, and her butterflies intensified.

"I missed you, too."

He took another step toward her.

"You wouldn't want to go get dinner or something, would you?" he asked hesitantly.

"Yes, but I think we really should talk first," she answered. "Is it okay if we just go upstairs?"

"As long as you're comfortable with that."

"I am. I trust you, Rick."

He led the way to the lift.

***

He purposely kept the conversation centered on food as they walked into his kitchen.

"I've got stuff for sandwiches, and... that's about it, actually," he admitted with a shy grin as he scanned the contents of his pantry and refrigerator. "Haven't gone grocery shopping in a while."

"Sandwiches work just fine," Faith told him as she sat on a barstool at the counter.

He began pulling the items needed and setting them on the counter.

"Would you like something to drink? I have tea made."

"I think something just a bit stronger. You want one?" she asked.

"I'll take a whiskey over ice."

"I'll be right back, then," Faith replied, and made her way to the bar in the living room to pour out two tumblers.

***

The conversation was light as they sat at his kitchen table and ate. She filled him in on what had been happening at her workplace, and he shared that he'd brokered a deal with several schools in the area to supplement their summer reading programs with new books.

When the meal was over, they moved to the living room and sat down on the couch.

She took a sip of whiskey, then set her glass down, turned to him, and spoke.

"I'm sorry," she began. "When you told me what you did, I completely freaked out and I ran away, and that wasn't fair to either one of us."

Rick watched Faith's face intently, his expression betraying nothing.

"I thought that if I stayed away and just... ignored what I was feeling for you, it would all work out. That it would go away."

She sighed, stood and moved to the fireplace.

"But it hasn't. I can't get you out of my head, Rick. And the more time passes, the more I feel like I missed a chance to have something really great in my life. I know I hurt you when I ran, and I am so sorry. I feel grateful you're even willing to speak to me anymore."

He stood and walked over to her and started to speak, but Faith kept talking.

"I just...I know you probably hate me now. I know I blew it and there's no chance for us at all anymore..."

Her voice trailed off as her eyes brimmed, and she turned away from him in embarrassment.

She closed her eyes when she felt his hands on her shoulders.

"And you underestimate me, a great deal," he said softly as he turned her to face him, then gently wiped the tears from her cheeks with his thumb.

"You captivate me, Faith, heart and soul, not just body. From the instant I saw you, I felt like I was finally able to breathe again, to feel again. To *live* again. That doesn't just go away." He kissed her lightly on the cheeks and forehead before he tenderly pressed his lips to hers.

And his understanding, his gentleness, the look he gave her that showed he truly did know firsthand about dying on the inside is what undid her.

He caught her as she slid down, took her in his arms, held her and comforted her while she purged over a year's worth of pent-up grieving and heartache from her soul.

***

She had no idea how much time had passed. All Faith knew was that she was emotionally and physically exhausted.

She had run out of tears.

Rick stroked her back, her hair, and rocked her gently to try to soothe her wounded spirit.

In a small voice she finally spoke.

"I bet I look amazing right now. Waterproof mascara, my ass."

Rick laughed and tilted her face up to his.

"You're beautiful, no matter what your makeup is doing. You're even more beautiful without it. But it's not run as badly as you think."

"I need to freshen up, and you probably could use a dry, makeup-free shirt."

Faith pulled herself upright and headed to the bathroom. At the sink, she ran cool water, wet a washcloth, and ran it over her tear-stained face.

And watched Rick in the mirror as he passed her, shirtless, to the closet.

There's that well defined six pack, I just knew he had one.

He walked back toward her, pulling a snug fitting t-shirt down around his midsection, and stopped when he saw he was being watched.

"What?"

"Um. Nothing. Got any aspirin? Making a complete ass out of myself in front of a cute guy brings a headache every time. This one's a doozy."

"I imagine your head must be killing you right now. And for the record, you didn't make an ass of yourself," he said, and handed her two Excedrin. "How do you feel, other than the head?"

"Drained," she said. "I didn't realize how much stuff I had pushed down and not dealt with, I guess. Quite a litmus test for you, I bet, dealing with me ugly crying. Are you sure you still want to be around me?"

"More than ever. You really think I'm cute?"

"More than ever."

"Good. Stay with me tonight, Faith. Not sex," he added hastily, hands up. "Just, stay. Rest. We can talk more, watch TV, sleep. Please."

She went to him and took his hand.

CHAPTER THIRTEEN

They snuggled up on the couch, Rick's hand tracing lightly up and down her arm.

"I'm sorry about before," she said sincerely.

"For what?"

"When I said I wanted it to mean more than just hopping into bed. That hurt you when I made it sound like that's all you wanted. I saw it did. But I didn't get that vibe at all from you; I still don't. That was me trying my damnedest to find enough bricks to build enough of a wall you couldn't knock down. So that you would give up, go away."

"I know."

She sighed, puzzled.

"How is it you know me so well already? How did you manage that?"

"Because, Faith, I built walls too. Different catalysts, same result."

"I'm sorry too, for what you went through. That must have been devastating."

"Yes," he sighed. "It was. I wouldn't wish it on anyone."

She shifted around so she could see his face.

"You meant what you said, didn't you?"

"All of it, but which part are you referring to specifically?"

"That you're broken too."

"Yes, I am. But for the first time in a long, long time, I know what and who I want, and I am hopeful."

And he kissed her temple.

They fell silent again, watching the fire casting shadows around the room. Faith yawned.

"It is getting rather late," Rick noted. "If you'd like, you can take the bed, I can sleep out here."

"I'm not kicking you out of your bed. That's rude. Besides, I kind of like snuggling with you. I've missed that more than I thought I would."

"Well then. I promise to keep my hands to myself. Sincerely," he added, looking into her eyes. "We will go as slow as you need to."

He stood up and took her hand, pausing at the doorway to his bedroom.

"I have some extra pajamas in the closet, let me get them for you."

"Okay."

Faith moved to the far side of the bed and sat to remove her boots. He returned with an oversized US Navy t-shirt, and a pair of plaid flannel pajama bottoms.

"Here you go," he offered.

"Thanks. I'll just, um, step in there for a minute," Faith said, pointing to the bathroom. She closed the door behind her and leaned against it for a moment.

***

He's different, she sighed. *He truly is. Never met a man like him, ever.* Her self-preservation radar was still pinging, though not sounding the alarm nearly as loudly now.

Her mind whirled a million different directions at once as she removed her jeans, sweater, and bra, stacking them neatly. She pulled on the pajama bottoms, tied the drawstring, then slipped on his t-shirt.

Smells like him. And it made her smile.

She brushed out her hair with long practiced strokes as she talked to herself in her head.

I still can't believe someone like him would want someone like me, her wounded self said.

What do you mean, 'someone like me?' her warrior side shot back. *You make yourself sound defective. You're not. You're smart, funny, pretty, driven. And there's a gorgeous man in the next room who is totally into you, who totally gets you, who is willing to move at whatever speed you want. You're only defective if you* don't *see where this goes.*

"You know what?" Faith whispered to her reflection. "You're right. I do deserve to be happy."

***

She came out of the bathroom, standing with the light behind her highlighting the silver streaks in her dark hair. She turned off the light, walked slowly toward the bed, and he was awestruck once again. She looked so natural, so right, wearing his shirt. It took his breath.

"Jesus," he said out loud before he could help himself.

"Hi," she grinned.

"Hi," he grinned back. "You really look good in my shirt."

She blushed as she made her way to her side of the bed and got in. "Thanks."

"What time do you want to get up?"

"I need to be out of here by six so I can go home and get ready for work."

Rick reached and adjusted the alarm clock, then turned out the lamp.

"I'd forgotten what it's like to have someone in bed with me," he admitted in the dark. "Been a really long time."

"For me, too," she answered, then said, "oh, wow...." as she looked up.

The skylights over the bed lent the perfect view to thousands upon thousands of stars spilling like diamonds onto the ebony carpet of night sky, and a glorious moon, bathing where they lay in a calming subtle light.

She turned her head to see his profile partially shadowed.

"Cool, isn't it?" Rick said and turned to look at her.

"It's breathtaking," Faith replied, turning her face to the sky again. "Reminds me of when I was little. We lived in an old farmhouse out in the country about an hour north of town. No city lights around.

At night, we'd go lay in our front yard in the grass and just look at all the stars."

She sounded peaceful, relaxed, filled with wonder.

"Rick, look! Shooting stars."

He smiled, put his arm around her as she snuggled up and laid her head on his bare chest. "You have to make a wish now."

"You do too," she said.

"No need. Mine already came true." He kissed her hair, feeling her cheek get warmer against his skin.

She's blushing again, he realized.

It melted his heart a little, that she could react so strongly to simple truth. To tenderness. It tore at him just how hurt she'd been. Instinctively he started to wrap his other arm around her.

"Rick?"

"Yes?"

"I think mine might have, too."

She raised her head, then shifted her body so that she was slightly over him, her left leg draped between his.

"I'm still on shaky ground. I know that. But it sure feels less shaky with you, Rick. I'm still scared, but I want to see where this goes."

"Good to hear," he replied, and kissed her gently. "I don't want to keep just existing, like a half-alive shadow. I want to get back to living each day to the fullest. With you."

They fell silent, and in that lovely twilight of pre-sleep, she heard him whisper to her.

"Faith."

"Hm."

"What's your last name?"

"Thomas." And she chuckled.

He held her closer and they watched stars until they drifted off in each other's arms.

CHAPTER FOURTEEN

A gentle buzzing, buzzing.

Faith, eyes still closed, cocked her head towards the sound. And frowned, furrowing her brows. It didn't sound familiar. She opened one eye, startled at first.

This is not my room. Where am I?

Then she remembered, and relaxed. Turning her head, she noticed Rick watching her, a smile curving his lips, his eyes sparkling.

"Good morning, beautiful," he murmured sexily.

"Morning," she said shyly.

"How did you sleep?" he inquired, stroking her cheek.

"That was nice," she said. "Peaceful. Is it six already?"

"I'm afraid so."

"Dammit." She sighed. "I guess I'd better get going then."

"Are you sure you can't stay?"

"Unfortunately, yes. Not on such short notice. But at some point," she added, as she reluctantly rolled away from him and out of bed, "I'll take at least one day when you don't open the store and spend it with you. Deal?"

"And when will that be?"

Faith tilted her head, grinning.

"Let me get quarter-end closing done, and we'll plan something," she called out from the bathroom where she'd gone to put her clothes back on and pull her hair back.

She came back into the bedroom, handed him his pajamas back, slipped her boots on, and put her purse on her shoulder.

They headed to the lift.

Rick walked her toward the front door of Book Keepers, then grabbed her and kissed her tenderly.

"When can I see you again?" he asked, brushing his lips with hers.

"When do you want to see me again?" Faith asked playfully, feeling sixteen again.

"I don't want you to leave to begin with," he nipped her bottom lip. "But that's your call."

"Hm," she responded. "How about dinner Friday night, after you close the store? My house. I want you to know which townhouse is mine."

His smile was a mile wide. "Ah. Progress. I look forward to it."

He unlocked the door, opening it for her.

"See you later, Faith Thomas. Have a wonderful day."

She grinned, then started for home.

***

Rick locked the door and returned upstairs. Ordinarily, he'd have rolled over and gone back to sleep if he'd woken at six a.m. on a Monday.

But this one had been special. He had awakened to his future lying beside him, and the mere thought of that had energized him. He was wide awake and revved.

He fired up the coffeepot, then his computer.

***

Faith arrived right on time to work. As she made her way toward her office, Jan, the receptionist, called out, "Hey, Faith, looking great today! How was your weekend?"

"Fabulous," Faith replied, with a million-watt grin.

***

Tomorrow's just too long until I see you again, Faith. I'd love for you to come over for dinner tonight, Rick said when he emailed her Thursday morning. *Around eight?*

I'll be there. Anything I need to bring? she replied and smiled to herself as she hit 'send'.

The answer was immediate.

Just your beautiful self.
***

When he met her at the front door of the bookstore, he noticed she had a little backpack slung on her shoulder and was smiling secretively like she had something up her sleeve he wasn't privy to – yet.

As they stepped off the lift he said, "I need to check on dinner."

He took her hand and they walked to the kitchen, and he gestured to the cozy two-seater table, then to the barstools lining the opposite side of the countertop from where he pulled open the oven door.

"Pull up a chair, your choice."

"Something smells amazing. What are we having?" Faith asked, as she once again appreciated the long, clean lines of marble countertops accented by beautifully built wooden cabinets in a cherrywood finish.

"Thanks," Rick replied. "Keeping it simple tonight. Angel hair pasta with chicken and mushrooms tossed in garlic and olive oil. And fresh bread. The buy-and-bake kind from the market," he grinned.

He tested the pasta and nodded. "Perfect. Time to drain."

He did that, then pulled the bread out of the oven and started assembling the pasta to bring to the table.

"Want some help? I can slice the bread," she offered.

"Sure," he said. "Already have butter, salt, and pepper on the table, so bread, the pasta, and us and we should be ready to eat."

She found a bread knife and sliced several pieces from the still warm loaf, placing two on each plate. Then she filled two glasses with ice and sweet tea and set them on the table.

Rick brought the bowl of pasta over, set it on the table, then pulled out her chair for her and lit the tall candle in the middle to complete the table before being seated himself.

"Faith, I'm happy you're here."

"Thanks. I'm happy you invited me."

He took a drink. "I have to tell you - I was pretty nervous about this. First real chance I've had to show off my culinary skills in over four years."

"Really?"

"Really. But I figured we click so well I'd take a chance on it."

"Smart move, this looks and smells fabulous. Pass the butter please?"

"Sure." He scooped some pasta onto his plate, then grabbed hers and did the same for her.

"Thanks."

She twirled up a forkful, stabbed a sliver of mushroom and chicken to go with it, and closed her eyes, savoring the flavors.

"Rick, this is really, really good."

"It's one of my favorites. Like I said before, I was stationed in Sigonella, Italy for a while. Learned to make it there."

"So how was your day?" he asked.

"Funny you should ask. We got hit by a ransomware virus at work yesterday afternoon, and all hell broke loose," she replied. "*Everything* is down. The boss has called in an outside IT group to work with our guys to see if anything can be done."

"I'm pretty good with tech," he reminded her. "Happy to take a look, if you guys need me to."

"I appreciate that. Hopefully, they'll be able to get it sorted out soon. How's your day been?"

"Got another set of files from Max this afternoon, and I can already tell this one's gonna be a doozy. I'm jazzed. Ready to get started on it."

Finally, Faith put down her fork and sighed.

"I want more, but I can't take another bite."

Rick laughed. "Me either."

They worked in companionable silence side-by-side to clean up after the meal.

When the last dish was dried and put away, she said, "Hey, you don't mind if I crash here again, do you?"

"Careful, Faith Thomas, or I might think you're sweet on me."

"Well in that case, I'll just use your bathroom right quick, then head home."

She went into the bedroom and shut the door, and Rick mentally kicked himself for being a smartass.

He was standing in his living room trying to figure out how to apologize for being a jerk when he heard a strange rustling noise and looked over.

She stopped in the doorway between his bedroom and the living room, and he gawked.

Faith had taken her hair down and was wearing an extremely sensual floor length black silk robe, loosely tied in the front. He could see just enough to see she wasn't wearing much else.

"Faith. Are you sure?"

"I'm sure."

"I don't want to rush you."

"You're not."

CHAPTER FIFTEEN

Tranquil. Satisfied.

Home.

That was her first coherent thought later, as she came back to herself with his arms around her in their safe place under the sky.

"Mmm," she hummed as Rick's hand ran lightly up and down her back, caressing.

"Mmm, yourself," he said, overwhelmed by her.

"That was...."

"Agreed."

"I never knew it could be like that."

"Me either."

"What time is it?"

He turned and looked. "Almost ten."

"Huh," she said. "We have some night left."

"That we do. What did you have in mind?"

"Oh, I was thinking TV, maybe surf the web...Ooh! I know! Naked hide and seek downstairs in the store," Faith grinned mischievously.

Rick lifted a brow and grinned back. "Why, you naughty thing you."

"Or," she continued, "we could enjoy that jacuzzi tub together."

"There it is. Your secret's out. You're just with me for my book selection and cool tub," he said in mock seriousness. "I'm hurt."

They laughed together.

"Seriously, though, a soak does sound good."

"Consider it done, baby. I'll go set it up. Give me a couple minutes."

He untangled his body from hers and walked into the bathroom. She watched him go, eyeing him like a hungry predator.

Inspiration struck, and she headed through the living room to the kitchen. She grabbed the wine, two glasses, the candle off the table, and a matchbook she found in a drawer.

Faith strode back into the bedroom as he came out of the bath. Rick grinned as he saw what she was carrying.

"Gonna get me drunk and take advantage of me?"

"Absolutely," she said with her best come-hither look.

She saw the flames of lust in his face again.

"But first, the tub."

She stepped over the threshold, sat the wine and glasses down on the wide corner next to the wall.

"Climb in," he said. "I've got this."

"In just a minute. Have to do something first."

She walked to the counter, grabbed her brush and a hair tie from her purse, gathered up her hair and placed it back into a high bun. He watched her every movement, fascinated.

Their eyes met in the mirror, and she smiled. "Now I'm ready."

As Faith eased down slowly into the steamy water, he lit the candle, set it on the counter, poured out the wine for each of them and handed her a glass, then turned out the light and lowered himself in across from her.

"And now," Rick said, "bliss." And pressed the button for the jets.

"This. Is. *Awesome*," Faith murmured, sinking down and leaning back, wine glass in hand.

"Yeah," Rick said. "This thing came in real handy during the renovation process. It was the first piece I installed up here after I got the walls put up and the flooring down."

He chuckled, remembering.

"You should have seen the looks on the delivery guys' faces when they brought this thing and then realized I was not cool with them just leaving it at the curb for me to wrestle inside alone. A hundred-dollar bill each later, they helped me not only bring it up, but place it where I wanted it to go. After a long day of swinging tools and working on this place, I would get so knotted up I couldn't sleep unless I spent some time in here first."

He paused, gazing at her.

"But seeing you in it, with the way you look in candlelight, takes it from just functional to sexy as hell."

She smiled softly at him.

"You don't know it, do you? You truly don't realize," he murmured.

"What?" she asked.

"How effortlessly sensual you are. It's striking, partly because you have no clue about it. You're just...you."

Now she frowned, sipped her wine.

"Sensual. That's not a word I would have ever picked to describe myself."

"Interesting, because that's the first word that came to mind when you walked into my store."

"Oh." She wasn't sure what to say. "My take on the word 'sensual' was that it's meant for someone, well, younger and in way better shape than me, for starters. First word that comes to my mind to describe myself is average."

Twenty minutes later, after Rick had demonstrated his belief that she was far from average, they padded back to the bedroom hand in hand, Faith pulling at the tie in her hair to let it down as she yawned. Then they tumbled into his bed together, legs intertwined, and slept.

***

Friday morning found Rick and Faith much as they'd been when they'd fallen into bed Thursday night – legs intertwined, snuggled up and sleeping soundly in each other's arms. Daybreak peeked in at them through the skylight, stirring them to wakefulness.

"Hello, gorgeous," he said, as he kissed her good morning.

"Hi there," she murmured sleepily and returned the kiss. "What time is it?'

He craned his head around to look. "Eight-fifteen. Faith! You're late for work!"

"Nope," she confirmed. "When that virus took us offline the owner put us all on standby. If they need me to come in, they'll call me. Can't do much right now anyway. Now. Your bookstore opens at ten, right?" she asked.

"Yep."

"Well, then, guess we'd better get moving at *some* point," she remarked dryly. "I'm headed for the shower."

"Want some company?"

"You know it."

***

The shower took a very erotic detour, so getting out of it had been delayed a bit. Faith was still smiling as she finally stepped out and into the oversized towel Rick was holding out for her. She tilted her face up to his and planted a noisy kiss on his lips.

"Definitely the most fun shower, ever," she pronounced.

He grinned in response and patted her on the butt as she walked past him toward her little backpack.

"How does bacon and waffles sound?"

"Sounds perfect. For some strange reason, I have a very healthy appetite. It's almost like I burned a million calories recently or something," she said cheekily, wiggling her eyebrows at him.

Rick roared with laughter. "Me too. I'm starving."

He dressed and went to the kitchen to begin making breakfast. She toweled her hair as dry as possible, pulled it up and put her clothes on. Then she picked up her phone and sent a quick text to Jandy before joining Rick in the kitchen.

***

Jandy was waking up slowly with her first caffeine jolt of the day when her phone buzzed with a new message. She yawned as she picked it up and scrolled lazily to read.

"Explosive and earthshattering, wasn't that what you predicted?" her baby sister Faith had sent. *"Well, it was, a million times over. Great guess! I just love it when you're right"* followed by a ton of very big smiley faces.

Jandy chuckled. "Good for you, baby sis. Good for you." And typed a reply.

CHAPTER SIXTEEN

Faith saw Jandy's response and laughed. *OMG DEETS!!!,* it said.

She texted back *call you later,* hit send, then dropped her phone into her purse and turned her attention back to the extremely attractive man in front of her.

"What can I help with?" she asked.

"I've got it under control," he responded, moving bacon around the pan. "But the scenery in here just improved exponentially," and leaned over to kiss her.

"You know," she reminded him, "we are supposed to have dinner tonight at my place."

"I haven't forgotten. And I know what a big step that was for you to take."

"Kind of pales in comparison to last night, I'd say."

He pondered that a moment as he pulled crispy bacon out of the pan, setting it down on paper towels to drain a bit.

"You know what? I don't agree. Here's why."

He paused as he made sure the waffle maker was heated up and ready to go.

"I think that a lot of times, physical intimacy is easier than emotional intimacy. It's harder to trust than it is to roll around naked with someone new, since just rolling around usually can't cause as much hurt as trusting can."

He looked intently at her for a moment.

"So, I still think you offering to let me see where you live was a pretty big deal all its own."

The look on her face made his eyebrow go up.

"You okay?"

"Yeah," she said honestly. "Just trying to wrap my head around the fact that you're in my life. I wasn't expecting you. I wasn't even looking. But here you are. You're gorgeous, built, smart, funny, passionate. And for some unknown reason, you want me. Pretty much everything I had hoped to find but had given up on."

"Oh, honey," he said, and kissed her gently as he handed her a plate of food.

"Seriously," she said. "And I cannot get my head around it. It doesn't feel real. I keep expecting a camera crew to peek out from somewhere and yell "PSYCH!" or something."

She grabbed the syrup and poured some on her waffle before she sat down and continued, "Like this is all someone's idea of a really elaborate and horrible joke."

He stopped what he was doing, came to her, cupped her face in his hands and rested his forehead on hers.

"No joke, baby. Not even close to one. You are where I am meant to be. I feel it down to my core. I know how badly you've been hurt, so you need to ease into this. I totally get that. It's okay. Just know, I am all in, and I am not going anywhere."

He kissed her, then released her to attend to the waffle that was beginning to smell close to overdone.

And to lighten the mood a bit, he teasingly added, "And don't think I didn't notice that 'gorgeous' and 'built' came before 'smart' on your list."

She grinned.

"I wanted to see if you were listening."

***

After breakfast, they headed downstairs together.

"I am going to run home for a while. I want to check in with my boss, see the status of things with that damn virus," she told him.

And she winked at him, then kissed him before heading home.

Back at her townhouse, Faith changed clothes, and called her boss. And the news wasn't good. Zero forward progress made. As more time passed it would become more and more difficult to undo the damage. Evidently, the virus wasn't just a ransomware, it also replicated through its host environment; the damage was multiplying exponentially.

The IT group had also discovered that it had embedded itself in the company's website. This meant that anyone even navigating to their site could have the virus transmitted to their systems as well, even if nothing on the page was clicked at all.

Faith put her head in her left hand as she held her phone in her right, listening to her boss tell her all the bad news. Then he said the thing she'd most dreaded hearing.

"Faith, we may not come back from this. The IT group is overwhelmed, they've never seen anything like it before. They're recommending we call in the FBI."

"Sir," she offered, "my brother happens to be an FBI agent up in Virginia. If you like, I can call him and get his advice on what to do next."

"Please do, and keep me posted," her boss replied despondently. "Forty years in business, Faith. I built this thing from the ground up. Now I think it may be gone. I hope I'm not right, but it doesn't look good."

"Let me make some calls, and I will call you back," she said firmly, trying to be reassuring. "We'll get to the bottom of it."

She hung up, took a deep breath, and called her baby brother.

***

"Hey, Faith! What's up?"

"Nathan, I need some advice."

She quickly walked him through what had happened at her company.

"I'm on it," he responded immediately. "Call you back in just a few."

Having gotten his IT man's take on it, Nathan rang Faith back ten minutes later and passed on Mitch's direct number.

"Call him right now, Faith. Mitch thinks he can still fix the damage, but he'd have to move quickly."

"Nathan, I owe you huge for this! Love you. Gotta go."

***

Faith called her boss back and passed on the data. She could hear the renewed hope in his voice.

"Keep me posted, sir," she said. "You're welcome, sir. Bye."

And felt renewed hope herself.

I was always fearful of my baby brother being a lawman, she mused. *But man am I glad he followed that path.*

Now, she could concentrate on the main reason she'd come back to her house, which was to get the meal for tonight started. Good old comfort food. Roast with carrots and potatoes.

She figured Rick hadn't had that in a while – roasts always seemed way too big to bother with cooking for just one person – and it was one of her favorite meals to prepare.

She rubbed some seasoned salt and black pepper onto the meat, then browned it on all sides in her cast iron skillet before placing it gently into the crock pot. Her next step was to place wedges of onion around and on top of the roast. Finally, her secret weapons – cream of mushroom soup, and brown gravy mix. These she whisked together with water and poured over the meat.

She checked her watch. Ten-thirty a.m. Rick wouldn't have the shop closed until eight p.m. She put the lid on and set her crock pot for low power for nine hours. The roast would be done to a perfect fork-tender in about seven hours, with two left over to add in the carrots and potatoes so that they wouldn't overcook. It was a rhythm she'd perfected over time through trial and error.

Satisfied that dinner was handled, she glanced around her house. Everything was tidy already; it just needed a couple of minor housekeeping items done.

So, she dusted, and she swept, and she made sure the bathroom was clean and presentable, with fresh towels. She changed the sheets on her bed, putting on the satin set - *look at you, putting on the sexy set,* her inner voice teased and made her blush – and took the ones she'd stripped off to the washing machine.

Her phone rang as she was starting the washer.

CHAPTER SEVENTEEN

"Girl. Did you forget me?" Jandy asked pointedly, then laughed.

"Sorry, got distracted with work stuff," Faith replied, and brought her up to speed on that stuff first.

"Geez," Jandy exclaimed. "I hope that Mitch guy can fix it."

"Me too. Now, about last night," Faith began, and shared a very, very broad overview of the previous night's events; basically, that it had happened, and it had been amazing.

She'd always been close-mouthed when it came to sex, but she realized she *really* didn't want to share details this time, not because she was by nature shy, but because she felt like that would be very disrespectful to Rick. She told her sister as much, and it surprised her a little when Jandy agreed.

"I know I said DEETS in my text, but I was kidding, hon," Jandy told her. "Bedroom stuff between a couple needs to stay between them. When I was younger, I didn't realize the importance of not breaking that trust. I guess that's one of the wisdoms I've gathered over the years."

She paused.

"Anyway, sounds like you've got yourself all four pillars, kiddo. I'm so happy for that."

"Four pillars?" Faith was confused.

"Four pillars. Mental, emotional, physical, spiritual. When you have all four of those categories in your relationship in a positive state, in a happy state, that's a healthy and loving and well-balanced relationship. What some might call 'soulmates'. I refer to it as the four pillars."

"Four pillars," Faith repeated. "I really like that."

They talked a bit more, then Jandy had to run. "I've got a conference call with my biggest fabric supplier in about ten minutes. But listen, Faith. Stay open to this new relationship. I know it's probably a little scary, but it sure sounds worth it."

***

Down the street, Rick was wading through his quickly moving day. Summer break had just ended, and the success of the book exchange program had led to becoming a supplier for the schools year-round.

He'd spent a large portion of his day printing off the exchange lists emailed over from the schools and packing boxes for each campus to come pick up.

Faith came back by around two in the afternoon and brought him lunch. It was a welcome break. He displayed the "be back in an hour" sign in the window, locked the door, and they went upstairs.

She filled him in on what was going on with her work as she made their plates and sat with him at his kitchen table.

"That sounds promising," he nodded encouragingly. "Hopefully they can get you guys back on track quickly with minimal loss."

"I sure hope so," Faith said. "How are things here today?"

"Pretty good," he responded before biting into a chip. "I have fourteen orders packed up, eight left. Every shipment should be picked up by around six tonight."

"Cool, and we are on target to be able to eat whenever you arrive," she told him. "Which reminds me."

And she handed him a slip of paper.

He smiled as he read it. Her name, address, phone number, and email.

He got up and went into the living room, returning with a business card that he handed to her.

"So," she quipped. "I guess we're an item now. No more "Contact Us" through the website to communicate anymore."

"An item?" he tilted his head and considered her for a moment, then grinned. "Yeah. I like the hell out of that."

"Me too," she said, grinning back.

They finished lunch and headed back downstairs.

"I'll be over a little after eight."

They paused at the door.

"Okay, so, see you tonight," she said, and kissed him.

I love you, he almost said.

But he honestly didn't know what her reaction would be to that just yet.

So instead, he just said, "Looking forward to it," and kissed her back.

***

Rick checked his watch. *Seven-thirty*. Almost closing time.

The school reps had all been punctual, for which he was grateful. All orders were gone by six as expected. Now he started the pre-close activity - running a dust mop over the hardwood floor, filling out the nightly close sheet. The next half hour passed quickly, and he was able to lock the door.

He texted Faith, *See you in twenty*.

He went upstairs, took a lightning-fast shower, and dressed, then checked his watch as he locked the front door behind him.

Eight-seventeen. Not too bad.

He made it to her door by eight-twenty as he'd predicted and pressed the doorbell.

"Hi there," Faith said, leaning forward to kiss him. "Come on in. Dinner's ready."

"Something smells incredible."

Rick closed his eyes, sniffed, then got a nostalgic look as he opened his eyes.

"Roast? Aw man. That's one of my favorite comfort foods ever, haven't had it in ages."

Faith smiled proudly.

"So, it sounds like I guessed well for tonight."

He wrapped his arms around her, grinning. "You hit a grand slam with this one, baby."

***

Faith and Rick sat at her kitchen table talking, letting the food settle a bit before dessert.

"Lemon bars from Mama J's," she said. "I know you like those, and since I didn't think to ask about any others you like, I chose to play it safe." And winked at him.

He stretched and ran his hands over his midsection.

"I am going to need a while before I get into the lemon bars," he stated. "The roast was fantastic, so tender and so much flavor. What's your secret?"

"Cream of mushroom soup and brown gravy mix," she told him.

"Really. I would never, ever have thought of that. But man, it's amazing. You brown it on all sides before you crock pot it, right?"

"Yep. My mom told me years ago that doing that locks in the juices."

"Mine did too," he grinned at her. "And she was right."

She made coffee for him and tea for her, and they talked as they moved to the living room.

"By the way, Faith, I like your place," he said. "It suits you."

She glanced around the room, trying to see it as he did.

An overstuffed armchair, the slightly worn couch she'd spent so many Saturday nights on, the rows and rows of books lining the wall all around her TV set.

"And I see the Robb series holds the place of honor," he pointed at the bookshelves.

"Of course. Not only are they my favorite series ever, but they're the first ones I started to collect," she replied. "Which reminds me. I bet being the owner of a bookstore, where literally any title you want you can get a hold of, is particularly satisfying."

"It is, no question," he answered. "That and other perks, like being able to have book signing events. Some of the books in my personal collection upstairs are autographed already. Now that I have a store, I can add to those with much less chance of having to travel to obtain them."

"Speaking of traveling," he smiled and took her in his arms. "Want to show me the upstairs?"

***

Before they could take too many clothes off, they heard Faith's doorbell ring, followed by loud knocking.

"Who the hell could that be?" Faith panted, putting her shirt back on.

"No clue, but their timing sucks," Rick muttered, buttoning his pants up again.

The barrage of noise continued as they went downstairs to the front door. She looked through the peephole.

"What the hell?"

She swung open the door.

"Good evening, ma'am, sir. I am looking for a Faith Tucker."

CHAPTER EIGHTEEN

"It's Thomas," she corrected, a bit harshly. "And you're looking at her. What's going on?"

"I need to talk to you, ma'am," the man said, and showed her his detective's badge. "May I come in?"

"Sure," Faith gestured to him, completely confused. "Would you like some coffee?"

"If it's not too much trouble."

"Not at all," Rick answered, pouring him a cup.

She and Rick sat together at one end of her kitchen table, and the detective took the seat opposite her.

"Ms. Thomas, I'm Detective Mitchell, Dallas PD," he said. "I need to ask you a few questions about your I am guessing now ex-husband, Kevin Tucker."

"Oh, Christ," Faith said bitterly. "What the hell did he get himself into now? Did he get caught bouncing on someone else's wife?"

"I suppose that could be a possibility," Mitchell said, "since he was murdered yesterday."

Faith and Rick's mouths dropped open. In any other situation, they'd have looked comical.

But this was not any other situation.

Rick put his arm around Faith's shoulders as she shook her head.

"What? Did I hear you right?"

Detective Mitchell nodded in affirmation.

"His body was found about one-fifteen this morning up in Philly. Coroner estimates he was killed sometime between six p.m. and ten p.m. Tuesday night. Philly PD pulled up his records and he still has you listed on everything. Next of kin notification, emergency contact, all of it. Naturally, they asked us to come talk to you."

"Detective, the last time I saw Kevin was over a year ago. The thirtieth of May, to be exact. That's the day I found him screwing another woman in our bed."

And the image flashed into her head like she was right there again, in real time. Every sound, every heartbreaking thing about that moment came rushing back. It made her nauseous.

She started to tremble and felt Rick's arm tighten a bit in silent support. She paused for a moment, regained her composure, and continued.

"Trust me, if I were going to kill him, I would have done it right then. He didn't even have the balls to show up to our divorce hearing last August. And I certainly haven't sought him out since. I don't miss him, or the bullshit being with him brought me. I am sorry he was murdered, Detective, no one deserves to go like that. But I cannot in all honesty sit here and pretend to be sad that he's dead. I won't," Faith finished, eyes dry and head held high.

"I understand completely. I'm just here to make the notification, and ask a few questions, that's all." He leaned his elbows on the table and held her gaze. "So, for the record, I do need to ask you where you were Tuesday between six and ten p.m."

"I was here, alone."

"Ms. Thomas," the detective continued as he made notes, "can you think of a reason why Kevin would still have you listed on everything?"

"Detective, I didn't know I *was* still listed on everything, but I do know exactly *why*," she said, maintaining eye contact. "He was extremely lazy, and he truly believed tedious little life tasks like paperwork were beneath him. I handled any and all legal and financial matters in our marriage. If not for me, he wouldn't have built up any assets at all. So, it doesn't surprise me at all that he never changed anything, despite the fact his lawyer probably strongly advised him to."

She didn't know it, but she'd just confirmed Kevin's divorce attorney's comments when he'd been interviewed up in Philly earlier in the day.

"Well," the detective rose. "That should do it. I appreciate your time. I'd say sorry for your loss, but..."

"In this instance, my loss occurred over a year ago."

"Yeah, sounds like." He shifted on his feet. "Like I said, Philly says he has you listed on everything still. Don't be surprised if you get contacted by his lawyer, the life insurance company, or both."

"Thanks for the heads up, Detective Mitchell. If Philly has any more questions for me, please tell them I will help however I can. I didn't kill him, I have nothing to hide, and I am not going anywhere."

"Quite a statement, ma'am."

She shrugged.

"I'm an accountant. OCD is part of it. Details matter when you're trying to solve something. And that also means ruling out the ones that don't fit the puzzle. Besides, what I just said is true."

She saw him to the door, then turned back to Rick.

"You all right?" he asked as he crossed to her.

She sighed.

"Yeah. That was a little surreal to hear. But I'm not upset. That part's weird. I was with him for twelve years, married for ten. You'd think I would feel...something. But nope. It's like hearing about a complete stranger's death. No emotional reaction at all."

She looked at him. "Is that wrong? That I don't feel anything?"

"I personally think that there's not a damn thing wrong with that. He cut you deep once upon a time, Faith, and for your own safety, you banished him. It's a natural reaction, and the result is, the feelings go too. Maybe not instantly, but over time, they go away too."

***

Philly Homicide Detective Munoz was at his desk at seven a.m. on the dot.

His desk phone rang.

"Munoz," he answered, then listened. "Wow, that was fast. I'll be right down."

He made his way to booking, where a nineteen-year-old kid had been picked up on carjacking charges, and whose prints were found at the scene where Kevin Tucker's body had been found.

Not even an hour into the interrogation, the kid cracked. He'd tried to steal Kevin's car as part of a gang initiation. There'd been a struggle, and Kevin had been shot and left in the alley. The kid's prints were both inside and outside the car, he'd changed clothes but still had spatter traces of Kevin's blood on his Air Jordans, and he'd tested positive for gunshot residue.

Police were still looking for the 9mm handgun that had been used, but other than that, police had an open and shut case against him.

The kid had never even heard of anyone named Faith. This was a straightforward carjacking gone wrong, no conspiracy, no planning.

Once Munoz had all his reports typed up, he sent them and the kid's confession to the DA's office. He also sent a formal statement of findings to the life insurance policy representative he'd reached out to the previous day. Then he erased the case from his whiteboard and wrote in the data for his next.

CHAPTER NINETEEN

Saturday morning also saw Rick and Faith enjoy waking up together, this time in her bed.

"I love waking up with you," he whispered, stroking her back as she lay on his chest.

"Mm, the feeling is very mutual," Faith whispered back, tracing little kisses across bare skin.

He lifted his head to look at her alarm clock. "Eight-thirty," he said. "Don't have to be at the store until ten."

She lifted her head to look into his eyes.

"My turn to lead, then," she said against his mouth before doing just that.

**

Not too long after Rick left extremely satisfied and with a mega-watt grin, Faith's phone rang. The caller identified herself as a Mary Mullins with Prudential, and could she please speak with Faith Thomas Tucker?

"Speaking," Faith said. "But it's just Faith Thomas these days."

Mary proceeded to fill her in. She was sure Faith had received the sad news by now, blah blah, the data her office had received indicated no reasons why the claim could not immediately be paid out as prescribed in the policy. They just needed to confirm her mailing address and would be overnighting her papers to sign, and upon those pages being returned to the company, the policy proceeds of two million U.S. dollars in a certified check would then be sent overnight.

Faith confirmed her address, ended the call, and sat on her bed, hands shaking.

Two million dollars.

She'd had no idea this was coming. She'd known about the policy, of course; she'd been the one to handle setting it up.

But she'd had no clue until Detective Mitchell mentioned it that Kevin had been his usual lazy self and failed to follow through with taking her off the policy.

Which also meant, she was probably going to have to be the one to handle all his other stuff, too. Unless the lawyer was willing to handle it all.

It was like she'd sent a summons out into the universe. Her phone rang again, and it was the lawyer she'd just been thinking of.

"Hello again Faith, how are you?" Marty said.

"I'm good, Marty, how are you?"

They'd always gotten along. Marty hadn't been Kevin's divorce lawyer, because Faith had moved faster and had gotten to him for that piece of business first. But Marty had previously done all their final expense planning and wills and was very familiar with the whole layout of their financial world during their marriage.

"I'm good. Faith, I'll get right to the point. This is straightforward stuff here. He never changed anything, even though that other lawyer that represented him in the divorce suggested it more than once. The will states you get it all. My question is, what do you want to do with it?"

"Sell it all, Marty, I don't want to keep anything. Bad juju. Just sell it – house, cars, whatever – and send me a check please."

"Let's do this, keep it all official. I will be sending you, via courier, a copy of the will, along with a complete detailing of all his assets, and any monies he owed to anyone. You look that over, send me back instructions in writing, okay dear? And we will proceed from there."

"Sounds like a plan."

"Good. Now, dear, we need to talk about the next piece of business. The coroner's office will be releasing his body to you, as next of kin per all his paperwork."

She closed her eyes. This was the part she dreaded.

"As you know, his will states he wanted to be donated to science."

"I remember, Marty. What I don't remember is, can we just arrange for the coroner's office to transport him directly? I don't want to see him. I don't want to even be near him."

A pause on the phone.

"To be honest, Kevin's my first client that's chosen donation," he said. "So, I'm not sure. I can find out, though, and include the data on that in the packet."

She breathed a sigh of relief. "Thanks, Marty."

"Anytime, kid. For what it's worth, I always thought he was a complete schmuck, running around on you like that."

She laughed. "Me too, Marty. Me too."

They said their goodbyes and she hung up the phone.

Restless, she called her boss for an update.

"The FBI team arrived just a while ago, with that Mitch guy leading," he informed her. "They're setting up some gear and it looks like it won't be long before they hit it running."

She was glad to hear the hope in his voice.

"That's great," she encouraged. "From my end, the Accounting stuff is as updated as it can be at this point. We'll have a really, really solid place to restart from if needed."

"Good to hear," he said. "Hey, why don't you plan on just enjoying yourself until Wednesday, then plan on coming in at eight. We'll get all the managers together, and we can revisit all this and see where things stand."

"Are you sure?" Faith asked him.

"I'm sure. Faith, I appreciate that you've been willing to be on standby through this, but really, until these guys can get us some solid answers, I don't see the need."

"Your call, boss. If something comes up and you need me to do anything before Wednesday just let me know."

"Will do. Take a breather."

"Huh," she mused as she hung up the phone. "What am I going to do with myself until Wednesday?"

Rick's store hours meant that he would be working every day of the weekend. Unless she could convince him to take a break.

Her eyebrows arched as she contemplated it.

She had no idea what his financial status was. It simply hadn't come up yet. She felt bad at the thought of asking him to play hooky with her if the lost revenue would mean problems for him. She paced a bit and thought some more. She wouldn't know unless she asked, now would she? Only one way to find out.

So, she'd wander down to Book Keepers. It was lunchtime anyway, and she was betting he'd be ready for a break. She packed up the leftover roast and some additional items and headed his direction.

Stepping into Book Keepers around one p.m., she was welcomed with a smile and a kiss.

"Thank God you're here," he said. "Faith, you're the first person through that door today since I opened."

"Ouch," she winced, and immediately felt even more guilty for what she was about to suggest.

***

He saw something flash across her face but couldn't quite put his finger on what it was. Before he could ask, she piped up and said, "I brought roast for sandwiches, if that's okay."

"That's totally okay," he answered, and he flipped the sign and locked the door before they went upstairs.

Once they were situated in the kitchen with plates filled, he looked at her directly, and said, "So, okay, about before. I mentioned you were the first person to come in today. I saw you wince, and then something else flashed over you. What were you thinking just then?"

CHAPTER TWENTY

"Wow, nothing gets by you, does it?"

"Nope. Not only am I naturally observant, but the Navy also honed it to a fine point."

"Touché," she said.

"So, what's going on in that beautiful brain of yours?"

"Well, I talked to my boss earlier. The FBI team is onsite and gearing up to look at what's going on. He said there was no point in being on standby and gave me off until Wednesday."

"That's great! So why the face?"

"Well," she stumbled, "I planned on asking you if you wanted to take a long weekend with me, but I was worried about you losing income if the store was closed. Then I get here, and you said I was the first customer all day, and I felt even more guilty for wanting to ask you to come goof off with me."

"You are so sweet," he told her sincerely, and kissed her. "But there's nothing to worry about. I own and run Book Keepers because I *want* to, not because I *have* to work."

"Really?"

"Yes, really," he confirmed. "Actually, I don't *ever* have to work again, if I don't want to. I could live just fine off of the interest I make."

"What are you? A millionaire?" she teased.

"Actually, I am," he answered seriously, and chuckled when her eyes bulged. "Why? Is that a problem?"

She laughed, loud and long. "That's perfect. I'm so relieved."

Rick looked puzzled. "Why?"

She filled him in on the conversations with the life insurance company and with the lawyer.

"Sounds like you're going to be wading through lots of legal documents soon."

"Yeah. But it will be good to get it all done and move on. Except the donation part. No clue how that works." She frowned, looking and feeling stressed.

"I do," he said, and when she turned to look at him, he shrugged his shoulders and continued, "well, I didn't think I'd ever have anyone in my life again to miss me, so I changed my will to donate my body to science. It's a pretty simple process, really."

"What happens?"

"The coroner's office calls the facility the body was willed to and lets them know that person has passed, and that facility arranges transport. Which means," he covered her hand with his, "no, baby, you won't have to see him or be anywhere near him. I know that's the part of this that was freaking you out the most."

She let out her breath.

"You're exactly right, that one piece of this whole thing just tore at my gut. Even though he's dead, I don't want to be anywhere he is. At all."

"I figured," he said gently, reassuring her. "And you won't have to."

"So, back to the original topic," she said. "Wanna play hooky with me?"

"Are you kidding me? Of course, I do," Rick grinned. "We can start now, if you want."

Faith laughed. "I was thinking a mini road trip starting tomorrow afternoon, actually. I feel the need to stick around for those two overnight packages to show up. Sooner I get that stuff in motion, the sooner it can all be over with."

"Agreed," he nodded. "And it gives me time to pick a perfect place for our first getaway together."

"Rick Connor, you hopeless romantic," she teased, batting her eyes at him.

"Only for you, Faith Thomas. Only for you," and he swept her into an ardent kiss.

***

Like the leaves turning, more things had changed in Faith's world by mid-November.

She'd received the package from Marty the second week of September and gone through the numbers with a fine-toothed comb.

Between the stocks, cash accounts, and the sale of that gaudy, overpriced chunk of glass and steel that Kevin had called his 'dream home', she would get another $1.5 million once the estate was completely settled and taxes paid. The life insurance proceeds had already been duly deposited into an interest-bearing savings account.

Rick had been right about the donation to science part of things; the coroner's office had dealt directly with the clinic it had been willed to, so she was able to stay out of that completely, which was a huge relief to her.

The little company she loved working for had had to start completely over, pretty much from scratch. Although the FBI techs tried everything they knew, the electronic records just weren't recoverable.

The last week of September, the owner had informed the management team that permanently closing the business was looking more and more like the inevitable outcome.

But she believed in the company and its people, and she'd made it a point to meet with the President again that afternoon after making some calls and checking some figures.

She'd disclosed her recent good fortune to him, then offered to put one million dollars in working capital down to back the rebuild of the company they both cared about so much. She'd also reminded him that rebuilding would be slow, but not impossible.

"Sir, you and I both know our storage warehouse has never, ever been cleaned out," she had pointed out. "Remember? I'd been here a month, and suggested it, and I thought you were going to shoot me, and you said you'd 'prefer not to shred anything at this time'?"

He chuckled, remembering. "That's *exactly* what I said."

"You probably have every single customer record, order, PO, whatever you need from the time this place first opened all the way through now, to rebuild with. It's just in paper form, not electronic, that's all."

She saw the light come on in his eyes, so she'd kept going.

"So, we bring in people, sir, and we roll up our sleeves, and we enter that stuff into a new, clean, virus-free accounting software on a new, clean, virus-free server. It may all have to be done manually, and it may take extra people on extra shifts. But we can do this. We shouldn't have to reload absolutely everything from the beginning to be able to reopen, just the year-to-date stuff on the sales side and AP for now, and the customer histories. For inventory and AR, it's even simpler. Beginning balances. I know we can do this, sir. This company is too damn good to just fold."

"I see where this is going, Faith. And yes, it's a viable option to closing. But why would you want to put your own money in? What's in it for you?"

"Sir, I believe in this place, and its people. I'm willing to stake an investment in my belief. If I'm right, make me a minority shareholder, up to the value of my investment, or make payments back to me once the company is sustainable, take your pick."

"And if you're wrong?"

"Then we'll know sooner rather than later, and it becomes a write-off on taxes," she'd said with a twinkle. "But we both know I won't be wrong about this. We were kicking ass and taking names in this industry before some jackasses set a virus loose on us. And we can do it again."

***

Now they were almost finished with the fourth quarter, and the company had battled its way back. Some things were still left to do, but Faith's personal financial gamble on her professional life had paid off in a big way.

Through long hours, they had rebuilt an entire electronic accounting system, with all customer records, inventory, you name it. Total down time from virus being unleashed to doors open again for business was about five weeks, and Faith's capital infusion covered the payroll dollars and new computer systems needed to make it happen.

A follow-up project was planned to scan all older papers into an electronic storage configuration, but after those physical papers had saved the day even Faith was reluctant to part with them entirely. The whole experience had given her a renewed appreciation that traditional methods were still very valuable in their way.

CHAPTER TWENTY-ONE

Rick and Faith lay tangled and exhausted in her sexy satin sheets.

"We need to be careful, or we may wind up getting hurt one day," he managed, winded.

"There are definitely worse ways to go," Faith replied, still panting a bit. "But if we keep this up, I'll need to start doing yoga so I'm more flexible."

Seeing the lustful gleam in Rick's eyes reignite at that comment, she patted his ass. "Down boy."

And they grinned that grin that lovers share afterward.

Rick laughed, and his guard was down, and it was out before he knew it.

"I'm so in love with you, Faith Thomas."

She stiffened, sat up.

"What?"

He couldn't take it back. And he didn't want to. So, he went all in and pressed ahead.

"I said, I'm in love with you, Faith Thomas. Utterly and completely."

"Um," she stammered.

"Um?" he parroted, an eyebrow raised, waiting.

"I...I...," she faltered. "I..."

It hurt, but he understood.

"Too soon," he said dejectedly. "In fairness, I've felt it since the very first time I saw you. But I figured you weren't even close to ready to hear it, so I've tried to keep it to myself."

Now he rolled out of her bed, looking completely embarrassed and unsure of himself.

"Maybe I'd better go."

She closed her eyes and listened to her heart.

"No. Wait. Rick, just wait."

He stopped at the foot of the bed, pants halfway up, eyes searching her face for any clues.

"I...I...," she took a deep breath, continued. "I'm in love with you, too."

And she felt the last chains of the anchor of hurt she'd been carrying fall away. She opened her eyes, saw the love and the joy in his shining back at her.

Now she smiled, said it again to him, more steadily this time, and she realized this heart that was meant to love her was healing hers. Jandy had been right once again.

"I'm in love with you too, Rick Connor."

"Really? Truly?'

"Really truly."

***

Faith and Rick were talking logistics over pizza the week before Thanksgiving.

"Why don't you just move in here with me, baby?" he asked as he reached for another slice. "It makes way more sense. You said yourself your lease is up in January."

"Yeah, I know," she admitted. "It would make more sense. I mean, I spend almost as much time here as I do there."

Still, she hesitated. Yes, they were a couple. And yes, they'd said the "L" word.

But the townhouse was her final bastion of freedom.

Or escape hatch. Admit it. Call it what it is.

Rick knew exactly what she was thinking. And he knew she'd decide when she was ready. So, he let her off the hook and switched topics.

***

Six weeks later, Faith Thomas was white with shock. She hadn't been feeling well but had attributed it to work stress and all the exertion lately.

She'd finally decided moving in with Rick was the logical choice; they had finished placing the last of her things they didn't plan to use right away in storage, and the few remaining boxes they'd finished moving to his place the previous night. All that remained regarding the townhouse was to clean it and turn in keys.

Now she stared in disbelief as her pregnancy test showed positive. At thirty-six.

"Oh, my God."

"What?" Rick called from the living room.

She closed her eyes, braced against the sink.

"Honey, what's wrong?" he asked, now in the bathroom doorway. He noticed how pale she was and moved closer, concerned.

Without a word, she showed him.

"Whoa."

"Yeah," she managed. "I didn't think I could even *get* pregnant. I am totally blown away right now. I don't know how to feel about this."

"Well, let's figure it out together. Okay?" He pulled her to him and hugged her tight.

***

Within a week the decision was made for them. Faith woke up around two a.m. to horrible cramping and blood everywhere.

Rick gently loaded her into the car, and they went to the emergency room.

It seemed like forever until the doctor came out to talk to him.

"Hi, Mr. Connor, I'm Dr. Davis, the surgeon," he said.

"Surgeon? What's going on?"

"Faith has an ectopic pregnancy, and if I don't go in, it could rupture the fallopian tube."

Rick was silent, eyes closed.

Dr. Davis paused for a bit to give Rick time to absorb what he was hearing. Then he continued.

"Mr. Connor, there's more. When we did the sonogram to see what was going on, we also saw a large mass on her uterus. There's a possibility that we may have to remove her uterus entirely, depending on what we find once we get the surgery underway."

"Does she know this yet?"

"I just spoke with her about it all."

"Take me to her. Please."

Rick walked solemnly beside Dr. Davis. The doctor pointed to the exam room Faith had been put in.

"I'll be along shortly. We'll need to get her into surgery within the next hour or so."

Rick opened the door the doctor had pointed to and walked into the room.

She lay on the bed, tears streaming.

"Faith," he said gently, taking her hand and stroking her hair.

"It's tubal, no way to save it," she sobbed. "And he said they found a mass."

"The doctor just filled me in."

"Rick, I'm scared."

"I know, baby."

"I was so shocked that I could even get pregnant. You know? But then it was kind of exciting, the idea of being a mom finally. And now, they may have to take everything out."

She wiped her cheeks.

"I have to ask you, Rick. If they do have to take it all, do you still want to be with me? I won't be able to give you children. I don't want you to throw away that chance."

"I'm not going anywhere," he told her earnestly. "I want *you*. You're who and what I want."

He leaned over and kissed her very gently.

"But right now, I am much more concerned with making sure you are okay. Okay? We will deal with the rest as it comes."

"Okay," she sniffled, as the anesthesiologist came in to introduce herself and start the pre-op medication.

"I will be right here when you wake up. I promise."

"Call my work for me, call Jandy too."

"You got it. I love you, Faith."

He held her hand and walked beside the gurney all the way to the doors leading into the surgery area.

Once they closed behind her, he headed to the surgery waiting room to make some calls.

665 | P a g e

CHAPTER TWENTY-TWO

Jandy arrived a little before four-thirty a.m.

"Any word?" she asked, as she hugged him.

"Not yet."

"Everything's going to be okay," she reassured him.

Rick left a message for Faith's boss while Jandy contacted Sarah and Nathan to let them know what was happening.

Then they settled in for the wait.

***

A little before six a.m., Dr. Davis came out to talk to them.

"Okay," he said, sitting on the little table in front of them. "Here's what we found."

Rick and Jandy grabbed each other's hand and looked at him expectantly.

"The mass we saw in the sonogram was solid, not a cyst as I had hoped. I thought we might be able to just remove it, but its location and size meant we had to take the uterus completely, along with her left fallopian tube that contained the ectopic pregnancy. The mass did look suspicious; we'll be testing to see if it's a malignant growth."

Rick winced. Jandy squeezed his hand.

"How soon before we know anything?" he asked.

"We should have the biopsy results back within three days."

"How...how far along was the baby?"

"I estimated four, maybe five weeks, at the most." Dr. Davis cleared his throat. "I'm so sorry."

"What do we need to know about her after-surgery care?" Jandy inquired.

"Well, we were able to do this laparoscopically rather than making a long incision in the abdomen; three incisions total, that aren't much bigger than about a half-inch each. She shouldn't lift anything weighing more than three pounds for the next couple of weeks, and we will be sending her home this afternoon with incision care instructions once we're sure all the anesthesia is out of her system."

"She'll need to come in for a post-op checkup in a week," he finished. "If there's any good news here, it's that her ovaries looked just fine. Which means no hormone therapy needed, and that's always a positive thing. Less disruptive on the body."

He looked at them. "Any other questions, concerns?"

Rick and Jandy looked at each other.

"I don't think so, except, how soon can we see her?" he asked.

"The nurse will come get you guys once we get her settled in the recovery area."

"Thanks, Dr. Davis," he said, extending his hand. They shook, the doctor shook hands with Jandy too, then walked away.

Rick held his head in his hands, his mind reeling.

"A lot to process right now, I know," Jandy reassured him again. "But we will all get her, and you, through it. Neither one of you have to walk this by yourselves."

"I can't lose her, Jandy," Rick said despondently. "I just can't."

"I know, hon. We just have to stay upbeat, for her sake, and hope that biopsy gives us great news. It's all we can do. And we've got to be there for her. She's going to be devastated when she hears what they had to do."

Twenty minutes later, a nurse approached.

"For Faith?" she asked.

They confirmed, stood, and followed her back to recovery bay seven.

***

Faith was floating in and out of awareness quite a bit. In a moment of lucidity, she noticed Rick's face close to hers.

"Hi, gorgeous," she murmured, then went back to sleep for a bit.

The next time she surfaced wasn't as happy.

"I lost the baby, didn't I," she stated to him, tears trickling.

"Shh, baby, get some sleep, we can talk about that a little later. Okay? I love you."

And she was out again.

***

Around two p.m., they discharged her. Jandy went and picked up Faith's prescriptions. By the time she arrived at Rick's to help get her sister situated, Faith had been gently settled into bed and was sound asleep again.

Rick and Jandy went over the discharge instructions together.

Then she said, "Do you need me to stick around? I can, you know."

"I've got this, for now," he replied. "But if you could come be with her tomorrow for a while, I'd appreciate it. I will need to make some calls, get the schedule lined out for the part-time guy I just hired."

"You got it, brother of mine," she said, and gave him a big hug. "I'll be back here by ten a.m. Okay?"

"Thanks, sis," he said, and made her smile.

***

Faith and Rick were settled in on the couch watching television when her cell phone rang. She answered it nervously.

"Hello? Yes, this is Faith Thomas."

Rick muted the TV and watched her face as she spoke.

"Just a moment, Dr. Davis," she said. "Let me put you on speaker so we can both hear you."

She did so, then said, "Go ahead."

"Faith, we have your biopsy back. Great news. No malignancy."

She and Rick both closed their eyes in relief.

"Thanks, Dr. Davis."

"You're welcome. I'll be seeing you as scheduled for your follow-up. But I wanted to tell you the results as soon as possible; I know you've both been worried."

"You're right, Doc, we have been," Rick chimed in. "Thanks."

They ended the call and looked at each other. He hugged her tightly.

"Baby I am so relieved to hear that," he told her. "Waiting to hear has been brutal. I know it has been for you, too."

She blew out a long breath. "Yeah. Dodged a bullet there."

Her face took on a pensive look.

***

Rick knew what she was thinking about. She hadn't mentioned the lost pregnancy at all in the last three days. And he wasn't sure how to bring it up so she could talk about it if she wanted to, or if he even should bring it up at all.

Now she took a deep breath, leaned her head on his shoulder, and opened her heart up to him about it.

"It all still seems so... surreal," she sighed. "Does it feel that way to you too?"

"Kind of," Rick agreed. "I mean, it's me and you, and we're coasting doing our thing, and then the test was positive, and you were freaked out a bit and so was I. And then before we could even get our feet under us, wham."

"Exactly," Faith said. "And I really wanted that. To get our feet under us about it. I mean, it would never have been a question of keeping it or not, in my mind."

"Honey, mine either," he told her earnestly. "I wasn't even considering keeping versus not keeping. I was more meaning like, adjusting some future planning, like that. You know?"

"Yeah, I know. And me too," Faith nodded. "It was never even a question of not having the baby. My mindset was like you said, figuring out stuff like, are we living in the best school district? Would I work up until the baby was born then just take maternity leave, or would that have been a good time to launch my own thing like we've talked about? Would we still be able to travel now like we wanted to, or would we have postponed that until the baby was older?"

"I've never had to stop and consider children in any of my plans before. Until this, I thought I could never have kids, so that kind of planning never came up."

She sighed again.

"But it would have been nice to have had the choice and the chance to do that."

CHAPTER TWENTY-THREE

"For what it's worth," Rick said gently, "I honestly thought when I lost my kids that I would never even have a *chance* to be a dad again. Like you, I was used to planning based around it being just me to worry about. Then I met you, and it changed. And I agree – it would have been nice to have had that choice and that chance. But if we decide we want a family, we can love an adopted child just as much, Faith."

He kissed her.

"Right here, right now, I'm just glad that it wasn't cancer, that you are here, and you are going to be okay."

"Me too," she agreed. "Speaking of which, I need to get on the horn and let the fam know it's all good."

"You do that, and I am going to go get us lemon bars from Mama J's, if you like. To celebrate Dr. Davis's call."

"Sounds good. I will make you some coffee and me some tea to go with them and meet you back here on the couch."

Standing, she leaned over and kissed him.

"And I promise to behave about the whole three-pound thing."

He'd caught her earlier in the day trying to lift a full gallon of milk, which was more than five pounds over Dr. Davis's lifting restriction.

"You'd better," he said with mock seriousness. "Or you don't get a lemon bar."

"You wouldn't," she pouted, teasing.

"Try me," he teased back, and headed to the lift.

***

"YES!" Nathan said.

Noticing his wife watching him with a raised eyebrow, he held up his cell phone.

"Faith just texted. They heard back. No cancer."

"Oh, thank God," Bella exhaled. "That's great news. I wonder how she's doing with the rest of it."

"No way to know, really," he shrugged. "Of the four siblings, Faith and I are by far the worst about stuffing things and not dealing with them. But she's with Rick now. Something tells me he won't let her shut herself away like that very often."

***

Faith stretched and looked at her watch on a Friday afternoon four weeks later. Almost five o'clock. She and Rick had a date night scheduled right after Book Keepers closed.

And Faith frowned, which was totally unlike her when Rick was the subject.

He'd been acting strange ever since her health scare, and she had no clue why.

She didn't like it one bit. And if it continued, a very heavy conversation would happen very soon.

*Fool me once...*she thought, shaking her head.

***

Rick had indeed been very distracted lately. Faith had no way of knowing why because he'd done an excellent job of not giving anything away.

He hated keeping secrets. But the wait was almost over.

Tonight, he'd be able to finally confess to her, about everything.

He just hoped she'd understand.

***

A little after five p.m. Faith texted that she was on her way home. When she got there, Micah, Rick's employee, smiled and waved from behind the register.

That's odd. Rick didn't say anything about Micah being on today...

"Micah, can you watch the store for a little bit? I've got something I need to do," she heard Rick say, and she blinked at the nervousness in his tone.

What the hell is wrong with him? she thought as they walked to the lift together. *The tension is coming off him in waves.*

Then it hit her. The way he'd been acting for almost a month. The tone in his voice and the look on his face.

Oh, my God, he's breaking up with me.

The thought buckled her knees and welled her eyes.

Not again.

No! her inner warrior urged. *Do NOT fall apart in front of him. Don't give him that satisfaction. Whatever he's got to say, let him say it, then let's get the hell out of here. But NO crying until after you leave. Promise me.*

She pulled it together silently as the lift gate opened into their home.

"Would you like a drink?" he offered.

"Whiskey on the rocks," she said in what she hoped like hell was a calm and even tone.

***

Rick's eyebrows lifted.

Wow, okay, she almost never drinks whiskey straight.

But he obeyed, pouring her one over ice, and handed it to her.

"I'll be right back," he said, then abruptly turned and went into the bedroom.

***

She sank to the couch, grateful for a moment alone to try to figure out where the hell things between them had gone so wrong.

And she couldn't.

Faith couldn't think of a single damn thing that had happened between them that would result in her being emotionally gutted once again.

Well, she realized, *it must have been something on his side that shifted and killed his feelings for me.*

Maybe he decided he really does want children of his own, and he just hasn't had the heart to tell me yet?

Realizing that the best thing that had ever happened to her might come to an end through no fault of her own was like a stake through her heart.

She began to shake, but when she heard the bedroom door open again Faith tried her best to quickly calm herself before he noticed.

"Faith, we need to talk," he said, walking over to her.

"Yeah, we do," she said, focusing on the fireplace and fighting to keep her voice and emotions level.

"If your feelings for me have changed, if you don't want to be together anymore, I would really appreciate it if you would just say so directly."

Her voice broke a little, and she swallowed hard. "Please."

***

Rick turned white with shock. He kneeled in front of her, took her hand, and said, "Look at me. Faith, *please.* Look at me."

She raised her eyes, and it crushed him to see the tears building in them.

"Faith Thomas, you are such a dork. I'm *not* breaking up with you. I'm asking you," he paused, pulling the ring out of his pocket, "to marry me."

"What?"

"You're my adorable dork, and I'm in love with you, and I don't wanna break up. Marry me," he paraphrased. "Please."

***

She blinked slowly, sending tears down her cheeks. She was completely stunned.

Then it registered.

Not breaking up. Getting closer together.

"Yes," she whispered.

"What was that?" he asked.

"I'm in love with you too, and I don't wanna break up either, and yes, I will marry you," she said loudly, and kissed him as he slipped the ring on her finger.

He pulled back, grinning at her, then yelled out, "She said 'YES'!!".

***

The bedroom door flew open, and out poured Bella, Nathan, Jandy, Tony, and Sarah.

"OMG YAY!!!" Sarah yelled, running over with the rest right behind her to give them both big hugs.

Faith was dumbstruck.

"What the hell?" she asked Rick.

"This is why I may have been acting kind of weird lately. I wanted to ask you, and I wanted your family to be around for it. So, I kind of snuck through your phone and got their numbers, and I called and set this up."

He smiled sheepishly.

"I know it wasn't right, going through your phone without your permission, but I really wanted this to be a complete surprise."

"You know what? You're totally forgiven. I'm just happy I deleted those raunchy texts from Felipe, my cabana boy," she teased. "Because otherwise that would have been awkward."

"Make that my adorable *smartass* dork," he quipped, and kissed her as she chuckled.

***

Faith's family said their good-byes and left around eight p.m., and the newly engaged couple had the place all to themselves.

They opted to start the private celebration in the bedroom and end it in the shower. Then they relaxed in the steamy jetted tub and sipped the champagne that he'd bought just in case she said yes.

"I so love you," she murmured, letting the jets pummel her back and shoulders. "You're sneaky as hell though."

"I am truly sorry if my behavior lately made you question us at all. I just wanted to make it a really good surprise. But I can see how my being preoccupied might have made you think something was wrong."

He took her in his arms.

"And it killed me to see tears in your eyes like that and know that it was doubts about me that put them there."

Then he kissed her, long, deep, and slow.

"No more secrets. *Ever*. I promise."

The End.

*** *Bonus Story!* <u>*See Me Now*</u> *starts on the next page!***

See Me Now

Blake Jones – The big brother coming home on leave from the Navy at Christmas time. Eight years older than Mia, he adores her, and is very protective.

Mia Jones – Blake Jones' little sister who's not so little anymore. A stunning twenty-one-year-old with black hair, green eyes, and shapely curves, she's a tiny spitfire who barely comes up to Blake's shoulder.

Tanner Greysen – Blake's best friend since middle school. Although she was always hanging around, he never paid much attention to Mia growing up – she was always just his best friend's 'bratty little sister'.

Three adults, returning to their hometown of Mason Valley, Texas for the holidays. But sparks fly when Tanner notices just how grown-up little Mia has become. His attraction to her could cost him the best friend he's had for years – if Blake doesn't kill him outright first, that is.

CHAPTER ONE

Mia Jones sighed as she unlocked her apartment door.

"Thank God finals week is over," she muttered, tossing her backpack on the couch.

"I know, right?" her roommate Cheryl chimed in from the kitchen. "Brutal. So, when are you heading out? You have time to eat? I'm making spaghetti."

Mia checked her watch. Five-thirty.

"I told Mom I'd be there no later than ten a.m. tomorrow morning to help her get everything decorated and done. But part of me says hustle out of here and try to beat the storm that's coming in. Have you been outside today? It's *already* raining, and the temperature's dropping like a rock."

"And if you stay here overnight," Cheryl pointed out, "you might not make it out of Lubbock at all for a day or two."

Mia set her jaw. "I think I'll be okay. If I leave now, I'll get there by nine tonight. Good thing I packed already!"

Cheryl chuckled and shook her head. "Like that's a surprise. You're the most organized, plan-every-last-detail woman I know."

"I love you too, smarty-pants," Mia called out as she went down the hall to her room to change into yoga pants and a hoodie for the drive.

That accomplished, she brushed back her long black hair, pulling it into a ponytail before quickly braiding it and securing the end with a hair tie. The last piece she added to her ensemble was a baseball cap.

She took one last look around, making sure she had everything she needed, then hoisted her suitcase off the bed and headed back toward the living room.

"Tell your folks hi and Merry Christmas for me," she told Cheryl as she hugged her.

"Call or text me when you get there, all right? Please? You know I worry about you driving at night by yourself."

"Geez, you sound like Blake. Yes, Cheryl, I will text you. And I'll see you in two weeks, okay?"

***

Tanner Greysen frowned to himself as he poured coffee from his Thermos into his mug.

"Gonna be a long night," he muttered to himself as he watched the radar screen on his phone's weather app.

Earlier in the day the meteorologist had predicted the incoming storm could be one of the most severe in the area in decades.

That keeps tracking like it is, it damn sure will be, Tanner had thought with a grimace when the weatherman's predictive graphic had popped up during the six o'clock news.

And of course, this would be the week I tell Max I can cover the place for a few days while he's gone. No telling how many idiot people I'm gonna get to go rescue out in this stuff.

Now, perched on the stool behind the counter at Max's Garage & Towing, he could only bide his time until the inevitable calls for help started coming in.

Within the hour, flashing skies and the windsock standing straight out from its pole would let Tanner know the wintery beast had arrived – with teeth bared.

***

It was a little over two hours into her trip, and Mia's anxiety level was beginning to rise.

It was already nightfall when the radio broadcast had been interrupted to announce a winter storm warning. Not five minutes later, the rain at the leading edge of the stormfront overtook her.

The twelve-year-old Honda she'd nicknamed Gracie shimmied and shook as the winds picked up, and Mia cursed as she gripped the steering wheel harder to try to keep her little car on the roadway.

"This keeps up I won't be able to see at all," she muttered. Her windshield wipers were already operating at max capacity and losing the battle with each passing minute.

The green and white highway sign she could barely make out read *Pine Mills, 2 miles.*

Still over three hours away at least, and I'm barely able to maintain forty miles an hour in this rain, she realized, and sighed. *At this rate, I won't make it to Mom's before midnight.*

Mia hunched over the steering wheel, peering through the windshield as best she could. She reached out and flipped the air controls to move the blast of heated air from her torso and feet over to defrost, then shivered as the warmth retreated from her slender frame to focus on improving her visibility.

And then she heard it. The distinctive *tink, tink* of sleet pellets that had formed among the raindrops beginning to bounce off the hood, roof, and windows.

Mia patted the dashboard nervously.

"Come on Gracie, hang in there. You get me to Mom's safely and I promise I won't ever drive you in a storm this bad ever, ever again."

Gracie, ever temperamental in foul weather, responded to her owner's plea by sounding an ominous chime and flashing the 'check engine' light just as an enormous clap of thunder rattled the entire car.

CHAPTER TWO

"Oh, no. *No*, Gracie, not now, please God, not here," Mia pleaded even as she felt the power steering begin to fail, a sure sign Gracie was about to give up completely.

Just ahead she could see the exit for Pine Mills, and she wrestled the wheel and slowed her speed even further to take the ramp.

At least get off the highway, Mia thought to herself. *Safer that way.*

Gracie plodded her way up the incline, speed plummeting, Mia coaxing desperately as if Gracie could hear her.

Just as the ramp leveled out to the narrow service road above, Gracie belched and backfired once loudly, then flatlined, and Mia shrieked as her little car's headlights abruptly shut off, as well.

Unable to see anything in front of her in the pitch black, Mia tried her best to get as far over to the right as possible so she wouldn't block the ramp. With the power steering rendered useless, she tugged with all her might, her arms straining mightily to turn the wheel as far as she could. Then she coasted to a stop and shifted Gracie's transmission into park.

"Dammit!" Mia yelled in frustration and touched her forehead to the steering wheel in despair.

Think. What do I do now? Call Mom, see if Dad can come get me, I guess?

With trembling fingers, she dug her phone out of her purse, and cursed again.

Great. Just great. Twelve percent battery, and no freaking signal. So much for 'organized' and 'plan-every-last-detail'. I can't even remember to charge my damn phone.

Now what?

***

Tanner's prediction of a long night had become a stark reality. He'd already been on seven calls, assisting stranded motorists along the highway.

And for the last one, he'd been just in time. He'd no sooner loaded up their minivan on his tow truck, put the elderly couple in his cab, and gotten underway when an eighteen-wheeler driving much too fast for conditions jackknifed behind them, finally coming to rest right where the couple's vehicle had been only minutes before.

Wow. Damn good thing I was here, he told himself as the three of them watched the event unfold about a hundred yards away in his side mirrors.

"Oh, my! I hope he's all right," the tiny old woman exclaimed, her eyes as big as saucers.

"Me too," Tanner told her as he keyed his mic to call it in to the Highway Patrol.

***

With her only source of heat lifeless, Mia's teeth were already beginning to chatter from the cold.

I can't stay with Gracie, she realized despondently. *It's freezing in here, and it's dark, and I haven't seen another vehicle in at least twenty minutes. I need to go find help. I need to get to Pine Mills.*

Using her cell phone screen's glow as a flashlight, she clambered into the backseat and unzipped her suitcase, looking to add layers to her clothing. Out came the oversized sweatpants she'd packed, and she slid them on over her yoga pants. A thick pair of socks was added to the thinner ones she was already wearing before she shrugged her feet into her hiking boots.

She slung her purse's strap across her body, turned off her cell phone to conserve what little battery life she had left, and shoved the useless accessory down into her purse before putting her heavy coat on.

Then Mia closed her eyes, said a prayer, and stepped out of her car and into the storm.

A hundred yards ahead of her was the little two-lane road that crossed the now mostly deserted highway. She was already losing feeling in her fingertips – *gloves, dammit, I forgot my gloves* - by the time she reached it and read the sign that pointed to the right.

Pine Mills, 1.5 miles.

One and a half miles? There's no way I can walk that far in this! part of her mind protested.

Her survivalist side spoke up sharply.

You can, and you will. The alternative is stay here and freeze. You don't have a choice, so let's go. Get your ass in gear.

She tightened the drawstring on her hoodie as best she could with a baseball cap on.

There. That will at least block some of the sleet and rain from getting in my face, she thought.

Mia shoved her bare hands into her coat's pockets, turned right, and begin to walk as quickly as she could.

She trudged along, keeping the white line painted down the side of the road in front of her as a marker to guide her way in the pitch black. Each frosty breath she exhaled was immediately whisked away by the biting crosswind that had her struggling to stay upright.

Her heavy overcoat, while great for cold weather, was not waterproofed, and as it became saturated, she began to feel the immense weight bearing down with each step forward she took.

Mia set her jaw and railed against her situation in her head as she walked.

I will not let this beat me. I'm a Jones, dammit!

In a half-hour, she passed a sign that called her bravado into question.

Pine Mills, 1.3 miles.

I don't think I can do this.

CHAPTER THREE

Tanner dropped the elderly couple and their minivan off at their daughter's house in town, then headed back to the garage.

He had just unwrapped his sandwich and poured himself another cup of coffee when the garage's ham radio crackled to life.

"Say again?" Tanner said into the microphone, then listened.

The sheriff's office dispatcher repeated the announcement.

"That's only a mile from me. I'll go get it. Any idea where the owner is?"

Hearing the word 'no', Tanner frowned.

Someone just parked their car at the end of the exit ramp and bailed? Not smart. Great way to get your car totaled if someone else comes barreling up the ramp.

Tanner made a mental note to teach the owner a thing or two about roadside safety -once the owner was located.

He shrugged on his insulated coveralls again, poured the coffee back into his Thermos to keep it hot, and headed out to his tow truck to make another run.

***

As Mia walked, she replayed the way this trip *should* have gone. She should have made it home safely and on time with no issues, with plenty of time left over to help her mother hang the 'Welcome Home' banners and other decorations before heading out to meet her big brother's flight.

Blake Jones had made a career out of the Navy, and he was scheduled to arrive tomorrow for the first time in a long time to celebrate Christmas with them in Mason Valley.

Mia was so proud of him, and she'd squealed with delight when he'd called her the first week of October to let her know he'd be able to make it home this year.

"That's wonderful, Blake! I really miss you and I'm so ready to see you and spend time with you," she'd told him.

"I know, Mia. I've missed you too, kiddo. And I promise we'll hang out the whole week, okay?"

"Deal."

A particularly vicious blast of cold wind refocused her attention on her present predicament, and she heard Blake's voice in her head as clearly as if he was standing right beside her.

Come on, girly. Come on, Mama Mia, you can do this. I believe in you. Just keep going, and don't stop.

And because Mia had idolized her big brother as far back as she could remember, she took the apparition's urgings to heart and kept walking, even managing a smirk at the childhood nickname.

But Mia's sides flared with pain with each step she took, her breath rattling in her lungs. She could no longer feel her feet, and her hands had already become pretty much useless. Sheer stubborn force of will was what she had left, and even it was beginning to wane. Mia was exhausted to her core.

Stop, sit down, take a minute, an insidious whisper crept across her thoughts. *So tired... rest...*

NO! I have to keep going!

She shook her head fiercely and lowered her chin, straining with all her might to stay focused on following the white line toward help and safety.

When she noticed two lights approaching through the swirling murky black, she thought she was seeing things. Then as she realized her eyes weren't deceiving her, she stumbled forward, arms raised, crying out.

"Help!" she managed, waving arms that felt like lead. "Please... help..."

She barely registered the vehicle slowing to a stop before she lost consciousness and slumped to the ground.

***

What the hell? was Tanner's first thought when he saw the bundled figure suddenly appear in his headlight beams. He quickly braked to a stop and got out of his truck just in time to see the figure fall over.

He raced over and bent down, shining the tiny flashlight he carried with him.

"Can you hear me?" he called out over the howl of the wind but got no response.

He reached out and grabbed a shoulder, wincing at the water wringing out of his mystery guest's coat as he did so. Tanner tugged gently until the individual was lying face up, then loosened the hood's drawstring just enough to take a closer look at the stranger's face.

Holy crap, it's a woman.

What the hell is she doing out here?

Tanner slipped off a glove long enough to touch her cheek.

Ice cold. I need to get her out of this storm.

He scooped her up and carried her around to the passenger side of the tow truck, placing her in the seat as gently as he could.

Once he got back behind the wheel, he keyed his mic.

"Dispatch," he relayed to the Prism County Sheriff's office, "I think I just found your missing driver, over."

CHAPTER FOUR

Tanner watched her sleep, unwilling to leave her side since he'd arrived at the emergency room with her in his arms. He'd only stepped out long enough for the medical staff to remove her wet clothes and get her into a gown and under some heated blankets, then he pulled up a chair and made himself comfortable to keep watch over her.

At one point, she'd opened her mesmerizing emerald eyes long enough to pierce his soul with their beauty.

"Thank you," she'd whispered before she slipped into sleep again.

She looks so familiar to me, but I just can't place where I've seen her before, Tanner told himself again as he gazed at her shiny, coal-black hair, creamy skin and high cheekbones. *She's gorgeous, I know that much.*

She sighed, then moaned softly, and Tanner immediately was overwhelmed with visions of her in his bed, making those same sweet sounds as he kissed and caressed and claimed her as his own.

He flushed beet red.

***

Mia found herself in the middle of the strangest dream.

She was being carried by Tanner Greysen of all people, the man she'd been in love with since she was a child. In the dream he cradled her close to his chest and whispered words of comfort, then laid her down gently on a bed and began to remove her clothing. She reached up to run her hands through his hair and sighed when his lips met hers, tasting, exploring.

But the gentle caresses turned to tiny daggers just under her skin, and she moaned. Tanner's face retreated into nothingness.

Her eyes fluttered open, and she blinked rapidly, confused.

"Hello, young lady," a kind, older man said gently, and she turned her head to the right toward him.

"Where am I?"

"St. Claire's emergency department," he told her. "You were out in the storm. It's lucky someone found you, young lady. This is the worst winter storm we've had around these parts in a long while."

She looked down and frowned when she noticed she was on a gurney and wearing a hospital gown. "How did I get here? And where are my clothes?"

"The tow truck driver who found you brought you in. And you were soaked to the bone. We had to get you out of those wet clothes and get you warmed up again. How are you feeling?"

As the feeling in her hands and feet returned, the sensation of a million sharp needles made Mia moan with pain again.

"My hands and feet really hurt," she admitted with a grimace. "Like someone's stabbing them."

"I know it's painful, but it shouldn't last long," he informed her. "You had mild hypothermia. The tingling you're feeling is normal and it's actually a good sign. That means we're doing the right things to get your body temperature back where it should be."

"I need to call my mom and let her know where I am," Mia said. "She's probably worried sick. I …"

Her voice trailed off as she glanced to her left and saw who was sitting there.

"Hey there. You're looking better," the man who had starred in every fantasy she'd ever had said gently.

"How... how did you know I was here?"

"I brought you here," he answered, and looked confused.

Oh, my God. It's Tanner. Blake's best friend since the fifth grade.

And he doesn't recognize me.

Be cool, Mia. Be cool!

She managed to collect herself enough to smile and say, "You don't recognize me, do you, Tanner?"

"No. Should I? How do you know my name?" Tanner said, tilting his head to one side as he narrowed his eyes and scrutinized her face.

Mia saw the exact moment the light bulb went off for him.

"Oh, dear God. You're Mia," he breathed, and flushed deep red. "Blake's kid sister."

"Got it in one," she said.

"You... you look so different," he stammered.

"Yeah, well, growing up tends to do that," she teased, and lifted an eyebrow at his expression.

What is he blushing about?

CHAPTER FIVE

You've got *to be kidding me,* Tanner thought to himself. *This perfect woman, that I'm overwhelmingly attracted to, turns out to be my best friend's kid sister. Which means she's off limits.*

Right?

"Tanner? You okay?" she asked, and he shook his head to clear it.

"Yeah, I'm fine, Mia. It's been a long time, huh?"

She smiled and nodded. "Eleven years, to be exact. I haven't seen you since you and Blake graduated high school and you left town."

He smiled back even as he thought *yeah, back when I was eighteen and you were ten, and all knees and elbows and annoying as hell. When did you get so hot?*

"Yeah," he said again, raking one hand through his dark brown hair. "Went straight into the Marine Corps."

A silence fell for a moment, and Mia turned her attention back to the doctor.

"When can I get out of here?"

"I don't see a problem with turning you loose in a couple of hours," came the reply.

Mia scowled. "I need to get my suitcase out of my car."

"Is your car the one on the exit ramp?" Tanner asked her.

She shrugged. "Didn't have a choice of where I parked, Tanner. Gracie up and died on me. I was lucky I even *made* it to the exit."

She named her car Gracie? That's... adorable, some mushy part of his brain chimed in.

He cleared his throat.

"I'll go get it and tow it to the shop, then come back and get you."

"Thanks. I need to call my mom and let her know where I am and to come get me."

Tanner shook his head. "They've closed the highway, Mia. Too much ice. Tell you what. I'll call your parents and let them know where you are, and that you're staying with me until the roads reopen. In the meantime, I can take a look at your car, see what I can do to fix it. All right?"

"But... but... Blake's flight is coming in tomorrow," she protested. "It's the first Christmas in *four years* that he actually gets to come home and be with us."

"Honey," Tanner said, "they shut down all flights into and out of DFW Airport about an hour ago. I don't think they'll be resuming operations before this storm passes on through."

"And when will that be?"

Tanner hesitated, knowing the answer would upset her.

"Mia," he said softly, "they're saying that this storm could last another forty-eight hours."

Her crestfallen look made his heart ache, and he leaned forward and took her hand.

"Hey," he soothed. "One problem at a time, okay? Let's focus on what we can control. I can go get your car, and bring you some dry clothes, and we can go from there. Okay?"

"Okay," she whispered, and squeezed his hand.

Tanner watched the sparkle that came into her eyes as she smiled at him and felt his heart double-thump in response.

Oh, boy. I'm in deep, deep trouble.

Reluctantly, he pulled his hand back.

"Okay, then. I'm gonna go get your car. I'll be back in about forty minutes."

He felt those emerald eyes of hers watching his every movement as he turned and walked out of the room.

***

He called me honey!!! Oh my God!! Mia's inner fangirl raved. *The only thing that could have made that any sexier would be if I'd been wrapped up in his arms when he called me that.*

Mia rolled her eyes at her inner monologue before she could stop herself.

But he's Blake's best friend, and Blake is so protective of me. I don't know that us getting together would be a good idea.

Why not? fangirl retorted. *We're both single, consenting adults. Blake doesn't get a vote here – and you've wanted to be Tanner Greysen's girl for years.*

Okay, first of all, you're assuming Tanner Greysen is single, and that's a great big assumption, and you know what they say about assuming....

Yeah, yeah, yeah. Shut up. I saw no wedding band, at all, fangirl shot back.

And that means zilch, dear. He may still have a girlfriend or a fiancée. Hell, he could even be married and just not wear a ring for some reason. And we haven't even covered the obvious yet.

Which is?

What if he's not interested in you like that?

Party-pooper.

CHAPTER SIX

She is off limits. She is off limits, his brain chanted in the background as Tanner drove to the highway, pivoted, then backed up in front of her little Honda.

But why is she off limits? She's an adult, and I'm an adult, he reasoned.

You know how Blake is. You mess with Mia and he finds out, he'll skin you alive. And then, he'll get really *mad,* came the answer. *Besides, she may not be single.*

I saw no ring of any sort, bro.

Doesn't matter, bro, his conscience echoed. *She may be in a relationship. And since when do you talk like a surfer?*

"Gah," Tanner snarled as he hooked up the car and pulled the lever to move it up onto the flatbed.

He continued the internal discussion all the way back to the garage, where he backed the rig into bay one and lowered the garage-style door.

At least do the stand-up thing, and talk to Blake first, his conscience pointed out. *Not to get his blessing, necessarily, just so he's aware of how you feel about her.*

"How *would* that go, if I talk to him and he shoots down the idea?" Tanner mused out loud, then immediately dismissed it.

If I do that and he gets mad, it might strain our friendship. And if I don't give him a heads up and I pursue her and he finds out, that might strain our friendship, too.

Dammit.

Not to mention – how do *I feel about her?* he asked himself as he climbed into his four-wheel drive pickup truck and turned the key.

The question dogged his steps all the way back to pick Mia Jones up from St. Claire's.

***

Tanner had been back by her side for about twenty minutes when the nurse came in.

"Here's your discharge paperwork, honey," the woman said. "Get somewhere warm and stay there for the next couple of days, all right? And go easy. Light activity only."

"Yes, ma'am," Mia said.

Once the nurse left, Mia asked, "Tanner, can you set my suitcase up here on the bed, please?"

"Sure."

He did as she asked, and she unzipped it and rummaged around.

"Huh. These will have to do, I guess," she said, pulling out a sweater and jeans. "My sweatpants and overcoat are soaked."

"We'll put them in the wash when we get to my house," he assured her, and she nodded.

"And I brought you this," he continued, and held out one of his coats.

"Thanks! That looks toasty," she grinned, and he grinned back.

"I'm gonna step out so you can get dressed. Holler when you're ready to go and I'll get your suitcase for you."

"Okay. Did you call my mom?"

"Just about to," he replied, waving his cell phone at her.

He walked out into the hall and dialed the Jones residence.

"Hi there," he said to Gladys when she picked up.

"Tanner! What a pleasant surprise! How have you been?"

"I've been doing well, Mrs. Jones, thanks. I wanted to call and let you know that Mia's car broke down, but she's here in Pine Mills, and she's with me. She's fine, but with the weather like it is they've closed the highway."

"Well, I have no doubt you'll take good care of my baby," Gladys responded immediately. "I take it she's aware that Blake's flight got cancelled."

"Yes, ma'am, I let her know that the airport shut down."

"Well, not much to be done but hunker down and wait it out, I suppose. What's wrong with Gracie?"

He chuckled. "I'm not sure yet, but my plan first thing in the morning is to start running some diagnostics. But no worries, Mrs. Jones. If for some reason I can't get Gracie running, I'll bring Mia home myself once the weather clears."

"Well, you could come along either way, dear. We'd love to see you, and I know Blake would, too."

"Thanks, I think I'll take you up on that."

"Tell Mia I love her and I'm glad she's safe, and that I'll talk to her in the morning."

"Yes, ma'am. Good night."

He disconnected the call and tucked his phone in his pocket, then knocked on the door.

"You ready?" he asked.

The door swung open to reveal Mia standing there with his coat buttoned up to her chin, and he grinned when he noticed that the waistband hit her mid-thigh.

She spun in place, then put one hand on her hip, smiled, and asked, "How do I look?"

She's so tiny! The top of her head barely comes to my shoulder, he thought as they stared at each other. *And she's gorgeous. I wonder what she would look like in my pajama top... and nothing else...*

I am in such, such trouble.

With effort, he broke eye contact to move to the bed and grab her suitcase and the two plastic bags that the medical staff had supplied for her wet clothing.

"You look great," he said softly. "Let's head home."

CHAPTER SEVEN

They rode in silence, and Tanner's full concentration on the road conditions gave her a chance to check him out, so Mia took full advantage of the opportunity.

He's taller than I remember, she realized, her eyes surreptitiously scanning his long, lean frame. *And he's definitely got more muscles than I remembered, as well. He's even more of a hottie now than he was back then, and I didn't even think that was possible.*

She felt her cheeks get warm as she imagined what it might be like to have those strong arms wrapped tightly around her. A picture of tangled sheets, murmured endearments, and soft caresses popped into her head next, and she cleared her throat and turned her head to stare out the passenger side window at the storm swirling around them.

Get it together, girl!

"You okay?" Tanner asked in that smooth baritone that made her knees feel all wobbly.

"Fine," Mia managed to say. "Just... a little tired."

Yeah, right. A little tired of not having your hands all over me, is all...

Oh my God shut UP!

She narrowed her eyes and focused on the sleet and rain pattering against the window to distract herself from craving him.

***

They turned onto a gravel road that wound back through the trees for a quarter mile, then opened into a small clearing where a rustic cabin greeted them.

"You live here? It's beautiful," Mia said quietly, straining to see through the rain and sleet. "I can't wait to see it in daylight."

Tanner grinned.

"Built it myself," he said proudly. "Took me over a year."

He pulled up in front of the cabin, angling his truck so that Mia would only have to take two or three steps to reach the porch.

"Sit tight, let me come around," he told her, and climbed out of the truck to grab her things.

He carried them to the porch and set them down, then returned and opened her door for her, holding out his hand.

She smiled and took it, then gasped as she stepped out onto the running board and slipped. In a flash, Tanner had scooped her up into his arms and shut the door, then carried her up the porch steps and set her down gently.

He unlocked the door and gestured.

"After you."

As she crossed the threshold, he grabbed her luggage and bags and followed her, flipping on the light with his right elbow.

"Washer and dryer are just through there," he pointed to the other side of the kitchen, and she nodded and took the plastic bags from him.

"I'm going to take your suitcase to the bedroom. Be right back."

Mia piled her wet clothes in the dryer and turned it on.

"Bathroom?" she called out.

"Back here," came the reply, and she followed the sound of his voice.

"I need my brush. And you don't happen to have a blow dryer, do you? My hair is still wet."

"I don't, sorry. But you're welcome to use a towel."

"Okay, thanks," she answered as she unbuttoned his coat and took it off. "Where does this go?"

***

He poked his head out of the bathroom to see what she was talking about, and his jaw almost hit the floor.

Little 'all knees and elbows' Mia grew some serious curves, and I am digging it, he thought before he could stop himself.

Her dark blue sweater flattered her build and accentuated her breasts, and the jeans she had on drew his eye downward to take in nicely proportioned thighs.

Heaven help me, I can't take much more.

"Um, here, I'll hang it up," he managed, and took the coat from her. When she turned around and he noticed that the denim showed off her toned butt like he thought it might, he almost groaned aloud with want.

Off limits off limits off limits, he chanted in his head almost as a talisman to ward off his impure thoughts about his best friend's little sister.

"Are you hungry? I can whip something up," he offered as both a distraction and an excuse to put some distance between him and the tantalizing woman standing next to his bed.

"Starving, actually. What did you have in mind?" Mia asked as she deftly unbraided her hair, then moved to the bathroom to grab the towel he'd talked about.

"Omelet sound okay?"

"Perfect."

"On it. Make yourself at home," he told her, and was proud of himself that he left the room in a controlled walk.

CHAPTER EIGHT

Tanner started a fire in the fireplace, then moved to the kitchen to prepare their food.

After he started a pot of coffee, he diced up some green onion and ham for the omelets. He'd just turned the burner on under the pan when he heard Mia walk in from the bedroom.

"Ooh, a fire," she observed. "That will help."

He paused his movements, watching her walk across his living room in low-waisted yoga pants and a red tank top that she'd knotted at her hip. When she bent forward from the waist to brush out her long, silky hair in front of the fireplace, Tanner almost swallowed his tongue.

He closed his eyes and leaned against the countertop, silently willing her to stay across the room from him until he got his arousal under control. A slight whiff of smoke broke his concentration, and he opened his eyes to find his saucepan was too hot.

He moved it and turned the burner down, waited a few minutes, then started again, determined this time to focus on the meal prep.

***

Huh. I came out wearing the skimpiest thing I have, and not a peep from him, much less any action, Mia noticed, and just stopped herself from sighing out loud. *So much for that.*

She straightened up and finished brushing out her hair, then went back to the bedroom to put her brush away.

"That's as good as it's going to get," she muttered as she looked at herself in the mirror. Her hair still wasn't fully dry, but at least she'd gotten most of the moisture – and all of the tangles - out of it.

***

She walked back into the other room and stood next to his dinette table.

"Anything I can help with?" she asked.

"Wanna handle toast?"

Mia grinned. "I think I can manage that."

"Pantry is there, and the toaster's over here on the counter," Tanner told her, and she moved in the direction he pointed.

Within a few minutes they were seated at the table.

"Did you want some coffee?"

"Absolutely. No, you eat, I got it," she said when he started to stand up. "You want some too?"

"Yes, please."

"How do you take yours?"

"Two sugars and a splash of milk."

She poured it out into two mugs, added sugar and milk to each, then rejoined him at the table.

"Here you go," she said, and almost gasped when his hand brushing hers caused a surge of heat to flow through her entire system.

She sat, hoping her cheeks weren't as flushed as they felt, and began to eat. As she took a bite, her mind raced, trying to think of something safe to talk about.

"So," she began, "you said you went into the Marines. What was that like?"

"Intense, but rewarding," Tanner answered. "I thought about making it a career, and then Dad got sick right around the time I was supposed to reup. I opted to leave and come home to help take care of him instead."

"I remember hearing something about that," she murmured. "How's he doing?"

"It was a tough battle for a while there. But he's been in remission for a little over a year now," Tanner replied. "He and Mom actually sold their house and bought a motorhome, and they travel a lot now. They chose Florida for Christmas this year."

"So, what will *you* do?" she asked. "Got any plans with anybody?"

"Nope," he confirmed. "Matter of fact, your mom invited me over when I called to tell her where you were."

"Did she? Well, I know they'd love to see you. Blake would too."

"Yeah. I haven't seen him in a long time. Not since graduation night, actually. And I haven't seen your parents in a couple of years, either."

He took a sip of coffee.

"So, Mia. What about you? What's going on in your life?"

"Well, I just finished my finals. I have two more semesters and I'll be done with my Criminal Justice degree."

"Nice! What do you plan to do after you graduate?"

"I'm thinking law enforcement, actually."

Tanner's eyebrows raised.

"What?"

"Sounds dangerous, Mia."

She shrugged. "I can handle it."

"Does your boyfriend like the idea?"

She gazed at him for a long moment.

"I don't have one."

"Oh," Tanner replied, and suddenly seemed very interested in his plate of food.

"What about you? Seeing anyone?" she countered.

He lifted his eyes and pinned her with a look that took her breath away.

"No, not for a long time now."

"Oh," Mia said, secretly pleased.

Not that I have any clue why I should be happy about that, since he's obviously not into me, at all.

"What are you thinking right now?" he asked suddenly, and she swallowed hard.

CHAPTER NINE

She got up abruptly and took her plate to the sink, starting to tremble when she felt and heard him walk up behind her.

"Mia," Tanner said softly, and she set the plate and fork down and turned to face him.

"I... um.... nothing... why do you ask?" Mia stammered, her cheeks turning a dusky pink as she self-consciously chewed on her bottom lip.

And she noticed his gray eyes darkened as they traveled down to her mouth and lingered there for a moment before slowly returning to hold her gaze again.

"What?" she whispered as he leaned in closer.

Tanner placed his hands on the counter on either side of her, ducked his head, and planted a kiss on her that curled her toes.

Oh....my God... he kisses just like I always imagined he would...

She sighed, contented, and moved forward into his frame, pressing her petite body against his and wrapping her arms around his neck to pull him closer.

Tanner responded by circling one muscled arm around her waist and fisting a hand in her hair as he plundered her mouth with his.

The next thing Mia knew, he'd lifted her off her feet. Her legs parted and wrapped themselves around his waist, and he uttered a low, primal growl against her mouth as he pivoted and carried her through the doorway to his bedroom.

When he reached his bed, Tanner laid her down gently, then pulled away, and Mia whimpered, immediately missing the heat his body had radiated against hers. Without breaking eye contact, he slowly removed his shirt, and the sight of his bare chest and arms, all chiseled muscle, made her mouth water.

He crept forward, a sultry smile playing on his lips, his gray eyes dark with lust, and loosened the side knot she'd tied in her tank top. Mia grabbed the edges and whisked it over her head, throwing it to one side.

"Mia," he said again, his voice strained as he took in the sight of her sprawled on his bed, her black lace bra and yoga pants enticing him to explore her from head to toe.

"Lose the jeans and come here," she purred, and he obliged, then stretched his long frame out beside her, and reached for her again.

When his hands caressed her skin, her eyelids fluttered closed, and she moaned, lost in the feel of his strong hands roaming her body.

He slipped an arm underneath her and rolled her toward him to attack the fasteners that held her breasts captive in their lace confinement, then slowly slid the straps down her arms, and pulled the undergarment out of his way.

"You're magnificent," he whispered, kissing down the side of her neck as he slid down to pay homage to the perfect breasts he'd laid bare.

Mia moaned again and arched her back when his mouth made contact with the left one, digging her nails lightly into his shoulders.

Then his right hand traveled down and cupped her, and her whole body shivered.

Tanner chuckled, his breath on her skin fanning the flames of her want.

"Like that, huh?" he whispered.

"*More*," she whispered back.

"You know," he murmured against her flesh, "you're *supposed* to be taking it easy. Light activity only. Remember?"

"I know what they said. I don't care."

"Hey, I'm just trying to make sure you don't overexert yourself," he teased. "Maybe we should just stop right here."

Mia growled.

"Stop teasing me, Tanner, and take me," she said huskily, and watched his eyes smolder with passion.

***

He took hold of the waistband of her yoga pants and gently slid them down, nodding his appreciation when black lace panties that matched the bra came into view.

He'd just reached for them when his cell phone began to ring.

"Ignore it," Mia pleaded as he pulled away from her again.

"I can't, baby. It might be the sheriff's office needing me to go help somebody else caught out in the storm," he told her, raking a hand through his hair in frustration before he stood and rummaged through his jeans pockets to find his phone.

"Tanner Greysen," he barked into it as he seared Mia with a lustful look.

"Tanner! Thank God! Where's Mia? Is she okay?"

Tanner closed his eyes and shook his head, then opened them again and glanced over at Mia, who had tilted her head in confusion.

You've got to be freaking kidding me. What, he's psychic now?

"Yes, Blake," he said, never taking his eyes off Mia, "she's fine. She's right here."

***

Dammit, dammit, dammit. I finally have my chance with Tanner, and Blake calls?

My brother's timing sucks. Seriously.

Tanner held out the phone and Mia grabbed it.

CHAPTER TEN

"Hey Blake! Sorry, I forgot to charge my cell phone again," Mia said, scrambling off the bed to go pull her phone and charger cord out of her purse.

He laughed.

"That's a total shocker, let me tell ya," Blake answered. "So, what happened with Gracie?"

Mia shrugged, raising an eyebrow when she noticed Tanner's visible reaction to her moving around his room in just her underwear. She licked her lips seductively at him and grinned when he groaned.

She fought back a giggle to concentrate on the phone call.

"I was driving down the road, and she did that weird thing she does sometimes where it feels like I'm about to lose power steering," she told her brother. "Only this time, it actually happened. Not just that – *everything* stopped working. Even the headlights."

"Wow. Not good. Bet that was scary."

"Not as scary as having to go hike for help in the storm," she admitted, then winced and pulled the phone away from her ear as Blake bellowed.

"Mia Diane! Are you nuts? You could've really been hurt."

"Okay, *Dad*," she snarled as her usual acceptance of her brother's protectiveness vanished into thin air. "I wasn't able to control the car, Blake, and I had to park on an exit ramp, and it wasn't safe to stay there. I waited almost half an hour, and no one drove by, and so I decided to leave Gracie to go find help."

He started to speak but she cut him off.

"Now, I need to call Cheryl, who I am sure by now has called out the National Guard to search for

me. You two would be *perfect* together, by the way –
she's another one who doesn't think I'm capable of
handling myself. Here's Tanner," she snapped, and
thrust the phone a shocked Tanner's way before
scooping up her clothes and storming out of the room
to plug in her own phone.

***

Mia sat on the couch, muttering to herself as she
untangled her yoga pants enough to shove her legs
back into them.

"Unbelievable. He's got some nerve," she hissed
under her breath as she stood and bounced, working
the fabric back up over her hips, then grabbed her bra
and put it on. Last came the tank top. Once it was
back in its proper place, she stalked to the kitchen
counter and pulled up her messages.

"Huh. Only four missed calls and six texts this
time? Cheryl must be slipping," she snarled out loud,
and dialed, tapping her fingers impatiently on the
countertop.

"Thank God you're okay," she heard her
roommate say, and Mia closed her eyes and tried her
best not to lash out.

"Hi," she said. "I'm okay, I'm fine, but Gracie left
me stranded."

"Oh, no! What happened?"

Mia walked her quickly through the night's
events.

"So, let me get this straight. You're stuck alone
with the man you've crushed on for years? Oh my
God, girl! What the hell are you doing on the phone
with me then? Go have some fun. You're fine, I'm
fine, and I want details later, Mia. Like, *lots* of them."

Mia giggled, her roommate's enthusiasm taking
the edge off her anger at her brother. "I fully intend
to. I'll call you later, all right?"

***

"What the hell did you say to her, Blake? She's seriously pissed right now," Tanner murmured.

Blake sighed. "I know. I know she's a grown woman, and I do trust her ability. I just... it's my kid sister, man."

"Trust me, I'm aware," Tanner said, but not quite neutrally enough.

"Dude. Tell me you didn't."

"Didn't what?"

"Put my baby sister onboard the Tanner Train."

"The '*Tanner Train*'? What the hell does *that* mean?"

"You know damn well what I'm talking about. You forget, we go way back. I know your *history*, 'Good Time Greysen'," Blake sneered. "Stay the hell away from her."

"Okay, first of all, she's a grown woman and can make her own decisions," Tanner growled at him. "And second, that was back in *high school*, man. I'm not that guy anymore. Besides, you weren't exactly pristine yourself, so don't you dare bring that shit up to me. You played the field just as much as I did, and you *know* it."

A long silence, then, "You're right. And I know Mia can make up her own mind. But I don't trust you with her, Tanner, I'll tell you that right now. Hurt her and I'll break you in half with my bare hands."

The next thing Tanner heard was dead air as Blake hung up on him, and he closed his eyes as the most hurtful words his best friend could have possibly said hit him like a punch in the gut.

I don't trust you with her.

CHAPTER ELEVEN

When he finally walked out into the living room, Mia closed the distance between them and flung her arms around his neck.

"Where were we?" she whispered as she stood on tiptoe to try to kiss him again.

Tanner gently slid his hands from her shoulders up to her hands and removed them from around his neck.

"Wait... what... I don't understand," Mia stammered, her heart pounding, her green eyes welling with hurt. "I thought we..."

"I was wrong, Mia. We can't do this," he told her, and took two steps back to put some distance between them.

"Why not? We're both single, right?"

"It's complicated."

She crossed her arms over her chest and narrowed her eyes.

"What did Blake say to you?"

Tanner just shook his head.

Mia lost the tenuous grasp she held on her temper.

"Dammit, Tanner," she snarled as she paced, stomping from one end of the room to the other. "One minute you can't *wait* to get into my pants. Then Blake calls, and suddenly you're looking at me with disgust like I'm some sort of freak? *What the hell did he say to you?*"

Tanner's eyes widened in surprise.

"What? No! I don't think you're a freak, Mia, I just..."

"Let me guess. Blake ran his big fat mouth about my crush on you and then he told you I'm still a virgin because I've been saving myself for you, right?"

Mia was confused when Tanner's jaw dropped wide open.

"What? Why do you look so surprised? Didn't Blabbermouth Blake tell you that?"

"Mia... Blake didn't say *any* of that," he answered quietly.

Mia stopped mid-pace and flushed scarlet all the way to her hairline.

"Oh," she squeaked.

Now he took a step forward, a tenderness in his eyes that managed to make her melt and feel pitied all at once.

"Baby. You've been waiting? For *me*?"

"You know what? Forget I said anything," she babbled, mortified, a single tear cascading down her cheek as she backed away from him.

"Mia, I..."

"*No*. Stay away from me. You're not into me now for whatever reason. It's fine. I don't understand it, but whatever. I'll just keep waiting for another man, is all, one who *actually* gives a shit about me. I refuse to be a pity screw on top of being a freaking idiot all these years. But don't worry, Greysen, you're blameless. The only thing that's happened tonight is you've opened my eyes, and now I can finally see it clearly."

"See what clearly?"

"The fact that you don't deserve me," she whispered, and she turned and fled past him to lock herself in the bathroom and cry.

***

Tanner Greysen stood as still as a statue in his living room, shocked to his core, and processed everything she'd just said to him.

She's been waiting. For me, his brain repeated, and the burst of emotion that flooded his heart both soothed and unsettled him.

I... I had no idea. How could I? The last time I saw her was over a decade ago, for Christ's sake. Just Blake's bratty little sister. I never looked at her any other way, until tonight.

And as he pondered it all, the reason for Blake's blunt comments, as hurtful as they might have been, hit him like a thunderbolt.

I get it now. She doesn't take this lightly; she will jump in with her whole heart. And Blake's afraid I'm going to treat Mia the same way I used to treat every girl I got involved with. He doesn't know I left all that behind me years ago.

He hung his head.

I've got a lot to prove, and I need to make amends. Starting with Mia.

He walked slowly through his bedroom and stopped outside his bathroom door. Just as he raised his arm to knock, the sounds of her sobbing wrapped tightly around his heart, then tore it completely in two.

Overcome, Tanner retreated to the living room, pulled on his coat, grabbed his keys, and left.

He drove to the garage, parked, and pulled out his cell phone.

"Don't hang up, please," he said when Blake answered with a snarl. "I need to talk to you."

***

Once she'd pulled herself together, Mia splashed water on her face, then cautiously opened the bathroom door, listening intently.

"Tanner?" she called out softly as she crept forward.

But he was nowhere to be found.

She turned and retreated to the bedroom long enough to grab a pillow and blanket, laid down on the couch, and watched the flames dance in the fireplace, tears streaming freely again, until she fell asleep.

CHAPTER TWELVE

"So, talk," Blake snapped.

Tanner sighed.

"I never told you about Amber," he began.

"Who's Amber?"

"She's a girl I dated right before I left the Marines," Tanner revealed. "And I fell for her. *Hard.* I started planning to buy a house and marry her and start a family with her. The whole nine yards. I really thought she was the one."

He heard curiosity creep into Blake's voice.

"So, what happened?"

"I came home early one day, and she was in bed with another guy," Tanner said simply. "She played me, Blake, the same way you and I used to play with girls' hearts in high school. And it crushed me, and it made me sick to my stomach to realize that I had put others through that exact same kind of hurt."

"What did you do?"

"I packed up my shit and I moved out and I haven't looked twice at another woman since. That was almost four years ago."

"I'm sorry, man, I didn't know."

"I know you didn't. I didn't tell anybody, not even Mom and Dad. I figured it was the karma bus running my ass over the way I deserved. And I've been alone since then. Until tonight, when I stumbled across Mia."

"So, she's not just another good time to you."

Tanner closed his eyes, searched his heart, and replied.

"No," he answered honestly, the realization flooding him with joy. "No, Mia's not just a good time at all, Blake. She's so, so much more than that. And if she's willing to let me be a part of her life and give me the gift of her time and attention, I swear to you that I will never, *ever* take it for granted."

There was a long silence.

"You there?"

"I'm here," Blake said. "I just... I'm sorry for what I said earlier, Tanner. It was uncalled for."

"It wasn't out of line, Blake. You were one hundred percent right. I was a complete player back then. I don't deny it. But I also can't change it. All I can do going forward is to be the best man for Mia that I possibly can be – if she'll even still have me, that is."

"I probably shouldn't tell you this, but she's had a thing for you for years."

"I know," Tanner chuckled, "she let it slip earlier, thinking you'd already spilled the beans about it."

He sighed and his tone turned serious.

"And right now, she's sobbing in my bathroom, Blake. After our phone call, I told her that I'd changed my mind and that she and I shouldn't be together. I didn't mean *ever*, I just meant take things slow, not rush in. But she thought I meant *at all*, and lost her temper before I could explain, and, well, I think she hates me now."

"Ouch."

"Ouch, indeed. And I don't know what to do."

"Actions speak louder with Mia. They always have. If you truly care about her, don't just tell her, Tanner. *Show her*."

***

Tanner crept back into his house and headed for the bedroom, confused when he didn't find Mia in the bathroom or in bed.

It wasn't until he returned to the living room that he noticed her, curled up in a little ball on the couch, shivering in her sleep. And he could see the streaks on her face where her tears had dried.

Oh, baby. I'll spend every day making up for making you cry, Mia.

He moved back to his room and turned down the covers, then returned to the couch. As gently as he could, he scooped her up, carried her to the bed, and tucked her in.

The last thing he did was turn off the kitchen and living room lights before he put on pajamas, climbed into bed, and snuggled up next to a still asleep and shivering Mia to try to keep her warm.

***

A few hours later Mia woke, startled, and started to pull away from him.

"What the..."

"Shh, baby. You were shivering on the couch, so I brought you in here."

He tightened his arms around her.

"Can we talk? Please?"

He felt her trembling against his chest as she responded in a shaky voice.

"Okay."

Tanner took a deep breath and spoke honestly into the dark.

"Mia, I don't know how much you remember about me back in the day, but...I was not a good person," he began. "I was a player, and I hurt people."

"I remember your nickname. 'Good Time Greysen'," she admitted, and he flinched, then sighed.

"Yeah. Well, I was a complete ass back then. And your brother thought I was still like that, so he warned me to stay away from you."

Silence.

CHAPTER THIRTEEN

"Go on," Mia urged softly.

"Long story short, about four years ago I got a massive dose of my own medicine," he confessed. "And it tore me up, but it turned out to be a blessing in disguise, because it also opened my eyes to what a horrible guy I used to be. I'm not that guy anymore, Mia. But I realized that maybe I was meant to be alone, as a fitting punishment for all the hurt I'd caused. I didn't like it, but over time, I managed to make peace with it."

He pressed his lips to her hair.

"And then I found you on the side of the road last night, and everything changed, Mia. You're the first woman in four years to even turn my head, much less make me *feel* something."

"What are you saying?"

"When I told you last night that I was wrong and we can't do this, I wasn't talking about being with you, Mia. I simply meant I didn't want to rush things. I want to slow down and do things right. You're worth that. Taking my time and doing things right."

"Oh," she said, in a small voice.

"Honey," he murmured, "you're worth all that and so much more to me. You were right. I don't deserve you, Mia, but I *do* care, very much. I do, Mia. And I am so sorry I made you feel like I didn't. I just... I want to do right by you. I want to..."

She lifted her head and whispered.

"Tanner."

"Yes ma'am?"

"Please stop talking and kiss me."

"Yes, ma'am."

He dipped his head down, and as he softly grazed her lips with his, he tasted the salt of her fresh tears.

"Mia. I'm so sorry. Please don't cry, honey."

"It's all right, baby. These are happy ones," she murmured, and kissed him back before sighing and laying her head against his chest again. "Can we talk more in the morning? I'm exhausted."

"As much as you want. 'Night, Mia."

"'Night," she whispered.

He ran his hand lazily up and down her back as he listened to her breathing become deep and even, and he smiled as he too faded back into sleep.

***

The storm was still raging outside when Tanner woke up and eased out of bed so he wouldn't disturb her.

He padded to the kitchen to start a pot of coffee, then called his friend Pete with the Prism County Sheriff's office.

"Any more trouble spots?"

"The weather's gotten bad enough that they've suspended *everything* county-wide at this point, Tanner."

"Damn. That *is* bad."

"I know, right? That hasn't happened in at *least* twenty years. It's just too risky, even for our emergency crews. Hell, half of us camped out up here last night just so we wouldn't have to try to drive in today."

"Well, keep me posted. And if something does come up, let me know. I'll help if I can."

"Will do."

He disconnected the call and set the phone down, then turned toward the refrigerator.

I wonder if Mia likes French toast.

Whistling under his breath, he got out two pans – one for the French toast and another for bacon – and got to work.

***

Mia stretched and yawned, then reached out to her left searching for Tanner.

Did he get another call for help?

She rose, then shivered, and stumbled over to her suitcase to add a sweatshirt and thick socks to her attire before heading to the bathroom. Once she'd freshened up, she brushed out her hair and braided it, then headed toward the living room.

"Good morning, gorgeous," she heard Tanner say, and she blushed with pleasure.

He set down the spatula in his hand, closed the distance between them, and lifted her off her feet to kiss her sweetly before setting her down again.

"Are you warm enough? I can build the fire back up."

"It *is* a little chilly in here," she admitted.

"I'm on it. Take over at the stove for me?"

"Sure."

She took a peek at what he was making and smiled.

"French toast! I *love* French toast," she called out.

"Good call on my part, then, huh?" Tanner quipped back.

"I'd say so. You want some coffee?"

"Sure, I'll take another cup."

"So how many calls do you think you'll get today?" she asked as she added milk and sugar to his mug, then poured one for herself.

"Zero," he said as he fed logs into the fire he'd gotten going again.

"Zero? Really? But Tanner, the storm is crazy outside still. People are gonna need help if something happens to their car," Mia said, her voice full of concern.

He walked back over to the kitchen and stood behind her, wrapping his arms around her waist and resting his chin lightly on the top of her head as she turned the bread over in the pan.

CHAPTER FOURTEEN

"I talked to my friend Pete with the Sheriff's office a little bit ago. According to him, not only are the roads closed, but all services have been suspended until the storm passes, as well. It's just too risky for *anybody* to be out there right now."

"Wow. I don't ever remember that happening before around here, do you?"

"Nope. Weatherman said this could be the worst winter storm this area has seen in decades. I think he may have been right."

She scooped the last piece of French toast out of the pan and turned off the burner, then pivoted in his arms and looked up at him with troubled eyes.

"Tanner," she said, "this should all clear out soon, right? What if Blake can't get home?"

"I honestly think this storm will blow itself out sometime tonight or in the morning. And I bet the temperatures are back up in the fifties by this weekend, so I'm sure you'll be able to see Blake for Christmas."

"I hope so," she sighed, laying her cheek against his chest. "I miss him so much."

He stroked her back.

"I know you do. And don't you dare tell him I said this, but I'm kinda looking forward to seeing his ugly mug, too."

She laughed.

"You grab the syrup and meet me at the table," she said, then wriggled out of his grasp to pick up the two plates of food.

Once they were seated, Mia said, "I'd like to talk to you more about last night."

"Absolutely," he told her. "Anything you want."

"I want to apologize for yelling at you."

"No apology needed. I deserved it."

"No, you didn't."

"Yes, I really did," Tanner replied. "Things between us were getting heated and then all of a sudden I was distant, and I did a really crappy job of explaining why. I can see how that made you think what you did."

She concentrated on her breakfast for a while before she blurted out, "I still can't *believe* I told you all that."

He grinned as he watched the color rising in her cheeks.

"Caught me by surprise, I'll admit it," he told her gently.

"Me too," Mia admitted with an embarrassed smile. "As soon as I said it and then realized that you didn't know all that yet, I wanted *so bad* for the floor to just open up and swallow me."

"Do you regret telling me?"

"In a way," she said shyly. "I mean, it probably sounded stupid and childish, and I never meant for you to know about it in the first place, so..." her voice trailed off as she swallowed hard.

"Mia."

"And now that you know, I don't want you to feel... obligated. Or trapped. Or whatever," she finished on a whisper.

He reached over and took her trembling hand in his.

"Mia," he said softly.

She slowly raised her eyes to his.

"The moment I saw you I was completely captivated by you. I had no idea who you were at the time. All I knew was that I'd found this mesmerizing woman that I just *had* to spend more time with. Had to. There was never a doubt in my mind. The moment

I picked you up and held you in my arms, I knew taking you to the emergency room and then walking away wasn't even an option," Tanner revealed, and she gasped.

"And then when I recognized you, part of me was worried, because I didn't know if my friendship with Blake would survive this or not."

"He *is* overprotective," Mia chimed in.

"Boy, is he ever. But here's the thing, Mia. I decided it would just have to work itself out somehow, because I'm not willing to walk away from you."

"Really?"

"Really. And the *only* reason I waited to kiss you had nothing at all to do with your crazy older brother."

"Then why did you wait?"

"Simple. I didn't know if you were involved with someone else, and I didn't want to make things difficult for you if you were."

"So what I said...about..."

"Just makes me even more certain that I want to be the man that you deserve. I want to be the one that makes you laugh, that you can tell your dreams to, that you can depend on. I'm telling you right here, right now, that I will wait as long as it takes for me to truly earn that precious gift you've saved for me – but I want so much more than just sex with you. I also want to win your *heart*, Mia. Please don't think I'm here out of obligation. I am exactly where I want to be, and that's with you," he finished.

Her brilliant smile made his heart do a double thump again, and he felt himself breaking into a goofy grin.

"Now," Tanner said after he'd leaned over and kissed her gently, "how about a movie marathon?"

"Good call. What were you thinking?"

"Go check out the collection," he indicated. "I bet we can find something."

A few minutes later she called out to him.

"I can't decide which one to watch first. Wanna start with *Goodfellas*, or *Guardians of the Galaxy*?"

He stood, dumbfounded. Out of over a hundred titles he owned, she'd just picked his two favorite movies on the planet.

"Damn," he breathed. "Mia, you really *are* the woman of my dreams."

***

Twenty-four hours later, the storm had finally passed, and the temperature rebounded into the mid-fifties, as Tanner had predicted.

They drove to the garage so Tanner could try to figure out what was wrong with Gracie. Mia passed him tools and asked questions and shrieked in fright when a large, burly man appeared beside her.

"Max, this is Mia. Mia, this is Max, my friend and boss."

"Pleased to meet you," the giant said shyly, and enveloped her dainty hand in his large one as they shook in greeting.

"How was the deer lease?" Tanner asked him.

"Cold," was all Max would say before he scooted Tanner out of the way and took on troubleshooting Gracie's woes himself.

Tanner grinned at him.

An hour later Max grumbled, "I have no idea what's wrong with this thing. It's like your little Honda just decided you really needed to stop in Pine Mills."

"Sounds right to me," Tanner murmured as he took Mia's hand. "What do you think?"

"I think that sounds *exactly* right."

EPILOGUE

On Saturday morning, Mia, Tanner, and Mia's parents waited anxiously in baggage claim for Blake's flight number to appear on the monitor. As soon as it did, the carousel came to life. Mia turned and began scanning the crowd of passengers entering baggage claim.

When she saw her brother coming toward them, Mia ran, arms outstretched, and jumped into his arms.

"Hey, kiddo," Blake said, smiling as he hugged her tightly.

The moment he set her down, she doubled up her fist and punched him as hard as she could in the shoulder.

"*Ow!* What was that for?"

"*That* was for interfering in my love life," she announced, then flung her arms around him again. "And *this* is for loving me enough to watch out for me like that."

***

The following August, Tanner and Blake sat next to Gladys and Phil Jones and clapped as Mia crossed the stage in her cap and gown and shook hands with the university's dean, then accepted her diploma.

Tanner leaned over to Blake.

"Think she'll be surprised?"

"I *know* she will."

When the ceremony came to a close, she made her way over to her family for hugs and congratulations.

Tanner held back, letting her parents and brother enjoy the moment with her first. And he grinned as Mia introduced Blake and Cheryl.

Wow, look at the sparks flying between those two, he noted, then refocused his attention on the brunette that had claimed his heart. He waited, biding his time until her back was turned to him, then got into position.

***

"I'm starved. I was thinking Italian," Mia told her mom. "There's this great place about a half-mile from here. Tanner and I can meet you there. Right, Tanner?"

When Mia turned to look at him, she gasped in surprise, tears coming to her eyes.

The man she'd loved for half her life was down on one knee, holding open a velvet box with the most beautiful diamond ring she'd ever seen.

"Mia Jones, I'm in love with you, and you're my world. Will you marry me?"

"Yes," she stammered, tears streaming and a megawatt smile on her face. "Yes."

***

That evening, after they'd packed up the last of her things in the apartment, she wrapped her arms around his waist, and murmured, "So, I've been thinking."

"About?" Tanner replied as he kissed the top of her head.

"I don't report to work at Prism County until next Monday, and I was thinking since we're engaged now, I could come home with you, and..." she looked up at him with a sultry smile, and finished, "you can finally open your gift."

Tanner lifted her off her feet and kissed her.

"Get ready, woman," he growled with passion, "because we're about to get back to Pine Mills in record time so I can take you up on that."